Elliot Perlman was born in Australia in 1964. He has received numerous awards for his writing, including the Betty Trask Award and the Fellowship of Australian Writers Award for *Three Dollars*, described by the *Daily Telegraph* as 'a brilliant first novel' and praised in the *Times Literary Supplement* as 'a sad, angry, disconcertingly funny reflection on the way we live now'. He is the co-author of a screenplay based on *Three Dollars* which has been made into a film. He lives in Melbourne, where he works as a barrister.

Further praise for *Seven Types of Ambiguity*:

'Remarkable . . . Perlman builds up an unsettling, often sympathetic but always memorable picture of [his characters'] emotional lives, and of the coldly mercenary world they inhabit.'
Sunday Times

'My novel of the year . . . Captures the *Zeitgeist* of contemporary Australia every bit as powerfully as *The Corrections* anatomised that of America.' Jonathan Bate, *Sunday Telegraph*

'This book's true size is in its scope, its ambition, its emotional richness . . . Certainly, no novel has made this reviewer feel quite so sane in a long time.' *Herald* (Glasgow)

'Elliot Perlman has many things working in his favour as a novelist: curiosity, erudition, daring and a gift for seducing readers into going along with him for the ride. He'll get you where you want to go . . .'
Washington Post

'This is a love story in the nineteenth century tradition, the kind that makes the real world seem a bit dim . . . George Eliot down under.' *Kirkus Reviews*

'Motives are tangled, perceptions unreliable, and outcomes unexpected . . . [Perlman] has created a novel with just the right amount of meaning, intelligence, and beauty.' *Boston Globe*

'Perlman writes with such convincing simplicity – his sentences read like whiskey-fueled confessions . . . We can't trust ourselves because Perlman makes us care too much.' *Esquire* (US)

'Terrific . . . A cerebral dazzler of a psychodrama about obsessive love. This exhilarating novel contains multitudes.'
Entertainment Weekly

'A relentlessly driven story . . . Think Grisham by way of Franzen.' *Publishers Weekly*

'A sophisticated psychodrama.' *Wall Street Journal*

'A brilliant book, written in the unadorned style of Raymond Carver, but with the wild metaphysical vision of a Thomas Pynchon. It is that most unusual thing – a novel that is both intellectually fun and spiritually harrowing.' *Baltimore Sun*

'Worthy of Dickens or Doctorow . . . Almost impossible to put down.' *Bookpage*

'Fast-moving, relentless but suspenseful . . . Perlman succeeds in illuminating the ambiguity inherent in lust, personal relationships, psychiatry and the law . . . Smart and edgy.' *Booklist*

'An all-too-rare literary page turner.' *Library Journal*

'Brilliant, absorbing . . . The scope of the novel is breathtaking but so intimately involving and densely plotted that it becomes that anomaly of a literate and urgent page-turner.' *New York Post*

'In literature, England has always looked down on the States, which have thanked God for Australia. With *Seven Types of Ambiguity*, Elliot Perlman is about to puncture America's supposed superiority . . . The payoff for [the reader] is nothing short of eye-opening.' *Dallas Morning News*

'The Great Australian Novel.' *Pages*

'Read it . . . A tour de force.' *The Age* (Australia)

'It is a pleasure to read a book that is so intelligently engaged with our time . . . and [whose] characters are so convincing.' *Australian Bookseller & Publisher*

'An elegantly constructed, wise and compassionate fable for our times, full of twists and turns and insights into the corners of human desire.' *Sunday Age* (Australia)

'This is a novel that can make you feel you are entering the lives of the people sitting either side of you in the morning traffic . . . It does what novels once did but rarely can nowadays: It brings the news.' *Sydney Morning Herald*

'Perlman sees with painful clarity. Insights from a writer of this calibre are worth sharing.' *The Australian*

'*Seven Types of Ambiguity* makes much Australian fiction of the past decade look wan and unambitious.' *Herald-Sun*

'An achingly humane, richly layered and seamlessly constructed masterpiece.' *Canberra Times*

'One of those rare works of art that makes you realise the world is both a simpler and a more complex place.' *Evening Standard* (Books of the Year)

BY THE SAME AUTHOR

Three Dollars

The Reasons I Won't Be Coming

elliot
perlman
seven
types of
ambiguity

faber and faber

First published 2003
in Picador by Pan Macmillan Australia Pty Limited
First Published in Great Britain
by Faber and Faber Limited
3 Queen Square, London WC1 3AU
This paperback edition first published in 2005

Printed in England by Mackays

All rights reserved
© Elliot Perlman, 2003

The right of Elliot Perlman to be identified as author of this work has been asserted
in accordance with Section 77 of the Copyright, Designs and Patents Act 1988

*This book is sold subject to the condition that it shall not,
by way of trade or otherwise, be lent, resold, hired out or
otherwise circulated without the publisher's prior consent in
any form of binding or cover other than that in which it is
published and without a similiar condition including this condition
being imposed on the subsequent purchaser.*

A CIP record for this book is available from the British Library

ISBN 0–571–20722–7

2 4 6 8 10 9 7 5 3 1

For Debbie

God has pity on kindergarten children.
He has less pity on school children.
And on grownups he has no pity at all,
he leaves them alone,
and sometimes they must crawl on all fours . . .

YEHUDA AMICHAI

part one

part one

He nearly called you again last night. Can you imagine that, after all this time? *He* can. He imagines calling you or running into you by chance. Depending on the weather, he imagines you in one of those cotton dresses of yours with flowers on it or in faded blue jeans and a thick woollen button-up cardigan over a checked shirt, drinking coffee from a mug, looking through your tortoiseshell glasses at a book of poetry while it rains. He thinks of you with your hair tied back and that characteristic sweet scent on your neck. He imagines you this way when he is on the train, in the supermarket, at his parents' house, at night, alone, and when he is with a woman.

He is wrong though. You didn't read poetry at all. He had *wanted* you to read poetry but you didn't. If pressed, he confesses to an imprecise recollection of what it was you read and, anyway, it wasn't your reading that started this. It was the laughter, the carefree laughter, the three-dimensional Coca-Cola advertisement that you were, the try-anything-once friends, the imperviousness to all that came before you, the chain telephone calls, the in-jokes, the instant music, the sunlight you carried with you, the way he felt when he spoke to his parents, the introductory undergraduate courses, the inevitability of your success, the beach houses, the white lace underwear, the private dancing, the good-graced acceptance of part-time shiftwork, the apparent absence of expectations, the ever-changing disposable cults of the rural, the family, the eastern, the classical, the modern, the post-modern, the impoverished, the sleekly deregulated, the orgasm, the feminine, the feminist and then the way you cancelled with the air of one making a salad.

You would love the way he sees you. He uses you as a weapon

against himself and not merely because you did. He sits in his car at traffic lights on his way out sometimes and tries to estimate how many times he has sat here, waiting at these traffic lights on his way somewhere without you, hoping to meet someone with the capacity to consign you to an anecdote, to be eventually confused with others. He thinks of you when the woman lying next to him thinks he's asleep. It would not surprise you that there are many women. Do you remember you thought him beautiful? You never told him. He had to assume it. He was beautiful and is now, some nine years later, even more so. The years have refined him so that once-boyish good looks have evolved into a clean smooth charm. Not always though. First thing in the morning or after he's been drinking the charm goes missing. The drinking is not really the problem at the moment though, not right now. Of late it has been no more of a problem with him than it is with your husband, which is to say, of late the quantity itself is no cause for alarm. But there is a secret need in both men to have their inhibitors inhibited. In Simon's case this is merely the tip of an older and more fundamental iceberg.

It is often almost too much for Simon to undertake even basic daily tasks: to shower and shave, to dress, to wash his clothes, to feed himself and Empson. He runs out of all but the most essential of foods and doesn't do anything about it until there's nothing for the dog to eat. You couldn't know Empson. Simon got him as a puppy. He would be about three and a half now. He used to take him to school with him. This was the sort of thing he would do. The children loved Empson almost as much as they loved Simon. You loved him too. I can imagine he was a wonderful teacher. You might remember that Simon's father, William (or did you call him Mr Heywood?), was disappointed that Simon was going to be a teacher, particularly a primary school teacher. He felt that this was not a sufficiently manly occupation for his son and that Simon would be wasted. Ironically though, had Simon still been teaching, William may not have felt the need to contact me.

It was very late one night. I could tell by his voice that William was embarrassed. He was at home and I was, of course, in my rooms getting the last little bit of my dinner from the bottom of a cup. I don't know why he thought I'd still be there. He almost whispered into the telephone that he was calling on his son's behalf but without his knowledge. For all his embarrassment, and I have since learnt that this is characteristic of him, he very soon got to the point. He told me he had a thirty-two-year-old son who lived alone with a dog in a flat by the sea, in Elwood. He told me that his son, always obsessed with poetry, seldom went out since losing his job in the first wave of the downsizing epidemic. In getting directly to the point, William missed so many others. Simon has said that the reason his father has no time for poetry is that he is afraid of the messiness of life. Poetry feeds on all that spills over the boundaries of the usual things, the everyday things with which most people are obsessed, so William has no time for it. He cannot think of anything more unnecessary. What about you? What's your excuse?

2

The conversation must have lasted about half an hour—most of it taken up with William's examples of his son's lack of interest in things other than poetry and perhaps 'the damn dog'. He seems to have had no idea of Simon's continuing interest in you and everything about you. He told me that Simon was severely depressed, from which I concluded nothing much except that William wanted me to think that he thought his son was severely depressed. He told me that I had been highly recommended to him by someone or other and that he was willing to pay for Simon to see me. I found that an interesting way of putting it. He was willing to pay for Simon to see me—as opposed to him being willing to pay *me* to treat Simon. His wife knew nothing about all of this and he asked me in advance to forgive him if she came into the room unexpectedly and he was forced to hang up, suddenly, without saying goodbye. William has spent much of his time planning to cope with people doing things *unexpectedly*. He would probably not recognise that he has ever done this, let alone the futility of doing it. He certainly would not recognise the utility of preparing for the *expected* just that little bit more—and planning for the unexpected just that little bit less. His wife didn't surprise him at all, not then.

At first there was nothing to be done because, as I explained to William, Simon had to *want* to see me. I couldn't call him up and say, 'Your father thinks you're disturbed in some way. How's Wednesday at four?' Since he had never broached the subject with Simon, I really didn't know what he thought I could do. We said goodbye and that, I thought, would be the end of it. Clearly, it wasn't.

About a month later William and Simon's mother, May, were out for dinner with Henry and Diane Osborne. You may remember the Osbornes; they are Simon's parents' closest friends. Simon assures me that Henry's contempt for poetry is probably second only to his father's. It was a Friday night and the Osbornes had taken Simon's parents to a French restaurant to celebrate William's retirement from the bank that very day. As they were leaving, having been feted by the owner, a drunk Simon literally walked into his parents, apparently by chance, with his arm around the waist of a very attractive young woman. The two older couples, seeing the short-skirted advertisement for herself that she was, guessed her occupation fairly quickly and were clearly embarrassed. William started to apologise to everyone as though he was responsible. Henry tried to make light of it, asking the young woman if she had ever eaten at the restaurant before. Simon was trying to hail a taxi and the young woman, who said her name was Angelique, told him she had eaten there many times and that the owner was a client.

On the Monday Simon called me. He told me the whole story and explained that it was a condition of the rapprochement with his parents that he arrange to see me. It was a brief conversation. He said that he would rather we didn't meet in my rooms and gave an address at which I was to meet him one evening. It was summer then and he said to come around the back into the garden where he would be waiting. I wouldn't normally ever agree to an arrangement like this, but something in his voice, an intelligence, and the honesty with which he told the story about his parents, the Osbornes and Angelique—a disarming honesty—made me agree. And, if I am to share the honesty I admired in Simon, I needed another full-paying private client. I still do. My wife and I have recently separated.

3

It is quite well understood that a clinically depressed person will show little, if any, interest in constructive activity concerning future events or outcomes. In this respect, Simon has only flirted with depression in its definitive or clinical form. But if that is all that depression required, then I could say without much hesitation that Simon has always been, other than for short periods, too involved in things to be clinically depressed. William really knows very little about what's on his son's mind. What he and many people don't understand is that there is more to depression than a sometimes overwhelming feeling of inadequacy and hopelessness and profound sadness. When people are depressed they are sometimes very, very angry. They are not just quietly miserable. They can be filled with great passion.

Simon was sitting on a chair under a sun umbrella in a large well-cared-for garden with an inground swimming pool in the centre and birches and firs along the perimeter. He got up and we shook hands and introduced ourselves. I was struck by his clean handsomeness and by his calm. One rarely meets anyone who makes a better first impression than Simon. Do you remember? He thanked me for coming, saying he realised such a meeting was probably unusual. I said something banal about having to expect the unexpected in my line of business and then he quoted someone, some verse about surprises or chance, in that soothing voice of his. I don't know why, but I was a bit nervous. He asked me questions as though he was interviewing me and making mental notes: middle-aged, separated, lives inner city, et cetera. I must have passed because he seemed to take a bit of a liking to me, albeit with some reserve. Perhaps I didn't fit his stereotype of a psychiatrist. I don't know. He told me not to completely ignore whatever it was his father had told me about him, saying his father's description of him no doubt contained what Simon called 'that dangerous element of truth', just enough to make me suspect that everything else his father had said, and would ever say, was true.

He was utterly charming, witty, and seemingly quite relaxed and intelligent. I was a little surprised he hadn't offered me at least a drink, but I didn't comment. We Europeans are instinctively better hosts, whether we have personality disorders or not. I didn't know him and perhaps he would never again be so forthcoming. It's not that I expect patients to entertain me but the circumstances here were quite unusually informal. And I didn't want to interrupt him. Perhaps he felt a little uncomfortable offering me his parents' alcohol. I figured a place of that size with the inground pool, the tennis court and the satellite dish had to belong to his parents. They must have agreed to go out for the evening as part of the deal.

'I *am* a thirty-two-year-old out of work teacher living on my own in a flat in Elwood,' he laughed, 'but just because I don't work doesn't mean I'm broken.'

Then, after some small talk, he started telling me about you. At first I didn't realise how long it had been since you had been together. It wasn't clear, so I asked him.

'It finished nine years ago,' he said, 'and you want to know why I'm still talking about it, right?'

'No, I didn't say that,' I responded.

'No. You didn't, but only because my father is paying you not to tell me I'm mad, or at least to tell him first. I think it's admirable what you guys do but, shit, it's embarrassingly primitive, wouldn't you say? What do you really know? And in any particular case, in my case, what do you really *want* to know? I'm afraid it won't make sense to you. I really mean that. I am genuinely afraid it won't make sense. I am not trying to sound casual or smug.

'Listen—all that she was then, all that she is now, those gestures, everything I remember but won't or can't articulate anymore, the perfect words that are somehow made imperfect when used to describe her and all that should remain unsaid about her—it is all unsupported by reason. I know that. But that enigmatic calm that attaches itself to people in the presence of reason—it's something from which I haven't been able to take comfort, not reliably, not since her.

'It's like the smell of burnt toast. You made the toast. You looked forward to it. You even enjoyed making it, but it burned. What were you doing? Was it your fault? It doesn't matter anymore. You open the window but only the very top layer of the smell goes away. The rest remains around you. It's on the walls. You leave the room but it's on your clothes. You change your clothes but it's in your hair. It's on the thin skin on the tops of your hands. And in the morning, it's still there.'

4

Now can you imagine it? I am sitting in a large manicured garden at the back of someone's renovated turn-of-the-century symbol of success. The sun is getting ready to call it a day but it is still quite warm. I think I can see mosquitoes hovering over the edge of the pool. The outdoor furniture is comfortable even if it is some of the ugliest I have seen. The air is still, so it's easy for me not to dwell too much on the prospect of the umbrella dislodging from the table and impaling someone.

This charming young man is eloquently expressing his quite legitimate doubts about the science or discipline that has brought me to him. He seems to have a fairly common and not necessarily unhealthy antagonism towards his petit-bourgeois father, who it appears has a somewhat authoritarian personality. They don't understand each other. They value different things but not different enough for the father's alarm bells to ring hollow with the unemployed aesthete in front of me. It gets to him. But not as much as you do. He's a romantic, focusing on some idealisation of the past. He could have offered me at least an iced tea but I was getting paid and he was, after all, the kind we dream of: one of the incurably worried-well. He was a little melancholic but not completely without some justification. There was no reason this could not go on for years. I thought he was normal, a bit unhappy—pretty much like everyone.

We heard someone walking up the side of the house towards us. Maybe it was more than one person. Suddenly Simon grabbed me, putting his hand over my mouth. He was quite surprisingly strong. There was a hysterical efficiency about him. I thought he was going to kill me. I didn't say a word. He dragged me behind some bushes near the edge of the garden where we both hid. He seemed to know where to hide, as though he had done it before. I was ready to jettison my first impressions of him. I was now convinced he was psychotic. We looked through the bushes at a man, your husband, entering the house with your son through the back door. It was your house.

Simon had meant to show me he was serious about you. He had been to your house many times without anyone ever knowing he was there. Bringing *me* there was his way of demonstrating that he was willing to take me seriously, or at least try. When your husband and Sam were inside, Simon and I crept out. He took me to the Esplanade Hotel in St Kilda, opposite the beach. We went in his car. I had never been there before. We have since been there many times. That first evening was my initiation into Simon's life, the one he has kept hidden from his family. Within an hour I had witnessed a fight, heard a frenetic country singer ('rockabilly grunge' he said it was) and someone had tried to sell him what they promised were amphetamines. I had also been introduced to his friend Angelique.

When you left Simon he was angry with you. There was a tremendous sense of betrayal with the shock of your leaving. He could not understand you not wanting to share a common future in which, together, you would observe the world in all its sad and beautiful guises. The way he describes it, you could have been in different rooms and been able to predict the other's response to something because it would have been your own response. You respected the same things—aesthetically, politically, morally. He felt the two of you were co-conspirators. You wanted the same things and laughed at the same things. But you ultimately needed different things. Simon was a phase. You began to find his optimism, opinions and his touch too predictable and tiresome, stifling. You stopped wearing his t-shirts. You put them back. You pretended to be obtuse. Some nights no one could find you. Where were you? When his father, who never noticed anything, noticed your absence he blamed Simon and then, after a while, so did Simon himself. William was never so warm as he was to you when you had gone, while May would look out on to the street through the venetian blinds as though she was waiting for you. The other sons had gone, all good men too, now with their own silent wives and good jobs, velour-clad children and brand new axes to grind.

Simon tried to find comfort in his reading but one can only turn so many pages before the anaesthetic wears off. He had hoped the two of you could survive and maybe even correct a few of the world's imperfections. Perhaps his romanticism was always his biggest problem. Your inexplicable leaving was literally breathtaking.

William came home from work one night and found Simon speaking out loud to himself in his bedroom. It was nine years ago. At his desk, he was talking to himself. William stood at the door and listened:

> And would it have been worth it, after all . . .
> To say: 'I am Lazarus, come from the dead,
> come back to tell you all'—
> If one, settling a pillow by her head,
> Should say: 'This is not what I meant at all.
> That is not it, at all?'

For a man so obsessed with words and language, it is interesting that Simon remembers perfectly what it was he was memorising that night but not what was said between him and his father which so quickly led William to strike him. He remembers clearly the seconds before the force of his father's hand became a very personal heat in his lip and jaw. They said nothing more about it. He also remembers the breeze of his father's moving hand and the cold of his wedding ring. Not long after, Simon left home. You met your husband at about this time.

5

It was an accepted view for many years that pain avoidance and tension reduction are the major sources of a person's motivation. This was challenged (principally by Maslow) with the suggestion that more meaningful or more subtle conclusions with respect to human motivation could be reached by examining people's strivings for growth, for happiness and satisfaction. To this end, a distinction should be made between a person's *deficit* (or lower) needs and his *growth* (or higher) needs. The *deficit* needs are the more powerful and tend to take priority over the *growth* needs. A starving person will be little concerned at the possibility of other people seeing the lengths to which he may need to stoop in order to eat. However, the identification of a person's higher needs is more revealing. Moreover, any attempt by someone to satisfy his or her higher needs will suggest a state inconsistent with clinical depression. It is only when a person has at least partially satisfied most of the lower needs that he can begin to experience the higher needs and then attempt to gratify them. Such attempts at gratification are very likely to produce tension, but this tension is constructive; it is positive.

Not long after Simon left home, he started teaching. It was his first permanent class. He was so full of enthusiasm for his new life that he sometimes couldn't sleep. He had so many plans for his students and for himself. There was very little communication between him and William although he spoke quite regularly to May. He still thought of you but the pain was not acute. He was contemplating a Master's in either education or English. Education would have helped his career but there was still that unrelieved passion for literature and especially for poetry. He was thinking of writing something on the work of his hero, the literary critic William Empson. You might remember Simon going on about Empson, the author of *Seven Types of Ambiguity*.

Simon has tried to explain to me what is so fantastic about what he calls this landmark in the history of literary criticism (which, incidentally, is also the way it is described on the back of the book), but it's all lost on me. He bought me a copy. To put it simply, or perhaps simplistically, it seemed to be an analysis of the effects a poet may achieve, consciously or not, through the use of ambiguity. I couldn't get through the book. I suspect Simon knows this. As far as I was concerned, there were more important ambiguities than the ambiguity of poetic language that Empson talked about. There's the ambiguity of human relationships, for instance. A relationship between two people, just like a sequence of words, is ambiguous if it is open to different interpretations. And if two people do have differing views about their relationship—I don't just mean about its state, I mean about its very nature—then that difference can affect the entire course of their lives. Interestingly, this is not a subject Simon has ever wanted to talk about despite the number of times I've broached it.

In any event, what was of greater interest to me than Empson's work (everybody's got to make a living somehow) was that he published it at the tender age of twenty-four, and, more particularly, that Simon mentioned this several times. I think this is significant. But of course, as Simon told me, Empson, who was later knighted, had the constant encouragement of his supervisor at Cambridge. William denigrated Simon's efforts and early interest in teaching. His son's love of poetry was a complete anathema to him. No one in the family, with the exception of May when he was a little boy, had ever encouraged Simon. You did for a while, didn't you?

Although the longing didn't stop, he had for a time forgiven himself for whatever it was that he had done to lose you. He had left home and it was impossible to stop him from talking to his friends about his children, as he called his students. He told May and even his brothers all about them, the twenty-two eight year olds in his charge, the noisy ones, the naughty ones, the scraggly ones with one jumper and two shirts, the fast ones in runners, the pretty ones with skinny legs who followed him everywhere and the very quiet ones who still were not used to having been born. There were twenty-two hopes to encourage and foster, little *people* to surprise and delight every day, to teach and to make happy with visits from Empson and, of course, to tell stories to. Can you imagine how they loved the way he told stories, with every word a song?

It did not take long for the parents to come and see who it was that their children were talking about. Naturally, they fell for him too, some of the mothers quite literally. It would often begin with spurious concerns for a child's progress and end in a proposition. Simon delicately rebuffed all such offers. It wasn't that he regarded married women as sacrosanct. (Anyway, they were not all married.) It was more his commitment to the children. They were, each one of them, human beings, not devices for someone's gratification. They were the future, not theirs or his, but everyone's. You don't sully the future, knowingly.

Anyway, as you can imagine, his libido was being satiated elsewhere or, should I say, everywhere else. If one didn't know him, one would call Simon a liar, but everywhere he went, he was almost inundated with propositions from women of all ages and backgrounds, many of which he accepted. He didn't have to do anything. Indeed, it quickly got to the point where he had difficulty telling his friends what he had been doing because an honest account would sound boastful. It seems he got into conversations with women in shops, cafés and even on public transport. There was an exchange of telephone numbers and the rest was usually fairly predictable and not so interesting. It is of interest, however, that he never formed attachments with these women and never permitted them to develop any legitimate expectations as to the future with him. He had a set speech, something like an emotional disclaimer, which he recited beforehand. Of course it did nothing to prevent recriminations on the part of the women, but it enabled him to stake a claim to the high moral ground and, as long as he required this (a higher or *growth* need), he cannot be said to have been clinically depressed. But, of course, it's of concern in itself that he was unable to form close emotional attachments with other women and that he needed the flattery. You remained unreplaced. You wouldn't let him move on. His self-esteem was completely immune to his carnal successes. They had no currency for him that wasn't immediately devalued upon attainment.

It was both the complications from the casual trysts and a certain amount of guilt that led him to Angelique. You would like her. I do. They have been friends for a couple of years now. The night she met his parents and the Osbornes was their first night together. An escapee from a feud with her Lutheran family in Adelaide, she had run away to Melbourne and landed on a one-time school friend whose boyfriend was a part-owner of a nightclub. Together they introduced her to the city's nightlife and when the free drinks and free passes ran out, so did her pride. She met Simon on her first night working the streets. He became a regular client, but it was very much on his terms. He told her that she was never to stay the night, never to call him without him having called her first, and always to accept full payment at the time of her visit, no credit. His conditions were designed to avoid any complications or emotional ambiguity.

Simon discussed you with Angelique from the beginning. The very first time she came to his flat she saw photos of you and said that she thought you were beautiful. She knows all about you, even the story of how your father left his family in Italy to be with your mother. Simon recruited her as he recruited me.

She asked lots of questions about you and about William and May. She knows all about Simon's childhood, his brothers and the family holidays with the Osbornes in Sorrento. She enjoyed hearing about his students from the days before he stopped teaching. Angelique would like to be a mother some day. As you might know by now, she has met Sam. She has met your husband too but, I'm afraid, it wasn't through Simon.

Although perhaps even this, in a funny way, was through Simon. As you would expect, Angelique has had some quite terrifying experiences in the course of her work and, although Simon was trying to prevent any romance or dependency developing between them, he couldn't hide his concern. He eventually convinced her that she would be safer (marginally, in my opinion) if she got off the street and worked in a brothel. I don't know the mechanics of this but I could ask her. It's not important. Presumably one goes for some kind of interview. Maybe the more successful brothels use management consultants like you for this. Excuse me. I don't mean to be flippant. I really don't know. But I did learn, and this I must say surprised me, that some of the more up-market agencies are on retainers to certain corporations, some of them very large. It seems to be a prerequisite for being publicly listed. It is put on the company card like a meal or tickets to the tennis. The brothel she's now attached to services several merchant banks and stockbroking firms. This is how Angelique first met your husband one busy Christmas. I am sorry but I really must tell you everything. It was quite an incredible coincidence without which everything would have happened differently, or perhaps not at all.

6

I won't ask you how much you already know. I don't wish to deal here with the grievances you have against your husband, even the fundamental ones. He is by no means the worst of her clients. This might not surprise you. He is quite expansive. This might. You see, Angelique has no qualms about breaching your husband's confidence and we learn quite a lot more about you from him than we ever could from simply following you.

Of course, Simon did not always follow you. There was a time, a time I have spoken of earlier as a time of forgiveness, when Simon forgave himself for all that he was and all that had happened to him. He was teaching and knew he was good at it. He felt good about himself. Although he tried to fight against it, like most teachers (and parents), Simon had his favourites. Simon's favourite one year was a little boy, small for his age and very quiet. Whenever Simon brought Empson to school, this little boy was always the last to come and play with him. His name was Carlo. He was shy. Although not really disliked, he was too quiet to be popular with the other children and Simon thought he could see the beginning of a life of pain for him. He, perhaps arrogantly, thought he could change this. Simon likes to rescue people whenever he himself is not in need of rescuing. Do you remember?

Carlo's shyness made it difficult for Simon to assess accurately his reading and comprehension skills. He wasn't sure whether Carlo's slow reading was a reflection of poor ability or of his fear of reading out loud. He wanted to know what could have made this little boy so afraid anyway. He arranged for Carlo to stay back after school a couple of days a week. Simon would read to him, children's stories and rhymes. Afterwards Carlo would read back to him. Sometimes he even sang to him. Slowly Carlo was improving. Simon noticed he was even slightly more extroverted with his peers during the day.

Unfortunately, Carlo's story became public knowledge after this. You may not remember his name. Simon had always stayed in the classroom with him until his mother came to pick him up. Carlo's father worked nights and slept during the day. His mother worked in a clothing factory. There were other children in the family, but because of the private tuition Carlo got from Simon, they would leave earlier than Carlo and go home together. Carlo was the only one to be picked up by his mother after work.

One day Carlo's mother was working overtime. She instructed Carlo not to stay late with Simon that day but to leave with the other children. It will always haunt Simon. Carlo didn't leave school with his brothers and sisters but, saying nothing about his mother's overtime, he stayed back as usual with Simon. When they had finished their reading, the two of them went to check on Empson. Carlo wanted to go to the toilet. After about ten minutes, Carlo hadn't returned and Simon thought the little boy might have had an accident and be too embarrassed to come back to the classroom. He gave it another ten minutes or so before starting to look for him. The little boy was not in the toilets or with Empson. Simon could not find him anywhere in the school yard. He ran around calling for him but the whole school was empty. It had never been so empty. As you probably know from the newspapers, he still hasn't been found.

This was the beginning of Simon's decline. He was devastated by the little boy's disappearance. He felt responsible for it. If anything, and you mustn't take this the wrong way, he actually felt a certain relief when Carlo's abduction turned out to be the first of that series of child kidnappings in Melbourne. In addition to the trauma and his sense of guilt, Simon was briefly, you might remember, the subject of some pretty tacky tabloid publicity. The other teachers even began to regard him warily. What had been initially regarded as admirable enthusiasm became an unhealthy pedagogic zeal.

I found him very forthcoming about this whole period. It might have been at only our second or third session that he discussed it with me. I think he was rather hoping that this would be all that he had to tell me. It *was* very important to him, I'm not denying that, but I think he was, in a way, glad he had it to tell me about. Have you ever expatiated on a particular experience to give a new acquaintance the impression of instant intimacy? It is not an uncommon form of flattery.

But I'm not so easily satisfied and Simon is not so easily intimate. In addition to you, and the disappearance of Carlo, he spoke quite readily about his father. It's fashionable. Simon rarely said anything much about May. One day I told him that I *wanted* him to tell me about his mother. He said there wasn't all that much to say. We were at his place, which was not unusual during his housebound, curtain-drawn days, and I insisted that he speak about her for an hour before I would listen to anything else. Simon said I was being ridiculous and that I could leave immediately if that were the case. I ignored him and got us both another beer from the kitchen and started playing with Empson. I gave him his drink and sat down.

Then Simon talked for three hours. I didn't think it would work. My theatrics and feeble threats seldom work. I'm not much of a hypnotist either.

As a child, Simon found what was happening to his mother very frightening. She could at one moment be very loving, gentle and caring and then, seemingly quite suddenly, very angry. Or she would completely shut herself off. She just wasn't available. She would go into her bedroom and stay there. Sometimes Simon would creep in and hide under the bed or in a wardrobe while she was asleep and just watch her, keeping his breathing as low as possible. She would not speak at these times. Her silences could go on for weeks. What happens to a child born to a mother who is depressed?

One woman in four becomes quite seriously depressed in the twelve months following the birth of a baby. But this went on well into Simon's childhood. His brothers always seemed to be outside breaking something or training for some event or else out camping. They were away. Simon was always there. He remembered, and it amazed him to remember, one summer afternoon in Sorrento with the Osbornes. William and May had been arguing fiercely. He doesn't remember what it was about. The older boys were on the beach playing cricket. William had stormed out. Simon had earlier slunk away from the screaming to shelter in his parents' wardrobe. He had fallen asleep there and was awakened sometime later by the sound of May's sobbing and heavy staccato breathing. He peeked through the crack in the door and saw her lying on the bed in her half-opened robe, her face and hair being caressed by Diane Osborne. Did he ever mention this to you?

He is amazed that he could have forgotten this. He remembers not understanding, being very frightened but not being able to take his eyes off his mother and Diane. There was, in that small space, the extreme austerity of an almost empty mind colliding with something sweetly frantic and wrong between the many breaths, and an indifference to what would happen when the breathing was quiet again. After a while, he could hear William coming down the passage. The women were with each other and didn't hear him coming. Simon didn't know what to do. He wasn't supposed to be there. He knew things were in some way wrong but he was unable to speak. He didn't know exactly what was wrong. Wasn't everyone a friend? William pushed open the door and found the women together. He grabbed Diane by her hair, pulled her off the bed and hit them both, May in the mouth and Diane in the stomach, knocking her to the floor. Then he picked her up as though she was a piece of furniture, placed her back on top of his frightened wife, who had fallen back onto the bed, and madly exhorted them to continue.

Simon saw all of this from the crack between the doors before he passed out and everything went black. As he fell to the floor, his body pushed open one of the wardrobe doors. He had always felt vaguely that somehow none of this would have happened had he not fallen asleep in the wardrobe. He wouldn't have seen it, and it would not have happened. He wasn't supposed to be there. It was never mentioned. Surely, he had thought, this was what you did with things that were never supposed to have happened. You don't mention them. Simon was crying when he finished telling me about his mother. Then he asked me another one of those questions I'm never sure I am supposed to be able to answer.

'What is it about men that makes women so lonely?'

7

When a child feels in danger, it will defend itself, hold itself together, possibly withdraw. We do not spring fully grown into the world. We have to develop or create our own sense of self. When we have people around us who threaten us in various ways, perhaps by punishing us or leaving us, abandoning us, then our sense of self can seem to fall apart. That is the greatest, the most terrifying fear. We all experience it to some extent as small children and we grow up trying to defend against this fear. Some of us have to work harder at it than others. People won't talk about it. They think they don't have to and, unless it persists, often they're right.

Simon has tried on several occasions as an adult to reach May. He has done it as much for himself as for her. When the whole business with Carlo happened, Simon went to her. What could she say? A child disappears. It is so obviously a tragedy for those involved. But she couldn't understand the full extent of Simon's involvement. It wasn't so much what she could have said as the fact of her saying it, saying anything. But she hardly said anything that showed even the thinnest empathy, and Simon felt rebuffed. Their relationship continued to consist of polite obligation fulfilment. One Mother's Day he included a poem by Robert Lowell with his traditional card. Not long before this, May had confided to him that, with all her sons grown and gone, she was sometimes quite lonely. She said nothing about her marriage or about William directly but he felt she didn't have to. For Mother's Day he copied out Lowell's 'To Speak of Woe That Is in Marriage' and gave it to her. Do you know it?

> *The hot night makes us keep our bedroom windows open.*
> *Our magnolia blossoms. Life begins to happen.*
> *My hopped up husband drops his home disputes,*
> *and hits the streets to cruise for prostitutes,*
> *free-lancing out along the razor's edge.*
> *This screwball might kill his wife, then take the pledge.*
> *Oh the monotonous meanness of his lust . . .*
> *It's the injustice . . . he is so unjust—*
> *whiskey-blind, swaggering home at five.*
> *My only thought is how to keep alive.*
> *What makes him tick? Each night now I tie*
> *ten dollars and his car key to my thigh . . .*
> *Gored by the climacteric of his want,*
> *he stalls above me like an elephant.*

Of course the parallels are very imperfect. The husband of the poem is almost as much one side of Simon as he is William. But Simon was hoping it might touch her in a way that could clear a new path for some kind of genuine dialogue or exchange. May never referred to it. He regretted giving her the poem. He wondered how she could say nothing about it, even if it was just to say that the husband of the poem was not her husband at all. Simon would even have been heartened by some obvious and dutiful defence of William, some acknowledgement that William did not cruise the streets for prostitutes, that the lust of the poem's husband was not William's.

Simon still has that boyhood reluctance to talk directly, even in a therapeutic situation, about his father's sexuality. I think you might know something about this from Sorrento, from that time at the beach house. Do you? It was towards the end, early one evening. Simon had taken the car to buy a few things before the shops closed. May was in the kitchen. You had just taken a shower. It was almost sunset. Do you remember? You were in the midst of putting on a change of clothes for the evening and you looked out the window to watch the sunset. You were playing with a bracelet Simon had given you. There were problems with the clasp. Were you already planning to leave? Maybe that was what William was wondering as he

19

watched you? The door wasn't completely closed. We know you did not know this. Obviously it was an accident, not an invitation, but it enabled William to watch you there. And through the accident of the open door and the disposition of the light, the silhouettes of both of you were visible to Simon when his car pulled up. He saw you looking out of the window and he saw William watching you; everything was still and no one hurried to see less.

8

In the time I speak of as the time of Simon's decline, there was a change of government. The new government decided to stimulate the economy by terminating the employment of thousands and thousands of teachers. You may remember this. Your husband and William voted for them. Perhaps you did too. Simon was stimulated out of his school. Given the size of the cuts, he would have stood a fair chance of losing his job even had he not stood out within his school. As it was, after Carlo's disappearance, it was a certainty. His unemployment accelerated the decline. There were the bouts of drawn-curtain days in bed. He slept and listened to the street sounds. His friends, who had kept their jobs and were trying to keep their marriages, had nothing in common with Simon anymore. He didn't have the resources to maintain these friendships. They stopped calling. May would call him occasionally but William could no longer bring himself to talk to Simon on a regular basis.

The sounds of his neighbours talking to each other, getting ready for the day, the sounds of their dinner parties where the guests arrived with several bottles and well-rehearsed greetings—these sounds hurt him. How do they know so many people? Can you imagine, there was nowhere Simon had to be at a certain time every day, or any day. There were no *certain* times except those marked by his neighbours' sounds or by the birds announcing the end of another night he'd been unable to sleep.

Things wore out imperceptibly until they broke, one by one: the clothes dryer, a heater, the collar of a shirt. And the neighbours would not shut up. He heard them, always laughing, as his bills came in, reformatted with their new corporate logos, the crowning achievement of micro-economic reform, and looking like invitations to a child's birthday party when they were really the philistine calling cards of the new society; the standard form ones and then later, the threatening ones, threatening to withhold some or other service, or else to commence legal proceedings.

You wouldn't have wanted to see him this way. You don't know anyone like this. Your husband has seen to it. In the morning Simon would add a little milk to the scotch and at first it all seemed ridiculous, staying in bed till anytime, watching TV on the couch. But there was no contrast, no friction, nothing to call for any resistance. Two bowls of cereal and scotch and ice per day can become one bowl, easily, and then just milk, scotch and a sliver of ice before lunch. No one said a thing and it wasn't ridiculous anymore. It became unremarkable and surely that *was* false laughter, forced semi-hysterical laughter coming from next door. He thought about you. He thought of killing the people next door. He wondered whether you would hear that he was out of work? Would *you* ever be out of work? He decided that no matter how bad the economy became, you would never be out of work. When every last management consultant was trying to get work waiting on tables or mopping floors, you would still be many floors up in the city, surrounded by glass, perfectly pleated, going to meetings and making unfounded recommendations. Was he jealous? Certainly he was jealous but more than that, much more than that, he was lonely. He was one of the loneliest people you don't see anymore.

Again, it did not take long for him to blame himself. We spend our time watching things like this happen in other people's lives and attempting to divine what it is they have done to bring it on themselves, what it is that we would never do. So when it happened in his life, Simon was ready to accept that he had brought it on himself but he didn't know how he had done it.

It may be said that, in some sense, we create our own reality through the way we choose to perceive the external world and, like anything that is created or constructed, it can collapse. Does this mean anything to you? You think you are happily married and then you discover that you aren't. Your whole perception of the outside world, as it pertains to you, just suddenly collapses. This is terrifying because our perception of ourselves in the outside world and our sense of self are the same thing. What was Simon in the world but a young man getting older on a couch, without a job, running out of time, running out of scotch, with all the cruelty of unrealised potential, and the bitter aftertaste of misplaced hope. Thus does he walk into furniture at two o'clock in the morning while outside the place next door there is a slamming of car doors and more wild laughter. Will they ever shut up? After a while you don't mess around. No ice. And surely it didn't have to be like this?

I should say that at least in the early days of my association with Simon it was really Angelique who kept him from taking his life. She got involved. She breached the terms of their agreement and he was in no position to enforce it. Angelique would visit him without an appointment, without an invitation. At first he would try to send her away, explaining that she should not take it personally but he could no longer afford to see her. How can anybody not take something personally? As soon as you take it, it's personal. She didn't listen to him. She brought him food and cooked for him. She would ask him to read to her, insisting it was a new deal. He had to read to her in return for her company, no credit. She asked him questions about whatever he was reading to her and in doing this she made him, in a small way, touch his former self. She held him when no one else was even calling.

It might be easy for you to dismiss all of this between them as simply Simon taking advantage of her, using her. But he had gone out of his way to institute those artificial procedures to stop her from falling in love with him, relenting only at her insistence, and so it would be unfair of you to characterise it like that. Whatever blindness or timely self-deceptions led you into your husband's arms, you did not find yourself completely without hope of anything in your life ever changing for the better, and still you chose him or allowed yourself to be chosen by him. Your membership of society was never under any kind of review and you never opened a newspaper to find the quintessence of your despair seasonally adjusted. Look at what was denied to him: love and work. It is asking a lot of a person to maintain a healthy self-esteem in the absence of both of these. And if his self-esteem is gone, how can you expect him to muster any reserves with which to make what are, after all, fairly subtle moral judgments, and then to act on them, harming himself, perhaps fatally?

The period in a person's middle years between, say, twenty-five and forty-five, is usually the period of greatest productivity. It is then one establishes oneself in a vocation, brings up a family and creates a reputation in the community. The ability to work effectively, along with the ability to love, of course, is a sure mark of maturity but Simon was living part of these prime productive years at a time when society denied him the opportunity to work in his chosen vocation, chosen, it must be said, with the most noble of intentions and in the face of his father's profound derision. So, yes, he permitted her to cook for him and to hold him, to take him for walks. He never permitted himself to tell her the lie she wanted to hear more than any poetry or prose. Despite this, she kept him going anyway, single-handedly, at least until I earned his trust.

One afternoon in bed, after a walk, she asked him how he could be so sure that he did not love her. Was she brave or stupid, do you think? Can you imagine you asking a question like that? Simon said that he *did* love her and that she should know it, but that he was not *in* love with her. You can forgive her, under the circumstances, for thinking he was off on another semantic frolic of his own. If he hadn't been so forthcoming she might have taken comfort in the ambiguity.

'In spite of all that I unfortunately am now, or more accurately all that I am not, I am still far too cautious, too careful with you, to be in love with you. That's how I know, I suppose,' he told her.

'You know you're in love with somebody when you wake up next to them, comfortable despite your breath smelling like week-old water at the bottom of a vase, when you are terribly excited to see them, to talk to them again, having missed them after all that sleep. You can fall out of bed into the shower and, still comfortable, burp or even fart while trying out various keys in which to sing the theme to a Peter Greenaway movie that you both hated and have never seen.'

When she asked who Peter Greenaway was, he could only say 'Yes' more or less to the ceiling and run his fingers through her hair, all the way along her face and down until he had to alter his position in the bed. He would probably agree now that she saved his life. She loved him unconditionally and there is nothing more sustaining than that. But for her there was nothing more dangerous. She was there for him no matter what he did and you were never there anymore, no matter what he did.

All his warnings and strategies did nothing to protect her from falling in love with what was really just his *need*, and his diminished responsibility only exacerbated his diminished sensitivity to her feelings. If I have been starving I am in no fit state to consider the needs of the hand that feeds me unconditionally and forewarned. Maybe Angelique needed to save his life but she could have done without much of the rest. Simon will admit this. I know her well now too and we are agreed; with her strength, all her vitality and that mix of almost naive optimism in spite of all she has seen and experienced, she is really a very special woman. Your husband would agree. I don't doubt it. He has taken great comfort from her.

She actually loves Simon to the point where she can become incredibly frustrated that she lacks the eloquence to express it. She makes a lot of money now, working for this up-market brothel. It's aimed at the corporate sector. Men like your husband unwind in her company and with her assistance. They pay her to dress in a manner that doesn't shame them and to undress in a manner that does. She would certainly be earning more than me now, but that's not terribly hard. Please don't underestimate her. She wants to get out of it too. She wants to be, of all things, an e-commerce entrepreneur when the market picks up, and a mother. She wants to be a mother when the market picks up! She's talked to Simon about having a child with him. Don't laugh. Whatever vestiges of middle-class sensibilities have stayed with Simon, and there are many, it is not these that keep him from Angelique. It is you, the myth of you. So please, don't laugh at him or at Angelique. You have, perhaps, become shy around empathy. It makes you uncomfortable now. You can live without it in the elaborately designed artifice that surrounds the swimming pool Simon and I have sat by. You do really live without it. Perhaps people ought to feel with more imagination.

Even before I had started getting through to him, Angelique had got him out of bed, out of his room. They went for long walks together, often taking Empson. They would talk about you. She told him everything that happened to her, everything your husband said. Simon's reactions varied. She could even make him laugh. After a while he was getting out on his own sometimes, shopping a little for basic food supplies or just walking around with Empson. Sometimes he would catch a train and stay on it for a couple of hours, reading or looking out of the window. You must understand how positive this was under the circumstances.

9

The circumstances and under them: he was in a shopping centre, walking by himself, when he saw you and Sam. It was afternoon. He had never seen Sam. You had just picked him up from school and the two of you went into the jeweller's on the corner. It is unlikely things would have turned out the way they have had it not been for his chance sighting of you and Sam that afternoon. Had *you* seen *him* things might have gone differently. But you didn't and this was no coincidence. He didn't want you to see him. From Sam's school uniform Simon could work out the school Sam went to and he figured that you must live in the area to be shopping there and sending your son to a local school.

He crossed the street and looked through the window from the side street. You were explaining something to the jeweller. Sam was turning a mobile watch display. It was taller than him. Given that Simon was afraid of you seeing him, he was undoubtedly taking an unnecessary risk in looking through that window. But it was a calculated risk. He was fascinated to see you, as an adult woman, a professional woman in a suit being served by the jeweller while your little boy played with whatever was on hand. For Simon time had stood still. He had heard that you had a little boy and had wondered what he would be like. What would he look like? His curiosity gave way to a kind of excitement.

Does it sound funny? Looking through the window from the side street as you handed the jeweller your bracelet for him to examine, Simon watched you looking at your son. He was pleased to see you both together like that. The little boy came to you with something in his hand from the display, a watch. You gently admonished him and told him to put it back, all seemingly without sound in that darkened little corner shop. When Sam had done as you asked, you ran your fingers slowly through his hair and Simon thought that it must have felt good to Sam, to have done the right thing, to have known what to do and to have been able to do whatever would elicit even the briefest manifestation of your affection for him.

The jeweller took his time examining the bracelet under a lamp on the counter. He took what looked to Simon like a tiny screwdriver and began playing with the clasp on the bracelet, Simon's bracelet, the bracelet he had bought for you from this very jeweller years before. You still wear it. You can imagine the effect on him when he realised this. He was desperate enough to take something like this as a kind of omen. Maybe this strikes you as sad? Perhaps it *is* sad but before you close your eyes to him, I ask you to remember the last time you took something as an omen or saw something as a metaphor for something else. You can't remember, it was a long time ago? But you *are* functioning, aren't you? You're never in any danger. He took you, that elegant woman he saw in the jeweller's with her little boy, as hope, for him, for everyone. Sam was the future and here was the future looking to you for warmth and for guidance. If he put the watch back in the display cabinet, there would be no uncertainty about your response. He was loved unconditionally and, at least when you were with him, he knew it, it showed. Simon knew where you had come from and it filled him with hope that you and your young son could look the way you did now. After all, weren't you born together, you and Simon, back in your early twenties, summoning up all that you could from the first two decades or so of games and rehearsals before finally inventing yourselves as adults in each other's image?

You left the bracelet with the jeweller along with your name and telephone number. Sam wanted an ice-cream. We don't know whether he got it. Simon remained undiscovered. But you were fortuitously rediscovered, halo intact. I told you that you would love the way he sees you. Are you going to tell me you don't understand any of this?

Angelique said you were cold. Simon wouldn't have it.

'You wouldn't say that if you'd seen her,' he said, pouring them both a drink. 'You're just going on her husband's need to rationalise his own behaviour. His infidelity needs a perception of coldness in her almost as much as it needs you. And the little boy, you should see the way she is with him, and the way he looks at her.'

'Sam, that's his name,' she said, unimpressed.

'Does he talk about the little boy?'

'Not much,' she said.

'You've never said he's said anything about him.'

'He hasn't said much about him. Think about the circumstances in which I see him. He's hardly going to bring out snaps of his family.'

'But he has said *something* about him to you, apart from merely that he has a son and that his name is Sam. You told me.'

'He's six and very bright. Takes after her. He admits this,' she said matter-of-factly.

'Well, he certainly looks like his mother.'

'Simon, you saw him for a moment through the window of a darkened shop. You don't know what he looks like. You wouldn't recognise him in a group of kids.'

He's right though, isn't he? Sam *does* look like you. We know this now. He's a very calm little boy, calm but inquiring, always investigating. Were you like this as a child? I suspect you were. Somewhere along the way, we lose our curiosity until we accept and then expect that we don't know, that we cannot really explain very much at all. Just as he idealised you, Simon idealised your son and this is where it starts. Well, this is where the recent chronology starts, the one that leads me to you.

Simon began walking to your son's school in time for lunch, not always, but often, just to watch him while he played. He didn't do it every day. He wasn't able to. The downward mood swings led him back to his bed. The near euphoria he experienced seeing you by chance in the jeweller's was soon met with waves of an equal and opposite mood. A pedestal always doubles as a measure of sorts. If you invented your adult selves together, that is to say, if you were in some sense born at the same time, why was he following you and your son in this pathological way, humiliating himself to himself and, potentially, to you. What if you did see him one day? How could he explain himself, all that he had become? Would you blame him for it? What would he do if you looked at him with horror in your eyes? The papers tell it every day, there's no work anywhere and, anyway, teachers are just leeches on the public purse. Right? What if you bought this line too? You dress as though you do. Forgive me. I don't mean to be insulting. I simply want you to see yourself as he sees you.

If you weren't inspiring him, intriguing him and getting him up out of bed, you were destroying him, holding up to him the cruellest double-sided mirror imaginable. On one side there was the Simon as he was when you knew him, with all his promise—and on the other side, a stagnating man with a sorry taste for late liquid breakfasts.

On those days when one of us got him out, he often went to see Sam. There is a definite calm about Sam. Simon keeps coming back to this. Sam is very comfortable with himself and this probably enhances his attractiveness to other children. At an age when boys are either trying to outdo each other, trying to be the boss of the game or else simply content merely to be included, it is extremely rare for the sheer presence of a little boy to have such an effect on the others as to have them nominate him their leader. But this has happened. Simon has seen it.

From just outside the school ground he saw some little boys attempt to arrest the natural chaos that threatened their enjoyment of a football. A boy, taller than the others, talked above the rest. Perhaps he owned the ball. He jumped excitedly as he spoke so that he seemed even taller than he was. He ignited the collective imagination with an idea. It must have seemed inspired: leave everything up to Sam. Soon most of the other little voices were nominating Sam for captain too. Sam, Sam. The way Simon tells it, they didn't fully understand the concept of a captain in the context of sport since they chose only one. He was to be the captain of both teams. They were crudely electing someone to organise them, to make the rules governing the use of the ball. They chose Sam as their captain. Why? It wasn't even his ball.

He is a handsome and capable little boy, not the fastest nor the tallest, nor even the smartest, but he is still tall, fast and smart. But more than this, he is quietly assured and very curious about the world around him. He likes to be able to make sense of things and, usually, he can. He is used to experiencing what he expects to experience. He has received more than the usual positive reinforcement from his teacher and from you and your husband, albeit all of you variously motivated. Simon attributes Sam's balance and calm to you. He said that the combination in Sam of an absence of both fear and arrogance is what marks him clearly as your son. You see how he remembers you? I told you. There is so much to be learnt about someone from the little they remember and label 'the past'.

You have heard Sam read. You must have. Does anything strike you? Not about his reading; he reads well. Does anything strike you about *what* he is reading, about its content? If you pick up the thin volumes from which children are taught to read, you will see short, simple sentences such as: 'Tom can run. Tom can jump. Run Tom run. Jump Tom jump.'

Think about this: the act of learning to read. A child is being made, almost certainly to some extent against his or her will, to sit still, pay attention and to concentrate on the symbols, the letters. The teacher, if at all successful, will have stimulated a certain curiosity in the child, the satisfaction of which both requires and is the reward for his unnatural stillness. What does the child feel if he or she is obedient? What does he or she learn from the discomfort of the stillness and the concentration? Tom can run but he can't. Run, Tom, run. He has to feel discomfort in order to hear of someone else's good fortune. The words describe Tom being told to do something pleasurable, which the young reader is being denied permission to do by the teacher.

Simon describes this as the first dichotomy in a child's education, the dichotomy between that which is *taught* as good or right and that which the child actually knows to be true in his or her experience. Of course, for a highly motivated child like Sam, this is hardly a problem. The praise he receives merely for the mechanical act of deciphering the symbols makes the effort worthwhile. But surely, after a while, he will have to become self-motivated. One hopes his curiosity will be enough to keep him going. One day the praise won't be there.

Simon identifies another problem with these readers or primers, as they used to be called. In the socialisation of a child, the first people with whom he or she must learn to interact are the mother and father. Shouldn't it be the case then that these texts present realistic scenarios encouraging legitimate expectations of parents in the child? What does the young reader get? There are never even the slightest differences between the parents. They never disagree. A child will know soon enough that something is wrong somewhere. There are two logically attractive alternatives. Either the stories are not true to life or else there is something wrong with the child's parents. In either case the difficult act of reading has let the child down; it was not worth it. The child was conned.

It is also one of the earliest sources of myth, the myth of eternal parental availability. Mother is always there. She is never preoccupied. She has no job and no desire for one. Her role is a cross between that of God and a slave. She is never tired, never suspects her husband and never thinks that another man might just bring back the zest she knew briefly, a little boy's lifetime ago before Tom could run. She sees Tom run but he sees nothing and, you see, there's another lie.

Of course, nobody can always be there for a child. We have to leave them just to provide for them and—maybe even to sneak in some sort of a life for ourselves. Please believe me, I am not being critical. If you can afford it and your housekeeper is good with children or not bad with them, even Simon wouldn't criticise you for taking some time for yourself. But, of course, it wasn't Simon or me that you were worried about.

10

Your husband doesn't always get told the whole truth. But Simon doesn't hold that against you either. It's just that gradually he has been gaining the impression that you have invoked Sam as a device for gaining some kind of secret autonomy from your husband. Simon's concern is that Sam is not benefiting from this. I'm sure you've rationalised this to some extent. Don't tell me. It goes along these lines: if *you* are happier this will somehow trickle down to Sam and maybe even to your husband; the *trickle down* theory. Well, of course it sounds foolish once it's actually articulated. Simon didn't know exactly what you were doing on those days when your sister, your mother or housekeeper was picking up Sam from school. He couldn't be in two places at once so he stayed near Sam, knowing that, sooner or later, you would return to him, smiling as though, *and* because, whatever had just happened had not happened.

But you don't need my doubtful insights to see the possible consequences of leaving Sam with others. Your housekeeper picked him up from school one day. They walked home. Sam was sucking on a frozen Sunnyboy she had bought for him. Do you remember Sunnyboys? Simon does. It was a hot day and he walked slowly, kicking cans and stones as he went, whatever was in his way. It takes longer to get from A to B if you do this and by the time they had reached your house at the end of this particularly hot day, your housekeeper was just barely managing to hang on to her patience. Perhaps you have never seen her in this state. You should never hire somebody just because they smell like Johnson & Johnson's baby powder. She told him to finish the Sunnyboy outside. It was melting and Sam was already sticky. He was really a bit of a mess with the sticky liquid on his hands and down the front of his school shirt.

When he was finished he carefully put the empty Sunnyboy wrapper on the grass near the edge of the pool and began kicking a plastic ball around the back garden by himself, back and forth. Simon felt tired just watching him. His energy seemed limitless, even in the heat. He kicked the ball from one end of the garden to the other and across, meeting it at the other end. He was puffing but showed no sign of stopping or even slowing down until, perhaps inevitably, the ball landed in the water. The momentum of the last kick took it away from the edge of the pool. He couldn't reach it.

It was obvious to Simon that Sam had been thoroughly warned about the dangers of going in the pool without the supervision of an adult. He was by no means a timid boy but, nevertheless, throwing off his clothes and retrieving the ball from the water himself was clearly not an option. He became increasingly frustrated. There didn't seem to be anything around that he could use to reach the ball even just to tap it to the edge. He called to the housekeeper but she was in the kitchen preparing dinner. The sliding door was closed and she had the radio turned up. The music and the smell of onions frying poured out of an open window. Sam, almost crying in frustration, leaned over the edge and paddled the water with his hands to create a current. The ball began to move but it moved away from him so he ran to the other side of the pool and began the same scooping motion from there. He had created a current strong enough to start sending the ball against the earlier current and back again. He began to work faster with his hands, impatient for his ingenuity to reward him. The radio played Roy Orbison. Sam was still calling your house-keeper's name, angry with her, working furiously and breathing hard. The ball was nearing the other side.

Was it 'Only the Lonely'? The repetition of her name, the heavy breathing and the angry little splashes of his paddling in the water gave way to a new fury of hands flat against the surface of the water, slapping the water. It was like this. He was in. He fell. His school shoes were certainly heavy on him. He swallowed in fear, in terror, until the water surrounded him, inside and out. He had never known such distilled terror. Do you tell her what to cook each night in advance or is it ad hoc? Does she have a general idea of what's required? She's to prepare dinner and leave Sam alone to grow up—a separate person—like you, sink or swim. Only the lonely could know the way I feel. The onions were frying. She's at the fridge. She's somewhere. Where are *you* while your son is drowning in one of those tangible manifestations of the medieval bargain struck between your husband's accountant and your parents' ambitions for you?

He holds Sam upside down by his legs with one hand. He beats him on the back with the other hand. Nothing is happening. He beats him harder. The water comes out in spasms like projectile vomit. There is the faintest orange tinge to it. It keeps coming. Simon lays him down on his back. He wipes his mouth. Anything. In panic, he tries mouth-to mouth but he doesn't know how.

Even if his estimate was inaccurate, it would still be interesting to know how long Simon *thinks* he waited before pulling Sam from the pool. Can you imagine him behind those trees in your garden? Initially frightened that the ball is going to lead Sam to find him, he watches Sam's frustration with the ball and with your housekeeper. He sees the splash, or maybe just hears it, but he has no idea whether Sam can swim. He has no idea, from his vantage point behind the trees, whether your housekeeper has been watching, constantly, intermittently, or at all. His own absurdity stings him in those inert moments between the thought that perhaps your son was drowning in front of him despite his own stretching, pulling and gripping movements to reintroduce oxygen to the boy's lungs. However long Simon waited, it was long enough for it to dawn on him that Sam's rescue was not inevitable. Nobody knew Simon was there. If he had not been there, what then? Would Sam have died? And what about you and your husband?

He had Sam lying on his back with his head tilted back. He had breathed into his mouth. Sam was very quiet. He looked up into

Simon's eyes. He calmed very quickly, exhausted. Simon stroked his forehead and looked down into his eyes. He made some soothing sounds, they may not have been words, and found the parting in Sam's hair with his fingers.

'Lucky your mum had asked me to have a look at the garden, my friend, or we don't know where we'd be. You're a bit of a tiger, aren't you?'

Sam looked up at him. Simon didn't think he had understood him but it didn't matter. The terror was going from his eyes and the sun was just beginning to dry his hair. They were your eyes. There was another song on the radio. Sam seemed about to cry. Something must have been added to the onions or they would have burnt by then. There was a fresh sizzling of something from the kitchen, something with a lot of moisture in it.

'It's alright, just a big fright, that's all. You'll be alright, won't you, Sam?'

'Yes,' he said quietly.

'Mum will be home soon.'

'Why are *you* here?' Sam asked.

'I'm here . . . for the garden.' He combed the boy's hair with a gentle rhythm. 'You can cry if you want to, Sam. It might be a good idea.'

He kissed the boy's forehead and left the garden.

I am sure you are thinking several things. There is no need for you to be feeling guilty about this, if you are. Sam was alright. If you are feeling guilty, I would ask you to put it aside for now. Maybe there is a time for it but not now. Angelique almost convinced Simon to be angry with you. That says a lot about her, wouldn't you say? She thinks she'll handle her affairs differently when, having made it as an entrepreneur, she becomes a mother. I shouldn't be flippant but sometimes I am amused by the transparency of people's motives. Anyway, there's something noble, isn't there, in planning to protect your unconceived child from swimming pools? No, she wasn't just talking about swimming pools. Simon said that she was almost able to convince him to be angry with you because she spoke as an expert, about abandonment, the first signs of it.

Have you ever taken a train at eleven o'clock on a weekday morning, a suburban train, and travelled for three hours, only to return to the station you got on at? You have not, by all accounts, shivered with cold and self-loathing on a warm day, or looked out the window of a train and wished the tunnel would never end. Have you ever affected a microscopic examination of the pattern on your automatic teller machine card while you waited for the woman at the bank to confirm your closing balance?

Simon was shaken after the swimming pool afternoon. Although he had rescued Sam, he periodically felt somehow an accomplice of sorts. No, I can't readily provide an explanation for this, not one that wouldn't cause you to cast a truckload of aspersions on my particular version of a trade. He felt what is felt by many witnesses to accidents or traumatic events. Was there something he could have done? But what makes this so difficult to understand is that he did the very thing, the *only* thing, that stood between Sam and disaster. So, in what way could he possibly have been an accomplice?

It frightened him. His drinking picked up again. He didn't shave, couldn't sleep, kept irregular hours, generally approximated clinical depression. Perhaps it was in part the thought that, after all these years, he might have re-entered your life one hot day as the man inexplicably holding your drowned son. He's made much of the heat of that day when we've discussed it. I tried to find out more about this 'accomplice's guilt'. He would not always acknowledge it, changing his story. I asked him on these *denying* days why his drinking had picked up so much. He said it was a hot summer. It was. I remember. Simon had been out of work for some time by then. He said he found the heat humiliating.

Were you ever a silly girl with your head full only of laughter and serious boys who visited your attention with their stern adolescent dumbness? Try to remember. It would have been before you decided to choose between various styles and ideologies, and well before you chose to stop choosing. You see, if you are now the finely honed product of all those years of choosing, what were you before this, before choice? Can you remember how old you were when you ceased to be a tabula rasa? Maybe not precisely, but there had to have been a time before the choice, the choice to speak in a certain tone, to mix a kind of polite forthrightness with a certain reticence.

It would have been some time in early adolescence. Something, some event you may not even remember at first, would have launched you into the orbit of choice that led you to be the person you are now. Perhaps you were greatly impressed by something you saw or someone you knew, something you felt? Was there a vaccine, some ampoule of humiliation, that immunised you against whatever it was that the girl no one chose to sit next to was riddled with? Do you remember when Sam began to define himself?

When did Sam start coming home with notes from his teacher and poor results? I caution you against putting too much store on the academic achievement of such a young child. It's far too early for ominous predictions, no matter what some of my colleagues may say. It's the reports of the change in attitude that I would want to remind you of and, insofar as the change in his academic results (if his school progress can be called that) is important at all, it is not the results but the change itself. He was (and is) clearly a bright little boy. He used to do well most of the time. By this I mean he was attentive and picked things up quickly. He was well liked by the teachers and the other children. Then, quite suddenly, he was *failing* most of the time with only the occasional mediocre mark in maths and spelling. He stopped picking things up, he lost attention quickly. Why did he decide to fail? I am suggesting that it was almost a conscious decision, as rational as any decision you or your husband might make. I would hazard a couple of explanations, both of them perhaps equally obvious.

To learn means to grow up (as Bettelheim tells us). If a child stops learning he can, in some way, retard his growing up. Why would he wish to do this? Many children see growing up as the incremental discarding of their mother and of the need to *be* mothered. Why did Sam find himself craving you again like a very small child? This was the boy others chose to organise the game, a quietly industrious little boy running on his own success. Suddenly he is disruptive, he is failing. Why? What is he feeling?

The decision to fail is often made in the pursuit of attention. It's a kind of depression in a way too (and don't tell me children can't be depressed, or have you forgotten everything?). There is some anger that he is internalising. He hurts you by hurting himself and, if he hurts himself sufficiently, surely you will notice. I am broken. Look. Can you bear it?

It is probably clear to you by now that I do not provide Simon with much in the way of what might commonly be thought of as advice. It's not my role, not professionally, despite the popular view.

I can't do it anyway, not even as his friend. His thoughts come faster than my wisdom. I am hoping that I can't be blamed for this. Angelique can be judgmental. Most people can. My position has always been that the mere provision of a sounding board must be of some help. Simon has trusted me from quite early on. We have never experienced what psychiatrists call transference, where the patient transfers a particular emotional reaction, positive or negative, to somebody in his earlier life to the therapist. Perhaps it is the opposite, some sort of reverse transference. I wanted *him* to like *me*, not for his treatment—well, not only.

In some way, I suppose I tried to guide him, but gently; he is able to resist. What is there to resist, my occasional sporadic outbursts of benevolent common sense? Of course, he needed more than this. He was already hiding behind your husband's trees long before William ever called me. I didn't try to stop him when I found out about it. That is true. But I didn't know he planned yet another visit to that jewellery store on the corner. How could I know that?

What was he thinking? Yes, that is supposed to be where I come in. Clearly, I don't know everything. Knowing everything is not my area. It isn't even supposed to be. I don't know why you left him nine or so years ago. He doesn't know. We speculate. Some of at least one of my children's education has been paid for from the proceeds of speculating why you left him. He said it was sudden. But there's no other way to leave someone, is there? You are always with them right up until you're not. Yes, William's been paying for this wisdom. And he's supposed to be shrewd in matters fiscal.

How could I know Simon planned to return to your corner jeweller, let alone what would follow? He wanted to see the bracelet, to touch it, as though it was an abiding and tangible manifestation of the link between the two of you nine years ago and now. Maybe it is. Why do you wear it? It's old and inexpensive with a clasp that you can't rely on. I am sure your husband would have courted you with much better pieces. But you wear it and when it breaks you take it to an elderly man with an accent in a corner shop and he makes promises to you for which you pay, willingly.

Does the bracelet remind you of Simon or of the person you were when you were with him? Perhaps you just like the bracelet, simple as that. You haven't been one for hanging on to things that are no use to you. Somewhere between my wife's place and my rooms there's a wall on which someone has painted: 'Nostalgia isn't what it used to be!' We are in heated agreement.

Even remembering his obsession, I don't know quite what he had in mind nor whether he had anything in mind. What would he have achieved by paying for the repairs to the bracelet and then depositing it secretly in, for instance, your letterbox? He doesn't know either, but this is not what happened anyway. When he went to the shop and enquired after the bracelet, the jeweller told him that it had been picked up. Simon was a little embarrassed and said that he hadn't realised you had already picked it up. But the jeweller told him, with old-world European discretion, that it was not you but a gentleman. Simon feigned a familiarity with your husband, even describing him to the increasingly uncomfortable jeweller but, no, it was another gentleman.

Simon was so taken aback that he momentarily forgot himself and cross-examined the old jeweller as to what the hell you thought you were doing. The jeweller apologised, either on your behalf or, most likely, on his own behalf for giving this well-spoken young man news that so obviously distressed him.

Another gentleman. Nothing either Angelique or I could have said about you could have made the dent in your pedestal that the jeweller made with these words. For a while, it was all Simon would talk about. Angelique found him either expansive about it in a pseudo-scientific way or else steeped in a familiar melancholic reflection about whether or not you were seeing another man and, if so, why. Would you leave your husband for him and to what extent were your decisions informed by considerations of Sam's interests? Was it simply that he felt he had a grip on the concept of your husband, who he was, and that, in some sense, he even had his measure? A new man might threaten the order of things even if that order had been dysfunctional. Yes, but I think it was more. There was a quite genuine concern for Sam. Was it better for him to grow up with dissatisfied parents in a sterile marriage, with or without infidelity (the fate of most of us), or with separated parents and all the attendant problems (the fate of the rest of us), but in an atmosphere not without a modicum of hope for the future?

As always, I tried to discuss the absurd with him with the utmost seriousness. It's not absurd to imagine that you are having, have had or are about to have an affair, nor even, in spite of your husband's wealth, your lifestyle, your child and the sheer bother of it all, that you would some day leave your husband. What *is* absurd, I thought, was that Simon should imagine that he had some say in all this, some control. Most of us have to fight to gain some control over our *own* lives and here is Simon, for whom it is sometimes too much to shave, to wash his clothes, to feed himself or to walk his dog, contemplating whether a woman with whom he has had no involvement for nearly a decade should or should not stay in her marriage. I don't laugh. I have never laughed. That's how we know I'm professional.

And isn't it interesting to see how bourgeois he is? For all his rejection of his parents and their rejection of him, he is at one with them in thinking there is something intrinsically sacred about marriage, even a sterile marriage, one in which the husband gets more warmth from the prostitute he visits regularly than from his wife, one in which the wife has been too successful in utterly repudiating everything she used to be before she managed to get everything her parents had taught her she would ever want. And Sam. Simon is angry at the possibility that Sam might, in some sense, be abandoned as a consequence of your attempt to mitigate the damage of a hasty decision to marry a man as remote from Simon as you are now.

12

This, Simon told me, is what happened when Angelique walked in to his flat one afternoon. The door was open and she found Simon sitting on his couch with the customary glass of scotch, listening to music and reading. At first she just stood there looking at him. Empson was asleep.

'Is this it? Are you just going to sit here for the rest of your life listening to Stephen Cummings and getting yourself shitfaced?'

'I've got some Leonard Cohen somewhere around here.'

'Simon, okay, you *don't* have a job. It's not the end of the world. You sit around here drinking in this . . . museum, or . . . shrine you've built to an ex-girlfriend. That's all she is. Everyone's got them and everyone's out of work.'

'What's your problem today?' he interrupted.

'I don't have a problem. I've got plans instead. If I'm not happy with things I try to change them. Isn't that what you'd tell me to do?'

She stood with her hands on her hips.

'I never tell you what to do.'

'Well, that's bullshit for a start. You gave me all these *instructions* when I first started seeing you, how I wasn't to call you without you calling me first and all the rest of it.'

'You didn't listen to me,' he said.

'No, of course not. Who would listen to you? You're a boring old smartarse with an alcohol problem and a thing for a yuppie girl you haven't spoken to for ten years. You're pathetic, Simon!'

'Why do you visit me, Angel?'

She sat on the edge of the couch and took a sip of his drink. 'I like your dog.'

She patted Empson, refilled Simon's glass and drank from it. Then she moved closer. 'And despite all this, I still think you're beautiful . . . and you're funny.'

Simon put his arm around her.

'Funny! In what way funny?' he asked.

'You make me laugh. And you create things out of nothing. With just . . . words. You're entertaining and . . .' she gestured to the room around her, 'it's like a place I can escape to. You give me advice.'

'Yes, now is a very good time to get into property.'

She put the palm of her hand to his cheek. 'Simon! Look at you.'

'Wouldn't get much for me in my present state, I'll grant you.'

'You've got to start looking after yourself. You've really got to get some kind of life, get out more, drink less, eat better.'

'Now just a minute. I won't have a thing said against your cooking.'

'Simon, I'm being serious.'

He kissed her.

'Are you staying for dinner, Angel?'

'No. I'm on tonight.'

'Anyone I know? Or everyone I know?'

She got up. 'It's your favourite client, among others. You know, I think he suspects.'

'Suspects what?' Simon asked.

'I think he suspects she's seeing someone else.'

He stood up. 'What makes you say that? You haven't said anything, have you? Jesus, you haven't said anything?'

'You know she doesn't want any more children?'

'How do you know that?' he asked.

'He told me. How else would I know?'

'I can't *believe* the things he tells you!'

'Yeah, scandalous, isn't it?' she said, taking another sip.

'Well, it's not that it's private, hell, it's *all* private . . . but it's irrelevant.'

'Irrelevant! Irrelevant to what?'

'How the hell can he screw you talking about his wife and child?'

'I've told you. It's not all that crap you see in the movies. I don't

38

dress up in a uniform or any shit like that. Well, not for him. He's just one of those guys who spends every day talking nonstop about things that don't matter to people he doesn't like or people he's afraid of. He knows he can say anything to me. It's pretty common with the regulars. It's all part of it.'

Simon wasn't listening. 'He'll be another "only child"—lonely,' he said, pouring another drink.

'Who?'

'Sam.'

'Yes, an only child in a broken home.'

'A "broken home"—what's that, Angel? It's just a cliché. Anyway, she won't leave him. She knows when she's on a good thing.'

'He doesn't think so. He thinks she'll have an affair.'

'For Christ's sake, what do you two do—undress each other very slowly so there's time enough to speculate on *her* fidelity? I hope you charge him extra for the analysis.'

She ignored him and spoke very deliberately. 'He told me he thinks there's someone else. She's going away next week to some conference or convention or something.'

'Oh he's crazy, paranoid. He's really crazy. You're both crazy. People go away to conventions all the time. Even teachers do these days, or used to. He's just trying to assuage his guilt, or maybe it turns him on talking about it with you.'

'Simon, will you relax. So what if she's going away with someone? It's *his* problem not yours.'

'This is just part of the shit he spins you, Angel. You don't believe it?'

She stood up and met his eyes. 'He said he'd leave her if she's seeing someone else.'

Simon realises that maybe the penny has dropped for your husband—that your marriage is in trouble and that you've just found out. What kind of man is he? Will he try to save it or will he put on a brave face? Is putting on a brave face the only way he thinks he can save it? Or will he leave you?

Bravery. For better or for worse, men usually give it up after adolescence. Well, it's not really bravery at all, is it? It's a kind of childish pride that we, as a society, tend to idealise. We imbue our screen heroes with it, this 'cool'. And isn't it seductive—this apparent absence of vulnerability? It works. Don't women want to be desired by someone who doesn't feel pain, who isn't afraid?

But it's an act. Anybody who doesn't want or need something is dead. And anyone who does need something can be hurt. They can be afraid. We teach men this act, to perform it all the time. And subsequent to their emancipation, women now have to pretend too. But your husband is so well conditioned he's not aware it's an act. He's been doing it all his life. That's how he attracted you in the first place and, after years of marriage to you, he's still playing invulnerable. But is he right to? Is the only truly happy marriage one of detachment and respect? Your husband needs you so badly that he won't talk to you in the hope that you'll respect him all the more for his silence. What if he did talk to you? What if he told you the truth? He sometimes cries in the cinema and he flirts with the fifteen-year-old girl at the dry-cleaner's? He thinks the men that service his car break some new part every chance they get. When he can't open a window in your house at the first attempt, he contemplates his mortality. He regrets opening a joint account with you. He wants you to watch him when your sister is around. He's not totally comfortable with the fact that your father is Italian. His eyebrows displease him, they always have and, on the rare occasions that it's relevant, sometimes he hastily stimulates himself secretly in the bathroom before going to bed with you so that he might stay the course for you.

It's hard to be certain exactly where Angelique's fondness for your husband stops and her desire to taunt Simon with him starts. She is certainly fond of him. He makes her feel needed with his confessions and, as you can see, because of his confessions, Simon also makes her feel needed. For as long as Simon is obsessed with you, there will always be a place where your husband will be welcome. But if Simon was well, if he had a job, if he could forget about you and rejoin the nine to five rate-paying dinner party guests, the commuters, the opinion-polled, if he was somebody's target market—where would Angelique and your husband be? And where would you be? Where will you be if you do leave him? Will Sam finally catch a first glimpse of some exhausted rapprochement between you and your by then ex-husband at his twenty-first birthday, just before the speeches when, as you stand together, you look honestly at this man with a shame you could never bear to put into words, a shame that only hindsight can deliver? And in the light of what your husband has become since you left him, in the light of his fall, will you regret your inability to say, 'I'm sorry I was not there to catch you'?

The need or striving for a sense of control is generally considered healthy. People's behaviour is often determined, to a large extent, by the amount of personal control the individual believes he or she has. Indeed, clinically depressed people do not attempt to alter their circumstances at all. And the longer they do not attempt to intervene, the greater their problems become. But here is the critical point. To be healthy, it must be *their* circumstances that they seek to change. There is no merit in attempting to control other people's lives. I never counselled any kind of Machiavellian desperation. Simon came up with this on his own. In theory, we don't drum up business.

Was he looking out at the street through the venetian blinds when reason momentarily turned away from him as though it had become as tired of him as he had himself? Reason has always been an early riser. It's always the first to leave. To be honest, it was not really a flight from reason so much as a perverse confluence of events. Simon learnt from Angelique that your husband had an early meeting nearly every morning, but there was one particular morning that especially interested him, the morning of the day you were to fly out for your conference. If the meeting had been later, Simon could not have left a message for your husband without speaking to him. If Angelique had not woken him for breakfast he might have been too late. But it was all as if it were on some kind of 'just in time' schedule.

Your husband was having a 'busy time', often working back late, always starting early. You remember. Why don't you ever ask anybody questions? Well, I suppose you will now. Think about it. It's a depressed market. They're not going to pay people to work those kinds of hours anymore and you don't earn commission if the phone doesn't ring. There was no busy time at all, except maybe with Angelique, but he did have a breakfast meeting that morning. Simon assures me that one day well-dressed people will start having breakfast at home again. But the dollar had been up to no good while your husband was with Angelique. It went down on him, through the floor, and this necessitated a lot of urgent consultation. There is, apparently, an excess of coffee but a shortage of croissants at these breakfast meetings, Angelique tells us. More importantly, Simon knew from her exactly when your husband would be unable to receive calls, so he could leave a message for him without the risk of speaking to him, a message ostensibly on your behalf. Your husband could have called you back and been put straight at any time throughout the day. Or you could have *really* called him, to clarify something or even just to say goodbye again, to say anything. Simon would not have known. He was taking a risk but, when you think about it, what was he really risking? After all, what would have happened if your husband had not received Simon's message and had arrived at the school in time to pick Sam up?

In the event your husband didn't call you. He didn't need to, he had everything straight already—pick up Sam from school, take him to dinner at your parents, pick him up at lunchtime on Saturday, leave some money out for the housekeeper. The shopping had been done. It was only for a weekend. And you didn't call him either. Calls during work are kept to a minimum. Instructions are issued in the morning and they tend not to be queried in the absence of any major ambiguity. You had your briefcase and your overnight bag already packed, sitting in the boot of the car at the bottom of the tower where you work. You could go directly from drinks to the airport. You weren't going to call him during the day—not this day.

Simon has yet another theory about children I haven't mentioned, theory No 6017, which I would say has almost no validity but which, yet again, I found interesting. This one he formulated on the basis of his observations from the perimeter of a school ground but I don't think he really accepts it. (It has all the hallmarks of a psychological theory, doesn't it?) He says that, as a rule of thumb, one can correlate the amount of time a child spends on the school premises after the final bell has rung for the day with the degree of domestic dislocation to which the child is subjected. Why is a child still at school after school hours? If he or she is being detained on account of bad behaviour, who is the child rebelling against, or emulating? If the child is receiving extra tuition, why is it that he or she isn't able to learn at the same rate as the others? If he or she is loitering around the grounds after hours, perhaps home is an unpleasant place to be.

It's pretty simplistic stuff and, as I said, I don't think he really believes it. What about after-school sport? And what about art, craft, music, drama and smoking behind the bike sheds? All of this attracts them to school, for many a cross between a temple and a marketplace. This is where it all happens and we must be careful not to discount the importance to them of these things merely because we have forgotten about so much that was important to us.

There are brightly painted red and white posts that designate the beginning and end of children's crossings. Have you noticed how each of these posts subtly comes to a point, but somehow it's not sharp? We can touch it, a palpable manifestation of our collective anxiety for our children. The wire mesh fence inclines towards the school building with lush green foliage on the inside of it forming a raised plantation, ideal for jungle warfare and general hiding. The building itself is in different sections. The central part is just over a hundred years old with reddy-brown bricks, white window frames and a roof of slate tiles rising to a spire. Next to this are extensions such as the library, with much lower roofs and brick of different shades of red reflecting subsequent spasms of public funding.

There is a sign on the wall of the library just below the guttering which reads: 'WARNING. KEEP OFF. THIS ROOF HAS A SECURITY CAMERA CONNECTED DIRECT TO A SECURITY COMPANY. TRESPASSERS CAN EXPECT IMMEDIATE ARREST.' Out of the highest external brick wall comes a two-tiered wooden fire escape leading to an asphalt basketball court. There is an old rusted ring at each end, but no backboards. Do boys play netball? Beside the court is a big green dump-bin surrounded by smaller silver rubbish bins, some of which are chained to each other. Others are dented, having been used at critical times to demarcate one area from another.

Not far from the bins are the cricket nets, the wire sagging at the ends, and next to them the small concrete field for the teachers' car park. The classrooms are of different sizes, each with a different feel inside according to the age of the class and the age of its teacher. Some have tiny plastic tables facing the blackboard, and wooden chairs with denim and gingham chair bags hanging from them. Others are lined with collages of animals, fashion models and dairy products. There are charts, Where Rain Comes From, Where The Sun Goes. Nothing else sounds like the bell and the children spill out on its instruction at a rate that bears no relation to their individuality which, if you attempt to ignore in any other context, will only confound you further.

In the seconds before the bell rings, the parents, grandparents and assorted guardians mill around the fence near the gate. They don't come in. Some talk, others just wait. It is interesting that children of the same ages are met by adults of such different ages and backgrounds. Young women and much older men, from southern Europe, the Pacific and South East Asia. How old are the children before they refuse to be hugged in front of their peers? How young are they when the accent of a waiting guardian engenders a shame they will, years later, remember with a fresh and much richer shame? Some of the children are not met by anyone. They might walk home alone or in groups. They try each other's bikes. Perhaps they are going to meet a parent at work? Some of them are in no hurry to end the day's commerce. They hang around.

Ball games start and children of all different sizes are lost to them. There's a kid with crazy eyes and a big bag of marbles smoothing the ground in front of him. He's wearing a black t-shirt emblazoned with the image of a steroid-enriched body-builder, naked to the waist, clutching an assault rifle. The kid holds a marble in the air between his thumb and forefinger and calls out, 'Hit it and you win it,' in a slow dragging voice as though he was selling papers. The teachers' car park is emptying of its small red, white and yellow cars. The younger women, fresh from teachers' college, are getting into cars decorated with furry cartoon characters wrapped around the rear-view mirrors and stickers on the back advertising radio stations now in liquidation and seaside resorts the young women went to with their slightly older young men in bigger cars. The kid with the crazy eyes has a small crowd of boys in front of him. 'Hit it and you win it.'

Sam was thinking about it. He stood with his hands in his pockets watching the other boys, some of them older. His school bag was on the ground and he wasn't looking for anyone.

'Sam.'

He heard his name called but ignored it. He was watching the boys and the marbles. Hit it and you win it.

'Sam,' Simon called again.

Sam turned around.

'Do you remember me?'

He shook his head.

'Yes you do. Do you remember that awful day when you fell in the pool at home?'

'You're the gardener!' he said.

'Yes. I'm the gardener. Do you like to play marbles?'

'Yes. Sometimes,' Sam answered, looking back at the others.

'Listen—Sam. You know your mum won't be picking you up today?'

'Yes. Dad will.'

'Well, he was going to, Sam, but he can't now. He's got something at his work that is going to make him late home. He asked me to come and tell you that—and to look after you. Is that okay?'

'Yes.'

'Do you like chocolate milk? I do.'

Simon knows about empty school grounds, about looking in them for someone, calling out with a dry mouth and a machine-gun pulse. Your husband would have looked everywhere. He would have gone through his pockets looking for the message in the hand of someone else's secretary, the message from you that Simon had left for him telling him that Sam was on an excursion and would be back late. It wouldn't have helped anything to have found it but he would have felt he needed to see it. Without it, he would have wondered whether he had dreamed the whole thing. You can imagine. The walk becomes a nervous trot. Can you picture it? He is still trying to deny what is happening. He loosens his tie and then he runs, unashamedly, in terror. Nothing can prepare him for this. He cries his son's name to stop the world. You must know all of this by now.

14

Angelique was looking for the use-by date on a packet of drinking chocolate. The cupboard was filled with tins of soup, chocolate, canned fruit and packets of mashed potato, much of which she had bought for him over the last few months. There were some saucepans in the kitchen sink with the remnants of tinned soup congealing on their sides. She was pleased to see this. It showed that he was getting through the supplies. There were some newspapers piled up on the floor and some empty bottles stacked neatly in a row beside the rubbish bin. There were not as many as there used to be.

'When did you buy this drinking chocolate?' she called to Simon in the lounge room.

'He doesn't want *hot* chocolate. There's some chocolate topping in there somewhere near the front. I bought it yesterday,' he called back.

'I was making it for *us* but if it's stale I'll throw it out.'

'I didn't know drinking chocolate went off but maybe the new improved stuff comes with state-of-the-art environmentally vindictive obsolescence. You can't stop progress, you know . . . can't stop anything,' he added quietly.

She boiled some milk to go with the chocolate topping for two mugs of hot chocolate and poured some more chocolate topping into a glass with ice-cream and milk. There seemed to be so much milk.

'I don't know what these will be like. I've never made hot chocolate from topping before,' she said, carrying all three of the drinks into the lounge room and placing them on the coffee table. The television was on but turned low, almost inaudible. Sam was lying on the carpet with a pillow underneath his head and a blanket over him. Empson was asleep next to him. Angelique sat down next to Simon with her hot chocolate.

'Do you know what you're doing?' she asked.

'I'm not certain I do. People who are certain they know what they're doing are very dangerous. I'm not dangerous.'

'You're crazy, Simon. What do you think is going to come of this? Nothing good, you know that.'

Simon put his mug down and got up to adjust the blanket around Sam. He knelt on the floor and made sure no part of him was uncovered below his chin.

'Angel, you're probably right, but like the guy said when he jumped off the Rialto building and got to the twentieth floor: so far so good.'

She smiled weakly. Empson sighed. The television showed a police car in a narrow alley. She looked around the room, for so long a cave of inert chaos, now sparely littered with several neat piles of mess, newspapers and books mostly. Her gaze came to rest on Simon with your sleeping son beside him.

'I want you to know . . . I love you, Simon. I know everything you've said. I know I am . . . *forewarned*, as you say, but please know it—remember it, no matter what. I love you even though . . . I know you're crazy. You're the softest man I've ever met. Too soft. *He's* smarter than you,' she said, pointing to Sam, still sleeping.

'He may well prove to be smarter than me. He's already a lot wiser.'

'They're going to find him here. You know they will. They'll figure it out,' she said.

'They'll find him happy and safe if they do, with a chocolate moustache.'

'What do you mean *if*? They *will* find him, it's just a question of how soon. They'll both be frantic. It's not going to take them long.'

She got up and went over to him on the floor. He held her in his arms and they looked at your beautiful son gently breathing half into the pillow.

'When will they find him? They won't be that fast,' he said in a low voice. 'The emotions are not skilled workers.'

She repeated the line to herself after a moment's thought.

'Is it Eliot?' she asked. He shook his head.

46

'Dylan Thomas? No. Yeats, isn't it?'

'No,' he answered, running his fingers through her hair.

'Who wrote that, "The emotions are not skilled workers"?' She put her head in his lap.

'That's a story in itself, Angel. It *is* a beautiful line, isn't it? Attributed to a man who never said it, by two men who wrote it and then pretended they were a third man who never existed.'

'Wait just a minute. Start again. Tell me slowly.' She closed her eyes and repeated softly, 'The emotions are not skilled workers.'

'In 1944,' he began, 'a very young editor of a fairly radical literary-cum-arts journal received a letter from a woman enclosing a couple of poems she had found while going through her late brother's things, poems she said her brother had written and never shown her.

'Her brother was born in Liverpool toward the end of the First World War and, when his father died of war wounds a couple of years later, the family moved to Australia. His mother had family here. They lived in Sydney where he went to school till he was fifteen, when his mother died. He hadn't done very well and his sister was powerless to keep him from leaving school and getting a job in a garage at Taverner's Hill.

'He kept the job for a couple of years but became restless and moved to Melbourne when he was about seventeen. His sister didn't hear much from him for a long time. Eventually someone she knew met him and reported back. They told her he was living in a room by himself somewhere in South Melbourne, by the sea. They said he was selling insurance. Worried about his health, he had always been frail, she wrote to him to re-establish contact, but didn't receive a reply for quite a long while. Finally, she got a letter from him. It was 1940. The war was still young. He wrote that his health had improved and that he was making some money repairing watches and doing odd jobs.

'After that, she didn't hear from him again until the year he came back to Sydney, the year he turned twenty-five. She got him to come home and it was then that she realised that he was ill, although his stamina concealed for a time the extent of his illness. Eventually, he told her that he knew what was wrong, that he had Grave's Disease. He said he would die from it.

'In the weeks before his death, his agitation and irritability gave way to a kind of calm in which he would talk to his sister almost as to a confessor. It seemed he had fallen in love with a woman in Melbourne but it hadn't worked out. He was by now very weak and often incoherent. He died in the winter of that year.

'His sister found the poems some six months later while going through his effects. She showed them to a friend who thought they had something to them and that she ought to try to have them published. So, along with a covering letter and postage for their return, she sent them to the young editor. Now literary editors who are at least half serious about their work and aren't just in the job because they didn't know what else to do with their lives dream of receiving an unsolicited gem through the mail, a collection of words that can move them, that can excite a very positive response. This editor, who was only in his early twenties, was no different in this respect. But he was in other ways. For a start, he was a poet himself. But the poetry he was interested in was modern, avant-garde. It wasn't accepted by the mainstream till much later. In addition to being a poet and a modernist, he was a "crow-eater", like you.'

'A South Australian?'

'Yes. He was born in Mt Gambier and later moved to Adelaide. If all of this didn't make him different enough to the Establishment, he was also a Jew. So, you've got this impossibly young modernist editor, a rural South Australian Jew, and he reads these poems written by a lonely young man without much formal education, a man who knew he was dying. Imagine him, Angel, discovering gold. He shows his colleagues the poems the sister had almost not found and it was decided that these poems ought to be published.'

'What were their names, the poet and his sister?'

'Ethel and Ern Malley, not such romantic names. But then they never existed, either of them. They were the products of the collective imagination of two more conventional poets of the time who claimed to have set up the whole thing as a hoax—as a kind of experiment. They believed that, by promoting modernism in poetry, the journal, and particularly the young editor, were promoting poetry which was bereft of any meaning, structure and craftsmanship. They regarded modernist poets as nothing more than con-artists.

'The hoax was an experiment to determine whether the critics who lavished praise on this kind of poetry were capable of distinguishing it from deliberately concocted nonsense. They invented Ethel and Ern Malley and Ern's life story as part of the experiment. The poems themselves were said to have been produced in one afternoon by the two poets through the random choosing of words and phrases from whatever books they happened to have lying around, such as the *Concise Oxford Dictionary*, a dictionary of quotations and some American report on the drainage of the breeding grounds of mosquitoes. They had Ern Malley attribute to Lenin the line, "The emotions are not skilled workers", but this was also false.

'The Ern Malley hoax, as it became known, was reported in the mainstream press around the country and ultimately in the *London Times* and *Time* magazine. Poetry was on everybody's lips. People all over the English-speaking world delighted in the humiliation of the modernists, whom they had never previously heard of but whose denigration, it seemed, gladdened their hearts. The editor was made a laughing stock and worse was to come.

'In late 1944, seven of the Ern Malley poems were deemed by the South Australian police to be "indecent advertisements" and the edition carrying them was alleged to be "indecent, immoral or obscene". The young editor was charged and put on trial. As insane as it may sound, he was found guilty.'

He looked down at the part of her face that was exposed. 'What is it, Angel? Does my memory frighten you or have I bored you to tears?'

She was crying silently. He held her closer against his chest. She took deep breaths, trying to get the air past her throat. Empson and Sam exhaled almost in time with each other. They were all of them on the floor in one corner of the room. The television showed the flag of an oil company blowing in the wind. This is how it all looked and this is what you would have heard in the last moment before the door was kicked in. They pushed it in with one kick, although it was locked. There were three of them, uniformed police, two men and a woman, with a warrant for Simon's arrest. They didn't need to kick the door in. He would have opened it. By the time they got to Simon's place you would have been well and truly contacted. Your husband would have reached you by then. How did you feel? I have never been paged at an airport. You know how it is. It's always someone else.

15
___

So this is where we are now—all of us *separate* people. William has been calling me but I haven't returned the calls. He hasn't gone to see Simon yet. He's got to blame somebody before he does anything else. First things first. He's got me in his sights. And why not? He's got to get something out of this. I think he knows he can't get his money back. I don't have it. We drank it at the Esplanade. He probably wants me deregistered, if not arrested.

It had occurred to me that it would not be possible for Simon to get you out of his system without actually seeing you again, without establishing contact. My thinking was, with respect, that you could not help but disappoint him now. This would have hurt him very much in the short run. It might even have driven him back to his darkened bedroom. But after a while his despair over the reality of you, as opposed to the idealisation of you, would evaporate, and with it a lot of other things. I told him this. I think he was coming around. I think it could have helped him. You could have—just by being the person you are, with whatever fears and weaknesses you have, just like the rest of us. You could have told him you remember it all fondly—at least that. It would not have taken much. He nearly called you several times. You weren't to know. He nearly called you last night.

They really do get one phone call, like on television or in the movies. He was scared. He called me. He said he didn't know whether they were going to keep him in the lock-up or send him to the Melbourne Assessment Prison so I don't know exactly where he is going to be after today. I don't know how they knew where to find Sam so quickly either. There's a lot I don't know—but I do know that your son had never been in less danger. And I also know that you're the only one who can help Simon now. You're the only one that can save him. Simon told me as much just now on the phone. He said you've got to tell them that he is your lover, that he had your permission to take Sam. That is the only course that can save him. Why would you want to save him? Because he's ill and because he's never stopped loving you. Among other things, he is ill *because* he's never stopped loving you. I'm not saying you owe him anything beyond that which we all owe each other but—when we are all finished being told that everyone out there must take responsibility for himself—what's it like when we get home? What's it like inside? He had been cast out and he had never done anything wrong, till now. You think it would be the end of everything to help him like this but it would only be the end of some things. What are you going to do? You're involved. You are finally involved, after all these years, and there is no way out of it. There are a few people you can help now. I nearly called you last night.

part two

1

I am irritating her. Again. I can sense it. Without even seeing her face
I can sense it. Over time I have learnt to register the signals. It is there
in the slow exhale of sulphurous breath in the morning as she lies
beside me in bed staring at the ceiling, or else in the way she turns
away to one side. It is there in the way she stays and stays on the same
page of a book or a magazine, pretending to be reading. Anyone could
do this but not the way she does it. I cannot prove it but there is no
need to prove it anymore. To whom am I trying to prove anything? The
jig is up. I suspect it is up for both of us now. This is what we suddenly
have in common. After years of drifting apart, suddenly, we have this
in common—this and our son. Everything will come out now.

We check on him several times throughout the night, several
times each, never together. He sleeps but we don't, not properly. I
keep replaying everything in my head, stopping and then starting
again at different scenes, each with its own configuration of supporting casts. I am in all of them. Anna is in many of them. Sam is
in the last of them and now I know there are two other people with
him. One of them is a prostitute. I know her. The other is an old, old
boyfriend of Anna's. I don't know him. The police said Sam wasn't
harmed at all. The doctor said it too. He slept soundly throughout
the night and I have to believe them. I have to believe them and yet,
this is my son and I want to kill.

I want to kill. It's a brand new way of waking up, wanting to kill,
wanting to hide, wanting to vomit, wanting to start again. It isn't any
kind of waking up I've known before but then I didn't really sleep.
Neither did Anna, but for a long time now we have had the grace to
pretend that we don't know that the other is only pretending to sleep.

Anna is wearing something white, silky, shiny, brief. It mocks us. When she turns over it rides up to reveal her underpants, also white, shiny and brief. There was a time when this would happen and, quickly aroused, I would pull them down and be inside her before she had a chance to fully waken. There had to be a last time that this happened. Would I remember it as the last time? It might have been the morning she looked over her shoulder into my eyes as I entered, saying matter-of-factly, her eyes barely open, 'It's rape, Joe.'

Her stomach is unsettled. I am offered this through closed lips as the explanation for the displeasure that has landed and is nestling on her face.

'Would you like a cup of tea?'

'What?'

'Would you like a cup of tea? It might help settle your stomach.'

'No . . . only if you're having one.'

She says this and somehow manages to cover each word with a semi-permeable viscous membrane of bitterness. I don't really want a cup of tea but because as a child I was brought up to believe that cups of tea helped, although even then I knew it was the offer that helped, and because I know that there can be no commerce between us until her stomach is settled, and because now we really have to talk, I get out of bed, go into the kitchen and make us both a cup of tea.

I put on the leather slippers she had Sam buy me for Father's Day. I put on the robe I had bought for myself, the Armani. This robe really should have made Anna suspect I was seeing someone. Isn't that what the magazines tell women to look out for? A husband comes home unexpectedly carrying a designer bathrobe. Anna didn't say anything about it. She's told me to pick it up on occasions when I've left it on the floor. I didn't buy it because I was seeing someone. I needed it. I needed a new bathrobe. She would never have noticed that I needed one. I wasn't seeing anyone. I sleep with whores.

When I bring the tea back to the bedroom she says nothing and does not look at me. I set her cup down on her bedside table, get back into bed and start to sip mine. This draws her attention. She looks at me for the first time this morning. How can she possibly blame me for all of this? She can't, but a wave of contempt splashes across her face for an instant. It is involuntary. I have sipped too loudly, reminding her that she should never have married me. And still I ask her, 'How are you feeling now?'

2

My mother wanted me to become a priest. The really funny part is that I actually thought about it. I was ten years old, maybe eleven. My father was away, the second time. Maybe it wasn't the second time. I remember it was around the time I started bringing my mother cups of tea. The cup would rattle in the saucer. I couldn't keep it still. The television would be on. It was always on. The girls watched cartoons as soon as they got home from school and Mum always had to watch *Temptation* with Tony Barber. Seven or seven-thirty. She called it *Great Temptation* but that was the name of his old show, the one that had been on during the day. We watched it with her if we were sick and she'd let us take the day off. Getting sick was about the best way to get some time alone with her, without the others.

But not without Roger. He was almost always there after she'd realised that school wouldn't do him any good. She would take the afternoon off and I'd sit beside her in Dad's black chair, the big vinyl one, the one we all fought over every night, and Mum and I would watch *Great Temptation*. Tony Barber asked the questions and the lovely Barbie presented the prizes while Roger lay on his back, eyes rolling around wildly inside his head. He breathed too loudly when you were trying to watch TV, always farting or whirring like the sound of a broken washing machine that no one could fix. We had a washing machine like that. It stopped in the middle of every cycle so it took twice as long to finish. We put it out on the nature strip. No one would take it so we brought it back in and Roger would impersonate it. Bubbles of saliva would come out of his mouth as he lay on the floor and, just for the half-hour of *Great Temptation*, without pronouncing upon it, Mum would let us ignore him.

I would bring the two of us a cup of tea, two sugars each, and we would watch.

'Who am I?' Tony asked rhetorically. 'I was born in Italy in 1898. As a designer of racing cars, my name has become synonymous with speed and style. I was president of the company I founded which came to be known around the world by my name.'

'Do you know that one, Joseph?' she'd ask me.

Roger would be mixing his spit with the threads of carpet he'd lifted with his fingers from the floor.

'Who am I? Anyone?' Tony asked.

I slapped the side of Dad's black chair and made the sound of a contestant's buzzer with my mouth.

'Yes, Joe?' my mother would ask.

'Ferrari!'

'No takers?' Tony said. 'Enzo Ferrari.'

'You knew it. Aren't you a clever boy, Joe!'

When the program was over the transmission of our lives would continue as normal. I would feel the cold on my feet. My toes would find the heads of the nails through the carpet. She would carry our empty cups and saucers back to the kitchen to wash them and I'd take the opportunity afforded by her absence to give just one quick perfect boot to Roger's chest, just to hear the sound it made, just to shut him up, just to do to him what he did to all of us every day, in all the ways he could never and would never understand.

I think there were times when I blamed Roger for our father's absence, although it would have been more reasonable to blame Dad for Roger. He had made him too quickly, in a hurry, in one of those regular tourist-like visits to our house in which he would stay for just long enough to tell us that the spongy, black vinyl chair in front of the television was his chair, just long enough for the checked, fleecy-lined jacket, his browny-orange lumber-jacket, to hang on the peg in the hall covering all the things we had put there first. For a time I was the only one who could reach that peg. Mum used to tell the others to get me to hang up their coats or hats there for them. There was only one peg. I told him that during one of his visits. He said he knew it, who did I think put it there? Who did I think brought the winter inside? Some nights Sarah or one of the others would wake me at three or four in the morning to get their coat from the peg. They were too cold to sleep.

Sam is warm. He is still sleeping. Usually he's awake before me, on the weekends anyway. I finish my tea before Anna. Neither of them has ever been cold in the place where they sleep. There are many coats and many places to hang those coats in this house. And I always come home. So why does she have such trouble looking at me? Maybe it's *because* I always come home. What day, what time did I become so hateful, so contemptible? Is it familiarity that bred her contempt, and how precisely did she go from sublime excitement to comfort to boredom to contempt to the arms of some other man? And how do you get from there to a suburban police station to collect your son after he has been stolen by a man she first met a long time ago, a time before I was able to afford new carpet for my mother's house?

She will have to look at me. She might even want to and, if she does, will I be able to look at her? I have never considered what I've done to come under the rubric of 'infidelity'. But seeing an old boyfriend, the last one before me, that is infidelity, and over a protracted period. It has to have been over a protracted period because otherwise how would he know such intimate details about us, about Sam? How would he know where Sam went to school? How does he know Angelique? How do I know her? Am I going to have to explain all of this to Anna?

I watch her sipping her tea. How can someone so beautiful—I can still see her that way—have made me feel so unworthy? Are we going to have to tell each other the whole truth, starting from the time things here just shut down? Everything in our bedroom is white. Even Anna's nightwear. She could have finished her tea by now if she'd wanted to. It's deliberate, this slow drinking of her tea. If she could just admit that, just start with that. Imagine if I told the truth. Where would I start?

3

I met Angelique through Dennis Mitchell. That's not true. I met her *with* Mitch. Sid Graeme sent us there one Christmas as a sort of pat on the back, a sort of bonus, a gift. Well, actually, he didn't send me there. He told Mitch that there was credit waiting there for him and some of his colleagues or his friends. Mitch and I work together more and more. We might even be friends. I like him. I think he likes me. Mitch is quiet, especially compared to most of the dealers, but he's probably the best or certainly one of the best analysts in the research department. Unlike a number of the other analysts, he seems to have no interest in ever becoming a dealer, at least none that he's ever talked about with me. I think he would tell me.

I'm a good dealer. A good dealer is someone who consistently provides his clients with good information. Mitch has been responsible for much of the information I give my clients. He is, in a sense, responsible for much of this house, for the cars downstairs, my bathrobe over there, for the white silk around Anna now. I once suggested to him that we were each other's alter egos. He smiled. I'd say we were friends.

Mitch is a quiet achiever. Even compared to the other analysts, who are all quieter than the dealers, he's quiet. But the management committee knows he's good. Gorman himself told me this privately one Friday night at drinks and he's the MD. Mitch doesn't need Gorman. He could get a job with any broking house in the country. The firm needs Mitch, or analysts like him. He's got the instincts and the contacts. I need him. We're a team, unofficially. Officially, there are no teams, just analysts and dealers, the demi-gods in corporate finance and the management committee. But I know Mitch gives me his best stuff, or, at least, he gives it to me first. He's never said anything but I think it's because we're just about the only Catholics in the firm. I never felt so Catholic before I started working there. The other guys all went to school with each other, all to the same handful of schools, the ones their fathers went to, the ones their sons attend, the ones where they all learn to hate Catholics.

Mitch is about my age. I think he was married but is now divorced or something, maybe even a widower. I don't ask. I haven't asked. He doesn't normally stay back long for drinks on Friday nights, something only someone with Mitch's track record could get away with in a firm like ours. But this one Friday night he seemed to be putting it away with the best of them. I don't know, maybe it was on account of the festive season. He'd been having a great year and, perhaps because he so rarely stays back on Friday nights, a lot of people, including Gorman and some of the other guys on the management committee, were coming up to him and complimenting him. Some of the dealers appeared to be sucking up to him. I don't know whether it was the alcohol or the praise that so took him out of himself, but when I brought him back a beer and we found ourselves alone for the first time that evening he told me about Sid Graeme's Christmas present.

He asked me what I was doing later that night. For a split second I honestly thought he was propositioning me. That sounds ridiculous now but at the time it didn't seem so much more out of character than inviting me to accompany him to a brothel. That night was the first time we went there together and the first time I had ever been to a brothel at all. It wasn't long before I no longer needed Mitch to come along for the ride.

It is difficult to imagine two people more different than Sid Graeme and Mitch. That they managed to find each other is a tribute to the market. Sid Graeme was one of the few entrepreneurs who managed to come out of the eighties with greater credibility than he took into them. It helped that he wasn't yet that well known and that he wasn't yet that big. But it was more than this. He had a dual strategy that was very clever. Firstly, he had managed to get himself on all sorts of boards, commissions and advisory panels, in the arts, in various sports, in entertainment, in hospitality, transportation—including aviation—and, perhaps most importantly, in government. Over the course of approximately ten years he became almost ubiquitous. Not only did he come to know everyone at the top end of town but they all came to know him.

He was also amongst the first to hear of even the slightest change to the most trivial regulation, whether it was in banking, superannuation, insurance, the Stock Exchange, the corporations law, consumer protection or any aspect of government, including the auditing of government expenditure. A man like this didn't have to pay for his own dry-cleaning. People were fighting each other to have that opportunity. This included politicians. It was invaluable to Mitch to be taken into this man's confidence.

Secondly, Sid Graeme realised, after the crash of '87 but before NASDAQ and the overnight rise and fall of the dot-com aristocracy of the 'new' economy, that there was still a way to make a few bucks out of the 'old' economy. If you were confident that your sources in government were good enough, you could invest in a forthcoming window of opportunity before the house containing it was even built. All you needed was capital and some reliable information. Sid Graeme had plenty of both.

On the strength of his borrowings he became a major share-holder in a number of private hospitals. Sticking with health care, he subsequently bought into a health insurance company, what the Americans call a health maintenance organisation or HMO. In a cab on the way to the brothel that Christmas, Mitch filled me in on Sid Graeme's rise to eminence in the industry.

'Impressive. But what does Sid Graeme really know about health care?' I asked, not entirely innocently.

'He's a majority shareholder in a couple of hospitals. He's frequently consulted by both the state and federal governments,' Mitch answered.

'Yeah, but what does he actually know about hospitals and health care?'

'He knows how to make money out of them.'

Mitch was nervous, not because of my questioning but because of where we were going. He obviously hadn't had as much to drink as he needed, or else the reality of reading the address of the place to the cab driver from a scrap of paper he pulled out of his coat pocket had had a sobering effect on him. I was nervous too but I didn't want Mitch to know and I didn't want him to lose his nerve. Talking about Sid Graeme seemed the best way to take his mind off the journey. I pretended to be as interested as I would have been had I not been drinking too much, had I not been nervous, a little guilty and, I suppose, excited.

'So does he make much money out of it?' I asked him.

'Sid Graeme?'

'Yeah.'

'Well, for a start, as CEO of the health insurance company he earns around three million.'

'Three million? You're kidding?'

'No, I'm serious. That's what he tells me. That's for starters.'

'And why is he telling you all of this?' I asked him.

Mitch smiled. 'I strongly suspect he might want the firm to underwrite a share issue one day.'

'By which of his companies?'

'Joe, does it matter?' He started to laugh.

Then we laughed. How we laughed. We were scared. We paid the cab driver and walked into the foyer of the place like we'd been there a thousand times, still laughing. I'd never seen Mitch laugh like that as we stood on all that red carpet in the foyer and a glamorous slightly older woman stood behind a marble counter and addressed us with a broad smile, like she was in on whatever it was that Mitch and I were laughing about. I suddenly felt really thirsty. 'Good evening, gentlemen,' she said. And we were scared.

I'm afraid now but this was different. The woman asked our names. I didn't want to tell her so I laughed and she laughed and Mitch laughed. Without thinking I told her my name was Mitch and that my friend's name was Joe. Then Mitch and I laughed again. Whoever would have thought I'd be so scared?

'We're guests of Mr Graeme,' Mitch told her.

'Mr Graeme?'

'Er . . . Sid Graeme,' Mitch said a little hesitantly. He didn't have much bravado to exhaust.

'Oh, yes,' the glamorous slightly older woman said, now smiling in a welcoming, reassured way before asking in a let's-get-down-to-business manner, 'Have you been here before?'

I felt like I was fifteen and I didn't know why. It was good and it was bad having Mitch there. It was bad because he'd obviously never been there or anywhere like it before. He looked nervous and when you're a fifteen-year-old cock of the walk you don't want to be with someone who smells nervous. It was good because I wasn't alone. There were two of us to look at, two of us to distract her from each other, and from the juvenility of the pretence that the hasty, breathy, impetuous, entirely self-indulgent marriage of sex and commerce was an acceptable semi-regular option for an intelligent, hard-working, white-collar father and husband. It was reasonable for me to be there. I could reason it. I could fathom it. I could understand it. I still understand it. Anna never will.

She'll drink stone-cold tea before she understands it. No one has ever taken such small sips. She will have constructed a perfectly blameless version of whatever it is she has been doing with the sick man who stole my son last night. She always manages to be right by the end of any strict logical analysis of the sounds that make up the words that we leave hanging in the air.

The room we were ushered into continued the foyer's theme of very red carpet from one gold wallpapered wall to another, with mirrors behind a bar at one end and a pool table at the other. And it was full of women. It was overpopulated by women. Most of the people at the bar, in chairs, on couches watching television, playing pool or just walking around, were women. At first I couldn't look anyone in the eye. I was afraid of being seen by someone I knew. It seemed there were lots of reasons to be ashamed and they all came flooding out, slippery, hard to hold on to. The machismo reasoning of my school-yard football-playing adolescence held that there was something wrong with you if you had to pay for it. In my late teens and early twenties financial prudence dictated one was better off with a magazine, some Vaseline and a box of tissues. Better to keep your 'ready' for something tangible. But by the time I walked in with Mitch I was making good money, better than I had ever dreamed I would, and these women were certainly tangible. Anyway, this was a free introductory offer.

Their business was lust and its satisfaction. They were soft and curvaceous in the places where decades of magazines, billboards, movies, music videos and the fashion industry said they should be. It was impossible to leave your home without being told a thousand times that this was what women should look like, that this is what we want and, one way or another, if you have money, you can have it. You need never be thirsty again.

We sat down and, in ones and twos, they gradually came up to us. Some were dressed more revealingly than others but none more than was necessary to stimulate your imagination. A tallish young woman came up alone and sat beside us.

'Hi, boys,' she said, and in the hearing of it we completed the regression back to boyhood.

'Hi,' I said, trying to be politely unafraid.

'Evening,' Mitch said.

'You just come in? What's it like outside?' she asked and we, who had already had our weather memories completely wiped by adolescent expectations, could not give her a straight answer.

'You like men as well as girls?' she whispered as she went to touch me with a hand which, though smooth, was just much too large.

I recoiled in panic, backing away as if he had the plague. My new companion took the cue and walked off entirely unfazed. Mitch was involved in some still semi-respectable conversation with a buxom redhead. I don't think he noticed the violence of my reaction. He certainly wouldn't have noticed that she was a man.

4

Anna puts the cup down and, suddenly, with freshly-minted fear, as I hear the sound of the china touching her bedside table I wish it were full to the brim all over again. With her thick hair, huge eyes and olive skin, sometimes I catch myself looking at her anew, looking at her as I looked at her in the early days when I hoped she would be the mother of my children and dilute forever the cesspool that resides in my family's genes. I dare not look at her as she puts the cup down. I hear the swish of her silk against the covers. I feel the displacement of heat as she moves. I smell her scent. Though I had been thinking about it all night I have no idea where to start. Do I accuse her or do I apologise to her?

'Anna, what's going on?'

'Joe, we have to talk.'

'This guy Simon, you know him?'

'You know I know him. You've met him.'

'I've never met him.'

'You have.'

'Have you slept with him?'

'He's my ex-boyfriend.'

'So you *have* slept with him.'

'When we were going out. We went out . . . I don't know . . . ten years ago or something. I'd just finished going out with him when *we* met.'

'You hadn't.'

'What?'

'You hadn't finished going out with him when we met.'

'Jesus Christ, Joe, what are you talking about?'

'You hadn't quite finished going out with him.'

'Joe, I had.'

'Anna, don't you remember? I remember.'

'What are you talking about?'

'Are you sleeping with him now?'

'No.'

'Are you seeing him now?'

'Seeing him? No.'

'You're fucking lying, Anna. You're lying.'

'No, I'm not.'

'He says you're in a relationship.'

'Who? Simon?'

'Simon says, "Fuck your ex-boyfriend behind your husband's back and steal his son."'

'Hey, don't talk to me about "behind your husband's back".'

'We're talking about Simon here.'

'Oh, are we? Have you talked to him?'

'No, I haven't fucking talked to Simon.'

'So what are you talking about?'

'The police.'

'The police?'

'The cops said you were fucking him.'

'Bullshit! Now *you're* lying. They didn't say that.'

'They said he says he was picking Sam up from school, picking up my son from school, because . . . because you asked him to. They said he claims to have had your permission. Now why would you give an ex-boyfriend permission to pick him up from school? Because you're still on with him.'

'Stop shouting. I'm not *on* with him. You'll wake Sam.'

'I'm not shouting.'

'You are.'

'You're fucking this Simon guy.'

'That's bullshit, Joe. I'm not.'

'Well, what's he doing picking up Sam ten years after you split up with him?'

'I don't know.'

'Oh, for fuck's sake, Anna, do you really expect me to believe that?'

'Sshh! Stop shouting. You'll wake Sam. It's true, Joe, really. It's true.'

'How can you look at me and lie like this? Do you think that I'm that fucking stupid? Do you think you're *that* much smarter than me, that this is all it takes, a piece of crap story like this?'

'Let go of me. Joe, let go of me.'

'I'm not touching you. Christ, who could *that* be?'

'Let go of me.'

'Answer the phone, for fuck's sake. I feel sick.'

I want to believe . . . something. I want to believe anything that takes this sick feeling away. Someone please take me back to before and whatever I have done to deserve this I will not do. I swear. Either way I lose. If this Simon had permission to pick Sam up from school then Anna gave it to him, and if she gave it to him she's having an affair with him. Otherwise I'd know about him. If she's not having an affair with him, I still feel sick. It means some mad bastard stole my son. He stole him when I should have been there. They say he wasn't harmed but none of it makes any sense. How can she be talking on the phone now? She doesn't seem worried. It must be true.

Sam is standing at the doorway. He stands in his pyjamas and looks in at us. His mother looks up at him from the telephone. I hold out my arms. He understands that this is an invitation to run to the bed and jump up into my arms so that I can assure both of us that everything is alright.

'Dad.'

I hold him to my chest. My love for him is the only unequivocally good thing I know is always there inside of me. It is the reason I should be spared all that is coming, the only reason.

'How's my little man this morning?'

Either way I lose. Either way I want to kill this Simon.

Anna's telephone conversation registers with me for the first time. 'Well, you *can*,' she says into the telephone, 'but we don't know our plans yet, exactly.'

She runs the fingers of one hand through Sam's hair.

'No, he's fine. He looks fine. He's had a good sleep,' she says looking at him.

She puts one hand over the mouthpiece and turns to me. 'It's your mother,' she says. 'She's read about it in the paper. Hold on,' she says, returning to my mother. 'Hold on and I'll get Joe for you.'

In the paper. Which one? It would be a stupid question so I don't ask it. It's the only paper my mother ever reads. She reads it every day. I know her routine. On Sundays, for example, she picks it up after mass and goes home to make herself some toast and a pot of tea to have while she reads it. Then she goes to visit Roger. She has to take two buses. She can't drive. They didn't have the money for it to be an issue when we were young and now she says she's too old to learn. She's too scared to learn. I have given her a cab-charge card but she seldom uses it. 'Save your money,' she says. She still thinks that the wretchedness of poverty can be mitigated by frugality. Even my father knew better than that. He just didn't know what to do with the knowledge. But today, from her daily paper, my mother has learned something new. Her grandson was kidnapped last night. I read the same paper.

'I don't know, Mum. No, I'm still in bed. No, I haven't read the paper but I can tell you he's fine . . . Well, how should I know? They don't know . . . The police don't know . . . Well . . . They didn't say anything about that to us.'

'What?' Anna asks in a whisper. I am listening to my mother telling me what a tabloid newspaper says about the theft of my son while he crawls headfirst under the covers to get to the foot of the bed.

'Mum, I don't know anything about that.'

'What? What's she saying?' Anna whispers again. I put my hand over the mouthpiece.

'She says the paper says your Simon is a serial child-stealer.'

'Oh, that's complete crap.'

'How would you know? You haven't seen him for ten years . . . Sorry, Mum, I got distracted . . . Sam's . . . Sam's playing cave explorer in the bed . . . No, he's fine . . . Sure, I don't see why not.' Again I cover the mouthpiece to speak to Anna.

'She wants to see him,' I tell her. Anna closes her eyes in momentary exasperation before answering, 'Whatever you want.'

I arrange with my mother to bring her over to see Sam before taking her to visit Roger. Sometimes she wants to go there on a Saturday. There is nothing I can do. Anna isn't happy about it but she knows that taking my mother out to visit Roger is the last thing I would want to do. Everything is surreal now. It doesn't help having my mother in the house to check for herself that Sam is well no matter what was said in the paper about the alleged history of his kidnapper, her daughter-in-law's former lover. Does the paper mention Angelique? What is she doing in all of this?

5

Mitch kept talking to the buxom redhead. He was like a stock-market Scheherazade delaying the moment of execution, all on Sid Graeme's tab. The redhead was quite sexy both in appearance and in the way she spoke. What made her all the more so was the fact that it was Mitch and not me that was talking to her, engaging her, flirting with her. I was close enough to be able to listen and observe the goings-on in the rest of the room. I found it exciting to see men and women discreetly leaving the room together.

What I found was that the women there were, for the most part, pretty, sometimes quite pretty, and all, including the transsexual I had so quickly and instinctively banished, were in their own ways enticing. But none of them were, on close examination, what a discerning man would call beautiful. You would not necessarily notice them on the street.

They had the prettiness of the airline stewardess who stands out a little from her colleagues and is serving the people in the seats diagonally opposite yours. You notice her without really being conscious of it at first. Then you catch yourself hoping that your seat falls within her allotted area and being disappointed when it doesn't. Is she really beautiful? No. Do you want her to notice you? For a hungry moment you want this more than anything else. Why do you want this? You don't know. It makes no sense. You're a number to this woman if you're ever anything to her. You're the chicken not the fish, you're the guy next to the old lady with the extra blanket. You want her so much by the time the plane begins its descent and yet, by the time you're removing your briefcase or jacket from the overhead locker, you have forgotten her. She is suddenly no more memorable than the safety instructions she and her colleagues issued at the start of your mind's round-trip from reality to her and back. You have forgotten her and have no appointment to remember her and you don't. Until one night in bed, five or so days later as you listen to the sounds of your wife disrobing and abluting in the en suite, preparing for another night of sleeping alone beside you. Then you remember that airline stewardess and your favourite useless part starts to come alive.

You would know what to do with it if only there was time. You think that there might be time and you start. You need this time. You remember the way that woman helped someone with his pillow and how it could have been you if you'd played your cards right. But this is alright. This looks like it's going to have a happy ending. You're thinking about that uniform, how she had to put it on and would have to take it off. You think you can remember her breasts. And everything is going to be okay. You're going to be free and no one will ever know. But then the light changes in the corner of your eye. It's over in the en suite. Your wife is back. You're not finished but you have to pretend you're asleep. You can't even exhale as deeply as you would like in your own bed. This is what it's come to. And through small tears that have replaced the light in the corner of your eyes, you thank Jesus there are places you can go and pay for the airline stewardess to set you free.

I think I chose Angelique because she didn't choose me. She was sitting at the bar talking to the barman or the security guy or whoever he was and she really wasn't interested in meeting me or getting her cut from making me feel nineteen again. When Mitch finally went off with the buxom redhead, probably choosing her because it would have been impolite not to after talking to her all that time, I went up to the bar and interrupted the conversation Angelique was having because I was bored, embarrassed and in a place where women just could not reject you. Every woman in the place was attracted to me by market forces and so I chose the one who seemed to most approximate the outside world, the one with her back to me. In this respect she could have been my wife. And in another respect too.

She was by far the prettiest woman there, pretty enough for me, under other circumstances, to have wanted to see her in my real life. When she took me upstairs she seemed in complete control. Having satisfied herself through the intercom that I wasn't required to hand over any money, her demeanour changed and she started to talk to me like a woman, albeit a young woman, that I would perhaps want to talk to when this was over. She asked me what I did for a living. I hadn't expected this. She spoke with an engaging confidence, friendly without being sycophantic, like someone I could meet through work, at a meeting or a conference. I remember that after I told her what I did she asked me whether she should put her money in stocks or property. Then I saw her naked.

I don't see Anna naked anymore. I can but I have to arrange it. This is not something she has commented on. She might not even realise it but she's taken to dressing and undressing in the bathroom if I'm in the bedroom and in the bedroom if I'm in the bathroom. All of this began even before Sam was born. If I'm going to be honest it happened after the first one and before Sam. We had a baby, a boy who died on the seventeenth day of his life. They don't know why so they put it down to SIDS, which is an acronym for 'we don't know why your baby died but it did and you're on your own now'. Anna took it worse than I did and then, for a time at least, seemed to hold that against me, the fact that she had taken it worse than me. It wasn't that I wasn't devastated by it because I was. But she'd carried him for nine months. It was she who was breastfeeding him, she who was watching him for most of her waking hours during those seventeen days. I was back at work. It was she who discovered him. I had gotten up to go to work while both of them were still sleeping. I thought they were both sleeping. At nine-thirty she called me. She called me. She called her parents and her sister. She called an ambulance. In panic she even called the police. Our son is dead. I was just coming out of a breakfast meeting. I can't underestimate what it must have been like to find him. She must not underestimate what it's like to run around a school yard at dusk screaming till you're breathless, screaming the name of a son who is a little person, a perfect little boy you've known for six years. Then I found out her ex-lover had taken him.

There's more. To be honest, there's more. The baby we lost, I don't know why now, but at the time I thought maybe there was something wrong with him. I hate saying it but he looked a little odd. There was something funny about his eyes. It made me think of Roger. I didn't say anything about Roger when I mentioned it to Anna but she was furious anyway, wouldn't hear of it. I wanted her to reassure me. I was his father.

We had some counselling for a while afterwards and we took a holiday to Fiji. After that, no, it was on the holiday, during it, she started being . . . what? Reticent. She said it was too soon. I could understand. It got a little better, not much. It didn't really improve until she got pregnant with Sam. She said some outrageous things before she got better, things she should never have said. I can't help Roger. I couldn't help the way the baby looked. Sam is all we have in common now.

Sam is six years old, almost seven, and already he's learnt to humour my mother. She's brought him boiled sweets and, as he did the last time she brought some boiled sweets, he'll have one in front of her and leave the rest. Confectionery grows up as you do. As you progress through your youth it takes more to satisfy you and the manufacturers seem always to be able to deliver. They work hard to increase your expectations. At least that's the way I remember it. I remember wanting more than just the boiled sweets and I remember remembering when she would reward us with boiled sweets and it was fine. It was enough. There were other times, as I got older, when, just for a moment, I felt cheated. Had she never heard of chocolate? Had she never heard of nuts, caramel, nougat? Small and round, you know where these boiled sweets would fit?

Sam is following Anna around. His grandmother has lost his attention. The boiled sweets sit there on the coffee table. My mother looks at them for a moment before turning to look at her spotted hands nervously playing with the metal clasp on her handbag, fake crocodile, opening and closing it.

She still feels uncomfortable in a house like this, even though it's her son's house. She used to ask all the time whether I had paid it all off yet. She sits in it uncomfortably. She acts like it's stolen. Anna offers her food and something to drink but my mother says no. We had better be going. Anna follows my mother and me to the front door. Sam has his arms around Anna's thigh. There's an unfinished jigsaw in front of the TV. Somebody had him last night. I can't stop thinking about it. Anna says something to him about the jigsaw as I'm closing the door. She is good with him. Sweet Jesus, we're never going to be able to clean this up.

6
_____

Why does my mother have to sit in the front passenger seat like she's never been in a car before? I'm looking at the road but I know she's holding on to the handle on the inside of the door. I'm not even driving fast. I should have said no to this. I can't see Roger today. I can't face that place.

'Is this the car you always had?' my mother asks me.

'What?'

'Is this the same car you always had?'

'I don't know what that means.'

'When did you get it?'

'The car?'

'Yes.'

'I've had it . . . I don't know . . . six months, maybe.'

'What do you call it?'

'What do I *call* it?'

She closes her eyes. She might be crying. 'You know what I mean, Joe.'

'It's an Audi, Mum. An Audi TT, a Roadster.'

I used to go with her on the bus to see Dad, a bus to the city anyway. We all went but I went the most. I'm the oldest male, the only male with an IQ over sixty. The car park here always reminds me of those visits to my father. We always did as we were told, presenting ourselves at the south gate at Urquhart Street. My mother would press the buzzer. At the counter you gave them the name of the person you had come to visit. You were asked to sign the visitors' book and identify yourself. You were given a card and had your hand stamped. All your personal belongings were placed in a locker. We were directed to proceed through a security metal detector doorway and asked to follow a straight continuous blue line until we reached the visit centre. At the visit centre you were asked for the card that had been handed to you previously. You were asked to identify yourself again, and, after being entered in a visitors' register, you were directed to the actual place of the visit within the visit centre. Then you saw your dad.

I never got to see where he slept, so I didn't know what he saw at night when he was thinking about us. He said he thought about all of us at night. What did he think about in the days? We brought him photos. I wanted to see them at subsequent visits. I remember that. I was afraid someone was defacing them. I don't know why. It just occurred to me one night. I brought him my Little Athletics ribbons. He wasn't allowed to keep them. He told me to have pride in myself.

'You're not ashamed, are you, Joe?' he asked me at one of the visits, holding my face between those two great hands. 'There's nothing to be ashamed of. As long as you tried. You did your best.'

'The ribbon's blue, Dad. I came first.'

'As long as you don't lie down. Can't change anything if you lie down. You've got to have the courage to strive for what you want. I wasn't afraid to go for it. I gave it a damned good shake. That's how I manage to hold my head up, even here.'

We would take a tram and a couple of buses home to the blocked-up plumbing and the neighbour's stomping on the ceiling. We would take it in turn to polish his boots. She made us do it as part of our chores, even though he wouldn't be home for another three years. He was holding his head up.

I've seen where Roger sleeps. When we see him today they've got his hair parted recklessly near his left ear in a manner calculated to make him look as far from anybody's measure of normal as possible. He is sitting on a chair, in a browny-orange fleecy-lined lumber-jacket, staring at other people sitting on chairs staring at people. Children can be very cruel to people like this. Roger has grown to my father's height. Here they are all 'clients' now. How's Sid Graeme going to make a buck out of this?

We walk into a large open room—the day room they call it—past all manner of intellectual impairment and psychological dysfunction. A man is smoking a cigarette and rubbing himself on the back of someone else's chair. My mother greets him. She comes here every week, usually having just thanked the blessed Virgin before waiting for the first of the buses.

'Hello, Leon,' she calls, and then to me: 'That's Roger's friend.'

Roger is smiling when he sees us.

'Hi, Roger-Dodger,' I say to my brother, shaking his hand. Someone stole my son last night.

There are people here who look like horses. Some are staff, some are clients, patients, inmates. We trust Roger to their kindness. We have no choice. Not for a moment will Jesus let my mother wish my brother had never been born.

'Do you want to hear the radio?' I ask her on the way home.

'I don't mind. Whatever you like. If you want,' she says.

With one hand on the wheel I play with the radio tuner, searching for a station she might like, easy listening, hits and memories, syrup, schmaltz. It can make you want to kill. We must be about due for a retrospective of the Ray Conniff singers. My mother joined the World Record Club many years ago. I remember the shiny catalogues on the kitchen table. I don't ever remember her not being a member of it. She must have cut out a coupon from a magazine before I was born and filled it in. The Ray Conniff singers, Paul Anka, Neil Sedaka and Al Martino; she got them all for a little bit less. And she got those round coloured boiled tasteless sweets.

'Joe, is he the one who stole that Eloise and the . . . the Chinese girl? That's what the paper said.'

'What? What did the paper say?'

'They said the man who kidnapped Sam might've been the same one who took those other kids.'

Matt Flinders is singing 'Picking Up Pebbles and Throwing Them Into the Sea'.

71

7

When we get back to her place she asks me to stay for a while but I can't even go in. I can't go home either. I have to stop off somewhere. Anna's parents are coming over. Or is that tomorrow? They'll come and they'll talk dago when they think I can't hear and they'll never leave. Do I want a coffee? I want a coffee or a juice. I wish someone would tell me. There's a place on Chapel Street with incredible wait-resses. One of the guys at work was talking about it. What was it called?

I'm too old for the music they play here. Christ, it's not even music. But once you're here you can't ask them to turn it down. You're lucky if they serve you after that. You're paying for it, for everything. I pick up a paper. Usually the best parts are missing. What are the best parts? Maybe I should eat something? I wish someone would tell me.

'Can I help you, sir?' the waitress asks.

I don't know if this is the place they were talking about at work but if it isn't *I* might start talking about it. She can't be more than fifteen. Already so nasty, even as she offers to help me. Every year they bring out a new model. I'm depreciating, done too many miles. It's unfair. She could help me.

'What juice seems to hit the spot today?' I ask her with a smile.

I hear myself ask that question. It doesn't actually make sense. It doesn't mean anything except that I have already begun rehearsing. I have begun rehearsing for a role as one of those middle-aged arseholes who saunter into trendy coffee shops and cafés alone on weekends wearing veined brown leather jackets, with a recalcitrant newspaper tucked under one arm and ostentatious car keys tossed and caught and tossed and caught in the other hand, calling too loudly to a girl, 'What juice seems to hit the spot today?' which doesn't actually mean anything. It doesn't mean anything except that I'm a God-awful lonely prick whose very being or way of being has ulti-mately put off anybody I've ever gotten close to, leaving me alone with a nice new smartarse haircut and the weekend paper, all alone to talk too loudly in a café, reeking of aftershave and divorce.

Does she think that I don't know that, this little double-breasted midriff with a serving pad, swishing her ponytail around like it was some kind of . . . pony's tail? Does she think I can't see what's ahead of me? She makes no suggestions. She reels off the juice list from the blackboard menu on the wall. I could've done that. Doesn't she want a tip? Doesn't she know how it's meant to go? And she'll wonder why I pay for it. She'll feign outrage to hear I pay for it. I have to pay for it.

'Oh, excuse me . . . Could you put some ginger and lemon grass in with that?' Damn right, it's not a problem.

She's gone. She's away clearing another man's table. He is about her age or certainly closer to it than I am, closer to it than I ever was. He is unshaven. I find him ugly. She doesn't. Actually he repulses me. But not her. What does he drive? What does he make? What can a man so young possibly make that he can sit here and get her to smile like that, sit here without a trace of panic. He'll have to pay for it one day. Sure as night. I can't hear what they're saying. I can't understand what they're saying. She can tell that I pay for it. What can she tell? I have a son. Please don't clear the table so fast. I have a son.

I have a son who was taken as part of the most bizarre conspiracy imaginable, a conspiracy between my wife, an old boyfriend of hers and a prostitute that I have been seeing, to be honest, for quite some time. Longer than I care to remember. So don't tell me you'll be with me in a minute and then laugh with that man over there when, plainly, I need you now. She'll come and go and come and go until, finally, she leaves altogether for another phase of casual employment, casual everything, no benefits, only to be replaced by another one, who will know instinctively how to come and go and come and go and go.

I never want to leave him again. I am trying to reconstruct how this happened. There had been a message left for me at work telling me to come late for him. Who left that message? Anna gets to make toasted sandwiches for him. Cheese and tomato and cheese and ham. She makes soft-boiled eggs for him, four and a half minutes. He can't grow up without knowing that I know that it's four and a half minutes. She cuts off the top of the shell. The cut is always clean. There are no jagged edges. I could do that but I've tended to tap it with the back of a teaspoon till the shell smashes. Then I peel it off. There are often tiny pieces of shell that I've missed. He always finds them.

But it's faster my way. It's quicker to use the back of a spoon to smash the eggs which, incidentally, I've got to pay for along with the sandwiches, the marbles and bicycles, the heating, the school uniforms. Anna says it's faster to cut the top off the egg.

The nasty girl-child with the ponytail and the skin-tight t-shirt sees my platinum credit card. I pretend I'm out of cash because I want her to see the card. I want to see her wonder whether she's missed out on a tip because she wasn't more attentive. There's a momentary flicker in her eyes, the sullen realisation of a missed opportunity that's disguised as a smile, which leaves her face as soon as it arrives. Of course I tip her generously. I might be back here again and, anyway, there's no point having the card if you don't tip well.

I know, once it's over, that wanting the young waitress to acknowledge the privileges attached to my credit card is a pitiful sign of my discontent and insecurity. But the realisation always comes too late. As it's all happening, I want her to see the card, to see my reflection in the shiny part that not everybody gets. I want her to see the car but there's no reason for her to look at it before I come in and afterwards it's too late. Too late for this time. I parked a little too far south down Chapel Street, out of her view.

I am walking to my car, remembering a sour-tasting fragment of a nightmare in which Angelique is in league with Anna's ex-boyfriend. I almost walk into a couple nursing the sharp-cornered carrier bags of the designer stores. They hold the bags in each of their outside hands and their inside hands clutch each other. But how firm is the grip? Is he, on closer examination, slowing her down? Do the bags contain an apology or do they hold a bribe? Do they expiate guilt? Do they obfuscate? Is there anything more to their relationship than the contents of the bags? Do these people speak to each other now only through the labels?

Years ago when Anna and I first started seeing each other she used to chide me for my poor taste in clothes. We made a date to go to Country Road so she could choose some things more to her taste. Nothing too radical—shirts, pants, jacket and shoes, a whole new wardrobe. Actually, it wasn't prearranged. We'd just come out of an afternoon movie. Those were much better times. She still wears the same perfume but its smell is different now. Every now and then I can smell it as I did then. I can smell it that way right now. I dragged her into Country Road to choose some clothes for me. She'd said that she didn't care what I wore but she often joked about it, that my clothes were out of date or else that I kept wearing the same things over and over. So when we came out of the movie that afternoon and I noticed the store, I suggested this was the time, right then. She could mould me, put my money where her mouth was.

We went inside and I followed her around to the shirts and pants. She pulled items out and held them up to me. Then a young salesman came and offered to help. Anna pointed at me and the salesman looked me up and down for a moment. Before showing me anything he asked me questions. What did I have? Where did I want to wear it? How about something more like this? I didn't know the answers to these questions. I looked to Anna but she was gone. At first I didn't know where she was. Then I saw her way down the other end of the store. She had quit. I called out to her. 'What about these?'

She didn't answer. I called again and saw her from a distance fan away the air in front of her face, briefly and dismissively, just once, and then return to whatever she was looking at. In the car she denied it but something had happened, something had snapped or clicked inside of her. She'd had to leave. She could not have the sales-man or maybe the other people in the store see us together with me depending on her completely for my wardrobe. Suddenly, perhaps for the first time, I was pathetic to her.

We argued bitterly about it. She kept denying what seemed obvi-ous to me, that the shopping had induced an almost chemical reaction in her. Irritation, shame, contempt—I'd delivered them sub-cutaneously. From then on I knew it could happen at any time without warning and there would be nothing I could do about it. I had the capacity to look ridiculous and pathetic to her. All my life, all my efforts, my defences, my skills, my wiles, they had all been devoted to distancing myself from the hapless son of an often absent drunken father and a sad, ineffectual mother who thought that tasteless boiled sweets could hide from her children the threadbare nature of their miserable existence, a family even Jesus had aban-doned. But Anna had found me out. She took a still picture of me that day which she cannot get out of her mind. This was way back, before we were married, before we were even engaged. This was before the seventeenth day when our first son stopped breathing one morning, before I started sleeping with whores and before Anna went back to Simon, that teacher I think she wishes she had mar-ried, a man who took my son.

8

I am walking to the car and it's taking forever. I cannot feel my own face. Then suddenly I can and it feels flushed, hot, burning. It warms my hands as I stop in the street to cover my face to get the temper-ature right and to see if I might not feel like an orphan anymore when I take my hands away. But when I take them away, they get cold again and my face stays at a temperature that would fry an egg. I don't know how I'm going to be able to do normal things anymore.

I can't remember what I've got to do. There's a corporate retreat coming up. Have we got the Sheeres tonight? No, that's in a fortnight. Anna wasn't going to be here this weekend. That's why the Sheeres are in two weeks. Is that why? Who else is coming? Will Donald Sheere get to hear about this, about all of it, about Angelique and me? What would Sheere say if he knew everything? The commission I have made trading for Donald Sheere alone would have paid for our house twice over. More. It started with his wife. Two or three years ago Gorman called me into his office with great solemnity. I thought I was going to lose my job. He asked me what I knew about Donald Sheere.

It was a rhetorical question. Gorman already knew what I knew about Donald Sheere. Sheere has been in the financial pages for at least the last fifteen years. His family has been in the social pages more or less since the beginning of European settlement. It didn't matter if you didn't know quite how or when the Sheeres made their money originally. Your children, their babysitter and the foreign woman who cleans your house would know who and what Donald Sheere is.

Sheere is a man for whom the acquisition of money is an autonomic activity. It is to him like breathing air is to all of us. We do not notice we are doing it unless we find that the air is unclean, in short supply or unless we find ourselves falling through it. Donald Sheere has never found money unclean or in short supply. He regularly falls through it only to land on a thermal and soar even higher. I have seen him do it. I have since helped him to do it. He is always grateful, charmingly grateful, charmingly, patricianly, Protestantly, unexuberantly grateful. If there is any physiological change in him upon the attainment of some objective, it is undetectable to the people he employs. Perhaps that's what they mean by breeding.

At the end of Gorman's question—what did I know about Sheere?—was the announcement that I had been chosen to be his wife's broker. I had been working my way up through the private client division and this, he explained, quite unnecessarily, was an opportunity to get to the very top of that division. But I'd have to do the right thing by her. I'd have to service her to within an inch of her life. I knew that too. There was a time not so long ago when a woman like Elizabeth Sheere would have occupied herself with charity work. She was still involved with a number of charities and volunteer organisations but now only as a patron or honorary president, with no administrative involvement other than to be reminded to consult her diary for luncheons and balls. Elizabeth Sheere had become a brand name eagerly sought by a panoply of organisations that collect money on behalf of people and causes she paid someone to brief her about. But now that her children had grown up, and she a little with them, this had all become rather tiresome. She owed her standing entirely to the wealth and success of her husband. That the success had been his and not hers had not mattered to her before. But now it did. She wanted her own. Not wealth. Donald had assigned her enough of his. She wanted success. She wanted to play the market. That's when Gorman called me.

I took her out to lunch a few times and flirted with her just enough for her to enjoy it but still be unsure whether it was actually happening. This takes great skill. Then I made her a lot of money. This took less skill, at least on my part, but she was left in no doubt that it was actually happening. She wanted the excitement and the success. And in something that would engage her husband's interest, something that had a more than ephemeral and ornamental connection with the world that occupied his day-to-day attention. It wasn't just that she bought appreciating stocks, and in large parcels, and not always blue chip either. I also had her sell against her feminine intuition right before certain collapses. How did I do this? How did I know when to come in and when to go out? I didn't know. I guessed. But it was an educated guess. Who educated me? Dennis Mitchell, the prince of analysts.

When Elizabeth Sheere started making money out of stocks no one had ever heard of and, even better, selling stocks everyone else was enamoured with right before they crashed, her husband suddenly found her as interesting as he had when they were courting. That's when Donald Sheere started calling me. He called me directly. There were no preparatory visits to Gorman's office. One afternoon I'm at my desk. The phone rings and a beautifully modulated, crisp, older man's voice, a gentleman's voice, asks, 'Is that Joseph Geraghty?'

'Yes, it is.'

'This is Donald Sheere.'

I came home that night, parked the car in the garage, took a shower, had a drink, and told Anna that we'd be moving.

She told me not to get my hopes up but I could tell she was impressed, at least momentarily. We moved. We bought and renovated an old two-storey house near the beach. We put in a pool and tennis court. I delivered as I'd said, and so did Donald Sheere. I became his personal broker for pretty much everything he traded: stocks in the old and then also the new economy, futures, options, hedge funds, anything going that Mitch so much as winked at. Then Sheere started recommending me to his friends.

When this began to happen, Gorman had no choice but to shelter me from the mum and dad investors who can rob a dealer of his time, his most valuable asset. I say rob because they call up and slowly ask a million questions all based on the unarticulated proposition that the law of gravity does not apply in the commercial world. When you have finally convinced them of the invalidity of this deeply held conviction, they want to know why, if you know so much, you cannot make them into Bill Gates in the next week or two. They never buy anything, not in any substantial quantities, not these long-talking, inquisitive ones, but you have to keep smiling and talking over the phone as you age rapidly, all in the knowledge that these are the people standing between you and a healthy retirement. They don't really want to talk to a dealer. They want a social worker with stock tips. The ever-so-slightly rich Volvo- and Saab-driving new-moneyed ones are the worst, worse than the retirees. They're always on about corporate responsibility and ethical investment, which is all very well. I just don't see why I have to talk about it every day while I'm trying to pay off my house. And they love to mouth off about Donald Sheere or Rupert Murdoch like they were still at university. Little self-righteous new money hates big self-satisfied old money more than either of them are hated by never-had-any money.

9

We are having the Sheeres to dinner in a couple of weeks. Anna begged me not to invite them. She said she couldn't stand the pressure of an evening with them and people like them. People like them! I thought she wanted to be people like them. If not, which people did she want to be like? She used to want to be people like them. I think she did. We seldom have sex. Never kiss. I make her cups of tea sometimes on weekend mornings and she leaves notes in large print for the foreign woman we employ, telling her the food I like. She no longer takes my hand under the table when we're out. She no longer reaches for me at night. She can have the Sheeres to dinner. I've paid for it, many times over. They're busy people. It's taken a long time to arrange it. It's taken my whole life. I would ask Mitch if I thought he'd come.

On my way to the car, the telephone rings shrilly in my pocket. I ought to throw the thing away.

'Hello.'

It's Anna. Sam is crying in the background.

'Where are you? You've got to come home,' she says.

'What's wrong? Why is he crying?'

'There are journalists photographing him through the windows.'

'What?'

'Can't you hear me?'

'What are they doing?'

'It's the papers, Joe. The phone hasn't stopped. People want to see him, interview him.'

'Interview Sam?'

'Or us. I can't get rid of them.'

'Have you called the police?'

'I'm calling you, Joe. Are you coming home?'

You buy a house in spring. The warm air, smelling of blossom and daphne, reawakens that tentative mood of hope which winter so nearly extinguishes every year. You try not to be influenced by anything the real estate agent says but you fail in this. His words, chrome-plated, reflect what you already hope to see in the house. You had not counted on spending this much, but the position *is* great and it does have so much potential. You and your wife have so much potential. You've got to take risks. Surely you will grow into the mortgage. You can see it now. Knock down that wall for an extra bedroom. You will drive your car into the three-car garage at the end of the day. It will never rain here. You will never speed into the driveway and screech to a stop in the hope that you have arrived in time to catch and assault a man who is trying to photograph your crying little boy.

'Hey!' I call out, slamming shut the car door.

He is around the side. Anna hasn't called the police or else they haven't arrived. The photographer looks at me and doesn't try to explain who he is or what he is doing. He can see that I know. He runs now, calling out something, some kind of apology, but he is only running further into my property. A skinny man who has done this before, he tucks the camera under one arm as he runs. What does he think is going to happen? He runs along the side between the fence and the trees. I have never moved so fast.

'You fucking prick!' I say, breathless. By now we have reached the back yard and I lunge at him, using him to break my fall. His camera drops to the stone paving around the pool.

'Mister, there's been a mistake,' he says, breathing hard and trying to get me off him.

'No mistake here, you fucking cunt. That's my son in there. He's crying.' I have my knee on his throat. 'You want to sell papers with that? He was kidnapped and you want everyone to see it, to make money from it for your boss. Quite a coup. Well, you won't sell this.'

He is gasping. His face is turning red as he grabs my balls.

'I'm going to fucking kill you,' I scream at him. I am punching his face repeatedly, left then right again and again against the smooth stone paving and I am going to kill him. He is squeezing tighter. I am killing him. I am trying to kill him as Anna is pulling me off. She has her arms around my shoulders. She uses all her strength to drag me off him. Sam is crying inside. He can see everything. The moment Anna has enough of my weight off the photographer he rolls over to where the camera has fallen. Seeing this I break out of Anna's arms. The photographer is on his feet. He holds the camera in one hand and I lunge at him again.

'Joe, are you crazy?' Anna calls out.

But I am. With my right arm I knock the camera from his hand and it falls on the stone again. He jumps back to get away from me. His face is bloodied and I am smashing his camera.

'Joe!' Anna calls out.

I jump on his camera till it is unrecognisable, till I am unrecognisable, so that no one will ever recognise Sam from the papers as the boy who was taken, like Eloise and the Chinese girl. I am shouting. The photographer runs past me. He is bleeding and wants to get away. I know how he feels. He makes it out to the street.

'Have you lost your mind?' Anna says.

Sam is crying and I shiver by the swimming pool in the mid-afternoon sunlight that the real estate agent had promised would hit my back yard at about this time. I shower and wash away the adrenalin and some blood to reveal cuts, strains, sprains and the beginnings of some bruises. I work out twice a week. Anna thinks it's three times a week but the third visit of each week is a phantom. That's when I used to see Angelique. But twice a week I bench press, cycle, work on my abs, pecs, biceps, quads, so I'm in pretty good shape. But I don't fight anymore. I haven't been in a fight since I played football towards the end of school. So while I'm not in bad shape for an Audi-driving husband and father who smiles at people from the neighbourhood when he sees them in the supermarket or at the dry-cleaner's, I am out of shape when it comes to using my hands to kill a man who has seen me coming and does not want to die in the course of his sordid job of photographing a little boy through the windows of his house.

The hot water stings. I nearly vomit. After the shower I notice that the veins in my arms and feet are horribly distended. I go to bed but not before washing down the analgesics with some vodka, which I keep by the bed. Anna doesn't notice this. She hasn't noticed it yet. She's playing with Sam. I am too tired to return the bottle to the freezer and I wonder if she'll notice it. If she notices the vodka will she say anything about it and if she doesn't say anything, will that mean something?

The leaves of a tall tree caress the outside of our bedroom window. I am utterly alone. There is no sound coming from downstairs. Perhaps Anna has taken Sam to the park. My eyes are closed but I cannot sleep. Someone should really come and check on me. I bought this house and I am Sam's father. These cannot be said to be bad things. No one can say that. How does a person come to be so alone? One is born in it and, somehow, despite parents, siblings, girlfriends, colleagues, a wife—despite finding a wife—I can't shake it.

Dennis Mitchell took me to a brothel. He doesn't judge me. He looks out for me. He has a fine mind. I look forward to seeing him on Monday. I often do. I've just realised that. Has he read about it in the paper? Is he aware that the little boy in the news is my son? I should take Sam to work one day, show him off again. Not yet. Let things calm down. I wish I could sleep now. Maybe I can. Maybe I will if I just close my eyes for long enough. It will happen.

She is here. I don't believe it. In my half-sleep she is here saying something about Sophie, her younger sister, taking Sam to the park. We are alone in the house, in the bed. My eyes are closed. She is running her hand along my skin. It is cool and gently touches the places where I hurt. My muscles are calmed. She seems to know where I ache. She can feel it better than I can. Sliding into bed, she is in her underwear. She whispers something. I can't hear her properly but she's not angry with me. I know this much from her tone. Now she reaches for that part of me I thought she didn't care to touch again. Her voice is quiet. She speaks slowly. I can just make out her words now that she is under the covers. She is admitting that I was right to do what I did to him. I know who she means—I know what this means. She speaks in waves and in between the waves she takes me in her mouth. I don't move. I can't remember when she last did this and it is as though she knows that this is what I'm thinking because she tells me as she takes me. She tells me between breaths that she is doing this because of what I did to that man. She sees me differently now, like she used to, and I don't move in case something changes. She is on top of me. She is younger than she was this morning. My eyes are still closed and I lie still, listening to the sounds she is making. It is like the sea. I take deep surreptitious breaths. I won't hold for much longer. I want to see her do this. I will need to store it. I want to look but if I move she might stop. The slightest change and it could all be over. I might spoil it. But if I am to see her down there I will have to look soon. I want to shiver. I can just imagine how she looks with her hair, beautiful thick hair forming a veil behind which she has me in her mouth, in her hands, in her mouth. She moves her tongue along the sides, one then the other, with the flat of her tongue. I will have to look. Soon. Now. I start to raise the covers, slowly, gently. She is not disturbed. Perhaps she hasn't noticed. A little more. I look down barely moving my head, just slightly off the pillow. My eyes are still largely closed. It is dark down there. I see her hair. She is still going. How much longer will we be able to inhabit this moment? She looks up for a second or two and I'm afraid I have spoilt it. But through the dark I can see her smile. She is smiling, then she licks her lips. She looks younger. Now she goes back down. I slide along the bed just a little. She looks up. She is younger. I can see her face and it's so like Anna's face but not the Anna I know who sips her tea. She smiles again and it is not Anna. It is Sophie. Oh God. Oh, sweet young Sophie. I am gone like a train. It's all out of my control except that now I ache there too. When I stretch out I feel all the other aches. They have matured. I feel them when I exhale but that is all I can feel. On the other side of the bed the sheets are stone cold. Below me it is wet. I open my eyes. No one is here. Not Sophie, no one.

10

The front door unlocks, opens and then closes downstairs. I hear Anna and Sam with what sounds like Sophie. Things are put down on furniture: car keys, coats or jackets, bags, a ball, maybe a kite.

'Do you want coffee, Sophe?' Anna calls from the kitchen, and then, 'What kind of juice, Sam? . . . Sammy, what kind of juice do you want, sweetheart?'

Upstairs beside me on the bedside table the vodka is unmoved. I can't put it back in the freezer now without them seeing it. Why the hell should I be ashamed of it? Why should I be ashamed?

'Do you want some help, Annie?' her sister calls.

Right from the beginning I have liked Sophie. I have always wanted her to admire me.

'No. I'm fine. You stay with Sam and I'll bring it all in. I've got a surprise for you, Sam,' Anna calls.

What has she said to Sophie? This has changed everything. That bastard has changed everything. I splash some water over me and throw on some loose-fitting clothes. I can't be a prisoner in the house I bought. What have I done wrong? Decent men do what I did. They don't steal children. I want it to be Monday already.

'Sophie, how are you?' I kiss her on the cheek.

'Better than you from the sound of it. You poor thing.' She gives my shoulder a gentle squeeze.

'Has Anna told you the whole story?' I ask her, not yet knowing the whole story myself.

'Yes,' she says, sympathetically, indicating she doesn't know the half of it.

We look at each other for a moment across the coffee table. We're alone. Sam is in the kitchen with Anna. Neither of us knows what to say. Sophie looks like a slightly fairer Anna. She smells beautiful, sitting there, and I imagine telling her my side of the story, all of it. I have certain needs. Do you remember Anna's boyfriend? What do you remember about him, Sophie? His name was Simon. Did you like him, Sophie? Well, Anna has been having an affair with him. At least, I think she has been. Otherwise why would he tell the police that he had permission to collect Sam after school? It is something that is so easy to verify, and he was, he is, a bright guy. Isn't he? So why would he say it? Have you known about this, Sophie? Have you been coming to my house, to my son's birthday parties, knowing what Anna was doing? Do you like this house? Do you want it? She doesn't want me, Sophe. Hasn't for the longest time. I don't have affairs but . . . has Anna told you? You'd like her. It's not sleazy. We talk and everything. I see the same one each time. It's not the way it sounds. You'd like her, Sophe. Yes, of course we've done everything you can imagine, but sometimes I just hold her. Women like that. She's someone I can talk to. You could talk to her. She can be really funny. She remembers things I've told her, weeks before, months before. She's always asking questions. It's like having a secret friend, whom nobody knows about, and this secret friend wants nothing but good for you. I know what you're thinking. I don't understand it either. Do you know whether Anna can tell us? Does Anna know what Angelique was doing there with Simon when the police came? Sophie, do you know? I'm going to miss her. Do I look foolish to you?

Neither of us knows what to say, so nothing is said and Sophie looks at me. I can feel tears gathering. I pick up the packet of boiled sweets from the coffee table. No one has touched them since my mother left.

'Do you want one of these, Sophe? My mother brought them and I can't seem to sell them, not for love or money.'

Sophie always has a different boyfriend. They're all lucky to know her, even briefly. Any man would want her. I don't meet them. She'll settle down with one of them sooner or later, for children if for nothing else. I want to know her children. They will hear about me. I will be an outline to them. That's Sam's dad, the one over there.

Neither Anna nor I could have hosted the Sheeres tonight. We are too tired even to accuse and counter-accuse in the privacy of our bedroom. It happens that each of us, independently of the other, has a glass of water and a sleeping pill by our beds tonight. Perhaps hers is a tranquilliser. I am in bed first. She turns out the light. Tomorrow her parents will come. The veneer of my life is on fire. It's dark in here. We have our backs to each other. Our eyes adjust to something like the world of the blind and I wish she would touch me. We breathe the same air. Soon it will be midnight. Has she already fallen asleep?

'Anna,' I whisper.

The wind taps the tops of the branches against the outside of our window.

'Anna.'

'Mmm,' she says eventually. Most of it is air.

'Anna, her name is Angelique.'

The house is still. Outside the branches are at rest. We are both so tired. Perhaps she hasn't heard me. She does not move and then I hear her whisper.

'I know . . . Go to sleep, Joe.'

Mitch, you have to love him. At work everybody seems to know that the little boy in the weekend news was my son. The young woman who sits in reception looks at me with a gentle pity I can't remember anyone ever bestowing on me. She knows that it was Sam. She even remembers seeing him once. This particular news story has captured her, it has impregnated her and it swells inside her. It consumes her. Throughout the weekend she has told everyone she knows that the little boy on the news, the one who was kidnapped, is the son of one of the guys at work. In the morning before she left for the station to catch the train to sit at reception all day, taking calls and signing for deliveries, she looked at herself in the mirror as she dabbed a little perfume under each ear and on her wrists and she tried to work out what she would say to me about it when she saw me. But when she does see me she can't bring herself to say anything. Having lived it herself the whole weekend she is exhausted by it and can only say, 'Good morning, Mr Geraghty.' Shyly, for I am suddenly a celebrity, albeit one to be pitied.

Gorman calls me into his office. He wants to commiserate but commiserating is not something he is good at. It is not a skill he has developed over the decades he has been summoning people into his office. To commiserate properly you need to know how to empathise with another person, or, at least, how to pretend to. Gorman doesn't. He finds the whole thing unpleasant, not the other person's misfortune so much as the socially mandated response. Never has he had to find the words to express the response he is meant to have to the kidnapping of someone else's child.

'Joseph, Joe, come in. Sit down. What a terrible business. How is everybody?'

'We're fine.'

'And . . . er . . . Simon?'

'Simon? Do you know . . .'

'Your son.'

'Sam.'

'Oh, yes, Sam, of course. Sam. How is he?'

'Thanks, he's well. Probably better than we are.'

'Really . . . really,' Gorman offered. 'Yes, you do look a little . . . er . . . Do you . . . would you like to talk to someone in Human Resources or . . . ?'

'No, I'm fine thanks.'

'Well, we've got the retreat coming up. That will . . . er . . . that's something to look forward to.'

There are tiny beads of perspiration on Gorman's forehead. He looks for relief in the handling and contemplation of his letter opener.

'Your figures are good, Joe. Keep it up. Can you keep it up given . . . what's the . . . given the circumstances?'

'I think so.'

'If you need any time . . .'

'No. I'll be fine.'

'Because we can always find someone . . .'

'Find someone?'

'Someone for you to talk to.'

'No, I'm happy enough talking to clients.'

'Well, we're here if you . . . we're behind you, Joe. Keep up the good work.'

This is something I have to go through. I now have a new social obligation—to give people the opportunity to offer their respective renditions of an appropriate response to the kidnapping of a colleague's child. It's boring, uncomfortable and time-consuming. That's why you have to love Dennis Mitchell. He doesn't say anything about it. He doesn't even know.

Mitch would feel obliged, like everybody else, to say something if he knew. Perhaps he hasn't read the paper. He never does what everybody else does. He doesn't even talk about what everybody else talks about. When people finish whispering about my family's descent into the world of tabloid crime, the talk of the office is the internet start-up Numero-one.com, the Silicon Valley wannabe whose modest pre-float claim was that it would change the way most people did most things. Whatever this meant on closer examination, it had resulted in an exponential rise in the price of the company's shares. Its appeal to investors lay in its offer to its customers of a free .com, .net or .org domain name for use in setting up a personal customised website.

Within a year Numero-one was to have signed up three million customers by acquiring the domain names en masse from Wide World Names, the domain name registry of a state university's publicly listed I.T. spin-off. Over a weekend the deal between Numero-one and the university's I.T. spin-off fell through. I don't know why. It was never my stock. It just had a smell about it. That's what Mitch had told me, quietly, in the tearoom. 'Don't touch it,' he said. The following Monday morning, within approximately twenty minutes, the price fell from seventeen dollars to one dollar sixty.

When something like this happens, there is usually at least one person in a firm like ours who will come as close as a human can to breaking apart without the application of physical force. Sometimes, not often, you can see it happen before your eyes. If a man puts enough clients in touch with a rising stock he can drive off into the sunset. If he puts enough of the really big boys in touch with a rising stock he can put a deposit on the sunset. Peter Laffenden did exactly that. There was talk that, at twenty-nine, he was going to retire on what he'd made from Numero-one. This morning the sky fell in on him.

I was talking to Gorman when it happened. By the time Gorman had been reminded of my son's name, Laffenden was finished. After lunch we'd be able to watch the security camera's transmission of Laffenden in the underground car park trying to fit all his files into the boot of his Alfa Spider.

Too much too soon? People will say that. But it's not my business, only my concern. I could have sold it but I gave it the 'Dennis Mitchell' test and I'm still here taxing Gorman's sympathetic nervous system on the occasion of the abduction of my son. Laffenden, whom they called Laughing Boy while he was making a killing, is in deep trouble. It's over for Laffenden.

Mitch will, sooner or later, find out what went wrong with the Numero-one–Wide World Names deal but he'll keep it to himself, store it for use in the future should the need arise. Right now he's not bothered about it enough even to momentarily warm himself in the glow of having been proved right or to nourish himself for an instant on the fresh steaming schadenfreude on which some of the others will be feasting. To Mitch, Laffenden is a casualty of the vicissitudes of the market. There is nothing more to talk about. But the others are talking about it, slyly, quietly. They are wondering whether Laughing Boy is going to fall on his sword or whether he's going to have to be *walked out*. There is more to see if he's walked out. The word is that he will be walked out but that's only because people want him to be walked out. Although not even the biggest fool, the dumbest loud-mouthed cowboy, could think that what's happening to Laffenden couldn't happen to him, they all want to see him walked out. I do.

Many people here have never liked Laffenden. He's young and loud, he's made a lot of money and he's told everyone about it. In this he is like a lot of the people in the firm. Many people here have never liked many people here. When, years later, Laffenden remembers all those eyes watching him carry his boxes from his work-station by the window, down the passages formed between the desks, past the photocopy machine and the water cooler, past reception to the lift; when he remembers certain half-whispered comments from colleagues who he would not have expected to so relish his demise, comments he was only half meant to hear made in the near orgasmic relief that it is Laffenden and not the maker of the comment that is dead, comments made to themselves, rather than to him, which attempted to explain why this was happening to him and not to them—when, years later, Laffenden remembers all this, he probably won't remember that many people here never liked many people here. He won't remember that it was nothing personal.

Dennis Mitchell has other things on his mind. Forget Laffenden and Anna's boyfriend. Mitch wants to see me. He wants this to happen immediately. Mitch is on heat. He wants to talk privately, out of the office, and so we meet for coffee downstairs.

'You've heard about Laffenden. I never liked him. You probably guessed that. Is this about Laffenden?' I ask him.

'Laffenden's through,' Mitch says dismissively.

'I know. Do you know what happened?'

'The deal fell through over the weekend,' he says as though nothing could be less relevant to us, as though he is hurriedly going to humour my need to pay lip service to the topic.

'I know it fell through. Do you know why?'

'No. Do you know?' Mitch says shifting almost nervously on his seat on his side of the booth in the coffee shop.

'Mitch, what's this about?'

He looks around the room. No one, including the waitress, pays us any attention. I have escaped to this place many times, though never with Mitch. I come here for the continental style coffee scrolls. I shouldn't, but it's the icing and the chopped walnuts. The radio plays songs for my mother. Nothing momentous was ever meant to happen here. Mitch hunches over, puts his hands together on the table in front of him and then raises his eyes from his hands to my face.

'Sid wants to see you.'

'Sid Graeme?'

'Yeah. He wants a meeting. This is pretty big, Joe.'

'What's it about?'

'Look, Joe,' he says, almost in a whisper, 'this has got to be between you and me. It's more than a matter of commercial discretion. This is a political hot potato.'

'Sure, Mitch, no one can know. Now what the fuck are you talking about?'

My body suddenly begins taking messages from its outskirts. The cuts, the sprains and the bruising around my ribs, from my attempt only days earlier to kill a man on the stone tiles around my pool, are losing patience with Mitch.

'Joe, this is as big a thing as you've ever been involved in. You can't even tell anyone in the firm about it. Not yet.'

'What do you mean? You want us to do something involving Sid Graeme and you want us to do it *outside* the firm?'

'No, of course not. Just don't tell anybody till after Sid Graeme has filled you in on it and we've discussed it.'

'Jesus, Mitch. What's this all about?'

'Are you in, Joe?'

'You know I am. I'm always in.'

12

Between talking to Mitch and my meeting with Sid Graeme later in the afternoon, I wish to hide from Gorman, from my clients, from the other dealers and from reception. I wish to be left alone to contemplate making enough out of whatever Graeme has in mind to buy off the past, to relegate it to having existed only to make everything sweeter from now on. The damp threadbare childhood home that a frightened ageing mother cannot bring herself to leave; the mostly absent twice-convicted father they let out just in time to die somewhere, anywhere other than on the system's watch; the two siblings absent without leave and the overgrown damaged one I can never forgive or sufficiently apologise to; the dangerously intelligent and dissatisfied wife with the widest eyes, the smoothest skin, the softest shock of hair, who looks upon me as a vulgar aberration in her life, an aberration with whom she made the mistake of having a son she wants to share with an old boyfriend. How much money does it take to be impervious to this? And will it help when you're an object of curiosity, even for people who do not know you, because your son was taken?

Of course I am not left alone. I take calls from clients but my mind wanders more than usual. What had Mitch said about me?

How come it's me and no one else that's in on this, whatever this is? Laffenden is finished.

Were his eyes always such a pale blue? I could never look in them when he was on top. I can look now. We all look. We have to look. He had a loud mouth. Of course we look. If we could, we'd look way past his carriage of the boxes, down the corridors, past the car park into the first of many bars. If we could, we'd be there at the bottom of each glass as the contents further drained the blue from his eyes until they had the egg-white cloudiness of the eyes of an old dog. We would be there when he tells his young wife how she has never understood the pressure he's been under. She will try to understand exactly what has happened but she will always think she doesn't understand because when he finally, reluctantly, explains, it will all sound too simple. She had always assumed her husband's job was far more complicated than the manner of his losing it made it sound. But she will immediately understand his shortness of temper, why they must stop frequenting the restaurants where the maître d's squeezed her husband's hand and kissed her on the cheek as they arrived. She will understand when an agent forgets to warn her in advance that the young couple he brought through the day before would like to be shown through the house a second time. If we could, we'd be there when she throws a vase at Laffenden and, in a voice that would cut glass, tells him that he is useless. We might even want to be there when she calls up an old boyfriend.

Anna, you won't believe what happened to Laffenden today. She won't believe it. She won't ever hear about it. She won't understand that I won. I'm still here, watching *him* leave. Anna won't remember ever having met Laffenden at a firm Christmas party. So I make a mental note to find someone I can talk to. Anna, was there a day when you thought we would be friends forever? On that day, you would have wanted me to have someone to talk to if you weren't around, not in preference to you, but just in case you were unavailable. You wanted the best for me. How long is it now that you have been unavailable? That's why I went to her every week. I swear it. Okay, not at the beginning, and we didn't just talk. Christ, no. But sometimes we did, sometimes we just talked. But now even she is gone. Now I can't even talk to her. Anna, why did you take even her away? Why did you condemn me to solitary confinement? If my thoughts, my feelings, never get any fresh air, if they stay locked up in that dull, plodding, thick head that I have to lug around everywhere, how is it any different from solitary confinement? How did you do it, Anna? How did you manage to co-opt Angelique?

If I am to stay sane I will have to talk to someone or at least imagine that I am talking to someone. It has been a long time since I have even imagined confiding in Anna. But Angelique, until Friday, I thought I could confide in her. I would have told her everything. That's the truth. I would have told her about Sam and Anna's boyfriend, about Mitch and Sid Graeme.

13

Four days after Sam was taken, Mitch arranged for me to meet Sid Graeme at the head office of Health National, Graeme's health insurance company. At the top of Collins Street, it was a new building with a renaissance façade. Façade is everything.

'Joseph, I'm glad you could get away.'

'I got the impression I would have been mad not to.'

'Is that what Mitch said?'

'More or less.'

'I've heard a lot about you, Joe.'

'I'm sure it's not true. Don't believe everything Mitch tells you.'

'Oh, but I do. Don't you?'

'Well, actually, I do. We work pretty well together.'

'That's what I've heard. Pretty well and pretty close.'

'That's true, Mr Graeme.'

'Sid. If we're going to go ahead it's got to be Sid. Okay?'

'Okay, Sid.'

'Are we going to go ahead together, Joe?'

'I would say so but I don't know anything about it yet.'

'What do you know about me, Joe?'

'You're very successful. You've got a large and diverse portfolio. You're the chairman and majority shareholder of this health insurance company. You're on the boards of lots of listed companies. And you're a member of the federal government health care advisory committee.'

He smiled. He was waiting for more.

'You donate to both parties although more to one than the other.'

'Well, they're the government more often.'

'You're connected at the top in one way or another to the opera, the ballet, the MSO, the Arts Trust, the Young Leaders Program, the Children's Trust, the Casino and the AFL. Have I left anything out?'

'If you have I don't remember it either. Do you know how I got started?'

'No, I don't. I don't think you inherited it.'

'No, Joe. I didn't inherit it.' He poured us both a scotch. 'My father was a salesman. He sold parts for cars, new and used parts. When I was nine years old, my father walked out. This happens all the time, I know. A man has a midlife crisis, meets a younger woman, starts a new family. Or else he gets some business opportunity and takes off. It's terrible, isn't it? I mean that, I'm not trying to be . . . funny. But that's not what happened with us. My father didn't meet a younger woman. He didn't meet any woman. He didn't take up any business opportunity, didn't get a new job. He went out one day when I was nine and he never came back. Eventually, we found out that he'd moved five miles down the road. He didn't want to have anything to do with us.

'When I was seventeen I joined the air force. You ever in the services, Joe?'

'No.'

'I joined the air force when I was seventeen.'

'What did you do in the air force?'

'I was stationed at Sale. I was a waiter in the officers' mess. You're probably wondering how I got from there to here.'

'I'm sure it's interesting.'

'I used to go into the radio room. I wasn't authorised to go in there but I'd sneak in. You know there are oil rigs off the Gippsland coast there?'

'Yes. I've even seen them.'

'Well, I used to go into the radio room and intercept the signals from the rigs. That's how I learned the results of the drilling. Then, knowing which company's rigs had done well, I'd get every cent I could beg, borrow or steal and buy into the stock before the information got to the market.'

'You did well?'

'I did very well. And I learned that information, the right knowledge at the right time, makes all the difference—that, and the right contacts.'

'The right contacts,' I said quietly, as though it was new and wise.

'Mitch understands this. I think he understands it as a matter of instinct. He said you understand it too, the importance of contacts and of timing.'

I kept telling myself to have patience, that I would understand what he was talking about as soon as he decided to stop promoting himself and tell me exactly what he had in mind. He was not a tall man. He was not a thin man. He used all his power not to be short and squat and he almost pulled it off. But in the context of his life, some fifty or so years, his power would have been too recently acquired to protect him from the particular wounds and inarticulable cruelties you suffer after a father, unannounced, moves away and leaves you crumpled on a chair, as though you were a jacket he had tried on for a while and had not liked the feel of. At least my father's absence was the consequence of failed attempts to help us in the only way he thought he could. Sid Graeme had soft hands, almost pudgy, good for an entrepreneur, but not for a waiter serving air force officers in the mess at Sale thirty years ago. To look at his hands, you could see the accidents, the fumbling, the humiliation that is the inevitable consequence of hands like that. Yes, he talked too much about himself but sooner or later he would get to the point because the point was where the money was. As he sat there talking out of his suit, so controlled, with me waiting to understand what this was all about, I had to admire his anger, the purity of his anger. It was there with him, even when he was quiet. It was definitely there and it had been there way before the money. I recognised it. It meant business.

'I'm the majority shareholder in Health National. We want to buy a number of private hospitals.'

'How many?' I asked.

'As many as we can, as soon as we can.'

'I thought private hospitals weren't doing too well at the moment. Aren't they . . . aren't they sort of struggling?'

'They are, Joe. At the moment they are but the government wants to pass legislation that will facilitate the introduction of US-style managed care. Managed care would make private hospitals very profitable. Managers run things more efficiently than doctors. There's a lot of fat to be trimmed in health care and medical people have no interest in doing it. I would do it, and the more hospitals I owned the more opportunity I'd have to do it, obviously.'

'What exactly is managed care?'

'Managed care is a system of health provision that is nothing short of a revolution, Joe, a triumph of common sense. It involves a commercial relationship, a contract, between the health insurer, such as Health National on the one hand, and participating private hospitals and private specialist doctors on the other.'

'I thought we had that already.'

'Commercial relationships between health insurers and health providers have been creeping in steadily over the last ten years or so, but there are obstacles to their legal enforceability. The proposed legislation will remove these.'

'Okay, but isn't this just a technicality?'

'Not at all. If the relationship between the health insurer and the participating private hospitals and private specialist doctors were contractual, it would transcend the relationship between a patient and his doctor or hospital.'

'What do you mean, transcend?'

'It would take precedence over the doctor/patient relationship. In fact, it would only be on account of the relationship between the doctor and the health insurer, and the relationship between the patient and the health insurer, that there would be any relationship, or at least any commercial relationship, between the patient and the doctor at all. This benefits everybody.'

'Why is that?'

'Well, the benefit for the patient, personally, is that the health insurer pays all the health care bills directly to the providers, the doctors and hospitals. Without managed care, the patient gets billed directly by the service providers and then afterwards has to recover whatever costs he can from the insurer. The benefit to society is that it allows huge cost reductions to the health insurer and to the private hospitals. It's been found, not surprisingly, that non-medical managers and accountants working for the health insurers and the private hospitals can manage health care in ways that greatly reduce costs and make the whole system more profitable.'

'How do they do that?'

'Well, they can do it in many ways. Nurses can be directed to do some of the work of doctors. A lot of it's very routine. There's a saving right there. Non-specialist doctors can be directed to do some of the work of the specialists. Specialists charge more. Cleaners can be given some on-the-job training to do some of the work of nurses. A lot of nurses' work is pretty basic. In many cases, in-patients can be discharged much earlier. Participating doctors can be contractually obliged . . . guided, with respect to the treatment they're advised to undertake—and also with respect to the fees they're able to charge. You see, Joe, if a contract is drafted properly, a doctor would be in breach for merely informing a patient of treatment not offered by a particular insurer's plan.'

'An insurer like Health National?'

'Absolutely. Why not?'

'But how does the health insurer know in advance which procedures are necessary in any given case?'

'That's a good question, Joe. It's not a stab in the dark for us. It could obviously prove completely disastrous if what we did were not medically legitimate, and that's where statistics come in. By rigorous use of statistics, we can actually know what's likely to be necessary for the treatment of any particular illness or injury and also, how long we can reasonably expect a patient to need to be in hospital.'

'And if they need longer?'

'They rarely do.'

'But if they do?'

'Then they can either go somewhere else or else pay out of their own pocket, on an ascending scale, of course. But the staff and the whole system would be encouraging the patient not to lapse into the ways of the bad old days. Everybody wins, Joe, and we're able to cap costs. Even ancillary procedures such as pathology, x-rays, ultrasound and magnetic resonance imaging can be tightly controlled and restricted to keep costs down. You ever had one of those?'

'One of what?'

'An MRI?'

'No, not yet.'

'Quite right too. I tell you, Joe, they're as scary as all hell. You don't want one,' Sid Graeme laughed.

'Let me understand, Sid. Private hospitals, which are not currently profitable, will be profitable soon and that's why you want to acquire them?'

'That's right.'

'There must be other interested parties who also want to buy up private hospitals.'

'You'd think so, wouldn't you?'

'I would think so . . . but you're going to tell me I'd be wrong.'

'Right again, Joe.'

'Well, don't other people know about this legislation and the profitability of managed care?'

'Yes, they do, but—' he paused significantly.

'This will be good,' I thought and, inadvertently, said. At least I meant it, even if I hadn't meant to say it. This wasn't always the case.

'It's thought that the government's legislation facilitating the introduction of US-style managed care in private hospitals won't get through.'

'It won't get through?'

'The Opposition have said consistently that they're going to block it in the Senate.'

'If the legislation is going to be blocked in the Senate why do you, why does Health National, want to buy as many private hospitals as you can?'

Sid Graeme looked at me with a smile. Here at last was the point, the point where the money was. He put his glass to his lips and swirled his scotch around in his mouth for what seemed like forever. When he finally leaned in close to my face to whisper the answer, I had to inhale the calm in the words that rode on his anaesthetised breath.

'The legislation will get through. It's going to get through.'

'What do you mean? You just said—'

'The Opposition is going to have a change of heart. Nobody knows this but they're going to support the bill. They understand that in order to be electable they can't fight the market. Oh, sure, they've got a few troublemakers but those guys are in the minority within their own party and, anyway, this is a matter that involves figures. It's all too hard for them. They don't really understand this stuff and they know that themselves. If they get a soft and fuzzy win on some environmental issue, they'll lie down. The pragmatists are just working out an acceptable form of words.'

'And nobody outside knows?'

'I do. Mitch does, and now you do.'

'How do you know this?'

'I have a contact. I have many contacts, Joe, you'd know that.'

'So you want to buy the hospitals as fast as you can before the bill gets through and before anyone suspects that private hospitals are going to start being profitable.'

'That's right. If I move fast enough, we can get them for a song.'

'How fast is fast enough?' I asked him.

'It's hard to say. It isn't just a question of the legislative timetable. The news could break before the bill is voted on.'

'What's going to stop it getting out now?'

'You're right,' he swallowed. 'It could get out any time. Except that the leak has come from the Opposition parliamentarians themselves and they're not likely to want to draw attention to how they're intending to vote.'

'Why not?'

'Well, even though everybody knows this sort of reform is inevitable, they won't want to draw attention to their one hundred and eighty degree policy turn. It'll look bad, like they're reneging on their principles or stealing the government's policy. And it'll give their extra-parliamentary membership the opportunity to rally to block the about-turn. Clearly, the sooner we buy the hospitals the better, because if the information does get out, their price will skyrocket.'

'And why are you explaining this to me?'

'Because I would like your assistance. I need your assistance.'

'Go on.'

'I need to raise money, a lot of money, in a hurry, through a share issue by Health National. I'm in this unusual position of needing investors to rush the offer, only . . .'

'Only what?'

'Well, because of the sensitivity of the information, I can't tell them why they should.'

'You can't tell them about the plan to buy up private hospitals or about the Opposition's backflip on the managed care legislation that will make these hospitals profitable?'

'That's right. And that's where you come into it.'

'How do I come into it?'

'I need the issue to turn investors on without telling them why it should. How am I going to do that?'

'You want some kind of rumour?'

'No, that's too dangerous. The truth could get out.'

'Sid, I think I've followed you all the way up till now but I don't see how I can help you.'

'Joe, I need a blue chip, high-profile, high net-worth, established and establishment investor to get the world's biggest hard-on for Health National as soon as possible. From what Mitch tells me, you can help me get him. You know who I mean?'

'Donald Sheere.'

'Can you get me Donald Sheere? Mitch says he likes you. He says he trusts you.'

'I think he likes me.'

'Mitch says he does. If Donald Sheere starts pouring money into Health National, everybody will. He's precisely the sort of investor who creates a buzz all on his own.'

'Why would Donald Sheere start putting his money into Health National?'

'Because you're going to tell him to.'

'Sid, Donald Sheere knows nothing about this whole health care industry.'

'So you teach him, Joe. I'm sure he's a fast learner. Here's a chance for a few people to make a lot of money.'

'Do you know him?'

'I know him socially.'

'Sid, I'm going to have to tell him. It's not going to happen if I don't tell him.'

'Tell him what?'

'About the legislation the government wants to introduce, the Opposition's forthcoming about-turn on it, and, as a consequence, its assured passage through the Senate, the whole managed care private hospital thing.'

'Jesus Christ, Joe, I *want* you to tell him. I want you to tell him everything, then I want you to arrange for me to tell him, and all as soon as possible, before any of this has a chance to get out. We just have to make sure Sheere understands that even his hearing about this is contingent on confidentiality. I can't have him talking about this to anyone or it's all over.'

'Well, he understands the need for confidentiality. He's not a talker, Sid, but . . .'

'But what? What, Joe?'

'I can't just tell Donald Sheere . . .'

'You can't tell him that he has to undertake to keep this quiet or you won't tell him anything? Now, listen to me, Joe. What the fuck are you afraid of? He's old money, yes, but it's still only money. If he wants to make a lot more in a hurry then he needs you. What's he going to do? Don't be afraid of him, Joe. This is your family's future. You can see that. Run after it, for Christ's sake. Grab it and embrace it, Joe. Your future does not have to be an enemy stalking you. This is an opportunity.'

I wondered how many times he had said that before, how many times it had worked and whether he knew before I did that it was working on me.

'Are you in on this, Joe? I've now told you everything you need to know. This kind of opportunity . . . well, you've been around long enough to know it doesn't come along every day. Gorman will thank you. Sheere will thank you. And you'll thank me. Will you get him for me, for him, for yourself?'

'You took a risk sharing this with me.'

'I made an investment, Joe. I invested this information with you on Mitch's advice. He said you were the man I needed. He said that not only do you have the ear of Donald Sheere but that Gorman thinks highly of you too.'

'Really?'

'That's what he said.'

'Gorman?'

'Don't be so modest, Joe.'

'What's Gorman got to do with it?'

'You'll have to sell the whole thing to Gorman if the firm's to underwrite the issue.'

'Sid, you didn't say anything about underwriting.'

'Mitch doesn't think that will be a problem, Joe, not with the two of you selling it to him.'

'To Gorman?'

'To Gorman, to whoever you need to get it past in order for the firm to underwrite the share issue. Mitch doesn't see a problem with that. You're going to help, Joe, aren't you? You're not going to let this go?'

He knew and Mitch knew I was not going to let this go. Sid Graeme squeezed my arm at the biceps as we shook hands. I turned to go but I stopped when he started to say something I couldn't quite catch.

'I know all this . . . a bad time for you, Joe.'

'I'm sorry, Sid, I couldn't quite hear you.'

'What with the . . . er . . . loss of your son.'

'He's not dead, Sid.'

'No, of course not. Look after him, Joe.'

14

One day when Sid Graeme was nine his father moved five miles down the road to another suburb without telling anyone. The repercussions of an event like that do not abate with time. They are the engine of Sid Graeme's commercial enterprise still. And on top of that, he is a talented man. I have to admire him.

Driving home I was tempted to take the fact of this opportunity, the fact it was me that was acting as the intermediary between men like Sid Graeme and Donald Sheere, as a measure of my competence, my skill. Mitch had recommended me. Gorman thought well of me. He'd even told Sid Graeme about me, an asset to the firm by all accounts, now with a golden opportunity falling into my hands. If I could just take Sheere with me on this. But in any event, here was I in this beautiful purring car, thinking about getting these two men together while Laughing Boy Laffenden had been home for hours trying to explain to his wife how it all fell apart.

I was tempted to think how much I deserved where I'd got, how I'd worked for it, worked hard to get a reputation, worked to win the trust of men of such high standing in the financial world. Most of the drivers in the cars around me were not wearing suits. They appeared content to drive dented cars with leaky exhausts and prolapsed mufflers, content to cling to hairshirt salaries which would never keep them from shivering each night in expectation of the debts delivered each day in the mail to their unpaid-for houses.

I was tempted to think all of this when, at a traffic light, I caught sight of my own face in the rear-view mirror. I had got older. I noticed my eyebrows. My father had one continuous eyebrow which lent him a Cro-Magnon quality that was amply confirmed whenever he spoke to you of his plans. Since childhood I had kept tabs on my eyebrows to make sure they were not turning into his. In the days when Anna commented on such things, she would laugh, pointing out how, after a shower or after I had washed my face, I would unconsciously comb each eyebrow with my finger. Stopped at the traffic light, I saw that in between the two still well-behaved, separate eyebrows, a long, curly, wayward hair was growing chaotically from the bridge above my nose. The lights changed and I thought suddenly of Laffenden.

Would I be able to get Donald Sheere to invest in Health National? I felt a little tightness in my chest. I loosened my tie and kept fast-forwarding the tracks on the Phil Collins CD, looking for one I wasn't sick of. I'm always forgetting to put other CDs in the car. I thought about my father's hands and about Sid Graeme's hands. I thought of Sam's eyebrows and was grateful that he looked like Anna and not like my brother Roger, who was everything my father's genes had threatened taken to the ghastly extreme my mother took two buses to visit each week.

Anna would ensure there was none of my father or Roger in him and if she did that and only that, maybe I could stand her affair with this Simon of hers. But he can't touch Sam. Perhaps Laffenden wasn't home at all. Perhaps he hadn't come home yet. Maybe his wife still didn't know that her husband was finished. How do you tell your wife? The eyebrow grows and grows and you can't do anything about it. We'd have to get the firm to underwrite the Health National share issue. Mitch could do it. Mitch could get Gorman on side. I'd do what I could to help him. Laffenden could have helped him to do this just as much.

The meeting and the traffic made me late. I turned into our drive with a thin disk of pain in my head. Removing the key from the ignition finally stopped Phil Collins from telling me again that you can't hurry love. Great version, just like the original, but please, some other time. I'd have to put something else in the car.

My mother's boiled sweets had not moved from the coffee table. They sat there in their cellophane bag, a little shrine of sweet anachronism, unwanted. Anna was standing in the kitchen, reading the newspaper while eating a bowl of stir-fried something or other. It was late, late for dinner, late for any semblance of cosy domesticity which, on reflection, we only contrived in company anyway. When I asked about Sam, she managed to make a simple statement of fact sound like an accusation.

'He's upstairs. I've just put him to bed.'

'I'll go up and see him, kiss him goodnight,' I heard myself say in a voice that asked permission. We have looked at each other differently since Sam was taken. We watched each other and waited to see which one of us would break first, which of us wanted to know, needed to know, the prime details the other had been hiding.

'How's my little man?'

'Dad!'

He was reading *Winnie-the-Pooh*. It is impossible to say how much I love him. It continually astonishes even me.

'Watcha reading?'

'Winnie-the-Pooh.'

'Oh, that's a good one. Haven't you read that? Haven't you read that before?'

'Yes, I like it, Dad.'

I gave him a kiss on the forehead. 'How was school?' When I asked him this, he turned back to the book.

'Sam? Sammy, how was school?'

'Okay,' he said without turning from the book to look at me.

'Sam, listen, little man. Can I put the book down for a sec?'

'Oh, Dad.'

'Please, Sam,' I said, taking the book and putting it on his bed-side table. 'Sammy, can we have a little talk?'

'Yeah.'

'A little talk . . . a father and son talk?'

His eyes were getting heavy as he answered, 'Yes, Dad.'

'Just a little talk between a dad and his son, which we won't tell Mum about . . . 'cause it's just between us. It's something between the boys and we're both boys.'

'Yeah,' he said. His eyes were closed.

'Sam, you remember last Friday when you got to visit the police station?'

'Yeah,' he said quietly.

'You remember the man that picked you up from school?'

'Yeah.'

'You were a brave boy, weren't you?'

'Yeah.'

'Were you ... Sam ... did he ... did that man ... touch you at all?'

'Yeah.'

'He *did* touch you?'

'Yeah.'

'Where? Sam, where did he touch you?' He didn't answer. 'Are you sleepy, Sammy?'

'Mmm.'

'Where did he touch you?'

'We ... we had chocolate milk, Dad.'

'Sam. Sammy, does Mummy know?'

'Mmm.'

About a week later, Anna told me he was having trouble at school.

'What do you mean, *trouble*?'

'His teachers have commented his marks are lower.'

'Lower than what?'

'Lower than they were before.'

'Before what? Before your boyfriend molested him?'

'Joe, I don't know if you're capable of having an adult conversation anymore.'

'Yeah, and I don't know if you're capable of speaking without condescension anymore.'

'Joe, we've got our problems, separately and together. We're angry at each other. But this is Sam and he's unhappy. You've been burying yourself in your work even more than usual and, don't say it, I know it's for all of us but ...'

'Okay, Anna, okay. You're right. Tell me what his teachers have been saying.'

'They say he's not paying attention in class.'

'Well, he's got to have inherited something from me.'

'I'm serious, Joe. You know he used to pay attention in class. He used to be near the top of the class.'

'I know.'

'They even mentioned ADD.'

'What's that?'

'Attention Deficit Disorder.'

'Oh, that's bullshit, Anna. He gets plenty of attention. Is this since the . . . the night he was taken?'

'That's not what ADD means, and anyway, they say it started before that.'

We looked at each other guiltily. My eyes grew moist and I didn't know why. Perhaps it was the way she was speaking to me. She had not spoken to me in that gentle soothing tone in the longest time. It was how she still sounded when she was alone with Sam. How in God's name was I meant to know how to be married? It had seemed enough once just to know how to choose a wife. I think she knows that I am forever fighting the sneaking suspicion that it is all my fault. But if she knows it, how does she justify using it against me in that self-righteous holier-than-thou way? How cruel is that? If she really is so superior she ought to be able to see that whatever it is about me that has made her change her mind about all of this is beyond my control. She mustn't be so hard on me for her mistake.

'Joe, I know you don't believe me but I have not been having an affair with Simon Heywood. I've barely seen him since we got married. Actually, I don't think I have seen him at all since we got married. I know things haven't been so good between us for some time, but this whole business with Sam and Simon is a crazy nightmare for me too; it's as much out of left field for me as you say it is for you.'

'As I say it is? What do you mean? Do you think I knew something about this in advance?'

'No. But—'

'But what? Jesus Christ, Anna! It was your ex-boyfriend that took him.'

'That's true,' she said quietly. 'That's true, Joe, but who was he with?'

She was right. The police found our son with her old boyfriend and a woman I saw regularly for sex. I could not explain that. Perhaps she really could not explain Simon Heywood. Whether she could or not, I felt ashamed. I have certain needs and these needs do not, of themselves, make me a bad person. I have no choice with respect to them. People make a big deal of it but it's just like eating, sleeping or going to the toilet. What if your wife wouldn't let you go to the toilet? You cannot force your wife to want you. In the beginning, you choose a woman who wants you but if she changes and you're the last to know and you're married, what do you do? I'm sure she tells Sophie everything. How long has Sophie known that her beautiful big sister married a mistake?

'Do you still have sex?' Sophie would have asked.

'Hardly ever.'

Hardly ever. Almost never. Just a bit of comfort, even a caress would have been a sign of hope. If you have these needs and you cannot force your wife to want you, what do you do? I have been seeing a woman, the same woman, a lovely young woman, every week for what must be well over a year, maybe two years. We talk. I have made her laugh. She's bright, funny. Sometimes I concentrate on her pleasure. Sometimes she focuses on me. I pay her. I pay the house, and I tip her. Over time you grow to know each other, a little anyway. This was never meant to affect my son.

'Joe, I have to know this.'

'What?'

'When you see that woman, is it . . . are you protected?'

'Of course it is . . . was. It always has been.'

She didn't say anything.

'Anna, you do believe me?' It was true. Angelique likes the slogan, 'If it's not on, it's not on.' She remarked on the cleverness of the same words meaning different things but being clearly understood by everyone. I don't even try. I tried once. She wouldn't agree to it, and she was right. It made me feel better about seeing her regularly because I knew then that she was safe. A small momentary frustration ultimately kept me coming back. It was good business.

We were in our bed. Anna had not spoken for a while. I had just tried to assure her that I was safe, that I was clean. I never thought I would have to do that.

'Anna, I had always hoped that you'd want me again . . . unprotected and I . . . wanted to be . . . ready. I wanted to be safe for you.'

'What did you do?'

'What do you mean?'

'With the woman . . . with the prostitute, what did you do?'

'Oh, Anna. Let's not talk about that.'

'I want to know.'

'No, you don't.'

'Don't you think I've got a right to know?'

'Oh, Anna. Let's not talk about rights. I'm your husband.'

'Is it too private?'

'Shit, I don't know. Yes.'

'What, it's just between you and her?'

'Anna!'

'What do you do?'

'Anna, this humiliates both of us.'

'You mean both you and her?'

'Anna!'

'Do you do it all positions? Does she let you do it anally?'

'Anna, I'm not answering this.'

'Do you get her to dress up?' She was crying. I leant over to comfort her but she recoiled and her voice grew louder and raspier through her crying.

'Do you hit her, just a bit? Does she piss on you?'

'Oh, Anna, please!'

'Does she piss on you?'

'Oh for God's sake, Anna! Let's not do this to each other.'

She threw the covers off her side of the bed in one quick agitated movement and leaned halfway up on her elbow.

'She does, doesn't she?'

'Anna!'

'You won't answer the question because she does and you can't even lie straight in bed.'

'Anna, you're getting hysterical.'

'Just answer the question then.'

'Will you calm down if I do? Why are you asking these questions? You're the one who turns her back on me. How long has it been, Anna? How long?'

'Fuck you, Joe. Answer the question.'

'Once. Once she did. I didn't ask her to. She just did it.'

'You're disgusting. Get out of my bed!'

15

Years ago, in the period after our first son had died and I was trying to rejuvenate an intimacy between us, I had once, during a thus far unsuccessful lovemaking session, suggested that she sit on top of me and just let herself go. She was horrified. I was just casting around for anything that might spice things up, just trawling my mind for anything at all, flailing around, desperate to ignite her. What was wrong with that? I didn't particularly want it. I thought she might like it. She didn't and obviously she had never forgotten it. But it was a random, private sexual suggestion from a husband to a wife made in an attempt to catch a spark. It was wrong to convict a man for something like that. I didn't take other people's children.

On reflection, her questioning seemed consistent with the position she had taken from the moment Sam was returned to us. I could not really believe that she hadn't been having an affair with Simon Heywood. Everything pointed to it. Her anger, her indignation, was clearly genuine but it would have us both at fault in order to mitigate what she had been doing for years.

Other than neutral questions—'Are you making coffee?'—or innocent statements of fact—'My car is making that funny whirring sound again.'—all our more lengthy conversations since Sam was taken ended in shouting and the verbal equivalent of one of us hanging up. The more I thought about it the more I became convinced that she had been seeing Simon. Looking back, there had been signs. I can't remember what they were anymore but I remember the idea of her seeing someone flickering across my mind. Did it bother me? Of course it did but you content yourself with the uncertainty. In all likelihood, I would not have given her the benefit of the doubt had she been a stock I was advising on, but I gave myself the benefit of my doubt about her just to put it out of my mind. Even if it was just for the sex, she had to be seeing him. We never slept together anymore and, despite these cold troubled phases, she was essentially a passionate woman. Even during those times in the past when she would have nothing to do with me, say between our first son's conception and Sam's, even then, she used to satisfy herself, at least occasionally, with a battery-operated toy I had bought her once from a little dive in St Kilda. She'd ducked into a cake shop and I told her I'd meet her at the car. When I showed it to her at home, she pretended to be shocked and embarrassed, but I know she's used it. She thinks I don't know.

I was even sceptical about the conference she was meant to be going to the night Sam was taken. But then, that had to be genuine because she couldn't have been off for a weekend away with Simon the night he took Sam. And he had planned it. He had chosen the day carefully. It wasn't an accident. Unless she was meant to meet him at his place with Sam? That was unlikely. It didn't make any sense. And where did Angelique fit in? You lie down with dogs, you get up with fleas.

Neither of us was sleeping much in the period after Sam was taken. I tried to tell her that there was something exciting, something big I was working on at the office, something potentially career-advancing. She was as polite as one could be and still exhibit unequivocal indifference. It had been years since she had once or twice shown any real interest in my work, or even in the market generally.

'Isn't it exciting?' she had once said. 'No one really knows what's going to happen.' This was before we were married. Now she couldn't care less. Occasionally she spouts some undergraduate nonsense about the environment or the homeless or something, as if she, or any of us, could be players in those arenas. She has said that she regrets not studying further. The money she makes is not bad at all for a second income but we don't really need it. We haven't needed it for years, not that I ever discouraged her from doing a postgraduate course even when we did. She's not serious about it. I secretly suspect Anna is afraid, like most people, that she's an idiot, which is crazy. It couldn't be further from the truth, but of course I wouldn't tell her that, not anymore.

There is an old fire station near us that was recently turned into an art gallery. She thought that was a good thing. We argued about it. She called me a philistine under her breath. I heard it.

'Well, if I'm such a philistine how come a man like Donald Sheere respects me? He's on all these boards that you have respect for, patron of the arts, a regular Medici.'

'He respects your capacity to make money for him.'

'You know this, do you? Anyway, listen, you can do worse things for somebody than make money for them.'

'He called today, you know.'

'When? Donald Sheere called?'

'His office called. The Sheeres send their apologies. They can't make the dinner party.'

'What are you talking about?' She could not have said anything that would hollow me, gut me more immediately.

'Something must've come up. I don't know.'

'No reason? Why didn't you tell me?'

'They just called today. I'm telling you now.'

'You know this is important to me, to all of us, and you're giving me shit about art galleries . . . about the community's need to express itself. Jesus, Anna!'

I had been trying to talk directly to Sheere ever since my meeting with Sid Graeme but he had been, even for him, unusually hard to get. Mitch had been calling me repeatedly to find out what Sheere thought of Sid Graeme's plans for Health National and I kept having to tell him that I hadn't been able to get hold of Sheere. It was embarrassing, bad enough in front of Mitch, but Sid Graeme was positively strung out when he called. 'Were you the right man for the job?' Sid wondered aloud. I started to wonder too. Sheere had always returned my calls fairly promptly and never before had I so stressed the urgency of my need to speak to him. I started to doubt the 'special relationship' with Sheere that had led Sid Graeme to rely on me. How could I get people so wrong, or had something changed? Had I inadvertently done something to offend him?

The funny thing was that my disappointment, each time I put in a call to him and was told that he would call me back, was tempered by a certain calm. It was a calm born not of confidence but of relief. I was calling him about as often as I could without stalking him. I was doing my job up to that point. As long as he was unavailable for me to pitch the Health National managed care thing to him, he couldn't reject it. And I couldn't fail. But it was the postponement of a failure that would in a short time itself become a failure.

The dinner party was my insurance policy. It was my guaranteed opportunity to pitch for Sid Graeme. It had also been the only thing I could offer Sid and Mitch to placate them. When Anna told me they had cancelled I was suddenly at sea.

'How much do you need, Joe?'

'What?'

'How much money do you need to make? When will it be enough for you?'

'Anna, what the fuck are you talking about?'

'Well, Don Sheere doesn't actually need any more and you have the house you wanted, the car you wanted. Yet you're so agitated when a couple pulls out of a dinner party.'

'Jesus, Anna! It's not just any couple.'

'You don't really like him, Joe. You don't really even know him.'

'Anna, what do you know about what I know? You sure as hell don't know what I like.'

'No, I'd have to be a prostitute to know that.'

'Why are you trying to goad me? You want an excuse to run off with the school teacher? You never needed one before.'

'How many times have I got to tell you? I haven't seen him in almost ten years.'

'Anna, you were meant to see him the night Sam was taken. You knew all about it. That's why you weren't worried about him.'

'Wasn't worried about him! Are you out of your mind? I wasn't meant to see Simon the night Sam was taken, not that night or any night. You're paranoid, Joe.'

'I'm paranoid, am I? My son is stolen by my wife's ex-boyfriend only to be found by the police—'

'Joe, the police—'

'Let me finish. The police say that the ex-boyfriend's story is that the two of you are lovers. That's what they told me when I picked Sam up from the police station. When I ask *you* about it, you continue to deny it and when I have my doubts you say I'm paranoid. But you don't offer any alternative explanation. Really, Anna, with intellectuals such as the two of you, I would have thought you'd get your stories straight. You'd better talk to him.'

'He's in prison.'

I looked up at her. She looked horrified at her own words.

'You tried to talk to him.'

'No.'

'You tried to get your stories straight.'

'No. Of course not.'

'Well, how did you know he was in prison?'

'The police told me. Anyway, it's in the papers.'

'You asked them.'

'Yes, I asked them. I wanted to hear it from them. Someone taking Sam without our permission, I wanted to be sure I knew where they were.'

'You were talking to the police?'

'They called today. They want—'

'Have you told them everything?'

'What the hell does *that* mean?'

'Did you tell them you were on your way to a conference the Friday Sam was taken?'

'Joe, they didn't call to—'

'You'd better at least get your story straight for the police. If I could find out, so could they.'

'Find out what?'

'You had no conference to go to. There was no conference.'

'Joe, the police called for *you*.'

'What do you mean they called for me?'

'They want to talk to you.'

'What about?'

'I don't know. They wouldn't say. Why don't you ask the prostitute?'

'Anna, just tell me the fucking truth.'

'The truth is the police want to talk to you.'

16

I put on my jacket. It was about eight o'clock at night when I got into the car feeling suddenly and quite wrongly like I had nothing to lose. Anna probably thought I was driving to the local police station. I don't know what she thought. I didn't particularly know what I was thinking either but I straightened my tie when I stopped the car outside the ivy-covered walled city that was Donald Sheere's Toorak house. I took a deep salesman's breath.

Would he offer me a drink? I needed one. All those manicured shrubs and stepping stones, ascending quasi-ancient pillars of rock off to the side of the stepping stones, all from some place Jesus never reached. They did their job on me as I waited, first to finally press the doorbell and then for someone to open it. The security camera was perched high in the corner above the doorway and to the right of one of the two Roman columns that guarded the front door. Who was it that looked down at me on a screen? Were Elizabeth and Donald Sheere in the same room? Were they watching television? What programs did Donald Sheere watch? Were they home?

A middle-aged foreign woman I assumed to be a housekeeper opened the door. When she had trouble repeating my name, I reached into my wallet and gave her my card. She read it slowly, mouthing the consonants of my surname incorrectly, almost in a whisper. Ger-ag-kh-tee.

'For Mr Sheere?'

'Yes, that's right,' I said, trying to hide my lack of patience, my exasperation, my nervousness. I was still saying it when she closed the front door.

I stood waiting outside his front door silently rehearsing my spiel. If he was busy I could come back later, but I had something to talk to him about that I really thought he would want to hear. The ring of my mobile phone startled me. I had forgotten to turn it off. The caller display indicated my mother's telephone number. Why was she calling me on my mobile? I let it go through to my voice mail. Sorry, Mum. I'm working. Why did I feel as though I were auditioning for something? I was trying to make the man some money. He could only say no. That was the worst he could do. I could survive that.

I wondered what my mother wanted. I turned my back to the door and looked at the shrubberies and the Sheeres' own little

Stonehenge. I thought of our fathers, Donald Sheere's father and mine. The distance between them was reflected in the time it was taking for the housekeeper to come back to the door. She could've just told me he wasn't at home. That wouldn't have taken so long. I would've gone away having done all I could have done to get hold of him and maybe more than I should have done. He would have learned that I had visited his home at night. Surely that would have made him curious enough to return my call. I started to wonder if the housekeeper hadn't forgotten me. I couldn't just leave in case, after all of that, he was available. I was wondering what I should do, if it hadn't been a huge mistake to go to his home like that, when, without warning, the door opened.

The housekeeper invited me in and asked me to wait in the foyer. I'd been there before but nothing looked familiar. The floor was mottled white marble. On one side of the front door was a winding staircase and on the other was a bust on a pedestal, presumably of some dead family member. Behind it the wall was almost entirely taken up by an oil painting of a bear being torn apart by five or so wolf-like dogs, with some seventeenth-century-looking men thrusting spears into the bear for good measure, all of it encased in a thick baroque frame. I was straining to see the name of the artist when I heard his voice.

'Joseph, what a surprise.'

I turned around and we shook hands.

'Is everything alright? I owe you a couple of phone calls. I'm sorry, it's been one of those weeks.'

He was dressed, without a tie, in a still-crisp white business shirt and in the pleated trousers of his suit. He led me to his study, all wood panels, leather chairs, plaques of his achievements and donations, telecommunications equipment in neat formations on the mahogany desk, and on the wall another painting depicting the dismemberment of a large furry mammal somewhere in Europe. He pushed a panel in the wall to reveal a well-stocked mirrored bar. As he poured us both a drink I looked at him and tried to calm myself. We mostly spoke over the phone. His hair had more silver-grey in it than I remembered but it was, as usual, perfectly shaped above his collar at the back of his neck and around his ears. He looked like he never sweated, never shouted and had never met anyone resembling my mother or father. Even the lowliest of his employees would have had greater continuity of income, would have experienced greater certainty in their day-to-day lives, than my parents. His father had been on the board of banks with branches my father had held up, unsuccessfully.

These were not helpful thoughts to have at a time like this. I was about to make my pitch for the Health National issue and thoughts about my origins and about the precariousness of my standing both in the firm and in that room, those sorts of thoughts, are audible in a man's voice. I had to think of the money, the commission, the houses, the cars. Thinking of the money had always worked for me before. What did that guy say? 'Picture success.' I bought the book but didn't read it. It was something Anna had said. But the title works. I'll give him that much. Nothing Anna can say about that. I was trying to think of the money when Donald Sheere turned around with a drink in each hand, one for each of us. I tried to meet him halfway but somehow our hands missed. One of us was a little uncoordinated.

'I'm sorry to barge in on you like this but when you hear me out I think you'd agree that it's pretty important.'

'That wasn't your son, was it, Joe?'

'Yes, it was.'

'Oh, I'm sorry. That is awful. Is he alright?'

'Yes, he's fine, thanks.'

'And . . . er . . . your wife—Hannah, is it?'

'Anna. She's fine.'

'That must have been terrible for you. The paper said they've caught the guy?'

'Yes. This isn't—'

'Terrible business.'

'Yes, but that's not why I had to see you.'

'No?' He seemed to stiffen.

'No, I need to talk to you about an investment opportunity that is potentially a huge winner.'

'Potentially?'

'I think it's excellent. If it wasn't, I wouldn't have been stalking you like this.'

He laughed, just a little, but he laughed. Here was the crack in the door and through it I could see the money. When he asked me what all this was about I cleared my mouth with my ration of his single malt and I started to sell the concept of managed care and what Sid Graeme's Health National was going to do with it. I was off and running. This is what I did. This is what had got me to where I was. It had got me into the man's study for a private audience after hours, and with a show of confidence, careful breathing, eyes on the prize and the sweet love of Jesus, there was no telling where it would get me.

Managed care, I began, refers to a health care system that is based on a commercial contractual relationship between the health care insurers and the health care providers, the private hospitals and doctors. I explained its commercial attractiveness—how, by allowing control of available services, it reduces costs sufficiently to transform the provision of health care into a profitable industry. He was still listening. I continued.

The attraction for the patients is that the insurer pays all the bills directly to the health care providers. It replaces the traditional fee-for-service system in which the doctors and private hospitals bill the patient directly and then the patient seeks to recover some or all of the costs from the insurer.

When I felt that he had understood managed care, at least as well as I did, I turned to Sid Graeme's Health National and his confidential intelligence concerning the government's proposed managed care legislation. The government wanted to introduce legislation to make managed care legal in private hospitals. The Opposition, ideologically opposed to managed care, was expected to block the legislation in the Senate. But Sid Graeme had a reliable contact in the Opposition who told him, in confidence, that despite party policy, there was actually majority support in the Opposition party room for the proposed legislation. Knowing this before anyone else in the industry, Sid Graeme wanted Health National to acquire as many private hospitals as possible. Private hospitals had been struggling up till now but the introduction of managed care would make them hugely profitable.

'How does he want to fund his acquisition of private hospitals?' he asked.

'Through a share issue by Health National.'

'And Graeme wants me to subscribe, and quickly, before the news gets out that the Opposition is going to pass the legislation and the price of private hospitals shoots up, right?'

'Exactly.'

Sheere refilled both our glasses before speaking. He was clearly thinking about it. He had got it in one. He hadn't thrown me out. Even if he said no, I hadn't made a fool of myself. I suddenly realised how utterly exhausted I felt. The bulk of the pitch was over but this was the dangerous part. This was the time in a sale when you desperately want to relax. I could have fallen asleep. But he was going to ask me questions, the answers to which would determine whether or not he was in. I had to be word perfect with the answers. Donald Sheere wasn't some talkback radio caller who had really wanted gardening advice but had missed the gardening segment and so had popped a question to the local investment guru.

'So managed care is really a scheme which takes the ultimate control of patients' health care from the patients and doctors and puts it into the hands of their health care insurers?'

I wasn't too sure that was the best way of putting it. 'Well, ultimately, I guess you could say that.'

He sipped his drink before speaking and I sipped mine.

'What's the profit margin of the hospitals Sid Graeme already owns?'

'Well, he owns two of them. One has a margin of five per cent and the other nine.' Mitch had told me this and I'd remembered it because sometimes I am really good at my job. People are always relieved when you can quote figures. Even bad figures can help them to trust you.

'Five and nine!' Sheere continued. 'No wonder they're struggling.'

'No private hospitals do much better than that at the moment. Most of them do worse.'

'Yes, I read about that one in the LaTrobe Valley.'

'But that's why they'd go for a song.'

'Yes, that makes sense.'

'But when managed care comes in, he'll triple nine per cent.'

Sheere thought for a moment before speaking. 'I suppose he wants an answer as soon as possible.'

'That's right.'

'Who's his contact, Joe?'

'In the Opposition?'

'Yes. I'd need to be very sure about this if I'm to move quickly.'

'Would you want to meet him?'

'I think that would be best, don't you?'

'No question. That's wise.'

'Who is it?'

I didn't know who it was. Mitch hadn't told me that. I didn't know if he knew. Sid Graeme hadn't deigned to tell me and I had not thought to ask. Would this sink everything? Put a spin on the truth. 'Sid hasn't told me but he said he'd tell you if you're interested in going into this.'

'He said that, did he?'

'Yes.' He hadn't.

'He might be a cowboy but he's smart. I'll give him that.'

Thank you, Donald. I wanted to sleep more than anything in the world. I would have given all his money to be able to lie down with my feet under the bleeding seventeenth-century European mammal and my head under his desk.

'Tell Graeme I want a meeting with his contact as soon as possible.'

'Sure.'

'Gorman is happy to underwrite this?'

'Yep. Absolutely,' I told him. The words came out of me like projectile vomit. It was not a matter of thinking about it. We both heard me say it at the same time. He had thought to ask me the question but no thought went into the answer. I had no idea how Gorman felt about this. We had not spoken about it. Nor had Mitch spoken about Gorman since Mitch had first broached the Sid Graeme matter with me. Had I just lied to Donald Sheere? I didn't know yet.

'What proportion of the private hospital market does Graeme anticipate he can own?'

'Between fifty and sixty per cent.' Thank Mitch again.

'Joe, if Graeme's contact is reliable and Gorman is willing to underwrite it, you can tell Sid Graeme I'm in.'

I was getting there. I was almost there. It was contingent on two things, both of which I had, more or less, lied about. Firstly, Gorman and the firm's risk committee had to agree to underwrite the share issue. Secondly, Sid Graeme had to agree to divulge to Sheere the identity of his contact who then had to agree to a meeting with Sheere as soon as possible.

My mobile phone rang again. This time I turned it off without first checking the identity of the caller. I was not yet out of the door and I wasn't taking any calls. Donald Sheere was thanking me for bringing the matter to his attention and apologising for not having got back to me sooner. In addition to my exhaustion I had started to experience terrible gripes in my lower abdomen. I could hear this inner turmoil and was certain that Sheere could as well. Worse than this, I was worried I was going to lose control. It occurred to me to ask him where the toilet was but that seemed a bit crass. As I struggled to remain continent and coherent, I jettisoned completely the idea of unburdening myself in Donald Sheere's home. The way I was feeling, even a fleeting moment alone on one of his thrones was bound to linger longer in his consciousness than my mini-tutorial on managed care. And who was to say it would be fleeting? But the contractions were becoming more frequent. I had to get out of there.

'Oh, Joe, I'm so sorry about your dinner party.'

'No, that's fine.'

'Have your girl call my office and we'll reschedule. I'm afraid I hadn't expected to need to be in Zurich.'

Surely he wasn't serious. In my parlous condition, for a moment I took his expression 'your girl' to mean Anna, and the thought of her response to being described that way almost made me lose it all in a convulsive voidance over the white marble. But then, as yet another spasm subsided somewhere below my navel, I realised that he meant my secretary. He would not have known that I did not have a secretary, just a telephone and a screen in a work-station that was fixed yet moveable. Laughing Boy Laffenden knew all about it. I had started to sweat before we shook hands.

17

The quiet winding streets of Toorak with their great walls and cast iron gates guarding manicured gardens and mansions by turns Tudor, Spanish, Georgian, Victorian, art deco and space age, are the enemy of a wayfaring interloper with a dire intestinal need. By the time I had parked my car and dashed into a cubicle at the back of a bistro on Toorak Road, I could not fairly be held responsible for anything I did. But a moment or two after my muscles relaxed and the beads of sweat on my forehead had begun to cool me, I slumped forward with my pants around my ankles and gave thanks for all that I was about to receive.

With everything that had been happening I had not noticed two unanswered calls on my mobile phone in addition to the call from my mother. When I listened to the message I found that one was from Anna telling me my mother had called and please, wherever the hell I was, could I call her because she sounded distressed. No surprises there. The other call was from the police. They wanted me to call them.

At first I assumed the police were calling to check out my version of something Simon Heywood had told them in an attempt to diminish the enormity of what he had done. I didn't know and could not imagine what I could tell them that Anna couldn't tell them, but then it struck me, suddenly, that their enquiry might not be related to this at all. I looked at my free hand, the one not holding the phone to my ear. It was my father's hand. Perhaps the photographer was going to press charges for assault. It had been a little over a week and I had heard nothing, but there was no statute of limitations. He could have been hospitalised until now.

When I thought about it I could still feel him underneath me on the stone paving beside the pool. The truth is, I had liked hitting him. I could still get myself worked up just thinking about him trying to take photos of Sam. So why shouldn't he want to press charges? Would I press charges in his circumstances? I don't know. Maybe. Maybe it wasn't even up to him. Perhaps his employer, the newspaper, wanted to boost sales with an exclusive twist on the latest victim of Anna's serial child stealer. That would explain the delay between that Saturday and these calls from the police. He had been off work trying to recover from the beating I had given him, and it was only after he got back that his editorial colleagues had become aware of the extent of his injuries and decided that there was a story in it, and an even better one if the police were involved. Editorial colleagues or not, the police were involved.

There was no question I had hit the man mercilessly. I had lost control. But he was trespassing. He was trying to get a shot of my son's distress. Someone was trying to make a profit out of it. My son had just been taken. So I hit him. But I hit him for much longer than any normal man possessing reasonable self-control would have. What was there to plead other than guilty?

Can I plead evolution? If aggression advantages survival, then perhaps the aggression which I inherited from my father and which I visited on the photographer that day was determined by evolution. That is how I might have tried to explain my assault on the photographer to Sam had he not been crying hysterically, had he not been convulsing in Anna's arms. Of course, had he been older still he might have considered that evolution can never be a defence to anything.

My father always said and acted as though he had no choice, as though *we* had no choice. For people like us, circumstance had to be grabbed by the throat. We had to make our own luck. He sure made his luck and I suppose I always believed that he made our luck just as he had made Roger, hastily and on a slow burn to catastrophe. But perhaps I am too hard on him. Perhaps things were different then. Now it is possible for a person like me to transcend his origins legally. I was invited into Donald Sheere's house. I did not have to break in. I am a stockbroker.

The police would like to talk to me.

There was no need to imagine how my mother must have sounded when she spoke to Anna. It was all there on the message she had left me. She was sounding like that more and more. Either that or I was noticing it more. I thought it was her. I know it now.

'Joseph, Joe? What phone is this? Is that you? Am I recording now? I can't take him, Joe. Not now. I'm too old. I can't do it. Are you there?'

Then it cut out. When I called her back it was as though no time had elapsed between her call and mine, as though she had continued the conversation between the calls.

'I can't keep him, Joe.'

'Mum, what are you talking about?'

'I know you won't take him, but, Joe—'

'Mum, take a deep breath. Let it out slowly and then tell me what you want to talk about.'

'I heard it on the talkback.'

'Heard what?'

'Most of them say it's a good thing and the expert did but I—'

'What did you hear on the talkback?' How do you keep her away from the radio? 'Is this about Sam?' I asked her.

'Not Sam—Roger.'

'What did you hear on talkback about Roger?'

'They say it's a good thing, calling it re . . . reintegration, but I—'

'Reintegration?'

'They'll close down the cottages and he'll have to live with me, Joe, but I—'

'Mum, what are you talking about? They're not going to close down the cottages.'

'That's what they were talking about on the talkback and they said it was a good thing because then people like Roger can get reintegrated. But, Joe, you know Roger . . .'

'Mum, take it easy. They're not going to close down the cottages and—'

'Why not? How do you know?'

'Because . . . because they're not. It's run by the government. They wouldn't do something like that.'

'Why not?'

'Because there would be an uproar. People wouldn't like it. And even if they did, which they never would, but if they ever did, he wouldn't have to live with you.'

'Well, you wouldn't have him. You said Sam was scared of him.'

'I didn't say that.'

'Yes you did.'

'No, Mum, I said the place, the cottages, would be a bit scary for Sam while he's still little.'

'Sarah wouldn't have him either, Joe. You know that and even if she would, she's interstate and I wouldn't want him so far away. I'd never see him like I never see Sarah.' She stopped at Sarah. It hurt her too much even to mention Megan and no one had heard from Denise since around the time we lost our first son. Talkback radio was bringing it all back home to my mother over her tea and sandwiches.

'Mum, it's not going to happen, but even if it did I'd see to it that he'd have a nice place to stay. He'd be alright.'

'Oh, Joe, he can't be out there. He can't be on his own. Who's going to wash his clothes? Who's going to get the dinner? He can't have a knife. He can't be with gas or fire. It's too late for all that and I can't . . . I'm too old, Joe.'

'Mum, it's not going to happen. Mum . . . Mum?' She was crying. 'Mum, are you there? Do you want me to come around?'

18

I told Mitch about my impromptu meeting with Donald Sheere and he seemed impressed. That was making it happen, going out and winning the business. He was not worried about Gorman and the risk committee. He said he thought that between the two of us we would have Gorman eating out of our hands and that if you had Gorman, you had the risk committee. Mitch said we just needed to 'do a Kissinger'.

'What do you mean?'

'Kissinger used to get all sorts of high-powered adversaries to the table by telling adversary one that he'd better be there because adversary two was going to be there and was very keen to meet him. Then he'd tell adversary two that he'd better be there because adversary one was going to be there and was very keen to meet him. So we tell Gorman that Donald Sheere is definitely in and you tell Sheere that Gorman and the risk committee are definitely in.'

Mitch was a well-rounded man. He'd read up on all sorts of things, not just finance and the market. He could have done anything with a mind like his. He just didn't have the personality for sales. With his poker face Mitch was, ultimately, an acquired taste. He did not instantly come to mind when one was putting together a dinner party guest list. It was not that he was colourless or phlegmatic. I knew he was enthusiastic about this deal but it was reflected more in determination than in excitement. I saw the determination in his eyes when we talked about Sheere's other precondition, a meeting with Sid Graeme's contact.

'This one's yours, Joe. You'd better fix it.'

Do you or don't you invite Mitch to a dinner party? For a start, he is very guarded about his personal life, so much so that I don't even know whether he is married or divorced. Second, I don't know if he can be trusted not to say what he thinks. I admire the way his mind works, but he is an analyst and not a dealer, which means he values getting it right above all else. At a dinner party, you have to allow your most important guests to be right even when they are wrong, to instruct you even in what you already know. The call for these deceits is the criterion that determines the right people to invite. I have never been sure Mitch understands this.

There is another reason for not inviting him. He would find my small talk and ingratiating manner quite nauseating and, in front of him, I would be ashamed of the fatuousness of my conversation. What did I talk about at dinner parties? I talked about the dollar. I talked about the mark, the pound, the euro, the yen, interest rates, the Dow, the FTSE, the Nikkei and the Hang Sen. I regaled people with little bits of information from journals I had begun to read but had stopped, distracted by the thought of the young woman from the dry-cleaner's sitting on top of me or by that perpetual question, the one that would not be resolved no matter what I did, 'Am I any good?'

Anna seemed to take the Sheeres' unavailability as a gift from God. She cancelled the dinner party citing, to the other invitees, the shock of Sam's kidnapping and of course everyone she spoke to, usually the wives, was nothing but sympathetic. Instead she put her efforts into planning a birthday party for Sam. She was going to invite all the children in his class, and organise games and prizes, the full catastrophe. I could not fault her with Sam.

Sid Graeme told me to forget it. Was I out of my mind? There was no way his contact would meet with Donald Sheere. He said the man would not even agree to be identified. I told him that was a shame because it killed the deal.

'Joe, you obviously don't know what these guys are like.'

'Well, isn't there any way around this?'

'You want me to make it worth his while?'

'I didn't say that, but I've got a very interested Donald Sheere. He likes it, Sid. He likes the sound of it very much, for Christ's sake, but he needs a little comfort. You can understand that. If he's going to put in the kind of money you want, it's only natural he'd want some assurance.'

'Joe, my guy won't talk. It's bad enough that he talked to *me* that time. If it ever got out that he was discussing the party's health policy with Donald fucking Sheere, the man is dead. No future, you know what I mean?'

'Wait a minute, Sid. You said he's talked to you *that time*. You mean you've only spoken to him *once* about this?'

'No, that's not what I mean.'

'Well, how many times have you discussed it with him?'

'How many times? What does it matter?'

'You want me to get Sheere to pour a vault of his money into Health National on the basis of one throwaway line capable of misinterpretation?'

'Joe, you're out of line.'

'I'm sorry, Sid. I really don't mean to be rude and I think you know that. Shit, I'm not casting *anything* on *anyone* but, Jesus, Sid . . .'

'How many times have I got to tell you, he doesn't like to talk about things like this to guys like us.'

'Guys like who?'

'Me and Sheere.'

'How many times *have* you talked about their policy turn-around?'

'I don't know.'

'More than once?'

'Yes.'

'How many?'

'I don't know. A few. Listen, Joe, call Sheere and see if it's enough for him to talk to me.'

'No offence but I can tell you it won't be.'

'Joe, call him. Let him prove you right. Tell him the guy has to think about his future. He'll understand.'

'Sid, he'll tell me to tell *you* to take care of his future. Tell the guy the future is not an enemy, it's an opportunity.'

'Joe, please, give it a try. Call him. See if it's enough for him to talk to me.'

I did not give Donald Sheere a 'try' because I knew what he would say. And however much I stood to gain if I could get Sheere to take up a substantial part of the issue Sid Graeme was planning, I was still Sheere's broker and it was decidedly not in my interest to alienate him. So if I needed to exert any pressure to bring these men together, it had to be on Sid Graeme not Donald Sheere. I gave it a little over ten minutes and then I called him back.

'No deal, Sid. I hate to say I told you so but he wants to hear it directly from your contact.'

'Well, then . . . I'm fucked, Joe. This guy, he's . . . he's a family man . . . and a good Catholic.'

'So am I. What the hell does that mean? You've got to tell him that talking to Donald Sheere is not like talking to the devil. He's already talking to you.'

'No, Joe. I mean if he's ever called upon to swear on the Bible and give evidence about who he'd been talking to and what was said, this guy will tell the truth.'

'Good for him. Very admirable. It's never going to happen. And if it did, any such meeting, if indeed he remembered one—and even then the best Catholics have memory lapses, Sid—any such meeting was a social one between a politician and some prominent members of the business community. At this social meeting, if he has to remember it, there were many things discussed: the weather, the football, Bananas in Pyjamas, a family trip to Sea World and certain aspects of the Opposition's health policy. Tell him that he's not doing anything wrong, that it's all innocent or Donald Sheere wouldn't be in it.'

'And neither would I be.'

'And neither would you be. Tell him all that, Sid, and then ask him if he likes sailing.'

'Sailing? Why sailing?'

'Because if he does, you should buy him a fucking boat.'

I still don't know whether the man sails or not. But everybody needs to be sold something. I needed to sell Sid Graeme the story which he needed to sell to the Opposition contact to make him agree to a meeting with Donald Sheere. In selling it to him I was also delivering what Sheere needed in order to go ahead with the whole Health National deal. The meeting was, after a torrent of calls back and forth, scheduled for late afternoon the next day. I felt a million dollars.

The police had called me at work but I hadn't taken the call. I had been too busy. That was true. I wasn't just avoiding them. Sheere could testify to that. Sid Graeme too, if it came to it. I tried not to think about it and found that easy to do most of the time, particularly after my success in arranging the meeting between Sheere and Graeme. But whenever I did catch myself thinking about the police, I always assumed the worst—that it was the incident with the photographer that they wanted to talk to me about, not Simon Heywood, and I felt something in my stomach, some small baseline anxiety that would eventually course through my veins when the shit hit the fan in some detective's office. My father's stomach was stronger than mine. You can't choose what you inherit.

There was another semi-hysterical message from my mother on the voice mail of my mobile phone. What time would I be picking her up to bring her over to our place for Sam's birthday party? And if

Sarah's husband lost his job, would I be able to get him another one? What the hell did that mean? Had he lost his job?

The meeting took place in a private room in Sheere's club, an impressive ivy-covered Regency building that ran off Collins Street at the Spring Street end. I was there first but wasn't admitted until Sheere arrived and signed me in. He had brought with him a young lawyer, Buchanan, who shook my hand with a sudden force which told me that irrespective of where we stood in relation to each other concerning the business at hand, sooner or later one of us would have to get rid of the other. There was not room for both of us in Donald Sheere's stable of upwardly mobile acolytes. We'd actually met before. I could see he remembered but he wasn't going to be the first to acknowledge it. Neither was I. Buchanan's hair was slicked back and he wore a pastel purple shirt with a louder tie than any Laffenden had ever sported. He looked like one of those brash teenagers one sees wearing an earring after hours in bars and nightclubs. But if he did wear one in that kind of place, he didn't have the guts to wear it in front of a man like Sheere, and of course, his judgment was a hundred per cent correct in this. I wanted to kill him.

Meretricious lawyers like Buchanan mostly came from the right secondary schools, the same schools that produced the majority of the people in our firm. From there they went to law school where they majored in coke and 'e' and sex with the honey-skinned daughters of their father's friends. As a kid I had seen them on the 69 tram, acting up for those more English than the English schoolgirls who wore their hair in ponytails and their tunics short and smoked ultra-mild menthol cigarettes. I only ever took that tram to play football. There were wealthy Catholics at the end of the line in Kew but we didn't know them.

Buchanan was already a partner in Sheere's favoured law firm. He had been brought along to scrutinise the deal, to 'legal' it, to perform a snap 'due diligence'. Given that it was not he that was putting the deal together, the only way he could promote himself in this was to find something wrong with it.

'Pleased to meet you,' he said, keeping hold of my hand long after he had delivered the line.

The choice of venue for the meeting and the unnecessary presence of Sheere's blond and tanned lawyer, not to mention the barely animated suit Sid Graeme felt the need to bring along, could not have been calculated to make the ageing Opposition backbencher more uncomfortable. Mitch was there too and I was glad he was. The backbencher sat frozen in his chair like a frightened rabbit. He looked like one of those people you see outside polling booths handing out how-to-vote cards that nobody takes.

Sid Graeme and I got the small talk going as best we could in an attempt to relax the frightened backbencher, but it didn't work. He drank his scotch like a dying man, holding on to the glass with both hands. He wanted it all over. But when we got to the Opposition's health policy, he sang right on key. Graeme had obviously rehearsed him. Mitch and I were silent as Sheere asked a few questions that called for him only to reiterate what I had already told Sheere. The man was humming along nicely and I thought it was all about to end when Buchanan felt the urge to remind us that he was there. He started to cross-examine the rabbit and my heart sank.

'Are you really saying there is no opposition at all to managed care in the parliamentary party?'

'No, I said no effective opposition.'

'No effective opposition? What does that mean?' Buchanan fired back.

'What little opposition there is will not prevent us from passing the bill.'

'Why is there *any* opposition to it?'

'Ideologically, the party has always held that medical care is not rightly a for-profit industry, a state of affairs which managed care is designed to facilitate. It's only recently that . . . well, how can I say it? Pragmatism has begun to prevail over this view and in favour of managed care. But not everybody is in favour of it.'

'Why is that?' Buchanan snapped.

'It's a political party, Mr Buchanan, not a board of directors. We accept a diversity of opinion and some members have, I suppose, been successfully targeted by those elements within the medical profession who are opposed to the implementation of managed care.'

'Who are those elements?' Buchanan came back.

'Oh, come on, you're not in court now,' I said angrily.

'Give the man the opportunity to answer,' Sheere intervened on Buchanan's behalf.

I thought he wouldn't know, but he did.

'There's a psychiatrist who is vehemently opposed and he has written a number of position papers on the matter. I would imagine that most doctors would be opposed to managed care to a lesser or greater extent but this guy is fairly passionate and vocal.'

'What's his name?' Buchanan asked.

'Alex Klima.'

'Is he alone in this?'

'No, there are others who've written about it but he seems to be the . . .'

'The ringleader?' Buchanan asked.

'Well, he's the most vocal. We've all been lobbied by him. But we'll be passing the legislation anyway. I think even Dr Klima knows that.'

'He knows?'

'He doesn't actually know,' the backbencher continued, 'but as I was saying before, he would have a fair idea of how few of us really believe it's as bad as he says.'

As it turned out, despite Buchanan's best efforts, the answers given by the backbencher did nothing to diminish the attractiveness of the idea to Sheere. If anything, they added to the urgency of the deal. If this psychiatrist, Alex Klima, had an inkling that the legislation would get through then the longer we waited the more chance there was that other people would get to know. If people knew, the acquisition cost of private hospitals would rise sharply. So it was agreed that night. The backbencher returned to his hole and Sheere and Graeme instructed Mitch and me to do all that was necessary as quickly as possible.

When everybody left, I walked Mitch back to his car primarily to ask him whether he thought we would have any problem getting Gorman and the risk committee to agree to underwriting the issue. He smiled and told me that he hadn't let me down. We had them all, Gorman, the backbencher, Sheere and Graeme. I could have hugged him. I didn't but I asked if he had chosen anyone to room with at the corporate retreat.

'I thought you'd never ask,' he said, 'but that's not . . . When is that?'

'Oh, it's not for a couple of months but the form came around today. You know what they say about the early bird.'

'Joe, that makes me a worm.'

'Hey, Mitch, forgive me my insensitivity. I'm not used to asking men to sleep with me. Now what do you say?'

'I think I can trust you.'

'We should have a drink to celebrate this Health National thing.'

'I'd love to but I've got to be . . . we've both got to be there extra early tomorrow morning and, to be honest, the tension has taken it out of me. Remember, you're the dealer, not me. I'm the back room type.'

You had to love Mitch.

20

Elated all the way home, it did not hit me until I pulled up in the garage and stopped thinking about the deal. I was late. I was very late on a day I had, days earlier, promised to be home extra early. I had missed his birthday party. I knew that the deal I had just facilitated would come to mean more to Sam's quality of life, and even to Anna's, than being there for his seventh birthday, but they would never see it that way. I would have hurt him by breaking my promise to be there. It was the sort of thing children grow up never forgetting. They grow up with the taste of that kind of crushing disappointment only a father can dispense permanently stuck under their tongues and you grow old smelling it on their breath whenever they talk to you. And the only way to get rid of it is to do something worse.

The house was quiet. Bizarrely, like something out of the Twilight Zone, a long children's party table had been laid but nothing, or almost nothing, had been touched. I wondered if I hadn't got the day wrong. I could live it again. But then Anna would not have put everything out, including jellies and cut-up watermelon, twenty-four hours early. Why would she have done that?

I was walking up the stairs when the thought first came to me. I wanted to scream. It was something he would never forget and it would overshadow my lateness and there was nothing I could do about it. Anna, her mother, Sophie, and perhaps even my mother, had prepared a party for him, invited everyone in his class and a bear from a children's television program. That had to count for something. There were tears in my eyes that my eyelids crushed out onto my face when, on reaching the top of the stairs, I realised none of the children had come.

Anna had him in the bath and when I opened the bathroom door she turned around and they both looked up at me. I knew I was right. From a class of twenty-eight, three children had turned up. The other twenty-five had not come. What had his parents done? Like me, Anna had been crying and I wondered if she had been able to hide it from him. Downstairs in the living room on the coffee table near the television my mother's boiled sweets remained untouched.

We had two gifts for him which we said were from both of us but that was belied by the dissimilarity of the gifts, a dissimilarity that was a reflection both of the difference between his parents and of the fact that they had nothing in common anymore but him. I had spent a lot of time researching the market for the dream toy of a seven-year-old boy and finally settled on the Capsela 200, a motorised science construction kit with ballast, flippers and seventy-two inter-locking parts. You could see the gears work and you could add to it as he got older. I would have loved something like that as a kid. We took it outside the next night, set some of it up and watched the flippers splash in the pool. For over half an hour my little boy tried to hide the fact that he didn't really like it. Even Anna seemed moved by his valiantly but thinly disguised lack of interest. She had got him an exotic aquarium. In the weeks that followed, he would just stare at it, silently, the life in him having been stolen.

About nine weeks had elapsed since Simon Heywood had taken Sam. The new issue had started to sell well after it was leaked that Sheere had bought in heavily. Everything Sid Graeme had planned was working. It was Friday night and we had just had the traditional Friday night drinks at the firm. The next day we were going on the corporate retreat. At work, Mitch and I were favourite sons, men of the hour, for an hour. At home I was a widower. I had drunk too much again, stayed too long, eaten corn chips and salsa instead of dinner. There was no one home.

Anna had taken Sam to her parents' place. She was there for dinner but he was staying the night with his grandparents, his *nonna* and his *nonno*, or whatever the Italian is for grandmother and grandfather. I went up to his bedroom and watched the fish. I lay on his bed. How did we make him so sad? Anna said he had been fright-ened by the television bear at his birthday party. She had had to get the bear alone with the two of them upstairs in our bedroom so that Sam could see the person inside the bear costume. There was a time when that would not have happened. There was a time when all his classmates would have come to his party. What had happened with him and Simon Heywood? What kind of person takes a child?

Simon Heywood. I don't think I ever met him, Anna was wrong about that. The paper said he was a teacher, an out of work teacher, but he was not a teacher yet when Anna was with him, when she was with him publicly. She will be with him publicly again when he tells a jury about their relationship. There will be an artist's impression of him in the paper and photographs of Anna and me leaving court. I thought of the photographer.

Some nights I can't bear to be so alone. This was one of them. You get to a certain age and you realise that you have been spending your working years on life-support being transfused against loneliness and only pretending to be alive. And except for the occasional tabloid photographer, nobody is really looking as you get into your car, into your fabulous car, already too drunk to drive, and you drive to a bar where no one knows you, so that you can listen in on the other people who don't have to be there alone. All of this can happen in your home town. It can happen to anyone.

I don't know why, but I picked up the cellophane bag of boiled sweets my mother brought Sam the day after he was taken and I put it in my pocket. Still in my shirt and tie, I put my jacket back on and got into the car. I pulled out of the driveway, aware that my wife's lover, Simon Heywood, was in prison. Now there was an opening line with which to strike up a conversation with a stranger in a bar. But I was content just to watch and listen and drink, for a while anyway. I had had a few beers when my mobile phone rang in my pocket. I almost didn't hear it and when I did I thought it was someone else's phone, and when I realised that it was mine, I almost let it go. It could only be Anna and what was she going to tell me? That she hasn't seen him in nine or ten years?

'Hello, Joe?'

It was a man's voice. It was Sheere.

'Joe, we've got problems.'

'Donald?' I could barely hear him.

'I've just had some disturbing news, Joe.'

I left my drink and went outside to try to hear him better.

'It's that psychiatrist, Joe.'

'Psychiatrist?'

'Alex Klima. I've just been told he has a letter in tomorrow's paper attacking managed care. He says . . . I've been faxed a copy . . . he says "managed care is a cynical system of health care which treats health like any other commodity. It sets up administrative and bureaucratic structures to control the provision of medical and hospital services in a way that ensures profits for the insurers and private hospitals, usually to the detriment of the patients' health". How do you like them apples?'

'I don't. But I wouldn't worry about it. This guy Klima, he always says that. He's been railing against it for years. Nobody listens to him.'

'They will this time. He's let the cat out of the bag, Joe. He goes on to say he has it on the authority of an Opposition senator that their caucus intends, contrary to declared party policy, to support the passage of the managed care bill in the Senate.'

'Jesus Christ!'

'Precisely. There is a lot of hostility to managed care among Opposition supporters and party members, you know, they're pro-welfare state and anti-business, and this disclosure will give them the opportunity to force the parliamentary wing to back off. Joe, the managed care bill isn't going to get through.'

'You don't know that—'

'Listen to me, Joe. First thing on Monday I want out of Health National.'

'Now, wait a minute. Don't you think—'

'Sell it all, Joe. It's over. The Opposition won't pass it now.'

'You can't be sure.'

'I can't risk it. Get me off the *Titanic*.'

'But it's only one letter. Who's ever heard of this Alex Klima? It's all decided by the New South Wales right. They never upset the market. You know that. This managed care . . . it's inevitable. They'll pass it.'

'They probably will pass it eventually, Joe, but not this session. I won't risk it. You'll get me out first thing Monday. Tell Graeme it was nothing personal. Joe . . . Joe? Are you there? I'm serious. This is an instruction. Sell it all, as fast as you can.'

'That's not so easy. You know we can't sell them till the Stock Exchange grants quotation to the new issue.'

'I don't care about the technicalities, Joe. Just sell them. Call up one of the banks and borrow an equal number of tradable Health National shares and sell *them* on the market first thing Monday.'

Sheere was right of course. The way around the problem was to borrow an equal number of quoted and therefore immediately saleable shares from a financial institution such as the trustee company of a bank, and then sell these. In return, the bank would get an equal number of the newly issued shares which, while not immediately tradable, become tradable once the issue is granted quotation, plus a fee.

The trouble was that the market would become aware that a

large number of Health National shares were being sold, and on Sheere's behalf. Their market price would plummet and the new issue would be undersubscribed. And our firm, as the underwriters, would have to take up the shortfall at a considerable loss. I had to get hold of Mitch. If we didn't do something we were dead. We were Laffenden.

'How did you get hold of the letter, if you don't mind my asking?' Despite the shock, I had to know, not that I didn't already have a pretty good idea.

'I've had someone watching the whole thing, a watching brief you might call it.'

'Someone from the paper called you?'

'No, no, no. I got a call from Buchanan. He just faxed me the letter a few minutes ago.'

21

I tried Mitch at home but there was no answer. Was there a way out of this? We had till Monday morning to change Sheere's mind. I couldn't think clearly. This was a nightmare coming to me live, via a mobile phone, in a bar in St Kilda. I sat there just staring at the phone in my hand. Some kid came up to me and asked for money.

'Get a fucking job.'

He picked a bad time, he could not have picked a worse time. This was a very bad time. The firm had underwritten the issue. Sheere had to change his mind. We had to change his mind. The firm's corporate retreat was tomorrow. We had to keep this from Gorman. I tried Mitch again. Still no answer. Buchanan. Buchanan was hanging on to my right hand. In one of my pockets I felt the bag of boiled sweets. I couldn't get rid of them. My parents are in me, in me and in Roger. No one ever had a watching brief for us. The ones with the real money, if we didn't work for them, they ignored us. And if we worked for them and stumbled, they abandoned us.

There was a person who didn't ignore me, who used to listen to me, but you abandoned me too. I got in the car without knowing where to go. I thought of Mitch but I didn't have his address. The phone rang while I was driving. I didn't know whether to take it.

This had to be Anna. I couldn't have her preaching, not then. Again I almost let it go but I didn't. Perhaps it was Sheere. He could have had second thoughts.

'Joseph Geraghty?'

Another male voice, not Sheere's this time, was trying to cut through the swathe of cloudy, half-formed thoughts that fired randomly behind my eyes in the dark of the night, bleeding, coagulating, just short of ideas capable of being articulated.

'This is Joe Geraghty. Who is this?'

It was the police.

'You're calling *now*? You're calling me *now*?'

'I'm sorry, Mr Geraghty, but we thought you'd want to know as soon as possible.'

'What?'

'Your mother was found in a distressed state about half an hour ago pacing up and down on a traffic island on the Nepean Highway.'

'Oh fuck!'

'She's alright.'

'Where is she now?'

'We took her home. She was very confused. We asked her if there was anyone we should call and she said she had two children in Melbourne, you and your brother, Roger. We couldn't reach him so we thought we'd better call you. Does she have any history of senility or mental illness of any kind? She kept singing.'

'Singing?'

'Something about Jesus, I think. Mr Geraghty? Hello? You're breaking up.'

The police thought it was something about Jesus. Blessed are the meek, Mum, for they shall inherit the earth, including the Nepean Highway. For thine is the kingdom, and the power, and the glory, forever, Amen. What a friend she has in Jesus. I found myself shouting this from inside my car. The man driving the car alongside mine stared at me. She has the gift of faith, a gift which has always eluded me. My dad and I, we had mixed feelings about Him. She had wanted me to be a priest but to me, even as a kid, the one universal truth about Christ was that he always stuck to the roof of your mouth.

So, when you think about it, where was I going to go? Where else but here? What a friend I have in you. Angels came and ministered unto me, right? You were the only one who could possibly answer any of my questions. It had been a little over two months. The son of man hath nowhere to lay his head. Did you think I wouldn't be back? Forgive and forget? Surely you knew me better than that? Didn't you think I would want to get to the bottom of this? How many times did you betray me before the cock crowed?

The woman at reception did not miss a beat. It was nice to see me again. I asked for you and told her I wanted to meet you in the room. When you got there, I had my shirt off but my pants and shoes were still on and I kept them on. Weren't you surprised to see me? You were frightened. I saw you look at the door. I saw you look at the intercom. How could you not trust me after all this time?

'Joe!'

22

Even afraid, you are mouth-watering. So round with youth, your eyes, your mouth, your breasts, your soft cushioning cheeks. Nothing weird, I just want to talk while we do it. I want to tell you what it feels like when you can't find your son, when you run around an empty school ground shouting his name. You didn't know I'd already lost one son. I've got so many questions for you. Have you seen him lately? Do you visit him in prison? Which one is it? No, you take it all off. I'm going to keep my pants on. It's the way I want it just now. Tell me about him and Anna. We've been having some communication problems lately. Don't look like that. You've been in more bizarre situations than this. Yes, I've been drinking but you'll get paid. That's on top of the thirty pieces of silver from him. Don't you love my son? I always told you he was cute. On your front please, arse in the air. I haven't been so happy lately, you know. Face down on the pillow, that's the way. There's a guy I met, Buchanan. You'd like him. Face down. Good girl. Buchanan's got this incredible handshake. He doesn't let go. He's *still* got one of my hands. So perfectly round. I'd forgotten how perfect it is. He's got one of my hands. The other, in my pocket, will have to do. Isn't it written that when thou doest alms, let not thy left hand know what thy right hand doeth? Here's a little something for your trouble. Rolled up it will fit perfectly. It's only what I owe you. Things are a little rough for everybody right now. See, fits perfectly. Surprised? I can see your face in the mirror.

Now you can imagine how I felt.

part three

Part three

1

'Surprise! Isn't this a surprise? It's me.'

He had been drinking. He was stripped to his waist and I could smell the alcohol on his breath as soon as I entered the room.

'Have you missed me?' he continued.

I didn't know how to play it. Who would know how to play a situation like this, as it's happening?

'Did you think I wouldn't be back? The son of man hath nowhere to lay his head. Did you think I would just let this go? Surely you know me better than that? How many times did you betray me before the cock crowed?'

'Hey, stranger. Good to see you.'

Of course I didn't expect him to really believe that I was pleased to see him. I just had no idea what to say.

'Nothing weird. I just want to talk. I just want to talk . . . while we do it.'

But it was weird. The whole situation was weird. It was frightening, surreal from the moment I saw that it was him. I have been in many difficult, even potentially threatening, situations before but this was unlike anything I had ever faced or ever imagined facing. I had never given a moment's thought to what must have gone through Joe's mind once Sam was safely home and he knew that Simon, the man who had taken his son, was his wife's ex-boyfriend and the current lover of the woman he had been seeing for so long. Because I was only ever thinking of Simon, I never considered what must have gone through Joe's mind about us, about me and Joe.

'I felt like feeling you. All of a sudden that's what I felt like.'

'You've been drinking.'

'I felt like . . . I want you to feel . . . I want to tell you what it feels like when you can't find your son, when you run around an empty school ground shouting his name. You didn't know I'd already lost one son. Did you know that?'

'Joe!'

'I have so many questions. Do you visit him?'

'Who?'

'Have you seen him lately? Do you visit the prison? Which one is it anyway? I'm going to keep my pants on, if that's alright.'

'Are you okay, Joe?'

'Oh yeah, I'm okay. It's just . . . that's just the way I want it now. Tell me about her.'

'Who?'

'You know who I mean.'

'No, I don't.'

His eyes took hold of me. He looked unwell.

'Tell me about my wife.'

'Joe, do you want to sit down? I don't know what you mean.'

'Tell me about Anna.' It was a shouted demand.

'Joe, I don't think—'

'Tell me about her. Tell me about my wife. We've been having some . . . communication problems lately.'

'Joe, what do you want? You're unhappy.'

I picked up his shirt from the floor, but he shook his head.

'Leave it . . . but you . . . Take it all off.'

We were never what anyone would call 'friends'. The girls are always talking about whether it's even possible for a client to really be a friend. If a man speaks nicely to you, if he is gentle to you, if he tips big, showers you with gifts and offers you stock market advice—within the walls of a brothel it is all done around the sex that he is paying for. The sex takes place entirely for his pleasure and any beneficence on his part is only an accompanying fetish. Part of his titillation is having an attractive woman think that he's kind. Her gratitude turns him on. Gratitude will have this effect on most men. Some don't have the stamina to earn it on the outside. These men get a simulated version for an hour if they pay. I've discussed this with Alex, a psychiatrist friend of mine. He didn't disagree.

As fetishes go, it's the one we wish for and we encourage it by exaggerating our gratitude and 'friendship'. But Joe and I, we were almost friends. I thought he wasn't such a bad guy. He could even make me laugh. The first time that happened he stopped what he was doing and looked at me in amazement. I can fake a lot of things, but not laughter. I eventually got it out of him, the explanation for that look of amazement. Why should he look at me like that just because he had made me laugh? His wife didn't laugh anymore. That was why. He could not remember the last time he had made his wife laugh. A little thing perhaps, but Alex says I might be better placed to gain access to a man's unconscious than he is, with all his psychiatric training. He's told me to watch for the little things. People tell you more than they think they are telling you. Simon wanted me to do that too, to watch for the little things, at least he did with Joe, the man who could not make his wife laugh. The woman Simon describes and the woman Joe could not make laugh were not the same woman, different in every respect except that she had sent them both to me.

'You . . . take it all off.'

'Joe.'

'Don't look like that.'

'Joe, you've been drinking.'

'Drunk or sober . . . I'll pay you. Thirty pieces of silver I believe is the standard . . . the market rate for these things. That's ten from me, ten from him and ten from Anna. Don't you love my son? I always told you he was cute.'

'Joe, if you want to talk—'

'Oh, I want to talk but . . . not just talk. I want you . . . on your front please . . . arse in the air . . . Oh, so round.'

'Joe, I can tell you, I will tell you what happened, but not here. Not like this. You're clearly upset.'

'You're right. I haven't been so happy lately. Face down on the pillow. That's the way.'

'Joe!'

'There's a guy I met, Buchanan. You'd like him.'

'I think we should talk first. We need to talk, Joe.'

'Face down. Good girl. Buchanan's got this incredible handshake. He doesn't let go. He's still got one of my hands.'

'Listen, Joe, he was asleep most of the time. He wasn't hurt a bit.'

'So perfectly round. I'd forgotten how perfect it is.'

'I can understand you being upset. I didn't know Simon was going to take him, really . . . I didn't.'

'He's got one of my hands but the other one is . . .'

'Joe, what are you going to do?' I asked him from on all fours. I'd never seen him like this.

'The other one is in my pocket and . . .'

'Joe, he didn't tell me that he was going to take Sam. I was there

when he brought Sam home, back to his place but I promise you I . . .
Do you want it . . .'

'You are blessed. Perfectly round. It's a gift,' he said, stroking my
cheeks.

'Do you want to do it first, Joe? Then we can talk. Is that what
you want?'

'When thou doest alms, let not thy left hand know what thy right
hand doeth.'

'Why don't you come inside for a while, Joe. Might relax you. This
way?'

'Here's a little something for your trouble.'

'You're not going to do anything silly, are you, Joe?'

'Rolled up it's a perfect fit.'

'Jesus Christ! What are you doing?'

'It's only what I owe you.'

'Joe! What the hell . . . ?'

'Well, things are a little rough now. Fits perfectly.'

'Jesus Christ, Joe!' I said in horror, pulling out the suppository of
cash and recoiling at it in my hand.

'Now you know how I felt, you fucking bitch.'

'I think you'd better leave.' I was gagging. I was frightened. It's
only when they know you, even slightly, that they can really humiliate you. That is why the regulars continue to hold the biggest threat,
no matter how long they have been pretending to be kind. People
might think that it's safer with regulars. I used to think so. Someone
new is, by definition, completely unknown. They could block the door.
But if they block the door and you're on the bed they can't touch you.
If they leave the door, you go for it or else for them. They could cut
you but you're likely to see that coming and call for help, not that a
new guy is more likely than a regular to decide that a gaudy room
alone with a naked you is exactly the place he would like to have a
violent psychotic breakdown.

On the contrary, it is the regular who is more dangerous than
someone new. The regular is the more dangerous for two reasons.
Firstly, no matter what you know or have been taught or how long
you've been doing it, you are most likely to let your guard down with
a regular. When you are tired or maybe a little sad, when you are
lonely or some part of your life is hurting, a regular, a clever one, a
smart one, can have you trusting him. You might, just for a moment,
need to think that you are friends. Secondly, someone new is usually
much too scared to try to slap you or cut you. And if they're not, you
can sense it. You can smell the mental illness on them, on their skin,

in their hair. And even if you can't, they are still unlikely to go too far before you get out or get help. But a regular, a smart one, a long-time remember-your-star-sign one, he can humiliate you. He can take what it is that you do day in, day out, and hand it back to you in front of your face, at eye level, so that nobody can pretend that there is anything professional, therapeutic or glamorous about it. He can make you feel foolish for ever thinking that you are anything but a slave to the need of every man with the price of your enslavement nestling snugly in his wallet next to the photo of his wife and kids, or else tight inside a white-knuckled fist along with the car keys. However dimly he discerns it, this is the humiliation that only a regular can bring.

It had gone far enough. I didn't know what else he was going to do. Barely getting myself upright I slapped the intercom attached to the wall and called for security.

'Hey!' he said with hands in the air, as if responding to a stick-em-up command in a cartoon robbery. 'You didn't have to do that.'

'I think you had better go.' I was shaken.

'But we've got so much to talk about.'

The door burst open. I covered up as two of the boys came in and picked him up, one under each arm.

'Come on, mister.'

'What's going on here? I've paid. I fucking paid. There's no problem here. I fucking paid.'

2

I would have reacted faster if I hadn't felt guilty. The way he looked at it, I had breached a code. The problem was that I knew this as soon as I saw his face. He was drunk, angry, and the betrayal he felt was genuine, more genuine than anything else in the room, and on seeing it like that in his face, for the first time I realised how deceived he must have felt. My pity and my guilt blinded me to the menace in his eyes, in his voice and in the way he stood there, naked to the waist. If ever any of them turn nasty you never waste time feeling in any way responsible. You're out of there or on the intercom before they know what they're doing. But with Joe I knew too much about him. I knew he was connected, in one way or another, to people I care about. Well, connected to Simon. I think of Simon all the time, even though I know where his thoughts are. I can't see him now.

I was under the impression we were making progress, progress as a couple. We were. We were sharing more. I have never been as close to someone. I was sure I was helping him too. And then he goes and does something crazy, so crazy that now I can't see him. I had no idea that all his questions, his incessant questions about every aspect of their lives, were designed to facilitate the kidnapping. The police didn't believe this and Joe was even less likely to believe it.

There are plenty of men, one-hit wonders, Christmas party-goers, teenage premature ejaculators and, of course, regulars, whom you could imagine hurting or harming in some way. These are the men whose grotesque or just stupid faces, insensate faces, you see when you wake in a sweat, the men whose putrid breath lodges in your nostrils for hours, for days, whose skin smell stays with you no matter how much you shower or how vigorously you scrub, the men that make you dry-retch till even the viscera you thought they could not touch are bruised. Of course, after all those showers, the soaps, shampoos, conditioners, moisturisers and deodorants, body sprays or perfumes, the physical basis for the smell of these men has gone. The molecules containing their essences have all washed down the drain. But the scent is lodged in your memory and the soap and water can't get there, not to your memory. Nothing is as evocative as smell, nothing can as quickly or as certainly take you back somewhere. But Joe was not one of those men whose scent was material for a nightmare. I didn't dislike him at all.

Kelly, my housemate, even suggested I get stock tips from him, if not for me, then for her. She wanted to play the market with his advice, not just once or twice but seriously, regularly. She thought his expertise could be her ticket out of the industry, and mine too, if I wanted one. But she will never have a ticket out. She will leave when the market kicks her out of bed.

'Why couldn't *I* get a stockbroker as a regular?' she complained. 'You should really make use of this. Get him talking about his work. Milk him for all he knows.'

'Jesus, Kel, now you sound like Simon. He's always telling me to do that.'

'No I don't. I only want to know what to buy, what to sell, what are the good dot-coms, that sort of thing. He wants to know . . . I don't know what he wants to know. He wants to know everything about this guy and his wife, doesn't he?'

'Well, yes, he does.'

'Angie, I hope you don't mind me saying this. I mean, it's staring you in the face really, but . . . your boyfriend is a little crazy.'

'Yeah, he is,' I had to agree. 'What's wrong with that?'

'No, really, sweetheart, I don't mean . . . you know . . . just a bit of a dreamer. He's a little . . . unhinged, isn't he, with all this . . . ? It's like spying.'

'Hey, Kel, whose boyfriend wants to videotape you doing it with a dog, for fuck's sake, a dog, and then use the tape to kick-start a career in pornographic movies?'

'I don't see him anymore.'

'Really?'

'No.'

'Since when?'

'Since I told him I didn't want to see him anymore.'

'Pity. Cute dog.'

'Yeah. Wasn't even his dog.'

'He stole it?'

'No, he borrowed it. Told me it was his, though, when he saw how much I liked it.'

'A liar too?'

'Such an arsehole,' she concurred.

Kelly is a little younger than I am but she has worked in the industry for longer. I like her a lot. It was she who took me under her wing when I started and we've come to look out for each other. She's sweet but I doubt whether she has ever felt deeply about anybody. Or ever will. In letting her talk about my relationship with Simon I am humouring her. She and I are different in so many ways and Simon is one of those ways. If I am less childlike than her, less childish and less childlike, then it is due to Simon. There is nothing special about me, save for knowing him. She will never know anyone like him.

But before Simon and I were close, there were times when Kelly seemed to be the only one I could talk to and for that she will always be dear to me. She is the only one I can talk to now, and Alex, I suppose, but I feel a little awkward talking to him. I do now, anyway. Not because he's a psychiatrist but because he is Simon's psychiatrist. At least he was. Maybe he still is, if they let your private psychiatrist visit you in prison. I'm half expecting them to fall out too.

Actually, it was well before Simon took the little boy that Alex and Simon had become more like friends than like psychiatrist and patient. Alex would meet us for a drink at Simon's place or else at the Espy. The two of them would go for walks around Elwood or St Kilda. Sometimes I went with them. I liked just being there. I remember the three of us walking along the St Kilda pier one day. It was overcast and windy and I caught myself feeling about as good as I have ever felt, without really knowing why. It was before what I subsequently took to calling, at least to Kelly, my 'inconvenience'. Simon was holding forth, as he often did, and I tried not to distract him with how good it was to be there.

'You read a novel in which the hero or the anti-hero, the one you like, or simply the one whose progress you like to follow, well, this character commits a crime, say, a violent act. Who do you feel sorry for? You should feel sorry for the victim of the crime but you don't. Why don't you? In your normal life you condemn violence of any kind yet you don't condemn this act of violence, even though it's brutal. Perhaps you dislike the victim. Or perhaps you don't actually dislike him but you don't actively like him either. So where will your sympathies lie? Who will you feel sorry for?'

'Who? The perpetrator?' I asked.

'Partly. He has to live with the moral and practical consequences, the guilt, the mess and the fear of detection. But who else?'

'I don't know. Who else?'

'You, the reader, Angel. The reader will feel sorry for himself.'

'Why, because he has been tricked into thinking the violent scene is somehow morally ambiguous when, of course, it isn't really?' Alex chipped in.

'No, because he has identified with his preferred character, the perpetrator of the crime, and therefore shares his guilt and his fears.'

'I don't get it,' I said. As we walked Simon tried to explain.

'The thing is, readers usually identify with one or other of the characters in a story so that they can the better escape from the problems and boredom of their own lives. That's why most of them read fiction in the first place. They need to identify with some character in a story, or with different characters at different times if the story is true to life, in order to be drawn into it. And they need to be drawn into the story, to be pulled along by it, because they want a break from their own lives. This is a need, a need that is recognised at least unconsciously by every reader and—'

'You can't recognise something unconsciously,' Alex interrupted.

'Why not?' I asked.

'Think about it,' Alex said kindly. 'If it's unconscious, you are not recognising it. You are not aware of it.'

'Oh, right.'

'Simon,' Alex continued, 'you used two expressions just then: "pulled along" and "drawn into".'

'Oh, Alex, don't give me that Freudian slip bullshit. The point I'm making is valid, for once.'

'Well, in any case, I think you are wrong. Not all novels are purely escapist, to be read only for entertainment. Fiction, at least some fiction, can also confront us with truths we might otherwise never have encountered. It can provide us with insights we would never have gained elsewhere.'

'Yeah . . . I guess you're right . . . I don't know. These days I often don't know.'

I had never known people who talked like this socially, as distinct from in a literature tutorial. I didn't know what a Freudian slip was back then, not exactly. They were aware I was struggling to keep up with a conversation that even then I suspected was for them just a throwaway verbal joust, not something they took seriously. But they took me seriously. They took me more seriously than anybody else ever had. The three of us got along and the two of them got me through.

'For all that, you might have something, Simon,' Alex continued as my understanding dropped in and out like the reception on a mobile phone.

'If the writer is able to properly convey to the reader the social and psychological forces acting on a character whose behaviour is unacceptable—and isn't it the mark of a good writer that he can?—then the reader might well end up feeling sorry for the character, and insofar as he identifies with him, sorry for himself. Of course, you realise this gets rid of the bad guy in literature?'

'Oh no it doesn't,' I said with a confidence born out of nothing but joy. 'There's still a bad guy. The writer, for making the reader feel sorry for himself.'

At that the two men stopped to look at each other for an instant before laughing uproariously. Then Simon took me in his arms and held me so that the wind stopped. By that time we had reached the end of the pier.

I have tried to think of that moment, to preserve it exactly as it was. Being with him made me feel that I was okay, that there was nothing wrong with me or with what I had done with my life, that I was clean. It wasn't just his intellect, it was the kindness and under-standing he showed me. His kindness wasn't the product of some New Age relativism, as he called it, that refused to judge anything. That was itself one of the things he railed against. He could get angry although he never got angry with me. Even now it is not anger, not really. And though we laughed all the time, he never laughed at me. He didn't think I had ruined my life, that I had done anything irreversible. He thought it was not out of the question that I could study, or get a job in one of the new e-businesses. In his opinion I was okay. But I've ruined that now.

One night, not long after we first met, he took me for a long walk along the bank of the Yarra, not near the city, but between Hawthorn and Kew, past the backs of what he told me were the houses of the wealthy. I was still fairly new to Melbourne and he told me that if I was planning to support myself sleeping with the husbands, fathers and sons of the well-heeled, I ought to see where they lived and what their houses looked like. We walked and talked for quite a while without touching. It was a very still night and the moon was full and perfect. I was sure that he felt like I did, that this was not at all a booking but a date, the kind you have when you're very young.

Standing at ridiculous angles to each other by the river, near midnight, we silently interrogated each other. He looked so vulnerable. He was afraid, afraid of getting involved with anyone after Anna, afraid of getting hurt. And I was elated. I had always hoped that one day I would meet someone who could make me feel the way he made me feel. Everyone does. But I had found him and he even knew what I did. I had found him on the street. What are the chances of that? He has said he wasn't looking for a girl, that he was just walking. When I started talking to him he didn't know I was propositioning him for money. That's what he's said anyway. For me, meeting him was the beginning of the end of a terrible time.

He will say it is because of me that this is a terrible time for him, and it is true, this is a terrible time for him. But it is not my fault, no matter what he says. What I did was done out of the deepest feelings I have ever had for anyone. Maybe one day he will understand that. But now I am in pain. My sleep is fitful and I wake up screaming. The muscles in my legs ache from thrashing about. I have to force myself to eat. And I can cry suddenly when I think I see him in the street, which is not infrequently.

I think that I see him crossing the street but I know it's not him, that it cannot be him. And if I look closely I can see that it doesn't even look like him. More and more it now takes only a distant or faint outline of a youngish man for me to think I see him and for me to ache. I remember the luxury of being able to tell him I'd seen him somewhere, or thought I had. I will never be able to do that again. He has all but assured me of that.

I cannot convey the extent of my pain. Even if I could adequately explain to another person the things he gave me—the calm, the confidence, the joy, the knowledge—even if I could get this across to another person, it would only be the first step. Then I would have to convey what it is like to have had all this, even if only by chance, and then to have lost it. But if in all the world I had a handful of people still with me at this step, I would surely lose them at the next one. I could not expect them to imagine my pain when he says that it is all my fault, that I am responsible for his arrest, for his incarceration. When I tell him that I was only trying to protect him from himself, he tells me that I had no right to interfere in his life. But in truth, I had no right not to. He taught me that. He was forever telling me that benevolent intervention was a moral imperative. I was only putting it into practice. I called the police because I didn't know how long he was going to keep that little boy. Simon was not completely well; he hadn't been for a long time. He needed help. You didn't need to be a psychiatrist to know this. What he did could not have been done by somebody who was well. I thought that sooner or later he would come to his senses and agree with me. The sooner it ended, the easier it would go for him. So I called the police because it wasn't ending. I was thinking only of him. I have never even told him about my 'inconvenience'. That's what I called it then, my 'inconvenience'.

3

I had not been in Melbourne long when we met. I had fled Adelaide weeks, certainly less than two months, earlier, and already before then my life had taken several unexpected turns, turns my parents would not have planned for me. They knew I was in Melbourne but I wasn't giving them any return phone numbers. This was in part because I didn't want them to know how often I was moving. In part it was because I just couldn't handle their constant harping on the scandal, as they put it, that their beautiful, privileged daughter had landed them in. And in part it was because I hated my father.

As scandals go, it pales against those of the real world but it was not in the real world. It was only in my parents' world, the world of the parents of the sons and daughters who went to a handful of Adelaide private schools, the world of my father's old boy network and of the regular customers who came into his pharmacy. My father had been a local football hero and had represented the state once. It was an honour that accompanied him every day thereafter. My mother was a trophy wife upon whom he had quite successfully engraved his pride, his values and his world view. And his will.

In the distribution of *their* trophies, I got her fingernails, their strength and beautiful shape enhanced by the manicures I have to have to get the better paid bookings, particularly when escorting. Men notice a woman's fingernails when they meet her. And they notice them when they are paying. It's all you need in a forty-second introduction. My mother took care of her fingernails for quite different reasons. We share more than her fingernails and this has always infuriated my father. He says I am too much like her but I think he's wrong about this. I have her face and her figure but everything else, really, is his. My father and I are both pretty stubborn and maybe that's one reason we get on so badly. It didn't help that he hit menopause around the time I hit puberty. When I started to look like a young woman instead of a little girl, the woman I looked like was the young woman he had chosen to marry at the time his choices were the widest he'd ever had and ever would have. My mother, after four children (I had three brothers), didn't look like that woman anymore. Only I did. He seemed to lose his balance around then.

We argued about everything when I was a teenager. Although I was an above-average student, a member of the debating team and something of a dancer, I hated the school I went to. But my father insisted I stay there. Everything that hurt had to be good for me. We lived right next to it. A large private school, it was Victorian in architecture and in culture. Heavy uniforms, khaki ribbons in everyone's hair, detentions for the wrong underwear, mandatory sport after school, sanctimonious hypocrisy from the staff whose vigilance and severity never seemed to detect or curb the cruelties and humiliations the popular girls visited on the weaker ones; this was all next door to me. It was always there, even on weekends, when the out of town girls, the boarders, reigned supreme. I could see and hear it all. It was next to where we lived and this was what my father thought was good for me.

'But you have friends there, Angela. I know you have. I've seen them.'

He had seen them alright. At the end of our house were two rooms that backed onto the school grounds. One was my bedroom and the other was a sort of playroom where I kept my birds. I bred birds. I can remember coming home from dance class at about eight one night to find four girls sitting in that room smoking. One of them said they had been there since around three-thirty. I knew them but they weren't my friends. They were slightly older girls, boarders, from the country mostly, who used to sneak into our back yard to smoke, gossip, read magazines, anything, just to get away from the mindless puritanism of the school. Whenever I saw them there they would briefly pretend to want to know what I was up to. They'd pretend they were my friends. But they were never really my friends. Except for Suramia, the Sri Lankan girl. She was different.

That evening I found them inside the house. My father had turned a blind eye to their smoking even though he would have killed me for it. Why had he not rebuked them? There were too many of them? They were someone else's and too threatening, too forward and too voluptuous to reproach? Perhaps they were also too exciting for him? Maybe that was why he had made them tea and coffee. As far as I was aware, he had never made tea or coffee for anyone before in his life. That had always been one of my mother's duties.

My father's hospitality to these girls was entirely out of character, or so I thought then. Ironically, it was his particular interest in Suramia, the Sri Lankan girl, that contributed, albeit indirectly, to my break with him and my leaving home. Suramia responded to what she perceived as the warmth of my, or more accurately my father's, hospitality with an innocent gratitude that was disarming. Tentatively at first, at least on my part, we became friends.

That was the first of what were to become fairly regular visits by the girls on weekends. Remarkably, my father continued to treat them with the sort of bonhomie he usually reserved for his old football cronies. He was especially attentive to Suramia. True, she was striking to look at. But then he had often expressed views on immigration that you could be forgiven for believing were, as Simon put it when I described them to him, inspired by the Nuremberg Race Laws.

My own friendship with Suramia developed independently of these weekend schoolgirl incursions into our back room. We went to the movies together, and when the weather allowed, for walks along the beach. I even went to her place for dinner one evening. I say even because she was reluctant to let me see her family's modest home circumstances. She was ashamed, she told me later, not of their relative poverty but of the sacrifices she was allowing them to make so that they could keep her at a private school. It was not that they had to pay her fees—she had won a full scholarship including board—but even the cost of ancillary items such as uniforms and the interstate excursions and social events the school prided itself on, even that was more than they could afford. Her parents were unassuming, even self-effacing, but not enough to hide their warmth. Her brother, Romesh, a couple of years older than Suramia and doing a computer science degree at university, was rather reserved but still charming in a subtle way. I liked him. Perhaps it was because he seemed somewhat more mature than the boys I was used to. Although my father knew about my friendship with Suramia he never commented on it. At least not while she remained at school and she and her friends used our back room as an occasional refuge.

When I started an arts degree at university more than a year later, I ran into Romesh again. We began seeing each other quite a lot. A very good pianist, he took me to classical concerts, which I enjoyed, and I took him to plays which he pretended to enjoy but, I suspect, didn't really.

I'd had boy friends and boyfriends since my early teens. My father was not aware of most of them, even the ones he met. They were his pharmacy delivery boys, the sons of his friends or, occasionally, the son of someone connected to his former football glory. And there were others. No doubt I was cruel to many of them but I was just coming to terms with being a girl that looked like me. We had all met at the wrong time. It wasn't our fault. It was an innocence we all had in common. Another thing at least they all had in common was that they didn't threaten anybody's established order, certainly not my father's. My father reacted savagely to anything that did. He reacted savagely to my friendship with Romesh.

It wasn't that Romesh was Sri Lankan, he insisted. Oh no, my father wasn't a racist. It was just that we should stick to our own kind. And these people should stick to theirs. 'You see, I'm not treating them differently.' He would not let up. We argued bitterly all the time.

Partly, I think, because of Romesh's loneliness and partly because of my father's bigoted hostility to him, our relationship after a time became physical. It was evident that Romesh was a virgin and although I wasn't, my idea of contraception owed more to roulette and the Vatican than to oestrogen and progesterone pills and condoms. Early in the second semester of my first year at university I found I was pregnant.

For a while I became an expatriate in the state of denial. Fine for a holiday, it was no place to live, and after two months I resumed residence in the real world. My father's response, when I finally managed to tell him, was utterly predictable. How would he be able to face his friends, his customers, his associates at the club? Oh yes, and an illegitimate child wouldn't actually be in my interest either. But he didn't insist I have it aborted. At least not till I succumbed to his relentless questioning a week or so later and confirmed what he had suspected and feared.

My father went completely berserk. A bastard was bad enough, a coloured bastard was the ultimate violation of all his cherished prejudices. Raving and ranting, he demanded that I have an abortion. The racism that spewed from him was all the more obscene given his undisguised salivation at his non-accidental encounters with Suramia in the back room a year or two before. His insistence on an abortion was rabid and remorseless. Eleven weeks into my pregnancy I stopped resisting.

There were six or seven women sitting around the waiting room, waiting. Three of us waited on our own. A woman opposite me was there with her husband or boyfriend and their young son. The little boy kept running back and forth to the TV set in the corner and they, clearly embarrassed, kept telling him to be quiet.

'He's pretending it's a computer screen. Crazy about computers,' the man said softly to the room.

Romesh never even knew I was pregnant. I thought that if I didn't tell him it would be as though it had never happened.

My regret and my shame were immediate and they were unassuageable. And so was my anger at my father for driving me to do it. He came into my room that night and found me crying into my pillow. Perhaps my mother had heard me and sent him in. Had she come in instead, things might have gone differently.

'You know how much you have upset me by all this, Angela. But you would have upset me much more if you'd had his child. You did the right thing, the only thing.'

We were in the dark. I lay on my front sobbing. I didn't say a word, hoping he might, just once, tell me, even if he didn't mean it, that how I felt mattered too. Had he turned me over, had he put the bedside light on, had he got me upright to tell me that, to tell me anything, he could have seen that my face was covered in vomit. But he didn't. The reach of my father's empathy did not extend beyond the skin that contained him and I hated him for this, his overweening concern for himself to the exclusion of everyone else, as much as I hated him for his racism and his hypocrisy.

I wanted to get away from him, from the abortion, from the guilt, from Adelaide, from everything.

4

By the time the house had begun to stir in the weak light of the following morning, before my mother had cut up the fruit she put on top of my father's cereal and boiled the water for his coffee, before she had collected his newspaper from the porch, I had already left. I had thrown all that I thought I would need into a suitcase, caught a taxi to Keswick Station and was on a train to Melbourne, a place where no one knew me, no one, except one of the girls of the clutch of boarders who had made the outskirts of my home their second home.

I had been told she was living in Melbourne. I got her phone number from the directory and to my surprise she agreed to let me stay with her for a while. She was working in promotions for her boyfriend, who was part-owner of a nightclub. Through the two of them I met a lot of the so-called glamorous people, dropped a lot of 'e', snorted a lot of cocaine and slept with as many men as I thought I needed to sleep with to help me forget Adelaide.

I couldn't get older fast enough. I never paid for my drinks and seldom for my drugs. I moved around a lot, staying with the people I met, men and women, for a few days or even a couple of months. They all had great places, in Prahran and South Yarra. Some lived in the centre of the city. Everything was new. Anyone I was still sleeping with ten days after the first time became my boyfriend and I made my boyfriends pay for everything. I caught up on my sleep during the day and did everything else at night.

I was sleeping with a man called Steve when the last of my savings and my Visa credit ran out. Steve asked me what I planned to do for money. It could have been an innocent question but despite the fact that I had not been his guest for very long, I feared it contained an impatience I didn't want to exacerbate. I told him I thought I would go back to dancing or maybe get a job as an aerobics instructor. He said that he had a friend who was always looking for dancers and that he could set up an appointment for me. When I found, as I should have guessed, that it was table-top dancing he was talking about, I said no.

'Give it a try.'

'No, I'm not doing that. What do you take me for?' But I knew what it was he took me for. I was out of money and out of contacts. The doors of my newly old haunts were closing to me and their denizens were already forgetting we had met. Where once they could all recognise me across a crowded dance floor, now they didn't see me. When I called out to them they couldn't hear me.

I took the job at Steve's friend's club. I lasted two nights. I couldn't do it. I was too embarrassed. Even now I couldn't do it. I do more than wriggle around on a table now, but it's in private and the onlooker is naked too. There's a certain equality about it, even an upper hand. There's nothing empowering in having to gyrate high on a table, naked but for stilettos, in front of a bunch of lecherous drunks. On my second evening there I kicked a drink all over a paralytic slob who was trying to lasso my leg with his tie. He complained and I was immediately dismissed by Steve's friend's manager. By the time I was dressed and my cab had reached Steve's place, Steve already knew that I had lost the great job he had got for me.

'That's what you're there for. That's what the men do.'

He was furious and told me that I had another think coming if I thought I could keep sponging off him. I had no work ethic. I disgusted him. He wanted me to move out, the next day. I made him sick. He was going to bed. I could sleep on the couch. I didn't know what I was going to do. I lay in the dark on his couch for more than two hours wondering how I had got into this situation. I thought that if I could revive his interest in me it would at least buy me some time. So I crept into the room. It was dark except for the light of the clock radio.

'Steve,' I whispered.

'Steve.'

I tripped over some shoes that were scattered on the floor and fell forward toward the bed with my arms out to protect my face. He sat up on the other side of the bed with a start and I realised that my hand was resting on someone else's ankle. The other person didn't move but Steve got up and dragged me all the way back to the couch in the lounge room. He slapped me a few times in the dark as we banged into the furniture. He told me I was a walking disaster, an irresponsible slut who had let him down to his friend. And then he raped me.

Steve kept snorting like an animal, cursing and hurting me. He was obviously high on something. The woman in his bedroom ignored my screaming but came in when she heard me sobbing after he had finished and gone into the bathroom. The lamp on the sideboard went on. I looked up and saw the spaced-out, heavy-lidded, bewildered face of the girl from school who had put me up when I first arrived in Melbourne.

The next day I checked into a motel at the end of Carlisle Street in St Kilda. It was the cheapest motel I could find. I was completely out of money. When the sun went down that day I found myself on the street offering men in slow-moving vehicles a hand job for forty dollars. When exactly did I become a prostitute? I don't know. Some time between the back of my parents' house the time my father first played host to the girls from my school and the street corner in St Kilda that evening it just happened. After I was raped I figured that since they were going to get it anyway, I might as well get paid for it.

5

I've talked to many businessmen since I started working as a prostitute. Many of my clients are in business. They differ physically and psychologically and in what they want from us, but there's one thing they all say: find out what people want and you'll never be hungry. I was hungry for a moment there, hungry in their sense of the word, but it hasn't happened since. I know what half the population want. I knew it then. But I still do not really know why. I've talked to Dr Klima—Alex—about it. He's a psychiatrist. He ought to know.

'Oh,' he laughed when I asked him. 'Angel, there is no simple answer to that.'

'Okay then, don't make it simple.'

'There is not even a single discipline within whose purview the answer lies.'

'What do you mean?'

'Well, anthropologists would fight amongst each other for the answer . . . biologists, psychologists and psychiatrists, neuro-psychiatrists . . .'

'Shall I tell you what I think?'

'Yes, why don't you tell me what you think.'

'I mean, I've seen enough men, right?'

'I would imagine you have.'

'You said before about man's need to . . . what did you say?'

'To propagate himself, to continue the species.'

'Right. I understand that but I see them hour after hour, right?'

'Yes.'

'Let me tell you, the ones I see are not thinking about continuing the species.'

'Well, I wasn't talking about individual men.'

'But that's what I'm looking for, the reason why individual men go looking for it and will pay for it, why they sometimes do the most extraordinary things for it. Why are they coming in the door one after another, not just to us but all over the city, in fact probably all over the world?'

'Certainly,' Alex agreed.

'And they have been since . . . I don't know when. The dawn of time, right?'

'I have no doubt.'

'I mean, they break up marriages for it. They do it even when they actually still love their wives. I see men who I believe genuinely love their wives yet they'll risk their marriages for it, their children. They'll risk humiliation for it. Some men don't want it *without* humiliation. So it can't be to make them feel good about themselves, not for those guys anyway.'

'So, what do you think?'

'I think it's like a drug with them.'

'In what way?'

'Alex, you talk like you're not one of them.'

'Hey, Angelique, leave me out of this. In what way do you say sex is like a drug to men?'

'It enables them to escape from everything.'

'Okay, I can accept that.'

'It's not just the orgasm that does it, though, it's the whole thing. The before, the during, the after. But the actual drug is the orgasm. They're using the orgasm to escape.'

'The orgasm is the medication?'

'Exactly, it masks their pain. It's like a natural painkiller or even a tranquilliser. The reason they want it so badly is that it's a kind of natural tranquilliser. You can see all their anxiety just lift when they come. I see it all the time. I try to watch them when they're coming, without them noticing. I don't want to make them selfconscious.

'It's really quite an amazing thing and it happens every time. I think it does. Sometimes I forget to pay attention. Other times I can't see their faces without making it obvious, so I miss it. But I would say pretty much every time. No matter what has happened before, either in their day or in the room, there's this complete lifting of anxiety when they finish. I've even been in frightening situations where some huge mountain of a man, all very polite at the introduction and early in the booking, starts to get a crazed irrational look in his eyes as he surges closer and closer to finishing. He'll be sweating and groaning. You can't stop him. You can't even communicate with him. It's just before orgasm and he's almost animalistic, grunting and shaking. He could snap me in two. Crush my windpipe and there wouldn't be a lot I could do about it. He's in some kind of fearsome trance. And then he comes and all the tension is gone instantly. He might want to bury his face in my neck and sleep, or just do nothing but lie there and breathe. At that moment, it's like he's helpless. Suddenly I could do anything to him.

'They all get that way when they come, they're all so vulnerable at that moment, all of them, old or young, black, white or Asian. Sometimes I feel quite tender towards them then. It's like, at that time, you see each one of them as a sleepy little boy. That's what they want, whatever it is that gives them that sleep or the need to sleep. It's not always sleep but it is always a release from stress.

'That's what I think it is, anyway. I know it works in other ways too. It's good for their egos to be treated as though they are attractive and good lovers, and by good-looking women. But there's more to it than that. Why will they pay to do it even with older, unattractive women? Because, as long as no one sees them, it doesn't matter who it is that's bringing them to the boil. What they are all always begging for, though like rats they don't even know it, is the promise of an instant, even if only fleeting, total release from anxiety. What do you think, Alex?'

'Like rats?'

'Sure, why not?'

'Interesting.'

'But what do you think? Do you think there could be something in this? What's the scientific explanation, the biological explanation?'

Alex thought for a moment. 'Orgasms, their physiology, let's see. They're not something I've given a great deal of thought to recently.'

'Alex, I thought you didn't want to get personal.'

'Angel, do you want the benefit of my training or my experience? And before you answer that, take my advice and choose the training, on this matter anyway.'

'Okay, let's play doctor.'

'The arousal in a man—we're talking about men here, aren't we? Okay, the arousal, the erection, is governed by what is called the parasympathetic nervous system. The heart rate is slowed and the contractility of the myocardium is stifled.'

'Alex, English, please.'

'Sorry. The heart muscle contracts, squeezes, less forcefully. It's not working as hard as it did before arousal. Now the bronchioles, the extensive air passages in the lungs, constrict. As a result the concentration of oxygen in the blood is diminished.'

'Is this for or against my theory so far?'

'Well, if anything, I suppose it's for. You see, if the concentration of oxygen in the blood is diminished, it puts a person, a man in this case, into a state of unavoidable relaxation. None of the conventional signs of excitement, apart from erection of course, is possible with a slow heart. You know it could be argued that even new thoughts are perhaps unlikely.'

'What do you mean "perhaps"?'

'Well, I'm thinking that oxygen-poor blood might even prevent a person from entertaining thoughts other than those he finds useful to support the arousal. You see, when the parasympathetic nervous system is dominant, blood is generally shunted toward the viscera to optimise the more peaceful and mindless of bodily functions. I'm thinking of peristalsis, salivation and the production of urine.'

'What about to the penis?'

'Yes, of course, to the penis as well.'

'So he's aroused, erect, with a slow heart rate, incapable of new thoughts. What happens when he comes?'

'Well, there is a sudden systemic shift with climax. Ejaculation is a phenomenon governed by the sympathetic nervous system. Cardiac output and the concentration of oxygen in the blood is maximised. Furthermore, if I'm recalling my med-school neurophysiology correctly, peripheral vessels and those in the viscera will contract, causing blood to be shunted instead to the heart and major muscles. Peristalsis and bladder function are at a minimum.'

'So he can't piss while he comes?'

'Well, no, he can't. And at the same time, there is an increase in the breakdown and the processing of lipids and glycogen in order to liberate glucose, fuel, into the bloodstream. It's conceivable, I suppose, that this represents a moment of complete and utter awakening, of crystalline clarity, a lucidity like no other.'

'Hey, wow!'

'You see, the sympathetic nervous system presumably evolved to serve primitive humanity in times of physical threat. You've heard of the "fight or flight" reflex, right?'

'I think so.'

'Okay,' Alex said, 'but what if there is no such threat, no one to fight and no one to flee from? Well, nonetheless, with sexual climax, you get all that energy, all that acuity in one sudden rush. No wonder climax is inevitably followed by the somnolence you described.'

'By the what?'

'The sleepiness, the desire to sleep. It's an exhaustion that comes as though the man has just escaped or fought a formidable foe.'

'It's usually a woman,' I said more to myself than to Alex.

'No, actually it's usually oneself,' Alex said.

'Is that your experience or is it your training talking?' I asked him, and he smiled. I had never really thought much about Alex as a sexual being. It would have been a lot like thinking of my father that way. Well, maybe not quite as sickening as that, but my mind never went there because he was a little like a father figure to me, maybe even to Simon. They certainly went beyond the normal, once-a-week therapist/patient relationship you hear about. At the very least they were good friends. We all were, but we never brought up Alex's personal life. Now it's something I do sometimes think about. Funny, everything has changed. Everything has changed and I feel so afraid. I feel afraid all day, from the moment I wake to the moment I fall asleep. No one ever told me that deep sadness feels so much like fear.

'But their brain,' I persisted. 'What do you think about my theory that there is something drug-like going on at the moment of orgasm that causes that complete release from anxiety?'

'You know you've put this to me before.'

'And you still haven't answered me satisfactorily.'

'Well, since you asked me last time, I've looked into it.'

'Alex, thank you. Did you look up stuff just for me?'

'Yes.'

'And?'

'It's not as conclusive as you would like but you might be on to something. Neuroendocrine patterns are difficult to gauge experimentally and the studies, at least the ones I've been able to find, yield inconsistent results. But there are some studies that suggest, at least indirectly, that endogenous, that is, naturally occurring opiate-like peptides such as endorphins may play a role in providing the subject with a sense of pleasure associated with orgasm.'

'Endorphins, as in the exercise high, right?'

'Right.'

'But what exactly . . . I mean, I sort of know . . . What exactly are opiates? What do they do?'

'Ah, opiates, the mother of them all, really. Opiates are all things derived from opium, including heroin, morphine, you name it.'

'What do they do?'

'Well, on a molecular level they effect reactions leading to sedation, hallucination and euphoria. Perhaps more importantly, they're responsible for the most potent sort of analgesia we know.'

'Analgesia? You mean what you get with analgesics?'

'Yes, the abolition of pain.'

'So when a man comes, he might be releasing opiate-like . . . did you say peptides?'

'Peptides.'

'. . . which can lead to sedation, euphoria and even the abolition of pain?'

'Exactly. In fact, I came across one interesting study that showed an elevation in pain threshold in women who were actively masturbating to orgasm.'

'You're kidding. What a study!'

'Uh-huh. Some people can get funding for anything. It's a real talent.'

6

Simon. I had not been in Melbourne long when I found him. I had been in the motel in Carlisle Street, St Kilda for two days and two nights, afraid both nights of the ghostly teenagers who, hungry for heroin, are hookers the way the public wants its hookers. They are sick, underfed and desperate enough to suffer the abuse visited upon them by the procession of bored predatory sons out in their mothers' cars looking for easy prey. I was afraid of the girls because they needed heroin more than they needed food and shelter, and I had not reached that stage yet. I was afraid of the men in the cars, even the ones who were not abusive, even the ones who wanted straight, protected, non-violent sex. I had not reached that stage yet either.

I was lucky enough to find a young foreign guy who was so satisfied with the way I masturbated him against a dump-bin in a supermarket car park that he tipped me more than the cost of my service and even bought me a hamburger. He felt so ashamed that, in broken English, he tried to fool both of us into thinking it was a date, that he had met his first local girl. But I had to burst the bubble when, in the manner of a frightened teenage boy hoping for a second date, he nervously asked if he could see me again. I drew a rudimentary map of the streets around Barkly and Carlisle Streets on the back of a serviette.

'You can see me again. I'll be there,' I said, pointing to an intersection on the map. I'm sure I got the map wrong.

It was on my second night and after I had been moved to all sorts of corners by all sorts of people that I first saw Simon. He was alone, drunk and beautiful. He carried a bag, a little day pack.

'Are you looking for a date?' I asked, doing a B-grade movie-inspired version of the way street hookers are meant to talk.

'A date,' he stopped and said to me. 'Yes, I am looking for a date, young lady, I'm looking for my birthday, not the anniversary of my birth, mind you, but the original day itself. I'm looking for a lost youth. You might say that this is where all the lost youths come to age, where they all come of age, where they come and where they age, and you'd be right on each score. But I'm not looking for just any lost youth. I'm looking for mine. What about you?' he said softly. 'What the hell are you doing?'

He took my hand very gently and examined it carefully. Then he slowly turned my arm over so that the softer side faced upwards and examined that too. I didn't know what he was doing and I didn't know what I was doing either. I was tired and the only thing I knew was that I didn't want him to let go of my arm. I stood there with my eyes welling up with tears and I wondered if he could tell. It will sound ridiculous since I had only just met him, but I didn't want him to see me that way. I didn't want him to see me soliciting and I even thought of apologising. When he took my hand I felt different, not just from the other girls on the street but different from the way I had ever felt. It might have been the way he spoke to me, playing games with words the way he did, or it might have been the gentleness with which he took my hand and then my arm. It might have been the way he asked me what I was doing. He ran two fingers slowly down the inside of my arm. How can I describe what that did to me? It was gentle and completely non-sexual. He didn't want anything from me and as I closed my eyes and crushed the tears out onto my face he continued in that voice of his.

'You're *not* an addict, are you?' he asked incredulously, for he already knew the answer.

'No,' I said, embarrassed.

'Oh, please, miss . . . I don't know you . . . Look, it's none of my business and I've probably had too much to drink, but you shouldn't be here, you shouldn't be doing this. They—' he said, pointing around him, 'they think they have to. Maybe they do. I don't know. But you . . . you don't.'

I just stood there with my upturned arm in his hand, crying.

'Have you eaten, miss?' he asked me.

We walked to Acland Street where I let him buy me a bowl of pasta. He asked me if I preferred white or red wine. I wanted to tell him everything by way of explanation but he didn't want to know, not at first, anyway. He wanted to know if I read books.

'What . . . what do you read?'

This was surreal. I don't think anybody had ever asked me what books I read. I had been asked at school by disbelieving teachers if I had read or finished reading a prescribed book, but Simon wanted to know whether and what I read for pleasure. When I saw that he was serious about this I started to tell him. I do read for pleasure and I did even before I was with Simon but, still, I had to think about it. As I was speaking I felt as though a heavy weight was being lifted off my chest and I could breathe more easily. It was the way he spoke to me, and the way I responded to how he spoke.

He took me to dinner. We drank wine, perhaps a little too much, and talked books. He paid for everything. We went for a long walk from one end of Acland Street to the other, past the cake shops, the delis, the restaurants and bars, past Luna Park and all the people, down to the Esplanade and along the beach.

'What do I read? Lots of stuff. I like a lot of science fiction because they always deal with, you know, very clever ideas.'

'Who do you like?' he wanted to know.

'Isaac Asimov, of course. He's great. You've heard of him?'

'Actually, yes.'

'Who else do I like in science fiction? Let's see . . . Have you read *Footfall*?'

'*Footfall*?'

'Yeah.'

'No, who's it by?'

'Oh, it's great. It's by Larry Niven and Jerry Pournelle. They also wrote *The Mote in God's Eye*. Have you read that?'

'No. Do they write together?'

'They write together and separately but they're much better together.'

'Who else do you like?'

'Who else? Terry Pratchett—'

'Is he science fiction?'

'No, it's more humour, really black humour, you know?'

'No.'

'No what?'

'No, I don't know.'

'Are you making fun of me?'

'No, I was about to ask you the same thing.'

'What do you mean?'

'I've never heard of any of these people. Terry Pratchett—you're making that up.'

'I am not. How can you say that?' I said, laughing.

'What have you read of Terry Pratchett's?'

'Oh, come on! What is this? Some kind of test?' I said, gently pushing into him.

'Well, you can't call someone one of your favourite authors and then not be able to name one of their books. Makes you sound like an idiot.'

'I beg your pardon, mister. Who are you calling an idiot?'

'No one, yet. It's conditional. You have to earn it.'

'Oh, good. I like a challenge.'

'Well?'

'Well what?'

'Terry Pratchett, I want three titles.'

'Or I'm an idiot?'

'You said it, babe.'

'Okay. *Mort*, *The Reaper Man* and . . .'

'The pressure's on.'

'Shut up.'

'Can't you make up another title by an author you've just made up?'

'Shut up, Simon. I'm thinking . . . *The Colour of Magic*.'

'Oh, very good, very fast.'

'Am I an idiot?'

'No, anyone who can lie that fast under pressure . . .'

'Hey, more people have heard of my favourites than those . . . Frederick Exel and Stephen Swain.'

'Frederick Exley and Stefan Zweig.'

'Whatever.'

'Oh, and while we're correcting names, it's William Empson, not Roy Hampson.'

'Who's Roy Hampson?'

'He used to host excremental television shows aimed at my mother before you were born. You shouldn't even know about him.

This is not Terry Pratchett we're talking about,' he said, giving me a little squeeze.

'Simon.'

'Yeah.'

'I like you.'

'You *are* an idiot.'

We walked and he told me everything: about his brothers, about William and May, his parents, and about their marriage. He told me about Empson, the poet and critic, and about Empson the dog, Simon's dog. We talked about our schools, the one I had attended as a student and the one in which Simon had been a teacher. He asked whether I had heard of the spate of child stealing in Melbourne and I told him that I had. Then he told me about Carlo, the little boy he had taught, who was among the first to be kidnapped.

'Carlo was always the last to come and play with Empson whenever I brought him to school.'

'Why? Was he scared of dogs?'

'It wasn't that so much. He was just shy. He was small for his age and very quiet, too quiet to be popular. I think popularity requires a certain amount of extroversion, at least with children. Quiet kids can only hope to be forgotten. That's the best that can happen to them. That's what happens if they're lucky. If they're unlucky they get picked on. Don't you think?'

'I think it's possible to be quiet and popular as an adult.'

'Really?'

'Yes, if a man is rich or good at sport he can be popular even if he doesn't talk much.'

'And a woman?'

'She has to be pretty . . . or sexy . . . attractive in some way. If she's beautiful she doesn't have to be the life of the party.'

'I think you're right.'

'But you're right about little children.'

'Well, Carlo was young and little and neither of his parents had English as a first language. You could just see the beginning of a life of pain for him.'

'What did you do?'

'I tried to help him. You see, the kids read out loud to us and even though you try to do it one on one, the other kids listen, or at least, some of them do, and an anxious child—'

'Like Carlo.'

'Right, an anxious little boy like Carlo would have been acutely aware of any other kids listening so it wasn't easy to tell whether he was a slow reader because he was having difficulty actually reading or whether it was just that he was embarrassed to do it in front of the other kids. So I arranged for him to stay back after school a couple of days a week so that I could read to him and he could read back to me, all of it alone. I had to fix it with his mother.'

'Get permission?'

'Yeah. I had to get permission but I also didn't want her to think there was anything terribly wrong, because there wasn't. He was within the normal range. I just thought he could be higher within it. So I'd read to him and he'd read back to me. Sometimes I'd even sing to him. It seemed to be working. He was also more confident during the day with the other kids.'

'You sound like a dream teacher.'

'Wait till you hear the end of it,' he exhaled. 'You'll wish it was a dream. We'd had one of our usual sessions after school. Everyone else had gone, the school was deserted. When we had finished we went to check on Empson, to see if he needed his water bowl filled, that sort of thing. It was actually more of a reward for Carlo. Empson was alright but it was sort of a treat for Carlo to get to play with him without having to share him with the other kids.'

'That's so sweet.'

'Well, on this day, Carlo told me he needed to go to the toilet. So off he went and I waited for him. I waited about . . . I don't know, ten minutes or so and he hadn't come back. I gave him another ten minutes because I thought that maybe he'd had an accident in the toilet and he might be trying to clean himself up. He was five and a half or six. Kids would shit themselves at school all the time. It was terrible for them *and* for us. We should've got danger money. Anyway, I didn't want to check on him too soon because I didn't want to risk embarrassing him. I didn't want him to feel humiliated.'

'Well, after a little while I had to check because he still wasn't back.'

'And?'

Simon put the palm of one hand to his face and let it slide slowly from his forehead over his eyes past his mouth to his chin.

'And he was gone. He wasn't in the toilets or the changing rooms. He wasn't with Empson. I ran around the school yard calling out his name. My mouth was dry. I was absolutely terror-stricken. I've been over it a million times in my mind. That's the way it happened. That's the way I told it to the police. It might have been the worst moment of my life . . . and they still haven't found him. That was the last day I remember feeling really good about anything . . . over a sustained period.

'I can't believe I'm telling you this. I haven't talked this way to anyone,' Simon said with amazement.

'Do you blame yourself?'

'Well, I know I shouldn't but of course I do. My arrogance kicked in, my naïve liberal faith in intervention, in getting involved. I thought that by involving myself in the little boy's life I could do him some good, as though I knew something about . . . anything.'

'Don't you think people should get involved?'

'That's just the thing. I have always thought people *should* get involved with the problems of other people. People don't help enough. It's the . . . it's probably the closest thing I've ever had to a philosophy. A pragmatic philosophy. You see it every day. Most people are too . . . they're not evil. They're just . . .'

'Lazy?' I volunteered.

'Apathetic.'

'You're sure they're not evil?' I asked him.

'Some people are definitely, unequivocally evil, but most people are not. Most people are simply apathetic, unaware and frightened. A lot of bad gets done by people who are not bad people. Maybe it's always been this way but I think it's more so now than ever. I saw a documentary about the sixties on TV the other day. They showed all these people in their twenties and thirties sitting around holding candles singing "We Shall Overcome". They were protesting against racism and the Vietnam War. It's not that people in their twenties and thirties then were better or smarter than people in their twenties and thirties now.'

'So, what is it?'

'It's the times. The times, they have changed. Where once people were told that the answers were blowing in the wind, now it's they who are blown by the wind, the wind generated by the market. The ruthless pursuit of the bottom line is the siren song of the times and the song is played over the public address system in banks, in stores and supermarkets. It's played when you are downsized because your company can replace you with somebody in another country for two dollars a day. And it's played whenever you call up anywhere needing assistance and they put you on hold because they've cut back on staff in order to increase their share price.'

'But people have always been obsessed with the bottom line. Why is it any different now? Hasn't money always been the siren song?'

'It has never been so loud. It's never been so ubiquitous. It has never before so routinely, so blatantly, ousted and nullified citizenship and notions of the common good, what was once called the common weal. It has never before so successfully colonised men's souls.'

'Except yours.'

'Except mine. Not just mine. I know that. But you see, if you are not with this Zeitgeist, if you are a victim of it or if you resist it, you're out in the cold. You are left to sell crafts at weekend markets.'

'What do you mean?'

'I mean you don't belong, you're marginal, you don't count. You live hand to mouth off intermittent piecework or part-time work. Or you're on welfare. You are ignored by the mainstream. You are part of that nation which is the less fortunate of our two nations and the other nation doesn't want to know about you.'

'What two nations?'

'The rich and the poor. It was how Disraeli described nineteenth-century England.'

'And which nation do you belong to? The marginal one?'

'I think so.'

'Ever since someone took Carlo?'

'That's when I first realised it. What about you?'

'Me? Am I marginal?'

'Yeah.'

'Oh no. I'm gonna make money.'

'Well, you're doing a great job so far.'

7

I had never met anyone like him before. He was sincere, passionate, intelligent and yet humble. He was an intellectual but he didn't think that made him better than anyone else, quite the contrary. I still haven't met anyone remotely like him, with the possible exception of Alex, but he is more formal, in a European sort of way, less relaxed and, anyway, he is almost old enough to be my father. The way Simon spoke, what he said, the way the words sounded when shaped by his voice, made me feel as though I had spent all my life till then in a deep sleep, a sleep interrupted occasionally by a nightmare.

His honesty about himself was breathtaking, especially later when he talked about his unemployment, about his drinking and about what he called his failure as a man, his failure to approximate his idea of a man. Despite being a little drunk, this gifted and eloquent man seemed so sane. He seemed so fair. As we talked and walked, arm in arm after a while, more for comfort and support than for any kind of titillation, I waited for him to talk down to me, not by way of condescension but because he had thought so much more about things. Important things. He had read so much more than me. He knew so much more than me. I waited for it but it never happened. If anything, he became more self-deprecating with every hour. He talked about William, his father, and how he had accused him of being depressed. He stressed that coming from William, this was an accusation. For William, being depressed was egocentric, self-indulgent, weak and, most importantly, it was spiteful. I listened to everything he said and wondered what good deed, what kindness, I had performed that God or fate or whoever controls these things had led Simon to choose me to put his arm around, to talk to, to listen to, without expecting anything in return.

'You asked me if I wanted a date. It had been a long time since anyone had asked me out,' he told me much later.

Even in bad times, in the moments of decline, as Alex describes them, when I have had to throw the covers off his bed, shower him, and then walk him and Empson, he never turned on me. He was always gentle with me. He only ever attacked himself. Until now. He says that I've done it to myself. And though I don't think I have, Kelly has to wake me up at night when I cry out. I am lost now.

We had been together for hours, walking, talking, drinking, eating and sitting for long periods not talking, just looking at the sky. I didn't know how the night was going to end. I hoped that it wouldn't end. I was scared I hadn't done or said the right things, the things that would make him want to see me again. Although I had never experienced anything like that night, what was special about it, what was always special about us as a couple, was him. It was a fairytale night that I was afraid would end when he kissed me and turned me back into a whore he had met on a street corner.

The streets had not changed in those last few hours. They were still wild with the noise, the mess and the shove of unregulated street commerce. The gawking tourists, the crowded ice-cream shops and bistros, the hookers, the young men wearing back-to-front baseball caps, their families only recently arrived from the Middle East or Eastern Europe, in their family sedans with the thud thud thud of African-American music flattening the ground beneath them, they were all still there. The difference was that now I could observe it without being part of it.

'Take it easy, bitch,' I heard one call out. But it was not to me, because I was with Simon and our body language suggested we were a couple, not a whore and a lonely guy. We too often laughed at the same time to be a whore and a lonely guy. Laughter protected us from what other people were doing to each other. It protected us from everything except Simon's parents.

We were laughing when we met them coming out of a restaurant with another couple. Simon changed instantly. He stiffened in an attempt to hide how much he had drunk. Everyone was embarrassed. The way I was dressed did not help. There were some perfunctory introductions and that's when, for the first time, I went from Angela to Angelique. I did it myself, capriciously.

'Angelique, is it?' said the older man who wasn't Simon's father. 'We've just had a lovely meal here to celebrate William's retirement. Have you ever eaten here? You should, if you live in the neighbourhood.'

'You're absolutely right. The food is great. I often eat here. The owner is a regular client of mine.'

'Henry, let's go!' the man's wife said, grabbing him by the arm.

'It's alright, Dad, we're leaving,' Simon said from the kerb, trying to hail a taxi.

'What did you want a taxi for?' I asked him later when we were back at his flat.

'I wanted the two groups of people to be separated as soon as possible and you can never hail a helicopter in Fitzroy Street at that time on a Friday night.'

'Were you ashamed to be seen with me, a prostitute?'

'I didn't think you really were a prostitute.'

'Were you ashamed to be seen with me anyway?'

'No. I was ashamed long before I met you.'

His flat was a sea of books and newspapers, magazines, photos from his past, CDs and video cassettes onto which he told me he had recorded years of movies and documentaries. It was quite a collection, an archive of a world still foreign to me. Then there was the cuddly Empson. The dog had Simon's often sad eyes but he was easier to amuse than his owner. When Simon took him outside for a pee, I looked inside the pantry in the kitchen. All it contained was tea, coffee, cereal, scotch, canned soup, two-minute noodles and dog food. The fridge was empty except for milk, beer and some sad fruit. I felt immediately comfortable there, at home. It needed a woman's touch to brighten the place up a little but it felt like a sanctuary. By the time Simon had brought Empson back in, I had made us both a cup of tea. It was very late but I told him all about my life in Adelaide, about my dancing, my brothers and my parents. I told him about our house, how it looked onto the prison for young ladies that was my school, about Suramia and the other girls, about my father and about university. I told him about Romesh, about the abortion and about coming to Melbourne. I told him about the habitués of the city's night-clubs and about Steve. But I didn't tell him about the rape.

Shortly after four in the morning, after we had finished watching a video tape of Simon's about a revolt on some Russian battleship, I worked up the courage to ask him about the woman in the photos. I hoped without much confidence that he would tell me it was a sister or a cousin or something but of course, it wasn't. It was Anna, the great Anna. He was a little tentative talking about her at first, more tentative than he had been talking about anything else, but then he began to warm to his subject, a little too much. I already had the picture. I understood how important she had been to him and when he paused for breath or else because the gravity of the subject demanded it, I leant over and kissed him. We made love slowly and quietly on his couch. Then, as we were falling asleep, he took me to his bed where we slept for hours.

The next morning, or rather it was early afternoon, I woke with a start and realised that my suitcase with all my belongings was back in the motel in Carlisle Street and that not only had I missed 'check-out time' but I didn't have the money to pay for even the night I had just spent at Simon's place, let alone the nights to come. He was in the kitchen feeding Empson when I came upon him with my problem.

'It's no problem, unless of course someone has stolen your suit-case. Drink your tea and then go and pay them. You'll get your suitcase out.'

'Are you kicking me out?'

'Well, no I'm not, but . . . what did you have in mind?' he asked me.

'I don't know, I just thought . . . you know . . . after everything that happened last night . . . and anyway, I don't have the money to pay for the room.'

'Yes you do,' he said, pointing to my handbag. I didn't remember leaving it there. He must have brought it in from the living room.

'What are you talking about . . . what's this?' I said, holding two fifty dollar bills he had put in there. 'What the hell is *this*?' I asked him.

'It's money, Angela. What do you think it is?'

'I know it's money, Simon. Why the hell are you giving it to me?'

'Calm down, will you. I've made you a cup of tea.'

'I don't want your fucking cup of tea. I don't want anything from you. Look, last night . . . I wasn't . . . I hope you . . . I wasn't your whore, you know.'

'Will you calm down.'

'What the hell do you think—'

'Please! Please sit down. Let me explain,' he said.

'I know what you think and—'

'Angela, please. Here is what I think. Okay. I think that last night was a wonderful night. I think that you are virtually penniless and that all your earthly goods, or at least everything you own in this part of the earth, is currently in the care and custody of the proprietors of one of the sleaziest motels in town. I think that you owe those proprietors money and I think that you have the best chance of getting your suitcase back if you pay them as soon as possible. This is the best and the quickest way of getting your suitcase back,' he said, pointing to the money.

'So the money, is it a loan?' I asked him tentatively, wanting more than anything for the answer to be yes.

'No. It's not a loan.'

'Why not?'

'Because . . . I don't want it back.'

'Why the hell don't you want it back?'

'Look, Angela, Angelique, Angel, I've just paid my rent for the next month. I need much more money than that hundred dollars to make the slightest bit of difference to my life. You, on the other hand, are about a hundred dollars between vagrancy and whatever else the rest of your life holds. It's worth a great deal more to you. You should have it. You would have earned much more than that last night had I not kidnapped you for a cameo role in the endless desperate self-indulgence that is currently my life. I owe you more than that in boredom money alone. Call it a "disappointment" fee. You had certain financial goals last night, which were thwarted entirely by me. But every minute you wait your tea grows colder and the chance of you getting your suitcase gets smaller.'

'Where will I go?'

'What do you mean? Don't you know the way from here?'

'Simon, where will I go when I have my suitcase?'

'Well,' he said, 'I was expecting that you'd come back here. You don't have to but I didn't think you had anywhere else to go. Try not to be too long though. I really owe Empson a walk.'

It is difficult to describe my relief on hearing that. I felt that things might be starting to work out for me, just a little. My suitcase was behind the desk at reception and when I gave them the money

I owed, no questions were asked. Money has that effect. When I got back Simon and I had breakfast, showered, and took Empson for a walk. It was during that walk that Simon made the first of his many pleas for me not to work as a prostitute. I told him that I would only do it until I had enough money to get a little settled. Of course, aiming to get a little settled graduated into aiming to get a car, to put a deposit on a place, and ultimately, to start a business of my own. The irony is that now, just when I am being forced to stop, he goes and shuts me out of his life completely.

8

Simon begged me not to work the streets. It was, he said, in addition to being very dangerous, also illegal. Brothels and escort agencies are legal in the State of Victoria. I hadn't known that. I looked through the yellow pages and phoned some places that charged three hundred, five hundred and even a thousand dollars an hour. That was what I wanted. If I was going to do it, why not do it for a thousand an hour? Simon said I could stay with him for a few days which became almost three weeks. In those three weeks I met Kelly, Simon started seeing Alex Klima, and I started earning real money.

The first place I called was the thousand-dollar-an-hour escort agency. I had a lot of embarrassing misconceptions about the whole industry, embarrassing to me now. I expected to find a sun-tanning bed, manicurists, a team of people to set you up and do your hair and make-up so that you would go on expensive bookings looking like you were some kind of model, but it wasn't like that at all. If you wanted to look that good you had to do it yourself. I had expected it to be a team effort. I thought they would have standards, a reputation to protect. They didn't have very much to protect at all.

I sat in the waiting room as the other girls came and went. Many of them knew each other. I just sat there. I was scared every time the phone rang. It wasn't that the manager was favouring the other girls. It was that they kept trying to send me to two-hundred-dollar bookings and I was holding out for at least a five-hundred-dollar booking. I didn't really know if I was going to be able to go through with it or, if I could do it once, whether I was going to be able to do it again. If nothing else, I wanted to come away from the night with a clear two hundred and fifty dollars after the agency's cut. I hadn't taken into account the driver's cut.

Finally, after sitting in the waiting room for four hours looking at a TV screen, trying to pretend I wasn't nervous, the manager came up to me. 'We've just got a five-hundred-dollar booking to a hotel in St Kilda Road. Will you take this one?'

She spoke to me as though I was a little princess, too precious, not really interested in working. It was time for me to put my money where my mouth was. Or some permutation thereof. I said I'd take it.

My stomach was churning. I trembled a little in the back seat of the car on the way there. There was a part of me that couldn't believe I was actually going to go through with it, and it is possible I would have had cold feet had it not been for Kelly.

It was a two-girl booking and we met in the foyer of the hotel. My first thought on seeing her, as though it mattered, was that she was prettier than me. She was certainly much more relaxed. We introduced ourselves. For some reason I was even nervous talking to *her*. She commented that she hadn't seen me before at the agency. I was tossing up whether or not to tell her that I hadn't ever done this before when she said, 'You're new at this, aren't you?'

'First time,' I conceded.

'First time! Okay, let's have a drink before we go up.'

Kelly was great, really comforting. She need not have been. It can be a very catty industry. She took me to the bar and bought me a glass of champagne. I was dressed in a very conservative blue dress, not very hookerish at all. It was a dress that one might normally wear to the theatre or something like that. Kelly later said it was a mistake to show no cleavage and to cover the knees. I looked shy rather than wanton. It mattered less than I could have imagined.

Kelly told me to relax, she would look after me. Then she bought me another glass of champagne. This would be fine, she said, no problems at all. I asked her how she knew and she said, 'Oh, it's two Chinese guys.'

'Why is that good?'

'They'll be clean, polite, and perhaps not so fluent in English so you won't have to talk much. And they'll be small.'

'Small?'

'Dicks. Won't hurt. Women are generally five and a half inches deep, you know. Anything bigger than that on a man, if it's used badly, can really hurt, especially on some young rammer who's really proud of his equipment. These guys, Chinese business types, possibly shy, they'll be easy. They'll swim in you. It's money for jam.'

'Small? What about those sumo guys, the really fat ones?' I asked.

'Sumo wrestlers? That's Japanese, and anyway, there's one part of their bodies they can't beef up. Either they've got it or they haven't, and, believe me, Asian guys haven't. No, trust me, honey, Asians, especially Chinese, that's really good. They all look the same so it's hard to get an ugly one. I'll do the talking, tell them you're the new girl. They'll treat you well.'

'Why?'

'A new girl, she's . . . she's almost a virgin, she's special. They'll feel lucky, like all their new years have come at once. And they'll be gentler with you. We often tell guys it's our first time. Everybody's happier.'

'I don't get it,' I told her. She explained.

'It's like they'll feel special being your first ever client and they'll want you to think well of them. You can use that.'

'But it *is* my first time.'

'Then it *is* special. It's the last time that will ever be true.'

She could see that I was still scared and she took my hand.

'Honey, if you get in there and you don't want to do it, you can call me. Here's my mobile number,' she said, copying it down and putting it in my bag.

We went up together. I stood beside her as she knocked on the door. When it opened Kelly did the talking. She explained in a friendly but firmly patronising way to the two men in their late thirties or early forties that we were there to show them a good time but first we needed to get the matter of money out of the way. The man who had opened the door pulled a credit card out of his wallet. I stood there nervously trying to avoid eye contact with the other one, the one I just assumed was mine. Neither of us was comfortable doing the talking. This was something we had in common.

Kelly took the other man's credit card and phoned the details through to the agency. As she waited for the agency to complete the transaction, she must have seen me looking like a little girl on her first day of school. That was how I felt. I wanted to go over to her side of the room and stand behind her as she spoke on the phone. Kelly discerned my discomfort and turned it to advantage by announcing rather loudly, their broken English being to her indicative of deafness, 'It's her first time, you know. You work out between you who wants me and who wants the new girl.'

After a minute or two that took forever, Kelly signified the payment had been accepted. It was really going to happen. I tried telling myself that I had a job to do and that it had to be done before I could go home. I just had to say a few things, not many, do a few things and permit still other things to be done to me. The voice inside me shouted at me not to be afraid. If I wanted the money I had to do whatever it took. That was my plan. The words came into my head, screaming to the exclusion of any other thoughts. 'Just do it!' How strange were the fruits of the children working in the factories of Asia, Simon mused when I subsequently told him.

There was an urgency to that instruction. It had no time for second thought, no stomach for anticipation and no mind for wisdom. Ultimately, I could not be held responsible for what I was about to do. I would only be following orders.

Kelly left with the holder of the credit card and I was alone with my client. As I sat down on the bed he took a bottle of champagne out of the bar fridge, opened it and poured me a glass. Then he told me that he was going to take a shower. He seemed pleasant enough, certainly not *un*pleasant. His shower and drying time was thirty minutes. I timed him because it was a one-hour booking and I couldn't believe how long he was taking. It occurs to me now that perhaps he was masturbating in the shower to lengthen his performance with me. Men sometimes try things like that. It's something Joe Geraghty told me. I was concerned that this guy might dispute the time.

He came out of the bathroom in a dry towel. I didn't know what to do, how to start, but he had clearly done this many times before. He lay naked face down on the bed. For a moment I just looked at him. He was the first Chinese man I had ever seen naked. Then I started to massage him and once I'd started the massage, everything was okay.

I relaxed. He seemed to be enjoying the massage and I just went into boyfriend mode. You learn early from experience that a boyfriend will often want sex when you don't. And it doesn't even take a boyfriend. It can be someone you met in a bar or at a party, the territory of the one-night stand. You want to meet new people, to be admired. You feel relaxed after a few drinks. Then you suddenly find yourself somewhere thinking, I don't really want to go through with this, not anymore, but it's easier to go through with it than to back out. So you go through the motions. You pay lip service to the act. You don't need to be a prostitute for this to happen. The only difference is that we take money for it up-front. If everyone knew how easy it really is, after the first couple of times anyway, we'd earn less than waitresses.

I put a condom on him and he took five minutes. I timed that too. He turned over and I gave him another massage. He barely spoke. It was a great introduction. If only they were all like that. He didn't even try to kiss me or bargain for any extras. We call them 'extras', whatever else they can think of. When we quote, what we are really quoting for is basic or straight sex. We charge more for any fetish or aberration. But you soon learn that sexual aberration is largely a myth or, rather, a misnomer. It is 'normal' sex that is a myth. Aberration is the norm. The fetishes, the games, the role play, costumes and equipment, they are so common. If every woman knew *that*, we would certainly earn less than waitresses.

Alex says a man's fetish begins at a moment of conjoined anxiety and stimulation when, for some reason, the man is made to feel that if he expresses his sexuality at that precise moment, he will be breaking some rule and love will be withheld from him. He says fetishes are about the search for love. I'm not sure about this. I am sure that I could have earned considerably more if I'd been more willing to help them revisit their moments of conjoined anxiety and stimulation but, as much as I've wanted to make money, the 'extras' can play games with your mind. Kelly is stronger than me. Simon thought I was mentally strong, stronger than him, but he never really knew Kelly. She's the strong one. He was constantly amazed that I could walk out of a place and wipe the booking from my mind. Nor could he understand how I could leave the safety of the brothel to do escort work. He thought, like most people, that the kind of work I was doing was likely, sooner or later, to lead me, through alienation and depersonalisation, to a sense of what he called 'agonising aloneness' and despair. But he was quite wrong. I got there through love.

Kelly introduced me to the brothel where she worked most of the time. She said that the management there looked after their girls better than they had to. She was right. They have looked after me well. They've helped me get well-paid escort work when I've wanted it, although they try to discourage their 'career' girls from escorting because they say it's more dangerous, wears you out and is usually the refuge of girls who wouldn't be able to attract bookings from men who have a choice of women they can see. Fran, the manager, said a girl as pretty as me didn't need to take the risks inherent in escorting but that she would get the work for me if I really wanted it. Kelly was pretty enough not to have to escort but because she was obsessed with making money, she did it on the side. She freelanced with the other agency, the one I had picked out of the phone book. She chose them in order not to alienate Fran. Somehow I think Fran knew about it.

This was the beginning of a time that Alex calls my 'golden age'.
I was earning good money for the first time ever. Kelly had taken me
under her wing and was showing me the ropes. We hit it off almost
immediately. I felt that I could trust her and she obviously felt the
same way because she invited me to live with her. We found a two-
bedroom place to rent with security doors, high ceilings and French
windows looking onto a little courtyard where we would often sit and
have coffee. I got a little car and a little self-esteem.

And then there was Simon. He was always trying to give me
money even though, within a week or two of starting work, I had more
money than he had. He had hardly any but he would take me out to
second-hand bookshops and buy me the books he thought I should
have. Poetry particularly excited him. He said that if you had books
you need never be alone. But of course, during that time, during the
golden age, I never was alone. I bought him food and I cooked for him.
We went for walks with Alex and Empson, went out for coffee, for
drinks. I read many of the books he fed me and he was right. When the
words dance privately for you it is possible to feel not alone. I didn't
pretend to understand all the words but Simon explained how they
wait for you inside the covers, how they wait for you to need them. I
know, since Alex brings Simon's books to him, that he is using them
now. But it seems my best words have been spent. The only words I
have left are not able to describe what has happened to me, to us.

9

Sometimes Simon would talk about Anna. Occasionally, he'd show
me photos of her I hadn't seen before, pulled from boxes in cupboards
or drawers. Of course I was curious at first, but eventually I saw
more photos of her than the satisfaction of my curiosity required.
She is pretty, very pretty. You can see the Italian in her. I thought for
a while that maybe that was the part of her that was so special to
him. I felt very Anglo, very white compared to her. At other times, the
way he talked about her made me feel stupid, or, if not stupid in the
sense of unintelligent, then uncultured. Whatever I read, and most
of what I thought about, Simon had introduced me to; it was all just
a regurgitation of things he had told me. While this was a kind of

membership of the world that was important to him, it was not a full membership and I didn't really belong. She did. She hadn't needed to be taught. She had come to him educated and sophisticated.

And so when it emerged that the Joe Geraghty I was seeing once a week was her husband, I thought Simon's fascination with their lives was understandable. Perhaps it was even to my advantage. Here was Joe, the husband of the great and lovely Anna, the woman who had rejected Simon, and Joe was cheating on her, weekly, preferring me, Simon's girlfriend, to her. The fairytale life of the affluent young couple in their half-acre home by the beach was a sham and I was in a position to bring him fresh and intimate reports of just how much of a sham it was. What spurned lover would not find this interesting?

I saw this interest in their lives, in Anna, Sam and even in Joe, grow into an obsession. For a long while I repressed what I was seeing. When that became impossible, I coped by telling myself that if it were an obsession then at least it was one that required my input, one that I was, so to speak, a part of. There were times, however, when something Simon had said about her a day or so earlier would come to mind and my eyes would fill uncontrollably and without warning. I always meant to ask Alex if that was a *sympathetic* or a *parasympathetic* response, or if it was just part of my 'inconvenience'.

I was at home catching up with the newspapers. Simon was an avid reader of newspapers. 'For all their biases, their hypocrisy and their remorseless conservatism, it's your world they're writing about. We have an obligation to care about it and you're really not going to learn anything from television news,' he'd told me. Kelly said she'd known a lot of men in her time but never one who set his girlfriend homework. But I didn't mind. It helped me to understand what he was talking about and I felt good that it mattered to him that I knew what was going on. He would ask me what I thought about something and in this way he got me to think about things I had never thought about before and I got him to talk about the world, important things, and not just *her*.

'Have a close look at the sort of things that get into the paper,' he told me. 'What does it tell you about newspapers, or the media more generally?'

'I don't know. What does it tell you?'

'Think about it. What gets into the newspapers?'

'I don't know, stories, news. Things the papers think are important.'

'Or things they think will sell papers. Or things they think will swing public opinion in a certain direction. And who are the newspapers?'

'I don't know, journalists, editors?'

'And who employs them?'

'The owners of the newspapers?'

'Exactly. But do you see what that means? The selection, the head-lining, placement and length of items, and the way they are slanted are ultimately influenced, albeit sometimes only indirectly and subtly, by the commercial and political concerns of the proprietors.

'That this is true in general, at least to some degree, is indu-bitable. But of course it is not always true. There are certain defiant journalists that tell it free of the party line. They're usually featured in the op-ed page, which most readers never reach. If you want an instant incisive fix on the headline news, stick with the cartoonists.'

'So why do you spend so much time reading newspapers?'

'Look, it's not that you can't learn a lot from them. You can. You just have to know how to navigate between the lines.'

It was very hot and I was in my underwear reading the newspa-per and having a cup of coffee. Kelly wasn't home, not at first. She worked more shifts than I did. Sometimes she would work a full day in the brothel, have an hour and a half off, then start a night of escorting. She said you could still escort if you were tired because it didn't matter, within reason, how you looked. Once they had waited for you to knock at the door, they were very unlikely to send you away because underneath your make-up you looked a little tired. They were too polite to mention it, if they noticed. There were things Kelly would do in a booking that distracted the client from her make-up, things I never used to do.

I had been thinking that my eyes were getting worse. I owned read-ing glasses I hardly ever wore, but that day I was having trouble focusing. I went to my bedroom and got the glasses to make it easier to read. There was an item with the headline 'Beijing considers ban as poor sell body parts'. It claimed that advertisements from poverty-stricken people trying to sell their own body parts were appearing on Chinese websites. The article cited some of them. 'Cornea from healthy person with sight: 1.5 million yuan—urgent sale because of poverty.' I squinted as I read it. I remembered that months before I'd had trouble reading in bed. I'd mentioned it in passing to a pharmacist and when he'd asked me which eye was the problem, I found that I couldn't remember. It hadn't been the purpose of my visit to the pharmacy.

'Well, it can't be too much of a problem then, can it?' the phar-macist had said.

I remember feeling embarrassed and angry at his response. He had spoken in that supercilious patronising manner that older men affect either to cover a clumsy attempt to flirt with you or to punish you for being young and out of reach and prettier than any of the women they had ever had more to do with than pass the time of day. You were an attractive young woman. Was there any malice you did not deserve?

Another advertisement, this one apparently from a place called Yangchen, read 'A kidney from living human body—two million yuan'. The newspaper said this was equivalent to $50 000. Human marrow was going for $10 000.

The blurriness was not going away. I went to the bathroom and got some eye-drops, which the old bastard had sold me for my sins. They stung and were past their use-by date. Anyway, the blurriness was not the same as the problem I had experienced before. It was, as Alex Klima would say, qualitatively different.

Trade in human organs had previously been monopolised by the Chinese Communist Party. The medical system had made huge prof-its from selling the organs of executed prisoners to well-educated Party officials who would then in turn sell them on the open market to people in Hong Kong, Taiwan and Singapore. Two thousand pris-oners were executed each year for harvest. The state wanted to crack down on the impoverished entrepreneurs who were driving down the price with their website advertisements.

'The triumph of e-commerce!' Simon had said later when we dis-cussed it. 'See, Angel, it's bringing democracy.' But that day I couldn't finish the article. The light was dazzling my eyes. I was physically unable to. When Kelly came home I was lying on the couch with my eyes closed. She was preoccupied with the day she'd had.

'You don't want to know about the day I've had,' she said.

She was right. I was distressed about my eyes, but she told me anyway.

'You know they still won't give me a loan.'

'Who, the bank?'

'Yes. The bank.'

'Have you told them what you do?'

'No. Why should I?'

'Because they're not going to lend you money if they don't know whether you're going to be able to pay it back.'

'Angelique, I've got $60 000 for a deposit. I've told them I just want a home loan. Nothing else. It's not for a boat, for fuck's sake. Why do they have to give me such a hard time about it?'

'Kelly, you can't seriously think they're going to give you a home loan when you won't tell them what you do for a living?'

'And *you* can't seriously think they're going to give me one if I do. Jesus, Angelique, sometimes you're so—'

'Kelly, be really careful with the next word you choose to utter.'

'That's right, we can't go upsetting the princess as she gets her beauty sleep on the couch.'

'Kelly, take it easy. I've got something weird going on with my eyes.'

'You're just reading too much of that poetry shit your boyfriend gives you.'

'No really, Kelly. I'm serious. There's something wrong with me. I don't know what.'

'You want to hear something wrong?'

'No, not really. Not right now.'

'So, I'm at the bank, right, and they're showing me into the office of one manager after another and it's taking forever. I'm there much longer than I thought I'd be. I stay till they're finally finished getting each one of their managers to tell me that I'm not a suitable candidate. Can you believe that? Candidate. It's a bank, not a fucking popularity contest. I just want to be a customer like all their other deadbeat customers who take it up the arse from the bank and quietly pay for it every month regular as clockwork with all those hidden fees and charges and that . . . what is it? Financial institutions duty. You ever see that on your statement?'

'That's a tax.' She was stopping me from cooling down. My eyes had got worse.

'What did you say?'

'Financial institutions duty—it's a tax. It's the government, not the bank.'

'You're not defending the banks now, are you?'

'No, I'm just saying . . . I've actually asked about it and—'

'Well, shut the fuck up and listen to the rest of my day. So I'm kept at the bank completely forever and by the time the last dickhead has said no, I'm late for Radji—'

'Who's Radji?'

'You know, Radji, one of my regulars.'

'Don't know him.'

'Oh, Angelique, don't be difficult, you do. Radji, Radji Radjadurai, the stocky dark guy, face like the wet end of a cigar.'

'What kind of name is that?'

'I don't know—who the fuck cares? Indian, Sri Lankan, Afghani, it's not the point of the story.'

'You *are* in a bad mood.'

'Listen and I'll tell you why. So, because of the bank I'm late for Radji and nobody thinks to tell him to just sit in the corner with a magazine like a good little Indian. No, nobody tells him I won't be long. Nobody ever watches out for you.'

'Maybe they didn't know when you'd be back.'

'Well, maybe, but listen to this. The new girl—'

'Who, Chantal?'

'Chantal, the new girl, she tells Radji that she'll look after him—'

'Kelly, she's new. Maybe she didn't know—'

'Will you listen to the story and you'll know why I'm so upset.'

'Okay, I'm listening. But my eyes are weird.'

'You don't need your eyes to listen. What you need to know about Radji is that for the last year and a half he's been after me for a—'

'Don't say it. You've told me. It's disgusting.'

'Yeah, he's wanted to do it to me ever since—'

'Kelly, I can't listen to this right now.'

'You have to. We live together. You see, I use these stilettos and dildos on him.'

'What do you mean *on* him?'

'He's straight but he likes things up him and he's always asking for a—'

'Stop, will you!'

'It gets worse. He wants to do it on me, *to* me and I keep saying no.'

'Like the bank.'

'That's not funny, Angelique, and anyway, unlike the bank, I don't give a blanket no. I just keep putting the price up and up and he just keeps asking for it. I even thought maybe that was all he wanted, just the thrill of negotiating. So, over the last year and a half, I'd got him up to $2500.'

'You're kidding!'

'No, for $2500 plus my usual hourly rate he could do it.'

'Oh, Kelly, that's really disgusting!'

'Will you listen. It gets worse. So Chantal, the new girl, sees I'm not there and she offers to show him a good time. They go upstairs and, surprise, surprise, he starts in on her for his fetish.'

'What a creep.'

'Listen, Angelique, he asks her—and she lets him!'

'Oh my God, that's horrible.'

'For fifty dollars.'

'What?'

'She only charges him an extra fifty dollars.'

'You must be joking.'

'I'm not joking. I don't know what the world's coming to. I really don't. I've been working this guy for a year and a half, and this new girl . . . I'm sent on a wild-goose chase at the bank and when I get back the new girl has stolen thousands of dollars from me. Of course he won't come back to me now. You know that, don't you?'

'I hate to say it but . . .'

'You're not actually going to defend that grasping little whore?'

'No, but . . . the whole thing is disgusting, Kelly, and there are worse things going on in the world than having the new girl out-deprave you.'

'This is really not a good day to give me a lecture.'

'I'm not giving you a lecture but . . . I just read an article, Kelly, in the newspaper, about people in China who are so poor they try to sell their own body parts to get the money to survive.'

'What's your point, Angelique? That's in China.'

'The other day I read something in the paper about these African refugees who've been living in tent cities for ten years.'

'So? Why don't they do something about it? You make your own luck.'

'They fled wars and hostile governments and armies and teenage militias only to live in tents for ten years.'

'Well, why doesn't the UN or somebody do something about it?'

'The article said the UN is investigating a people-trafficking racket run by some of its own officials. It said they take $10 000 per person to resettle them somewhere else.'

'Ten thousand? That's a high-roughage week with Radji.'

'Kelly, what's wrong with you?'

'What's wrong with *me*? You're the one lying on the couch in your underwear with your arm over your eyes bringing me the news from the Third World. Is this the sort of shit your boyfriend makes you talk about? I spent half the day being patronised by these dickhead bank managers who knew, who must've figured out, how I get my money, but they wanted to make me say it. They wanted to humiliate me within the offices of a bank and that was the only way they were going to give me the money. They wanted to be able to go home and tell their wives they had a whore come and see them today. I wouldn't do it and they wouldn't give me the money.

'Fuck them! What I'm going to do is lend what I've got to the brothel at ten per cent. Fran says they've got huge problems with the Tax Office. Ten per cent is better than you can get from the bank. The bank can go fuck itself.

'And then, after all this, when I finally get back to work, one of my regulars has been stolen by the fucking new girl and nobody, none of my esteemed colleagues, says anything. Nobody does anything to stop her and this is just the thin end of the wedge. Where will it stop? A regular is a cash cow because some of the money you'll get next week comes from the work you did last week and all the weeks before, from all the times you got him to believe that you look forward to his visits and only to his visits, that you miss him between visits, that you're thinking of him and that he's the only one you enjoy it with. That's the bulk of what they pay for, the illusion that they matter and that they're desirable to a pretty young woman. And if you can get them to believe that then you don't have to do much in the room with them. You're like a brand name. A loser buys a t-shirt with a fashion logo on it and even though, other than the logo, it's just a crappy old t-shirt, it makes him feel better about himself when he wears it. Well, a regular's whore is the logo he wears when he's with all the untouchable women who see him the way the mirror sees him. We are to him the logo on the t-shirt. We make him feel better about himself. It's all smoke and mirrors. It's marketing and once you've reached a certain level, the brand keeps selling itself. I'd reached that level with Radji and she undercut me. And for what? For fifty lousy dollars. I mean . . . it's not even a thousand. She's only hurting herself in the end. She's hurting all of us, not just me. But does anybody say anything? Does anybody explain things to her? No, no, it's everyone for himself. And when I get home I've got the princess from the Adelaide private school system giving me a fucking lecture on everything her boyfriend taught her about the Third World.'

'Kelly, I know you don't want to live with me forever but why do you need the money so badly?'

'I don't need it so badly. It's just . . . it's the principle of the thing. You're really on your own. You never stop having to defend what you've got, never stop having to look over your shoulder. You see, a regular is like an asset, the way a bank would see it if they weren't so hypocritical. And I just lost an asset today . . . but I suppose you're right. I don't really need the money so badly. I know what to do if I ever needed a lot of money in a hurry.'

'Oh, you're talking about another tour of duty as part of the Sultan of Brunei's harem?'

'No, those days are over. Miss America fucked that up for everyone.'

'What do you mean?'

'Well, she pretended she didn't know why he was paying for her to go over there and then she sued him. It's a shame because they always wanted new girls and you could earn great money for just being there on call. You didn't have to do anything. A white girl can always make pretty good money in Asia and the Middle East, though not with the good old Sultan anymore. But it's still possible to make great money fast if you're really desperate and you know where to go. I've never been that desperate.'

'Here or overseas?'

'I meant here, but you can probably do it anywhere, any city in the world I'd imagine.'

'You're talking drugs, trafficking, right?'

'No, nothing to do with drugs.'

'Well, are you going to explain what you're talking about or are you just going to—'

'What's your problem, Angelique? Did you have a fight with Simon?'

'No, I'm sorry. I just . . . my eyes are . . . they're strange.'

'Honey, you've got lovely eyes.'

'Thank you, Kelly. Now, how do you earn great money fast, short of trafficking or letting some freak use you as a toilet? What scheme have you got in mind this time?'

'Oh, it's not *my* scheme. I wouldn't do it. It's really dangerous. But I know where to go if I ever change my mind.'

'Maybe I don't want to know.'

'Believe me, you don't.'

I told Simon the stories Kelly had told me. He seemed either sceptical or uninterested in most of what Kelly had to say. I don't think he believed much of it. He had always thought Kelly a dubious source of any information.

'Your flatmate gives prostitution a bad name,' he once told me.

10

I didn't mention the trouble with my eyes to Simon and, looking back, I can only guess why. I was, even then, a little afraid that it might be serious. To cope I told myself that it was probably nothing. So what if the letters on a page sometimes went a little blurry around the edges? I didn't want to think about it, and telling Simon meant thinking about it. He would have asked me a million questions and then chastised me for not paying enough attention to my health. Perhaps I had another reason, although this one sounds like something Alex Klima would have come up with. Simon had known from the beginning that I was neither highly educated nor particularly well-read, not like him anyway. What if he found out that it might even be a waste of time trying to teach me anything because I was visually impaired as well? Perhaps I could not bring myself to tell him that reading, the activity which he believed was the way to the stars, could become physically difficult for me. Whatever the reason, I didn't tell him.

It happened again at the end of a booking, in the shower and lasted well into the period in the waiting room between bookings. I was trying to read a trashy magazine when I noticed that the movie stars and supermodels kept coming unstuck. Famously strong marriages were falling apart without warning. The background was more prominent than the letters resting on it. Nor were they resting. I went to see what I thought was an ophthalmologist. He was actually an optometrist, a distinction that wasn't important to me then. He checked my eyes and assured me there was nothing wrong with them. He updated the prescription for my glasses and told me to wear them more often. I felt reassured.

At about this time I noticed that Simon was asking me more questions about my work. In light of what has happened it is hard to understand how I could have been blind for so long to just how sick his obsessive questioning was becoming. He would ask me about Joe Geraghty, about his working day, what kind of man he was, what he liked to do with me, what he liked to do with his wife, with Anna. He asked a lot about Anna. What could I tell him about Anna, what was she doing now? Stupidly, I thought, or preferred to think, he was finally succumbing to a certain voyeurism which, out of embarrassment, he was trying to pass off as some sort of overarching concern for Anna and Sam, her son, that was rooted in Simon's personal history.

I had got to know about so many male obsessions, quirks and fetishes that it was fairly easy to overlook an over-zealous interest in the life of an ex-girlfriend, especially if one was motivated to. What I hadn't got to know, what Simon didn't tell me for quite a while, was that he had taken to following Anna and Sam after catching sight of them one afternoon.

Despite all this, and despite not living together, we were seeing more and more of each other. We were intimate with each other, not only but also physically, and exclusively so, excluding my work. We shared our most intimate thoughts. He read to me, explained things to me, showed me things, introduced me to the music he liked. I remember in particular a Billie Holiday CD he bought me around that time. She was one of his favourites. It was something he had played me that unforgettable night we first met. I'd heard the name but didn't know it belonged to a black woman and that she was a singer. I certainly had no idea, before he told me, that Billie had been a prostitute before she was a singer.

We went for walks together and out for drinks, usually to the Esplanade. I cooked for him and fed his dog. I knew all about him, his parents and his brothers. When things were really bad I talked to his psychiatrist, and I know that Alex thinks I was good for Simon. I have showered him and he has even said that he loved me. What if he took an interest in his ex-girlfriend's little boy?

And so it happened, through Simon's subterfuge, my need not to see it all, and Alex's own problems, that the three of us allowed Simon to get worse.

'Are you staying for dinner, Angel?'

'No. I'd love to but I'm on tonight.'

'Anyone I know . . . or *everyone* I know?'

'It's your favourite client, among others. You know, I think he suspects something.'

'Suspects what?' Simon asked, clearly alarmed.

'I think he suspects she's seeing someone else.'

At this he stood up. 'What makes you say that?'

'Well, they hardly ever have sex anymore. And she doesn't want any more children.'

'How do you know that?'

'He told me. How else would I know?'

'I can't *believe* the things he tells you!'

'Yeah, scandalous, isn't it?'

'Well, there's something that is particularly offensive about telling you that. It's not that it's private, *hell*, it's *all* private but it's . . . irrelevant.'

'Irrelevant!' I laughed, even though he hadn't meant it to be funny. 'Irrelevant to what?' I asked him.

'How the hell can he screw you while he's talking about his wife and child?'

'Simon, I've told you. It's not always the crap you see in the movies. I don't dress up in a uniform or any shit like that. Well, not for him. He's just one of those guys who spends every day talking nonstop about things that don't matter to people he doesn't like or people he's afraid of. He knows he can trust me. He can say anything to me. That's one of the reasons he keeps coming back. It's pretty common with the regulars. It's all part of it.'

Simon had long before come to a conclusion about my work. Whatever Alex Klima had confirmed for me about the drug-like effects of the male orgasm, Simon's view was altogether more matter-of-fact, more prosaic. Men, he said, were not paying me to have them come on demand. They were, for the most part, simply paying me to let them leave on demand.

Joe was not only just about my favourite client, he was Simon's favourite client too. Gradually, Joe had become the only one of my clients Simon wanted to hear about. One day I got two bookings in a row from twenty second introductions simply because I looked young. That was the sort of thing I used to be able to talk about with Simon, to debrief, so to speak. It had always been a great help to me for us to be able to discuss the bookings together in a sort of clinical, academic way, as though we were two anthropologists. We would talk about the bookings and also about my responses to them.

When the first of these bookings got me alone upstairs he told me, a little embarrassed, that he wanted me to dress as a schoolgirl. So when I managed to get the house school uniform from one of the other girls, I came back into the room intending to take on the role of the recalcitrant smart-talking seventeen-year-old slutty school-girl. But never a great actress, within five minutes I had regressed to a ten year old. Somehow I had become doe-eyed, docile and utterly submissive. This was not what he wanted. He wanted the loud, vulgar, slightly cruel, back-talking, promiscuous pretty girl he could never get when he was at high school and when, instead, he found himself alone and naked with a frightened little girl he was unable to maintain his erection. He felt like a paedophile and he left in a panic.

I had wanted to talk to Simon about him. And about the next guy, who had also been in the market for a young girl. This guy looked like he could have been my grandfather. He spent a lot of time stroking my face with the back of his hand, commenting on the soft-ness of my skin. I just sat there on the bed, letting him do it while the minutes, his minutes, ticked away. Both of us were naked, me and this old man who wanted to do this in his retirement. We were silent until he said without warning, 'You're young enough to be my daughter,' as though it had just occurred to him. The comparison did not stop him from taking his hand from my face to my chest and pushing me down until I was supine on the bed. Then he entered me. He had not wanted me in a school uniform but he had stayed and finished after comparing me to his daughter. How sick was that?

There was a time when Simon would have discussed all of this with me, but that time had passed. All he wanted to talk about, when it came to my work, was Joe or else what Joe said about Anna and Sam.

'He'd be an "only child" . . . lonely,' he said, pouring himself another drink.

'Who?'

'Sam.'

'Yes, he would be, an only child in a broken home.'

'A *broken home* . . . what's that, Angel? It's just a cliché. It's a term traditionally employed to keep mismatched people together through the pretence that the only thing their children need in order to be happy is their parents' misery to stew in until they are old enough to escape.'

'What's wrong with parents staying together?'

'Often there's nothing wrong with it. But you can't assume there never is and then make a value judgment when two people respond to circumstances they could not have foreseen in ways which might or might not be in the best interests of the children.'

'I didn't know you felt strongly about this too.'

'You've got to watch those clichés because when the chips are down and the devil's in the detail, the grass is always greener on the other side.'

'What?'

'I'm kidding but, really, many people do make the mistake of thinking that as long as there are two parents' names on the school enrolment form, that's all a kid needs.'

'And what does a kid need?'

'What we all need.'

'What's that?'

'Love, empathy. You can get both from the one person . . . if you're lucky enough to get to know such a person.'

'What do you mean, empathy?' I asked him.

'If you really want to help a child cope with life, you have to do more than just give it love. You have to empathise with children. You have to try to understand their anxieties, their terrors, their loneliness, you have to put yourself in their position.

'The mother of a little girl I was teaching came to see me once. She told me, with a mix of anxiety and exasperation, of her daughter's recent unreasonable behaviour one day when the two of them were out walking in a crowded city street. The little girl, who was around six, suddenly started to scream quite hysterically. She refused to cross the road even while holding her mother's hand. It was making her mother late and embarrassing her in public. The mother said she tried very hard to find out what was wrong with her daughter. She spoke softly to her and she spoke harshly to her. She tried to bribe her daughter.'

'And what happened?'

'She ended up dragging her across the street, with the girl literally kicking and screaming.'

'What should the mother have done?'

'Well, and I don't say that it's always easy to do this, she should have tried to imagine the child's terror, not necessarily what was causing it, that mightn't have been possible, but what it would have been like to experience it. She should have empathised with her.'

'Sympathised?'

'Empathy will work better. Sympathy is the capacity to be affected by someone else's pain. Empathy requires that you go close to experiencing that pain yourself. It requires that you project *yourself* into the situation and then introspect on how you feel. The mother has to imagine herself being as terrified as her daughter is. If she can do that she won't feel like hitting her.'

'Did she hit her?'

'I suspect she did. She said she almost did.'

'Why don't you believe her?'

'Because I used to be a child. It came naturally to me. I was an adult for a time too. That came less naturally.'

'Did your parents hit you as a child?'

'My father would probably like to hit me now. I was not an *only* child and my home was not broken in any way that would show up in a government census. There are an infinite number of ways to bring about the damage to a child that is connoted by the term "broken home". A full house with two parents can rob you of comfort, stability and self-esteem as fast and as surely as a crowd can rob you of company. Anyway, Anna won't leave him. She knows when she's on a good thing.'

'He doesn't think she does. He thinks she might be having an affair.'

Simon looked at me as though I had just slapped him. When he spoke it was not without anger.

'For Christ's sake, what do you two do . . . undress each other very slowly so there's time to speculate on *her* fidelity? I hope you charge him extra for the analysis.'

Sometimes I hated Anna for the reasons the wife of a widower might hate his deceased wife, for the time they'd had together, for the retrospective saintliness death has conferred on her predecessor. But the widower's new wife can at least comfort herself with the knowledge that there are some areas of her husband's life where a ghost won't do. In my case, the ghost was living. She had a son and a husband. She had a future as well as a past and so was all the more threatening. For the same reason, though, I could feel less guilty for hating her. And it was hate that formed the words I used when I stood up to tell Simon of a fear that Joe shared with him. And momentarily, but not for the first time, drunk on this feeling, I spoke without thinking and made one of my best ever mistakes, a mistake which, in retrospect, is at least as responsible for my current situation as is calling the police when I found Simon had taken Joe and Anna's son.

'You know, he told me he thinks there's someone else.'

It would be comforting now to say that I didn't know why I repeated this to him. But I knew. I thought that the suspicion of infidelity might tarnish her image, her halo, enough to allow us all to get on with our lives without her. I was completely wrong. It only fuelled his illness. After that he just about wanted me to take notes whenever Joe said anything. And without understanding the effect it was having on Simon, I did my best to comply. Only once did I keep something back. That was because it said more about me than her, more than I wanted Simon to know.

11

Joe and I were talking about cars, value for money in a new car, what to look for. Joe was in a good mood, telling me about his car. He was very proud of his car. We were joking about him taking me for a ride in it sometime and laughing with relief because we both knew it would never happen. I got on top of him when he asked. It was one of the ways he liked it. He had just had his car serviced and the joke mutated to a request for extra attention to take his mind off the mechanic's bill. He wasn't sure he could trust his mechanic, he told me as I guided him inside and started the moves. I went from small laughter to concern, whatever he was asking for, all the time gently moving the booking along, always appearing acquiescent and aroused. I was getting hot doing all the work when I began to experience the problem with my eyes again. It was hard to focus. Everything became a little flickery in front of me. Joe must have noticed that I was a little distracted because he asked me if everything was okay.

'You're doing a lot of work there, Angel. Don't think I don't appreciate it but . . .'

'What? I'm fine. I'm happy, aren't you?'

'You can take a break if you want to, come back to it later. You been having late nights?'

'Yeah, something like that,' I said unconvincingly, sliding him out of me. That's when it happened and it was unequivocal. I was still over him but we were disjoined. He lay on his back, his conversation going from the way I made him feel to the way his mechanic made him feel.

'Some people, I don't know . . . you can just relax with them. Then there's other people you just instinctively don't feel you can trust. Know what I mean? Hey! Jesus! That's . . . what is that? That's new!'

The really frightening thing was that I had no idea it was coming. I had never done it before when offered money to do it, and it was involuntary. It was not a lot but it was unmistakable. I had lost control and had peed on him. He laughed, a little surprised, but he didn't seem to mind. He was good about it but I was in shock. I had lost control of my body and it frightened me.

I made an appointment to see my GP and told her about my bladder problems, as I put it. She said it sounded to her like a urinary tract infection and took a urine sample from me before prescribing a short course of antibiotics. She asked me if I had been sexually active, to which I answered, 'Just a little.' She wanted to have me tested for sexually transmissible diseases but I assured her that I'd had a test a few weeks earlier. I did not, of course, explain that my work required me to have one every month. She smiled curiously, said she was pleased to hear it and that it was better to be safe than sorry. But she didn't outline what could be worse than being safe *and* sorry. She said the antibiotics ought to clear it up, but they didn't. When I called to tell her that, if anything, it was happening more and that I was unable to gauge the extent of the urge, she said she would send me a referral to a urologist. I told her that, in addition to my bladder problems, my eyesight was still flickery on occasions. She recommended an ophthalmologist in whom she said she had the utmost faith.

'But I've already seen an ophthalmologist.'

'Really, when?'

'I don't know, a little while ago.'

'And what happened?'

'He checked my eyes and increased the prescription strength of my glasses lenses.'

'Are you sure that wasn't an optometrist?'

'No, I'm not.'

'Did you need a referral to see him?'

'No.'

'I think you saw an optometrist. I'm referring you to an ophthalmologist.'

I thought to myself how grown up I was to keep going to work, to keep paying bills, to keep visiting Simon, to keep cooking for him, shopping for him, reading the books he seemed to think I needed to read, without ever mentioning to him or Kelly or Alex or to anyone the unstoppable fear growing inside me, a fear that was like an imbecile unable to speak of the abomination that was itself. That fear, which edged its way out of me and into the world every time the light flickered in no one else's eyes but mine, every time I would find myself unable to recognise faces until they came close enough, on a bad day, to be registered by scent; that fear cannot hold a candle to the fear I know now. I have lost him completely now. Back then he hadn't yet taken Sam.

I explained my symptoms to the ophthalmologist. When he first asked me what I did for a living, I was surprised. I almost said I was a dancer but instead I told him I was a student. What was I studying? I studied the books someone smarter and better-read than me thought I needed to read. The ophthalmologist smiled gently at this, mistaking for irony my attempt to be as honest with him as I could. He asked me whether the blurriness, the flickering, was more in one eye than the other. After too many moments I was embarrassed to say that I couldn't remember and then worried that this made me sound either dishonest or else stupid.

'You know when you've heard a rattle somewhere in your car,' I said, 'and you take it to the mechanic, and that's the only time you don't get the rattle?'

As soon as I'd said it I realised how imperfect the analogy was since he had not asked me to reproduce the blurriness, only to recall and describe it. This was my memory failing me, not the rattle in the car or, in my case, the illness, the problem that had me sitting in his office as nervous as someone on trial. But the ophthalmologist didn't comment on the analogy, instead preferring to pick up a black hand-held device he called an ophthalmoscope. He turned off the room light, told me to pick out a spot on the wall and looked into each of my eyes. They worked well enough to see the flicker of concern in his eyes when he had put the ophthalmoscope down.

'You've said it's worse after exertion, after exercise?'

'Yes, I think so.'

'But you don't really remember whether it's worse in one eye than the other?'

'No, not really. But maybe it is.'

'What about when you're hot? Does heat exacerbate it?'

'Well . . . I'm sorry, I haven't really concentrated often on these things and I . . .'

I couldn't bring myself to tell him what I was often doing when it happened and I hoped it didn't matter that I couldn't.

'That's okay,' he said. 'I'd like you to do something for me. It might sound a little strange at first.'

'Oh, no.'

'No, it's not that bad,' he smiled reassuringly. 'I'd like you to go down to the ground floor and out on to the street. Then I'd like you to run twice around the block.'

'Now?'

'Absolutely. As fast as you can without running into anybody. Then I want you to come back in here as fast as you can.'

'Around the block?'

'Yes, as fast as you can.'

I went out on the street and just stood there for a while looking at all the people going about their business. It felt ridiculous to suddenly start running around the block in the middle of the city. I felt ridiculous and I felt scared. The ophthalmologist obviously had something in mind and I wasn't at all sure I wanted to help him determine whether or not he was right. There had been a time when I thought I could have been a dancer. Before that I used to breed birds. Now I had a problem with my eyes and though I knew very well what exacerbated it, I couldn't bring myself to tell him because I didn't want to see the look in his eyes when I did. I didn't want to see the change in the way he looked at me.

It was warm outside as I ran around the block getting hotter with each stride despite the cold dread of that which would get a name only when I got back to the fifteenth floor, back to the ophthalmologist. I ran as hard as I could, weaving my way through the crowd, past the people who, had they ever needed to, could have told the ophthalmologist what they did for a living, what it was they did that made things go glittery before their eyes, hazy, out of focus; who, when he identified their problem, could probably have told their lovers or spouses without fear of losing them. Running around the block a couple of times, with tears in my eyes, dodging people, bouncing off a fire hydrant, it occurred to me that the double life I had led was not an adventure. It was not like backpacking in Paris or Nepal. Whatever was wrong with me was making me question whether I would ever be able to tell people the truth about myself. There are lines we cross, all of them pregnant with consequences. The gestation of the line I had crossed was nearing its term.

He looked into my eyes again, this time not with the ophthalmoscope but with a penlight which he shone into each eye. He spoke slowly.

'Do you have it now?'

'Yes . . . I think it's worse in my left eye,' I said, after closing each eye alternately.

'That's what I thought. Have you had any other health problems lately?'

'Like what?'

'Have you experienced any numbness or tingling sensations, any muscle weakness?'

'No, I don't think so. I've had a bladder problem which I took a course of antibiotics to get rid of.'

'What do you mean by a *bladder* problem?'

'I don't know . . . I've been a bit . . . a little . . . leaky.'

'Did the antibiotics get rid of it?' he asked, looking down at the notes he was making.

'No, not really.'

'Did they take a urine sample?'

'Yes.'

'And what was the result of that?'

'I didn't seem to have an infection.'

He continued writing it all down and didn't speak again until he had finished.

'I think it would be a good idea if you made an appointment to see a neurologist.'

'A neurologist? Why?'

'I think you might have a little optic nerve damage. You really should have a brain MRI.'

'I don't understand.'

'In women of your age with symptoms like yours, we have to rule out the possibility of demyelination. What I mean is, we have to rule out the possibility of multiple sclerosis—MS.'

'You think I have MS?'

'I don't know. I think you might have.'

Within two weeks a neurologist had confirmed what the ophthalmologist had suspected. Now my bladder 'inconvenience' had a name. MS explained the visual symptoms as well as the incontinence. He gave me a pamphlet on MS and told me that it wasn't as bad as it sounded. He wanted me to have a brain MRI every six months. I would have to see him regularly. If my visual problems got worse I'd have to have intravenous steroid treatment.

'There are probably lots of students that you see every day at the university, studying, getting involved in student activities, who, though you'd never suspect it, have MS.'

I'd told him that I was a student. I let him believe it. I let him believe I was somebody's daughter when he asked if I wanted him to talk to my parents. 'Thank you, but no.' I let him believe that I would tell my boyfriend. I let him believe I didn't know much about the disease. But I did. I knew about it from the clients who had told me what had happened to their wives, the young wives who had MS. Pallid and mute, I went home.

12

I will always wonder whether it was because of my own illness that I did not fully appreciate just how sick Simon was becoming. Were there clues in his behaviour, or in the things he said, that should have alerted me to what he was going to do? There might have been, but towards the end I was not able to give him the attention I'd given him before. Simon would be talking about William Empson and his contribution to ambiguity, about history being littered with good ideas getting ruined when taken to extremes, and I would be wondering whether I should tell him about my illness and whether he would leave me if I did, whether he would leave me if he knew, for example, that one in two people with MS need help walking within fifteen years of the onset of the disease. I would be wondering how I was going to support myself, and how I was ever going to mean more to him than Anna did when I couldn't even displace her in his hagiography when I was well.

So we drank more than ever towards the end and that and the different voices inside each of us blocked out most of everything else. Reluctant to interfere with our drinking, Alex Klima came in and out, joining us occasionally to drink more than was normal for him because, as I would learn later, it was helping him through the dissolution of his marriage and separation from his children. But mostly, Simon and I by then were practising to be apart, rehearsing together in the same room and often in the same conversation.

'So, picture it, Angel,' Simon said before taking another half-mouthful of scotch to quiet his turmoil, 'he's twenty-three, an undergraduate, and he reads to his tutor an essay he's written about ambiguity in Shakespeare. He's twenty-three and the tutor, who would never have heard anything like it, doesn't demolish him or make him feel stupid. He actually encourages him to write more. You can believe it. There is no necessary job at the end of it, just academic excellence.

'So Empson goes away and writes a bit more, about thirty thousand words more. He gets a first in English and a research fellowship. What happens then? Not long after this he gets turned in, handed over to the university authorities, after a college servant finds a packet of condoms in his rooms. And they expel him. They banish him forever because of the condoms!'

'Condoms are mandatory nowadays,' I volunteered my expertise.

'Yes, if they had to comment on them at all, they should have applauded their use. But this was at a time when chastity rather than safe sex was de rigueur for young unmarried people.'

'So he was thrown out?'

'Yes, he was thrown out. He went home and continued his landmark work which became *Seven Types of Ambiguity*.'

'Simon, you've told me about this. He's trying to work out what makes certain pieces of poetry beautiful, right?'

'Yes, he is, and even the fact of the undertaking deserves praise. He forms the view, maybe tentative at first, that it's the presence of ambiguity in a poem or in a line of poetry that makes the poem what we call "poetic".'

'Okay, don't laugh but what exactly *is* ambiguity? I mean . . . isn't it just what everyone thinks it is?'

'A dictionary will tell you that an ambiguity is an expression capable of more than one meaning.'

'And what does Empson say it is?'

'Well, he extends it a little to include any slight verbal nod, any nuance of expression that permits alternative responses.'

'What do you mean, responses?'

'Cognitive or emotional reactions to the words from the reader. He says most good poetry contains ambiguity. It permits alternative responses, more than one interpretation. Then he classifies this ambiguity into seven types. I've tried to explain all this to Alex but he's less than impressed. He thinks that there are far more significant ambiguities than the lingual ones Empson considered. The one he keeps talking about is what he calls the ambiguity of human relationships. He says that, just like a verbal expression, a relationship between two people is ambiguous if it is open to different interpretations, but that unlike most words, most relationships are seriously ambiguous. And, he contends, if two people have different views, not simply about the state of their relationship, but about its very nature, then that can affect the entire course of their lives. It's funny how often he talks about that. Seems to be a bit of an *idée fixe* for him.'

Alex's thoughts on relationships were not new to me. Nor were they something I wanted to grapple with right then. 'So for poetry to be any good, even clever, well-read people have to be unsure what it means?' I asked, not yet having given up pretending that I cared. If I gave that up he might see me for what I was. There were times when I had cared and had tried to follow everything. But I did not have that luxury anymore. I didn't have the strength.

'I think he's saying that there has to be more than one meaning. If the poem is any good we'll find them. Listen to this line from Swinburne, a very underrated poet. Have I mentioned him?'

'More than I can remember.'

'Very good, Angel. That's capable of more than one meaning right there. I won't ask for your preferred meaning. So, Swinburne, right? He has a verse in a poem called "In the Orchard", very sensual. You'd like it. It's something like . . .

> *Lie closer, lean your face upon my side,*
> *Feel where the dew fell that has hardly dried,*
> *Hear how the blood beats that went nigh to swoon;*
> *The pleasure lives there when the sense had died;*
> *Ah God, ah God, that day should be so soon.*

'The first thing you should notice, the thing that gets you in is the music in there, all achieved without a note, only rhythm and the sound of the words. Listen to the line . . . "The pleasure lives there when the sense had died." There's a melody in that line and that's even before we go in search of the meaning. "When the sense has died." Does he mean sensation or does he mean sense as in common sense or reason? Sensation and reason might even be said to be opposites. I think this might be an example of Empson's seventh type of ambiguity, one that allows alternative meanings that contradict each other.'

'Does he quote that example in his book?'

'Swinburne's line is a good example, but no, I don't think Empson discusses that particular poem.'

'So you've applied all of this to your own reading of poetry?'

'Well, I've tried to.'

'You haven't been wasting *your* time, have you?' The words escaped from inside of me and the pleasure briefly lived there when the sense had died. I regretted it more quickly than I had said it. 'Simon, I'm sorry. I get defensive. It's all hard work for me, you know. I don't want you . . . I never want you to think I'm stupid.'

'But you think I'm stupid because I turn my mind to things that will never earn me any money. My father would agree with you.'

'Simon.'

'But none of you knows how important it is to get to the meaning, the real meaning of things, of words, the truth behind the galaxies of obfuscation . . . of shit.'

'Simon, I'm not like your father.'

'You see many things the same way. You see me the same way.'

'No, Simon, how can you say that? I see most things through your eyes.'

'You, my father, Joe Geraghty . . . Perhaps it's not completely your fault. The good ideas mankind has come up with are nowhere near as familiar as the pathological extremes that are their progeny.'

'I don't know what you mean. I don't know what you're talking about.'

'Our capacity to come up with great ideas is exceeded only by our capacity to ruin them, to destroy what is good in them, to poison them, by taking them to extremes. You take literary criticism, take Empson. Poetry represents the most sophisticated use of language possible. It is able to inform us, and through its concomitant musicality, to move us. Language is what separates us from other animals. It certainly isn't our behaviour. Now, Empson pioneers a form of analysis of that particular use of language. I admire it. I test it privately in my spare time but since I don't have a way of readily turning it into income, most people laugh at me. But that's another story. Many of the people whose business is words, who earn their living from the study of words, have, in effect, taken the ambiguity of words in poetry, and by extending its ambit to cover all language, in all disciplines, they have devised a new kind of vandalism. It's called deconstructionism. You see, according to the deconstructionists, words, be they in any field, be they in everyday discourse, do not have relatively fixed, widely accepted meanings. For them, no interpretation of any "text"—that's the word they love to use for anything written or said—is privileged. If they were right, we'd never be able to understand each other at all. How something so patently absurd could ever get off the ground defies the imagination. But it did. Deconstructionism even denies meaning to itself, not that that's a problem. But what is a problem is that it also denies the legitimacy of all human communication and thought, the legitimacy of all that distinguishes us from animals.'

'Simon, you're drunk, sweetheart. I don't begin to know what you're talking about.' My haunted lover was drunk and railing against the world. I didn't want him to be upset but his anger was beyond my understanding and, as long as it wasn't solely directed against me, I thought I could survive it, anaesthetised as I was by my own problems. But I should have understood that Simon's ranting, what Alex Klima called his increasingly vehement tilting at windmills, signalled his weakening hold on reality.

'So they turn university English departments into cultural studies departments where you can't teach Shakespeare unless you sandwich him between Jacques Derrida and Wes Craven's schlock. Okay, most people don't think this matters. My father wouldn't think this matters. He would think you could get on very well without Shakespeare even though nobody tells us more about ourselves than Shakespeare. But then most people live in terror of knowing very much about themselves. They can barely stand their own reflection for too long.'

'Simon!'

'Okay then, let's forget Shakespeare, he who saw inside each of us. What about the outside of us, the collective outside of us? Sometime in the nineteenth century it was recognised by certain thinkers that the state should, as a corollary of the social contract implicit in the aggregation of people into a society for their mutual benefit, take more responsibility for the economic well-being of its individual citizens.

Good thinking! But what happens? The idea is taken to an extreme. More responsibility is extrapolated to total responsibility, total responsibility and total control by the state of all economic activity. The extrapolation is implemented in Russia and China and millions of people are imprisoned or die in its name. It comes to tyrannise half the world for most of the next century. Its opponents are killed or imprisoned and labelled insane. When it is finally so discredited that it is abandoned by its own advocates, we see its polar opposite blindly triumphant, and the emergence of a different tyranny. Total responsibility by the state for the economic well-being of individuals is reduced, not to partial responsibility, but to zero responsibility. One extreme gives way to an opposite extreme, a new madness, called neo-liberal economics or, euphemistically, globalisation, which insists that the state should not interfere with the dog-eat-dog working of the market. All talk of a common good is seen as intellectually suspect and the product of unhinged minds.'

What used to be occasional observations ostensibly for my edification were becoming increasingly frequent harangues.

'Simon, I still don't know what you're talking about but it's got nothing to do with us.'

'No, it has *everything* to do with us. I used to teach small children and I was good at it. Now the government gets told by some agent of the money market that if it wants a triple A credit rating it has to spend less on education and everything else. They're taking education out of the mouths of babes and taking me out of work. Children are the most important thing we've got and governments are stealing from them because they want to collect less tax in order to win elections and to attract investment. Investment in what? There's nothing more worthy of investment than children. And hardly anybody talks about this. You're made to feel utterly alone, that there's nothing you can do about it. If you think there are more important things for society to think about than an annual budget surplus, Angel, then you must be one of those crazy people wandering the streets with all the other victims of sound economic management. Heaven forbid you should ever spend a moment reading poetry when you could be out there taking it up the arse for a living and trying to convince yourself it's some kind of . . . way of life . . .'

'Fuck you, Simon.'

'Well, look what happened when you found out that I had wasted my time trying to examine Swinburne through the eyes of Empson. You make a smartarse remark suggesting that it's futile because there's no money attached to it.'

'I didn't say anything about money!'

'It was implied and unambiguous.'

'Well, we can't all be fucking poets, can we? Maybe Anna can come and start shopping for you? Maybe she can cook for you or would she just pay someone to take care of you? Oh, that would be me, wouldn't it? She could pay me to clean up the place while the two of you get off on Swinburne or Empson or whoever the hell.'

And if it was not already over, if we had not yet spun out of our orbit and into some new nightmare, I took a breath and made it certain. With hindsight, I see that now.

'You know, he told me he thinks there's someone else. She's going away to some conference or convention or something,' I told Simon.

'Oh, he's crazy, paranoid. He's really crazy. You're both crazy. People go away to conventions all the time. Even teachers do these days, or used to. He's just trying to assuage his guilt, or maybe it turns him on talking about it with you.'

'Simon, will you relax. So what if she's going away with someone? It's *his* problem, not yours.'

'This is just part of the shit he spins you, Angel. You can't believe it?'

I had wanted not to cry but the tears rolled down the side of my face one after the other, too fast to dry. I was angry. I was hurt. And now I keep trying to convince myself that I did not send him to prison with these few words, that my sentence was not his sentence, and therefore not my sentence either.

I regretted it before I had said it but I said it anyway; like a fool determined to take everyone down, 'He said he'd leave her if she were seeing someone else.'

The next time I saw Simon it was done. He had taken the little boy and there he was. A sweet little boy whose mother I knew too well from photographs and whose father I knew even better. I looked at the little boy and felt ashamed for all of us—for me, for Simon, for Joe and even for Anna, whom I had never met. Children can do that to you. They can make you ashamed of yourself. I don't know why. Perhaps by so effortlessly reminding you of yourself when you were still innocent, they force you to confront all the mistakes you've made since.

I was shocked to find him there and when Simon whispered to me, 'That's him, this is Sam,' it took me a moment to connect the sleeping schoolboy in the living room with Joe Geraghty's son. It is still one of those realisations that keeps hitting me the way the death of someone close to you does; you go to sleep exhausted by what has happened and wake up the next morning to have it happen all over again. Nobody was actually dead but I felt a sense of that deepest loss for which there is no preparation. Simon had taken their son from school and in doing this he had robbed me of the wisest, sanest man I had ever known. He had been grooming me for life but he had stopped before he had taught me how to protect him from himself. No longer could Alex and I pretend not to hear the alarm bells he was sounding. Perhaps that was his motivation. It makes as much sense as any other explanation.

Even though Simon was calm and the little boy was sleeping, and even though I knew Simon was not going to touch him at all, the whole scene made me feel sick. I didn't know what to do at first so I played along with what he'd done for a while, trying to hide my horror. In the freezer I found a box of icy-poles in Walt Disney shapes which Simon must have bought the day before. He'd planned the kidnapping. It was not a spur of the moment idea. It had crystallised in his mind when I told him that Joe had said he would leave her if she was seeing someone else.

When exactly did it occur to me that if Joe left Anna then Simon might leave me? I really don't know. I just remember being appalled at what he had done and how crazy it was. I knew he was not going to hurt Sam but, other than Alex, nobody else would know that. The sooner Sam was returned to his parents the easier things would be for Simon, and for everybody. I decided to call the police and tell them where Sam was.

During one of my now frequent and unpredictable visits to the toilet, I called the police in a frightened whisper on my mobile. Then I made some hot chocolate for us and a glass of chocolate milk for Sam. Simon and I were like two young kids playing dress-ups, pretending to be parents. He was Sam's parent and I was his. He was calm and I was nervous. I knew that soon he would know what I had done. I knew that everything had changed.

The police would be arriving any minute and it seemed like my last chance to tell him again that what he had done was insane. It wouldn't change anything but I had to tell him. And it was my last chance to thank him for, as Alex had called it, the golden age that would be ending for me at any moment. I had to tell him that too. My words tumbled out manically, compulsively. With everything that has happened to him since that day I am certain that he doesn't remember what I, or he, said, not the way I do.

But for me it holds the significance of last words spat out hurriedly without much breath or premeditation, rapid-fire words filling up the seconds before an execution, before our execution. If he does remember what I said, it clearly means nothing to him.

'I want you to know . . .' What did I want him to know? 'I love you, Simon. I know everything you've said. I know I am . . . *fore-warned*, as you say, but please know it—remember it, no matter what—I love you even though . . . I know you're crazy. You're the softest man I've ever met. Too soft. *He's* smarter than you,' I said pointing to Sam, still sleeping.

'He may well prove to be smarter than me. He's already a lot wiser.'

'They're going to find him here. You know they will. They'll figure it out,' I said.

'They'll find him happy and safe if they do, with a chocolate moustache.'

'What do you mean *if*? They *will* find him, it's just a question of how soon. They'll both be frantic. It's not going to take them long.'

'However little time it takes them to get here, it will have been long enough to have saved him. I did it for him.'

'You did it for him? Simon, are you completely mad? What are you talking about? What does kidnapping a little boy from school do for the boy other than scare him out of his wits?'

'Listen to me, Angel,' he said deliberately. 'This will stop his mother having an affair.'

'My poor Simon,' I said to him and to myself. 'You're even crazier than I thought.'

I got up and went over to him on the floor. He held me in his arms and we looked at Anna's son gently breathing half into the pillow.

'When will they find him? They won't be that fast,' he said in a low voice. 'The emotions are not skilled workers.'

I repeated the line to myself after a moment's thought. Was I meant to know that one? 'Is it Eliot?' I asked. He shook his head. They were coming for him. They were on their way. 'Dylan Thomas? No. Yeats, isn't it?' Just keep him talking.

'No,' he answered, running his fingers through my hair for the last time.

'Who wrote that, "The emotions are not skilled workers"?' I put my head in his lap. Maybe I'd given the wrong address. Maybe they wouldn't come.

'That's a story in itself, Angel. It *is* a beautiful line, isn't it? Attributed to a man who never said it, by two men who wrote it and then pretended they were a third man who never existed.'

'Wait just a minute. Start again. Tell me slowly. Tell me a story.'

201

I closed my eyes and repeated softly, 'The emotions are not skilled workers.'

I wanted him to tell me a story to get me to stop living the one about the out-of-work school teacher who drank too much, thought too much and felt too much for his own good.

They kicked the door in, kicked it clean off its hinges. We were in the other room but it sounded like a grenade, a short sharp shock to restore order. Empson started barking and the boy started crying for the first time.

13

When I was a child I had a night light. It was a small cube of soft orange light that just plugged into the wall at floor level. I don't remember it being given to me. It was always just there. Then one day, without warning or explanation, my father took it away. I remember lying in bed that night going through the events of the day trying to work out what I must have done to have had it taken from me. When nothing came to me I extended the search beyond that day back to the previous day and then to other days. The further back I went, the hazier the days became and the less I could remember. All I knew was that the light had gone and that everything was black when I woke up at night. And that I had somehow caused it.

There were two police cars. Simon and I went with two male officers who put us into the back of one of them while Sam was taken by a female officer into the other. We were the perfect suspects, caught red-handed, cooperative, only speaking when spoken to. I sat next to him in the back wondering whether he had already worked out that I was the one who had tipped off the police, that it was because of me that they had homed in on the sleeping boy in his cluttered flat so quickly. It was not going to take him long to figure it out but I wasn't going to tell him because the instant he realised it was me was the instant the night light would be snatched from the wall and everything would be black.

When the police treated us the same way despite the fact that I was the one who had called them, I found myself going along for the ride. Relieved to be able to cling a little longer to the fiction that Simon and I were in this together, I sat beside him in the back seat squeezing his hand and staring out of my window or looking straight ahead, past the policemen sitting in the front seat, at what was coming toward us. Only occasionally did I steal a glance at him through the corner of my eye and wonder which squeeze of his hand would be the last I would be allowed. The police radio kept cutting in and out. Externally, he was remarkably calm. It was only at the station when they shepherded us in opposite directions to different interview rooms that I looked back at him and I saw in his eyes that he knew. I heard the door close behind him.

One of the uniformed policemen who had come for us accompanied me into the room and asked me to sit down. He said that a detective from CIB would like to ask me a few questions. The detective would be in shortly. He looked me up and down when he thought I wasn't looking, but since it was a small room without windows and there were only two of us in it, he found it difficult not to stare at me. The seriousness of the offence and the formality of the situation were no match for his male curiosity.

'What's a nice girl like you doing mixed up in all of this?' he asked, but before I had a chance to say anything, the door opened and the plain-clothes detective came in, shook my hand and sat down opposite me. He started arranging some paper he had on a clipboard, telling the uniformed man that he would wait alone with me for another detective to join him. The uniformed man left the room without making eye contact with me. The detective, a broad man with eyes too small for his face, seemed to look at me furtively.

'Could I have your full name, please?' the detective asked me matter-of-factly as the door snapped shut behind him. He did not seem to know that I was the one who had called them. He had a flat, pasty face, blank and bovine. I had seen men like that before, standing naked in front of me in the middle of a working day when they were meant to be doing whatever it was they did for a living. These were the ones who wanted you to kneel and open your mouth while they remained standing. I won't do that for any money. Kelly told me about a man who had become a regular of hers. At his very first session with her he had her kneel down while he remained standing. He coiled his fingers through her hair at the back of her neck and then, pushing down on the back of her head, he had her deep throat him so deeply, so suddenly, that she vomited. It turned out that he was expecting this. He had done it before. It was what he had wanted to happen. He wanted it every week and she complied and charged more for it. Even when we were busy, all too busy to know what day it was, passing each other only briefly in the waiting room, everyone knew when this particular regular of Kelly's was due. She would be seen hastily gulping down a half-bottle of drinking yoghurt. It was easy to bring up. The face of this detective made me think of it. I don't know why. I don't think I would be able to pick out any of Kelly's regulars in a line-up. But something about this detective's face made me think of the way she would look at the clock on the wall and take her yoghurt. His face had the consistency of congealed milk.

Another detective came into the room, nodded at me as he sat down beside the milk-faced detective and introduced himself. They sat opposite me and I stuck out my hand to shake hands with the second detective, which seemed to amuse both of them. The second detective spoke.

'So . . . Angela. What's your connection to Simon Heywood?'

'He's my boyfriend.'

The second detective looked sideways at his milk-faced colleague.

'Your boyfriend?'

'Yes.'

The second detective gestured to the other one that he wanted to see him outside the room.

'Would you mind waiting here, Angela,' he told me and the two of them got up and left.

When they came back only a couple of minutes later the second detective, whose name I would come to remember as Threlfall, started asking questions before they had even sat down.

'So, Angela, you say you're the one who called this in?'

'I don't *say* I'm the one. I *am* the one.'

'And Simon Heywood—you told us Simon Heywood is your boyfriend,' the milk-faced one said.

'That's right,' I said.

Again the two of them looked at each other in code. The milk-faced one pushed his chair out away from the table.

'And the little boy . . . ?'

'His name is Sam.'

'Do you say that he's your son?'

'No, of course not.'

'Is he your boyfriend's son?'

'No.'

'Do you know him?'

'No, not really. No, I don't.'

'But you do know him a bit?'

'No. I mean . . . I've heard about him.'

'Who have you heard about him from?'

'Simon and—'

'And who?'

'Simon.'

'You said Simon *and*.'

'Yeah, and thinking about it I realised that it was really only Simon who had talked about him.'

'Who else could've talked to you about him?'

'I don't know. Everyone you know these days is always talking about their little kids and how cute they are or how smart they are. Well, they do to women, anyway. After a while you forget which cute story belongs to which friend's kid.'

'But you said he's not Simon's son.'

'No, he's not Simon's son.'

'Who is he, Angela?'

'He's a little boy. He's the son of an old friend of Simon's.'

'What's the name of that friend?'

'Anna. Anna Geraghty.'

'Is she your friend too?'

'No.'

'You seem pretty sure about that.'

'Well, I know who my friends are.'

'Is she your enemy, Angela?'

'Don't be ridiculous! I've never met the woman. She's an old friend of Simon's. I don't know her.'

'Does Simon talk a lot about Sam?'

'No, not really.'

'Does he want children of his own?'

'Maybe in the future. We haven't really talked about it. You should ask him that. Do I have to stay here?'

'What does Simon say about Sam when he talks about him?'

'I don't know. Nothing really.'

'What do you remember Simon saying about him?'

'I don't remember him saying much at all.'

'But you said he has talked about him. What has he said?'

'I really don't remember. He's a clever little boy . . . I don't know . . . once he fell in a pool.'

'What happened?'

'I wasn't there.'

'What did Simon say happened?'

'I don't know. He fell in a pool with his school clothes on. Simon had to . . . they had to pull him out and resuscitate him or something.'

'Did Simon resuscitate him?'

'I don't know. I told you. I wasn't there.'

'Was Simon there?'

'I don't know. Can I go?'

'Why did you call the police and tell them where Sam was?'

'I thought his parents might be worried about him.'

'Why should they worry about him?'

'I don't know.'

'Was there anything they should worry about?'

'No.'

'Were you worried about him?'

'No.'

'Were you worried Simon was going to do something to him?'

'No. Simon loves children. He wouldn't harm anyone.'

'In what way does Simon love children?'

'Oh no. This is too weird. He wasn't going to hurt him at all.'

'How do you know that?'

'Because I know Simon very well. He's the sweetest, gentlest man on earth. He'd be the perfect father.'

'But he doesn't have any children of his own, does he?'

'No.'

'And you didn't have any immediate plans to start a family, did you?'

'We already were a little family . . . in a way. We took care of each other. And we had the dog.'

'You're not married to him, are you, Angela?'

'No, but . . .'

'Did you have any plans to marry?'

'Well . . . not in the short term. What have these questions got to do with anything?'

'Why should Sam's parents worry about him being with a friend of theirs?'

'They shouldn't.'

'But you thought they might?'

'Parents worry about their kids.'

'Angela, you're not being completely frank with us, are you?'

'What do you mean?'

'You're holding back and trying to protect your boyfriend.'

'It's a bit late for that, isn't it?'

'What made you call the police?'

'I really don't know. I might've overreacted. I just thought they might be worried about him.'

'Wasn't Simon meant to have him?'

'I don't know. I think he was . . . or he thinks he was.'

'Don't you think he was?'

'I think he was but . . .'

'But what?'

'Look . . . Simon forgets things.'

'What sort of things?'

'All sorts of things, arrangements. Sometimes he makes arrangements and forgets them or gets them wrong.'

'Why does he do this?'

'I don't know, he doesn't sleep well. He has insomnia.'

'Does Simon use drugs?'

'No.'

'Does he drink?'

'Everybody drinks. Is that a crime?'

'Does he drink too much?'

'Sometimes he does.'

'Had he been drinking too much today?'

'You mean was he drunk when he picked up Sam? No, I don't think he was.'

'You were there when he picked him up from the school?'

'No.'

'Where were you?'

'I don't know exactly what time he picked him up. I was probably at home.'

'Can you verify that?'

'I'm not a suspect. I called it in, I called you.'

'Why did you call the police?'

'I didn't have his parents' number.'

'But you said Simon was an old friend of the family. Surely he would have had a contact number for them?'

'I'm sure he does.'

'Then why didn't you ask him for it?'

'Okay, I was afraid that . . . Simon doesn't sleep and he drinks more than I would like him to. He's unemployed and—'

'What was his previous occupation?'

'He was a teacher.'

They glanced at each other again, just briefly.

'Look, I thought he might've screwed up the arrangement and

that Sam's parents would be worried and call the police. I didn't want to embarrass him, I didn't want to humiliate him by either second-guessing him or having the police called by anxious parents . . . I didn't want to have the police burst in on Simon and the little boy. There was nothing dangerous or . . . there was nothing wrong, except perhaps with Simon's memory. I thought that if I told the police where Sam was you could tell his parents and then they could pick him up from Simon's place or Simon could bring him home. I wanted to protect him.'

'Protect him from what?'

'From everything that's happened. From all of this, actually. And I failed.'

'Who did you want to protect?'

'Simon.'

'You called the police because you wanted to protect Simon?'

'Yes. Sounds stupid now in light of this, I know.'

'In light of what?'

'In light of the front door of his house being kicked in and us being dragged in here like this.'

'Was it really Simon you were trying to protect?'

'Yes. What do you mean?'

'Wasn't it Sam you were trying to protect when you called the police?'

'There was nothing to protect Sam from. Look, I don't have to answer any more questions. I called you guys. I've talked to you. I'm not under arrest, am I?'

I stood up for the first time since they had brought me in.

'I want to leave now. I've done nothing wrong and I want to leave.'

Trying to hide my nervousness, I walked around the back of them, just a few steps towards the door. I heard one of them shift his chair back as I reached the door and then the milk-faced one spoke for the first time in a long while. The room was hot and stuffy.

'Where do you work, Angela?'

I stopped dead. 'Why do you want to know that?'

'We want to be able to contact you if we need to.'

'Can't I give you my home phone number?'

'We'd like all your contact details, please. Are you working?'

'I'm a student.'

'How do you support yourself?' the milk-faced one asked, looking directly into my eyes with the beginning of a smile in his. It was hard to focus. Everything became a little flickery.

'I'm a dancer.'

At home I tried to remember everything I had said to them but I couldn't. I was running late for work and even thought of calling in sick, but then I remembered that I was sick and therefore had to work as much as I could before the illness forced me to stop. The clouds of the rainy day for which everyone is meant to save were closing in on me. I tried to reach Alex, thinking he had probably left for the day. He hadn't left yet but the line was busy. I tried a few times but it was continuously busy. It occurred to me that Simon might be talking to him. A moment of relief was displaced by regret that it wasn't me he was calling. Perhaps he had tried to reach me while I was phoning Alex? I knew he hadn't.

At work nobody asked for their money back but they would have been entitled to at least a discount. I could barely talk. I kept wondering about the milk-faced detective and where Simon was and what exactly he'd been charged with. I was not sure I had done the right thing by calling the police. If Simon hadn't been going to hurt Sam, and I knew he was incapable of that no matter how unwell he was, why did I have to call them? Why hadn't I at least waited a little longer? I didn't even really know why he had taken him. I thought about all of this while the regulars and the flotsam and jetsam of a normal Friday night took off their clothes, touched me, played with my skin and put parts of me in their mouths. It was not until much later that night when I caught a glimpse of myself with a man, much like any other man, in one of the mirrors, that I started to cry convulsively, hysterically. I cried for myself in the mirror, for myself in Adelaide, for the foolish man, and for Simon, wherever he was.

I went home and had another shower before going to bed. I couldn't sleep. At around five-thirty I got up when I heard Kelly turning the key in the front door. She was just closing the door when I put the light on and startled her.

'Oh my God! You scared the hell out of me. What's wrong? You look awful.'

'What's the name of the guy you drink milk for?'

'What?'

'Yoghurt. The guy you drink yoghurt for every time before his booking. The deep throat guy?'

'Yeah?'

'What's his name?'

'The milkman? I don't know. Why? I didn't have him tonight. What's wrong? Did *you* have him? What's wrong, Angel? You look terrible. Did he hurt you?'

'Is he in the police force?'

'I don't know. Possibly. It's hard to ask him anything. We don't talk much. Why?'

'Simon's been arrested.'

I got to sleep at around six-thirty only to be woken by the telephone at nine forty-five. It was the second detective. He wanted me to come to the station as soon as possible. They had some more questions for me. It couldn't wait, it had to be that morning. He said they would come to my home to pick me up. It didn't sound good.

'That won't be necessary. I have a car.'

'How soon can you get here?'

'You've just woken me up. I'd like to have a shower and something for breakfast first.'

'You can have coffee here.'

'That's very kind. What's so urgent?'

'We need you to clear some things up for us.'

I was not at all interested in eating breakfast but I wanted some time to think, to try to figure out why they needed to speak to me again and so urgently. I had a hot shower and my eyes got blurry. I tried to call Alex but the only number I had was for his office. I didn't expect him to be there. It was Saturday morning. I called it as a matter of ritual, just so that I could tell myself I was doing everything I could do. I needed help. I wasn't smart enough to do this on almost no sleep and on my own. It was pointless calling him at work but I did and the line was busy.

I boiled some water for the coffee and then found we were out of milk. Kelly had only a professional interest in dairy products. These sorts of things were left to me at home. She got her fuel somewhere else. I have never really understood how she survives. At times she could finish all the milk and cereal I'd just bought in a single sitting. At other times I could go for days without seeing her eat anything.

With my hair still wet I went down to the corner just to buy some milk and found the nightmare had colourised the day. It had hit the streets. It was surreal. The blurriness was spilling out of me. Under the headline 'Another Child Stolen' was a photograph of Simon. It was a photograph I had taken. The police must have gone back to his flat. The photograph was an old one I had taken on a really good day. It was a portrait shot of two heads, Simon and Empson, given equal prominence. The papers had cropped out Empson. I had some time ago decided to take photos of us on good days for Simon to look at on the bad days, and on the days when I couldn't be there. I would ask strangers to take shots of Simon and me, much to his embarrassment. Sometimes I asked Alex, but Simon seemed even more uncomfortable being photographed by Alex. I had told Alex privately how I thought that perhaps the photos might help and he didn't disagree. I wanted our snaps to outnumber the ones of Anna. They were not meant for the tabloids.

I ran home, still blurry, and tried Dr Klima again. A woman answered. It sounded as though I had woken her but she roused herself enough to tell me I had the wrong number. I tried him again, paying more attention this time to the numbers my fingers hit. The line was no longer busy but there was no answer.

'Do I need a lawyer?'

'We just want to ask you a few questions,' Threlfall told me.

'You asked me questions yesterday. Where's Simon now?'

'We want to tape your answers this time.'

'Why?'

'We don't want to keep having to drag you out of bed,' the milkman said, looking away, unable to say it to my face.

'Do I need a lawyer?'

'It's Saturday morning, Angela. Do you *have* a lawyer?'

'Well . . . no.'

'We just want to ask you a few questions, pretty much like yesterday only with the tape on.'

'Can you tell me please where Simon is? Shouldn't I have a lawyer?'

'Angela, we do this sort of thing all the time. If you spend time trying to get a lawyer now and then have to wait for him to get here we'll all be waiting here for hours. If you really want, you can get a lawyer on Monday and everything we talk about now will be on tape so he won't be missing anything. It's just a few questions and then we can all go home. So, Angela, do you agree that it is now . . . eleven-o-five on Saturday morning?'

'Yes.'

'I want to talk to you in relation to the possible kidnapping of Samuel Geraghty. Do you agree that you know Simon Heywood?'

'Yes, you know I do.'

'What is your relationship with him?'

'He's my boyfriend.'

'How long has he been your boyfriend?'

'Oh . . . approximately two years.'

'Do you agree that you had a conversation with us yesterday in this very room at around six-fifty pm?'

'Yes, although . . . I mean, I don't know exactly what time it was.'

'Do you remember, Angela, that when you talked with us yesterday you told us you were a student?'

It was hot and my mouth was dry. The room was already stuffy.

'Do you remember telling us you were a student?'

'Yes.'

'Are you a student, Angela?'

'What has this got to do with anything? You woke me up and got me to come over here to ask me that?'

'Are you refusing to answer the question?'

'I'm answering.'

'Are you a student?'

'Well . . . sort of.'

'What are you studying?'

'Literature, politics, sociology . . . lots of stuff.'

'Where are you studying literature and politics and sociology?'

'At home . . . mainly.'

'Are you enrolled in any educational institution?'

'I was.'

'When?'

'About two years ago.'

'Are you enrolled in any educational institution now?'

'Not really.'

'Are you enrolled at all?'

'No, I'm not. You don't have to be enrolled somewhere to learn things.'

'Angela, are you really trying to assist us with our investigations?'

'Well . . . yes, I am but . . . I don't know why you're asking these questions about my studying.'

'You see, yesterday, Angela, you told us that you were a student but today you're telling us that you're not.'

'But I am . . . in a way.'

'Who is teaching this . . . er . . . literature and . . . what was it . . . politics?'

'Simon has been.'

'Are you saying that Simon Heywood has been teaching you literature and politics?'

'Yes, I am saying that. He's a teacher. I don't know what this is about. Do you think I could get a glass of water?'

'We'll get you one in a moment, Angela. Do you agree that yesterday when we talked to you at around . . . six-fifty pm you told us that you supported yourself as a dancer?'

'Look, I don't know what this has got to do with Simon or anything. Simon is a teacher. He's a big reader, a huge reader, and a natural-born teacher. He can't help trying to teach people, to pass on . . . ideas . . . It's a thing with him. If you're around him for any length of time—'

'Has Simon Heywood held a job in the time you've been involved with him?'

'No, he hasn't.'

'Do you know what kind of job he had when he last was in work?'

'He was a teacher.'

'Are you able to say what kind of teacher he was?'

'He was . . . he was a very good one.'

'Angela, are you seriously trying to assist with this investigation?'

'You've got him locked up somewhere. I don't know why you're asking me these stupid questions.'

'Are you able to say what kind of teacher?'

'He was a primary teacher. He taught little kids. You should know. It's in the papers. You told them.'

'Do you agree, Angela, that you told us yesterday that you supported yourself as a dancer?'

'Yes.'

'What kind of dancer?'

'I don't think I specified.'

'Would you specify now?'

'I don't think I want to. I'd like a glass of water now and I'd like you to tell me why I have to answer these . . . irrelevant . . . They're stupid questions . . . Are you going to get me a glass of water?'

'We just have a few more questions, Angela. Do you say now that you're a dancer?'

'I can earn good money as a dancer. I have earned good money as a professional dancer.'

'Is that how you're supporting yourself now?'

'Not right now, no.'

'When was the last time you worked as a professional dancer?'

'A while ago.'

'Angela, do you think that you're cooperating right now?'

'I'm here of my own free will first thing in the morning, second time in twenty-four hours, answering stupid questions when you already have my boyfriend locked up somewhere. You haven't let me see him. You won't let me have a glass of water. I haven't had any sleep. You won't even tell me where my boyfriend is. I hope the tape is getting all of this. They won't even tell me where my boyfriend is—'

'Angela, you earn your living as a prostitute, don't you?'

The milkman asked me that. This was when he looked me in the eye for the first time.

'Can I have a glass of water, please?'

'Angela, you earn your living as a prostitute, don't you?' he repeated slowly.

'It's not against the law. Not in this state.'

'Are you saying that you do earn your living as a prostitute?'

'What has this got to do with anything?'

'Angela, are you refusing to answer this question?' Threlfall asked.

'He knows the answer.'

'Are you pointing at Detective Staszic?'

'I've seen him there. I even know what he pays for. You should ask him a few questions. He's the disgusting one, not me.'

'Angela, you're not in any trouble for working as a prostitute.'

'Am I in any trouble?'

'It is an offence to hinder the police in the course of their enquiries.'

'How have I hindered you? I'm answering your questions. Am I in any trouble?'

'Not if you cooperate, Angela. Would you still like that glass of water?'

With a sideways look Threlfall got Staszic to bring me some water. Threlfall seemed to be in charge but this was not because of a difference in rank. Maybe there was something Threlfall knew about Staszic that made Staszic accept his authority. He didn't flaunt it. In fact, it was barely there. But it was there. Staszic came back quickly with the water. He didn't like giving in to me. Threlfall continued.

'Angela, you say Simon Heywood was your boyfriend?'

'Yes.'

'Do you live with him?'

'Not full time.'

'What do you mean, not full time?'

'I'm often there . . . at his place. I often stay the night. We hang out there, but I have my own place.'

'Did you have any plans to move in with him?'

'I don't know . . . at some time.'

'Did you have plans to marry?'

'How can these questions possibly have any relevance to anything?'

'We want to know about the relationship,' Staszic, the milkman, said.

'Do you have a common bank account?' Threlfall asked.

'No.'

'Did he help support you financially?'

'No, not really.'

'What do you mean, not really?'

'Well, at the beginning he tried to help me out but . . . you know . . . he was out of work. He wanted to give me money, he really did. He used to try to force it on me but it was pretty clear that I had more money than he did.'

'Did you help support him?'

'I tried to.'

'What do you mean by that?'

'He was like most men in this respect, I suppose. He felt uncomfortable accepting money from me and would have preferred to be looking after me.'

'But you looked after him?'

'I was working. I had money, he didn't.'

'And you gave him money?'

'Sometimes, not much. Usually I'd just buy him things.'

'What kind of things?'

'I don't know, anything, food, clothes, dog food. Sometimes I'd help him out with the rent. He got some money from his father sometimes but he didn't like to talk about it. What's this got to do with anything anyway?'

'Did Simon know you were a prostitute?' Staszic asked.

'Yeah, he knew. He didn't judge me for it.'

'You said before that you don't know Anna Geraghty.'

'No, I don't know her.'

'Do you know Joseph Geraghty?'

'Joseph Geraghty?'

'Yes, do you know him?'

'Could I have some more water please?'

'Would you answer that question please, Angela? Do you know Joseph Geraghty, Joe Geraghty?'

'That's the little boy's father, right?'

'Please answer the question. You're going to have to answer these questions in court so you might as well get some practice here,' Staszic said.

'I'm not going to court.'

'You'll have to go to court, Angela. The question is whether you go as a witness or as an accessory.'

'Accessory? I didn't know he was going to . . . Accessory to what?'

'Kidnapping, child stealing . . .' Staszic was getting warmed up.

'Angela, it really is in your interests to start cooperating.'

'I am. What do you want me to say?'

'Do you know Joseph Geraghty?'

'Yes, I know him.'

'How do you know him?'

'He's . . . he's a friend.'

'Is he a friend of Simon's too?'

'No.'

'Simon doesn't know him?'

'No.'

'So, let me understand the situation. You and Simon Heywood have been in a relationship for about two years.'

'Yes.'

'He's friends with Anna Geraghty.'

'Yes.'

'But you've never met her.'

'No.'

'And you're friends with Joseph Geraghty.'

'Yes.'

'And Simon's never met him.'

'No.'

'Angela, it really is in your interests to tell us the truth.'

'I know. I am.'

'How do you know Joseph Geraghty?' Staszic continued.

'I think I have to—'

'How do you know Joseph Geraghty?'

'Can I go to the—?'

'Angela, please cooperate. We are trying to help you. You don't want to be charged.'

'I really have to go to the toilet.'

'Does he pay you to have sex with him?' Staszic asked.

'No, I'm serious. I really have to go.'

'Angela, does Joseph Geraghty—?'

'Look, I'm not well—'

'Does Joseph Geraghty—?'

'You already fucking know. I have to pee. I'm serious. I'm not well.'

'Angela, if you just answer the question—'

'Oh, for fuck's sake,' Staszic shouted in disgust, pushing back his chair and angrily getting to his feet. His chair fell backwards. Threlfall turned off the tape.

'You filthy little bitch. Charlie, she's pissed on the floor.'

'I'm sorry.' I was crying by then. 'I'm not well. I have MS. I can't always tell when I need to go.'

'It was pretty convenient, wasn't it?' Staszic snapped.

My face was hot and red. I cried without any way back to dignity.

'You think I meant this? You think I chose to piss myself? You fucking, fucking piece of shit!'

'Okay, let's everybody take a break. Angela, why don't you go and clean yourself up,' Threlfall suggested.

15

I made my way to the women's toilet and looked at myself in the mirror. I went into one of the stalls and took off my sodden underpants. Not knowing what to do with them, I wrapped them in paper towels and threw them in the rubbish bin. I couldn't answer their questions, not like this, not without a clear head. I had to be careful not to say anything that would harm Simon. I couldn't just tell them the truth. It occurred to me that Simon might be in a cell at the back of the station. I wondered whether they would let me see him if he were. They wanted me back in the interview room. They would know, once I was there, that I was sitting naked inside my skirt or else squirming in my own mess. I called home hoping Kelly could drive over with some clean underwear but there was no answer. Either she had gone out or, more likely, she had slept through the ringing. Simon had once told me that in parts of Europe during the Middle Ages prostitutes were regarded as both socially and morally responsible in that they contributed to the defence of the established order. Their testimony was prized because they had seen so much of life and their place of business, the brothel, was sometimes even referred to as 'the city's house'. Seven hundred or so years later I sat in a different kind of house of the city, utterly wretched and humiliated.

I had run out of excuses for not going back to Threlfall and Staszic. I glanced at my feet on the floor. It looked as though someone had made a perfunctory effort to clean up my mess with the same kind of paper towels I had used to dispose of the material evidence. Simon didn't even know that there was something wrong with me.

'Okay,' Threlfall said. 'If you're feeling better, I'll start the tape again.'

'Shouldn't I have a lawyer?'

'Do you agree, Angela, that the time is now . . . ?'

I said yes. Even without looking at him I knew Staszic, sitting opposite now, was peering at me. I felt the cotton of my skirt on my skin. Cotton. 'What did you pay for that skirt?' Simon had once asked me about it. 'You know it was made in the middle of the night by children for a fiftieth of what it cost you.'

'But do you like it? Do I look good in it?' I had asked him, putting on some Billie Holiday. And I had looked good in it.

That day had gone. Now there was a thin layer of cotton between me and Staszic.

'Have you ever had sex with Joseph Geraghty?' he asked me.

'Jesus, I don't have to answer that.'

'Have you ever had an affair with Joe Geraghty?'

'No.'

'You've never slept with him?'

'This is none of your business.'

'No, I'm afraid it is. Have you ever accepted money from him?'

'From Joe Geraghty?'

'You've said you were friends.'

'Yes.'

'Friends sometimes help each other out.'

'What do you mean?'

'Has he ever given you money?'

'I don't know.'

'You don't know? Angela, this is the time to remember.'

'He . . . he might have. What does it matter?'

'Has he ever paid you for sex?'

'I told you, he's a friend.'

'Do you only sleep with people you don't like?' Staszic asked.

'Angela, your answers are important. The truth could help you. We can't help you without it,' Threlfall said.

'Look, I don't want to get the guy into any trouble.'

'You don't want anyone to get into any trouble, do you, Angela?'

'No.'

'But if you're not frank with us *you* might be in trouble.'

'Joe Geraghty is a client. So what?'

'Why didn't you want to tell us that?'

'I don't know . . . he's not the worst guy, and I didn't want his wife to know.'

'You don't like Anna Geraghty much, do you?'

'I don't know her.'

'But Simon knows her, doesn't he?'

'Yes . . . so?'

'Simon was having a relationship with her.'

'No he wasn't.'

'Are you sure, Angela?'

'What are you talking about? Yes, I'm sure. I'm his girlfriend. He'd had a relationship with her but that was almost ten years ago.'

'And when he renewed it you weren't too happy about it.'

'This is mad.'

'You weren't too happy about it and neither was her husband, Joe.'

'You're making this all up.'

'You told Joe about their relationship, didn't you?'

'There was no relationship.'

'When you told him about it he offered you money.'

'What are you talking about? Money for what?'

'He offered you money to call the police when the boy was with Simon and tell them that Simon had kidnapped him.'

'I don't know why you're saying all this.'

'He wanted you to help him end his wife's affair and you were only too willing to oblige.'

'Is this what Simon told you?'

'It's the truth, isn't it, Angela?'

'He would never have said that.'

'Isn't that what happened?'

'No.'

'You're in love with him, but he's in love with another woman. He's in love with Anna Geraghty, isn't he?'

'No. He isn't.'

'You didn't like it so you decided to end it and make some money for yourself at the same time.'

'That isn't what happened at all.'

'Well, why don't you tell us what happened. Don't you think it's time?'

My head was spinning. I kept telling myself that they wouldn't charge me because they had to know I hadn't done anything wrong. They were making this whole story up. They had to be. They certainly didn't get it from Simon. Hanging on to this, I was eventually permitted to leave without being charged. They would want to speak to me again. I got back into my car, crossed my arms over the steering wheel and buried my face in my arms. After a minute or two I called Alex Klima but of course there was no answer. Threlfall and Staszic would not let me see Simon. They wouldn't even confirm that he was there. I put the key in the ignition and saw that I had a parking ticket.

Simon and Sam had earned a place in the Sunday tabloids. A teacher had been arrested in connection with the latest child kidnapping. The man was the same teacher who had been in charge of the little boy who had gone missing from his school after staying back for remedial reading lessons some years earlier. The teacher had lost his job shortly thereafter and had been unemployed for a long time. He was one of the long-term unemployed. There were photographs of other missing children. The papers were keeping count.

Kelly worked most of the weekend, so I didn't see her nor did I go to work. I couldn't bring myself to go through all the questions the other girls would ask me about Simon and Joe and maybe even Staszic the milkman. I certainly couldn't bring myself to let anyone touch me. I kept calling Alex's office only to hear his voice on the outgoing message, over and over again. His machine wasn't taking messages. His voice and those few words in his Central European accent were the only link I had on tap, on call, to the calmer moments of the best part of my life. When he finally answered early on Sunday evening, I didn't know where to start.

'Jesus, Alex! You startled me.'

'Hello?'

'I didn't expect you to be there this time either.'

'Who is this?'

'Alex, it's me, Angel.'

'Oh yes, I'm sorry. How are you holding up?'

'I'm in a mess. What's going on?'

'They've charged him with kidnapping. They might charge him with other things too. I don't know. They haven't decided.'

'Alex, I called them. It was me who called the police.'

'I know. He figured it out.'

'Can I see you?'

'What, now?'

'What are you doing there? Are you working?'

'No, I'm . . . I'm spending more time here of late than my work requires.'

'Alex, can we meet for a drink?'

'I don't think so, not right now, Angel.'

'Where is he?'

'He's . . . he doesn't want to see you, Angel. Not at the moment.'

'I didn't think so. That's why I wanted to talk to you. I can't bear him thinking that I informed the police for money. That's what they are saying. They're saying that Joe Geraghty, Anna's husband, found out about an affair between Simon and Anna and then paid me to call the police when Simon had their son. Alex, I didn't know he was going to take the boy. I went over there on Friday afternoon and found the two of them together. I called the police because I was frightened. I was frightened for Simon. What was he doing with the little boy, Alex?'

'We shouldn't talk about this over the phone, Angel.'

'That's why I have to see you.'

'I really can't now.'

'Are you helping him, Alex?'

'As much as I can. I've spent the whole weekend trying to help him. I've talked to the police. I've examined him.'

'Is he alright?'

'Under the circumstances. I've talked to his father several times.'

'What about?'

'Lots of things. I want to see if he'll cover Simon's legal costs.'

'Will he?'

'As of today the answer is still no but he might come round.'

'Alex, *you're* not angry with me, are you?'

'No, I'm not.'

'Can I do anything?'

'No, there's nothing for you to do. I've done everything I can think of, everything he's asked me to do. I've even spoken to Anna.'

'Oh my God! Really? Why? What did you say?'

'We shouldn't talk about this over the phone.'

'Alex, you don't think they're . . . ?'

'Angel, I know you're upset but I really can't talk about it now.'

'Please tell me where he is.'

'Angel, he doesn't want to see you now.'

'Did he say that? Did he specifically say that?'

'Angel—'

'Did he?'

'Yes.'

'Oh, Alex.'

'Give him some time.'

'When can I see you?'

'I . . . I don't know. Can you call me tomorrow?'

'I can call you whenever you say.'

16

Simon had given Alex instructions, a list of people to call. He had instructed him to contact Anna, after all those years, and to not tell me where he was. I met Alex two nights later at the Esplanade. He looked terrible. That's when he told me about Simon's plan to have Anna say that they were lovers and that she had given him permission to pick Sam up from school that afternoon and take him back to Simon's place.

Alex sat calmly holding his drink as I explained how I had told the police that there was no relationship between Anna and Simon, that there hadn't been for years.

'But why did he take him, Alex? Did he tell you he was going to?'
'No, I didn't know.'

'You can imagine how I felt when I saw them there together and Simon told me who the little boy was. I was scared he'd really lost it. He didn't tell the police that I'd turned him in, did he?'

'But you did.'

'I called them, yes, sure, but I wasn't being paid by Joe Geraghty. How could I have been? I didn't know he was going to take the boy. How could I have known?'

'You couldn't have known.'

'Did Simon really tell them that . . . about me and Joe Geraghty?'
'I don't know.'

'Why did he take him in the first place, Alex? What was he trying to do?'

'I don't know. He's not well, Angel.'
'Please tell me where he is.'

'He's in a bad way, Angel. The police want to hold on to him. They're trying to link him to all the other missing children.'

'That's insane. Is it my fault, Alex? Did I start this?'
'No, it started long before you. We just didn't stop it.'

I called Alex every few days to get updates on Simon's health. He wouldn't say anything about his case over the telephone. Simon did not get bail. It was in the papers. They also said that he had been moved from the mainstream section to maximum security at Laverton.

'Why did they move him there?' I asked Alex.
'They said it was for his own safety.'
'Is that true? Is he in danger?'

'Everyone in prison is in danger. He's in more danger than the average prisoner.'

'Why, because he can't fight the others?'

'No, because of what he's charged with.'

'What do you mean?'

'It seems there's a hierarchy of offences you can be charged with, at least as far as the prisoners themselves are concerned.'

'Kidnapping isn't the worst thing you can do.'

'He's been charged with kidnapping a child. Anything to do with children puts you at the bottom of the pecking order in the prison community. It makes you the lowest of the low, whether you can defend yourself or not. Simon is what inside they call a "rock spider". Don't ask me why they chose that insect.'

'But he hasn't even been tried.'

'I know, but inside he's already convicted. So they moved him to the maximum security unit, ostensibly for his own protection.'

I drove out to the prison at Laverton. I was worried about how he would look and how he would receive me but I needed him to forgive me. He had to know I was still living every minute for him. I had never been to a prison before. It had a busy car park like a shopping centre. Families came and went. Small children clung to the legs of slightly bigger children. I had to put my bag and keys in a locker, write my name in a register, place my hand palm up under a blue light that in some way 'read' it, or measured the bone density, and then submit myself to two searches before being told, some forty minutes later, that Simon wouldn't see me.

'You his girlfriend?'

'Yes.'

'He's popular with the ladies, isn't he?'

I didn't know what this meant. The lawyer Alex had got for him was a woman, Gina somebody. She would have to see him a lot. Maybe that was it. I went another three times before he got the idea that I was not going to give up, at least not until he saw me once. The fourth time I went there, he agreed to see me.

Once inside, a man in a guard's uniform led me past rows of identical barracks, each of them surrounded by barbed-wire fences and all of them within a compound ringed by a huge stone fence with barbed wire on top of everything that didn't move. All you could hear was the gravel grinding under your feet as you walked. The guard, who seemed a little put out to have to walk all that way for only one person, said nothing to me after his initial request for me to follow him. There were light towers in every corner and guard towers just beneath them. The sun beat down and everything was still. Inside I could imagine an ocean of misery seeping through every vent. I thought about the nights there.

I was escorted into the maximum security wing that housed some of the most violent and feared prisoners in the state. Simon had been put there, Alex had told me, for his own protection. I signed my name in yet another register inside the wing's visit centre and was told to take a seat and wait. The visit centre was a big room about the size of a school gymnasium. At the far end were small rooms with plastic tables and chairs. All these rooms were full, presumably because they provided an element of privacy despite the windows in the doors. The rest of the room was full of prisoners in bizarre powder blue plastic gowns, fastened at the back like hospital gowns. They were sitting on plastic chairs trying to hold, to touch, the people who had come to visit them. They hushed their small children or bounced them on their knees like parents do. The older children crowded around vending machines to buy ice-creams or drinks. It gave the adults time to kiss and grip each other in ways forbidden by the prison and by the stares of other people, especially their children. But there were moments, seconds, when the grown-ups hid in each other in order to be alone together and the better to record the memory for the rest of the time, the long time, the real time when they were unremittingly alone separately. I watched a couple trying to steal the feel of each other when they thought no one was looking. They pressed as hard as they could, perhaps knowing it had both to end in seconds and to last longer than humans can store the touch of another, no matter how much they need it.

I had tears in my eyes before I had even seen him. And then I saw him. He looked terrible. The circles under his eyes were wider and darker than ever before. When he came over to me I gripped him as hard as I could and the tears came out unashamedly from as deep within me as I can plumb. He hugged me tightly for a moment and then sat down. It is the feeling of the pressure from within his arms that I ache for now.

'Simon, sweetheart.' I took his hand and squeezed it. 'I love you. I didn't know this was going to happen. Please believe me.'

He left his hand in mine but didn't squeeze back. I could see the beginning of tears in his eyes as I waited for him to speak.

'Angel,' he said, 'what did you think would happen when you called the police?' He was more sad than angry.

'I don't know, not this. You're the most important thing in the world to me. You know that. You still are.'

'But you called the police.'

'Sweetheart, I was worried about you. I was afraid for you. You weren't well. You haven't been well. I got such a shock to see their little boy with you at your place. I didn't know what to do. I still don't understand why you took him. I wanted . . . I only ever wanted to take care of you, to help you. Don't refuse to see me if I come to visit you. Please don't. You haven't been well. I wanted to help you get your life back on track.'

A tear shone on the side of his face. We were in hell and he withdrew his hand from mine and took my breath away as he whispered: 'Where the fuck do you get off giving anyone advice about anything? Your idea of having your life on track is being able to afford a Magna Executive in which to drive to an appointment with a man your father's age.'

'Simon, don't talk like that. You've loved me. You—'

'I've never told you that.'

'Simon, it's okay. You can say anything you like. I can imagine what you're going through—'

'You have no idea what I'm going through.'

'Tell me, tell me anything. Tell me how I can make it right. What can I do?'

'You've done everything you can do.'

'Do you want me to tell the police you were having an affair with Anna? I'll tell them that. I'll tell them anything that will help you. Alex told me—'

'I don't want to talk about it.'

'You don't really think I took money from Joe Geraghty, do you?'

'But you did.'

'For sex. He was a client. We never ever talked about you. You don't think I took his money to call the police? Think about it, Simon. I couldn't have done that. I didn't know you were going to take him.'

'You could've chanced it when you saw Sam.'

'What does that mean? Do you mean that I called the police when I found Sam with you in the hope of getting Joe to pay me later? Is that what you mean?'

He didn't say anything.

'Is that what they told you, Simon? Look at me, sweetheart. Is that what the police told you? They're trying to turn us against each other. You can't believe them. You know the real us. Don't let them—'

'They said you were jealous.'

'But I would never do anything—'

'They said . . .'

'What? Simon, what did they say?'

'They said I should have known that you . . . would do anything for money.'

'You didn't believe them. Sweetheart, you can't believe them. I'm nothing without you. I was nothing before you—'

'You have talked to them, haven't you?'

'I had to.'

'Did they arrest you too?'

'No, but . . .'

He put his head in his hands.

'Simon, I'm not capable of that. I couldn't do that to anybody. You know that. You know me. We've been in love for two years. I took care of you. Don't shake your head. You can tell them you love her. I don't care. I know the truth. How can I help you? Tell me what to say, what to do to make it right. I'm so alone without you.'

'Alone? Angel, take it from me, you *are* alone. Most people are alone. To not be alone somebody has to connect with you and you have to connect with them. I mean *really* connect. I mean that somebody has to make the emotional and intellectual effort to come with you as you ride the relentless waves of fear and hope, of pain and pleasure, of doubt and certainty that inhabit the sea of human experience.

'And you have to return the compliment. You have to project yourself into someone else's pain and, by absorbing, lessen it. Listen to me, Angel. I was determined to not go out entirely alone. There is nothing I can do to make someone ride those waves with me. I know that. But projecting myself into someone else's pain, that's up to me. That's why I took him. That's why I took Sam. I could feel his impending pain and it was that pain that I tried to pre-empt by what I did. You don't understand, do you? Nobody has even ridden these waves with you. And you have never made time in your busy schedule of lying on your back, eating and sleeping, watching television, to work at feeling someone else's pain. Angel, you're right. You are alone.'

'I don't know what you're saying.'

'Remember I said it. That's all.'

'You're talking empathy?'

'I'm trying to.'

'Simon, what you're saying isn't true. I've survived on your empathy. And I've certainly empathised with you. I'm the only one who's ever really listened to you. Nobody remembers more of what you say than I do.'

'Angel, I loved you. But I was *in* love with her.'

Which of us was more desperate? When later I repeated all that I remembered of this to Alex, he looked at me with a smile and said,

'He can't decide if he's Bettelheim or Hamlet.'

I didn't know what that meant. But it soon became clear to me that, as desperate as I was, Simon was more desperate. It was worse even than him believing that he was in love with Anna and that that made stealing her son defensible. He was in danger.

'Look over there, without letting them see you. To your right,' Simon whispered.

To the right I saw a hollow-faced man, a prisoner, with his arm about four inches from his chest in the permanent shape of the letter 's'. He rocked back and forth in a chair as an older man beside him wiped the traces of ice-cream from his mouth with a white handkerchief. When the handkerchief had been removed, you could see a dark triangular-shaped gap bordered by the man's lips, trembling slightly, as he gasped for air.

'He wasn't always like that. He didn't come in like that. He wasn't that way three weeks ago.'

'What happened?'

'Officially, he tripped and hit his head in the shower. But everyone knows what really happened. It's a farce. It's the only sphere of activity where people cooperate round here.'

'What happened to him?'

'One of the other prisoners assaulted him, stomped on his head,' Simon whispered.

'You're not serious?'

'Of course I'm serious. This is the maximum security wing. There are men here doing sixteen years, twenty-five years. There's a paedophile doing eleven years on fifty-seven counts of sexual abuse of children over a period of thirty years. There are murderers, rapists, armed robbers and drug dealers. Nothing should surprise you in here. They're not going anywhere. Where do they take their anger, their psychoses?'

'But you haven't even been tried for anything yet. Why are you here?'

'I was beaten up in the mainstream section.'

'What happened?'

'It wasn't as bad as it could have been.'

'Why?'

'Anyone charged with anything to do with children is fair game in the prison system. You're a legitimate target. The guards are even more likely to turn a blind eye to an attack on a rock spider. As far as these guys are concerned,' he said, gesturing around him, 'I'm a paedophile and not just with Sam. I'm a recidivist. I'm responsible for everything that has happened to all the children who have gone missing in the last ten years.'

'Why?'

'Because the papers, the tabloids, print my name and photo next to photos of every child that's gone missing in the last ten years. Because the public has a right to know.'

'Are you safer here than in the remand section?'

'That's the theory. It gets Corrections off the hook. But look at him. Does it look like he was safe?'

I looked at the man and suddenly felt that I might have to pee in a hurry. I shifted on my chair.

'Do they know who did it?'

'They know. Everybody knows.'

'Why him?'

'He was weak, had no alliances and he owed the other guy money. He was a prime target for extortion. But I'm a better one. I'm a rock spider. I'm the next one.'

'What are you talking about?'

'I've got till the end of the month to get a certain prisoner $30 000 or I'll be like that guy over there.'

'And if you pay him?'

'I can't pay him.'

'But if you could?'

'If I can he's meant to leave me alone.'

'Can you trust him?'

'I trust him to push my skull in if I don't get the money to him.'

'But you could pay him and then he could ask for more.'

'He could but I can't pay him anyway. So I don't have to worry about the strength of his word.'

'Why don't you tell the authorities?'

'In order to tell anybody anything I first have to get through to that man there and men like him who search me daily—mouth, underpants, arms—who watch me and mock me, who enjoy my fear for a living. Even if I was taken seriously by the Correctional Services Commissioner they couldn't really protect me even if they wanted to. There's always somebody stronger or able to bribe, threaten or blackmail someone. Sooner or later . . .' he exhaled, 'it would come.'

'Jesus, sweetheart! Simon. I've hardly got anything in the bank. I haven't been saving lately. What can I do?'

He looked at me.

'You called the police.'

> *The pleasure lives there when the sense had died;*
> *Ah God, ah God, that day should be so soon.*

Give me that day back. I am the whore that called the police to come and take her lover away. There is no sense in it. The sense had died.

I arranged to see Alex as soon as I could. Of course he already knew about the extortion threat. He had discussed it with Simon's lawyer. It seemed the law was unable to prevent a crime, even in prison. That's if the lawyer knew what she was talking about. Alex thought she did. Simon's assessment of the situation seemed to be borne out by what she had said.

'Then we have to find the money,' I said. 'You don't have it, do you, Alex?'

'Angel, I'm living out of my office at the moment.'

'What about Simon's father? I suppose that's our last hope.'

'It's both the last and the best hope.'

'But even if he hasn't got the money himself, he could easily borrow it. He was a bank manager, for God's sake.'

'William hasn't even visited him. I've got him to put some money into Simon's defence but I'm probably the worst person to approach him for money. He thinks he's already wasted two years of it on my fees.'

'Why wasted?'

'Angel, come on. When he started with me Simon drank a little too much and flirted with depression. Now he's in a maximum security prison charged with kidnapping his ex-girlfriend's son. I think that's what William would call a bad return. He thinks I spent too much time writing letters to the papers about managed care and not enough time thinking about his son.'

'Alex, he looks terrible. Why won't his father visit him? What kind of father would desert his son under circumstances like these? And where's his mother? Did he bring himself up?'

'Largely.'

'What the fuck is wrong with them?'

'They're regular, everyday people. They're ashamed. They've had the press around there. The mother, May, doesn't sleep. His brother's children have been teased at school.'

'Oh that's tragic, Alex.'

'Angel, I'm just the messenger. Simon feels frightened, threatened and very much alone. He's right to feel this way. We have all let him down.'

'And he thinks I betrayed him. He thinks I caused it all.'

I was barely sleeping and barely eating. I went out to see him again but he refused to see me. I started snapping at clients, which I soon learned was worse than peeing on them. I tried to pee after every booking, sometimes successfully, sometimes not. Even pressing on my abdomen was no guarantee that I would be safe twenty minutes later. Kelly tried to stay out of my way but the smallest things about her, things I might never have noticed before or never commented on, were driving me crazy. Her way of trying to help me was to stay out of the way. She left a t-shirt on the living room floor one day and when it was still there two days after I had bawled her out for leaving her stuff around the place, I ripped it in a fury. A couple of my regulars started seeing other girls. I was falling apart.

It was in this frame of mind that I found myself at work one night, sitting on the toilet pressing into my pelvis with my fingers, trying, as the doctor described it, to prophylax against a bout of urge incontinence, when one of the girls came and knocked on the door of my stall.

'Angelique. Angelique, are you in there?'

There was a regular waiting upstairs for me. It was Joe Geraghty. 'Surprise!' he said.

Had our relationship been the same as it had been two months earlier, I would have been tempted to tell him a little, if not about my real circumstances, then at least about what those circumstances were doing to me. He might even have offered me more than the usual fee and tip. We would have acted like old friends who enjoyed each other, because with his help and the help of those like him, I had learnt to have sex feigning pleasure there when the sense had died. And after he had finished, after his endorphin release, I would have been tempted to cry. I would have been tempted to tell him that I was not well and would not get well. I might have asked him what he knew about his wife's activities because my boyfriend got off on the two of them. I wouldn't have added that every time I thought I had a handle on his obsession I just made things worse. I might have told him that I had lost the only person who ever really listened to me, the only person whose talk was worth listening to, the only person who ever thought I could still amount to anything. I had lost touch with my parents, not that we had ever really been in touch. My brothers were strangers to me. They had not known me since I used to dance.

I was going to be a dancer. I used to breed birds. I had plans to breed them again one day: parrots, canaries, finches, doves, jarvis sparrows. I must have read forty books on them. I knew quite a lot. I was going to breed companion birds, sell them in twos. Now I needed a lot of money in a hurry, by the end of the month, more money than Joe Geraghty could fit inside me before I could call security.

18

'Hello?' the woman's voice said at the other end of the phone. I heard it but could not bring myself to say anything and I hung up. At first I only really wanted to hear her voice. She had to take her share of responsibility for all of this. I called again later that day and again I just listened.

'Hello,' she said. 'Hello? Who is this?' Then she hung up. It was a thin voice. I don't know why I was so surprised at its thinness, its reedy quality. It's just that anyone with a voice so thin should have been weaker, less hostile, especially a mother. I called that night before work and got him. I hung up.

The next day I poured myself a drink before calling again. Kelly was out. It was late morning when she picked up the phone.

'Hello,' she said again. 'Hello? Who is this? Hello? I'm going to call the police.'

'Mrs Heywood?'

'Yes. Who is this?'

All my rehearsals went out the window.

'Mrs Heywood, you don't exactly know me.'

'Who is this?' She sounded frightened.

'Mrs Heywood, my name is Angela. You don't know me but—'

'I know who you are,' she said suspiciously.

'I'm Simon's girlfriend,' I said after a pause. 'Do you have a moment to talk?'

'You're not his girlfriend.'

'No, I am.'

'No, Anna is his girlfriend. You're the . . . you're the whore.'

'Mrs Heywood, I am a prostitute and I'm Simon's girlfriend.'

'No, Anna is—'

'Mrs Heywood, Anna is the wife of the man whose child he took.'

'What do you want? I've got nothing to say to you.'

'Simon is in great danger.'

'I . . . I can't talk to you.'

'Just hear me out, Mrs Heywood. If you love Simon—'

'Of course I love him. He's my son. I love them all no matter what they do.'

'There's someone in the prison . . . one of the prisoners in the same section as him is threatening to beat him senseless if he doesn't get a certain sum of money by the end of the month. The man is a brutal thug. He's done this sort of thing before. I've seen one of his victims, Mrs Heywood. He's brain damaged.'

'How much does he want?'

'Thirty thousand dollars.'

'I don't have that kind of money.'

'Can't your husband—?'

'This is a trick, isn't it? The money is for you, isn't it?'

'Mrs Heywood, if you visited Simon you could ask him yourself. You could see the prisoner, the brain-damaged one. He just sits there with his mouth open. You couldn't miss him.'

She was thinking.

'My husband handles the money.'

'For God's sake, will you do something for your son before it's too late?'

It sounded as though she was putting her hand over the phone. Her voice sounded more muffled. 'No one, dear,' she called. 'No one. It's a wrong number.'

Then she hung up. Simon was an orphan.

Kelly had left the t-shirt I had torn draped over a lampshade in the living room. The gesture, I'm sure she thought, was the most efficient way of getting back at me. She never tired. She would sleep, but other than that she never stopped doing what she did to put off thinking about what it was she was doing, or why she was doing it. I was seeing less of her not only at home but also at work where I'd started doing less in-house and more escort work. Nobody said anything. They'd found me a little strange since Simon was arrested. I was not well. And then Staszic called.

'Do you agree, Angela, that the time is eleven-twenty am?'

'Do you agree, Detective, that I have spoken to both of you twice before at your request? This time I have a lawyer on the way to sit in with us and my lawyer has instructed me not to say anything until he gets here.' They looked at each other.

'Yes, but as a courtesy to you, Angela, we are seeking your comments at the earliest possible moment concerning certain information we've received.'

'What are you talking about?'

'Do you agree that the time is eleven-twenty am?'

'Yes, yes.'

'It's been said that you were acting in concert with Simon Heywood with respect to the kidnapping of Samuel Geraghty.'

'That's bullshit.'

'Are you denying any involvement in the kidnapping of—?'

'Absolutely, I deny it completely.'

'Do you deny also that you provided certain information to Simon Heywood concerning the whereabouts, activities and routines pertaining to Samuel Geraghty, Joseph Geraghty and Anna Geraghty—'

'This is mad.'

'—that would assist Simon Heywood to stalk all or any of these people?'

'Joe Geraghty is a client of mine, a regular. You can't possibly take his word.'

'Angela, for your own sake, the sooner you cooperate the easier it will go on you. We cannot stress that strongly enough.'

'Did Joe Geraghty come in here?'

'Angela, do you understand what is meant by the term "accessory"?'

'Why are you talking down to me? Is your tape still on? Is it recording us?'

'A person who commits an act with the purpose of impeding the apprehension, prosecution, conviction or punishment . . .'

'Who's the audience for the recording anyway?'

'Persons who conceal an offence for their own benefit are guilty of a separate offence altogether.'

'Benefit? Last time you said I was in it with Joe. Now I'm in it with Simon. Whoever's listening to this—'

'Angela, you should be advised of the effect of Section 323 of the Crimes Act. I have a copy here.'

'I'm glad you're taping this. No one would believe it. You're trying to intimidate me.'

'It says, "A person who aids, abets, counsels or procures the commission of an indictable offence may be tried, indicted or presented and punished as a principal offender."'

'Does your boss listen to this? Does the judge?'

'Angela, you could be punished as though you are the principal offender, as though you did it yourself. We know you weren't the main one. You should tell us what you know.'

'Tell you what I know?'

'That's right.'

'Is it on, are we recording?'

'Yes, get it off your chest. You'll feel better. Go ahead.'

'You know, ladies and gentlemen of the jury, this man here, Detective Staszic, pays prostitutes to vomit during the sex act. That's what I know.'

19

Insomnia extended every night, stretched it, lengthened it, and the sourness of each added moment made a home inside me—inside my mouth, in the crevices of my tongue. The nightmare continued into the day, while other people were at work, or in supermarkets, or at their hairdresser's, having on the way picked up the daily tabloid unthinkingly, as part of their routine. On the inside pages a barely intelligible sensationalised account of our mistakes, Simon's and mine, waited for them. At work they talked about it, thinking I couldn't hear. I heard but I was numb.

The full extent of the trouble I myself might be in only dawned on me when the police called, yet again. It was never good when Staszic himself called. Perhaps this time I would be arrested? This time I really would not go without my lawyer. They, and Staszic the milkman in particular, were eager for me to dig my own grave. I could hear it in his voice. He had some news, information that he thought I might want to have. It couldn't be discussed over the telephone. I said I wasn't coming down without my lawyer. No, this was sensitive, off the record, no lawyers. Did he think I was an idiot? He said he was trying to help me. He wouldn't tape the conversation. He promised. It didn't even have to be at the police station. I could choose the place.

So we met at the Esplanade Hotel. He was already there with a beer when I arrived. It would have seemed strange going there without Simon had everything else not seemed far stranger.

'Where's your partner?' I asked, sitting down nervously.

'He's not here. We thought you'd be more relaxed, more amenable to cooperating, if you met one of us sort of . . . one on one.'

'So he knows about this?'

'Angela, I'm the more senior officer. But thanks for looking out for me.'

'You must be joking,' I said, not entirely to myself.

'Listen, Angela, I meant what I said on the phone.'

'What did you say? Do you have some good news for me?'

'You're caught up in this, you know that?'

'What do you mean?'

'Each of these men accuse you of helping the other.'

'What are you talking about?'

'Joe Geraghty says you and Simon set him up. Simon says Joe Geraghty paid you to set *him* up.'

'Simon never said that.'

'You can't have done both. The problem is, a jury only has to believe one of them for you to be in serious trouble.'

'I should have my lawyer here. I'm not saying anything—'

'Now, wait just a minute, Angela. There might be a way out of all of this. There ought to be some advantage attached to a young woman with all your . . . talent.'

'What are you saying?'

'I could make sure that you're not charged with anything but I'd have to get something in return, you know.'

'I've told you everything—'

'It's not so much what you can tell me. Give me a weekend.'

'What?'

'If you gave me a full weekend alone with you, full service, all your charm, I think you'd find you wouldn't need a lawyer. We would just say that the evidence against you wasn't strong enough, that it was in conflict with other evidence, which it is really. You wouldn't be charged with anything.'

'I could report you for this.'

'It would be your word against mine. Who would they believe? Angela, be reasonable. You're up to your neck in this and I'm offering you a way out. Don't put on this outraged act. It's one weekend, for God's sake, one lousy weekend versus serious charges in a highly public, very . . . what can I say? . . . very emotionally charged case. I'd be sticking my neck out for you and you'd . . . you'd be doing the same for me. No lawyer you can afford is going to get you a better deal than this. A friend of mine has a place in the mountains, very quiet, very leafy. Do you like pancakes?'

'You can fuck yourself.'

I was still shaking in the car. I shouldn't have driven. My eyes were playing up and I thought that I would never again know how it feels to sleep through the night without waking several times to some dread. Later the dread would be displaced by panic.

It can never be predicted where your mind will go in the middle of the night when starved of calm and sated with fear. Once it's there you might be only minutes away from placing your hand on the telephone directory. Finding the right name and address can seem like a sign, an omen, if it is done under a small light in the dark. You hear the refrigerator hum and the ticking of a clock in another room but otherwise there is nothing to compete with the sound of your own unspoken voice offering counsel inside you. I would try to see Joe, try to talk to him. Not knowing where he worked, only where he lived, not knowing exactly when he would be home, I decided I would camp outside his home sometime in the late afternoon, early evening, and wait for him.

I had never really thought about where they slept. I had never thought about the furniture they had, the knick-knacks on the mantel, the art on the walls or about the family photographs that were used to convey the impression to friends, to visiting relatives, or perhaps to themselves, that they were not a collection of urges incapable of remembering when their particular coupling seemed like a good idea, but a fine example of what Simon bitingly described as the best micro-unit we have been able to come up with in thousands of years of trying to live together. It was an impression that Joe, at least, was still trying to convey. Even when he came to me week after week for his ego boost, for his analgesic endorphins, it was all so that he could go out there again, get back on the horse, keep going. He had to keep being someone's husband and someone's dad, otherwise he would be Simon.

Some part of him knew this and was determined to keep fighting for them and I had helped him. That was my job and I was good at it. If he knew that, then there remained the hope, however slim, however desperate, that he would be prepared to help me. I needed a chance to explain things to him properly, slowly. After all, what lasting harm had been done to him or to his family by me, or even by Simon? The truth was that Simon was not having an affair with his wife. What they had had was long over. The truth was that his son, rather than ever being in any danger, was for a few hours in the care of a very dedicated teacher who lavished attention on him. If Simon had done anything at all, he had drawn attention to gaps in their supervision of Sam. How easily something unthinkable could have happened to the little boy had someone else taken him, someone crazy in a different way. And for this Simon had landed in a maximum security prison, thirty thousand dollars and a few weeks away from permanent brain damage and disfigurement. Could Joe perhaps think of it as a loan? I could pay it back, with interest if he liked. He probably had almost instant access to that kind of money. He wouldn't feel it. That was the truth of it.

It seemed to make sense as I sat in the car parked opposite their house, watching the lights of their early evening routine go on and go off. I was wondering if I could really say any of this, or anything like it, when it occurred to me that she was home without him. How hostile would she be if I came to the door? Maybe she wouldn't be hostile at all.

The house, like many of the others around it, was two storeyed and imposing. Tall trees in the front garden obscured the view. Although all the houses had large garages, there was a line of sleeping European cars parked in the street, grazing on the fallen leaves. People around me were arriving home. When would he come?

A man walking a Great Dane slowed just a little to look into my car as he passed by. They seemed to sense that someone was alive inside this one. The street was quiet. The evening was fairly still and one of them, at least one of them, felt me, smelt me on the other side of the car door, my insides churning, my hand resting on the handle, squeezing it from time to time, a million miles away from them. What would the man do if someone he loved was in Simon's position? The dog relieved himself beside my car without warning. Perhaps I would have to soon too? As they started to move on the man looked back, for no apparent reason. That's when I saw him come home.

I saw him in the car he had talked about, a car I had only ever pretended to imagine. I was scared. I twisted the keys out from the ignition and opened the door. He had opened the automatic garage door. I slid one leg out of the car. It was possible to see inside the garage. He seemed to be taking his time. I needed him to. He was playing with a hose or something. Just as I stood up and closed the car door behind me Sam ran out to him from within the fortress. Joe pressed him, hugged him, with one arm against his leg. He was somebody's father. Then the automatic tilt door slowly swung shut and the garage swallowed Joe, his car and his son. I quickly got back into my car and pulled out from the kerb. The man and his Great Dane had not walked very far.

20

I had forgotten how to sleep. I would hear Simon's voice at all hours of the day and night and I would cry. It was the middle of the night when I heard Kelly come in and close the front door behind her. She wasn't even trying to be quiet. I looked at my bedside clock and saw that it was almost four. I got up and went into the lounge room just as she was turning on the lamp. The torn t-shirt was still on the lampshade and she was singing.

'Well, look who's here,' she laughed. She was high on something or other.

'Do you know what time it is?'

'Time you were in bed, Angelique.'

'What did you say?'

'I don't know. What did I say? Time you were in bed, Angelique.'

When she repeated what she'd called me, I suddenly saw her differently. I saw her the way they did. She was in a tight red body-hugging dress with a satiny feel to it and there was nothing she would not do. It was five in the morning and I was semi-delirious, suddenly furious at the sound of the voice of the spaced-out whore I lived with, calling me by the name I had chosen for myself.

'It's not Angelique,' I shouted.

'What?'

'What's my name?'

'What are you talking about?'

'You don't even know my real name, do you?'

'Will you calm down. You need to take something to make you relax. Ever since your poet got picked up for playing with little boys—'

'What's my name?' I shouted again.

'Angelique.'

'That's not my name, you fucking whore.'

I shouted at her and I cried. One of us knocked over the lamp. At some stage she started crying and somewhere in all of it the neighbours started banging on the walls to get us to shut up.

I asked her where she got the toughness. She pretended she didn't understand. Maybe she didn't at first, or maybe she had forgotten that to do the things she was prepared to do, to have them done to her, took enormous toughness, more than most people had. She said you just had to keep working on yourself until you didn't feel what they wanted you to feel, or anything else. By seven o'clock she had fallen asleep in my arms having said that she loved me and that she knew I was going through hell. She breathed like a little girl.

She slept and I held her. If she had not passed out when she did she might have caught a glimpse of how alone she really was, that is, had all that she had done over the years not dulled her sense of it, perhaps permanently. I have learned what hell is because I am not able to dull the sense of what I have done. Hell is the special pain that dwells in that loss which you yourself have caused. Exhausted, I fell asleep and when I awoke everything seemed so much clearer. It all seemed so simple. The solution was obvious and now I wonder how I could have missed it. Everything is going to be alright. In rescuing Simon I will have bought myself a second chance.

Kelly knew the way. The trick was to keep working on yourself till you didn't feel what they wanted you to feel. No fuss. I feel strangely calm now.

I'm looking out the window. It's a little chilly up here but it's very pretty, so many birds. He's playing my Billie Holiday CD. I brought it with me. I don't have to worry about getting the thirty thousand dollars anymore. Simon could be out on Monday, Wednesday at the latest. I understand there are documents that need to be filed. The pancakes don't smell too bad. He's even brought his own yoghurt.

part four

PART FOUR

'Picture a flat grey field in a wilderness somewhere, anywhere, on an overcast day. Where once there was vegetation, lengths of brightly coloured cloth attached vertically and horizontally to wooden poles to form crude but eye-catchingly vivid shelters now flap in the wind. Some of the people who struggle to live around there have been told about the colourful tents in the field and they tell the others until, before long, everyone has come to see what has grown inexplicably out of the dust that barely feeds them most months of most of their years. As the wind howls, the doors to the tents dance this way and that, inviting the people to hide from the dust that blows in their faces and to delight in all the fun of the fair.

'Two men, A and B, for a small sum each, are permitted to compete against each other in a game of ball. They each have to get the ball into a hole. The first to do it six times wins. Call it *palla* . . .'

'Why *palla*?'

'It's Italian for ball.'

'Are they Italian? Why do they speak Italian?'

'I'm getting to that. I thought you weren't meant to interrupt.'

'I'm sorry. Please continue.'

'The first one to win six rounds wins the game and a prize. But the game is stopped prematurely. Somebody's crops are on fire and A and B are required to help put it out. By the time they get back to the fair and to their game, the tents are being disassembled. The fair is moving to the next town. At the time the game was stopped A had won five rounds and B had won three.

'They want to continue the game but the fairground attendant won't let them. He's got to pack up and keep moving. If he falls behind he's no longer part of the fair. He's just a man with sticks, coloured fabric and some balls. But A and B, and even the people who had been watching them play in the tent before the fire, are out-raged. They feel somehow that they've been cheated.

'Well, the fairground attendant, as is the wont of all good fair-ground attendants, can see where this is heading. In order to escape with his life, liberty, posts, flapping coloured strips and balls, he gives the two of them the prize money, which the first to have won six rounds would have been entitled to had the game continued with-out interruption.

'They look at the money and complain to the fairground atten-dant, "That's the prize for only one of us", whereupon the fairground attendant tells them they are fortunate to get even that, which you might say they were. Remember, neither of them had actually won. It was only through a not so veiled threat that they got anything at all. "Whose fault is it that there was a fire anyway?" the fairground attendant asked.

'Well, it was probably a mistake asking these questions because it led the assembled folk to consider for the first time who it might be that was indeed responsible for the fire. They thought back to the way they had been distracted from their work by these strangers who had come from some far-off place to take their money and who they could see hastily packing up and preparing to move off as soon as the fire had been put out. "Here's your money," said the fairground attendant. "You divide it between the two of you. Make sure you do it fairly, according to who you think was going to win. Don't go fight-ing amongst yourselves." And with that he was gone, leaving them to determine how the winnings should be divided.'

'Why do you give the game an Italian name?'

'Because the question of how to divide the stakes in an uncom-pleted game, the whole matter of the quantification of probability, was first taken seriously by an Italian. In the fifteenth century the Franciscan monk and mathematician, Luca Paccioli, posed this prob-lem of predicting the probable result of a game of ball played by A and B, first to win six rounds wins the game, if the game is stopped prematurely when A has won five rounds and B three. Paccioli was a friend and contemporary of Leonardo da Vinci. Some say he helped Leonardo with perspective. Everybody needs help with perspective from time to time, right? Is that what you were going to say?'

'No, I was going to ask whether Paccioli was able to solve the problem he'd posed.'

'No, not even Cardano could do that.'

'Who was Cardano?'

'He was a slightly later, sixteenth-century Italian mathematician. His *Ars Magna* is one of the classics of Renaissance mathematics.'

'What makes you interested in these people?'

'I had a teacher when I was about fifteen who told me about these men. It was he who was responsible for my interest in probability. He used to humanise mathematics for us. I haven't thought about him for years. He died before I finished school. Anyway, Cardano attempted what was possibly the first systematic study of probability. He was a gambler. He was a gambler's gambler. He gambled every day—dice, cards, chess, anything. He recommended it for the relief of anxiety and grief even though he concluded, somewhat paradoxically, I would say, that the greatest advantage from gambling comes from not playing at all.'

'Is that why you've come to see me? Is it about your gambling?'

'I came to see you . . . for many reasons . . .'

'You needed someone to talk to?'

'Yes, that's undoubtedly true and you were recommended to me. A woman recommended you. I probably wouldn't have listened to her, I wouldn't necessarily have taken her advice on something like mental health but then . . .'

'But then?'

'Then I realised where I'd heard of you. I realised the psychiatrist she was recommending was the one who had campaigned so vigorously and publicly against managed care and I thought, what are the chances of that?'

2
___

'Why do you say you're here? Dennis . . . Dennis? Why do you think you have come to see me?'

'Why have I come to see *you* or do you mean why have I come, at this time in my life, to see a psychiatrist?'

'Well, I'd be interested in your answers to both questions but let's start with the general and work our way in to the particular.'

'I like to be called Dennis.'

'What do you mean? It's your name, isn't it? The message you left said Dennis Mitchell.'

'No, you're right. It's my name but . . .'

'Yes?'

'I don't hear it much. I haven't heard it regularly for a long time. At work . . . Actually, it was this way at school too, and even my wife—'

'You're married?'

'People who don't know me well . . . People who want to give the impression of knowing me well . . . I'm just thinking out loud, as I go.'

'That's a good start.'

'Please don't patronise me, Dr Klima.'

'I wasn't, and you can call me Alex, if you prefer.'

'Fine . . . Alex. You can call me Dennis.'

'What were you called at school and then at work by people who wanted to give the impression of knowing you well?'

'Although I have never, at least as far as I can remember, invited anyone to call me that . . .'

'What?'

'Mitch. People have always called me Mitch.'

'They abbreviate Mitchell.'

'Yes, and in doing so they give the impression to an objective observer of some kind of real intimacy.'

'And you're saying that it's been a long time since that intimacy was genuine?'

'Yes. I am saying that. And it's been a long time since there was an objective observer.'

'Is that why you're here? Is that why you've come to a psychiatrist?'

'I'm here, Alex . . . I'm here, I think, because I've been crying. Recently I've been crying in a manner and with a frequency that is not consistent with being a functioning adult male.'

'And how have you arrived at your measure of how much a functioning adult male ought to cry?'

'Alex, I'm really not here to see how smart you think you are. Maybe you can help me and maybe you can't. Maybe it was a big mistake to listen to her. I'll admit that I asked her. She's one of the few things I *don't* feel bad about. Nothing ever happened anyway.'

'That's none of my business.'

'Isn't it up to me to tell you what's your business?'

'I meant, Dennis, that I'm not here to make moral judgments.'

'Really?'

'Really.'

'What if you thought I was about to commit a crime?'

'Then I'd have to contact the police but that's for legal reasons, not for moral ones.'

'Or do you not judge me because *you're* one of her clients? No, wait, you can get out of the whole thing by insinuating that she's a patient and then refusing to confirm or deny it.'

'I can tell you, Dennis, that that's none of your business.'

'Brilliant answer. That's what I would say in your position. But in your position I wouldn't be able to resist moral judgments.'

'Well, you'll have to trust me.'

'Trust you?'

'To an extent.'

'Alex, I'm not very trusting these days. You'll forgive me.'

'Is that why you're here? Do you want someone to forgive you?'

'How many people would I have to have harmed before you would . . . before you couldn't help but judge me?'

'Are you about to confess to a crime, Dennis? Sex with a prostitute is not a crime.'

'I told you, I didn't end up doing anything with her.'

'Why do you think that's my business?'

'Dr Klima, do you have any idea at all who I am?'

'Barely. You seem to know more about me thus far.'

'Are you in touch with her?'

'I'm really not at liberty to discuss her.'

'You wrote those letters, you spearheaded the campaign to warn the public against the dangers of managed care.'

'Yes. Is that why you're here?'

'I worked to promote it. That was part of my job. I looked to promote my own personal interest through a complicated scheme which required the widespread implementation of managed care.'

'I see.'

'Do you still want to treat me? Are you able to treat me dispassionately?'

'Why not? As long as you are human I am licensed to treat you.'

'Please. Alex . . . Dr Klima. I'm serious.'

'So am I. There are various religions and political ideologies out there for people who can't help but judge before they understand. Psychiatry is neither a religion nor an ideology.'

3

'Are you a Catholic, Dennis?'

'I was brought up in a Catholic family but I'm not a practising Catholic, no. Why? Is this some sort of fancy detective work on your part or do you have a problem with Catholics? What are *you*? What kind of a name is Klima?'

'I'm a Czech Jew. Does that matter to you?'

'No. I've no problem with Jews.'

'Yet you tell me you have no problem with Jews and say nothing about Czechs.'

'I don't have a problem with Czechs or Jews.'

'What I mean is, I tell you I'm a Czech Jew and you focus on the Jew and ignore the Czech.'

'Is this the way it's going to be all the time, semantic posturing dressed up as therapy? You described yourself as a Czech Jew, not as a Jewish Czechoslovakian. The Czech qualified the Jew, not the other way around. Your choice of words.'

'That's a very good answer. It's intelligent and it places the responsibility back in my court.'

'Responsibility for what? Why are you grading my answer?'

'Responsibility for your anger.'

'My anger?'

'The anger you direct at me. You said you want to talk to some-one and I think that's right. But you also want to confess.'

'Is that why you ask me if I'm a Catholic?'

'That's not the only reason I ask.'

'You heard of Vatican II? We don't have a problem with Jews anymore.'

'The Pope doesn't.'

'Oh, and *I* do?'

'You've got a problem with this one but I'm not saying it's because I'm Jewish.'

'So why do I have a problem with you?'

'I don't know yet, Dennis.'

'What makes you say I do?'

'Because you're angry with me and I haven't earned that yet.'

'Yet?'

'We're still at an early stage in your treatment. You seem uncomfortable confiding your vulnerability to me but you persist. You are compelled to press on. You feel you need some kind of absolution but it's not for weeping like a child. That's just your ticket in here. Is it perhaps for seeing a prostitute?'

'We didn't do anything, for God's sake! Is this some kind of liberal revenge for promoting managed care or working in the market? If you'll just give me a chance to talk and take a break from your constant need to impress yourself with your own sophistry you might learn something. You don't need to punish me for managed care. I've been punished already. It's been taken care of.'

'Are you angry with me, Dennis?'

'Yes, I'm angry. I wanted to talk to somebody because I thought it would help me, and your idea of helping me—maybe this is all psychology is—is to look at my random choice of words and simplistically, pathetically, categorise me or my feelings and dispose of them with clichés. I didn't know and don't care that you're Jewish. I'm not hung up about sex. But I am highly sceptical of the value of psychiatry, the talking part anyway. It's a fraud not a science. Maybe you could just prescribe something.'

'For what exactly?'

'For the crying, you bastard. You have to keep making me say it. I wasn't always like this.'

'It's alright, Dennis.'

'Jesus! I'm . . . I'm so embarrassed. I'm forty-four years old. I haven't cried in front of someone, in front of another man, since I was a kid.'

'Tell me about your life as a child. Were you born in Melbourne?'

'Yes, and I finished school here. When my father was laid off my parents moved to Mildura. I didn't go with them. I stayed in Melbourne and went to university.'

'What did your father do for a living?'

'He was a painter. I said he was laid off. That's not strictly right. He used to do contract work almost exclusively for Carlton and United Breweries. He painted their pubs. He got older and slower and they got someone younger to be him.'

'Did your mother work?'

'No.'

'Why do you smile at that?'

'She didn't work while my father was painting. But when they let him go and my parents moved from Melbourne to Mildura it was my mother that found work for both of them.'

'What did she find for them?'

'Together they managed a caravan park.'

'You said you went to university here?'

'Yes.'

'What did you study?'

'I did a science degree and then went on to do a PhD in theoretical physics. I was seduced by the elegance of physics, by its generality and its economy of assumption. Stupidly, I also thought it would make me eminently employable.'

'What was your PhD on?'

'It was on photon fission in the electric field of a heavy atomic nucleus.'

'That sounds very impressive.'

'It's not really. Quantum electrodynamics allows you to calculate the extent to which light can scatter light, that is, the extent to which photons can scatter photons, and related to that, the extent to which an electric field can cause photons to split or to fuse. They're what are called fourth order effects and are very small. Anyway, such calculations are fair grist for the theoretical physics PhD mill.'

'What did you do after that?'

'I looked for a job in academic physics. I looked for over a year. In Melbourne, in other parts of Australia, overseas. I couldn't get one. The world was in recession and theoretical physicists were not wanted. Eventually, feeling utterly defeated, I went to stay with my parents for a while.

'I was the first member of my family even to go to university let alone to get a PhD, and where had it got me? Helping my parents manage a caravan park. Despite everything that has happened to me since, I still remember how hard it was to hold my head upright at the time. Education, intellect were of no value and, since I could not paint a house like my father could, I could not even join the men who had replaced him. I was useless.

'It was all a little surreal. The weather was warm and sunny and everyone got around in shorts and t-shirts. It was like a summer holiday, only one that I watched, not one I participated in. I was working but it was not my real life. Most of the time my mind was off somewhere else and eventually my parents came to understand this. It took a huge argument though, one that saw me clear the kitchen table with my forearm, leaving everything smashed on the floor. My parents had taken to introducing me to the town's people as Dr Mitchell, my father even calling me "Doc". They had not understood how much I had meant it when I pleaded with them not to do it, not even to mention to anybody the fact that I had a doctorate, to forget about it. They were just being good parents, proud as parents could be. But I was embarrassed and angered by the title; embarrassed because doctors, doctors of anything, do not manage caravan parks, and angered because learning and research will not furnish even a single room. Only the market will, and not just any market, the stock market. I know what you will say about the stock market—that you are appalled by what you see to be its mad randomness, its essential immorality. To you it's just a giant casino. But there's one thing about it you can't deny. As mad as it might be for the activity of that casino to be what determines the economy, it isn't mad for you to try to get a job as a croupier there. In fact, it might be argued that you would have to be mad not to.

'I got to driving my parents' ute to the Working Men's Club, getting drunk, sleeping it off in the front seat, and driving home just before dawn. I was doing this a couple of times a week and that is when I first saw Patricia, the woman I married.

'She was German, a tourist backpacking with her cousin, a couple of Bavarian cowgirls delaying the rest of their lives. She was pretty. I needed someone pretty and she needed some local colour to write home about. Neither of us at the time had any idea how much the other really needed. She had recently acquired a diploma in physical education, and before getting a teaching job she had set off with her only slightly less attractive cousin to see the world. Her parents, more particularly her mother, had made quite a bit of money through a chain of ice-cream shops. Her father was an inspector of schools with the department of education.

'Because of me, Patricia and her cousin stayed in Mildura and got jobs picking oranges. After a while her cousin got bored and moved on. Patricia remained at the caravan park, shacking up with the young manager, the owners' son. That was not the way she put it when she finally wrote home to her mother. Needing something to impress her with, to beat her with in their ongoing war, she told her mother she had become involved with a local physicist, a PhD whose parents were in the hospitality industry. In her next letter she told her she was pregnant.

'In the summer heat, with everyone telling me how pretty she was, no plans of my own, no genuine self-esteem to base any plans on, and Patricia wanting badly to have the child, as if to prove something to her mother, we married hastily before the child was born. I was never a practising Catholic but my parents were, and with them fearing the disapproval of a small town, it made just enough sense for just long enough for me to marry her. I want you to understand that.

'The marriage made it impossible to keep real life on hold. I was back in it with a vengeance, married to a pregnant German tourist with all sorts of needs and demands she was only learning to articulate. If you want to tell me what an idiot I am, now might be an appropriate juncture.'

'Dennis, I've heard of people doing far more self-destructive things than marrying someone impulsively out of a sense of obligation and perhaps out of a need for esteem.'

'What do you mean, need for esteem?'

'You said Patricia was very pretty?'

'Yes.'

'Well, in addition to being attracted to her, I am assuming that her attraction to you added to your self-esteem, particularly given the choice of men that she would have had and would have been used to having.'

'Yes.'

'It would also have felt good to have your parents and everyone else around you see how well you had done, the all-conquering hero, at least in one area. Didn't it feel good to bask in the reflected glory of her attractiveness when you went out somewhere with her?'

'Yes. Yes, it did . . . at first. I had almost forgotten about that.'

'You see, however much of a mistake you're going to tell me it was to marry her, however much hindsight suggests that, atypically for you, you didn't properly think through what you were getting into, I want to suggest how understandable it is.'

'I don't know that not thinking properly is so unusual for me, Alex.'

'Come on, Dennis. You've got a PhD in physics. You must have the capacity to think extremely well. You have to admit that.'

'A lot of good it's done me.'

'We'll get to that. You see, though, how all your roads lead you to self-blame and guilt?'

'Yeah, so? What are you trying to say? Are you saying I'm depressed?'

'Well, we have to consider the full battery of criteria, and I don't yet know whether they're met in your case, but—'

'But that's what you think, isn't it?'

'Dennis, let me put it this way. Depression is the most under-diagnosed illness in the western world.'

'How do you know that if it's so underdiagnosed?'

'Do you still think your reasoning is faulty?'

'You haven't answered my question.'

252

'How do I know depression is the most under-diagnosed illness in the western world? Occasionally I take public transport. Nobody who has ever taken the Glen Waverley line for even fifteen minutes could dispute it. But I want to get back to you. You mustn't be afraid to be diagnosed as depressed, or as having been depressed. If you are ashamed or afraid of the label we'll have to break that down as quickly as possible because that denies you even the possibility of relief, as for that matter does ignoring the mitigating factors in your apparently flawed decision to marry Patricia.'

'It's in your interest to say that everyone is depressed and it's in your interest to excuse me for marrying someone I didn't really know. You shouldn't marry someone you don't know. It's that simple.'

'Yes, you shouldn't marry someone that you don't know, I'll grant you that, but in return I ask you to suspend judgment on whether, at least in your case as you've described it, it is really that simple. Dennis, you use all the power of an admirable intellect to attack us both. When you refer to my "interests" you're referring to my economic interests. You don't really mean that. You have told me that you weep like a child. Maybe I can help you; I think I can. Maybe I can't. But either way you must know that your pain is not my investment. I have no chance of helping you if you suspect I'm trying to cheat you.'

'I'm sorry.'

'That's quite alright. Let's return to your marriage. I think you're being too hard on yourself. You shouldn't blame yourself too much for deciding to marry Patricia, given your circumstances at the time. Your reason was overridden by your emotion. It happens to all of us on occasions. Let me put something to you which, although obvious, might nevertheless help you see your decision to marry her in a kinder light.

'People tend to assume that there is a dichotomy between emotion and intellect. In fact, it's really more of a continuum, with emotion at one end and intellect at the other.

'As we move along this consciousness continuum, away from the emotions, we move further towards the self. The self is highly personalised, highly individualised. It consists of one's inner world, one's thoughts, memories, interpretations of memories, assessments of past events and of people one has met; it consists of all the information you have managed to retain. It includes extrapolations of the past that you use to predict future events and the outcomes of your interactions with the world. The further along the continuum we go, the less one's consciousness has in common with anyone else's. That's why no two people can have identical minds.

'There is, however, an irreducible emotional component present even at the cognitive end of this continuum. The structures fashioned by years of experience, contemplation and introspection will always be at least a little damp with emotion.'

'Why the fuck are you telling me this?'

'Bear with me, please. It might help. While there's an emotional component even at the cognitive end of the continuum, there's hardly any rational component at the emotional end. When you're frozen by panic, when you're wildly ecstatic, when you're driving and suddenly someone cuts you off, you're completely swamped by emotion. The more refined workings of your mind are so soaked that it might be said that, for an instant, you have lost your mind.'

'Are you saying that I had lost my mind when I decided to marry her?'

'Not quite. That's a little extreme. All I'm saying is your capacity to reason was certainly impaired by emotion.'

'How many years of study does it take to come up with that sort of wisdom?'

'Dennis, you were devastated after you got your doctorate to find that you couldn't get a job as a physicist. Your self-esteem was shot. And you were frightened. You were frightened for the future, your professional and your economic future. Fear is still fear even when it is fear of humiliation or of impoverishment. It doesn't have to be fear of being eaten by a wild animal.

Then along comes Patricia. Prettier than most, she flatters you. She excites many things in you—lust, hope for a better future. Her existence excites you out of your cognitive mind. When she tells you she is pregnant, all that is left of your functioning or rational mind is your sense of obligation to a vulnerable young woman far from home whom you have made pregnant.'

'This is a waste of time. This continuum of yours, this consciousness continuum, would allow you to excuse everybody's behaviour, and predict nobody's. What you've constructed is a simplistic fiction, and not a very useful one at that.'

'Dennis, I really am just trying to help you. Whether this continuum construct is useful or not is one thing. But as for it being a fiction, so what? It's probably no more a fiction than are your constructs in physics.'

'Hey, wait a minute. That's not true. Constructs in physics, the fundamental ones like length, time, mass, charge and so on, are all ultimately defined by specific operations and measurements.'

'Okay. Give me an example. How does it work? How do you define, say, mass that way?'

'Mass? Well, there's Mach's operational definition of mass. It's quite complicated, though. Do you really want me to try to—?'

'No, I don't, but you do make it sound like it's an elaborate abstraction rather than something you can point to or touch.'

'Well I suppose in a way, yeah.'

'And what about your elementary particles, your electrons and whatever?'

'Alex, that'll take forever.'

'I only want a vague idea.'

'Alright, let me see . . . I guess they're ultimately by-products of quantum fields.'

'Okay, and what exactly are quantum fields?'

'They're mathematically very abstract constructs which . . . Do you really want me to go into this?'

'No, that's okay. But Dennis, aren't you telling me now that the supposed ultimate constituents of reality are also only elaborate fictions?'

'I'm not saying that at all.'

'Look, it doesn't matter, really. My point is that many sophisticated sciences employ constructs that are essentially elaborate fictions. That shouldn't present a problem; it doesn't stop us using these theories to explain or predict. On the contrary, it's through the operations and measurements that define these constructs or fictions that these theories connect with the real world.

'The problem in psychology is not that the constructs we have are fictions but that they're not really measurable and that, consequently, you can't establish empirical relationships between them. I have to say it's not for want of trying.

'Unfortunately, Dennis, psychology is still pre-Newtonian. In its defence, though, you will admit that the behaviour of a person is a lot harder to predict than the behaviour of a rock in space.'

'Okay. Okay. Will you stop? I apologise for the fiction jibe. And yes, I'll admit rocks are more predictable than people. But even apart from prediction, this continuum of yours, with emotions at one end and the cognitive self at the other, still has a serious problem. As I said before, it allows you to excuse everybody's behaviour.'

'I've told you, I'm a psychiatrist, not a judge or a theologian. I'm not interested in blame. Dennis . . . why . . . why are you crying? Dennis, why . . . Do you know why? Wouldn't it be a relief, even for a moment, to be free of blame? Do you blame yourself for all that has happened to you?'

'You haven't heard the half of it.'

4

'So, tell me what happened. What happened after you married Patricia?'

'We moved back to Melbourne and she gave birth to our son, James. Needing a good job urgently, I started to apply outside physics for anything that paid well. Non-disclosure of my PhD proved a winning move and I quickly got a job as a money market trainee. Things looked as though they might be starting to improve.'

'What exactly is a money market trainee?'

'I was being trained to be a dealer in the short-term money market.'

'Is this some kind of banking? Were you being trained to be a banker?'

'Yes, in a way. I was a middle man buying and selling cash, bonds, commercial bills, that sort of thing. What's wrong? You look confused.'

'I'm not much of an investor, Dennis.'

'It's quite simple, really. At the end of every trading day some corporations have excess funds, money they don't need for immediate trading purposes. Other corporations may have an acute debt. They may need funds urgently to cover some contingency, some debt that's fallen due. We operated in the middle, borrowing from the corporations in surplus at a certain rate and lending to the ones in deficit at a higher rate. The margin, the difference between the borrowing rate we paid and the lending rate we got paid, was our livelihood. The lenders don't know where their money is going and the borrowers don't know where their money has come from. The loan might be for twenty-four hours and the rate could change during the course of the day. You didn't trade only with corporations. You could often make your best money from other dealing houses.'

'How does that work?'

'Your last chance to negotiate a deal was three o'clock in the afternoon. That is when the deals had to be in. It's ten to three and you've borrowed too much. You've got surplus cash that you haven't been able to lend. Another dealer from another house calls you in a panic. He's desperate. He has a client who needs funds urgently. He's been calling around but he can't find anyone who has any available. You tell him you borrowed at eighteen per cent, and so you'll be charging him nineteen or twenty per cent when you really borrowed at fifteen per cent. Now not only do you no longer have to lose money when you pay back the lender from whom *you* borrowed at fifteen per cent but you're going to come out four or five per cent on top. You'd go for more if it was really close to three and he sounded desperate. The trick in this situation is to make the other dealer really believe you borrowed at eighteen per cent.'

'Couldn't he check?'

'He doesn't have time to call around to too many other dealers. You have to persuade him, get him to believe you.'

'So you're lying?'

'Yes, you're lying, every day. The better you do it the more successful you are. That's the way it works. Of course, not everyone lied every time. Many dealers were straight and if you were a straight dealer yourself these were the first people you would call when you got into trouble. Of course the straight dealers didn't stay, they didn't last.'

'Why not?'

'The market didn't tolerate them.'

'Did it tolerate you?'

'No, I was too straight. There were no disasters. I did okay but I just didn't have it in me to hustle. I couldn't say things I knew weren't true, not in a confident way. The best of these guys, they live on their nerves. They drink too much. Ninety per cent of their marriages fail. My marriage failed too, but that was not because of what I did for a living. It was because of who I chose to marry.'

'Is that when you started gambling?'

'No, I started gambling before I was married. Why did you think that?'

'Well, you talked about living on your nerves. I would have thought serious gambling requires living on your nerves.'

'No, it's a totally different thing in many ways. If you're a dealer in the short-term money market you're still an employee. What distinguishes the employee from the sole trader, which is what a gambler is, is the capacity to be terminated not merely by the market but at the whim of another human being. It's a special kind of humiliation over and above losing money. Anyway, I was a different kind of gambler. I told you about that teacher who sparked my interest in gambling?'

'Yes.'

'Later, when I was at university, I read about these guys, physicists from California, who tried to use physics in Las Vegas casinos to predict where the ball was going to land on a roulette wheel.'

'Really?'

'Yeah, two of them played as a team. Only one actually played. The other was there to gather the data they needed. Both had tiny computers fitted into their shoes. The computers were programmed to calculate the final position of the ball given its initial position, its initial velocity, and the initial velocity of the wheel. The guy observing fed these initial values into his computer by pushing buttons with his toes. He fed in the initial velocity of the wheel, for instance, by pushing a button on each of two successive pass-bys of the zero. His computer calculated the final position of the ball and radioed it to the computer in the shoe of the guy playing. His computer then tapped his toe a number of times to tell him what position to bet on, all while the wheel was still spinning.'

'Remarkable!'

'What attracted me so much to this was that they weren't gambling. That's the part that hooked me, being smarter than the others and drastically reducing the odds until the bet was almost a certainty.'

'Is that your game, roulette?'

'No. I played a little of most things when I first started. Not roulette or slot machines or lotteries, they're mathematically rigged against the player.'

'Aren't they all?'

'No, there is one game in which it's possible for a player to gain an advantage over the house: blackjack.'

'Is that the same as "twenty-one"?'

'Very good, Alex.'

'Is this the game that has . . . that is the manifestation of your gambling problem?'

'I don't think I have a gambling problem.'

'Didn't you say . . . ? One of the first things you said to me was the gambling had got you into trouble. Do you remember saying something like that?'

'Alex, you really don't know who I am, do you?'

'I only know what you've told me.'

'Aren't you in touch with her at all anymore? Oh yes, I forgot. I apologise. You can't answer that. It's too personal. She's part of your private life and you're not going to give anything away about your private life.'

'Do you think she's implicated in your unhappiness?'

'You said I was depressed, now you say unhappy.'

'I said I thought you might be depressed but you won't argue with the description of yourself as "unhappy"?'

'No, I can't.'

'Dennis, what happened after you stopped working as a dealer in the money market?'

'Well, as I said, I wasn't actually doing that badly at the time. But I could see the writing on the wall. I knew I wasn't really a salesman and I thought I'd better do something pre-emptive before everybody else realised it.'

'What did you do?'

'I made an appointment to see the only director I thought had a sense of me. I told him I didn't think I was cut out to be a top dealer and that I could serve the firm better if I were transferred to another department, one I knew was having problems.'

'What did he say?'

'He seemed a little taken aback. Firstly, no one had ever gone to him and volunteered their comparative shortcomings as a dealer or as anything else. Secondly, I was absolutely spot-on about the problems they were having in their unit trust department. In fact, the board had discussed the very matter the day before and apparently had passed the sort of resolution that gets passed when a board is looking to hide the fact that it has no immediate solution to a particular problem.

'He said he could probably swing a transfer with the board but he warned me, somewhat ruefully, that a culture of excel or get out prevailed in the firm and that my admission of incompetence as a dealer, and even my very candour, would you believe, would be held against me at the annual performance review.

'His response rattled me. He hadn't told me anything I didn't know and it shouldn't have, but it did. They had this "rank and yank" policy of regularly terminating fifteen per cent of their employees after each annual performance review. Desperate to convince him of my value to the firm, I told him I had a PhD. I had never told anyone there that. I didn't want them thinking I was . . .'

'You didn't want them thinking you were *what*?'

'I don't know . . . too educated for my job. Although I knew how little the market valued education and science, they could still have thought I had wasted my . . . human capital.'

'Dennis . . . Dennis, why do you think you're crying now?'

'I don't . . . don't really know.'

'What are you feeling when you recall these things to me?'

'I don't know . . . frustration, anger.'

'Tell me what happened next.'

'Well, when I told him about my doctorate his ears seemed to prick up. I think he liked me. "So we can assume you're pretty comfortable with numbers, a lot more than most?" he asked. I told him that was a fair assumption and he told me to give him a couple of days and he would get back to me.'

'Get back to you with what?'

'He got back to me with what he seemed to regard as a Solomonic compromise. Implicit in it was the acknowledgement that I was effectively finished there. He had called in a favour owing to him and got me a job as an analyst at a broking house.'

'A broking house, is that like a stockbroking firm?'

'Yes.'

'And an analyst?'

'An analyst researches the market and provides the recommendations upon which the dealers base their hype.'

'Is he like an actuary?'

'Not at all.'

'But do you need some facility with numbers?'

'It helps a little but you sure as hell don't need to be a mathematician of any kind. What you really need is a facility for impersonating someone with the facility to sell ill-founded corporate speculation, hunches, to trigger-happy dealers, gorillas disguised as men.'

'I don't think you like dealers.'

'The dealers make the really big money off the backs of the analysts.'

'Well, that's reason enough.'

'Joe Geraghty was a dealer I worked with.'

'Joe Geraghty, why did you mention him . . . that name, in particular?'

'He was the dealer I worked with to promote managed care. If you think *I'm* evil—'

'Dennis, I don't think you're evil. Just because I'm opposed to managed care doesn't mean—'

'He's certainly a lot stupider than me. You misunderstood me before to have said something about not being here but for gambling. I wouldn't be here but for Joe Geraghty. He's an ordinary man and I don't mean that in a way that would appeal to someone like you.'

'What do you mean, someone like me?'

'Someone with your . . . socialist leanings.'

'Dennis—and I say this not because it's important to me but because it might be important to you—I'm not a socialist. Remember, I've seen first hand what socialism really means, one form of it, anyway. But what does this have to do with this Joe Geraghty?'

'He's not a man of simple tastes, he's not ordinary in that sense. He's ordinary in the sense that he'd be easier for someone like you to understand than I am.'

'There you go again with that "someone like you" business. Are you saying that a psychiatrist would find you hard to understand?'

'I suppose.'

'I'm reminded of the Latin *Homo sum; humani nihil a me alienum.*'

'I'm impressed as hell yet again. What does it mean?'

'I am human; I consider nothing human strange to me.'

'Give me a chance, Alex. I'm just warming up. You think you have a handle on me, some understanding of me: middle-aged, depressed you say, screwed up, unable to attract women without paying for it—'

'Dennis, they are all your words. You know, being angry with me will provide you with only temporary relief. You're too quick to have me jumping to diagnostic conclusions. I wish it were that easy.'

'I'm the first one in my family to go to university as well as being the first one to go to a psychiatrist.'

'I don't know what you mean. Are you linking the two? Are you equating the two? Is that it?'

'No one had ever littered a conversation with either of my parents with a little advertisement for themselves in Latin.'

'Oh, Dennis, I'm sure they had, often. At least once a week, probably on Sundays. What happened, Dennis? You took the job as an analyst. What happened?'

'Before I started I was interviewed by the MD of the broking house, an immaculate survivor, a veteran, a well-connected broker called Gorman. I don't know exactly what they told him about me but, even though I needed the job, I had a wife and child to support, I didn't want him thinking I had any experience as an analyst. I made sure he knew that but he didn't seem to care. The salary I would be starting on was low but it would rise if I could prove myself.

'Gorman was a no-nonsense sort of guy who nevertheless treated me with a certain deference. I thought he might have been told about my PhD.'

'What makes you think that?'

'I don't really know. Something he said, maybe. But perhaps he was like that with everyone. You know the type—so high up the food chain that he can afford to be courteous even to someone at my level.'

'Look at your reasoning, Dennis. Someone above you is respectful towards you and you discount it and attribute it to your relative unimportance. Perhaps he was a decent man who had been told good things about you.'

'He's not a decent man. He was doing someone a favour. You'll hear. He's not a decent man. I would appreciate it if, in your sessions with me, you manage to refrain from giving people the benefit of the doubt.'

'Even you?'

'You can't help yourself, can you?'

'Please, go on.'

'I had a week off between leaving and starting with Gorman. Patricia was by then working part-time as a receptionist at a gym. I thought I'd take my son to Mildura. See my parents. It was an unexpected bonus for them.'

'The new job?'

'No, the week with their grandson. I'd told them about the job but one of my jobs was like another to them. Once I had got into university, my parents stopped trying to understand what it was I was doing. I think my father was actually a little disappointed that I didn't make something someone could hold, something people needed, but he always acted proud at my graduations. I think as long as I had a job and a family, they were satisfied. As long as he had a grandson he could take out fishing.'

'Do you fish?'

'A little. Not as much as my father, living on the Murray. He was delighted to have the unexpected opportunity to take his son and his grandson out fishing. It was really quite sweet to see but he wasn't very good at hiding his disappointment when it rained.'

'It rained in Mildura?'

'Yeah, we got rained out. What are the chances of that? We came home a day early. Patricia wasn't home and the house was in a mess. There were a number of message pads around the telephone with times and dates scribbled on them. I took my bag into the bedroom, which was also a complete mess, like a bomb had hit it. The bedclothes were on the floor. There was a bottle of cognac out and a glass on each of the bedside tables. I felt like a weight had been dropped on my chest because I knew what it meant. A short time later I heard Patricia pull up outside. She would have seen my car. I was putting the cognac away when she came in. The first thing she said was, "You're a day early." That was a Friday. I was starting the new job on Monday.

'Patricia had been seeing one of the clients from the gym. It didn't matter what his name was or how long she'd been seeing him. I had to understand that. What mattered, she said, was that she had never been happier. I should be happy for her. I asked what she wanted to do and she said that my discovering the relationship was a good thing. It had forced her hand. I remember she was making the bed when she said, "I'm going." And she did. She packed a couple of cases and left. She walked out on my son and me.'

'How old was your son?'

'Almost eight.'

'How did you feel?'

'How do you think I felt? I felt as though all the air had been forced out of my chest.'

'Did you love her?'

'I thought I did.'

'So now you're not so sure?'

'No, I'm quite sure it was love. I just don't know who it was for. It was probably just a kind of love with the idea of being in love. I needed to be in love.'

'Why do you say that?'

'Because even then I didn't really know her. I didn't know what made her tick. She was pregnant when we bought the house. It was a new neighbourhood. I thought that under the circumstances she should find a doctor she liked, a GP. To be our family doctor, someone she could trust. She chose someone. I even saw him myself a couple of times.'

'What was wrong with you?'

'Nothing really. Nothing then. I was working hard, and though I was always tired at night I had a lot of trouble sleeping. He gave me some pills and told me I was working too hard. She was going down on him.'

'What?'

'She was having an affair or a fling with him, with the GP. She told me about this much later, said it wasn't serious, that it didn't last long. She said they didn't even have proper sex. They used to meet in the middle of the day. She described how she did it for him. I had made her pregnant, I had married her, but I had no idea who she was.'

'So she left the weekend before you started the new job?'

'Yes. I had to keep it all together, learn the job, get my son ready for school in the mornings, take him there and arrange to have him brought home by a neighbour with a boy at the same school. I was numb. I just wanted my boy to be okay. And he wasn't. He cried a lot, asked where she was. Time went slowly for him but for me the weeks just tumbled over each other, trying to get away from me as fast as they could. I tiptoed around at work unknowing and unfeeling. I was exhausted at the end of each day. Impersonating someone with self-esteem can be very enervating.

'About six weeks later my wife came around to the house in tears. The man she had left us for was married. His wife had only been overseas on holiday. Patricia hadn't known he was married.'

'You took her back?'

'I thought I loved her. She said it had been a mistake and that I had contributed to it by neglecting her, working too many hours. Look, of course it sounds like bullshit now but I didn't know then all that I know now. My son was crying every night. I had just started this job, an unfamiliar job. She was still his mother.'

'I'm not criticising you. I'm just trying to learn about you.'

'Interestingly, a few weeks after that, I read in the paper that one of the directors of the merchant bank I'd left, the one who'd helped me, had resigned. It was rumoured he'd been pushed.'

'Do you know why?'

'No, I don't. None of the other members of the board were prepared to comment. They stick together, those guys, maybe even more than you guys do.'

'What makes you think Czech psychiatrists stick together?'

5

'Essentially—for the last God knows how many years it's been now— my job has been to go out and see people from various companies, officers of corporations, managing directors, people whose task it was to tell market analysts like me what their companies wanted the market to think about their operations or about their share price. I would see people, talk on the phone, read the press, the industry reports, financial reports, formulate questions and try to get them answered. I would attempt to sift out the deliberate ambiguities and unequivocal lies and then I'd make recommendations to the dealers. It might be to buy, to sell or simply to hold. There's no commission for the dealers when a client holds. Dealers need turnover. People should remember that. It's a matter of simple logic that there exists an ongoing necessary conflict of interest between the dealer and the client.'

'And between the dealer and the analyst, I suppose.'

'Oh, I'll get to that, don't worry. Dealers are the interface between the reality of the market and the man in the street who sees it as an almost magical machine for the rapid creation of life-changing wealth. The man in the street hears the news or reads the paper, the stock reports they're pumping into his consciousness twenty-four hours a day, every day. He hears names, mostly unfamiliar names, attached to companies that trade in things he often either doesn't know or understand. And those names are in turn attached to dollar values, which the man hears are going up, way up. He's heard of other men who got on to all of this before he did and they don't worry anymore. They breathe easier. They've paid off their houses. They've bought new houses, new cars. These other guys have left our man for dead.

'Breathless, the man in the street, who usually doesn't know these other men, not just now, he *never* knew them and he never will, picks up the receiver of his phone and he dials a broking house. And no matter the words he chooses, no matter how he starts the conversation, no matter how polite he is, what he's trying to say, what he is screaming is, "Let me in!"

'And who does he get? Who is on the other end of the line when the man in the street wants out of the street and into some barely imagined stratosphere? He thinks he's getting an economist, a financial expert of some description, a calm and considered man, top of his class, with quick reflexes who speaks the impenetrable language of the market, a man who can simultaneously read it, translate it and, most importantly, who can predict where it's going. Is this what the man in the street gets when he calls a broking house? No, it isn't. Not at all. What he gets is a man like Joe Geraghty. Have I mentioned Joe Geraghty to you before?'

'You've mentioned him.'

'Joe Geraghty is the reason I'm seeing you. Forget gambling, forget my wife.'

'Tell me about him.'

'He's a dealer I worked with on the managed care deal, and I was a fool ever to have anything to do with him. Where do I start? He's a big man, tough, works out, prone to arrogance, vain, vacuous with a . . . a volcanic stupidity.'

'What do you mean, "a volcanic stupidity"?'

'It's generally dormant, but it erupts under pressure. He is the kind of man who wants you to think that he's got people on six other lines waiting when you're talking to him on the phone. He wants you to think he's surrounded by screens, receiving information from all over the country, from all over the world, and transmitting it to clients, tapping frantically but purposefully on his keyboard like a percussionist, or else that he's having seamless conversations through a headset with an attached microphone, like an air traffic controller, calling the money in to land, guiding it, making money for you even as he inhales. He wears ostentatiously expensive suits and too much aftershave. He drives some impractical smartarse foreign car and talks about it. He's proud of his car. He doesn't understand the inanity of having pride in a car. He thinks women like him and, because he is so utterly convinced of this, some of them always do.'

'What women?'

'Oh, I don't know, the women in the office. I've heard his wife is beautiful in a classy way. By rights she should be a plastic bimbo. I've never met her, so I can't say. But, you see, everybody likes him and he knows they do and that only makes it worse.'

'Do you think you're a little jealous of him?'

'Jealous! He's a buffoon. I don't want to be like him. Look, Alex, he is one of those people who makes huge sums of money off other people's backs.'

'Off your back?'

'Aren't you ashamed to charge for such facile analysis?'

'Dennis, you stop me if I'm characterising the situation incorrectly. Analysts, who do the research, are on a fixed salary while the dealers, who sell the results of this research to investors, are on a salary plus a commission.'

'Yes.'

'But you knew this was the way it worked when you started. Dealers make more money than analysts. Despite that, you didn't ever want to be a dealer.'

'No, I didn't.'

'So why do you hate them?'

'I don't hate *them*. I hate him. I know you'll say hate is a stupid word.'

'Do you think it's a stupid word or do you think I'm going to tell you it's a stupid word?'

'I think questions like that are stupid. I don't know how any remotely intelligent person can think questions like that can be beneficial to somebody's mental health and I fucking hate it when you ask them. You charge for this. It's unbelievable.'

'Tell me about you and Joe Geraghty. What happened?'

'Joe Geraghty sold things, chiefly himself. He was a dealer. His job was to sell whatever we recommended and, I have to admit, he was good at it. His figures were good, sometimes very good. He'd worked his way up as, I suppose, I had, but our methods were different, our modus operandi . . . what's the plural of that? You're the Latin scholar.'

'I don't know. You were saying, you went about things in different ways.'

'Most people are optimists when it comes to investing. Joe Geraghty made a name for himself by playing on that. He talked things up infectiously and got people to buy more, and more often. He was better at it than many of his competitors both inside and outside the firm.

'You see, people, investors in the market, spend ninety per cent of whatever mental effort they expend on their portfolio looking at the buy side of the story. It goes against the grain, for most people anyway, to put much thought into the selling side—what to sell, when to sell, for how much—it's not as appealing. And it's easier for the dealer to bring someone along for a buy than it is to bring them along for a sell. For a start, the investor has to already own the stock. And on top of that the dealer is more reluctant to push him to sell than to buy because it will feel as though the dealer's telling him, "You've made a mistake. You've done something wrong." Nobody likes saying that to the hand that feeds you, especially when the truth is that you don't know your arse from your head and are just mouthing the advice of someone you don't fully trust anyway, knowing, feeling somewhere between your heart and your hypothalamus, that the whole endeavour is always and everywhere largely speculative. It's gambling. And if the dealer does stick his neck out and convince the investor to sell the stock, there's always the chance that the investor will want a second opinion.'

'Is that bad?'

'Sure. Even if a second dealer confirms the first dealer's recommendation, the investor will most likely sell then and there through the second dealer. The first dealer loses the commission and is forgotten by the investor only to be remembered if he made the wrong call.'

'What does all this have to do with you and Joe Geraghty?'

'Because we were opposites we made a good team. It got to be that we acted de facto as a kind of team. He fell into the habit of listening to me, even when I recommended holding or selling. Because of me he would frequently recommend holding, selling, or not buying. If it worked in his clients' favour, it made him look particularly good, wise and knowledgeable. As a result, when he told them to buy something, they really listened. He could get people to pour buckets of money into something simply because he refused to get excited about every stock.'

'You said you were opposites. In what way?'

'In practically every way. He was forever talking, trying to promote himself by letting people know how much he knew, or thought he knew. I tried to survive by saying as little as possible because you can get it right for the wrong reasons too, you know. To some extent as an analyst, especially when you start, you have to wing it. It's the worst thing you can do but sometimes, to be frank, you just have to. You're under such pressure to come up with ideas. And it's not only when you're starting out.

'In the beginning you're out of breath every day just trying to keep them from realising how superficial your knowledge is of anything anyone is talking about. How many stocks do you think anyone can properly cover, anyway?'

'I don't know.'

'Guess.'

'I've no idea.'

'Well, what do you think?'

'Dennis, it's not my area. I'd be guessing.'

'I'm asking you to guess.'

'I don't know—fifty, a hundred?'

'A hundred! Are you out of your mind? I'm talking about knowing a company inside out. You have to work hard for a long time to know ten, twelve at most. I've seen kids come in raw, straight out of business school, the print on their MBAs still wet. They put everything into certain boxes, do a Porter framework on everything, and walk around their work-stations like they're some kind of guru.'

'Does it matter that I don't know who Porter is?'

'Not in the least. He's a professor of business administration at Harvard Business School . . . and that's just at the beginning. Sooner or later, if you're still there, you realise that you have to get rated because being unrated means your position is tenuous and your salary is pathetic. You need to be making a lot of money. So you keep an eye on what your competitors are doing, read their research if you possibly can, watch the surveys. You lie awake at night and worry about other analysts getting to your contacts when you're on holiday or when you're at home with the flu.'

'But you said it takes lots of time and effort to know even ten or twelve stocks.'

'Yes, and I also said you can get it right for the wrong reasons. Someone, without knowing anything, could get lucky, all while you weren't there. You'd be forgotten. When you're unrated, you go to meetings and look up to the rated analysts above you. You don't know how they do it. The MD calls them by their names but he doesn't know yours. You realise you have to make contacts and you have to get rated.

'Then when you are rated, you work on trying to improve your rating or else on just maintaining your current ranking. You lose sleep. You get used to not sleeping. When you go to meetings as a rated analyst, everyone is looking to you for answers, for recommendations. The MD knows your name now and the unrated nameless guys watch him make small talk with you before the meeting starts. They're trying to listen. They're trying to catch crumbs falling from your plate. They want your ranking. You see a thick band tautening around their temples, pulling at their eyes, making them smile in that way that reminds both you and them that we cannot, none of us, ever relax.'

'This must take its toll on your relationships, on your personal lives?'

'If you're referring to my marriage, sure, I was leaving early and coming home late, but Patricia . . . she was never going to be faithful, no matter what I did for a living. It was not the sex . . . well, not only. She needs what she misperceives as the reassurance, the reinvigoration of her self-esteem, that comes with each new conquest. She needs it like so many men do. I think that at some level she knows that the lust of a stranger won't ever cure her of her fear of rejection, that no number of men will ever erase the feeling of being unloved by her parents, particularly her mother. But she forgets it just long enough to take the bait, every time.'

'You sound as if you've forgiven her.'

'You think so? I'm nowhere near finished.'

'And what about Joe Geraghty?'

'Oh, that's clever, Alex. Touché. What the hell are you trying to suggest?'

'I wasn't suggesting anything. I'm just asking questions—'

'Look, what they have in common, *all* they have in common is betrayal, their betrayal of me.'

'I've heard it said betrayal and trust come from the same place. It's just a question of which gets there first. What do you think?'

'Oh, what sort of shit is that?'

'Well, in order for someone to be betrayed, he must first trust or at least rely on the betrayer.'

'Doctor, if you'll give me the antidepressants, I'll leave now and you can masturbate for the rest of my session *without* me in the room.'

'Dennis, what happened with you and Joe Geraghty?'

'We needed each other . . . or thought we did. I told you, he'd sometimes rely on what was often really just a recommendation hewn from the depths of my uncertainty. Based on what I'd tell him he'd frequently get his clients to do things which were, at least in the short term, not in their best interests. For example, he'd get them to hold and there's no commission in that. When it eventually paid off, his clients thought he was God and he started to think of me not just as a rated analyst but as his lucky analyst.'

'What made him take your advice even when it wasn't in his short-term interest to? Was it that he could see that it would pay off in the long run?'

'I don't know.'

'Why do you think?'

'I really don't know. I think . . . I think maybe . . . he just trusted me.'

'You said before that you needed each other.'

'Our skills complemented each other, or we thought they did. And then, for one brief shining moment, our contacts complemented each other as well. Our contacts needed each other. It was a perfect match. Everyone was going to come out of it with a lot of money. By the way, everything I say in here is confidential, right?'

'Of course.'

'Not that any of it isn't already known by anyone who is interested, I suppose . . . Joe Geraghty was the dealer of choice to one of the wealthiest men in the country while I, after years of talking and listening to a certain entrepreneur, was uniquely placed to assist that entrepreneur. My value to him was contingent on my relationship with Joe Geraghty. The way it was to work . . . I may as well mention their names. You'd work it out anyway.'

'Dennis, you'd be shocked to know how little I know about the world of the stock market but you can say anything you like in here. I'm not permitted to repeat it, even if I understand it.'

'Oh, you'll understand it, too well for my liking . . . It was widely known by anyone who cared that the government wanted to introduce legislation to make US-style managed care agreements legally enforceable. I know you know what that means.'

'Better than most.'

'Now, at that time, as you'd also know, the declared intention of the Opposition, which was ideologically opposed to this, was to block the legislation in the Senate. My contact, the entrepreneur I was close to, was Sid Graeme. Don't look surprised. I know you're not. Sid is, among other things, the chairman and majority shareholder of the health insurance company Health National. He also even then owned a number of private hospitals.

'Sid had been told in confidence by somebody in the Opposition that, despite declared party policy, there was, in fact, majority support for the government's mooted managed care bill in the Opposition parliamentary party room. Knowing that private hospitals, which weren't doing too well, would become extremely profitable with managed care, Sid wanted Health National to buy up as many private hospitals as possible. To fund the purchase he planned a massive share issue by Health National.

'Sid's problem was that he couldn't publicise either Health National's intention to purchase the hospitals—'

'Why not?'

'Because it would've immediately raised the price of the hospitals.'

'Yes, of course.'

'Nor did he want to publicly signal the impending policy repudiation by the Opposition parliamentary caucus and alert the large majority in the party's extra-parliamentary membership hostile to managed care in time for them to pre-empt the about-face. What he really needed was for it to be known that someone really big, somebody renowned for their commercial sagacity and huge wealth, had invested heavily in the share issue. That's where Joe came in. You can guess who *his* contact was. He was the dealer of choice for Donald Sheere. If he could get Sheere to take up a sizeable part of the offer, the price would skyrocket and every man and his dog would want in.'

'Hmm, I suppose so. It's obvious I don't play the market.'

'Plenty of psychiatrists do, Alex. I've known a few.'

'Yet you chose to come to me.'

'It was her idea. She spoke very highly of you.'

'You say that as though you have considerable regard for her, her opinion anyway.'

'Don't speculate about me and her. I don't know. I suppose it's the managed care thing, the coincidence of it. As I've said, what are the chances of that?'

'But you've also said this is not about gambling. That's not why you're here.'

'You're determined, aren't you, Alex? Determined to have me a sexually frustrated Catholic with a gambling problem, in need of confession?'

'What went wrong with the deal? The Opposition did let the legislation through. We *have* managed care now. Couldn't you get Sheere to invest?'

'It wasn't up to me to get Sheere to invest. That was Joe's job.'

'And he failed you. Is that the betrayal?'

'This is testing you, isn't it, Alex? You're having trouble remaining objective, aren't you?'

'No, I don't think so. Why do you say that?'

'Because this whole topic seems to make you . . . jumpy. You're quick to interrupt. It's as though you want me to hurry up, as though you want this topic over and done with.'

'I'm sorry if I'm giving you that impression. You should feel free to talk about whatever you like. Go ahead.'

6

'Joe and I got the firm to underwrite the share issue. It was me, really.'

'What does that mean? Is that like a form of insurance?'

'Yes, you can think of it that way. It means that in the event that the share issue is undersubscribed, the firm undertakes to make up the shortfall.'

'That sounds very risky.'

'Well, it shouldn't have been. After a little legwork, Joe eventually sold Sid Graeme's idea to Sheere, who bought in well and everyone was happy.'

'I think I can see where this is going.'

'Oh, you might think you can but you only see the beginning. Sheere got wind of your letter to the paper warning of an about-face on managed care by the Opposition.'

'What do you mean, "got wind of"? You mean he read it in the paper?'

'I'm sure he read it in the paper on the Saturday morning but he knew about it on the Friday night.'

'Really?'

'Yes, really. He knew about it in advance and he called Joe late that night to tell him to sell out of Health National, completely. Told him to sell it all first thing Monday.'

'Because of my letter? I don't get it.'

'He thought there was a risk, a high risk, that the disclosure would precipitate sufficient fury in the Opposition rank and file to force the caucus to back off from their intention to support the bill.'

'But they did pass the legislation. That letter, all the letters, all the protests, were . . . futile. We have managed care to care for us now.'

'They did pass the legislation but not then. They had to wait a while for the fuss to die down, for it to be replaced by something else the talkback callers could get their teeth into. Illegal immigrants, I think it was, something or other. Who the hell remembers? Whatever it was, when Sheere called Joe that Friday night with those instructions it meant, with one phone call, that we were finished. Sheere would sell. The firm would have to make up the difference and we'd bear the brunt of it. We'd be gone within the week.'

'But what about your track record?'

'That would be a matter of history, part of an anecdote for people to tell each other over lunch, if it was remembered at all. Press "Control Alt Delete".'

'Sorry?'

'It's what they say when you're iced, when you're terminated. "Control" plus "Alt" plus "Delete", like on a computer.'

'Yes, I see.'

'Now, Alex, this is where the real fun starts. Sheere called Joe on the Friday—'

'Dennis, I'm not quite sure how to put this. I've never had to say anything like this to a patient before but—'

'Like what?'

'Well . . . for the sake of your treatment I need to have only one role in your story, namely, that of your psychiatrist. I can't also be a protagonist, or worse, an antagonist in your life.'

'Look, I'm sorry, Alex, if I've been—'

'No, Dennis, it's not your demeanour. It's not a healthy situation for a patient to see an act by his therapist, particularly one unconnected with their doctor–patient relationship, as even partly responsible for the patient's negative circumstances.'

'You're talking about the letter?'

'Yes.'

'Alex, my business was to be the handmaiden of people whose business was selling units of stock in certain companies. We didn't care what the companies did. They could mine uranium, they could pollute rivers, they could insure against other companies being prosecuted for doing those things. We didn't care. It wasn't our business what they actually did. My job was to help them make money, and thereby keep my job so that my wife could keep buying things and I could pay off the mortgage.'

'You misunderstand me. I know you were a mercenary in the battle for managed care rather than a crusader. Come to think of it, so was everybody else. I believe it was a matter of supreme indifference to you whether the share issue you were promoting required the passage of the managed care bill or its rejection.'

'Hang on a minute. I hadn't finished. It's true that I had no views about managed care one way or the other while I was selling the selling of the share issue, but it's not true anymore. On the contrary, I'm now very sympathetic to your position on it—for obvious reasons. At the time no one at work ever talked about the human consequences of the legislation we were depending on. People don't express moral or political views in social conversation anymore.'

'No, you're wrong, Dennis. They do. But it's the same view over and over again, so you don't notice it. The problem, as your therapist, that I have with you does not relate to a possible difference with respect to managed care, but as I said, to you seeing me as at least part author of the problems you're wanting me to help you with.'

'In that case, Alex, let me put *your* mind at rest, and I won't charge you for it either. My domestic problems predate your letter by years. And as for my job, had the Health National deal not fallen over, sooner or later, and very likely sooner, another would've. Failure is systemic in the investment industry. I do not for one moment hold you responsible for the problem I came to see you about.'

'Alright then, I will accept that that's true, at least at the conscious level. Now tell me what happened after Sheere phoned Joe. Were you and he actually fired?'

'Within the week. Maybe not even that long. We had the weekend for Joe to get Sheere to change his mind. That's the way he put it to me first thing the next morning.'

'He called you?'

'Apparently he tried to call me but I'd already left for the firm's corporate retreat. Now, at that time, and I think it's still the case today, there existed a government requirement that companies with over a certain annual turnover had to spend a minimum of one per cent of their gross income on what they were pleased to call "staff development" or incur a tax hike. Millions of dollars had to be spent before the end of each financial year. And so a new industry of training brokers was born to service this requirement. Enter Dr Terry Brabet.'

'Doctor? What was he a doctor of?'

'I still don't know. He was not a doctor of medicine. I don't imagine he had a genuine doctorate in anything. What he did have was a Svengali-like ability to talk profitable companies into throwing their money at a snake-oil salesman rather than at the tax office.

'Gorman, the MD, had sent me and Joe and eighteen others, men and women, some of them from the offices of interstate affiliates, to something Dr Terry Brabet marketed as his Personal Effectiveness Program. We were meant to be flattered to be chosen. It was said to signify that we were part of the company's future. It cost the firm $8000 per person for a four-day course, so with twenty people, that's $160 000 in four days. Even allowing for the Spartan overheads and for his sad, obedient, doe-eyed, slightly overweight assistant, Helen, he had to be clearing at least a hundred grand for four days of total crap. "That's a talent," Joe Geraghty pointed out between moments of panic.'

'Panic?'

'Sure. The first time he'd seen me since Sheere had told him to sell was in the foyer of this guest house they'd booked us into. It was two and a half hours out of the city in the foothills of the mountains. They wanted us there by nine am. Terry Brabet couldn't wait to work on us, to start breaking us down. I got up at five-thirty on Saturday morning to be there on time. When I arrived I was ready to find the bed they'd allocated me and sleep for the whole four days. And how I wish I had.

'But Terry Brabet didn't have us up there to sleep. As he told us in the introductory session, if we let him he was going to help us find our true selves, even if it meant taking us outside our usual "comfort zones". I knew it was all going to be bullshit but I saw it as a few days off so I was prepared to sleepily go along with it. I was still asleep. But Joe Geraghty was red-eyed and ashen faced. He looked as though he hadn't slept.'

7

'"What's wrong? You look awful," I said to him as we signed in and received our nametags. For the first of what was to be countless times, speakers mounted everywhere blared the song "Celebration" lest you catch your breath or get lost in your thoughts. It was like a Maoist indoctrination camp in that regard. Light towers with speakers under them were everywhere and everywhere we heard this idiot's idea of a corporate mantra, "Ce-le-brate—Good times—Come on!"

'But Joe had known for twelve hours or more that we had nothing to celebrate.

'"Sheere called me last night. Have you read today's paper?"

'"You must be joking. I've been asleep at the wheel for the last two and a half hours trying to get here on time. What's up?" I asked him.

'My guard was down. I had relaxed and you can never relax, not in the business we were in. Certainly you do not expect to hear, first thing on a Saturday morning while registering at a corporate retreat in the foothills of the mountains where you've been sent as a pat on the back, about a development that will most likely cause you to lose your job within days. So when he told me about your letter to the paper and that Sheere, having got wind of it, had decided to pull out of the whole thing, for an instant I thought Joe was joking. It was too surreal. But Joe was not a good enough actor to look the way he did for his newsflash concerning our careers to be a joke. He looked about to cry. It was not a joke.

'The music was blaring and above it our names were being called out in what really amounted to a roll call, the first of many. I had started to contest the logic in Sheere's decision, to tell Joe that your letter did not source the U-turn by the Opposition to anybody authoritative, that it was simply rumour-mongering and that, anyway, sooner or later the legislation was going to get through, as it did. But Joe had already unsuccessfully put this to Sheere and before we could continue, we were separated and being told by Dr Terry Brabet that we each had chairs and that our chairs were our own personal responsibility.

'When the music stopped Terry Brabet introduced himself and his Personal Effectiveness Program. I should have punched him out then and there. He asked us to stand up and then he led us through some en masse stretching side to side. He walked around us, occasionally adjusting someone's stretch or whispering "good". He completed a circuit or two of the entire group, alternately directing his "good" to the individual he was passing and to all of us collectively. I kept trying to make eye contact with Joe.

'When we'd finished with the stretching he told us that we could be seated. Then he told us that in four days he was going to extend us beyond our previous limits and that, as a result, we would return to our workplaces, to our homes, to our loved ones—more *effective* people. He was going to get us to open up. We would be talking about ourselves, finding out some home truths and telling each other about them. We were going to be putting in, physically and emotionally. He recounted stories of previous participants who had run out of a particular session in tears and were better for it. A few people looked a little uncomfortable at this. Some looked at others, some at the floor. I looked at Joe. He sat like a stone version of himself.

'Then Terry said he thought it was only fair that he tell us a little about himself. He said, with a rehearsed laugh, that in his colourful life he had been a carpenter, an insurance salesman, a rugby player and physiotherapist. He never told us what he was a doctor of.

'"And I'll tell you something else," he said meaningfully, by way of both a boast and a confession, "I'm divorced and I'm a recovering alcoholic."

'There were to be no phone calls, no newspapers, no television or radios. When people complained that they needed to be in touch with their offices for work reasons, Terry Brabet informed us that for the following four days this *was* our work. Then he instructed Helen, his assistant, to walk among the group carrying a wicker tray on which people were meant to place their mobile phones. "See if you can live without them for four days. You'll get them back at the end of the program," he told us. Helen moved slowly, silently but for the sound of her feet barely lifting from the floor. She was a heavyish young woman with large breasts and dark hair which she wore tied back. She smiled a sad little smile, the smile of a woman who had played tag with a weight problem for too many years, barely keeping it at bay, a woman who now had a job picking up after and following the orders of a charlatan who possessed what she took for charisma. The effect of Terry Brabet's matter-of-fact instructions that we all relinquish our mobile phones, added to that of Helen's eyes and sad smile and the perfume on her neck above the outstretched wicker tray, was that all of us, without exception, silently yielded up our mobile phones without further protest.

'I must have been mad to comply. It's no excuse to say that I did not yet know that the rooms didn't contain phones because the truth is, I hadn't even turned my mind to whether they did or didn't. That wasn't why I gave it to her. There was a coin-operated phone in reception but I hadn't yet noticed that either. I'm ashamed to say . . .'

'What are you ashamed of?'

'Well, we hadn't been there an hour and although I realised that keeping my job depended on Joe Geraghty phoning Donald Sheere before Monday morning to try to get him to change his mind, I . . . I had just given away my phone. Everybody had. Joe had. The idiot! He knew the trouble we were in. He knew what he had to do. But he gave his phone away as well. I remember when she came up to me. Everyone was looking at me. I looked at her face, at her eyes. I can see her now. I know it sounds ridiculous, absolutely ridiculous. I could smell her perfume and I didn't want to . . . you know . . . right from the beginning be singled out as the guy who makes trouble. I did hesitate for a moment. I really did. I was thinking, I'm not sure I should be doing this, but she came a step closer and she smelled so surprisingly good and, as I said, everyone was watching. I took it out of my pocket, slowly, like a kid at school handing up a pack of cigarettes, and I gave it to her. Just like that.

'Terry Brabet explained that we had to be ready for physical exercise each morning at six am. Then we could shower, have breakfast and be ready for our first session. There was an expectation that we would complete all the designated exercises. This was work. The firm had paid for it. When the introductory session was over, we were given fifteen minutes to find our rooms, which were actually cabins, and to take our bags there. That was the next opportunity I had to talk to Joe. We were sharing a cabin. The first chance I had I told him, "You have to change his mind."

'"I tried. Believe me," he protested.

'"Well, you have to try again. You know what will happen to us if he sells."

'"Mitch, what can I do? I didn't know he was going to get spooked by a letter to the paper. How could I know that? It's not my fault," he said, closing the door to our room behind him.

'"Don't tell me it's not your fault. Just fucking fix it. Talk him round."

'"What should I say?"

'"Joe, you're the salesman. You're the one with the great relationship. Tell him he's got to trust you on this. Tell him that the legislation will get through, that it's still a great deal—"

'"Mitch, he's not stupid."

'"But, Joe, it *is* a good deal. Nothing's changed. Why is he so timid?"

'"He's not timid, Mitch. Look at it his way. He knows he can always buy in again later if the legislation ultimately passes. If he sells, the firm has to take up the shortfall for Sid Graeme and Health National gets to buy all the hospitals Sid wants for a song. Then when the legislation passes, Sheere can buy all the Health National shares he wants if the price is low enough. He knows he can't lose by pulling out."

'"No, but we can."

'"That would really worry him, wouldn't it?"

'"What about his relationship with Gorman? The firm would be taking the loss. Would he care about that?"

'"What do *you* think?"

'"Well, you've got to fucking try to get him to change his mind, Joe. You've got to at least try. How the hell could something like this happen?" I said unpacking.

'"Did he say this was for four days? I thought it was only for the weekend. I didn't bring enough clothes. Did you know it was for four days?"

'"Yes."

'"How did you know?"

'"It was on the memo."

'"Shit, I must've misread it. I've only brought enough clothes for two days. What am I going to do?"

'"For fuck's sake, Joe. We've got bigger problems than that."

'"Mitch, don't get mad at me. We're both in the same boat. Did you give her your mobile?"

'"Yes. I don't know what I was thinking."

'"I know. I gave her mine too."

8

'It was still a good deal. All your letter had done was to introduce an extra degree of uncertainty. But certainty costs money. You get a discount on uncertainty. Joe was right. However small the risk, after the uproar triggered by your disclosure, that the Opposition caucus would be forced back into line by the overwhelming hostility to managed care in the party as a whole, there was no reason Sheere had to take that risk. He just didn't need to. By then, because the firm had underwritten the share issue, even Sid Graeme didn't need him to. It occurred to me that we had been set up, that maybe Sheere and Graeme had spoken. But that was unlikely, given the timing of everything and, anyway, invoking Occam's razor, I realised it was a leap I didn't need to make. However the situation had arisen, if Joe couldn't get Sheere to change his mind before Monday morning, the firm would take the loss. And because Joe and I had convinced the risk committee that the whole deal was a good bet, he and I would be finished.

'Joe went to reception and tried to reach Sheere from the pay-phone. The husband and wife proprietors were talking animatedly about something, arguing, and Joe had to put one finger in his free ear to block out their voices. When I got there he was having trouble just making the person on the other end of the line get his name right. "Geraghty, Joe Geraghty . . . for Mr Sheere." Only when Sheere's housekeeper had got it right to their mutual satisfaction would she tell him that Sheere wasn't there. Neither was Mrs Sheere. Where could they be so early on a Saturday morning? I saw Joe scour the pay-phone for a return number, but after glancing at the arguing proprietors and then at me, he told the housekeeper that there was no message and that he would call back. He put the phone down heavily, heavily enough to interrupt the hostilities between the proprietors and prompt the wife to ask, in the manner of an accusation, whether something was wrong.

'"It's just not possible to have a normal telephone conversation with somebody here while the two of you are going fifteen rounds behind your little counter over there."

'It was at this point that the "Celebration" song started again and I took Joe in to Dr Terry Brabet and the others, apologising to the proprietors for my colleague's rudeness.

'"Oh fuck 'em, Mitch. What are they going to do, spit in my food? They won't even remember which one I am."

'I managed to calm Joe down by telling him that at the end of the session I was simply going to ask for my phone back. This gave us both sufficient peace of mind not to tear the place apart. There were large handwritten signs in coloured texta or crayon stuck all over the walls and every available space of what was called the rec room. The signs read: "Just Do It", "I Can Not Not Do It", "Choose An Attitude", "Live As Your Word", "Grow Beyond Your Comfort Zone", "There Is No Such Thing As Failure, Only Life's Feedback", "We Can Not Not Participate", "Win/Win—Go For It", "If It's To Be, It's Up To Me", and "Everybody Is Fantastic". This was how the sad young Helen paid her rent, by making kindergarten-like posters for Terry Brabet and sticking them on the walls. I should have ripped his head off then and there but we had to get through that session without causing any trouble if I was to get him to give me my phone back.

'The first session, Terry told us, was designed to illustrate "focus". He arranged everyone into same-sex couples and then had one member of each put their hand on their partner's shoulder. On a signal from him the partner was then to push down on the outstretched arm and try to force it to move from their shoulder. He tried this with couple after couple and each time the partner was able to displace the outstretched arm. When every couple had had its turn, he sent each of us back to our seats and told us to watch him intently. We watched him reach into a brown paper bag and pull out an orange, which he then placed on a ledge over by the wall. He called the first couple to come back out to the front and repeat the exercise, only this time, before starting, he instructed the person with the outstretched arm resting on the other's shoulder, a woman from the Brisbane office called Pamela, to concentrate all her attention on the orange he had placed on the ledge. He told this woman, Pamela, to harness the energy from the pit of her stomach and focus on the orange. The woman did as he instructed, her eyes never wavering from the orange on the ledge by the wall and, sure enough, her partner was unable to move Pamela's arm. Pamela and her partner looked at each other with something approximating awe. Then, as they turned to the rest of the group, they both broke into beaming smiles, like small children who had tied their shoes for the first time.

'One after another, Terry Brabet had the other couples come out to the front and try again, only this time with the person with the outstretched arm concentrating their attention not on the force of the other person's hand but, as Pamela had done, on the orange in the middle distance. For every couple the result was the same, even for Joe and me. The outstretched arms could not be moved. What was far more amazing than any of this was the group's response to the exercise, their exhilaration, their euphoria, to which Brabet contributed from the sidelines by exhorting us with slogans from the posters on the wall.

'"Good, Pamela, good. Grow beyond your comfort zone."

'At the conclusion of this session, we were granted a fifteen-minute break. It was at this time that I approached Brabet. I started by buttering him up, telling him how inspiring I had found the last session. He told me there was nothing more satisfying to him than hearing that. He said that this was what he was all about, empowering people, helping them to help themselves. He seemed to believe his own cant. As he walked toward the door with a hand resting on my shoulder, it was not hard to believe that he was genuinely delighted by this level of praise from a consumer at the end of the very first hour of clearing over a hundred thousand dollars in four days. But then I started to explain that I was involved in a very delicate matter at work and that I really would need my phone back. We both knew it was a request but I tried to dress it up as a statement. This is when his eyes changed shape, just briefly, as they looked into mine and registered commerce talking to itself. Brabet smiled a smile from the new economy where the customer is always riled. If he could have, he would have put me on hold so that Helen might fend off the request, but not before the disembodied voice of a third person had warned me that the request might be monitored for training purposes, that the enterprise realised my time was valuable and that my call was important to them. But this was a "live one-on-one" situation and he had to deal with it himself. He said he was sorry but I knew the rules.

'"But this is an extremely important matter, it's just arisen. A matter of great commercial significance to the firm."

'"Your personal effectiveness is of great commercial significance to the firm too . . . Dennis. Sorry, no can do, Dennis."

'By the time I had conveyed to Joe, through facial expressions and sign language, that my attempt had failed, I'd already decided that if we hadn't somehow got a phone by the end of the day I would leave Brabet's stalag to get one by hook or by crook and bring it back to Joe. With this decision made, I managed to keep my blood pressure down enough to survive the next session.

'You see, we knew we could leave if we had to—probably even Joe realised that—but before every session Brabet had Helen check everybody's names off the list, so leaving was a last resort, not a first one. Between asking Brabet and going AWOL, there had to be other stratagems we could try. During the break, Joe tried the public phone at reception again, only to find he didn't have enough change. You're smiling, Alex. They're small things, right? But small things can bring you undone. Anyway, you have to hear all this because it's what eventually takes me right here, right to your door, via her.

'The next session in his ascending march toward the nirvana of inanity was devoted to teaching us how to juggle. Yes, I'm serious, how to juggle. The purpose of it, insofar as I could discern any, was to demonstrate that life's difficult problems can be broken down so that they appear less difficult, something to that effect. Having juggled for us till we gasped at his skill, Brabet gave everyone, one by one, a turn at trying to do it with three red plastic balls in front of the rest of the group. Only one of us could. There was a guy from Sydney and he was much better than Dr Brabet. He was very quickly asked to sit down.'

'How do you do it?'

'You start with two balls in one hand and one in the other. You throw the two balls up in the air and the single ball in the other hand is thrown across to the hand that held the two balls. After a while quite a few of us were managing to pull this off, very slowly, maybe once every five minutes, but even this degree of success showed, Brabet claimed, that inherently precarious balancing acts could be broken down into manageable steps, steps which when undertaken quickly enough by someone practised, could not be seen to be discrete.

'The session went on for hours and with the cacophony of people's laughter, their cursing, and their chasing after spilled plastic balls, Joe and I had a chance to confer. Joe had a simple plan with which it was hard to argue. At a convenient time, which we didn't expect to arise until after the last session of the day, we would attempt to bribe Brabet's assistant, Helen, to give Joe back his phone. Joe said he would do it. He would try to sweet-talk her. He was a salesman. In between throwing and chasing plastic balls, we figured that between the two of us, we probably didn't have more than $220 cash on us. We both had credit cards, of course, but neither of us had planned on needing cash at a corporate retreat, much less needing to bribe someone. We just hoped the $220 would be enough.

'I told Joe that if it didn't work, I was simply going to leave the following day and bring him back a phone. The idiot praised me for my audacity. Can you believe it! He knew as well as I did the consequences for both of us of not getting Sheere to change his mind, but he was somehow intimidated by the school-like discipline of Brabet's regime. And he was far from the only one. You could see people stifling their resistance to hours of juggling; you could see them looking to Brabet for praise. Their rugged individualism, their enterprise, had completely evaporated, so successful had Brabet been in getting them to identify their participation and his approbation with career advancement and job security. Keeping a roll was important in this. Even though everybody could see that everybody else was there, by checking our names off a list each time, he was planting so many unspoken questions in our minds. What would the consequences be of missing a session? Who would get to read these attendance reports? What else was he noting about us?

'For the rest of the day and into the night Joe made a point of subtly ingratiating himself with Brabet's assistant. He chose to help her collect the balls when finally the crash course in juggling was over. When she took the roll after lunch, he engaged in some self-deprecating chitchat, the substance of which I couldn't hear but the tone of which was sufficiently audible to be nauseating.

'There were two sessions in the evening. Even by the start of the first one, people were getting fairly tired. Again, we were put into pairs not necessarily of the same sex and not necessarily with our room-mates this time. Helen made sure the lights were turned off and as Brabet spoke quietly in a voice that was intended to be calming or soothing, she lit small candles in glasses that had been placed strategically around the room, giving it an ethereal quality. This time there was not the usual blaring of "Celebration" announcing the beginning of the session but rather the tinkle of a triangle. They had done this before.

'In the first session, one of us in each couple was meant to lie on our back and the other was meant to massage our temples.'

'Isn't that a little invasive?'

'Oh, Alex, it gets worse. Then he asked us to do something to each other's ears . . . that's just too silly to mention.'

'Up to you, Dennis.'

'Well, the point is that by the start of the second session, which was also a candlelit one introduced by the tinkling of a triangle, people on the whole were so relaxed they were almost sleepy. This time, he had us sitting on mats in groups of three and four. People were too tired to question the fact that the chairs, each of which had been our personal responsibility, had been taken away from us, which is to say that in the space of twelve hours, twenty adults who had been deemed in some way above average had, with expert help, regressed to infancy.

'In the candlelight Terry had us kneeling and leaning forward so that our foreheads were touching. Then he went around in hushed tones allocating a topic for discussion to each group and the person to start it off. I could hear some of the topics he'd allotted: your childhood, your first kiss, the loss of your virginity. Terry, as though anticipating their reluctance to dive into their topics, walked softly around from group to group prompting them. Gradually they started talking, some so warming to their subjects that they couldn't stop. A woman in our group—Pamela, it turned out—had been the victim of child molestation. She began talking and was soon crying. Nearby groups stopped to listen to her. We were embarrassed. Our heads were still touching.

'A man in another group, a bald, stocky guy, started talking about the horrible time he'd had as a child, being picked on, and being rejected. He also started crying.'

'What did you do?'

'Me? I wasn't going to tell these people anything. There was a woman there in another group, kind of plain, not what you'd call unattractive but . . . you know . . . she didn't wear make-up, her hair was all over the place. I knew her, sort of vaguely. Well, she was talking about her failure to hold down relationships. We could hear her when Pamela's heaves became longer and more evenly spaced. The other woman, the plain one with the unruly hair, she was talking openly about how things tended not to work out for her romantically, but she seemed to be coping okay with the telling. That is, until Terry stopped by and started pushing her. "Why do these relationships always fail? What do these relationships have in common?" For Christ's sake, they have *her* in common. Well, after a while she was in tears too. I wasn't going to let Brabet anywhere near me, the real me.'

'What were you feeling when these other people were crying?'

'I was angry.'

'Angry?'

'You bet I was angry. I was angry with Brabet for doing that to all those people. I was angry with myself for being there in the first place. I was angry with Joe for pretending to go along with it all and for getting me in this shit with Donald Sheere. I was even a little angry at those saps for spilling their life stories like that. It was embarrassing. It was uncomfortable for everybody.'

'Did you think of doing anything about it?'

'Yes, and I did.'

'What did you do?'

'I tried to make Pamela feel better. Joe and I both did.'

'What did you say?'

'I told her to stop talking about what had happened to her. I told her she didn't have to tell us these things if she didn't want to.'

'And what did Pamela do when you said this? Dennis? . . . Dennis? Why does it affect you in this way to tell me this? Why do you think you're crying now? . . . Were your heads touching?'

'Yes. Yes, they had to be.'

'Why?'

'Brabet said they had to be. We had to lean in with our foreheads touching. I told you.'

'Did you touch Pamela when she started to cry?'

'Our foreheads . . .'

'Other than your foreheads?'

'No.'

'You didn't pat her or . . . ?'

'No.'

'Put your arm around her?'

'No. What's your fucking problem, Alex? What are you getting at?'

'I'm not getting at anything.'

'Well, if you're not getting at anything why are you asking these stupid questions?'

'Why are you crying, Dennis?'

'I . . . I told her to shut up.'

'Why did you tell her that?'

'Because I couldn't stand it. I couldn't stand hearing what was done to her. I couldn't stand the way she vomited it all out to complete strangers. Not only did she not have any shame, she didn't have any sense. It would get around. It would be known in the offices of every affiliate around the country. She was committing career suicide.'

'Career suicide?'

'Sure. Absolutely. People would look at her differently after that. They weren't going to promote her knowing what had happened to her. They'd tiptoe around her. They'd ignore her if they could. They'd see her as an unstable bomb . . . one that could go off at any time.'

'That seems grossly unfair.'

'Of course it's unfair but fairness doesn't enter into it and she should have known that. Within weeks of the retreat, she'd handed in her resignation. I don't know where she went.'

'Is that really the way you see your work environment?'

'Alex, have you been asleep? I'm telling you in minute detail the way I see my work environment. It includes Dr Terry Brabet reducing these people to tears one Saturday night in a dimly lit rec hall at the foot of the mountains. And I'm telling you they weren't going to get to me.'

'Okay, go on.'

'It was after midnight by the time the session ended. Even though everybody was exhausted, Brabet's little contingent of camp followers remained clustered around him. It was all Joe needed in order to get a moment alone with Helen. He told her that the last session had really taken it out of him. She said that that one always particularly affected people. I was listening in. He was pretty smooth. He started telling her about his son who had been kidnapped only a few months earlier and the effect it had had on his family. It was true. Someone really had taken his son.

'Well, this caught her interest. She'd read about it, apparently, and was very sympathetic. She asked him if he wanted to raise it at a session the next day. She could raise it privately with Terry first. And this is where he was particularly brilliant. He told her that he didn't know if he was ready to bare it all publicly but . . . and then he sort of stumbled as though he was a little embarrassed or nervous. He looked at her, then away and then back again before speaking.

'"I'm not sure what I'd say. I wouldn't want to break down in front of everybody and . . . I don't know that I'd be able to control myself. Look, I hope you don't take this the wrong way but . . . I don't know exactly why, but I feel I can talk to you. Things have been very difficult for me since it all happened. I have . . . I don't know if this is allowed but I have a little brandy that I brought up. I like to use it to relax at home when I don't have time to do all the stretching I should be doing. It's just that I haven't really . . . strange as it might sound . . . haven't really had anyone around that I felt comfortable debriefing with and—"

'"What about your wife?"

'"Well, see that's . . . I'm afraid to say, that's part of the problem. See, it was her boyfriend who took him."

'"You're kidding? Her boyfriend kidnapped your son?"

'"Yep. That's what it looks like."

'"That's incredible. I think I read something in the paper about this but—"

'"Helen, can we talk about this somewhere else? I don't know that I want other people to know. I'm not even sure I want Terry to know and that's one of the things I thought maybe we could talk about. Do you like brandy?"'

9

'There's no question that Joe is a great salesman. It's a gift. I couldn't have done that and that's why it wasn't absolutely impossible that, given half a chance—which meant, more particularly, given a tele-phone that could receive calls as well as make them—he might just have been able to change Sheere's mind. Of course, Sheere was no sweet-smelling sad little Rubenesque assistant to a charlatan, but Joe had a knack for pitching a customised line just to get his foot in the door.

'Helen asked where his room-mate was and Joe told her that I liked going for long walks before retiring. Can you believe that? He said it and she believed it long enough to start knocking back the brandy in our room.'

'What did you do?'

'Well, he got a chance to throw my coat to me through the door of our cabin and, huddled in it, I sat outside, on the ground, beneath an open window listening to Joe trying to coax the phone from her. The sooner he succeeded the sooner I could go to bed. They drank out of plastic cups. It was all we had. I heard him pour the brandy. He was smooth as he spoke, so fluent, it might have been the truth.

'"Things had been incredibly busy at work, still are. Maybe that's why I didn't twig to them. I had no idea she was still seeing him."

'"Still?" Helen asked incredulously.

'"Well, he was her ex-boyfriend. They'd gone out years ago, before we were married. I didn't think she'd seen him since then. We certainly never talked about him. She never mentioned him. In hindsight maybe that was suspicious in itself."

'"Oh, you poor man. It sounds like everyone's worst nightmare."

'"Yes, I suppose it is. My marriage is all over bar the shouting. I'm still kicking myself for not having seen it coming."

'"Doesn't sound like you have any call blaming yourself."

'"That's sweet of you to say, but I guess it was not enough just to get her the house she wanted near the beach and everything."

'"It sounds lovely."

'"You see, there were things happening at work . . . even now . . . I'm in the middle of something very, very big. If it comes off they'll probably make me a director. Another drink?"

'"Really, a director? That makes you a boss then."

'"One of them."

'"What do you do exactly?"

'"I'm a dealer."

'"Like a stockbroker?"

'"Exactly like one. The thing is, I really have to make some calls tomorrow and I have to be contactable to take them. Caught off guard, and to be perfectly frank, also a little overwhelmed by your perfume, I gave you my mobile phone when you came around this morning and I shouldn't have. I need it back or this particular deal could well fall through."

'"Sorry, Joe. Terry is absolutely adamant about outside contact. He really—"

'"Helen, if it's about money, I could—"

'"No, no. Joe, you're an incredibly sweet guy and I'd really love to help you but it could cost me my job."

'"Do you like your job?"

'"Yeah. I suppose I do."

'"You suppose?"

'"I used to like it more . . . "

'"Really? Why don't you like it so much anymore?"

'"It can get a bit predictable. I know what's coming and Terry—"

'"What about Terry?"

'"He doesn't treat me . . . as he used to."

'"He's lucky to have you."

'"Sometimes I think that too. I don't want to do this for the rest of my life."

'"Look, Helen. I don't mean to be coy about it, I really need my phone back. If I get it then I can steer this deal through and if that happens—"

'"You're a director."

'"Almost certainly. Then I can take people on. You know what I'm saying. An attractive intelligent young woman like you should be out there grabbing the future and embracing it. You know, the future doesn't have to be an enemy stalking you. This is an opportunity, right here in this cabin. Another drink?"

'"Are you serious? What kind of job would it be?"

'"What would you like to do? What are you interested in? Would you like to earn some really good money? That's always interesting. You could start as a trainee broker."

'"Really?"

'"Why not? Train you on the job. Base salary, plus commission with a start-up allowance. How does that sound?"

'"What's that for—the start-up allowance?"

'"It's a little signing-on bonus for clothes, shoes, general corporate grooming and, of course, a mobile phone account."

'Joe Geraghty knew how to close. It was an instinct with him, to know how to plant, tender, cultivate and then harvest. She waited till everything was quiet and then I heard her go to get Joe's phone. It was the absolutely perfect seduction. I ducked inside to tell him I'd heard the whole thing and to praise him for the delivery and for thinking so fast on his feet. He had used his celebrity as the father of a kidnap victim as bait, invented the troubled marriage business to hook her and had given himself a promotion contingent on her getting him the phone, after which he was going to give her a job as a dealer, to reel her in. Brilliant! Hearing her coming back I ducked outside again to freeze in my hiding spot.

'"Get rid of her fast, will you? I'm freezing out here," I whispered as I left but all he said was, "It's true, Mitch."

'"What?" I asked from outside through the open window. "What's true?"

'"I didn't make that—"

'"I don't think anyone saw me," Helen said, opening the door without knocking. The brandy must have emboldened her.

'"You said Motorola, right, and there were only three of them. I brought all three," she laughed. Joe immediately shushed her and then it suddenly went very quiet. Neither of them was talking and I couldn't hear anything at all. It took a moment before it dawned on me that the bastard was probably kissing her.

'Why in hell was he doing that? He had the phone. He didn't need anything more from her. Why couldn't he have just thanked her and promised to use it discreetly before simply saying goodnight. Perhaps he could have reiterated his promise to give her a job, anything polite just to get her out of the room. After all, I was outside freezing. Okay, so he kissed her as the first instalment of her start-up allowance. One kiss, something wrong exchanged for something wrong and then out she goes. But no, the silence gave way to heavy breathing and I was getting angry. He could have used me as an excuse to get her to go. Where on earth was I supposed to be walking to, Mongolia? He had forgotten about me.

'I didn't know what to do. It seemed to be taking forever and I was getting angrier by the second, and colder. I got up slowly and looked through the window. She had her top off and his hands were moving over her breasts like a milking machine in overdrive, methodically, until he'd removed her bra. I couldn't believe it. And then he proceeded to rub his face between her breasts furiously, manically. What did he think I was doing? He didn't care. He just kept fondling and kissing those huge breasts of hers, like a man possessed.

'She was putting up no resistance either. In fact, she seemed to be similarly aroused even though he was being quite rough with her. She ought to have been a little frightened. She didn't know this man at all. She had just stolen for him and risked her job for him. Now he was grabbing at her with all his strength and she was letting him. Still standing, he pushed her hard up against the wall opposite the window I was looking through. People in other cabins could have heard her forearms slap against the wall to keep her head from crashing into it. He lifted her with one hand and she just let him. Then he started pumping her like an animal. He didn't care about the noise they were making or the three mobile phones lying uncovered on my bed. He was just going for it with the little fat girl for no damn reason at all, just because he could, and he had forgotten all about me. He was risking everything and all I could do was watch it, this pointless, carnal, reckless risk-taking.

'Hell, it wasn't as though he didn't get any.'

'What makes you say that, Dennis?'

'He was always talking about it like a schoolboy, that and his car. It was like he never grew up. He apparently had this quasi super-model of a wife and yet he still had to sleep around. It was he who first took me to a brothel, you know. My wife was screwing anything that moved. She'd already walked out on me once and yet it was me who was shivering outside while he was gratuitously fucking the fat girl. What kind of justice is that?'

'What did you do?'

'I walked around to the front door, stepping as loudly as I could, and then I knocked on it. I knocked, I didn't tap or anything. It was too late to worry about the noise. He whispered loudly, "Just a minute!" somewhat breathlessly and then there was some more quiet whispering inside before he stuck his head out the front door and, still panting, said, "Give me a couple of minutes."

'"Fuck you!"

'"Sorry, Mitch," he said, closing the door.

'He seemed to be assuring her that I was alright, that she had nothing to fear from me knowing some or all of what had gone on. I was his partner. I was his friend. I was cool. I was cold, tired and sickened by what I had seen. You know, Alex, you can have your suspicions about your friends and colleagues, about what animals they can be, how stupid and utterly irresponsible they can be, but when those suspicions are confirmed, even cynics can be disappointed.'

'Were you disappointed?'

'He said he was drunk. I didn't want to talk to him. We had to be up at six the next morning. I'd been up since five that morning. He held his mobile phone up in triumph like it was a trophy. The truth was, he wasn't going to get through to Sheere and, even if he did, we both knew that there was no good argument to keep Sheere from selling. I told him he was pathetic and, you know, he agreed.'

'Really?'

'Yes. What is it they say about alcohol?'

'Lots of things.'

'Well, in this instance it had lubricated a slide from a kind of ado-lescent triumph to a kind of senescent self-pity. He started telling me his marriage was a sham, that his life was a sham. He said, God help him, that I was really the only friend he had.'

'What did you say?'

'I told him his life was a sham and that if he didn't let me sleep I'd ram the phone down his throat. He said he was sorry and that he would fix everything tomorrow. He wanted me to trust him to make everything okay tomorrow. Then he fell asleep, and not long after, so did I. I slept heavily, deeply, cocooned by my own body heat from the coming storm.'

10

'At six the next morning came "Celebration" pounding over the public address system, the reveille of the asylum. We were all to assemble for a series of stretches and exercises which included a one and a half mile time trial.'

'Running?'

'Running or jogging, whatever we were capable of, but Brabet was going to time it. People didn't know what to expect. It was still cold at six-thirty and barely light. Most of the group were standing around looking half asleep, bewildered, some still a little embarrassed from the last session of the previous evening. Pamela looked a little crazed. You know what I mean? She had an almost psychotic cheerfulness to her, greeting everyone like we all went way, way back, like we'd all graduated high school together and then served side by side in the trenches. She had snapped. You could see it in her eyes. At six-thirty in the morning she had her little pocket-sized camera with her and was taking shots of all of us. She kept this up all day. She was finished.

'Joe showed no signs of being hungover. In fact, he was buoyed by the night's conquests, which he saw as twofold: Helen, of course, and his mobile phone which, before we left our cabin, he tossed from one hand to the other, hamming up Brabet's juggling lesson. He patted me on the back as we closed the door and made our way to meet the others.

'"Sorry I kept you up, Mitch, but all you're going to remember when this day is over is that I'm the guy who got the phone back, got hold of Sheere and made him fall in love with Health National all over again."

'He probably believed that. I didn't say anything. But I have to confess that when it came time to run the mile and a half I found myself trying a lot harder than I would have expected. I used to run a lot at school.'

'What do you mean, you tried harder?'

'I wanted to beat Joe. He worked out and, although I didn't, I was determined to beat him, or at least try to.'

'Did you beat him?'

'No. Not a chance. He was fit. He stayed with me for a while, more or less jogging, telling me how he had it all worked out, how he couldn't call too early, it being a Sunday morning. Then he sped off. By the time I got back to the start he had Helen hanging around him so we were not able to talk even had I wanted to. I tried to keep away from him as much as I could through the morning but at the start of the noon session he sidled up to me, looking pretty pleased with himself, and told me that he'd spoken to Mrs Sheere, who loved him, would do anything for him, and she had promised to have her husband call him back within half an hour. I was saved having to answer by Terry Brabet clapping his hands together, seal-like, to get everybody's attention for the next exercise.

'He had us all outside again for what he called a "trust" exercise. He tended to volunteer some pseudo social-scientific mumbo-jumbo before every session. He wasn't capable of telling you to go for a run without first delivering a vacuous homily or reminding you who *he* was, "a personal consultant with a background in attitude change". Really, that's how he styled himself. The "trust" exercise, as he called it, was meant to demonstrate that, whatever the undertaking, if you had a united team backing you up, you had nothing to fear. Something trite like that. Something that people want to believe. And that isn't true.

'There was a flagpole on the lawn outside the dining area. Brabet had arranged to have a vertically positioned extension ladder attached to it. The top of the ladder was about twelve or thirteen feet off the ground. We were to take it in turns to climb up the ladder. Everybody had to take a turn at being what Brabet called "the climber", and stand at the top facing the flagpole. The distance between the rung you were meant to put your feet on and the ground was about ten feet.

'I was not the first climber. I was probably about the tenth. I might have been the last of the men. There were different signals you were meant to give at different stages of the exercise, in a sort of "Lord of the Flies" ritual. "Climber ascending" you were meant to call out as you went up the ladder. When you got to the highest or second highest rung you were meant to grab hold of a rope that was tied to the top of the flagpole. Grabbing hold of the rope was a signal to the rest of the group below, whom Brabet had told to stand in two parallel lines facing the ladder. When they saw the climber take hold of the rope they were to signal by calling "catchers ready".

'When you heard their call, when your fear had been overwhelmed by a desire to get the whole thing over with, to show that you're as much a man as anyone else there, when your anger at the people beneath you, at the world, and at the near certainty of your imminent unemployment had become the dominant reason for your shaking, when you had jettisoned even the most rudimentary laws of physics from your memory, you were to call out "climber falling", let go of the rope and fall backwards through the air onto a sea of hands and arms, heterogenous in height, musculature, rigidity and owner concentration.

'"Climber falling," I called, just as I had been told to.

'Brabet was wrong about it being an exercise in trust. It was an exercise in a man's capacity to clear his mind, even if only momentarily, of all reason and judgment. And since people have been doing this every day since we could walk upright—when we drink and drive, when we choose our jobs, when we go to war, when we marry—it didn't need to be proved. We are the living proof. I am. It wasn't that I trusted Joe Geraghty so very much. I just had not expected that he would be fumbling for his mobile phone as I was falling. What are the chances of that? What are the chances, Alex? An educated man would put his money on it *not* happening.'

'Dennis—?'

'Shut up, Alex. Of course I'm crying. You should hear me in the middle of the night. I howl like an infant. And no one comes in; no one turns the light on to see if I'm alright. Because I'm not alright. That's the reason I started calling her. That's the real reason, if you want to know the truth of it.'

'Dennis, I've told you, I don't care—'

'You don't care about the truth?'

'Yes, of course I care about whatever you say is the—'

'Then shut up and let me finish. I haven't yet. This is what it was all for, Alex. Can't you see that? Wasting my time training to be unemployable as a physicist, getting a job with the biggest game in town, climbing one corporate ladder after another, conniving with people like Sid Graeme and Joe Geraghty, it was all so that I could climb that last ladder, let go and fall backwards. My father never had to do that for a living.'

'You said he was a painter. He would have had to climb ladders in his work.'

'Yes, but nobody wanted him to fall, nobody instructed him to fall backwards. There was no missive from head office ordering him to commit suicide. His eyes, the eyes I inherited, were never inflamed and swollen, like mine are now, from months of spontaneous crying. He didn't earn very much, never had a bumper year. He used to get a little hamper at Christmas from the company, ham, mince pies, mostly tinsel. We thought how lucky we were when he brought it home. How lucky he was to be able to look anyone in the eye, anyone at all.'

'Looking people in the eye, why can't you look people in the eye? I don't understand, Dennis. Are you talking about morality?'

'I can talk about morality if you want. I never could but I can now. In the course of my job I used to have drinks, lunch or dinner regularly with people, usually men, who said things, who threw away lines that would have had average people outside the industry gasping with disbelief. I courted them. One guy—he worked in Emerging Markets—'

'What does that mean?'

'Investments in the Third World. He used to say that the best time to buy was when there was blood in the streets. That way you could get everything for half price. He used to tell me all about his trips to Thailand, Indonesia, Brazil, South Africa. He would fly in, get picked up at the airport in a bullet-proof limousine, get escorted through the streets by members of a private militia so that he could inspect one or other natural resource. He'd be talking on his satellite phone to Sydney, London, New York, Singapore, all within the space of a car ride that took him past row after row of tin shanties, open sewers and muddy children who, he said, stared at the car the way rabbits stare in the night at the beaming light of a torch. Occasionally, the dirt road might be blocked by an angry crowd demonstrating against this or that. The car would slow and before he had a chance to enquire about what they wanted, two or three of the closest would be shot by the militia. Then the rest of them would disperse and his car would pick up speed to make up the time. "Only two or three," he explained. "I didn't tell them to shoot," he said.

'On his way back he would pick up a couple of children and take them with him to his hotel. He would tell me all this the way people might tell you how they managed to get upgraded on a flight somewhere or how they got away with parking in a loading zone while they collected tickets for a show. I had lunch with this man regularly.

We used each other. Once, while we were eating lunch, he saw a destitute old man through the window of the restaurant. He said, "Look at that guy wandering around like that. They should take them all and slap great big advertising boards on them so that they'd be doing something useful as they shuffle around. It'd be a win/win move." My father would never have met anyone who talked like that.'

'Your father didn't have your aspirations.'

'My father didn't need them.'

'A certain amount of ambition is healthy.'

'Healthy! Look at me, for Christ's sake! Haven't you heard a word I've said?'

'Yes, I have, but I'm not clear who you're blaming for your present condition. Is it people like this lunch companion from Emerging Markets, Sid Graeme, Gorman, the managing director? Is it your wife, Terry Brabet—?'

'Don't leave anyone out, Doc.'

'Joe Geraghty, of course. Is that who you mean?'

'Now you're talking. What's-her-name, Pamela, took snaps and Helen stood in for her as a catcher. She photographed the fall and you can see him. She gave me a copy. I can barely look at it. He's the one, Alex.'

'I have one other scapegoat to put to you. You blame yourself, don't you? . . . Dennis? You think that what's happened to you is punishment for supping with the devil, don't you? . . . Dennis? Tell me what happened after you let go of the rope.'

11

'I fell backwards onto many different levels of hands. There were meant to be nineteen people standing there waiting for me, nine on my left, nine on my right and one in the middle to catch my head, thirty-eight outstretched arms with their palms facing up. But Joe Geraghty, in all likelihood the strongest person there, was distracted. Had he been responsible for catching my head, I might be dead already instead of just . . . wishing . . .'

'Instead of just wishing you were dead?'

'It was strange because at first I didn't feel . . . I wasn't in absolute agony or anything. I felt like I'd been punched in the back, like I'd received a huge punch square in the middle of my back from a heavyweight. I mentioned how it felt to Pamela and I remember she told me to tell Brabet, perhaps he could help and, slightly dazed, I did. He didn't say anything. By then he was ushering us on to the next exercise, another one involving ropes.'

'So you thought you might be hurt, but you continued anyway?'

'Well, I was a little spaced-out. The immediate pain of the impact was diminishing and I just thought . . . Everyone had seen what had happened to me and no one was acting like it was any big deal. They'd all done it by the end, even the most timid of them, and they all seemed alright. As I said, the immediate pain was diminishing. I suppose I was sort of in shock and I just followed everyone else to the next exercise.

'By suspending five feet of rope four feet off the ground, Brabet had demarcated an area which he called "jail". He divided us into two groups of ten and it was the task, in turn, of each group to get all of its members out of jail without going under the rope or even touching it. By the time it was my group's turn my leg was starting to stiffen up.'

'Dennis, I'm sorry, I have to interrupt you there. You said that at the moment that you were falling in the previous exercise, Joe Geraghty was playing with his phone. I think you said "fumbling". Was he taking the call? Was he talking to Donald Sheere?'

'No. That's what I thought too, but when I asked him afterwards what the hell he was doing with the phone he said he'd just turned it off to stop it from ringing while I was jumping. So that he would be there for me. Alex, he's full of shit. He'll say anything to avoid responsibility.'

'But you would have heard the ring.'

'Maybe. Maybe not. My head was fifteen feet off the ground and I was about to fall backwards. Maybe I did hear it and have forgotten.'

'Forgotten hearing it?'

'Sure, why not? After what happened to me.'

'But, Dennis, someone would have heard it. Brabet would have heard it and confiscated it. He would have rebuked Joe Geraghty, held up proceedings to make an example of him and to maybe find out how Joe got his phone back. You don't remember him doing any of that?'

'I'd just fallen backwards more than thirteen feet.'

'But you weren't concussed and you didn't then know the extent of your injuries.'

'Yeah, so?'

'So you would have been aware of any fuss being made if Joe had been caught with his phone. Since you don't remember that, it probably didn't happen. Joe might have been telling the truth. Perhaps he did turn the phone off in order to be there to catch you. Especially if Sheere didn't call him back—'

'Alex, he did. Sheere did call. I don't know exactly when. Maybe it wasn't then but it doesn't matter. The phone isn't important anymore. Joe couldn't talk Sheere around. I knew and even he knew he wasn't going to manage it. Sheere had nothing to lose by selling. By the time Joe told me about the call I was in agony. I didn't care anymore. I was packing to leave a day early, but it was all over.

'My leg had got increasingly sore. I thought it was a hamstring. I was limping around the cabin when he tried to tell me what Sheere had said. I didn't care anymore. I was furious with him. I was in agony and it was his fault and all he cared about was his job. I was swearing at him and he was telling me to rest the leg, to take a painkiller, telling me that we had to keep our heads. We had to keep cool if we were going to think of a way out of the mess. He's an unbelievable idiot.

'I drove home feeling every bump in the road, every loose twig, every atom of dislodged gravel. When I got home it was already early evening and I could barely get out of the car. I couldn't walk properly. I had to hobble, wincing, sweating, swearing through gritted teeth. I called a feeble collective "hello" to my family who must have been surprised to see me home so early, and headed slowly straight up to bed. Patricia came upstairs, curious about my unannounced and premature homecoming. The last time that had happened it had really inconvenienced her. This time, however, there was nothing to suggest any infidelity, although in my condition I would have missed the telltale signs she had taught me to notice. I would have missed a lover on the other side of the bed.

'She came upstairs and looked in on me dubiously, as if whatever it was that was going on with me, it wasn't going to be good for her. When I had finished telling her what had happened she put her hands on her hips and said that I was too old to be running around when I should have been working. I'd had a week off and now I'd come home, gone straight to bed and was looking for sympathy. She hadn't had any time off and she'd had "child care responsibilities", as she called it. It hadn't been a week. It had only been three days. And it hadn't been "off". She berated me with all the invective her vocabulary permitted. As she walked out of the room I muttered that very soon I would be losing my job. She didn't seem to hear.

'The pain was unrelenting. Unable to go to sleep, I just lay there in an immobile nervous sweat. At around one in the morning I limped to the shower. The heat felt good. But drying myself was difficult and by the time I had made it back to bed the palliative effect of the hot water had almost disappeared. I told Patricia I was worried. She had her back to me and didn't say anything but I know she was awake.

'"I'm in a bad way. I don't know what's wrong. I think I should go to the hospital."

'"Okay," she said. She didn't move.

'I slipped some clothes on. I couldn't put much weight on my leg so everything was done incredibly slowly and, despite the cold, I was sweating again by the time I made it to the car. The streets were quiet but not everybody was asleep. When I got to the Emergency Room it seemed most of the city was there as well. I was told there was a queue and I wouldn't be reached for five to six hours. I drove home and, having made it in the dark to the living room, stood there leaning against the wall over the ducted heating vent. It was then that I began this . . . crying, that I seem to . . .

'At eight-thirty the next morning I drove to the local GP and told him what had happened and that I thought I'd torn a hamstring. He examined me somewhat perfunctorily and said he thought the problem was with my back, not my hamstring. He referred me to a physiotherapist down the road who, the GP assured me after phoning him, would see me immediately.

'Now, Alex, you have to bear in mind how much it hurt just to get to the door of the GP's room, let alone down the steps of his building to the car. By this time the pain was constant. The physiotherapist watched the way I walked towards him and told me he wouldn't touch me without first seeing an x-ray. He thought my injury might be serious. I went somewhere else to be x-rayed and eventually I was diagnosed with fractures of the lower vertebrae, L4, L5 and S1 to be precise. In addition, I had a prolapsed disc which was strangling a nerve to my left leg. I didn't spend another night in my bed for three months. When I wasn't in hospital, I slept downstairs in the living room bent over a coffee table.

'The pain took control of my life. There were red-hot daggers piercing my back. I didn't eat or sleep for the four days that elapsed before I was given a shot of pethidine and admitted to hospital. The pain was so unbearable during those four days that the only thing that stopped me ending it then and there was my very incapacity. I was too physically incapacitated to do it. I don't think, in fact I'm quite sure, you don't understand the kind of pain I was in. The muscles where the calf attached to the shin were being pulled off the bone. They never extended. They were constantly contracting.

'The GP I'd first seen was on holiday for the next few days. The only other one we knew was the one Patricia had serviced all those years before when she was pregnant, and he didn't make house calls, at least not to us. I couldn't get into hospital because I wasn't deemed an emergency and there was a shortage of beds. By the time the first GP came back and drove out to see me with the pethidine, *I* would have gone down on him. He managed to get me admitted to hospital. I was there for eight days. The plan was to allow the prolapse to correct itself. I would have agreed to anything for the pethidine.

'In those first few days before I was admitted I touched hell. I remember lying face down over the coffee table in the middle of the afternoon crying. The rest of the house was empty and the phone kept ringing. The answering machine picked it up each time. It was Gorman's secretary. She was polite the first time but subsequent calls indicated she'd absorbed her boss's wrath. Gorman would have been furious with me. On Sheere's instructions, Joe would have got rid of the Health National shares and, in doing so, committed career suicide because the firm, as the underwriter, would have to bear the loss of the consequent undersubscription. Gorman would not have been content with just Joe's scalp, which I later learned he had within the week. No, Gorman would have wanted to drag me over the coals before having me walked out. My absence at that time would have looked deliberate, maybe wilful, and his secretary would, not least through his mood and his tone, be implicitly blamed for also being derelict in her duties, one of which on this occasion would have been to find me. So as the hours and then the days wore on and Human Resources were also put onto the case, Gorman's secretary would have grown to hate me. She could smell blood and it came across in the increasingly strident messages she left on the answering machine.

'I heard them only as a special effect in the soundtrack of the delirium I was living through. When Patricia heard them the first day she added to their censure by informing me that I was failing her as well. Sometime later, scared that I could lose my job for not getting back to them, she took it upon herself to tell them what had happened to me. By then I was in hospital.

'On the eighth day there, I was put in a huge back brace, given one last shot of pethidine and sent home. Within forty-eight hours the pain had returned, more vicious than before. I saw a neurosurgeon, who recommended surgery, but by then, because it was a work-related injury, it was out of the hands of my health insurer. Surgery had to have Work Cover approval. It took Work Cover six weeks to examine me, interview other people on the course, and finalise their paperwork. In those six weeks, I spent my days and nights draped over the coffee table living from one six-hourly dose of painkillers to the next. Patricia was furious with me, as though I had injured myself to spite her. She stopped preparing my food. "There is food in the kitchen. Get it yourself." Fortunately my appetite could not even remotely rival the pain. Occasionally, the local GP would come over and give me a shot of morphine.

'The surgery lasted seven hours, during which time they put a specially constructed metal cage, connected to the pelvis by rods, around the bottom three vertebrae. They took bone from my hips and grafted it onto the eleven fractures in my spine. I came out of the anaesthetic to find a tangle of tubes sticking out of me. I wasn't allowed to eat for ten days. The night before the surgery, I'd been told that there was a ten per cent chance I wouldn't be able to walk again after the operation, a thirty per cent chance I'd have the same level of pain as before the operation and a seventy per cent chance that I'd have the pain reduced. Who could resist those odds? Right, Alex?

'For those first ten days after the surgery I wasn't in any pain because of the regular doses of morphine and, even though I had to wait to know the result of the operation, it was incredibly, unimaginably liberating to be so free of pain. The anxiety I had for my future registered, as you might say, almost purely cognitively, which is to say, I didn't *feel* anxious. The only food I took by mouth was the occasional ice-block, and that had to be held to my lips. Everything else I took by intravenous drip. They wouldn't let me eat until my bowel had reactivated after the surgery.

'My first four attempts at walking were unsuccessful. Not only did I have no control over my left leg but, having been on my back for so long, I was overwhelmed by dizziness when I tried. It was at this time that I began having the intensive physiotherapy I'm still having. The hospital staff were very encouraging. The idea was to try to stimulate the muscles through massage, lifting the leg, bending the knee, rotating the foot, moving the entirety of the leg. But I was getting muscle spasms in it. Every part of me wanted to go to sleep except my left leg, which just kept dancing and no one could tell me when it would stop. I had lost fifty-seven pounds. I was in there for four weeks and it wasn't until the last three or four days that I realised I was going to be able to walk. That's when they took me off the morphine.'

'Did anyone visit you?'

'My parents came down from Mildura. Patricia brought James in once a week, Sundays, I think it was.

12

'Only towards the end of my stay in hospital was I able to get out of bed to walk to the toilet. I was in the neuro ward sharing a room with three other patients, all men. On my second day of walking to the toilet I was slowly pulling up my pants around my shaky leg when one of the other three, who'd had his head shaved and stapled all the way around, burst in on me. He grabbed me and accused me of having sex with his wife right then and there in the toilet. Then he thought I was her. He lifted his gown and tried to mount me. I pushed him away as best I could and it made him angry. He took a swing at me and I just managed to duck. I had to hold on to him to keep him from hitting me and to keep from falling. He was still hard. I could feel him against me. I was in agony from the movement. The whole time I was calling out for a nurse. One of the other patients in the room pressed the buzzer and two nurses came and got him off me.

'He did eventually recover enough to be remorseful about it. His wife must have heard about it because she was embarrassed too. It turns out they lived in Mildura. When visiting my parents recently I looked him up. He's on the dole now and living in a flat on his own. His wife has gone. He's lost everything. Used to be a teacher.'

'Did anyone else visit you?'

'Yes, there was a day not long after the surgery when I was visited by some of the people who had been on the retreat with me. Pamela was one of them. That's when she gave me these photographs, the ones she'd taken, including the one of my fall.'

'Are these the photos?'

'Yes. You can look at them if you like. I can't bear to. They even managed to drag Terry Brabet along. Can you believe that? Stoned as I was at the time, I couldn't believe it. He wouldn't actually come into the room, just stood at the doorway, raised his right hand in the air and tentatively said "hi". I should have said, "Look how far I've gone beyond my comfort zone!" Then he slunk off somewhere. Couldn't look at me for too long.'

'Did Joe Geraghty come?'

'He did, but not with them. He did and this I remember well. He came at night when no one was meant to be there. It was after visiting hours. The other three were asleep and, since I was always half asleep anyway, at first I thought I might be dreaming or hallucinating. He pulled up a chair so that he was sitting right next to me. When he leaned forward he was level with my head and I could smell his breath, heavy with alcohol. I pretended to be asleep but that didn't stop his whispering.

'"Mitch. Mitch, can you hear me? It's me. It's Joe . . . You poor bastard. What the hell has happened to you? I don't know if you can hear me . . . Mitch? I'm finished. Gorman had me 'walked out'. Sheere won't return my calls. I wish you were awake . . . I've got a lot of free time now, Mitch. My wife . . ."

'Alex, he was practically crying. I couldn't believe it. He had the audacity to creep into my hospital room half drunk and cry for himself, after all that had happened, after everything he'd done.'

'Dennis, when was the last time you looked at these photos?'

'I don't know. Pamela gave them to me in hospital. I looked at them then. I don't think I've looked at them since.'

'That was the last time you looked at this photo, the one of you falling?'

'Yes, I think so.'

'Have a look at it now.'

'No.'

'I think you should.'

'No.'

'I think you should.'

'Fuck you. Why should I? I know what happened.'

'You know the *consequences* of what happened.'

'For Christ's sake, Alex. What are you saying now?'

'Dennis, you told me earlier that Brabet said that for each "climber" there was meant to be nine people waiting on the left, nine on the right and one to catch the head.'

'Yeah. So?'

'Have a look at the photo.'

'No.'

'Have a look. There are nine on the left, nine on the right and there's the one to catch your head. Is that Joe Geraghty on the left?'

'Fuck you!'

'That's him, isn't it? His hands aren't in his pockets. He's not playing with a phone. His hands are waiting to catch. He was doing what he was told, wasn't he?'

'What sort of bullshit is this?'

'What I'm saying is that everyone did as they were told, including you. Joe was there to catch you. He let you down only to the same extent you yourself did. You're a physicist, Dennis. You should have known better than anyone that the whole exercise was flawed in its design, that it was inherently dangerous. Even with everyone doing as they were told, it was incredibly likely someone was going to get hurt.

'Look at the outstretched arms, Dennis. Look at them waiting to catch you, all at different heights, different degrees of rigidity. You are a man five foot ten inches tall weighing about one hundred and sixty pounds and you voluntarily fell backwards from an average height of thirteen feet just because a man whom you had already deemed to be a charlatan had told you to and because everybody else had done it. Just one or two arms giving way would have been enough. No wonder it felt like you'd been punched in the back. You don't need a PhD in physics to know how dangerous that was, but you had one and you did it anyway. Go ahead and cry—'

'Shut up! Shut the fuck up!'

'Swear at me, Dennis. Blame Joe Geraghty—'

'I rattle when I move. It feels like there's a fucking Meccano set in my back.'

'I can imagine how you feel.'

'If it weren't for three sessions of physiotherapy a week I wouldn't be able to walk at all. Do you know how many attempts it takes to get my legs into pants? I have a method for putting my socks on. I throw the sock on the ground and with my right toe pinning the sock to the floor, I basically grab hold of my left leg and push it into the sock. I had a rehabilitation specialist come to my house to teach me how to put my socks on but she's not there when I fall over. They're the worst times, especially when I'm alone. That's when I scream. That's when I throw things. I have a lot of falls. I'm lucky to get through a day without a fall and once I'm on the ground it's very difficult to get up unless there's something to hold on to. I fall over more now than I did when I was a toddler—'

'Go on, Dennis, see if you can make *me* cry.'

'You see, I'll be walking and my dropped foot catches on the ground. If I don't lift my left foot high enough then my toes drag along the ground. I have fallen down in public. That's when it's really embarrassing. Once my arm got rammed into my shoulder at the joint and ended up frozen that way.'

'It's terrible, and it's all everyone else's fault, isn't it, Dennis?'

'You're sick, Alex. You're a very sick man to do this.'

'It's Terry Brabet's fault, Joe Geraghty's fault. Listen to yourself, Dennis. You're not responsible for anything. You're lucky all this happened to you before managed care came in and limited your rehabilitation—'

'So that's what this is about, you miserable sick fuck. You should be struck off.'

'But I know my physics, don't I? Keep going, Dennis. I'm still not crying.'

'Is this how you shrinks get your kicks?'

'Come on, Dennis, you can do better than that. What about your wife, Patricia? You haven't mentioned her for a while.'

'She got tired of taking me to the physiotherapist. Said it was inconvenient. She refused. She was bitter about the whole thing. She said she felt cheated, robbed. It was getting worse, all this anger growing inside her, until one day . . . she just . . .'

'What?'

'Our son was ill. She'd had to pick him up from school early and just as they'd pulled up in the driveway, he'd vomited in the car. I was slumped over the coffee table in the living room. I heard her scream as she opened the car door. She stormed in the front door calling for the cleaning lady, who had been to clean that day but had already left. I suppose Patricia had wanted her to clean the upholstery in the car. I don't know. But after calling her name a few times she must have realised that the woman had gone. She saw that the vacuum cleaner had been left in the living room, that it hadn't been put away, and then she saw me lying there, as usual, looking up at her. She started telling me how James, "my son", was sitting in the car in his own vomit. She was beside herself with fury. It was as though she didn't know whether to shout or cry. Then she started on me.

'"If you think I'm going to be the wife of an invalid for the rest of my life, you've got another think coming. I had a real man once but, like an idiot, I came back to you. You're not a man. You're just . . . a useless cripple."

'She was shouting and she was . . . she was flailing at my face, hitting me, with the end of the vacuum cleaner. I was on the floor, covering my face with my arms, trying to get to the wall so I could pull myself up. And then I turned and looked back at her, back towards the door. I saw that James was standing there. He was standing behind her in his vomit-stained shirt. He had seen her hitting me. He had seen the whole thing. I called out to him. I just . . . called his name, and . . . he vomited again, just where he stood. That's more or less how my marriage ended.

'That wasn't the only time James had heard her call me a cripple. It wasn't even the first time he'd seen her hit me. I shudder to think what he's going to remember. Is he . . . Alex, do you think he'll remember this?'

'Dennis, what do you remember of your childhood? He'll remember. Where is he now?'

'He's with Patricia. She said unless I let her take him with her to Germany, she's going to hang me out to dry. She said she'd keep me in court till all the money had gone.'

'The money?'

'She means the house and whatever I get from the firm.'

'Are you suing them?'

'Yes, of course. That's the only reason they haven't got rid of me. They got rid of Joe Geraghty within a week but they don't want me to add a "wrongful dismissal" or some accusation of discrimination to my case against them so they've kept me on. They're hoping I'll just quit. They're doing everything in their power to make me quit.'

'What are they doing?'

'Everything. They've demoted me. I'm not working as an analyst. The head of Human Resources has an assistant. I assist that person.'

'The assistant?'

'I assist the assistant. When I was ready to try to come back to work Gorman told me that I could take off all the time I needed during the day for rehabilitation, physiotherapy, occupational therapy, whatever. Of course, he said, with me missing all that time I clearly could no longer work as an analyst. But I wasn't to worry, they would find something "appropriate" for me. "Appropriate" meant sixty per cent of my previous salary. They moved me into a cubicle in an open-plan office where not only did I not have any privacy, I didn't have any room. You see, I'm meant to divide every hour into twenty minutes of sitting, twenty minutes of standing and twenty minutes of lying down. When I complained about this to the head of HR, he told me to stop feeling sorry for myself.

'People walk past me. They try not to look but I catch them looking at me sometimes. They're embarrassed. They're embarrassed by the whole thing. Some of them have been interviewed about me by the firm's lawyers. But then, I'm suing the firm. You know, they're still doing it.'

'What are they still doing, Dennis?'

'They're still sending people on retreats. Since I was injured they've had two people hospitalised—one with a heart attack and one who collapsed from exhaustion. I don't really have any work to do there but they won't get rid of me until the case is over.'

'It must be unpleasant for you, the reduced circumstances, the lack of work. Why do you go in there?'

'Why do you think! I need the money. Did you think I needed the humiliation?'

'What part of what has happened to you humiliates you?'

'Only a psychiatrist could listen to everything I've been saying and ask a question like that. It's a vocation; there's no question about it. You sit there, session after session, writing notes in your book. Jesus Christ!'

13

'A day or so after James had vomited in the doorway of the living room, Patricia outdid herself. I told you she had found it inconvenient driving me to and from medical appointments.'

'Yes.'

'Well, I had to find a way of getting to them. There was no way I could drive myself at the time. Even now, though I can and do drive, I still prefer not to. I'm still fighting the pain. Sometimes it's worse than other times and I don't always feel confident behind the wheel. At first I caught cabs to and from but, given the number of appointments—medical, legal, physiotherapy, hydrotherapy, pain control—'

'And now here.'

'Sure, but I'm going back a bit.'

'Sorry.'

'Well, I was eating up my money in cab fares and needed some help.'

'With money?'

'No, not money. Alex, will you shut up? Will you just listen! I needed some help with transport. There was a couple who lived a few doors down from us with a son about the same age as ours. They'd seen my situation and had been very sympathetic. The wife offered to drive me to my appointments. It started as an offer to fill in for Patricia but gradually she took over from her. The woman worked in sales, said she was on the road anyway and could schedule her appointments to fit around me. It was incredibly good of her.

'Anyway, a couple of days after . . . that fight . . . Patricia came home and told me that for the last five or six months she'd been having an affair with that woman's husband. But she said that the relationship was over. They'd had a fight and she didn't want us to see them anymore. And, Alex—get this—to consummate its ending she told the neighbour's wife about it and about other relationships he had apparently told Patricia about. That was the day she ended *their* marriage. That was also the day she told me about all the other men she'd played around with.'

'How did you feel?'

'I was hurt when she left me years ago but after that . . . quite frankly, I knew what she was. It was just a question of how many times and in what particular way she was going to confirm it. In any case, what she did or said couldn't begin to compete with the physical pain that had taken over my life. As I sit here and hear myself tell you about her, I have the luxury of being horrified by the Patricia I'm describing, but the only way she can really get to me now is through my son. And also, I suppose, by tying me up in court. Look, we hadn't slept even side by side for months. We hadn't actually had sex since . . . I don't know when we last slept together. Until I went into the pain management clinic I wouldn't have cared if I'd never touched another woman again.'

'What happened in the pain management clinic?'

'They did more tests and $25 000 later I was fitted with a dorsal column stimulator. They inserted a wire to run down my spine with electrodes attached at regular intervals. The other end runs down to a device implanted near the hip. It's battery operated. When I switch it on, it sends electrical impulses into the spinal cord and masks the pain. They don't want me to use it too much but, I swear, I couldn't have made it this far without it. I wouldn't have made it here quite literally, because I wouldn't have met Angelique.'

'You mean you wouldn't have been thinking about sex?'

'That's right. But since it was installed . . . Patricia had left, and I thought there's got to be some advantage to all this.'

'So you phoned for a prostitute?'

'You know I did. You don't have to put it that way. It wasn't ever like phoning for a pizza. My wife had abandoned me. Suddenly I was pain-free, at least at times. So yes, after everything that had happened, I called up the place Joe Geraghty had once taken me to and Angelique was the one they sent me. I was overwhelmed by what I saw when I answered the door. She didn't seem to be too repelled either because within minutes she was naked on top of me upstairs in the very bed my wife had had all her affairs in. Picture it, Alex. There she was, so young and sexy and alone with me in the quiet of my house, naked and all mine. Can you picture it, Alex? She smiled in that way of hers where there's nothing but sex in her eyes. You know how she can look, Alex.'

'I thought you said you hadn't slept with her.'

'I thought you said you didn't care?'

'You don't need to tell me anything you don't want to but you shouldn't lie to me. You're only hurting yourself if you do. Whatever you tell me ought to be the truth. You're only interfering with the treatment otherwise.'

'Just give me the pills and I'll go. You can stick the rest of what you call "treatment" up your arse!'

'You didn't sleep with her, did you, Dennis?'

'Look how interested you are!'

'You brought it up, initially telling me you didn't, now you say you did.'

'You can believe what you want to believe.'

'Dennis, I don't have an interest in choosing a version of your life. I'm more interested in why you want to lie to me about this.'

'What makes you think I'm lying? Well? Now, *you* don't want to answer, do you, Alex? You just don't like the idea of me sleeping with her, do you? Admit it, you'll feel better.'

'That's not really . . . Dennis . . . Dennis?'

'What?'

'Why do you think you're crying? . . . Why do you think you're crying now?'

'Did she say something? What did she say? You've spoken to her? Is she alright? She won't return my calls. I leave messages. Alex . . . Everything I touch turns to shit.'

14

'I was nervous even looking up the number in the telephone book. I got in the shower as soon as I put the phone down. I was pretty nervous. It felt like a kid getting ready for a date.'

'But you'd done this before, hadn't you?'

'Why is that so important to you?'

'It's not, but I want to get everything straight so that—'

'Once. I'd done it once and that was years before. Joe Geraghty had taken me to that brothel, the one she worked out of. I didn't even pay and it wasn't like . . . having someone come out to your home. Maybe that's why I was nervous. For a time after I was dry I just sat on my bed in my underwear. I didn't know what to wear. I didn't know what to say when she got there, whether to have some music playing, whether to offer her a drink. I didn't have anything in the house. Patricia had always bought the booze. It occurred to me how much better at this she would have been than me, although, as far as I know, she'd never had to pay anyone for it.

'I wondered what would be waiting for me when the doorbell rang. What would she look like? What would she think of me, that is, before I spoiled it completely by undressing? Alex, I didn't feel I was any kind of man anymore. Each day when I get out of the shower now I try not to catch sight of myself in the mirror, of my buttocks and all the scars and the angles I make when I try to negotiate space. I squint at the mirror. I've caught myself squinting so many times that I don't try to hide the squint anymore, only myself from myself.

'I put on a loose-fitting shirt and a pair of casual pants thinking she, whoever she was going to be, would have to have seen worse than me, even me after the accident. Then I went downstairs and waited. My palms were moist. I would have paced but . . . well, you know. It's not practical is it? The doorbell rang. I made my way to the door and opened it. She was delightful. She was . . . well, of course, you know.

'I introduced myself and when she told me her name was Angelique, I made some facile star-struck remark about angels or something completely wet, befitting a shy teenage boy trying to differentiate himself from the pack. As much as I recognised that she had a beauty quite beyond that of even the prettiest tawdry working girl I could have hoped for, you have to believe me, lust was not my primary urge, not then. It was just good to be with, to be in such close proximity with, someone so lovely. That's when she said she had to ask me for the money.

'I offered her a drink and had started to pour it when she changed her mind. On second thought, she wouldn't have one. I must have turned around to face her a little more quickly than she had expected because I caught her face before she'd had a chance to change her expression . . .'

'It's alright, Dennis. Take your time . . . What did you see?'

'For a moment, a brief moment, I was on my way. I was getting a drink for a lovely young woman. I was on my way to fixing her a drink, Alex, and I had forgotten what that felt like, the anticipation, not sexual, or hardly, but that sense of being alive that comes with being in the glow or aura of a woman's beauty. You can almost touch the possibilities even if you can't name them. You can't articulate them because they're subliminal, almost primal. It is risible to even try. If your mind let loose the words, even unsaid, to enumerate what you might have within your ken: sex, yes of course, but also someone charming to talk to, to look at, to touch, to care for, to breathe in, to fill the emptiness, to give you back a sense of yourself; if your mind is given the chance to form the words for any of this then the words will no sooner take shape than they will mock you. You had better just feel it, keep it at the emotional end of your continuum.

'Well, I felt it. I was humming with it until I turned around too soon to find her pretending that she was not shocked. You see, she had just then noticed the drag of my left leg and her face said, "Oh no, I've got another gimp."'

'A "gimp"?'

'A cripple, a spastic, an aberration, something that was going to be abhorrent to her. It was the first time I had ever seen a woman direct that look at me, that mix of pity and revulsion.'

'I am sure you are exaggerating.'

'You mean I'm being self-indulgent.'

'Maybe that too, but that's not what I meant.'

'Alex, I saw how she looked at me. She's not a nurse. She's not meant to expect this . . . sort of thing.'

'Did she say something about it?'

'She didn't have to. She's a professional and she had a job to do. She asked me to take her to the bedroom. I let her walk ahead of me on the stairs, not so much in order to be able to look at her but more to minimise the time she had to look at me. Especially me walking up the stairs. When we reached the bedroom she suddenly needed the bathroom. It was very sudden. She rushed away and it occurred to me that perhaps the prospect of imminent intimacy with me was actually going to make her sick. So I listened to the sounds she made and it wasn't that. She didn't throw up, thank God.

'When she returned she'd regained her composure and offered me a massage. She told me to undress and to lie face down on the bed. I didn't say anything. I just did as she instructed. I knew this was the whole idea but I was still uneasy about her seeing me naked.

I guess being face down and not having to do anything to her was a good way to ease myself into it. She must have known that. When I buried my head as deeply into the pillow as I could, I felt the cool of her fingers tracing lines on my back. No one had touched me like that in years and, involuntarily, my eyes misted. I exhaled as though I'd been holding my breath for longer than I could remember.

'"Why don't you turn around?" she said after a while, almost in a whisper. When I did I saw that she was naked. I must have stared like a teenage boy who had never seen a naked woman before because she smiled at whatever my face was doing. Alex, I did stare. I know I did. She was sitting on top of the bed leaning back on her arms with her feet just touching my legs. Though I could see everything my eyes were drawn to her inner thighs, to the gate of shaved hair, and to the folds of pink beneath that I thought I would never see on any woman again. And the truth is, Alex, I won't ever see it again without paying.'

15

'I must have stared like a teenage boy and when she took one of my hands in hers and gently placed it on her inside leg and put her other hand on my inner thigh, I was gone, finished, spent, just like a teenage boy. I felt smaller than that and I apologised. She smiled, grabbed a tissue from the bedside table and cleaned up after me . . . like she was a nurse and I was a child.

'"I'm so very sorry. I'm very embarrassed . . . to have called up and dragged you all the way out here and then . . ." I stumbled.

'"No, really. There's nothing to be sorry about," she told me.

'"This must be . . . I must be the most pathetic . . . This is probably the saddest thing you've ever seen."

'"No, of course it isn't."

'"I mean, the saddest thing you've ever seen in your line of work."

'"No, you're still wrong."

'"You're very kind."

'"I'm not being kind, really. Dennis . . . It's Dennis, right?"

'"Yes. It's Dennis," I said.

'"I mean, I get the impression that you might be *feeling* sad, you know . . . inside . . . but really . . . from my point of view you're a guy who has some leg and back problems and you came too fast for your own good. That's just to look at you. You look like a nice guy who's had some bad luck—which everyone has at times—but this is nothing on the sad I've seen, even on the job."

'"Really?"

'"Absolutely. And while I've seen men who claimed to be the biggest, I have to admit I've never met one who claimed to be the saddest. Do you mind if I put some clothes on? I'm a little chilly. I can still give you a massage if you like."

'"No, you put . . . whatever you like."

'Alex, I felt so ridiculous, and not just because I had come like that. Even to be naked on my bed with this naked lovely woman whom I'd just met seemed absurd. I felt stupid. It was not the sort of thing I did.'

'You'd done it before.'

'Once. I'd done it once before, and not in my own house, which is, which feels entirely different. Why do you keep bringing that up?'

'I'm sorry. It's not important to me but—'

'But what?'

'Well, it is important that you don't kid yourself even about—'

'Even about sex?'

'About anything.'

'You don't like hearing about us do you, about me and her? Well, you've got nothing to worry about. She put her clothes on and I put on mine as she told me about the saddest booking she ever had.

'She said, "It should have been a dream booking. Probably a lot of girls would think it was. I was meant to be flattered to be chosen. The guy called the agency and said he wants the prettiest girl they've got, wants her young-looking, wants her to dress formally, wants her for six hours, the better she looks the bigger the tip. The agency chooses me. I dress up in a formal strapless thing and I drive to the address I was given. I was pleased to dress that way. I don't normally have much cause to. When I get there a young man opens the door, a very overweight young man, but not entirely ugly, and he's dressed formally too. He invites me in to this totally modern apartment—no expense spared, with a beautiful view overlooking Fawkner Park. The untidiness tells me I'm in the company of a spoilt rich kid, probably the product of a beautiful mother and a driven, possibly absent, rich repulsive father."

'"I know them."

'"Sorry?"

313

'"I know the parents."

'"Really?"

'"No, I mean I know the type."

'"Yeah, right. A friend of mine, a good friend of mine, would call the son a living, breathing tribute to Charles Darwin. You know what I'm saying?"

'"Sure."

'"Well, he was about twenty-one, in fact he was exactly twenty-one and really quite nice to talk to. He offers me a glass of champagne, real French, none of this 'methode' shit, and he tells me the deal. He wants me to be his date, to go out with him in public and pretend to be his interstate girlfriend. Seems in his circle he is, for all his money, something of a joke, an object of ridicule. So we drink champagne alone together for about an hour in his apartment while he tells me enough about himself, his history, to enable him to pass me off as his Sydney girlfriend, the model.

'"He calls a cab, really nervous, and on the way he tells me, as if it had slipped his mind, that the twenty-first birthday we were going to is his. There were at least two hundred and fifty people there, two hundred and fifty twenty-one year olds, so to speak. And his parents. He can't possibly have known them all. He says it is alright if I admit I am a little older than twenty-one. We settle on twenty-four, almost twenty-five. People keep coming up to me, mainly girls, to tell me that they really hope the two of us will last, that it is so good to finally meet me, that he talks about me all the time. His parents tell me that too.

'"He didn't seem such an object of ridicule that night. Perhaps it was the new role he was playing. We danced and drank. I think I did a pretty good job. I had to go back to his apartment with him and wait until the last of the 'inner sanctum' had gone home. He kissed me on the cheek, paid me twice what I was owed and asked if I'd be available when he turned thirty. A real gentleman. I didn't have the heart to tell him how familiar his father looked."

'"Was he gay?"

'"No, I don't think so. Why do you ask that?"

'"I don't know . . . rich guy, can't get a date, doesn't even try to—"

'"Dennis, you've missed the whole point of the story."

'And she was right. I had to laugh, Alex. Even after what had happened she could make me laugh, laugh at myself. All the while she was telling me the story she was holding me. Of course, after hearing it, I had to tip her too. So I guess I became another perfect booking. But it was worth it. You know what I mean? I liked having her there, just listening to her. So I started calling for her, booking her specifically. She would come to my house almost weekly. I found I needed it. I needed to see her.

'We didn't do anything. We didn't undress or anything. Sometimes she'd hold me while we watched television. I always paid her. This was an hour or two that she was meant to be working so I felt I had to pay her. I started confiding in her, telling her how I was feeling, about my son and Patricia, anything. It was in the context of all this that she would mention you. She'd quote you. I told her about my accident and gradually, perhaps reluctantly, she started telling me a little of her own story. I asked her why she did that kind of work. You see, I felt I could ask that because, although technically I was paying, I was really paying her just to come and see me. I wasn't really a client like the others. Like you, perhaps.

'She told me she was doing it for her boyfriend. That was a shock. I have to admit that. Didn't know she had a boyfriend, did you? Not so easy when you know that, is it? Her boyfriend was in some kind of trouble with the police and she needed money to pay for his defence. Apparently some cop had promised her he was going to fix everything up but—surprise, surprise—he double-crossed her and now her boyfriend was having trouble getting Legal Aid funding. She was reluctant to tell me the details. It all sounded very messy but the nub of it was that her boyfriend's trial was imminent and she needed a lot of money for his legal fees. She seemed pretty serious about him. I bet you didn't know any of this? Unless you're treating her. You wouldn't know it from sleeping with her, would you?'

'Maybe we should stick to *me* asking the questions.'

'I'm telling you everything . . . no matter how bad it looks . . . how bad it makes me look.'

'Go on.'

'I told her I would like to help her but I wasn't in a position to. And I would've but I didn't have any money, what with Patricia threatening to take James to Germany, threatening to hang me out to dry. But I did think about it. I wanted to help her. That's good, isn't it?'

'What do you mean?'

'You once said something to me about *lower* needs and *higher* needs. *Lower* needs were things like the need to eat, to sleep. *Higher* needs would include the need to help people. You said the urge to satisfy a *higher* need was a sign of health, that it was inconsistent with depression.'

'Yes, but—'

315

'That's what you said.'

'Yes, but it's not quite as simple as that.'

'No, I was thinking that even when you said it. But I really did want to help her. Is that selfish too, a way of making myself feel good?'

'That's the kind of selfishness we call altruism. Subject to certain qualifications, it's the best kind there is. It's also one of the more mature methods of dealing with a difficult situation or emotional experience.'

'Well, there you are then!'

'What you're looking for now is absolution.'

'Fuck you! I really wanted to help her. I'm telling you the truth. I break down in front of you like a child but I keep going. I don't care if you don't believe me. I really did want to help her.'

'You keep saying that but you don't say how.'

'The next time she visited I told her I had an idea.'

'An idea?'

'An idea of how she could get the money she needed.'

'You don't feel good about this idea, do you?'

'Alex, I don't feel good about anything.'

'But you're wrestling with yourself about this. You don't really want to tell me about it.'

'Dr Klima, you are full of shit! This is the reason I'm here, to tell you this.'

'So . . . tell me.'

'I offered to teach her to count cards in blackjack.'

'To play blackjack?'

'Not just to play it. To win at it.'

'By counting cards?'

'That was the idea. It was a skill I had, one she didn't have, which I thought I could pass on to her. She'd never played it at all. Didn't know the rules. I had to teach her from scratch.'

16

'"There's the standard way of playing and then there's counting. We'll just take it one step at a time," I tried to reassure her.

'"Dennis, I don't know anything about it," she protested. "The only times I've ever even been inside a casino I was there with clients and we never played blackjack."

"'A lot of men, wealthy men, treat call girls to a few hands of blackjack."

"'Yeah, I've heard of that happening, but not to me. I'll never be able to get the hang of it. I don't play cards. I'll never be able to count them. You're crazy. I don't even know how many cards are in a deck."

"'Fifty-two and they play with eight decks here."

"'Dennis, you're out of your mind. Fifty-two times eight is—"

"'Four hundred and sixteen."

"'How does anybody count four hundred and sixteen cards in their head?"

"'You don't, you don't even try. Some people try and they're almost as stupid as the impulse gamblers sitting there—"

"'What do you mean, impulse gamblers?"

"'I mean the ones who make impulsive decisions without a plan, the ones who double-down or split because of a rush of blood to the head."

"'Dennis, I don't even know what double-down means."

"'I'll explain it all to you slowly. There's the standard way of playing, and there's counting. Insofar as counting is concerned, there is not that much to understand or even to remember. The secret to it is, sure, to know what to do. But the real trick to it is to have the discipline to put it into practice no matter how you're feeling, confident or shy, bold or scared, you just have to stick to the rules I'm going to teach you and then it's not gambling. You have to pay attention to what's going on and divorce your emotions from your thinking."

"'I want to quit already."

"'Look, Angelique, you want to get the money to help him?"

"'Of course I do."

"'Then it must be worth at least hearing me out."

"'Dennis, I appreciate it but I'm not the kind of person who can—"

"'Just hear me out. Your boyfriend deserves at least that much, doesn't he?"

"'I'm listening."

"'It all sounds very daunting but it isn't really anywhere near as complicated as people think. Fear sabotages people's capacity to absorb a set of rules. That's all counting is, a set of rules. And they're really fairly simple. Let me explain them. There are only ever thirteen possible cards that are going to come out. Forget the four hundred and sixteen, just think of thirteen."

"'Okay, thirteen."

"'Three of those thirteen will be an ace, a two and an eight."

'"Yeah."

'"I want you to forget about them. You're not going to try and count them; they're irrelevant. They don't make it weaker or stronger whether they're in or out of the pack. This leaves what we call the low cards and the high cards. The low cards are three, four, five, six and seven. There are five of them. Treat all of the low cards simply as low. Don't try to distinguish among them. Now we're left with the high cards—nine, ten, jack, queen and king, these last three cards each being worth ten. Similarly, they're just high cards. Don't distinguish among them.

'"Now, when the cards are dealt, they might come out low, low, high, high. You see that, you take it in and you can ignore it. They've just cancelled each other out."

'"But they won't always cancel each other out."

'"No, of course not, but that's all you have to keep track of in your hand. You don't need to know whether there are thirty eights left in the pack or whether fifteen threes have been played. Just watch the highs and lows. Like this. High, low, high, high, low. That's one high card over. The way I do it, a high card is 'minus 1' and low card is 'plus 1', so if I've got one high card left over, all I have to remember is 'minus 1'. Now you do this one. Tell me what the count is. Remember, ignore aces, twos and eights. Just track the high cards and the low cards. So . . . low, high, high, low, high, low, high, low, low, high, high, high."

'"Minus 2?"

'"Exactly, you're counting cards. Faster or slower, that's the principle. For greater speed and accuracy, you just have to do it for hours and hours."

'"That's easy for you to say. I don't know the rules and I don't know what it means to count, to have a 'minus 2'."

'"Okay. I can teach you. It's not hard. If there were four more high cards than low cards, I call it 'minus 4'."

'"I got that bit."

'"If there were four more low cards than high cards, I call it 'plus 4'. But it can be anything, 'minus 10' or 'plus 14', whatever."

'"So?"

'"So this is what I call the *actual* count. It varies with each hand, with each card, and you use the *actual* count to get the *true* count."

'"The *true* count?"

'"The *true* count is the *actual* count divided by your estimate of the number of decks to come. If, for example, at the end of the first deck of cards, with seven decks to come, the *actual* count is 'plus 14', you divide 'plus 14' by the seven decks to come and you get a true count of 'plus 2'."

"'Whoa, Dennis! Hold it right there. Firstly, how the hell do you guess the number of decks left?"

"'You just look at the shoe holding the dealer's cards. It's not theoretical physics. Don't be afraid of it. Does the shoe look half empty, three-quarters empty? You look and you guess. You will have been there from the beginning when the dealer had a full shoe, if you're playing your cards right."

"'And even if I could correctly guess the number of decks left to come—"

"'Oh, Angelique, it's easy—"

"'Even if I could guess that and I remember what you called the *actual* count and divide the actual count by the number of decks to come and I get . . . whatever . . . 'plus 2'—so what? What the hell does that mean?"

"'It means you've got a *true* count of 'plus 2'. This is the basis for raising or lowering your bet. For each *true* count of 'plus 1', the odds shift in favour of the player by about two and a bit per cent. The starting point, the player's chance of winning any particular hand, without counting but using the standard system of playing, is about forty-eight per cent. At 'plus 1' you get to about even, so there's no need to increase your bet. When you're at 'plus 2' you've got about a fifty-two per cent chance of winning your hand. When you're at 'plus 8' you've got about a sixty-six per cent chance of winning your hand and that's worth backing heavily."

"'So you're saying the higher your *true* count, the higher your chances of winning the hand and, therefore, the more money you should bet on that hand?"

"'That's exactly what I'm saying."

"'But why don't we just bet on the good hands? Don't put anything on a hand where the *true* count is too low."

"'Well, firstly, they only let you play if you bet at least the table minimum per hand and, secondly, you have to be careful the way you vary your bets. Erratic betting behaviour will alert the casino to the fact that you're counting."

"'Is it illegal to count?"

"'No, it's not illegal, but it may as well be. If the casino catches you counting they'll ask you to leave, ban you or worse, because you're lessening the odds in their favour and they hate that."

"'Is it cheating? Are we stealing from them?"

"'It's not but they act as though it is. We're just playing their game by their rules better than most people do. Better than they expected us to. They normally have everything, absolutely everything you could think of and more, stacked against you in their favour and then here we are, using nothing but our minds, to take a tiny fraction of their money from them and they find it unbearable."

"'Dennis, I love the sound of it, but I've got to be realistic. I could never do it. I don't even know the rules, what you called the standard way of playing. I don't even know that."

"'Not yet. I could teach you. No one step is too hard. Listen and stop me only if you don't understand something or I'm going too fast."

"'Can I stop you now?"

"'Listen! All cards have numerical values. An ace is worth one or eleven. Whoever comes closest to a twenty-one without going over twenty-one wins unless the dealer has an ace and a ten. An ace and a ten is called blackjack and it's unbeatable. If the dealer has black-jack after they deal their second card and you have twenty-one, then you get a stand-off, that is, your original bet is returned to you.

"'When a dealer deals you a card there are only four things you can do. You can hit, which means you take another card. You can stay, which means you don't take another card, you can split and you can double-down."'

17

'Dennis, I have to stop you there because there's something I don't understand. You seem to have gone to a lot of trouble to teach Angelique everything you know about this. If you don't mind my asking, why didn't you just offer to do it yourself? For all the clarity of your explanation of the basic rules and counting, wouldn't it have been easier for you to do it on her behalf?'

'Yes, it would've been, and that's what she said. But there was a problem doing that. I used to do it fairly well and not infrequently. They knew me as a counter and I'd been banned. It is the highest form of flattery they can pay you. They don't want to have to pay you anything else.'

'Who is "they"?'

'The casino—'

'Yes, but—'

'Alex, what part of this are you having trouble understanding?'

'Well, in everything you've told me you have never mentioned this, not in detail.'

'I mentioned blackjack but I've never been addicted to it so there was nothing really to say about it till now. It hasn't been relevant until now. I hadn't been to the casino for more than a year prior to going with Angelique.'

'You've tried to play since being banned? . . . Dennis?'

'Yes . . . Jesus, Alex! That isn't the point. With all your facile speculations you're missing the point.'

'So, what's the point?'

'She is. She . . . Angelique . . . She thought that I was able but just unwilling to play for her. I tried to assure her that this wasn't the case, because it wasn't. Alex, I would have done anything to help her. If she wanted the money for her boyfriend . . . I didn't care. I didn't ever even ask her what he was charged with. But she said I was just like all the rest of them.'

'The rest of them?'

'Bookings. Men, I suppose. You.'

'What did you say?'

'Well, I finally managed to convince her that the casino has records of me, photographs of my face stored digitally. I'd been escorted out of there before, you know. She suggested I disguise myself.'

'You'd really impressed her with your counting.'

'Is that what she said?'

'No, I'm surmising. It impressed *me*.'

'Anyway, we were stuck. She needed the money faster than she could earn it. She thought counting was a good idea but she felt incapable of doing it herself. I thought . . .'

'What?'

'She was annoyed with me. I thought I would lose her.'

'Lose her?'

'I've told you. She wasn't a whore to me. I didn't touch her, and she liked me . . . I wanted to help her . . . still do.'

'So what did you do?'

'I didn't want to let her down so I came up with a compromise which in itself took weeks of practice. And in those weeks I wasn't paying her, even though she visited me often when she would otherwise have been working. But I suppose she . . . we *were* working.'

'What was the compromise?'

'We were to go to the casino as a couple. She would play at a table and I would sit behind her, barely speaking. I would sit behind her with my hand on her and by signalling with my fingers, I would play through her.'

'But wouldn't you be recognised?'

'I knew that sooner or later I would be, but the idea was to delay it as long as possible.'

'How?'

'Well, firstly, I wouldn't be seen to be playing, she would be, so provided I didn't say too much while she was raising her bets, she'd be more the object of attention than me. Secondly, she was to wear something eye-catching, something revealing. Most of the dealers and the pit bosses were men and you could bet your bottom dollar that the monkeys they've got upstairs watching the video monitors were men. They'd still be enjoying her cleavage before they realised someone was counting. There are no Einsteins up there working out who the master criminals are. They're no more sophisticated than your average nightclub bouncer.'

'Yes, but still . . . You said they had your face stored digitally.'

'Sure, but they'd have to connect her winnings with my face and that could take some time or might not even happen at all, especially if I hadn't shaved for a few days and was wearing glasses, which I was. You see, Alex, for all their technology, the greatest likelihood of being picked up as a card counter is by someone you know, a dealer you've spent hours sitting in front of. Remember that I hadn't been there in over a year. When I put it to her she thought it was worth a try. Neither of us really had much to lose by trying.

'For almost three weeks she came to my place in between her bookings. If she had just finished one, she would take a shower while I'd make her something to eat. Then, once she'd eaten, we'd get down to work. I was to be sitting close behind her with my hand just resting on her neck or part-way down her back. It doesn't take much pressure for her to feel the signal on her bare skin. Through a system involving the thumb and two fingers of one hand I would be telling her when to hit, when to stay, when to double-down and when to split.'

'And you were to be basing your decisions as to what to do on your own counting.'

'That's right. We tried using the fingers to signal when to raise the bet because the rest is useless if you don't know how to bet strategically—but it became a bit confusing. I decided to use verbal signals that would sound innocuous to any interested onlooker.'

'What were they?'

'I liked the idea of referring to luck because, while luck's got nothing to do with it, you'll find that practically everyone sitting at

had in common with respect to their interior architecture. She said they were both designed to eliminate context. Once you were inside there was nothing there to remind you of your outside life. The garish lights and the absence of clocks served to eliminate even space and time themselves, at least for people without a bladder problem.'

'She said that?'

'Something like that.'

'She has a point . . .'

'Yes, but it didn't apply to us. For one thing, I don't gamble, I count. I led her to a table where the minimum bet was $100 but ranged up to $10 000. The range was right for us yet it wasn't too exclusive. It still had a big crowd around it. I waited for the first deck in a new shoe before we took up our positions. I had her sit in the seat farthest to the dealer's right. From there it's easier to see over the table as the cards are coming out, easier to keep track and to keep count. It's also a key position in terms of influencing other players in the game. I sat right behind her with my hand on her back and we started.

'Her nervousness was actually good for us. She looked glamorous and nervous, which was totally acceptable to anyone around her, anyone who cared to pay her any serious attention. We were able to do quite well for a while before anyone did. The table had the usual array of characters. The guy next to us had dark hair, kind of short around the sides and slightly slicked back. Thirtyish, his chiselled face seemed in danger of cracking under the solid workout his gum chewing was giving his jaw muscles. His grimness wasn't matched by his ability. Nor was it mollified by the occasional win.

'Another guy, at the far end of the table, was busy convincing himself how friendly and fun-loving he was. Heavy-set, this man sat there in a t-shirt losing money, making quips and disc-jockey-standard gags chiefly against himself but always looking to someone, usually the dealer, for a response, especially when the dealer was a woman. There were times when the beating he was taking was simply brutal. I'd look at him between hands. You had to feel sick about it. He was hurting and you didn't want him to be. He was a likeable guy. Sometimes he seemed to be finding it hard to breathe. He was dropping thousands. God knows where it came from but the stayers at the table wanted him there. I used his poor "luck" to signal Angelique to increase the bet. We were doing well.

'We were up by about $4500 when she whispered something to me. I didn't catch it immediately, and concentrating on the game, I didn't ask her to repeat it. But she did anyway.

'"I need to pee."

'"Just hold on," I muttered.

'"Can't."

'"You have to," I told her. She was still in the middle of a hand but she didn't want to wait. She just stood up at the table with a twelve in front of her, brushed past me and left. I wasn't the only one to watch her as she ran through the crowd. This was trouble.'

'Why?'

'Well, firstly, it was distracting. It made it hard to keep focused on the count. Secondly, it attracted more attention to us than we needed and it left me sitting there in full view of everybody, including the "eye in the sky", the video camera in the ceiling. I had to decide whether to play for her until she came back or to drop out, take our chips and wait for her. If I played in her stead there was a greater chance someone would recognise me. If I dropped out and we left the game we'd have a long wait for circumstances to be right at another table.'

'What do you mean?'

'Well, we'd have to wait for a new shoe so I could start my counting again and, ideally, I'd have liked us to have the same position at the table, to the far right of the dealer. Who knew how long it would be before we found a table with all of that? In the meantime, even without playing we could attract attention.'

'Why?'

'There is this beautiful young woman, wearing almost nothing, who is doing very well. Suddenly she stops and literally runs away. Her companion is an unshaved Quasimodo with glasses. And you ask why?'

'What did you do?'

'Well, I had to make a decision while still trying to keep count. I decided to keep playing for her but to play reasonably badly. I was going to lose as little as I could until she came back. My thinking was that if I played badly and lost a little, I would decrease the likelihood that anyone would pay much attention to me, that they would pay less attention to me than to the two of us wandering around with our chips, an incongruous couple waiting for the perfect table.

'"Do you want me to take over?" I hurriedly called out to her before she'd gone too far.

'"Yes, take over," she called back, without turning around.

'We were, both of us, sweating by the time she came back and I'd lost her $800. It was the best I could do.

'"Sorry," she said, for everyone to hear, as she slipped back in.

'"He's the one who ought to be sorry," said the young shaggy-haired fat man in his t-shirt. "Your boyfriend's been losing all your money."

'Everybody laughed, as the fat man had hoped they would. I shrugged my shoulders in mock resignation and we went back to the way it had been before nature had forced her to run away. Gently, slowly, and with just the right amount of faltering, we started winning again, and attracting onlookers. I could tell she was enjoying it, often counting the chips between hands and joining in the chatter about cards or luck with the dealer, or the young fat man in the t-shirt, or the floating players who came in and out to bask in the apparent bonhomie of the table. The crowd was growing too big for my liking, though clearly not for hers. She was enjoying their enthralment. I had a sense that she was in part playing for them, playing to them, anyway. There was no opportunity to tell her to tone it down. Remember, we wanted to make the money as quickly and as inconspicuously as possible and then get out.

'Then, with $1000 in $500 chips riding on the next hand, a sum it had taken time to build up to, she started to play for herself. The crowd was closing in, jostling against me. We had a pair of tens against the dealer's ten. She decides to split. I didn't tell her to split. You don't split with a pair of tens facing a ten. You never split tens, never.'

'What exactly does it mean to split?'

'Splitting refers to splitting pairs. When a pair is split the player has to bet the same amount again on the split card so that now, he's playing two hands and betting on two instead of one. We had a pair of tens. Twenty is a good total to draw to. I don't know what she was thinking. She wasn't thinking. She wasn't listening to my signals. She said she was and her excuse made some sense. She said that I signalled for her to split. I suppose with the crowd pushing into us, pushing me into her, it is possible that my hand went into her back involuntarily. I don't know. I can't swear to it.'

'And what happened?'

'What happened shouldn't have happened. I don't know the odds but I could work them out. She got two more tens against the dealer's nine.'

'So she was right to do what she did? It paid off.'

'It paid off, that's for sure. By this stage we were about $15 000 ahead. But she was wrong to do what she did. It was crazy. She wasn't listening to me.'

'But, Dennis, you said she'd just misread her signal. Didn't the crowd push you into her and—?'

'Stop defending her, Alex. If there's one thing I know—perhaps the only fucking thing—it's the odds against splitting tens. But with the chips piled high in front of her she thought she knew it all. It was after this hand, the one that had us up $15 000, that the heavy-set man finally stood up and announced, "I'm out. Can't compete with that kind of luck." This appeared to unsettle her. She had liked him, or had liked having him there with his inane remarks. I can understand this. There's an almost irresistible tendency to think that the smallest thing is the only reason you're winning. It was like he was absorbing everyone else's punishment and thereby improving everyone else's luck. Other people were losing too, but not like this guy who sat there and took it, hand after hand. As hard as it was to imagine where his money came from, it was even harder to imagine what he was getting out of it.'

'A sense of community, perhaps?'

'No. We were the only ones left from the start of the shoe. Even the gum-chewing guy had quit by then. There was no community. He was living in some kind of world I've never been to.'

'You're angry with him, aren't you, Dennis?'

'Shut up! I'm angry with the whole lot of them. This guy was asking for it, like the woman at the retreat who told everyone she'd been molested as a child. There are some things you don't do unless you're asking for it.'

'Like jumping backwards off a ladder?'

'For Christ's sake, Alex, he played like someone who thinks you win if you play defensively. All he wanted to do was to never go bust, to just survive.'

'You hate him for that, don't you?'

'He didn't ever draw a card when he had a total of twelve or more for fear of going bust.'

'Dennis . . . Why does this make you so angry? Why does it make you cry?'

'Because this man is ignorant. His strategy is the fastest way known to lose money at blackjack.'

'You see yourself in him.'

'He lost every damn thing. You always draw to a hand under seventeen when a dealer shows a card from the seven to the ace.'

'You're not talking about blackjack, are you?'

'I am talking about blackjack. I'm talking about her, and why I'm here now. The heavy-set guy got up to leave and she got worried. Then the dealer changed, just because they change periodically, and she stood up. I thought she might want to stretch so I didn't say anything.

Then she grabs the chips and starts walking away from the table. I thought maybe she had to pee again so I followed her to ask her. It feels like everyone is looking at us as I drag my leg along the carpet trying to brush my way through the crowd to get to her. I thought she'd gone mad.

'"What are you doing?" I asked her when I'd finally caught up.

'"That table wasn't going to be good for us anymore."

'"What are you talking about?"

'"I didn't feel good there anymore with that new dealer. I didn't like the look of him. And that other guy, the big one. I liked him and he was going. Maybe our luck would go with him."

'"Angelique, how many times have I told you: this has nothing to do with luck. Have you forgotten? I've been counting the cards and telling you what to do. It's a system. As soon as you move away from the system, as soon as you move away from strict rationality, you're gone for all money. These people are fools. They're blind. They're throwing away good money after bad. Some of them know the odds and they're doing it anyway. There's no luck. There's nothing to ride. It's science or it's nothing. You've got to calm down. You've got to listen to me. Where are you going now?"

'She stormed away from me in the direction of the ladies' room and, seeing her head in that direction, I didn't pursue her, didn't even try to keep up. That's how she was able to get away from me.'

'Did you lose her?'

'Just long enough for her to veer away from the ladies' room towards a roulette wheel. I saw this and in horror I went after her. I got there in time to see her place $15 000 on the red. She said she felt lucky. I heard her say it just as I got my fingers to the back of her neck.

'"I'll stop here if I win. I promise," she whispered.

'The croupier called, "No more bets." In the time it took for the wheel to spin and for the ball bearing to revolve within it, I wished I'd never agreed to play for her. I wished that I had used her like all the others had. I should have been just another booking and made her do what she did with everyone else. Pay your money and get the service. No risk. Any other man, any that my wife would call a "real man", would have grabbed her, even hit her a little right then and there. It was Cup night. There were fifteen thousand dollars spinning around on a game with fixed odds, a suckers' game. No one would have denied I would have been justified in treating her the way anyone else would have, the way everyone treats everyone whenever they can. I should have forced myself to—'

'Dennis . . .'

19

'Well, that's how I felt, Alex. That's how I felt until it was me she turned around to hug. She hugged me, Alex, in front of everyone while everyone applauded. It fell on the red. She had doubled her money. We had walked in there with five thousand dollars, which I turned into fifteen thousand dollars, sweating on every dollar. In a fit of complete madness she'd risked all of it and won. She hugged me spontaneously for free in the garish light of midnight in front of anyone who cared to look, and many, many cared to look. I could feel the sweat of her as she held the thirty thousand dollars worth of chips.

'I'm telling you, Alex, when she held me like that, for one instant it felt as though everything had paid off. I don't care how many times any of you bastards have ever slept with her. None of you have ever known the joy I had that moment knowing that I'd helped get her exactly what she wanted and that she would never ever forget me because of that and because I was the one, the only one, who *hadn't* fucked her. I had helped her, helped her help someone she loved in a way that excluded me from being loved by her in that same way. And I'll be damned, Alex, if I was not more alive inside her embrace in front of all those people than I had ever been before. You see, others, maybe even you, have felt her sweat against your skin but it was only ever the sweat of her exploitation, not of honest exhilaration.

'We were giddy. She kept her word. That was it. She had her thirty thousand, and the two of us went to cash the chips. She squealed and we punched the air. The cashier pulled out one of those bound bundles of one hundred dollar notes fresh from the Reserve Bank and asked her if she wanted them counted in front of her. Angelique looked at me for a moment before answering, "No, no, it's alright. I trust you." She had just won thirty thousand dollars and was numb to a hundred more or less. I know how that feels. It's dangerous, Alex, it's deliciously dangerous. It's better than you imagine it to be and it's why you do it.'

'Yes, I can understand that, but why *don't* you do it?'

'What?'

'You said you hadn't done it in over a year. What stops you from doing it all the time?'

'Like I told you, I've been banned. Sooner or later they'd recognise me. And anyway, even if they don't . . . At the bottom end, fifties, hundreds . . . you can't feel it. The money, the amount at stake has to be higher and higher each time for you to feel anything.'

'And what stops you from making the amount higher and higher?'

'I can't. I can't do it. I don't have the nerve. You need the nerve of someone who doesn't see what can go wrong. I'm not Joe Geraghty. When it gets as high as I need it to get . . . I lose my nerve. Mind you, I don't know that I could do it now even if I kept my nerve. It would always remind me of a moment I can never recapture, and the struggle to rid my mind of that moment would screw my concentration. She . . .

'She had her arm around me all the way to the car. We had done it. She was still cheering as I started wondering about the future. She opened the car door for me. I got in and while she walked around to the driver's side I wondered whether now she might visit me on some sort of regular basis . . . you know . . .'

'For nothing?'

'Yes. She could visit me. I could make dinner for her. She got in the driver's seat still saying something about not believing her luck. I don't know exactly what she said. I was a little lost in my own thoughts by then. She pulled into the traffic. I wasn't really listening. She said she was hot. I started to worry about her reference to luck. What if she focused on the roulette? I mean . . . she'd have a real problem. She said something about her eyes. I didn't want her forgetting how we'd got, how *I'd* got, to fifteen thousand. It had been by counting, not by luck, Alex. I began to tell her that.

'It was just then that she called out, "Jesus, Mitch, my eyes!"

'She'd never called me Mitch before. I don't know where that came from.

'"They're blurry!"

'We veered slightly to the other side of the road and hit an oncoming car. Time stopped with a thud and the tinkle of glass and the hiss of steam. Then silence. She was hurt, Alex. Did you know that?'

'No.'

'Why do you think she hasn't been keeping appointments? Doesn't anyone follow these things up? Yours is meant to be a caring profession, isn't it?'

'Dennis—'

'I was just in shock, but she was out cold. An ambulance came and took her somewhere. I didn't know where. Maybe they said it but it didn't register with me. A second ambulance came a little while

later for me. They said I was slightly concussed. She was bleeding,
Alex. I'm not crying for myself, you idiot! If it hadn't been for me, she
wouldn't have gone there in the first place. I still don't know where
they took her. I've been leaving messages for her at the agency. It's
the only number I have. She hasn't returned them. I don't know her
surname, Alex. I don't know her real name. Tell me how I can reach
her. Her family's interstate.'

'You know I can't give you her details—'

'But you have them to give.'

'I'm sorry, Dennis. You know I can't answer that.'

'But it would help me to help her. I've got you there, haven't.I?
I've got you there on two counts. You're morally, and perhaps even
professionally, bound to help me help her, for her sake. And you're
both morally and professionally bound to help me want to, for my
sake. If higher needs are inconsistent with depression, that's what
you've said, then you are obliged not to subvert them.'

'I've also told you it's not that simple. Remember?'

'No, but it is. It is this time.'

'Dennis, wanting to help someone doesn't stop you from being
depressed. Perhaps I should have expressed it as a matter of probability. Someone capable of feeling a higher need and, more than
that, of trying to satisfy it, is less likely to be depressed. It does not
guarantee it. In your case your apparent need to be in contact with
her stems from the blame you inappropriately pin on yourself. Something undoubtedly bad, but beyond your control, has happened to
her and you blame yourself for it. You feel guilty. This is itself a classic symptom of depression.'

'You're fucking her, aren't you?'

'That's both ridiculous and untrue.'

'I don't care if you are. I only want to help her. You will admit I'm
at least partly responsible for her situation. I haven't lost the capacity to help people, you know.'

'Yes, that's good, but I couldn't give you her details even if I had
them.'

'You want to be the only one, don't you? You want to be the only
one capable of helping anyone, the great messiah, Herr Doktor, the
only one that everyone needs. Well, what about me? You're sure as
hell not helping me.'

'We have a great deal of talking to do if I'm to be of any help to
you, Dennis. There's a lot to get through here.'

'What the hell are you talking about now? Some sort of talking
cure, cognitive therapy or something? You think I'll feel better talking

to you? I don't like the odds, Doctor. I don't like the chances of all your wisdom, your speculation, your pre-Newtonian psychology, getting me through even the week. You know what I think you should do? Take out your prescription book. Write me a prescription for Prozac or Zoloft and at the bottom just write down her phone number. Go on, Alex, you know I'm right. Is that your prescription book there? Go on, Alex, for Christ's sake, pick it up. Write me a prescription. Everything I touch, Alex—'

'You should have both.'

'Both what?'

'Both pharmacological *and* talking therapy.'

'No, *I* need the pills, *you* need the talking. But if it's a matter of making a deal . . . okay, I'm in. Pick it up, write it out and I'll come back. I promise I'll come back, and dance to the tune of your psychotherapy or philosophy or whatever.'

'Yes, yes, Dennis, I know . . . There are more things in heaven and . . . Before you get this filled, we'll need to talk about dosage and about possible side effects.'

'What was that? What did you say about things in heaven?'

'No, don't worry about it, it was nothing.'

'What was it?'

'I was mumbling to myself.'

'What was it? You're not falling back on religion, are you?'

'No. It's from *Hamlet* . . . something a friend of mine . . . something her boyfriend might have said.'

'Alex, I know you'll help me.'

'I'm so glad to hear you say that.'

'I know you will. I have the money.'

'What money? Dennis, it's not a question of—'

'You will help me, won't you?'

'You know I'll do everything I can.'

'Yes, I know. I have the money, her money. I have her money. She left it in the car. Everything I touch, Alex . . . everything. You can see, you have to help me.'

333

part five

He is known as the Turk, or just Turk. Because of the tendency in this place to slavishly follow even the rules and traditions they themselves have developed, everybody here calls him that. Not only does he not hear his language, he doesn't ever hear his name anymore, not his real name. And I, the sensitive prick who always prided himself on being so finely attuned to ethnic nerve-endings, don't call him by his real name either. I'm not at all sure of his real name—Yakub, I think. I'm not sure. I call him Nazim, both because it is somehow comforting and because he doesn't mind. He even answers to it, though it's not his name, not his nickname, not something he asked to be called. I'm just doing what I can to endure confinement in a place designed, not with an indifference to your welfare but with a concern—a concern to crush the very best out of the very worst people, or perhaps just out of those who hadn't got away with it, whatever the it was. People here use names and all the weaponry of language they can get their hands on to bludgeon, impress, intimidate, insult, humiliate and control, in order to survive. And I am as guilty as they are.

When Alex asked me what books I wanted him to bring me, it was the Turk who reminded me to ask for the selected poetry of Nazim Hikmet, the best poet there is for one who will spend time in prison. It wasn't anything the Turk said. He thinks Nazim Hikmet is a Turkish friend of mine. I just happened to hear him address one of his children by the name Nazim in the visit centre one day just as Alex was asking me for a list of the books I wanted and, of course, I remembered Nazim Hikmet. Don't forget Nazim Hikmet.

One could get bored even with boredom here were it not for the fear that grows under every stone and between every brick. The fear reminds you you're alive. So I read and reread the selected poetry of Nazim Hikmet until I know it by heart. Once in the laundry, before I was put into solitary for my own protection, I tried reciting a poem by him to Nazim the Turk. It is called 'Some Advice to Those Who Will Serve Time in Prison'.

> If instead of being hanged by the neck
> > you're thrown inside
> > for not giving up hope
> in the world, your country, and people,
> > if you do ten or fifteen years
> > apart from the time you have left,
> you won't say,
> > > 'Better I had swung from the end of a rope
> > > > like a flag'—
> you'll put your foot down and live.
> It may not be a pleasure exactly,
> but it's your solemn duty
> > to live one more day
> > to spite the enemy.
> Part of you may live alone inside,
> > like a stone at the bottom of a well.
> But the other part
> > must be so caught up
> > in the flurry of the world
> > > that you shiver there inside
> > > when outside, at forty days' distance, a leaf moves.
> To wait for letters inside,
> to sing sad songs,
> or to lie awake all night staring at the ceiling
> > is sweet but dangerous.
> Look at your face from shave to shave,
> forget your age,
> watch out for lice
> > and for spring nights,
> > and always remember
> > > to eat every last piece of bread—
> also, don't forget to laugh heartily.
> And who knows,
> the woman you love may stop loving you.
> Don't say it's no big thing:

> *it's like the snapping of a green branch*
> *to the man inside.*
> *To think of roses and gardens inside is bad,*
> *to think of seas and mountains is good.*
> *Read and write without rest,*
> *and I also advise weaving*
> *and making mirrors.*
> *I mean, it's not that you can't pass*
> *ten or fifteen years inside*
> *and more—*
> *you can,*
> *as long as the jewel*
> *on the left side of your chest doesn't lose its lustre!*

It's easier to do if you keep the poem in mind. I've repeated it to myself so many times it has come to play the same role for me that prayer plays for others, even others in here. Especially in here. My mother will not come here. Perhaps she knows that the unanswered prayers get caught in the vents and make it hard to breathe. She is busy with the gardening. I can only imagine how ready she is to believe I've done even more than they've charged me with. She blames the drink, the shrink and 'that whore' and, no matter how much I protest my innocence, she thinks I took Anna's son without Anna's permission. She thinks I am guilty. Of course, about this, she is right.

My father wants to blame Alex, despite the fact that, apart from me, Alex has taken this harder than anyone. He doesn't have poetry to fall back on, only psychiatry, which he thinks has failed us. But I know it was I that failed us. Alex is shocked to see how I've adapted to solitary. Neither of us realised how well I had been preparing for it. But, alone in my flat, for years now, I would shiver there inside, when outside, at forty days' distance, a leaf moved.

Nazim the Turk didn't know it was a poem and I'm not sure he understood even one word in four, but he liked me reciting it. He liked that I was getting advice from a Turkish friend of mine. He liked that a lot.

'I eat every last piece of bread. I'll eat yours, you Fuck!' he laughed. When he saw me for the last time before they put me in solitary he grabbed my arm with one hand and the back of my neck with the other, using all the strength and recklessness of a truly uninhibited demented man. He laughed a loud staccato laugh for no apparent reason and then suddenly stopped the same way.

'Say again . . . the Turk words. Say again for me, Fuck. Please say.'

2

I was not the worst in my class, not the worst behaved, not the slowest, not the bottom nor the top, not even consistently, reliably, conspicuously quiet. I am easily forgotten, not remembered by anyone looking back. But as far as I can tell, I am the only one to have made it here. And I did it with one mistake, only one.

Alex thinks it was more than one. He thinks it was a mistake ever to invest such hope in her, not just now but way back then at university. Was that my first mistake? It was impossible not to have noticed her. I had watched the way she carried herself, the way she would smile. She moved in a manner that suggested she was completely comfortable in her skin, a manner that elevated a natural beauty untouched by artifice to a level none of the other pretty young women could hope to attain, no matter their expertise in front of the mirrors that hid the lotions and cosmetics in the many bathrooms of their fathers. Yet she was without affectation. You saw her and felt some hope. How cruel would it be to be shown her by chance and then be denied her, denied her because not everybody could know her, even a little.

But, as it happened, mutual friends, bit-players, introduced us. It was in a tutorial. 'This is Anna Traficante,' someone said and I thought, yes, I know. Don't let me be her friend. Let me upset the rhythm of her breathing just once the way she disrupts mine every time I see her. She was captivating and at the same time intimidating. Alex thinks the person I was seeing was a figment of my imagination. She was just a clever, pretty, middle-class girl enrolled in a BA in transit between school and a job and marriage to someone other than her university boyfriend. Not worth entombment for almost ten years inside a crumbling bayside flat. And not worth this more formal, tangible incarceration.

One early evening, acting on a tip from someone who used to say that she was in love with me, the police broke into my flat and arrested me because I had not given up hope in the world, or, more particularly, because I had not given up hope in Anna or in her son. What I did was wrong on many grounds. It was not only wrong, it was crazy every way you could think to look at it, except the way I looked at it just long enough to do it.

I have not been home since. I have not been free since. I cannot get the smell of prison out of my nostrils. When people outside are forced in an emergency to use public toilets they try to breathe in as little as possible for fear of gagging on the stench. Their eyes water and when they've finished they escape almost breathless back into the uncontaminated air. Here you are captive even to the smell. It's not so much the smell of human waste (although it too is here often enough and is never reliably absent), it's the smell of human misery and the pungent nauseating smell of the institutional detergent which I have come to associate with it. I can't get it out of my hair or off my skin. It is always all around me and has been ever since I entered the prison system almost a year and a half ago via what is called the mainstream section of Port Phillip Prison, one of the state's first fully privatised prisons. The detergent they use makes nothing clean. There is nothing here you would want to handle, nothing that feels comfortable to the touch, not the bed linen or the clothes they put you in, not even the food. Everything smells of it but nothing is clean. I am unable to breathe, even here in solitary.

There are only two things that have kept me going. There is Alex, of course, and there is the hope of seeing her, seeing Anna. I know I should be ashamed for her to see me here but shame is a luxury no one in prison can afford. The things you see, the things you do and that are done to you in this place, quickly make shame a distant memory, an archaic word from a language no one here speaks. I should have made use of it when I still had the opportunity. I should have made use of it when I was lying on the couch embalming myself with scotch. And I should have made use of it before I took her son from his school in a fleeting moment of what seemed at the time unparalleled clarity and not of the madness which, of course, it was. That was the moment I lost all hope of any kind of a future with her, or without her. Everything now is really just about trying to stay alive. If she doesn't tell them I had permission to take him after school I will certainly be convicted, and if that happens I will not be able to keep going. I am not like Nazim the Turk. It will kill me.

Nazim Hikmet advises prisoners to weave and to make mirrors but in this prison they don't let you have the necessary materials for that. It's hard to imagine how he was permitted to have them. Glass and twine are rightly considered weapons in here. Everything is a weapon, even language, even the tone of a man's voice. I would not have understood this before I was imprisoned. I could not have imagined all the ways there are to injure a person. Sure, a gun, a knife or even a club can kill instantly, but the tone of a man's voice can kill just as surely given enough time for its full effect to sink in, to penetrate the skin and then the mind of its victim until he is so afraid, so cowering, so utterly without hope, that one more bark and he will find a way to stop his own breathing. He will prefer this to hearing that tone in the voice of his tormentor ever again. I can imagine this very well. I know now when a question is a threat.

You can be looking at a spot on the wall to keep another prisoner from accusing you of making eye contact with him, because eye contact means you're challenging him to fight or to have sex—when suddenly a prison officer will come upon you. He might speak quietly in a baritone or he might shout but the question is so often the same one, part of the 'call and response' ritual that goes on here that everybody learns within two days.

'Any problems here, boys?' the officer asks and the prisoners, all of them, answer, 'All good boys. All good boys, Mr Greer,' or Mister whoever it is, and it's often Mr Greer.

'That's what I like to hear, boys.'

When you first hear this ritual, it sounds silly, infantile, puerile. You can, if you want to, and you will want to, take it to be evidence of a kind of institutional paternalism that may well one day be of help to you. But you won't be able to think that any longer after the day Mr Greer strolls casually upon an excited circle of prisoners who, upon hearing the question, 'Any problem here, boys?' break the circle revealing to him two bloodied men, one standing and one on his side on the ground in the shape of a grieving question mark.

'All good boys. All good boys, Mr Greer,' everyone says. Then the bloodied man still standing will move back into the throng of men who have formed the circle as Mr Greer takes this man's place in the centre of the circle.

'Any problem here, boys?' he asks again, this time more quietly than the first. This time no one answers.

'Any problem here? Do we have a problem?' he asks still more quietly.

'All . . . all good boys. All good boys, Mr Greer,' he hears wheezed through the holes in the question mark at his feet.

'That's what I like to hear, boys,' he says, and walks on.

While all of this is happening, you are breathing in the detergent-proof smell of human misery faster and more deeply than usual. It forces its way in and up your nose and into your head and it blends with the hot putrid smell of another man's breath, a man who is taking the opportunity afforded by the tightly packed circle of men to grab at your crotch and rub himself up against you.

The lawyer that Alex had found for me got me moved into maximum security after I was beaten up in the mainstream section of the prison. My arrest had been the occasion for a spread in one of the Sunday papers, almost a lift-out supplement on all crimes involving children, solved and unsolved, over the previous ten years. There was an article about me taking Sam from school—it purported to be a piece of straight reportage—which also mentioned the disappearance years earlier of Carlo, a little boy I had taught another life ago when I was a school teacher. The clear implication was that I was connected to both children in a sinister way. There was a photograph of me that Angelique had taken and below that a photograph of Carlo, the one that had been used to publicise his disappearance at the time. On the next page was a piece by a criminologist or a forensic psychologist on the type of person who commits offences against children. The offences covered in the article ranged from kidnapping to indecent assault all the way through to murder. It included photographs of many of the children who have disappeared or else been found dead in the state in the last ten years. By the time I had been processed into the mainstream section I was a rock spider, a child sex-offender, the lowest of the low according to prison lore and therefore in a category more deserving of contempt and cruelty and mistreatment than any other. The process by which a prisoner is deemed a rock spider does not require evidence and does not admit of appeal. One day I was told, 'You're gone.' Just the label is enough to damn you. I was gone even from what passes as the civil society of prison.

3

And so it was that I was placed in the maximum security section of the prison, not to protect the outside world from me but to protect me from the rest of the prison community. As if to not let this section down, a prisoner here threatened to cripple me unless I paid him $30 000 within the month. I am here with other prisoners who cannot be held in the mainstream units of the prison. These are prisoners who are prosecution witnesses and therefore liable to have contracts out on their lives, prisoners who are the subject of extortion threats, prisoners who have been assaulted more often than usual by other prisoners, convicted child sex-offenders, child killers never to be released, prisoners regarded by the prison authorities as a threat to the prisoners in the mainstream, and others known inside as plastic gangsters, who have requested to be placed in protection for fear of retribution for something prisoners in the mainstream believe them to have done. I live here with these men.

The majority of the cells are single-person cells although there are some double cells. They are all small. My cell is a single. It is exactly two metres by three metres. It has no natural light and no external air vent. There is a shower, a toilet and a handbasin. There is a very small single bed, a tiny desk and a chair. Each cell has a steel door with an inspection trap opened, of course, from the other side of the door. The cells are bugged but I don't know who is listening or what they're listening for. I am the only one here who is still awaiting trial. Everyone else has already been convicted.

There are double doors separating this unit from the rest of the prison and these are electrically controlled. The whole area is monitored by security cameras twenty-four hours a day. Each cell has a steel reinforced door which is barred, dead-bolted, and key-locked, and it requires two keys to open it after the appropriate switch has been flicked in the security office. The unit comprises twenty cells, which run along the perimeter of a room that constitutes the common area. There are about twenty prisoners in the unit at any one time. With three round tables, a table tennis table, a pool table and some fixed weight equipment, twenty odd people quickly fill the common area. You can immediately notice the extra space if someone new has been put in virtual solitary or else has died. I'm in virtual solitary. This means that, at my own request and for my own protection, I'm locked in my cell twenty-two hours a day. Had I not requested this virtual solitary confinement, I would have been beaten insensate when I failed to pay the extortioner.

For the others, the cell doors are opened at eight-thirty every morning and locked down at seven-thirty each night. Outside the common area is the yard, an empty yard six metres by five metres, about the size of a few cells put together. The prisoners are permitted to walk there when the cells are unlocked. Beside the yard is what is known as the small workroom, which is where inmates are permitted to undertake paid work if they wish. It's available on average about once a week and consists, always, of screwing nuts onto bolts one at a time. The nuts and bolts are always counted before and after sessions, to prevent inmates stealing them for use as weapons or in suicide attempts, but that doesn't stop them trying.

There is a small library containing a pitiful number of defaced books, some of a religious nature, some that are war stories, a book of Kipling poems, and an Ayn Rand novel. The library is open for an hour and forty-five minutes a week on Fridays between one pm and two forty-five. This is also the time at which courses are offered at the prison programs centre. There are just a few to pick from and they are pitched at an extremely basic level. They include Grade Seven standard English and mathematics as well as drug and alcohol counselling and anger management. The sessions are frequently cancelled, perhaps as a consequence of their Friday afternoon scheduling. Once every six months a programs officer is sent to the unit. She asks us what sort of programs we would like offered. People give her lists. Nothing happens and she comes back six months later disputing the items on the lists she got six months earlier and citing funding cuts which, she confides, may soon see her out of a job. In the intervening six months you can sometimes hear her name or else her title come up in prisoners' conversations as they compete with each other in suggesting the 'best' thing to do to her.

There is a larger yard with a basketball court and a swimming pool to which the unit has access for one and a half to two hours per day, depending on the roster. The water in the pool contains traces of blood and urine and, occasionally, excrement. I have never been in it. One of the prisoners in the unit is known to be dying. He has full-blown AIDS. He was given between two and five years to live but the smart money inside gives him two to two and a half. More than one inmate will take bets on the timing of his death. The odds shift according to rumour and speculation based on conversations and fleeting untrained observations by inmates with vested interests in the outcome. But the man must die from his illness. This is absolutely imperative. It's understood that there'll be no payout if the man dies from any intervening act. An addict who became a professional armed robber, he's appealing his sentence but the courts are said to be jammed and overworked. Nobody here is disconcerted by the prospect of a successful appeal. I've heard it said more than once 'the cunt will never die.'

There are five prisoners in the unit whom I know to have hepatitis C. Some of these are included in the group who take bets on the date of the HIV-infected armed robber's death.

This is my community. My twenty-two-hour-a-day confinement in my cell is essentially self-imposed and I have no wish to spend part of even one of those hours in the common area with the other prisoners. As it is, I still don't feel safe. My food is delivered by prisoners. I have two hours each day where I'm potentially a target. All it takes is for the relevant prison officer to look away at the wrong time. I keep expecting this to happen, even on my way to or from the visit centre.

I see Alex almost every day. It is not good for him that he comes so often. It must be destroying his life. Something is, but we never talk about it. He won't talk about his children or about his wife who is divorcing him. Instead we talk about my case, my treatment in here, my thoughts, my memories, my parents, my ex-girlfriend—always about me. I often wish he would talk more about himself, his children, his own childhood in Europe, because I am so thoroughly tired of me. Perhaps that is part of my problem, part of why I came to take Anna's son. I have always spent too much time hearing my own voice. It was always the loudest and the strongest. I know there was Alex and, of course, even Angelique, but they are much newer to the conversation than I am, the incessant conversation going on in my head. They have been like brief interruptions compared with my own voice droning on for as long as I can remember, driving me crazy with the idea that I, who was incapable of creating a mature and stable adult life for myself, could help the world, or could help anyone.

'But, Simon, you did create an adult world for yourself,' Alex tells me. He still tells me this, even after what I've done, even in here.

'No, I didn't. I drank too much, I rarely left the flat. I lost touch with people . . . I am an inadequate human being, a dreamer, who never grew up. People have worse parents than mine, people lose girlfriends, people lose jobs. They don't opt out of life. They don't borrow someone else's child.'

'Yes. It's true, you romanticised Anna and your relationship with her but it's only in taking her son that you fall off the graph.'

'You know I wasn't going to hurt him.'

'Yes, of course I know that. I told her that the night you took him. But even now you still haven't adequately explained why you did it. What, at the time, did you think you would be achieving?'

He has asked me this many times in many different ways since that day I called from the police station. That day, in my horror at the realisation of what I had just done, not to Sam or Anna or her husband, but to myself, and in my panic under another kind of questioning, the matter of 'why' seemed like something that could wait till everything else was over. But it's still not over and I find myself so infected by the misery of this place, so caught up in the battle for my own mind, the battle to stay sane, if you can call it that, and alive, that it is genuinely hard to remember the state of mind that made it all seem like a good idea.

But he keeps asking me and, though I keep avoiding the question, when he goes and when Mr Greer is satisfied that I am not concealing anything in any cavity of my body, the door slams shut and I try to remember my psychological state during the period leading up to the time that it seemed like a good idea. How did I come to place photos of her around my home? How many people around the world who have not yet fallen off Alex's graph are eating dinner night after night after night on their own? There are the divorced. There are widows and widowers, of course. We think of them as old. They are not all old but even those who are—are they in some way meant to eat dinner each night on their own? Do they deserve it? Have they earned it? How many nights must you spend alone for every night you were *not* on your own?

It feels ridiculous to make a salad for only yourself. You wash the lettuce, tear it apart, cut up the tomatoes, add a little dressing and wonder whether it will feel less ridiculous, hollow, artificial, with the passage of time. Don't add dressing. No one is watching. Try to cover the hum of the fluorescent strip light and the refrigerator with the radio. The radio is worse. It shouts at you, advertisements, drum and bass, little girl or boy groups voicing perfectly timed musical clichés to computerised accompaniments, right-wing shock-jocks with switchboards lit up by fear, hate and ignorance, or New Age flatulence masquerading as enlightenment. Turn it off and that just leaves you the hum and the salad. If you don't add dressing, it will be over that much faster. Then you try leaving out the tomatoes. I've mentioned this to Alex, even offered to let him publish it as his own, include it in the DSM IV, the idea that there is a definite warning sign for people living by themselves—the salad dressing stops appearing in the salad, then the tomatoes, then the salad itself. Then you're just left with a bowl which, sooner or later, you fill with cereal and milk and then—for the hell of it—you start to add a little scotch to the milk.

If now the market determines that your job ought to go the way of the tomatoes and there is no place you have to be at any particular time anymore, you will find yourself drinking alcohol dangerously, without any pretext. Some people drink to celebrate, others to unwind after work, others to lubricate social intercourse. This is not anymore why you drink nor why you drink so much more than at any other time in your life. At first, you drink because it's one of the last things that they, the others, the still-functioning, gainfully employed, socially participating others do that you can do. Maybe you drink for the taste. Then you drink as a dare. You dare yourself to have another one when it isn't really appropriate, to see whether anyone will notice. But there isn't ever anyone to notice and you drink upon the realisation of this. Then you drink to see if you can get from two-seventeen pm to three-fifty-five pm without noticing the time, without feeling it. The idea of slicing a tomato when you've reached this stage is completely out of the question.

No one calls and after a while you feel pleased with how long it has been since the last time you thought about how long it had been since somebody called. You can't remember when you last remembered. You must really be getting good at living like this. And it's just as well because when the phone rings by this time, even when it's a wrong number, a hang-up or a telemarketer, you don't want to speak to anyone. You're in no fit state to speak to anyone. It's not even a matter of sobriety. Even sober, you're in no fit state to speak to anyone. You're out of practice. When you do have to speak to someone, say, someone selling you bread, milk, cereal, toilet paper or scotch, you have trouble. You have to practise the words and the tone of the small talk and it always sounds stilted. You're either too vague or too focused or too polite. The person serving you looks at you strangely and you know you've done it badly. You can't do it anymore.

The neighbours can do it but not you. They're living your life for you on your behalf. They change their cars, their houses. They don't concern themselves with the problems of the world, its trouble spots, local and foreign. Places in which they don't live are potential holiday destinations which they will discuss with their local travel agent. On election day they vote not as their parents and their parents before them did but as their perception of their socioeconomic status demands. They read their newspapers in the thirty second bites through which they've been conditioned by TV to see the world. Not that it's ever quiet enough to read for longer amidst the amplified noise they continuously pipe through their houses. You hear it, whether you want to or not. You hear them laugh at night with their dinner guests. You hear them in their beds. The groans must be exaggerated.

You ask yourself if it was ever really that good. A little numbed, you turn on a small light in another room, go to a cabinet and to a drawer that you don't visit much anymore and fumble in the half-light for images. And there she is, lovely as ever. There are more images, deeper and deeper in the drawer. Ah yes, you remember. It was that good. Remember her skin, you weak bastard. Concentrate and you won't hear them. Smooth, olive, soft, a sweet scent on her neck, on the back of her neck and below her ears, and you burying your face in her hair. Remember her body. You never knew where to start. Remember the taste of her, how she would take you. Remember the different rhythms she had for you, the change in the tension of her body. Remember the tightness of her, the many ways she held you, the sweetness of it. Whatever they have next door is a far cry from what you and she once had. If you weren't so drunk, you'd call out. They would know who it was but to hell with them. No, not really. To hell with you, and when they do finally stop, your head is between two pillows and you are breathing in the alcohol from your own breath. They wake you in the morning. You hear them getting up. There is a point to getting up but for the life of you you can't find it until you see, through the mess you've made of everything, her. The photographs of her are still with you and you get up to go and look at them again.

The place is a mess. Things are wearing out all around you but she looks at you with those dark eyes and the memory of how it felt to look into them suggests that maybe only she is real and that everything else, the solitary existence, the unemployment, the whole damn mess, is imagined. She has to be real. There she is in the photographs as true as anything ever was and in some of them you are there with her. You remember when each one was taken, although sometimes you wish you didn't. In one she is sitting on your knee. You have your arms around her. Remember how that felt: her weight on your lap, your arms meeting around her waist. She is smiling. You are not. Something had made her smile but the smile was not for joy. Perhaps it was for you, because she knew you might need it afterwards. And perhaps you looked sad for the same reason, because you had guessed there would be an afterwards. As she sat on your knee and smiled, not genteely, but with that fierce warmth and intelligence shining in her eyes that you would never again find in any other woman, did you suspect she would leave you so soon? As you carry her now to the bookshelves, as you hold her, blow dust from her, or wipe your eyes, you must have known.

But she, as she was then, looks at you now, is there for you now, and you can't think of a reason this ever has to change. Why put those photos away? It's your past too, as much as hers. And . . . No, wait. It's your past more than it's hers. Alex says that's the whole problem or that's the start of it. You need her more than she needs you. You can admit it if you have to, but in all likelihood you won't ever have to because nobody will see her there propped up against the bookshelves. Nobody ever comes here. And anyway, where is the harm? You look back fondly on the time you were involved with this woman. It's as simple as that. To the poetry and novels, music and videotaped movies, to the list of things you call upon during difficult times, you add her, the memory of her, neuronal and photographic. Is that so unhealthy? People use all sorts of things to get by. Your devices are not immoral. They're not even illegal. Or they weren't then, before they became immoral and illegal, before they became unhealthy.

I have to have the chance to convince Anna that it was only *my* health that was compromised, not his. Sam was never in any danger from me. I was not the one abandoning him. I have already saved his life once. She doesn't realise how close he came to losing him. Her marriage is a mistake borne of naïveté and weakness but it produced a proud, intelligent, self-sufficient little boy. It was crazy of her to jeopardise all that he is, all that she has helped him to become, and all that he could grow up to be, by having an affair. Or was it crazy of me to try to stop her the way I did? Is Alex right? Am I really very ill and is what I have done a manifestation of that illness? Considered a risk to the wider community even before I am tried, I am refused bail and sentenced to be sentenced in the interim by the prison community who, with the wisdom and the insatiable blood lust of a mob, condemns me as a deviant who preys on children. So, I hide and wait for Alex to bring her to me. And I repeat to myself day after day after day:

> If instead of being hanged by the neck
>> you're thrown inside
>> for not giving up hope
> in the world, your country, and people,
>> if you do ten or fifteen years
>> apart from the time you have left,
> you won't say,
>>> 'Better I had swung from the end of a rope
>>> like a flag'—
>> you'll put your foot down and live.

But every day I gag on the misery.

On Alex's advice, I had retained the services of a Ms Gina Serkin, a criminal barrister of some twelve years experience who was what people in her world called a 'senior junior'. He said she was very bright, thorough and good in court but not too senior to be 'unavailable' for Legal Aid work. He knew her before this. Perhaps from other 'problem' patients. I wasn't sure. Since I didn't have any experience in this sort of thing and no one else was rushing to offer me help or to recommend anyone else, I took his advice.

She came to see me at the Melbourne Assessment Prison in Spencer Street immediately after he called her and began to work on my bail application. She warned me that the media frenzy tacitly linking me to every child that had ever gone missing, coupled with the general upsurge in publicity concerning crimes in which children were the victims, had made what should have been an excellent chance of getting bail very doubtful. I was shaken by this. It wasn't what I had expected. Nothing was. I had expected to see Anna. I hadn't expected the police. I hadn't expected to be charged and once I had been charged I'd thought bail would be little more than a formality. Why should the prosecution even oppose it? I didn't have a criminal record. I wasn't a danger to anybody. But the police and the prosecutor thought differently. Everybody seemed to know more about the procedure, the protocol and the grimness of my circumstances than I did. When Gina told me to be prepared to lose the bail application I somehow managed to convince myself that she was in some way trying to make a likely successful outcome look even better. I thought that perhaps she was marketing herself for future work. If I thought she'd pulled me out of the fire then I'd be more likely to use her in the event that the charges weren't dropped. If I was stupid enough to take Sam I was definitely stupid enough to believe nearly anything I needed to believe in order to keep going.

A guy in the same cell who'd been arrested for dealing wanted to talk. He looked like he knew the ropes. We spoke fairly frankly and he seemed to think I didn't have anything to worry about. It began like nearly all prison conversations with, 'What are you in here for?' It's often asked in a threatening tone, the answer being just one of the variables taken into account when determining your position in the food chain. But this man, an experienced trader in almost everything prohibited, seemed rather calm and his demeanour helped me to relax a little. It wasn't so much what he said but his manner of saying it that suggested that the criminal justice system was just another branch of government bureaucracy. With experience or, better still, sound advice, it could be negotiated until it was a mere annoyance. He was comforting in his way. Without confessing to anything in dispute, I did admit to him that this was my first time in trouble with the police, that I'd never been arrested before, and that I was having trouble believing I was there. In the course of my half-delirious rambling, I told him, quite incredibly, all about Anna and about her mistaken marriage to Joe. I told him how much I loved her and asked him if he had anyone. I don't remember what he answered because I was too busy telling him how ashamed I was to be there, that this wasn't me, that I wanted to start again, rewind my life. I told him that I just wanted to disappear. He would have been forgiven for thinking I was high. Maybe that is a way of putting it, of getting Alex to understand what it is like. You don't need to be seeing someone to be in love with her. You can have lost touch with her, she can have hurt you, even inexplicably. If you ever felt that you really knew her and that it was what you knew that you loved, and if you remember what it was you once knew, why is it so crazy to retain that love still?

5

We were in a small café at the very end of Glenhuntly Road, opposite the beach. The sky was grey and sombre and I had just made her laugh. An involuntary convulsion had gripped her body the way it would sometimes when she laughed, and her breasts had leapt a little and my mood with them. Not knowing any other way of going about it, I pulled out a small wrapped package from my coat pocket.

'What's this?' she said, by which time my mouth was dry.

'I don't remember anymore. I found it on the ground. You may as well open it.' It was a simple bracelet of linked silver, a series of interlocking Möbius strips.

'Simon, it's beautiful!'

'I hope you like it. It's very simple.'

'Oh, I do,' she said, putting it around her wrist.

'Really? I designed it myself.'

'You didn't?'

'Of course I didn't,' I said, but by now she had found and was unfolding the poem I had at the bottom of the box.

'What's this?' she said. It was Shakespeare's 'Let me not to the marriage of true minds' and she read it to herself except the last four lines, which she read out aloud.

> *Love alters not with his brief hours and weeks,*
> *But bears it out even to the edge of doom.*
> *If this be error and upon me proved,*
> *I never writ, nor no man ever loved.*

I knew the prosecution was going to call Detectives Staszic and Threlfall in opposing my bail application. I was ready for that. But when they mentioned the name Frederick Zwier, I had no idea who they were talking about. Even as he was sworn I thought that the face might be familiar but I really couldn't place him. He gave his full name and a prison address. He was the dealer who had shared a cell with me at the Melbourne Assessment Prison.

He told the magistrate that on a certain day he shared a cell with the 'applicant', as he knew to call me, and that he found me keen to engage him in various conversations in which I did most of the talking. He said that I had confessed to stealing the child, and that expecting to be granted bail, I was planning to abscond as soon as I could.

Gina Serkin had me wearing a suit and tie. I sat in the dock clutching at my collar, inserting the finger of one hand between it and my neck. Gina turned around to face me briefly and saw me shake my head to damn this man to hell. The police had bugged our cell. He had been placed there deliberately to get me talking. They had it all on tape. The prosecution had not planned to play it unless Mr Zwier's evidence was contested. He was the man who found the criminal justice system just another branch of government bureaucracy, ubiquitous in his line of work but a mere annoyance.

We got permission for Gina to 'seek instructions' from me.

'He's lying!' I whispered to her in fury.

'Was he in the cell with you?'

'Yes, but—'

'Did you talk to him?'

'Yes, but—'

'Simon, is there anything you didn't tell me but now wish you had?'

'Gina, he's fucking lying. I didn't say any of that. I didn't confess to anything. Can you make them play the tape?'

'Are you sure I should?'

'Gina, for Christ's sake, you have to believe me!'

'I want to be clear on this, your instructions are for me to get them to play the tape to the magistrate?'

'Yes, of course.'

'What's on it? What did you say to him?'

'I don't know, nothing important. We just talked. I told him that I'd never been in trouble before, that I felt sick about it. I didn't confess to anything. I haven't done anything to confess to.'

'Simon, I appreciate your instructions but we've no reason to believe Anna Geraghty is going to change her story. It'll be your word against hers, and now there's this tape.'

'There's nothing on the tape. I didn't say anything, nothing incriminating.'

Gina had them play the tape. Then she sought a short adjournment before putting Zwier through his paces. Alex was right. She was good in court.

'Mr Zwier, would you tell the court where you live.'

'Do I have to?'

'You don't want to?'

'Not really.'

'Why not?'

'Well . . . it's not relevant.'

'Its relevance may not be obvious to you immediately, Mr Zwier, but I'll ask you to bear with me and answer the question.'

'I . . . I'd rather not.'

'And that's because you don't feel comfortable with people knowing where you live, isn't it?'

'Well, I don't know who all these people are,' he said, gesturing toward the public gallery.

'Mr Zwier, you think you have good reason to be cautious about people knowing where you live, don't you?'

'I don't know.'

'More reason to be cautious than the average person?'

'I don't know. What's average?' he smirked.

'Ms Serkin,' the magistrate interrupted, 'do you know where you're going with this?'

'Yes, Your Worship.'

'Do you think you could take us there a little faster?'

'Yes, Your Worship. Mr Zwier, you know Anne-Marie Bellamy, don't you?'

'Not very well.'

'But you know who she is, don't you?'

'Hardly.'

'But you know her well enough to have slept with her, don't you?'

'Yes, like I said, I don't know her very well.'

'No, not very well. Not well enough for her to consent to sleeping with you.'

'No, that's not true. She consented.'

'Did she consent before or after you put something in her drink at the Amazon Nightclub?'

'I didn't put anything in her drink.'

'But the police think you did, don't they?'

'I don't know what they think,' he said dismissively.

'Mr Zwier, twenty-four hours before you had the taped conversation with Mr Heywood in the cells at the Melbourne Assessment Prison you were charged with administering a drug for the purposes of sexual penetration pursuant to Section 53 of the Crimes Act.'

'Yes.'

'And you were also charged pursuant to Section 19 with administering a substance capable of interfering substantially with the bodily functions of another, weren't you?'

'She said she was eighteen.'

'Did she volunteer that or did you ask her before you drugged her?'

'Objection! Sir, Mr Zwier is not on trial here,' the prosecutor protested.

'No, he isn't, Your Worship, but his credibility is,' Gina answered.

'Try not to get into an argument with the witness, Ms Serkin,' the magistrate said.

'She said she was eighteen but she's seventeen. What's a year? It shouldn't be a crime,' Zwier said.

'Is that your defence, Mr Zwier?' Gina asked.

'I don't have to answer that.'

'You were also charged pursuant to Section 71 of the Drugs, Poisons and Controlled Substances Act with trafficking in a drug of dependence, weren't you?'

'I don't know.'

'Too many charges to remember, aren't there, Mr Zwier?'

'They're not important.'

'All those charges, not important? Not important to you, Mr Zwier?'

'They've dropped them.'

'Are you telling the court the police have dropped the charges against you?'

'Most of them. Yes.'

'That must make you feel very kindly disposed to the police, does it?'

'They should've dropped all of them.'

'But they haven't, have they?'

'What?'

'The police haven't dropped *all* the charges against you, have they?'

'No.'

'You're still facing the charge of sexual penetration of a sixteen- or seventeen-year-old child, aren't you?'

'Yes.'

'Well, perhaps they're not quite finished with you, Mr Zwier.'

'They'd better be.'

'I wonder if you can help me get the timing of all this straight, Mr Zwier. You met Anne-Marie Bellamy on the Friday night at the Amazon Nightclub, right?'

'Yep.'

'You slept with her that night, right?'

'Yep.'

'You were charged with everything I just mentioned late the next morning, weren't you?'

'Yes.'

'About thirty-six hours later you find yourself sharing a cell with the applicant in the Melbourne Assessment Prison?'

'Yes, that's right.'

'Whilst there you have various conversations with him which the police have on tape.'

'Yes.'

'Sometime after that many of the charges against you are dropped.'

'Yes.'

'Some of the more serious ones, too.'

'As I said, they should have all been dropped.'

'They dropped trafficking in a drug of dependence, didn't they?'

'Yes, they did.'

'That's a good one to have dropped, isn't it?'

'Yes, it is.'

'Because a second conviction for that is likely to lead to some serious time inside, isn't it?'

'Yes.'

'And you've been convicted of that before, haven't you?'

'Long time ago, Your Worship.'

'Mr Zwier,' Gina continued, 'was that the time you were charged with "perverting the course of public justice" or was that another time?'

'Don't you remember the section for that one, you stuck-up—'

'Mr Zwier,' the magistrate interrupted, 'please limit your answers to the question put to you.'

'Yes, sorry.'

'Mr Zwier, you made a deal with the police to try to elicit information from my client, Mr Simon Heywood, and then to testify against him in return for certain of the charges against you being dropped, didn't you?'

'No.'

'Are you telling the court that's not what happened?'

'No, that's not what happened.'

'Mr Zwier, will you have a look at the transcript of the taped conversation between you and Simon Heywood.'

'Yes.'

'I'd like you to read it carefully.'

He pretended to read it but the temptation to demonstrate his contempt and his anger was too strong and he made a show of letting the pages drop from his hands as he sped through it.

'Have you read it carefully, all the way through?' she asked him.

'Yes,' he said and then added, 'I was there.'

'Is the transcript accurate?'

'Yes.'

'Can you read aloud to the court those sections of the transcript which you say record the applicant, Simon Heywood, admitting to you that he unlawfully took the child, Samuel Geraghty, and that, if he was granted bail, he intended to abscond.'

'Your Worship, I must object to this,' the prosecutor jumped up to announce.

'Yes, Ms Serkin,' the magistrate said, 'I would have thought that the witness's opinion or rather his interpretation of the conversation is not as important as mine. Wouldn't you agree?'

'Yes, sir, but I was—'

'I have the tape and the transcript and there seems to be no dispute as to its accuracy. Do you have any further questions for this witness?'

'No, sir.'

'You weren't planning any re-examination of this witness, were you?' the magistrate asked the prosecutor, which I took as a good sign. Gina knew better and thus I was introduced to those legal procedures that are never codified and, apparently, are never taught. I took the magistrate to be hinting heavily that he did not want to hear any more from Zwier, most probably because Gina had destroyed his credibility by indicating there was a motive for him to lie. I started to congratulate her but she quickly brought me back down to earth with her expression and then explanation.

'I have to say, I don't think it's looking good for us, Simon.'

'What are you talking about, you completely destroyed him. So much so that the magistrate didn't want to hear from him anymore, didn't want him re-examined.'

'That's part of what I mean. The purpose of re-examination is to allow the counsel who called the witness to fix up any problems that have arisen in cross-examination. When the court hints that re-examination isn't going to be welcomed it's like saying, "Don't worry about cleaning up the mess your witness just made. I'm going to find for you anyway. So don't re-examine, I want to get out of here."'

'But, Gina, the guy was so obviously disreputable and there are no confessions on the tape. You heard it.'

'Simon, I know, you're right. But that magistrate is backstage right now writing up the reasons for his decision. He's thinking a lot of different things all at once. He's pissed off with the police for not getting someone better, someone "cleaner" to "verbal" you. As a magistrate he's completely oblivious to the attempt by the media to blame you for every missing child since Mowgli, but as a person he's reading it, hearing it, watching it. Even if he's not buying it, he doesn't want to be the one to let the "child abductor", as they're portraying you, go free. He doesn't need the letters to the paper, the talkback psychos. He doesn't need the cutting remarks from his colleagues or his wife.'

'But he seemed to like you,' I said, bewildered.

'Oh, he does. He'll probably make a point of coming over to me at the Criminal Bar dinner in a few weeks to tell me what a good job I did. But he's not going to let you out.'

She was right. His written decision did not refer to any part of the taped conversation in which I was alleged to have confessed to taking Sam unlawfully, but it did make mention several times of the throwaway line I used to evince shame, namely, 'I just want to disappear.' Thus, out of my own mouth I became an unacceptable flight risk and this, plus the community's 'justifiable concern at recent crimes against children and young persons' led to my application for bail being refused.

The law permits more than one attempt at bail. After I was bashed in the mainstream section of Port Phillip Prison we tried again, this time in the Supreme Court. The prosecution countered that society's concern that I not abscond, not intimidate witnesses and not reoffend, as well as my concern for my own safety following the assault, could be met simply by placing me in the maximum security section of the prison. The court preferred this to what it described as 'the inherent risk' in granting me bail. And so it was that I came to be moved from the initial police cell at St Kilda to the Melbourne Assessment Prison in Spencer Street to the mainstream section of Port Phillip in Laverton and then to the maximum security section there.

Gina said it was an outrage, that I shouldn't have been in custody at all, that there was a madness in the air that had infected the court's decision-making. She said we were living through a time when society deemed all child-related offences so heinous that the mere accusation of them was sufficient to reverse the traditional presumption of innocence. Whatever madness was in the air Gina breathed, it was nothing compared to the fear, excrement, and disinfectant that was in the air we breathe here.

We tried a third time for bail once I'd been moved to the maximum security unit. The move constituted what Gina called the 'new facts and circumstances' we required to try again in the Supreme Court. She ran the argument that I was an unconvicted man completely without prior convictions pleading 'not guilty', a man who had been brutally beaten whilst in the care of the state and who was now being punished by being placed inside a maximum security facility with the worst criminals the jurisdiction had to offer and with an even greater deprivation of freedom. The prosecution argued that this new application should fail on the same grounds as those it had successfully argued in the two previous applications, namely, that the move to maximum security, while clearly regrettable, was for my protection, and that consequently my interests as well as those of society would be best satisfied by the court denying this third application. The argument completely ignored the reality of life in maximum security and, in court, away from the claustrophobia, the cavity searches, the arbitrary abuse, humiliation, the ever-present terror, the systematic degradation and the random cruelty and violence, it sounded a reasonable argument. It was a successful argument. The

law permitted more than one application for bail. It was society that
didn't permit their approval.

Alex suggested a fourth attempt when one of my fellow inmates
within maximum security gave me a month to have $30 000
deposited into a bank account of his choice or else be beaten to a
pulp. Surely, Alex reasoned, this extortion attempt constituted a 'new
fact and circumstance'? Gina said it did, at law, but there was a risk
in trying to use it because it would require me to give evidence of the
threat and to identify the prisoner who had made it. If I was denied
bail after 'squealing' I was effectively dead. She would try a fourth
time for me if I wanted her to. What did she think I should do? She
wouldn't say. It was my decision. What did she think my chances
were of getting bail this time? She said I would have to expect denial
of the threat not only by the extortioner himself but by everyone
else, other prisoners, prison officers and those further up the prison
hierarchy. It would be my word against everybody else's. So I should
expect to lose? Probably.

'If that's what she thought all along, Alex, why didn't she just
come out and say it?'

'I don't know, Simon. I suppose she, like me, visits you in here,
sees your distress and maybe she couldn't bring herself to advise you
not to take any opportunity to try to get out.'

'But if she didn't think it would be successful and that to fail
would literally kill me . . .'

'Simon, what are you suggesting? Believe me, I know this is hell,
but you can't start doubting her. You don't doubt her ability, do you?'

'No.'

'Well, you shouldn't doubt her integrity. She still hasn't been
paid for the third bail application.'

'Is that what this is about, money?'

'Simon, listen to yourself. If she advised you to try a fourth time
despite the danger you'd be in if, as is likely, you lost, you'd accuse
her of being motivated by money. And if she doesn't advise you to try
you think she's holding back because she still hasn't been paid for
the previous application. Either way, she's mercenary.'

'Not entirely . . .'

'Simon, this is her job. This is how she earns a living. You're not
her charity.'

'No, just yours. Right, Alex?'

I wondered whether he knew why he was coming to see me
almost every day. My father had long since stopped paying him.
What was in it for him? Why was he so determined to keep me going,

to keep me sane? It certainly wasn't doing *him* any good. But I never asked him. I never asked him why he kept visiting me and bringing me books, why he kept talking to me—about my legal situation, about my past, about literature, about the world, about everything that was or had once been important to me. I never asked him why he was acting as my agent, trying to liaise with my father and mother, with Anna, with Angelique and even with Gina. What if I asked him and he didn't know?

'It's just that I don't think she believes me.'

'What do you mean?' Alex asked.

I leaned in and the plastic of my one-piece sky blue prison uniform exhaled. 'She thinks I did it,' I whispered.

'You did,' he whispered.

'Don't say that, not here,' I continued, in an outraged whisper. It wasn't that I had forgotten how crazy it was for me to have taken the little boy. My circumstances reminded me every waking moment that it had been sheer insanity, however brief, to insinuate myself into Anna's life like that, thinking, in some vague ill-conceived way that I was also doing something positive for her son. The logic of it had been to leave her no choice but to save me by telling the world that I was, after nearly ten years, her lover again, her confidante, her conspirator, confessor, the person she most trusted. So of course I had her permission to do something as uncontroversial as pick her son up from school. In maintaining this line she would be aborting whatever relationship she had or was about to have with her putative lover and she would be bringing to an end her sham of a marriage to Joe Geraghty. She would be free to start again. She could reconsider me.

However mad this plan was, once I had acted on it I had no other way out but to persist with it if I wanted to get out of prison. Anna's permission was my only possible defence. I had to hope that she retained enough of a vestige of what she had once felt for me for it to be less insane for her to go along with what I'd planned than it was for me to act on it in the first place. Alex understood that, having acted irrationally, it was now rational, even essential, to act for all the world as though, as Anna's lover, I'd had her permission to take Sam and that it was only her second thoughts about ending her marriage and the humiliation of a public admission of the affair that was keeping her from speaking up and freeing me. I had maintained this line all along, to Staszic and Threlfall, to Gina, in fact to anyone who would listen. Alex knew this and, perhaps with a heavy heart, he went along with it. But he kept checking, prodding me to make sure I was hanging on to reality.

'Simon, we're trying to get you out of here, you and I, and we'll do and say what we have to. I can't get you well in here. But let's not forget that you . . . you took him without Anna's permission.'

'Yes, but . . . do you think Gina knows?'

'She hasn't said anything.'

'Either way?'

'No.'

'Do you talk to her about me?'

'Of course I have.'

'But *do* you? Do you talk to her regularly?'

'Well, I do. She wants to know how you are.'

'Do you talk to her about my mental health?'

'Simon!'

'What? She's my lawyer. Only things, matters, affecting my legal situation are of any relevance to her.'

'Simon, do you think I'm betraying your confidence to Gina?'

'I think you're seeing her.'

'You know I—'

'I think you're seeing her more than you need to on my account.'

'You think I'm seeing her socially?'

'Yep.'

'Do you think that concerns you?'

'I think that the word "concern" has more than one meaning. I think that whatever meaning you had in mind, the answer would be the same—yes. Yes, it concerns me, and I think that by responding with a question you've answered my question.'

'Simon, I am seeing her.'

'Jesus! I knew it.'

I don't know why this made me feel the way it did—afraid, anxious, like someone had hit me in the stomach. I hadn't thought I had any equilibrium left to disturb. I covered my face with my hands and leant forward on the chair. I wanted to vomit. Alex put his hand on my back and began to rub it.

'Were you seeing her when you recommended her to me?'

'No.'

'Was your . . . be honest with me, Alex—was your interest in her the reason you recommended her to me?'

'No.'

'Not even part of it?'

'No. I'd worked with her before although . . . never as intensely as this. When I contacted her about you I didn't know she was separated.'

'Separated?'

'Divorced. She's divorced. I'm separated.'

'Does she have kids?'

'Two, like me.'

'Alex, you've got to tell me—what am I to you?'

'Simon, why are you asking me—?'

'You lie with her—'

'Really, Simon, that's not your—'

'I don't mean *lay*. I'm not talking about sex. Look, Alex, you're worried about me losing my mind in here. You're worried I'll lose my grip on reality altogether. You remind me, rightly, that my defence is . . . a lie. I was not really having a relationship with Anna.'

'No, you were not.'

'I didn't really have permission to take him.'

'No, you did not.'

'Despite that, everything you've done, everything you've said to everyone since the day I called you from the police station has been consistent with that lie. I admit that. But now you have some sort of involvement with Gina. I know you. You would have told her the truth. You would have told her that I'm guilty as charged.'

'She can't act for you if your instructions are to mislead the court.'

'Alex, what does that really mean?'

'If she knows you're guilty she can't continue to defend you against the charges.'

'But, Alex,' I said, now looking up from my knees into his eyes and holding both of his hands, '*you* know.'

7

It was Gina who finally influenced Alex to stop trying to get me to agree to see Angelique again. Alex had been insisting that Angelique couldn't reasonably be blamed for my present situation. If she hadn't called the police, Anna or her husband, Joe, would have called them, sooner or later. In calling them so soon she had actually helped me by reducing the time Sam was away from his parents. If I was to be found guilty, having had Sam for less than three hours wouldn't look so bad when it came to sentencing me. Sound as it was, this argument was never going to get me to see her. The idea of being sentenced at all, even leniently, was and still is an anathema to me, the more so because nobody had been hurt, certainly not Sam, by what I had done. But more than this, I still hadn't completely given up the hope that if I could just talk to Anna alone, I might yet persuade her to tell them that I'd had her permission to take her son that afternoon.

Alex had also appealed to my sense of guilt. I am to Angelique what Anna is to me, only in Angelique's case it is more warranted. When I thanked him for flattering me he corrected me sharply.

'I am not flattering you, Simon. It's more warranted not because you're a worthier object of affection than Anna is. At least, that's not what I meant, although it's interesting that you interpreted it that way. Your feelings for Anna are based on an idealised version of a relationship you had with her ten or so years ago—'

'Idealised. You always have to say that, don't you? Is it not enough—'

'Angelique's feelings for you are much more rooted in reality.'

'Alex, how can other people comment on the "reality" of someone else's subjective feelings? Affections can be more real to someone than anything else in their lives. They can be the only things that keep you going, like religious faith.'

'Simon, don't play dumb with me. She, Angelique, was the only thing keeping you going. She cooked for you, talked to you, walked with you, listened to you. She drank with you, shopped for you.'

'You did most of that too, you know.'

'Simon. She held you. She made love to you. She misses you terribly. How can you punish her like this? It's not consistent with the person you are, the person you want to be. You owe her.'

'The person I want to be is the person who's not in here. You'll forgive me if I'm not at my most giving.'

'Simon, just because she felt more for you than you felt for her doesn't mean it was wrong for her to feel the way she did. It doesn't mean it was crazy.'

'But I suppose it's crazy for me to hold on to feelings for Anna that were once reciprocated?'

'Whether they were reciprocated once is not the point. You've had nothing to do with her for years. You've got no reason to believe they've persisted all this time.'

'She can't have changed that much, not the essence of her.'

'That's what you're counting on, isn't it? Her essential constancy. If she hasn't changed you're a free man. You're out of prison, this one, and the psychological one you've been in for ten years. But if she has changed . . . what then?'

'If instead of being hanged by the neck
you're thrown inside
for not giving up hope . . .
you won't say,
"Better I had swung from the end of a rope
like a flag"—'

'Who is it, the Turkish guy? Nazim Hikmet, is it?'

'Yes.'

'What a fine memory you have. But Hikmet is in prison because of the hope he retains in the world, his country, his people, while you are in prison only because of the hope you retain in Anna, in Anna as she was. It is indeed a heavy burden you impose on her. And even if she hasn't changed, if the essence of her hasn't changed, what if you simply misremember her? What if you've had her wrong for all these years?'

'I don't think I have.'

'You hold on to this memory of her the way a religious person holds on to his faith. There's no test for a theist that can displace his faith in God. If God fails there must be something wrong with the test or else with the theist's interpretation of the results. It's the same with a political ideologue too, a communist or an evangelical free marketeer. It's not ever possible to displace an article of faith.'

'But, Alex, I'm testing her now.'

'Simon, she doesn't come to see you. She's failed.'

'No, not yet. She *hasn't* come to see me.'

'Simon, listen to you! You're unable to design a test that allows her to fail.'

'If I can just get a chance to talk to her, I know she won't leave me to rot in here.'

'And if she does?'

'Then she's failed.'

'And if she doesn't ever come to see you?'

'Alex, I've designed the test. You have to help me get her to take it.'

'And, Simon, if I can't get her to, you stay in jail and she still hasn't failed.'

But just as he ultimately managed to talk me into agreeing to see Angelique another time, so he failed to persuade Anna to visit me even once. He had apparently spoken to her a total of three times since the day I took Sam to my house. He assured me that she understood what it was I wanted from her. Despite that, he said, I should be in no doubt that the 'essence of her' envisages herself negotiating her way through the rest of her life in the knowledge of my conviction for the kidnapping of her son.

8

The smell of disinfectant is everywhere. It burrows into my skull and eats away at the very idea of me. How am I meant to breathe? Perhaps I'm not.

It was Gina who persuaded Alex to stop trying to get me to see Angelique. In fact, Gina insisted that I not see her. She was horrified to learn that I had even seen her once. Angelique was a prosecution witness who could, herself, be charged and this, Gina argued, made Angelique at least potentially very dangerous. Neither Alex nor I had ever thought of her that way. Gina didn't know her but she said prudence required that we assume the worst with respect to her. It was possible Angelique could testify to a conversation we'd allegedly had in prison. She could say that I had told her what to say to the police or in court. Alternatively, she could say that I'd threatened her, or bribed her to change her testimony. It would be difficult enough with Anna refusing to corroborate my story. As far as Gina was concerned, no good could come of me seeing Angelique again. The woman was a young prostitute. She was extremely vulnerable to intimidation by the police. They might even persuade her to wear a wire. Who knows what deals she's made.

Alex was the one that needed convincing. I had not wanted to see Angelique. He'd been insistent to the point of anger that I did. It was the more pronounced because he had never come close to anger with me over anything, not even over me taking Sam. That day in one of the conference rooms in the visit centre, when Gina laid down the law with respect to Angelique, I just sat there and listened, but Alex argued with her. It became a little heated.

'Gina, I understand what you're saying but you don't know her.'

'I don't need to know her. I'm giving Simon my professional opinion. He can disregard it if he chooses but why would he want to give her more opportunity to fabricate something?'

'Gina, she's completely devoted to him. She's just a vulnerable young girl.'

'Fine. That only makes her more susceptible to pressure.'

'Gina, she was good to him at a very difficult time.'

'Alex, who knows what she'll say? The more he sees her the more rope they get. You can't give the prosecution a windfall like this, not another one. Especially when there's no need to.'

'You haven't seen her. The way she is—'

'Alex, there's no forensic need for him to see her. My job is to get him out. I don't care if he marries her once he's out. But right now he doesn't have the luxury of worrying about her feelings. Simon, *you* know I'm right,' she said, turning to me.

'I'm not arguing,' I said quietly.

'Alex, *he's* not arguing. It's his decision, his life, his girlfriend.'

'No. We were just . . . friends . . . really.'

'Strictly speaking, Alex, this isn't even any of your business. It concerns his defence. You shouldn't even really be here—'

'I can leave,' Alex said, standing up.

'No, stay. I want him here,' I shouted at Gina, but she wouldn't stop.

'It's just wasting time, this . . . your relentless advocacy on behalf of that . . . woman. Why do you do it?'

'Maybe we should take a break or something,' I volunteered.

'That's a good idea,' she sighed, looking at her watch. 'I need to call home.'

'Everything alright?' Alex couldn't help himself asking, but she had closed the door before she could answer.

When we were alone I told him that I had to agree with her. I just couldn't risk it, I wouldn't agree to see Angelique. But I suggested, and regretted it even before he could respond, perhaps he would stay in touch with her. Perhaps he could look out for her.

'Do you want me to try to keep her on side?' he asked.

'Well—'

'Simon,' he began quietly, partly in anger and partly in despair, 'I'm your psychiatrist and, against the best interests of at least one of us, I have become your friend . . . I am not your pimp.'

Against whose best interests was it that Alex had crossed the line and ceased to be purely my therapist? He had become a friend, maybe even a little of a father figure who also just happened to be a psychiatrist. We had both known this for a long time. But, as a friendship, it was plainly unequal. In what way had I ever helped him? Before I took Sam to my place, before my incarceration, we would often have long conversations that seemed to have nothing to do with me, at least nothing to do with Anna, my past, my family or my mental health. We would discuss the news, politics, history, his concern about disturbing tendencies in health care. I would hold forth on literature and recommend movies, and even music. We traded ideas and shared enthusiasms. But the friendship was always unequal when it came to our personal histories—I still know very little about his past or his private life, about his children, or about the breakdown of his marriage. And since coming here it has become even more unequal. My long-time emotional palette of shades of melancholy has degenerated into a kaleidoscope of raw extremes— extremes in which I flirt briefly but intensely with paranoia, anger, self-pity, self-doubt and a sense of hopelessness. To assault Alex with one of these moods whenever he comes to see me is not what one does to a friend. It is what one does to a psychiatrist.

His visits saw the evolution of a minor ritual. After greeting each other, the first thing he would do was ask me about the hours since he had last seen me—how were they spent, how did I get through them, how had I slept? And while he was asking I would be apologising abjectly for some outburst the previous day or even days before. And I really was sorry. I couldn't be more sorry. Alex was about the only good thing my father had led me to, the only friend I had in the world. He was my family now. Even Angel, whatever her motives, had turned on me. I had engineered this situation myself with an act that was as irrational as it was futile and as a result I was more alone than ever. There was absolutely no one else to hear me except Alex. I was not myself anymore. Or else I was too much myself. The relationship, initially of therapist and patient, and then of enquiring minds in the service of lacerated souls, had turned full circle. Something about me had helped to distract Alex from some deep, black, lachrymatory hole that hid within him, but not anymore. Now the help was all one way. And he had to drive out to Laverton to give it.

The Turk has gone crazy. That was the word around and the word would always reach me somehow, often in the gap under the door along with the smell of the disinfectant. He had smashed in the cheekbone of some other prisoner. Some said the prisoner had taunted him about his wife; others that he had just repeated something one of the guards had said. Some said the wife was sleeping with a lodger; others that she was sleeping with men for money. The Turk had been confined to his cell. It was for a week; it was for two weeks. Wherever the truth lay, Nazim the Turk's wife was appearing less and less in the visit centre.

And who knows,
The woman you love may stop loving you.
Don't say it's no big thing:
It's like the snapping of a green branch
            to the man inside.

9

'Then why doesn't she come?'

'It's not that she doesn't care.'

'If she cared she'd come.'

'It's hard for her.'

'It's harder for me.'

'She'll never stop caring about you but . . .'

'She's ashamed, isn't she? Admit it, Dad, you both are. It's obvious.'

'Well, I'd be lying to say we're . . . proud. You always had to be . . . I mean we knew you were always different. You had to be different. I don't know where it . . . certainly not from me. It's very . . . the papers . . . the stories in the papers. It's very hard for her. She has to . . . she hides from people she knows, hides in the supermarket when she sees someone she knows, goes from aisle to aisle. It's very hard for her . . . and your brothers. They send you their . . . their kids have been teased, you know, at school.'

'Dad, the worst thing I did was to have an affair with a married woman. And not just any married woman. It was Anna. You both know her. You liked her. She asked me to pick up her son from school one day. The arrangements got confused and the relationship was found out. She's been unhappily married for years. End of story.'

'No. It's not the end of the story. Do you think we're idiots? Why won't she admit it?'

'She should. I think she will.'

'Simon, are you mad, stupid or blind? It's been months. She's not going to admit anything. You always had ideas above your station.'

'What the hell does that mean?'

'Do you think she's going to leave her husband for you? She didn't want you back then.'

'Fuck you!'

'Yes, yes, that's right. Fuck me, fuck everyone with a good job, with a marriage, with prospects. We never understood anything, did we? Only you did. You read poetry and looked down on the rest of the world, on your brothers and on me, and now look at you. You've made your bed—'

'I didn't look down on Mum. I was the only one. Why won't she come?'

'Your mother tried . . .'

'Tried what?'

'She tried to get Anna to tell them . . . what you want.'

'What did she do? What happened?'

'It wasn't something she'd talked about, at least not with me. I don't know where she got the idea . . . what put it in her head. She phoned there a couple of times. Must've looked up the number in the book. She said she knew the name from the newspaper reports. A woman answered, an older woman with an accent, a foreign accent. Well, your mother had to hang up each time. Hearing that woman's voice just broke her up. She figured that it had to be the boy's grandmother, Anna's mother, and she started to imagine how it would feel, having your grandson kidnapped. I guess she would have put herself in that woman's position, imagining it was one of her grandchildren, one of ours. I can imagine how it affected her hearing the grandmother's voice just saying "hello". She didn't give her a chance to say more than that before having to hang up.'

'She was empathising with the housekeeper.'

'What?'

'Anna's mother was born here. That was the housekeeper she was talking to.'

'Well, she didn't know that. I don't think we ever met them, did we?'

'I don't think so . . . no, of course not.'

'We would have if you'd married her, I suppose.'

'So what happened?'

'She stopped calling. Didn't want to be a nuisance.'

'That's it? That's what she did?'

'No, no . . . she did more than that. She got their address out of the phone book.'

'Oh my God.'

'She was thinking of you, Simon.'

'I know. There's much to be thankful for.'

'Look, it was hard enough on her when that other little boy was taken—'

'What other little boy?'

'The other one, the Italian one.'

'Carlo?'

'The one you were meant to be in charge of.'

'Carlo. His name was Carlo. I was his teacher.'

'Terrible business for her when that was in all the papers.'

'Yes, it must have been impossible for her.'

'That's what you're good for, isn't it? Always been good for smart-arse remarks, sarcasm and rudeness.'

'What happened?'

'She probably blames me.'

'No, I mean what did she do with their address? Did she go there?'

'Yes, she went there. Drove there herself. As I say, she didn't say anything to me about it. She would have looked up how to get there in the Melways, I suppose.'

'Yes, I suppose so.'

'She parked the car. It's not far, really. Lovely house, she said. They've done well.'

'I know the house.'

'Yes. She went to the front door and rang the doorbell. She waited for a long time and nobody answered.'

'Maybe there was nobody home?'

'She said there was a car in the garage, the garage door had been left open and she could see—'

'What happened? Is that it?'

'She rang the doorbell again after a while.'

'You're drawing this out. Why are you deliberately drawing this out?'

'I'm not doing any such thing. You're so . . . quick to jump. You have to imagine how difficult this must have been for your mother. Eventually someone opened the door.'

'Probably the housekeeper.'

'No, it was a man. Your mother asked for Anna. He said she wasn't there. It was the middle of the day. She said he looked terrible, unshaven, red eyes, still in his bathrobe.'

'She should've turned and run.'

'He asked if there was any message. She said no, there was no message. He was closing the door when she said she was Mrs Heywood. He opened the door again, just to be polite, your mother says, because apparently he didn't place the name immediately. She took a breath and repeated it. He asked if she had an appointment to see

his wife and she told him, she had to tell him, that she was your
mother. He looked at her and . . . you know what? . . . he invited her
in. She walked into their house. How could you possibly doubt her
feelings? He took her into the kitchen and you know what he did?'

'No.'

'He offered her a cup of tea. She accepted. He made her a cup of
tea and while he was making it she started to cry.'

'Oh my God.'

'She apologised to Anna's husband. His name is Joe.'

'I know.'

'She apologised to him for . . . the whole mess. She said that
she'd been very upset. She asked after his parents. His father is dead
but his mother is alive. She doesn't live far from them either.'

'Either what?'

'What?'

'You said, "She doesn't live far from them either." What does that
mean?'

'Don't snap at me. That's all I need. I meant . . . didn't Anna's
parents live near there too?'

'Yes, they did.'

'Yes . . . you see. Although this house . . . it's in the "golden mile",
isn't it?'

'I know where it is. What happened?'

'He said his mother was very upset by what happened, said she's
very close to her grandson. Your mother looked around the room and
complimented him on the house. She asked what he did for a living.
He said he was a stockbroker. He said he was on leave. "Stress
leave?" she asked. He said it was something like that and she apologised again. She tried to defend you. She told him, quite wrongly in
my opinion, how close the two of you, you and Anna, had been when
you were students. She told him how much we had liked Anna. She
said that, wrong as it was, it was easy to imagine two people, "exes",
meeting up somewhere by chance, and then something . . . developing. She said she wanted to apologise for the pain the two of you had
caused. She told him that you say you had permission to take the
boy.

'He stood up when she said this. She put her tea down. His tone
had changed. She became a little afraid. I can't believe she did this.
She hadn't intimated to me she was going to.'

'What happened?'

'Well, you can't blame the man.'

'I can.'

'She comes into his house—'

'What happened?'

'He was angry, insulted no doubt. He told her that her son and the prostitute girlfriend had kidnapped his son and were going to demand a ransom. He told your mother that her son was depraved and that the whole family was going through hell. He took her to the door saying that he thought she should leave. He asked her if she'd come there wanting something from him. She said she hadn't meant to offend him. At the door he said he didn't have any money. She shouldn't make assumptions about the house. All he had, he said, was his son. He told her to tell you that he hoped they throw the book at you.

'She was in a terrible way when she got home. She wasn't even going to tell me she'd gone there but she was in such a state when I got home from golf, it all tumbled out.'

10

I remember growing up in my parents' house being aware of all sorts of ornate, delicate stuff stacked or leaning on every conceivable surface—figurines, crockery, cake knives, lace tablecloths and lace napkins, silver sugar tongs, silver tea pots, coffee plungers and brocaded tea trays—none of which we ever used. They were for occasions, circumstances, modes of being that my family never seemed to encounter. From the earliest times I remember this stuff accumulating, congregating around us, crowding us. I remember it always being in the way of the things we actually used to prepare and serve the food we really ate. Reaching into the cupboard for a plate my mother had bought as part of a slightly damaged set from Dimmy's, a set we were allowed to use, I had to crouch down and peer into the dark of the cupboard and be careful that my hand, my wrist, weaved between the vases, percolators and Bodum coffee plungers that were kept for 'company'. The decanters and smoked glass cheese platters with their clear domed lids stood there in the dark, silently, stubbornly waiting for 'company', always threatening to be chipped or broken, the collateral damage of a processed ham, processed cheese and processed white bread sandwich. The domestic consequences of chips, or worse, breakages, would persist insidiously long after the repair or replacement of these avatars of a longed-for but never enjoyed lifestyle. The mere presence of these things in our house promised my parents that one day they would, with practised formality, be entertaining people who shared their aspirations, not the least of which was entertaining each other with practised formality.

It was always a fantasy. It was never going to happen. When my parents die or are put in retirement homes, the stuff will be laid out in a long row and my brothers' wives will stand in an otherwise empty room and squabble over the 'choice bits' which they will mistakenly regard as valuable or as redolent of a time long ago which they do not realise they are still living through. The rest of it will be sent to charities for distribution amongst certain types of people we were never to have anything to do with because they were 'different'. In this way will the only objective manifestation of that difference be as the difference always was, nonexistent. Risibly, my father's insistence on the distinction between these people and us has been the closest thing he had ever had to a calling, to a religion. On her wedding day, my mother took a vow of silence in the service of this religion and the silence has extended to watching as the family was sacrificed at its altar.

And yet, when I found myself living alone in a flat in my late twenties and into my thirties without any stuff, I noticed its absence. I did not merely notice it, I found myself bothered by it. I became viscerally aware of the voracious accumulation of things by the people around me, other teachers I worked with, or their friends, friends who had sprouted into couples, women I went out with. I would find myself in their homes or see into my neighbours' homes through their windows and notice the way people construct shrines from a whole variety of objects, shrines to some not otherwise articulated long-term view of themselves which it is their ambition to resemble.

It wasn't so much their stuff per se that I envied, it was this long-term view of themselves of which it bespoke. As a child, and certainly as an adolescent, I had been ashamed of my parents' stuff, ashamed of what it said about the future to which they aspired. Then, as an adult, I grew to be ashamed of my lack of stuff and, worse, ashamed of my lack of any discernible future.

Maybe my father recognised this? How had the youngest son come to have so questionable a future? Questions were an insult to him, an apostasy. Maybe that's why he hated me? He had worked for the same bank all his working life. He had started as an office boy at fifteen, worked his way up to a teller and eventually to managing a local suburban branch. He never questioned bank policy or the implementation of initiative after initiative, reforms they termed them, that saw him lose staff as though bubonic plague was being pumped out of the air conditioning vents. He never questioned head office when they shifted him from branch to branch. And when they told him there would be no more transfers anywhere, when they said 'no', he didn't question their description of his downsizing as 'retirement'.

'Write this down. Have you written this down?'

Alex wanted me to keep a journal and to fill it with as many of my thoughts and reminiscences as time would permit. It wasn't my incarceration that made him suggest this. It was one of the things he said to me when I first went to him for help. He said everyone ought to keep a journal, that it was conducive to better mental health. I was unconvinced.

'Surely people's incoherent, internally contradictory, mental detritus is hardly worth chronicling. You'd have people less engaged in life and more engaged in the contemplation of their navels. Not only that, but it elevates egocentricity, the pursuit of the personal instead of the common good.'

'Is there any part of that you believe?' he had countered.

'I'm not really sure. What is there to recommend it?'

'Why do I recommend that you chronicle what you call your mental detritus?'

'Sorry, Alex, I know it's your stock-in-trade, but—'

'Are you quite finished?'

'Sorry.'

'Writing things down often forces people to clarify their thoughts.'

'Really? You obviously don't read contemporary literary fiction.'

'That's not what we're talking about, Simon.'

'Sorry. Please . . . I interrupted you.'

'Not always, but sometimes seeing one's fears written down, seeing them articulated, can reduce their efficacy. I don't mean that having them before you on a piece of paper causes them to evaporate but it can lessen their potency. You can go back and see that something that worried you deeply six or twelve months ago turned out to be a trivial problem or no problem at all. You can see before your very eyes how often worry robbed you of the capacity to enjoy the good things in your life when, in retrospect, there was objectively nothing to worry about. And if you can see that historically your fears were as a rule unwarranted, you can then extrapolate to the present and make the reasonable assumption that there's a high probability that you're unreasonably anxious now.'

'"Auto-immunisation against anxiety", it sounds like a good title for a self-help book.'

'That's the other advantage of writing everything down. You can turn it into a book.'

'I'll bet that's not infrequent. What do you say about it promoting egocentricity, promoting the pursuit of the personal rather than the common good?'

'You're kidding, right?'

'Am I?'

'Let's hope you are.'

'Okay. Why am I?'

'Simon, look at the world. Never in western history has there been less emphasis on the common good. What did Margaret Thatcher say?'

'"There's no such thing as society."'

'Right. I see it in health care. Neo-classical economics, that is, free trade and the rush to ever cheaper labour, deregulation, privatisation, the abandonment of government to the market—it's now sold under the feel-good euphemism of globalisation—has been rampant for the last twenty years. People not yet unemployed are shivering in their shoes from insecurity. They can't plan for their retirement, they can't plan for their children's education, they can't plan for next week. And all the while they and the untold numbers already unemployed are being made to feel inadequate because of it.'

'This is great, Alex. You sound like me.'

'Simon, you can't for a moment think that this massive erosion of the common good can be blamed on people who keep journals.'

'Do you keep a journal?'

'Yes.'

'Not just for your professional notes, I mean a private journal, a personal record?'

'I know what you mean. Yes, I keep a journal and it hasn't led me to care less about the common good.'

He had told me to record all my thoughts about Anna. Now, in prison, he talked to me about her, about my memories of her.

'Write it all down, the good and the bad. We'll talk about it.'

There was so much, too much, to talk about. One doesn't normally talk about the good times, not easily anyway. They're not inherently interesting except to the dramatis personae themselves. One feels silly, trying to explain exactly what it was one felt, and why it felt so good. But he insisted. I had to assume his reasons were valid but it made me uncomfortable. It trivialised it.

'Is that the point, Alex, to trivialise what you felt?'

'I'm asking the questions here. You were telling me, you were describing the mental images of her that remain with you.'

'This is ridiculous. There are too many. What's the point of this?'

'Go back to the one you were telling me about. You were alone together at your parents' beach house on the Mornington Peninsula. You said it was summer. You said you had the house to yourselves that time.'

'The house wasn't anything special, not like some of them there.'

'You weren't talking about the house. It was night.'

'It was night and we were in bed. We had been at the beach for much of the day. We had come home, showered and made love. It was a long, long session, long enough to encompass different shades of mood, different types of lovemaking. We fell asleep, read, showered again and made dinner. I barbecued lamb chops—she liked the taste of lamb—and she made one of her elaborate salads. We were drinking a little bit. After dinner we had some of my father's scotch. I started a crossword and we read a little. We took what we were reading to bed. I think we might have played around a bit, not another marathon session but . . . we were always hungry for each other. Then I slept for a while. I don't think Anna did. Maybe she did. I woke from my nap. She was beside me and I went on reading, I think it was Kundera. I felt I was the first person in the world to read Kundera, ahead of even the Czechs. Are people still reading him, do you think? I turned off the bedside lamp, the one on my side. Hers was still on and I remember just watching her, looking at her.'

'Why do you remember this?'

'I don't know. I just do. She looked beautiful. I remember thinking that.'

'Didn't you often think she looked beautiful?'

'Of course. I often did.'

'Why do you remember this time in particular?'

'It was the conjunction of things, I suppose. Isn't that what it always is? I looked at her on the other side of the bed. I drank her in. She lay on top of the bed, smooth olive skin, interrupted only briefly by the white silk of her underwear and the silver bracelet I'd bought her. She had a beautiful shape, full, not overweight but not scrawny either. Her breasts were . . . unambiguous. She was unambiguously female, not just feminine, but entirely woman. There was nothing androgynous about her. I keep seeing her eyes, huge black eyes. They swallowed you. You wanted them to. I did. She was wearing her glasses, the tortoiseshell glasses, with her thick nut-coloured hair tied back. I don't know why, Alex. I just remember it. She had a pencil in one hand, doing a crossword. The whole scene appeared to me . . . I remember thinking . . . I was experiencing a moment of perfection. It's not up to us to choose the visual images that stay with us. Everything I ever wanted just seemed to crowd into that instant.'

'Crosswords?'

'What?'

'You used to do a lot of crosswords.'

'Yeah, I was pretty good at them. I started doing them as a kid, the whole "word" thing. You know—puns, palindromes, anagrams. I must have been quite a pain in the arse. I graduated to spelling puzzles, crosswords, cryptic crosswords . . . "Rare ewes at 1, 3 and 5". Seven letters. Give up? "Unusual".'

'How do you get that?'

'Seven letters. Rare. Ewes, written as in sheep, but taken as a homophone to refer to the letter u, which occurs in the word "unusual" three times, at positions 1, 3 and 5. It fits.'

'That's very clever.'

'Yeah, like an idiot savant.'

'You were still doing crosswords when you were a university student?'

'Yeah. So? It didn't consume my time or anything. It was just a bit of fun, you know, a bit of—'

'You said Anna was doing the crossword.'

'She was reading something.'

'You said Anna was doing the crossword.'

'I don't think so. *I* was doing the crossword. She was probably—'

'You were reading Kundera, the first in the world ever to read him.'

'I don't get it. What's your point? So what if I said she was doing the crossword? What does it matter?'

'Simon, it only matters to you.'

'What are you talking about? Don't get cryptic on me, Alex.'

'Was she doing the crossword or not? It's *your* perfect moment.'

'I don't know. It doesn't change anything. Maybe she was finishing my crossword.'

'Simon, she never did crosswords, did she?'

'No, you're wrong. She did. I think she did.'

'Did she read Kundera?'

'She had to.'

'Did you take any of the same courses?'

'We took English and politics together. That's how we met. There was even a combined honours course we took in third year, "The Politics of Literature", two two-hour seminars a week. Drove me crazy.'

'Why, too much reading?'

'There was a lot of reading but it wasn't that. My suspicions about the nature of the English department were confirmed . . . it hurt. I took it personally.'

'What do you mean?'

'Let me give you an example. We had a visiting lecturer, a professor. Some escapee from the class of 1968, he comes in wearing a cravat—'

'Oh, I see, pompous?'

'He was pompous, authoritarian, but not in the way you'd expect. It was that new breed of pomposity that smugly masquerades as a kind of matey egalitarianism. You were explicitly invited, encouraged, to call him by his first name and to participate in class discussion, but you were implicitly forbidden to publicly disagree with him by his manner, his body language and his Sinaic delivery.'

'I see.'

'He was giving a seminar on George Orwell, and in particular the novel *Nineteen Eighty-Four*. At the back of the book, Orwell put an appendix outlining the principles of Newspeak, the language of the novel's totalitarian Big Brother. The idea posited in the book, one of them, anyway, was that by taking away the word for something you take away the concept. For example, Orwell has Big Brother outlaw the use of the word "bad" which is replaced by the word "un-good".

'The visiting professor, who subsequently made a home for himself in the department, rambled on asking the class a series of trivial questions which culminated in a consideration of what comes first, the concept or the word for the concept. Can "bad" exist without a word for it? When the class reached the conclusion, fairly quickly, that generally the concept comes first—we came up with the word "bad" to describe things that are bad—the professor triumphantly suggested that, together, we had proved Orwell wrong. Then I did what one was never to do. I objected to his characterisation of what we had, together, just done. I told him Orwell can't be wrong. He was a novelist not a social theorist. He can be a good novelist or a bad novelist, he can create a world which is more or less convincing, he can even devise an implausible conceit, misrepresent reality, but he can't be wrong. A novel, like poetry, can be more or less insightful, more or less profound. It can certainly be more or less moving. It can even be moral or immoral. But, being fiction, it cannot be true or false in the way that an empirical proposition is true or false.'

'Hold on, Simon. Isn't that a bit extreme? After all, fiction is usually anchored to at least elements of reality to give it verisimilitude. And insofar as these real elements are concerned, surely their representation can be said to be true or false even if the work of fiction as a whole can't be said to be true or false?'

'Yes, you're right, of course. But what do you expect from a child who had to disagree just to prove he was there. Anyway, the professor became flustered. His face grew red. He started shouting, accusing me of either not taking literature seriously enough or not taking politics seriously enough. The man was an idiot.'

'But why were you so hostile in the first place?'

'The hostility wasn't so much to him or to what he'd said. It was to what was happening to the English department. Like so many others in the country, it was in the process of turning into a cultural studies department, with all that that implies.'

'What does it imply?'

'Where do I start? It implies a rigid doctrinaire embrace of certain amorphous schools of thought often grouped together under the mantle of post-modernism. Now, you're probably thinking this is surely just another fad within the social sciences or the arts to which some people will subscribe and others won't. Who really cares?'

'That's not quite what I was thinking but if it had been, you would have put it very well.'

'The real and grave problem with this particular fad is what it includes and what it has come to exclude. When English departments become departments of cultural studies, it means that the decision-makers within them embrace, adhere to or, to put it more aptly, are under the sway of Jacques Derrida's deconstructionism. Do you know anything about Derrida?'

'Not much. Just that you rail against him nearly as often as you sing the praises of Empson.'

'Yeah. But do you know what he and his deconstructionist friends have to say?'

'To be frank, not really. Nor, for that matter, do I know why anyone should be so upset by it.'

'Well, Alex, that only confirms that you don't know anything about deconstructionism and the harm its wholesale adoption by the literary academy in particular has wreaked. And you don't need to be actively involved in the study of literature to find it pernicious.'

'Okay. Enlighten me.'

'Deconstructionism or post-modernism in so far as it pertains to language, is a doctrine originating with Derrida and others that asserts that every lingual statement, they call this a "text", has a large number of meanings rather than "a" meaning, that every text is essentially ambiguous.'

'Isn't that what your friend Empson was on about in *Seven Types of Ambiguity*?'

'No, not at all. Empson merely suggested that what separates much of the very best poetry from the rest is the latent ambiguity within it. He was only talking about poetic language. He didn't claim that all literature, let alone all texts, were riddled with ambiguity. For Christ's sake, don't ever confuse Empson with Derrida.'

'Sorry.'

'No, this is serious, Alex. Deconstructionists claim that neither the intention of the author, nor any putative connection between words and some non-lingual reality, will confer any more or less agreed definitive meaning to a text.

'They claim, on the contrary, that words only acquire any meaning at all by virtue of their relationship with other words, and these only with other words, and so on *ad infinitum*, and that this endlessly defers arriving at any agreed fixed meaning. Rather than arrive at "the" meaning of a text, all you can do, they say, is to "deconstruct" it, by which they mean to keep on endlessly uncovering the ambiguities and contradictions within it. The effect of this is that you are left with an infinite number of possible meanings or interpretations.'

'Okay, so they're wrong. But why do they make you so angry? I still don't understand why they make you so angry. After all, Simon, all they're doing is taking the observation that many statements are somewhat ambiguous and open to a number of interpretations to an absurd extreme.'

'No, Alex. Don't you see? What the deconstructionists are doing is much worse than that. By denying that there is a fixed correspondence between language and the world, and concomitantly, between language and meaning, they deny that there can be any objective facts or knowledge at all. Thus it is open to them to deny, for instance, that the Second World War occurred, to dismiss all science as just one of a limitless number of narratives, and to deny that Shakespeare's plays are more significant than Enid Blyton's stories.

'Deconstruction delegitimises all that man has accomplished intellectually, morally and aesthetically since he climbed out of the trees and began to walk upright. For them nothing is true or false, no political system is good or bad, no work of art is superior to any other.'

'In that case they're completely mad. But tell me, Simon, if, as they claim, complete ambiguity bestrides the world like a colossus and no text has a definitive meaning, then neither do the texts of deconstruction itself. It's hoisted on its own petard. Not only does it dismiss science and everything else, it dismisses itself as well.'

'Exactly, Alex, exactly. So you'll be stunned to learn the extent to which people swallowed it all. And no group of people swallowed it more than the academics in departments once devoted to the study of literature. These departments ceased being the home of literary critics and became the home of theorists of deconstructionist criticism who wrote about the "self-betrayal of the text". These new emperors of the humanities scorned literary excellence as elitist, entirely subjective and a reflection merely of the dominant paradigm. And with their clumsy, jargon-ridden opacity they succeeded in intimidating those students and scholars not already under their sway. The term "theory" came to be understood as "their theory".

'They all but refused to teach what had before them been regarded as the best that western literature had to offer. They argue that no work of literature, not Shakespeare, not Dante or Donne, not Dickens or Hardy, has any intrinsic value. "Value" is for them a term reflecting the political interests of a particular group or class. There's no premium on consistency. While they claim that it is impossible to discern definitive meaning in all the writings that distinguish us from the apes, including their own—which doesn't seem to embarrass them—they nevertheless claim that it is possible to discern the way these writings function to covertly influence society in accordance with the interests of the established elites.

'Alex, these doctrines have savaged the teaching of literature in universities. A lot of the very best art will barely ever come to you. You have to come to *it*. You have to work at it or you will go without it. And if you do miss out you will have all but lost in the never-ending argument with yourself over whether there is anything that redeems us.'

12

'It's hard for people outside academia to believe the deconstructionists took over a whole field of enquiry. They overran university literature departments like an army of ideological storm-troopers. Junior academics found it was much easier to join the party and trash a long-recognised classic in the name of deconstruction than to write something original and coherent about it.

'Perhaps worst of all for me, even worse than the realisation that I would have to teach myself everything I'd hoped to be taught at university about literature, was the obscene self-righteousness of these people. They labelled themselves socially progressive. This was what had become of the intelligentsia of the left. They were completely totalitarian, again.

'I tried to argue with them in lectures and tutorials. At times I was ignored, at other times I was treated like an oddity, some sort of mattoid. Mostly I was ridiculed or gagged. I was made to feel a fool, not merely a fool, but a reactionary fool. This is when I decided not to pursue a career in academia but simply to teach children, to try to save them from the meretricious cant their would-be teachers were being fed.'

'Where was Anna in all this?'

'Oh, she agreed with me.'

'How do you know?'

'We talked about it.'

'Was she also appalled by deconstruction?'

'Yes, she was. She was.'

'Are you sure?'

'Yes.'

'You're not so sure, are you?'

'She hated that little smug pompous visiting professor.'

'Did she hate the way he spoke to you?'

'Absolutely. She was very upset about it, angry.'

'Who was she angry with, the professor?'

'Of course.'

'She heard it all?'

'Everybody did. It was a public dressing-down. She was sitting next to me. It was embarrassing to see.'

'Embarrassing?'

'Very embarrassing.'

'Who exactly was embarrassed?'

'Probably everybody in the room, all the students.'

'Did anybody stick up for you?'

'No, the guy was a bully. People were too afraid.'

'Where was Anna?'

'I said. She was sitting next to me. What does that matter?'

'Was she afraid of this visiting Orwell-hating bully?'

'I'm sure she was.'

'You don't know?'

'I'm trying to think back . . . I'm reconstructing . . .'

'Let me help you—'

'What are you saying, Alex?'

'She's sitting in the seat next to you. There must have been some people in the room who knew that you were a couple.'

'Yes, so?'

'A man, an older man, a teacher, an alleged expert in something or other, visiting from somewhere or other, is expatiating on that something or other to the whole group. He's wearing a cravat, fancies himself as something of a raconteur. Everyone is listening politely to him.'

'Yep.'

'Until suddenly, someone challenges him, the authority.'

'Well, I would say that *he* was challenging the authority, the authority of the cultural canon.'

'Yes but he *was* the authority, at least in that room at that time.'

'Sure.'

'And you have to open your mouth, full of all your extracurricular reading, and disagree with him. You have to draw attention to yourself—'

'You know it wasn't like that.'

'Not to you, Simon. You didn't see it like that.'

'Oh, and you're saying that's how Anna saw it?'

'Everything had been just as it was meant to be. People were politely taking notes and then looking up, taking notes then looking up, asking the occasional almost rhetorical question. He was pretending to teach, they were pretending to learn, until suddenly you can't take it anymore. You can't bear not being noticed—'

'Alex, she didn't say that.'

'Okay, let's say she didn't think that. Let's say she gave you the benefit of the doubt, that this wasn't about your need to show off. Still, you have to confront this guy—'

'Hey, Alex, he was the one who was shouting.'

'He was the one shouting but not until you told him, in front of everyone, that it wasn't Orwell who was wrong, it was him. What did you think would happen when you did this? It was unequivocally confrontational.'

'Hey, he was the one who chose the Socratic method, questions and answers back and forth until he'd led us to a conclusion, his conclusion. Were we meant to just go along with him, nodding like mindless puppets?'

'Anna thought so, didn't she?'

'No.'

'What did she say when the pompous professor with the cravat started tearing strips off you? What did she say, Simon?'

'How can I . . . I don't remember exactly what she said.'

'You do remember. She didn't say anything, did she? . . . Did she?'

'She was afraid.'

'Really? I thought you said she was embarrassed.'

'She was probably both.'

'You're saying she was afraid lest a visiting professor somehow negatively affect her academic results?'

'He was made permanent.'

'Yes, but she wouldn't have known that then.'

'You had to be careful. Everybody did.'

'*You* didn't though, did you? Simon, listen to yourself. She didn't come to your defence and you're still defending her. Was it reasonable for her to be so fearful? And what was it that so embarrassed her?'

'Me. You're saying it was me. You're wrong, Alex. She saw everything for what it was.'

'She did when you explained it all, put it in context.'

'She's not stupid, Alex.'

'No, she's not. She just wasn't that motivated to stand up for the enlightenment, for western civilisation . . . for you. She wasn't that motivated and she wasn't that brave. But she was bright enough, shrewd enough to know which way the wind was blowing. You said she was appalled by everything that appalled you?'

'Yes.'

'And you would have read her essays?'

'Yes.'

'And you would have argued with her about them?'

'No, why would I have?'

'Because she found a way to come to terms with any intellectual fad, any passing "ism", any doctrine or dogma she perceived to be in vogue.'

'You make her sound like an intellectual whore.'

'Then tell me I'm wrong.'

'You're wrong. She wasn't an intellectual whore.'

'Tell me you never argued with her about her apparent accommodation with the school of thought that prevailed in the department.'

'We never argued about it.'

'Really?'

'Really.'

'And you're telling me the truth. You did read all her essays?'

'All of them.'

'Well, then, you've got me. Maybe she deserves more credit than I've given her.'

'No . . . no, no. No, Alex . . . .She doesn't.'

'What do you mean?'

'We didn't argue about her toeing the line in her essays because . . . because I wrote them.'

'You wrote them? All of them?'

'There wasn't an essay of hers in that course that I didn't write, plan or at least edit. Her father had health problems. She was distracted, needed at home and—'

'Didn't she complain when she got the essays back and the marks were bad?'

'Well, they were never all that bad. In fact, initially they were very good. I wasn't always controversial and even later on, they didn't want to make her grades so bad that she might be tempted to go outside the department and complain. And anyway, they knew who she was . . .'

'They knew who she was?'

'They knew . . . what she looked like. It didn't hurt.'

'You think she was marked up because of her appearance?'

'Oh, come on, Alex. Don't be so naïve. Even deconstructionists have hormones. They just don't have intellects.'

'And she was willing to let you do this?'

'It's not how it sounds. She wasn't lazy. She passed the exams under her own steam. Her father had had a heart attack. She wasn't stupid either. She completely understood my problems with deconstruction. She agreed with me.'

'Let me tell you how it sounds to someone who hasn't spent the last ten years mourning her absence. She was willing to learn without understanding and she would learn whatever was necessary to get by. No heroics for her. She didn't need them and, more than that, she didn't appreciate them. She privately deprecated them. Until one day—and didn't it seem sudden?—it wasn't private anymore. She was gone, gone with a pragmatist's alacrity. She was always a pragmatist. That's why she married—'

'No, Alex, you've got her wrong.'

'Simon, you must know, at least at one level, that your defence of Orwell that day, your virtual crusade against the intellectual tyranny of the department, your passion for literature, maybe even your passion for her—it embarrassed her.'

'No, Alex, you're wrong. She really agreed with me. And she did love me.'

'She really agreed with you? And she was faithful to your beliefs, all the way to the barricades? As for loving you, you were a young handsome aesthete worth killing time with while she was an undergraduate. But when the academic year ended and graduation approached, it was time to get real. There were no more essays to hand in. Her father had recovered. There was one more trip to the Mornington Peninsula, to Sorrento, and then she was gone. And you were left with *Seven Types of Ambiguity*, all the crossword puzzles she didn't finish, didn't even start, a box of unfinished compilation tapes meant for her, and a need, born way before Anna, a need to exalt an undergraduate relationship to within an inch of your life.'

'Alex, the sequence of events might be right but your interpretation is all wrong.'

'Simon, will you concede that it's at least possible that you're so emotionally involved that your interpretation of what happened might not be entirely trustworthy?'

'Memory of an intense emotional involvement need not be untrustworthy just because it was an intense emotional involvement.'

'But, Simon, you have clung to that relationship even though it ended many years ago. Why? Don't you ever wonder why? Anna predates Anna.'

'What does that mean?'

'If it was a special relationship, the most special thing about it was you. You're the one that was so . . . what are the clues? Rare.

Ewes at 1, 3 and 5. Seven letters . . . .unusual. Your passion, your morality, your intellect, even your coping mechanisms right up to now are exceptional. You read voraciously, you analyse and you recite Shakespeare, Eliot, Swinburne and that Turkish—'

'Nazim Hikmet.'

'You memorise them. You are able to remember each of Empson's seven types of ambiguity. You can, can't you?'

'I don't know.'

'Tell me them.'

'This is pointless. Anyway, you only want an excuse to launch into your spiel on the ambiguity of relationships.'

'I won't, I promise. Just tell me what Empson's seven types of ambiguity are—now—in this prison.'

'Alex, what does it prove if I—?'

'What are Empson's seven types of ambiguity?'

'Okay . . . Ambiguity exists when . . . this is stupid. I don't feel like indulging my pedantic obsessions right now.'

'Tell me, Simon. Wipe your eyes and tell me. Type one, the first type . . . go on.'

'The first type . . . exists when a word or grammatical arrangement of words is effective in several ways at once . . .'

'Go on.'

'The second type exists when two or more meanings constitute the single meaning of the writer. The third type exists . . . when two ideas are given simultaneously in a pun. The fourth type exists when different meanings combine to make clear a complicated state of mind in the writer . . . Alex, this is—'

'Go on. You're up to five. The fifth type of ambiguity . . .'

'Alex. I can't get . . . through this.'

'You can. Take a breath. You're a remarkable man. But okay, leave the fifth and sixth types. What about the seventh type of ambiguity?'

'The seventh type of ambiguity exists . . . when two meanings are mutually contradictory for the specific purpose of illustrating a fundamental division in the author's mind . . . Alex, what did you mean when you talked about the need that was born before Anna, to exalt my relationship with Anna?'

'Were you . . . what was it? Were you six years old—?'

'Once, yes, for about a year. What are you talking about?'

'You must have been older than four, surely. Maybe not. Your brothers were outside playing cricket on the beach. Maybe you watched them for a while or maybe you were already old enough to have given that up. They probably had friends with them or perhaps some kids from neighbouring beach houses. You weren't with them. That's the important point. You were already in prison.'

'Alex, what are you talking about?'

'You know what I'm talking about.'

'I don't.'

'You went there voluntarily, a four-, five- or six-year-old boy, wanting it to be more like a womb than a prison. But in birth as in prison, it's not uncommon to experience arbitrary violence and be slapped without explanation into a new awareness of some darker reality.'

'This is great, Alex, this stream of consciousness. You're riffing on my life. That's what they call it in jazz, you know, riffing. I'm in there somewhere, in the chord progression, perhaps? But the more you improvise, the more I lose the original melody . . . You're making this up as you go along. I'm impressed but I don't know what the hell you're talking about. Do you?'

'William and May—'

'My parents?'

'Your parents had been arguing fiercely. The older boys were on the beach, playing cricket. Your father had stormed out. You had earlier slunk away from the screaming to shelter in your parents' bedroom wardrobe. You had fallen asleep there only to be wakened sometime later by the sound of your mother's sobbing and heavy staccato breathing. You peeked through the crack in the door and saw her lying on the bed in her half-opened robe, her face and hair being caressed by Diane Osborne, the wife in the couple who, in your parents' mythology, are their closest friends. You were frightened but nonetheless unable to take your eyes off the two women. It was rare enough to see your mother naked, and now here she was physically and emotionally involved with the half-naked Diane Osborne.

'After a while you can hear your father coming down the hall. Something beyond pure cognition, something pre-thought, tips you off that the apparently inexplicable is about to become catastrophic. Should you warn them? There isn't time and, anyway, what are you warning them of? You don't even know what they're doing. You're not even supposed to be there. You can't speak. Your breathing quickens and you watch as your father comes in. You see another example of that which had sent you hiding in the first place. You see that we are not all friends. Your father catches the two women together. He grabs Diane by the hair and pulls her off the bed. You see him hit your mother in the mouth and Diane in the stomach, knocking her to the floor. Then he picks her up as though she were a piece of furniture and places her back on top of your frightened mother who is trying to get off the bed. He shouts at the women, exhorting them to continue what they were doing when he came in. This is where you faint, your little boy's body spilling out of your parents' wardrobe and crashing to the floor.

'You remember it, Simon. So do they, all of them—William, May, Diane Osborne—but they don't ever speak of it. Never. And how you wish they would because until they do there will always be a part of you that thinks it's your fault. Had you not fallen asleep in the wardrobe you wouldn't have been there to see it, and if you hadn't seen it then it would never have happened. It is as if, like Bishop Berkeley's God, looking at the tree in the quad when there's no one about, your looking caused it to be. But if they were to mention it, it would mean that *they* saw it and then you'd be off the hook.

'That little boy still thinks he caused it all. His brothers knew to play outside. That was the right thing for young boys to be doing, not listening to their parents argue, not listening to all that dissatisfaction pour out of their mouths like water from a fire hydrant that cannot be turned off. And even when he sought to hide in the dark where he would never be found, to hide inside a wardrobe in a room with the shades drawn, in a room meant for sleeping, a room where the grown-ups always went when it was time to be quiet—even then he couldn't escape from hearing and seeing it all. He was a witness, a witness who knew instinctively to keep his mouth shut. We don't talk about these sorts of things. We don't talk about our mother being with other women. We don't talk about our father's anger or the strength in his arms and his hands. But even at a tender age we sense the flimsiness of the line separating a witness who doesn't tell anyone what he saw and an accomplice. When your mother goes quiet each time, when she withdraws to her room, takes to her bed for a day or two or three or four, the boy thinks he knows why. But no one ever says anything and he just misses her. He wants her. She should have been his ally. She should have understood why he went to hide inside the wardrobe in the first place. But instead, she is either absent in bed in a dark room or absent in all but an impersonation of a mother who is like the other mothers. Not only is she absent but she conspires with her oppressor to be silent about the pain and to reject you, a leaf sensitive to the slightest breath of wind, the slightest drop in temperature, to the briefest look of bitterness across the kitchen table.

'None of this is fair and while you've always suspected the

unfairness of it, the older you got the more apparent it became. But even the little boy who awoke from a faint to find that his fainting itself had become the drama, even he saw the criticism implicit in the simulated solicitude behind which they all hid, and the injustice outraged him. Always too perceptive to be completely deceived, he wanted someone to tell the truth, someone to show genuine concern for his welfare. But no one did, so you took it upon yourself to expose their hypocrisy, their dissimulation, you took it upon yourself to protect that child. You would arm yourself with books, fortify yourself with knowledge. You would know so much more than them that they would have to admire you, respect you, even fear you, to make up for the love they were never going to give you. And it wasn't enough to save just that little boy, you were going to save as many children as you possibly could. You were going to save all the children you taught, all of them—the noisy ones, the naughty ones, the scraggly ones with one jumper and two shirts, the fast ones in runners and no socks even in winter, the pretty ones with skinny legs who followed you everywhere, and the very quiet ones who still were not used to having been born. You were in the process of saving the shy little Carlo when someone took him, stole him. And you were devastated, gutted.'

'And, Anna, where is Anna in all this?'

'She was the proof you needed.'

'Proof of what?'

'Proof that you had been saved, that you had grown up and were ready to succeed where your parents had manifestly failed.'

'Alex, sometimes . . . in here . . . I think of my mother now.'

'It's alright. Go on . . . Simon?'

My parents were united mostly by their mutual disappointment. Outside they put on a show for the few petit-bourgeois friends they had, but at home my father would lash out at my mother and she would withdraw into herself, emerging very occasionally to gnaw on her regrets. But the aspirations she had allowed him to thwart were never articulated. To mitigate the loneliness and frustration of her life with my father, she sought solace when she could in the company of another woman. Now, my generation combines its ignorance and its arrogance to conclude that she was ahead of her time. But it is still her time and she has never been ahead, ever. And she never visits me.

13

'Alex, did you tell her he was drowning?'

'Who?'

'Anna. Did you tell Anna that I saved her son from drowning?'

'Yes, I told her.'

'When?'

'When I told her everything, right after you were arrested.'

'Did she believe you?'

'I don't know. There was so much for her to take in.'

'She can't have believed you.'

'Why not?'

'I wouldn't be here now if she'd believed you.'

'You're still imputing feelings to her that she almost certainly doesn't have anymore, if she ever did.'

'Tell her again, Alex. Can you tell her again before the committal hearing starts? Tell her to come and see me . . . *I'm* drowning.'

But he couldn't. He was not to try to contact her in any way. Gina absolutely forbade it. I think they argued about it. How close they had become. Gina said it could be interpreted as an attempt to interfere with a witness. She said it could leave Alex liable to a charge of attempting to pervert the course of justice.

Inside, Mr Greer and all good boys had seen to it that the Turk would be quiet, at least for a while. Two hours a day outside my cell, even under supervision, allowed me more than enough time to discern who it was in my community that had dried blood under their fingernails.

> *I mean, it's not that you can't pass*
> *ten or fifteen years inside*
> *and more—*
> *you can,*
> *as long as the jewel*
> *on the left side of your chest doesn't lose its lustre!*

A week to go before the committal hearing and nothing had changed. There was still nothing to breathe that wasn't tainted, nothing to touch that wasn't soiled, nothing to hope for that wasn't hopeless. A week to go and Anna had not come.

Gina explained the purpose of the committal hearing. It would give the magistrate the opportunity to hear the prosecution evidence in respect of each of the charges and, on the basis of that, to form a view as to whether there was a prima facie case against me. The test, put formally, to determine whether I should be committed for trial on any particular charge was whether a reasonable jury, properly instructed, could at law convict on that charge. In the committal, as it's called for short, there's no jury, just the magistrate. There was a kind of poetry to much of the technical language Gina used to explain what was going to happen and what we needed to happen. Had I been merely a casual observer I might have enjoyed the rhythm and tortured syntax they use but I was the "defendant", also the "accused", except when travelling to or from the court cells to the prison, when I was the "prisoner".

'They'll call their witnesses,' Gina said, 'and we'll get a chance to cross-examine them.'

'Who will they call?'

'The cops, Threlfall and Staszic, Angela—'

'Why her?'

'She called it in.'

'What's she going to say?'

'I don't know. That's what we'll find out. Is there any reason we should be particularly worried about her?'

'No, not if she tells the truth.'

'There are lots of reasons she could stray from the truth, the most likely being some sort of deal with the police.'

'What could the police possibly offer her?'

'Some kind of immunity.'

'Immunity from what?'

'From prosecution.'

'But she hasn't done anything.'

'Oh, Simon, she doesn't need to have done anything. It's your case that *you* haven't done anything.'

'Yeah, but in my case Joe Geraghty is motivated by my affair with his wife to claim that I have. Why would anyone want to have Angelique charged?'

'The police could threaten her with it to make her a more compliant witness. She's the only one they've got who is capable of giving evidence as to your actions, and as to what you said, before the police found you with the boy.'

'Sam. His name is Sam. I had his mother's permission to pick him up from school.'

'His mother will be their main witness and obviously I'll be asking her about that.'

'What good will that do? She's denying I had permission. She's denying the affair.'

'Firstly, it gives her another chance to tell the truth, and in quite different circumstances. She will never have been asked that question in a court room under oath, with all eyes on her. Secondly, it gives her a glimpse of the dire consequences for you if she sticks to her denial. She'll see you in the dock with an officer on either side of you. It will give her the shot of reality she needs. I'll give her a middle way out as well. If she continues to deny the affair, I'll suggest that perhaps she had resumed a non-sexual, even non-romantic relationship with you and that she hadn't told her husband about it for fear of arousing suspicion, jealousy, anger, or just so as not to hurt his feelings. If I can give a jury an accurate picture of you, it will be seen as eminently reasonable to suggest that Anna preferred talking to you, confiding in you, rather than her husband.'

'I thought you said there wasn't a jury at the committal stage?'

'No, there isn't, but it's prudent for us to use the committal to set things up for the trial.'

Gina would not let me harbour any illusions that a magistrate would dismiss *all* the charges after he'd heard the evidence against me. She said I shouldn't imagine that I'd be going home at the conclusion of the committal hearing. Technically I didn't have a home to go to. I wasn't able to pay my rent and my father couldn't be talked into paying it. Alex had tried but having failed, all he could do was to pack my books and music into boxes and store them in his wife's garage.

'Are you saying you won't even be trying to get me off?'

'Not at this stage. I'll try to get the magistrate to throw out some of the charges but we won't be putting any case of our own. There's no point. We'll save it all for trial.'

'What will you be saying at the trial?'

'You need to remember that the burden of proof is on them. We don't need to prove anything. We'll be trying to raise a "reasonable doubt" in the minds of the jury. We don't have to actually prove that you and Anna were having an illicit relationship or even that you had her permission to pick Sam up from school. They have to prove beyond reasonable doubt that you didn't have permission. If we can cause the jury to have a reasonable doubt then they have to find you not guilty.'

'But what evidence do we have even to cast doubt on their case?'

'Mainly you.'

'Me?'

'You're going to have to give evidence of your relationship with Anna and specifically of her instruction to pick Sam up from school.'

'But it's just my word against theirs.'

'It's really your word against Anna's. At the trial, we will try to lead evidence to show how much she stood to lose by acknowledging the affair—the house, the lifestyle, her husband's income. If she persists in denying the whole relationship we'll just have to discredit her. Given that you don't have any incriminating letters from her—'

'What do you mean "incriminating letters"? You make it sound like *she's* on trial.'

'That's what we're going to have to do, create that impression, the sub-text, that she's on trial. We have to get the jury to understand how reluctant she must be to confess to the affair; the indignity, the guilt, the fear of losing her family. We have the letters she wrote to you in your university days when she was your girlfriend, when she wasn't ashamed of your relationship, when it wasn't illicit. We'll tender them as exhibits so the jury can see them. We'll do the same thing with photos of the two of you.'

'But she's not denying that we had a relationship back then, just now.'

'I know, and for that reason we'll have a fight on our hands trying to get them admitted as evidence. We'll be arguing that they ought to be admitted to show the improbability of the prosecution's case. We'll be asking the jury to consider how unlikely it is that after almost ten years of not seeing her, not being in contact with her at all, you would suddenly get it in your head to pick her six-year-old son up from school one Friday and give him some chocolate milk. We'll be making them see that she has very good reasons for lying, that the truth will destroy her whole world, her status quo. You, on the other hand, had no reason in the world to pick up Sam from school unless you were asked to.'

14

The protective services officers, the men who were in charge of transporting prisoners, in charge of guarding them on the way to court and back to prison, were not the same men who guarded us at the prison. The shelf company the state paid to employ them was not the same company that owned the prison and the men were selected from a completely different pool. For all that, there was no qualitative difference between them and the prison officers. They too liked to find out what it was the prisoners they were transporting were charged with. They too, like almost everyone else I had encountered since it all began, equated being charged with being guilty, the assumption being that the police wouldn't have charged you if you weren't. Where these men differed from the prison officers was the alacrity with which they let you know how much they disapproved of what you must have done to be in their care.

The prison officers had you captive every day and so they were in no particular hurry to exercise the power they had over you. They had the luxury of sitting back and letting prisoners take care of each other, intervening only when the de facto justice system within the walls of the prison demanded a little tweaking, a little ad hoc extrajudicial improvement. The officers who were in charge of prisoners only when they were away from prison, on the other hand, had to victimise you expeditiously. They had to take every opportunity to torment you, be it when they cuffed your wrists, when they pushed you into the prison van, when they ate their lunch in front of you after depriving you of yours on some flimsy pretext. They were small things designed to humiliate and intimidate. They were effective.

I sat in the dock, as I had for the bail applications, dressed in a suit and tie with an officer on each side. I stood like everyone else when the magistrate entered the court and sat down like everyone else when instructed. The room was filled with people I had never seen before, print and television journalists, and members of the public who had struck it lucky and got into the committal hearing of that guy, the one who took all those children. Alex was there sitting behind Gina and her instructing solicitor.

Gina had advised me to sit up straight and to look attentive, politely engaged, and never indignant no matter what was said. I was to make no sotto voce remarks but I could make notes with a pen and paper she had provided for me. I was to look neither too confident nor too afraid but rather, if I could manage it, sympathetic, intelligent. Ironically, the effort required to eliminate from my appearance all the extremes she had warned against as each person in the court room looked at me—some furtively, some feasting on me, convinced of my guilt, some not fully understanding the charges, some wondering what I had actually done to attract them—made it impossible for me not to grimace from time to time. She had told me earlier not to be afraid of the committal.

'This'll be a rehearsal. There's no jury. It's just an opportunity for us to put the prosecution and their witnesses through their paces,' she had said. I kept trying to remind myself of this. But I was afraid of their witnesses, one of them in particular. Alex was right. There was really no way of avoiding it. Anna was failing.

I looked at the magistrate, a not unpleasant-looking somewhat colourless man, so very ordinary. Did he like music? Did he read? Was he married and, if so, how had he met his wife? What had made her choose him? Did she consider him a reasonable man? Did he work too hard? Was he the type of man to equate any increase in the funding of state schools with a lamentable stifling of individual responsibility? And would we have been able to enjoy each other's company, to smile wanly at the sorry state of the world over a drink together, had I not ruined my life and taken an ex-lover's son home from school?

The prosecutor opened, his matter-of-fact style of presentation revealing to the close observer a studied theatricality that had no doubt assisted him in getting to this point in his career. As at the start of every high-profile case, his mouth was a little drier than usual, his palms a little moister and his patience a little shorter. He knew, as he stood behind the bar table and addressed the court, that given what the media are pleased to call their commitment to the public's right to know, he was addressing a far larger audience.

'Your Worship,' he began, 'Simon Heywood is charged . . .' and then, after he had formally and quickly recited all the charges, he went on to describe a stranger who, superficially, had much in common with me. This stranger had once been a primary teacher but had lost his job. He had lived on his own in a flat for many years. He was something of a dreamer and was chronically short of money. He had been seeing a psychiatrist for a couple of years. He had been romantically involved with a prostitute and had lived off her earnings. He liked to think of himself as something of an intellectual but, sadly, he had not apparently achieved anything that would warrant this self-assessment. Largely estranged from his family and with few if any friends, he was, in short, a man with some potential, but it was a potential that was entirely unrealised. I listened to the prosecutor describe this man, a man nobody could possibly have any time for, and though I am, I think, more honestly acquainted with myself than most people, I did not recognise him.

Alternately holding her own hand, nervously shifting up and down from toe to heel and back, as if for a ballet exercise, joining a thumb and middle finger around her wrist, or else leaning against the railing of the witness box as if exhausted, she looked like she was more afraid than I was. She was required to give her full name.

'Can you tell the court how long you've known the defendant, Simon Heywood?'

'I don't know exactly . . .'

'Approximately.'

'I've known him . . . approximately . . . two years. Something like that.'

'Two years?'

'I think so, is that right?'

'I can't give you the answers, just the questions.'

'I'm sorry.'

'How long had you known him at the time of his arrest?'

'About . . . I'd known him for about two years at that time.'

'Two years at the time of his arrest, so it's more than two years now?'

'Yes.'

'In what capacity did you know him?'

'What capacity?'

'What kind of relationship was it?'

'Good.'

'No, what I mean is—'

'Your Worship,' Gina rose to interrupt the prosecutor, 'I'm loath to interrupt my learned friend's examination of this witness but I'm concerned that, in his quite genuine and legitimate attempt to have the witness understand his questions, he might be about to lead her to the very answer he seeks!'

'Well, Ms Serkin,' the magistrate answered, 'Mr Henshaw hasn't yet done anything to warrant an objection so let's see if he continues that way. Mr Henshaw, you will not be suggesting the answer in your question, will you?'

'No, Your Worship.'

'There you are, Ms Serkin. Can we let him continue now?'

'Yes, Your Worship.'

'Thank you, Mr Henshaw. Continue with your next non-leading question of the witness.'

'Angela, will you tell the court the type of work you're engaged in.'

'I work in the hospitality industry.'

'Can you be more specific?'

'I work as an escort.'

'What does that entail?'

'I work for an agency. They . . . the agency sends me to meet different clients.'

'For what are you paid?'

'For my time.'

'What do you do with your time?'

'When I'm working?'

'Yes.'

'It varies.'

The prosecutor tried to hide his frustration.

'Your Worship, I sense some perhaps understandable reluctance on the part of the witness. I seek my friend's indulgence to lead on a fact not in dispute.'

'Well, don't ask, me Mr Henshaw. It's Ms Serkin's permission you need.'

With a wave of her hand Gina agreed to the prosecutor's request, adding, 'To establish one thing only.' The prosecutor nodded and looked back in the direction of my nervous young friend.

'You've been supporting yourself by working as a prostitute, haven't you?'

Angelique, who must have expected this to come out sooner rather than later, nonetheless went red. She turned to the magistrate.

'Isn't that a leading question, sir?'

The magistrate waited for the general burst of laughter in the room to die out.

'It is, but Ms Serkin has agreed to let him ask it.'

'Is it relevant? I don't mind talking . . . about the boy.'

'I'm afraid you have to answer it.'

For all that she had done for a living since I had met her, she had never stood up in court, in public anywhere, and announced it. This was the moment when she would confirm what her parents in Adelaide had perhaps tried their best not to suspect. How many people could I hurt in one fell swoop?

'What was the question again?'

'Do you work as a prostitute?'

'An escort.'

'Does that involve an exchange of money for sex?'

'Yes. Yes, it does. I'm the one who gets the money. Happy?'

'I'm sorry, I'm . . . not trying to embarrass you,' the prosecutor explained. She was testing his patience.

'Were you working when you met Simon Heywood?'

'Yes.'

'Was he your client?'

'No.'

'Then what was the nature of your relationship?'

'We . . . we were friends.'

'Friends?'

'Yes.'

'Your Worship, again I seek my learned friend's indulgence to lead the witness.'

'Ms Serkin?' the magistrate directed a questioning tone to Gina.

'Sir, the witness has answered the question. She's said my client and she were friends. I'm not inclined to indulge Mr Henshaw's taste for leading questions just because he's not getting answers that suit him.'

'There's your answer, Mr Henshaw. Do you have any non-leading questions for the witness?' the magistrate asked. Henshaw continued.

'Were you always friends with Mr Heywood, with the defendant?'

'No. I've only known him for a few years.'

'Have you ever described your relationship with him in any other way?'

'I don't know, maybe . . . You know, wishful thinking perhaps.'

'Are you saying that's how you described your relationship with him to the police the day he was arrested on the charges that bring us here—?'

'I object to this, Your Worship.' Gina shot up. 'Mr Henshaw is badgering his own witness.'

'And you're protecting her, Ms Serkin? Can't we get around this, Mr Henshaw?'

'I'm trying, sir.'

'Well, keep trying.'

The prosecutor was annoyed. He bent down to whisper furiously to his instructing solicitor. Then he returned to Angelique.

'The investigating detectives in this case will be giving evidence that you said to them—'

'Your Worship, I must object.' Gina rose again. Clearly no one had expected Angelique to make the prosecutor's life such a nightmare. Certainly not so soon.

'Was it a sexual relationship?' Henshaw asked.

'I must object to this.' Gina stood up again.

'On what grounds, Ms Serkin?'

'Relevance,' Gina answered.

'What do you say, Mr Henshaw? The relevance of either a positive or a negative answer to your last question is not immediately apparent to me.'

'Then I'm afraid, Your Worship, that I find myself in the unexpected position of being forced to make an application to have this witness declared hostile.'

'What do you say, Ms Serkin?' the magistrate said.

'I oppose my friend's application. In my submission it's entirely unwarranted.'

'Entirely?' the magistrate asked.

'My learned friend cannot expect to have his own witness declared hostile merely because he's having trouble with his questions.'

'You don't think the witness's answers may be construed as at least . . . problematic?'

'Only to his case, sir. At worst, the witness might be considered "unfavourable", but not "hostile", by the prosecution.'

The magistrate took the opportunity to adjourn early and give each side a chance to prepare a submission on 'unfavourable' as opposed to 'hostile' witnesses. The next day they were to argue before him which of these Angelique was. In the court cells, before I was driven back to prison, Gina explained the difference to me and what effect the ruling would have.

The first thing Gina said to me was, 'Your friend is either incredibly brave or incredibly stupid.' She ignored the possibility that Angelique was both. On reflection, she was right to. If Angel and the police had an agreement wherein she would testify against me in return for immunity, she appeared to be breaking it. Perhaps she was gambling on the charges against me being dismissed at the committal stage, in which case both of us would be safe. It was a risk but a calculated one. And even if I were committed to stand trial, the police might give her the opportunity to make amends at the trial itself. Angel wasn't stupid, something I was forced to remember when Gina explained what was going on.

'Henshaw wants to be able to treat her as a "hostile" witness because she's clearly being difficult on your behalf. She's deliberately making it harder for them.'

'She's not refusing to answer, not yet anyway,' I volunteered.

'She can't refuse to answer,' Gina explained, 'but she's clearly not providing him with what he wants, what he's no doubt been expecting given Threlfall's and Staszic's testimony as well as, of course, her own statements.'

'What do you mean?'

'She's told the police, at least at one stage, that you were her boyfriend, that the two of you were romantically involved, a couple. This helps their case. It makes it that much less likely that you were romantically, albeit illicitly, involved with Anna. It makes it less likely that you'll be believed when you say that you were Anna's lover and that you had permission to pick Sam up from school that day. Now she appears to be going back on that. She says the two of you were friends. There is every sign she's going to be unhelpful to them generally.'

'Okay, I see that, but what's the difference between an "unfavourable" witness and a "hostile" witness?'

'Well, to put it very simply, an "unfavourable" witness is a witness, called by a party to prove a certain fact or issue in favour of the party, who then either cannot prove it or proves its opposite. A "hostile" witness, on the other hand, is a witness called by a party who is not incapable but is unwilling generally to assist the party at all.'

'So it's just a question of degree?'

'Well, yes, but the ramifications of having a witness deemed "hostile" are huge. If the magistrate accepts their submission and she's deemed "hostile", Henshaw will be permitted to cross-examine her. He'll be able to ask her leading questions, to challenge her means of knowing any fact with respect to which she gives evidence, to challenge her memory, her perception. And he's angry with her, too. He'll be hard on her.'

'So, if you can get her deemed just "unfavourable" and not "hostile" you can protect her.'

'Yes, but more importantly, Henshaw will be pretty much stuck with her answer that the two of you were only friends. Oh, he can try to recall Threlfall and Staszic but it will just look, as she said, like she'd been talking up her relationship with you to the police.'

'Can we win this?'

'I don't know. I need to go back to chambers and read some cases. I've got a feeling the law is against us.'

I'd had that feeling for some time. I had it again when I was handcuffed and thrown back into the prison van. There were five of us in the van. It was dark and close. Sometime between being delivered to court in the morning and being taken back to prison, a prisoner had written something on one of the inside walls of the van in excrement. I complained to one of the protective services guards. He told me to be careful not to lean back.

Gina was right to assume the worst. She had marshalled as many cases as she could in our favour. She cited one in which the judge held a 'hostile' witness to be one who bears a 'hostile animus' to the party calling him. Angelique, Gina argued, had not demonstrated a 'hostile animus' to the police or to the prosecutor. But Henshaw countered this with other more recent cases with less narrow interpretations. The thrust of his argument was that the motive of the witness in question was irrelevant. Rather, what mattered was that the party calling the witness was unable to elicit the truth from the witness without recourse to leading questions and cross-examination generally because of an unwillingness on the part of the witness to tell the whole truth. The magistrate preferred Henshaw's interpretation. When Gina then argued that Angel had not demonstrated a general unwillingness to tell the whole truth but only a natural and understandable reluctance to admit to prostitution, the magistrate was against her on this as well. And so it was that Mr Henshaw, the prosecutor, began to cross-examine Angel.

15

'Detectives Threlfall and Staszic interviewed you over a number of days concerning the matters that form the subject of these charges, didn't they?'

'Yes.'

'In the very first of these you told them that Simon Heywood was your boyfriend, didn't you?'

'I don't know. I might have.'

'Yesterday you told the court that the two of you, that is, you and Simon Heywood, were merely friends.'

'Yes.'

'Were you lying then to the police or were you lying yesterday to the court?'

'Neither.'

'Your Worship,' Gina interjected, 'the witness ought to be given the opportunity to explain the apparent . . . inconsistency in her answers.'

'I'm sure Mr Henshaw has every intention of giving her that opportunity.'

'Yes, Your Worship,' Henshaw offered patiently before inviting Angelique to explain herself.

'I thought about this overnight, sir,' she said, facing the magistrate, 'because I know I caused some kind of trouble yesterday. I didn't mean to, and now it seems Mr Henshaw is angry with me and—'

'Don't worry about him. I'm giving you the opportunity to explain your answer now.'

'When I told the detectives that first time that Simon was my boyfriend, it was sort of true, at least it was to me, in the way that I felt about him. I loved him. I was in love with him. I wanted to believe that he felt the same way about me. I really did. Even now, after all this time, I'd still like to think that he loved me, but I don't think he was actually ever in love with me. I'd be fooling myself to think he was ever in love with me. He had photographs around his house of another woman! I mean, for God's sake—'

'Who was that other woman?'

'Anna Geraghty.'

'I see.'

'He'd had a serious relationship with her years ago and . . . I don't know . . . I couldn't replace her, much as I wanted to. They'd re-met—I don't know the details—but she was everything to him and he didn't hide it from me. He even told me that he wasn't in love with me. More than once. He would talk about how . . . troubled he was because of her marriage and—'

'Did he say that Mrs Geraghty was similarly troubled?' Henshaw asked.

'You mean Anna?' Angelique asked him.

'Objection, sir,' Gina said, rising again. 'Mr Henshaw's question invites an answer that's clearly inadmissible.'

'Why is it inadmissible, Ms Serkin?' the magistrate asked.

'He is asking the witness to say what the defendant, Mr Heywood, said Anna Geraghty said. If it is asked to establish the truth of Mrs Geraghty's feelings concerning her marriage, it is clearly hearsay and therefore inadmissible. If it is asked just to establish whether Mr Heywood ever mentioned the topic of Mrs Geraghty's guilt over her affair with Mr Heywood, it is irrelevant and therefore equally inadmissible.'

'What do you say, Mr Henshaw?'

'I'm content to withdraw the question, sir,' the prosecutor said before continuing. 'You also told the police, didn't you, that Simon Heywood loved children?'

'Yes.'

'You told them, didn't you, that he had no plans to have children?'

'Yes, not any immediate plans.'

'Well, you're not able to tell us about any plans he had to have children with you, are you?'

'No.'

'You were just friends, weren't you?'

'Yes.'

'And you don't know of any plans he had to have children with Mrs Geraghty, do you?'

'No.'

'You also told police that you and Mr Heywood were already "a little family", didn't you?'

'I might have said that . . . It's what I felt . . .'

'You also told the police that sometimes Mr Heywood drinks too much, didn't you?'

'I might have.'

'You told them that he suffers from insomnia, didn't you?'

'Yes.'

'And you knew that first-hand from staying the night at his home with him.'

'He . . . often complained of lack of sleep.'

'Are you saying then that you didn't ever spend the night with him?'

'No.'

'In fact you often spent the night with him, didn't you?'

'I don't know. What's "often"?'

'Several nights a week,' Henshaw offered.

'I'm a prostitute, Mr Henshaw.'

'Does that mean you've lost count?'

'Objection, Your Worship. My friend is gratuitously insulting the witness, a witness he called.'

'Yes, Mr Henshaw, I'm sure this is difficult enough for the witness,' the magistrate said before turning his attention back to Angelique. 'But perhaps you could clarify what you meant by your last answer.'

'Yes, sir. He asked me if I often spent the night with Simon. Well, as he seems to want everyone to know, I'm a prostitute. I work nights, mostly, anyway.'

'I see,' the magistrate answered, appearing to write something down.

'In all the time you've known the defendant he hasn't had a job, has he?'

'He's a teacher.'

'But he hasn't worked as a teacher in the time you've known him, has he?'

'No.'

'In fact you used to support him with the money you earned through your work, didn't you?'

'No, not . . . support him. I tried, where I could . . . to help him.'

'You gave him money, didn't you?'

'Yes, sometimes . . . a bit.'

'He used that money, the money you gave him, for food, didn't he?'

'Sometimes.'

'He used it for food, for clothing, rent, didn't he?'

'That sort of thing . . . dog food.'

'He didn't give *you* money, did he?'

'He tried to.'

'He tried to give you money, did he?'

'Well, he was unemployed. He wasn't really in a position to—'

'Why did he try to give you money?'

'He didn't often.'

'But when he did, why was that?'

'I don't know . . . a friendly gesture.'

'A friendly gesture?'

'Something like that.'

'Are you really telling the court that a chronically unemployed man tried to give you money as a "friendly gesture"?'

'Yes. What's wrong with that?'

'He didn't give you money in exchange for sexual services, did he?'

'No. You can't have it both ways. One minute you want me to say he was my boyfriend and the next minute you want me to say he was my client. What do you want me to say?'

'Please,' the magistrate started, 'let Mr Henshaw ask the questions.'

'I only want you to tell the truth,' the prosecutor intoned piously. 'On the day in question, you arrived at the defendant's home to find him there with Samuel Geraghty, is that right?'

'Yes.'

'Was this visit prearranged?'

'No.'

'What was your purpose in going there?'

'My purpose? I went to visit my friend.'

'And you found him alone with Mr and Mrs Geraghty's son, is that right?'

'Yes.'

'And you were surprised by this, weren't you?'

'Yes. Well, I didn't know who the little boy was. I'd never met him before.'

'There wasn't any reason you should have met him before, was there?'

'No.'

'You told the police you'd never met his mother, Anna Geraghty, didn't you?'

'Well, I hadn't. I still . . . I've never met her.'

'But you've met Mr Joseph Geraghty, haven't you?'

Angel exhaled a breath of exasperation. 'You're determined to humiliate as many people as you can.'

'I'm determined to have you answer my questions. You've met Mr Joseph Geraghty, haven't you?'

'Yes,' she sighed. 'Yes, I've met him. What have you got against *him*? You're not prosecuting him, are you?'

'Please tell the court how you came to know Joseph Geraghty.'

'Do I have to . . . answer this?'

'The sooner you answer the sooner it will be over,' the prosecutor said.

'You know, Detective Staszic once said something like that to me,' Angelique said.

'You knew Mr Geraghty through your work as a prostitute, didn't you?'

'Yes.'

'He was a regular client of yours, wasn't he?'

'Yes.'

'You saw him at least once a week, didn't you?'

'For a while there I did, yes.'

'And this while lasted for almost two years, didn't it?'

'Yes, something like that.'

'And you got to know him pretty well, didn't you?'

'Look, he paid me for sex. Are you happy? Have you got what you want? I don't see what this has got to do with anything.'

'After two years you knew what he did for a living, didn't you?'

'I only knew what he told me. He could've been lying for all I knew. A lot of them lie, especially the lawyers.'

'But he didn't lie when he told you he was a stockbroker, did he?'

'I don't know. Is he a stockbroker?'

'Yes, he is.'

'Then he didn't lie about that.'

'He told you the name of the firm he worked for, didn't he?'

'He might have. It wouldn't have meant anything to me.'

'He told you the kind of car he drove, didn't he?'

'Again, he might have. Cars aren't very important to me.'

'But you knew enough about him to have a sense of his socio-economic standing, didn't you?'

'You mean I knew what he made?'

'Among other things, yes.'

'No, I didn't really. Look, they often come in to boast, amongst other things.'

'But he gave you the impression he was well-to-do, well-off, didn't he?'

'I suppose so. I didn't really think about it.'

'You told the police, at least initially, that there was no relationship between Simon Heywood and Anna Geraghty, didn't you?'

'Yes. I was very upset. I was confused. I was scared to be . . . dealing with the police. I meant that there was no future to Simon's relationship with her. I was always telling him that. I told him she'd never leave her husband and, now look, she won't even admit to the relationship to keep him out of prison. That's not love.'

'You called the police and told them that Simon had the Geraghtys' son, Sam, didn't you?'

'Yes. Yes, I did.'

'And you did that because you were concerned for the boy's welfare, weren't you?'

'No. No, not at all.'

'Then why did you call the police?'

'As I said, I was very upset to see Sam there with him. It brought it all home to me, the reality of it.'

'Of what?'

'Of . . . of his relationship with Anna. I realised it had to be . . . more than a little serious if she had him pick up her son from school.'

'You told the police that you called them because you thought the boy's parents might be worried about him, didn't you?'

'Yes, but I told you, I was very disturbed. I was very emotional. I was . . . I wasn't worried about him. I was worried Simon had got the arrangement wrong, and that everything would spiral . . . out of control. I was worried Joe would find out and all hell would break loose.'

'You knew the defendant, Simon Heywood, did not have permission from the boy's mother to take him home from school, didn't you?'

'No, that's not right.'

'Why did you tell the police you thought the boy's parents might be worried about him if you also thought his mother had given Simon permission to take him from school?'

'I shouldn't have. I told you, I acted out of emotion. I acted out of . . . jealousy. I wasn't thinking.'

'Are you now telling the court that you lied to the police about your concern for the child's parents and that it was simply out of malice to the defendant that you had him arrested?'

'Yes. I was angry with him. I knew Anna wouldn't bail him out and I thought it would break them up if he saw her for what she was. I didn't think it would go this far. I just didn't think. I don't know whether you've ever made a mistake, an enormous mistake, because you were angry, because you were hurt, because you felt rejected by someone you thought you needed. You have to imagine being in my position, Your Worship,' Angelique said, turning to the magistrate. 'Really, sir, everything I said to the police, even the contradictions, especially the contradictions, can all be understood by someone, anyone, with enough . . . empathy.'

16

Gina had stressed repeatedly that in criminal matters the burden of proof was always on the prosecution. Now Angelique had introduced the burden of empathy, and she had put it squarely on the magistrate. It had been quite a performance. Even Gina had to concede that my young untutored friend had set things up for me at the trial. At the very least she had provided Gina with enough inconsistent statements to ensure that, if I was to be convicted at the trial, it wouldn't be through her testimony. What I hadn't understood from her cross-examination was why Henshaw was asking her questions about her knowledge of Joe Geraghty's financial state. Gina explained.

'One of the charges you're facing, what is called a section 63A kidnapping as opposed to a common law kidnapping, has, as one of its requisite elements, the intent to demand a ransom.'

'But I didn't demand any ransom. Even the police don't say I demanded a ransom.'

'No. They don't, but they don't have to. They just have to prove that you took Sam with the intention of demanding a ransom for him. It doesn't matter whether you, in fact, got around to making any demand.'

'That's crazy. How can they possibly prove that?'

'I don't think they can. The best they can do is to establish that you knew that Geraghty had money. That's why Henshaw asked Angela all those questions about Joe's car, where he worked, that sort of thing. I'm going to try to get that charge knocked out. I'll be arguing that they don't have the evidence to prove beyond reasonable doubt that you intended to demand a ransom. There just isn't enough on that one for a properly instructed jury to convict.'

'Can we win that one?'

'We really should be able to.'

'Hell, we've got to win something.'

'Actually, Simon, in the current climate, we don't.'

The next prosecution witness was neither unfavourable nor hostile, at least not to the prosecution.

'We had arranged . . . my wife and I had agreed that I was to leave work early that Friday and pick him up from school. She normally . . . It was usually part of her routine to collect our son from school and take him home or to swimming lessons or to wherever he had to go. But on this particular day I was meant to do it because she had a work commitment. She was going away, for a seminar, I think it was.'

'And what happened?'

'Well, I left work early and drove to my son's school. I parked the car and got out. There was hardly anyone around. I couldn't see him. I went looking for him. I must have gone into every classroom in the school. I mean . . . I didn't go into them. Most of them were locked. I mean . . . I looked into every classroom I could for him. I went to the bike sheds. I must have covered every inch of the place looking for him. There were a few kids, older kids, hanging around. I asked them if they'd seen him. I remember I described him. They hadn't. I went to the administration building. I ran around the school ground calling out his name . . . Could I maybe get a glass of water, please?'

Joe Geraghty was a well-built man. I had never seen him before nor had he ever seen me. We looked at each other. This was the man who had paid Angel so diligently. This was the man Anna had chosen to marry. I had no business bringing his private life into the open, no business even bringing it before his wife. I looked at him in the witness box while he lost his son all over again, while he admitted to his weekly arrangement with Angelique and then later, while he struggled with Gina's questions concerning the health of his marriage. But he looked most vulnerable, most bewildered, when he spoke about the failure of his son to be where he was meant to be and about the bogus message for him at work advising him to pick his son up from school later than originally arranged. He talked of his panic and that's when he almost broke down. When he talked of being taken for a ride, taken for a sucker, a sap, he grew angry, angrier than was good for their case. It made it easier to imagine disharmony within the marriage. Gina would have briefed him better than that had he been her witness.

> *To wait for letters inside,*
> *to sing sad songs*
> *or to lie awake all night staring at the ceiling*
>   *is sweet but dangerous*

All night I imagined her. Eyes open, lying on my cot in the dark, she was in my mind like a melody not entirely remembered. You remember loving the song but, truth be told, you don't really remember exactly how it goes. I waited for the sun to rise on what was not her first chance to rid me of the mess I had made for myself. Nothing the corrective services officers could do could get to me. The waiting had made me, at least temporarily, invulnerable. I had long stopped doubting that what I had done was mad. And yet, because I was tempted to interpret the stupid old bracelet she was wearing while she took the oath to tell every last bit of the truth as some kind of omen, the real truth was that I still was not completely well. Otherwise I would not have held out the hope that fluttered like a butterfly inside me.

'We went out . . . that is . . . he was my boyfriend when I was a university student, a serious boyfriend. We were together for a couple of years but then I lost touch with him. I didn't even know he was a teacher until that business with the schoolboy—'

'Objection!' Gina interrupted. 'I ask my learned friend to confine the witness to his question.' I had not thought Anna meant me any harm by this. But I fought the memory of Alex's characterisation of a theist as someone for whom there is no test God can fail.

'No, definitely not. We hadn't been in touch at all since the relationship ended. I was not romantically or in any way involved with him when he . . . took my son. He didn't have my permission. He couldn't have had it. We hadn't been in contact for ten years or so.'

'Do you know why the defendant took your son?'

'Objection! Calls for speculation other than that of an expert.'

'I have absolutely no idea . . . absolutely none.' That was the only time she looked at me.

17

Gina managed to persuade the magistrate to dismiss two of the charges against me, the stalking and the section 63A kidnapping charge, the charge that I intended to demand a ransom notwithstanding that I never actually got around to it. She argued that there was no evidence upon which a reasonable jury, properly instructed, could conclude an intention to demand a ransom. But the prosecution was successful with respect to the other charges. I was to be presented for trial as soon as there was a spot open for me on the court calendar.

Things died down for a while, for months, months that I experienced as years. The press reported that I had been committed for trial, that the accused had once had a love affair with the kidnapped boy's mother, that the kidnapped boy's father had been a regular client of the prostitute jilted by the accused, and that no other children had gone missing lately. Alex stayed in touch with Angel. He told her I wasn't angry with her anymore but, on my lawyer's advice, I still couldn't see her. He promised to act as a go-between and to keep her abreast of all that was happening to me and to the case. Then, a little later still, came school holiday time and Gina took her children away somewhere for two weeks. Alex's estranged wife took his two children away somewhere else for two and a half weeks.

It was around this time that I was informed by Legal Aid, who had been paying for my defence up until then, paying both Gina and her instructing solicitor, that a problem had arisen with respect to funding. The problem was mine, not theirs, although its origins were no doubt systemic, part of society's enchantment with a barbarism that those under its influence euphemistically called 'efficiency'. The gist of it, as far as I was concerned, was that Legal Aid had decided, subsequent to the committal hearing, that they would continue to fund me but only on the condition that I plead guilty. As long as Anna maintained that I did not have her permission to take Sam, Legal Aid considered funding my defence, if I pleaded 'not guilty' at the trial, tantamount to a waste of its limited funds, throwing good money after bad. They were only going to pay Gina to represent me if I pleaded 'guilty'. Then she would be paid to get me the lightest possible sentence.

Gina was away and we couldn't contact her. I was devastated when it sank in. Alex tried to convince me that we would figure something out, that I would be alright. But he stopped short of saying that Gina would represent me if I couldn't get funding. I didn't know how close they were. He never volunteered anything about their relationship and he didn't seem to welcome being asked. Whatever our friendship meant to him, it had to be wearing thin. I had become a bottomless pit of need and, for all his attempts to implicate my parents and the times we were living through, we both knew that with the one desperate, impetuous act of stupidity, I had really brought it all on myself. Why should Gina defend me for nothing? She had children to support.

Alex told me to delay my despair at least until Gina got back. We would figure something out, he promised me. As he talked to me about the possibility of one or both of us approaching my father for money again, I began to contemplate the ultimate fall-back option, the one we all have. But could I really go through with it? And how would I go about it? It occurred to me that I might have to enlist some assistance. The Turk would do it. He would help me. He understood. But for him to get to me we would need Mr Greer to turn a blind eye. We would need to have something to offer him in return. Alex didn't suspect the road my thoughts had taken but he knew I'd turned off. While waiting for Gina's children to return to school he told me how upset Angelique was after he apprised her of my problem with Legal Aid, so much so that it got her working at a scheme to fund my defence. She claimed she would have $30 000 within a few weeks. I had to smile when he told me this. She didn't tell him how she was going to get it; she just made him promise to tell me that she was working on it and that I would be alright. I would not be forced to plead 'guilty'.

I was a man of more than average intelligence seasoned by years of wide and considered reading, a man of not unpleasing visage and of some awareness of the mighty winds and faint breezes that move the world, a man sensitive both to the plight of the many and to that of the man in his shirtsleeves ambling through the leaves in the city park during his lunch hour, desperately trying to keep his own tepid inconsequence at bay with every short and timid breath. I had really wanted nothing more in life than to help this small man and perhaps thereby to make the world a slightly better place. But instead, I have, as if by careful planning, visited upon myself first a virtual state of confinement in a small flat without even the means to pay for the rent, and then an actual state of solitary confinement inside a maximum security prison without the means to pay for my own defence. Dostoyevsky was right. Money is coined liberty and so it is ten times dearer to a man who is deprived of freedom.

By accepting the lower scale of fees offered by Legal Aid, Gina had been discounting her usual fee all along, not that accepting a high-profile, perhaps career-making, kidnapping case required all that much selflessness. But now with Legal Aid threatening to withdraw its funding if I pleaded 'not guilty', I could not expect Gina to keep fighting for me. The children she wanted to protect were not an abstraction, not the children of the world. They were hers. She had to feed them. She had to take them away for school holidays. She had to make up for whatever it was that had led their father and her to separate. Just because Alex had adopted the cause of my well-being with a passion and madness that rivalled my own, didn't mean she had to. Nor did it mean he would ever ask her to.

It was as a consequence of my longstanding reliance on Alex that it felt completely unnatural to plan the last stage of my decline and fall without consulting him. As strange as it sounds, the decision to bypass him took more courage than the decision to kill myself, an enterprise I was confident my fellow prisoners would not be so cruel as to not assist me with.

I was figuring it all out. My conviction would confirm what I had long suspected—that I was just not cut out for the business of living at a time like this, a time when wondering, caring, dreaming . . . they were just not selling, they were uncool, unhip, not sexy, past their use-by date, and I was going to have to go down with them, all the way down, stopping all stations via the tabloids, my parents' shame and my little orgasms of mental instability. Some other time maybe. My life had been worth a try, a good idea at the time, in principle, but ultimately a waste of breath. It had all gone way too far off track.

I found myself frequenting an inchoate state between sleep and wake in which dream and fantasy took it in turns to grapple with dying. I would see myself speeding on an elevated freeway, and in trying to get ahead of the traffic, losing control of the car and plummeting through the barrier into a desert-like ravine, my frustration and anger when I couldn't get a break on the rest of the traffic giving way first to fear and panic as the car sailed into the air, and finally, just before hitting the ground, to 'oh well'. Oh, well.

A means to the end would always be near at hand if I wanted it badly enough. I'd heard of a man inside who had stabbed himself to death with his eyeglasses. My eyesight was too good for that. I would need the help of a sympathetic killer. I thought again of the Turk.

In one of my two-hour stints out of my cell I sounded him out about helping me should I need him to. We were in the exercise yard. It was noisy and crowded with prisoners kicking a soccer ball around. We were being watched. There was no time for small talk.

'If I want to die, will you help me?' I whispered.

'Hey, Fuck!' he greeted me. 'How do you do? You look like shit.'

'Nazim, if I want to die, will you help me?'

The more Alex became aware of the unrelenting flatness of my affect the more he insisted that we talk about it. Perhaps he suspected what he would have called my 'suicidal ideation'. That would certainly have explained his exhilaration when he came to see me in the visit centre.

'I have great news, Simon.'

Gina was back. They had finally spoken directly to each other after a couple of days of missed calls and phone messages. When he told her about Legal Aid withdrawing funding unless I pleaded guilty she had laughed.

'They can't do that and they know it. Why didn't somebody call the solicitor?'

It was a good question. I had not thought to check the regulations governing Legal Aid funding with the instructing solicitor. It had all seemed so hopeless. I took a while to understand precisely what Alex was telling me. Gina subsequently explained it better and more fully, but that afternoon there was no stopping Alex Klima.

'She said they can't do it. They have to fund you whether you plead guilty or not guilty.'

'Why?'

'It's because of a case, some case, a decision of the High Court called . . . What did she say? . . . Dietrich. She called it Dietrich. She said she'll have to make a Dietrich application for you.'

'How long will that take?'

'I asked her that too. A week to two weeks. She said she'll visit you in two days' time. She's in court before that.'

'Dietrich,' Gina later explained, 'stood for the proposition that an accused person has a right to a fair trial in accordance with law. And, in the absence of exceptional circumstances, an indigent person charged with a serious offence who, through no fault on his part, cannot obtain legal representation, will be taken by an appellate court to have been denied a fair trial in accordance with law by virtue of the absence of legal representation alone. I will make an application pursuant to the Crimes Act and the court will order Legal Aid to fund your defence.'

Somewhere in his personal journal Alex would have noted that he was not going to have to test Gina, not then anyway. And I in my journal? 'Thursday: I gag on the stench of the disinfectant they use here, again.'

18

And who knows,
the woman you love may stop loving you.
Don't say it's no big thing:
it's like the snapping of a green branch
        to the man inside.

'You can't ask someone to feel more. It's pointless,' Alex had once said to me.

'No,' I had agreed, 'you can only beg her.'

The first time I hugged her properly, really held her, really squeezed her tight within my arms, I felt an incredible release unlike anything I had ever known. That's how it started, the addiction. Where the release is great enough it can capture you and imprison you. Everything will always be more or less surreal after that. Even her leaving was surreal. Why did she leave all of a sudden?

'Can we . . . do you mind if we just talk for a bit before I try to . . . explain anything?'

'Yes, I suppose so. I've never been anywhere . . . like this before.'

'No, I . . . didn't think you had . . . How are your parents?'

'They're fine, thank you. Your mum came around but . . . I wasn't there.'

'I know. I heard.'

'You were . . . are a teacher?'

'Yes.'

'I read about that little boy.'

'Carlo.'

'Yes, that must have been awful.'

'Yes, it was.'

'I was going to call you but . . . I'm sorry I—'

'That's fine. I understand. You're probably very busy. How's your work?'

'Good, thanks. Busy. Too busy sometimes . . . sometimes I think that . . . This is . . . Simon, this is so weird.'

'What exactly is it that you do?'

'What do I do? Let's see. That's a good question. I suppose I'm what's broadly called a management consultant, but that's so . . . I mean whatever that used to mean . . . the job has changed so much even in the years I've been doing it.'

'So you work for a firm that recruits people for other firms and . . . counsels people who've lost their jobs. You help people.'

'Yes, but it's more than that now, more than just . . . what you said.'

'There's something I've never understood about that kind of work.'

'What?'

'Well, you said you counsel people who've lost their jobs.'

'Yes, people whose positions have been outsourced, or downsized, nearly always receive some counselling. I don't do that anymore myself but, yes, that's part of what we do.'

'But you're paid by the employer, right, not by the freshly out-of-work?'

'Yes, their employer . . . former employer, pays us for the counselling.'

'That's the bit I don't understand. Why would the employer pay you to do that? I mean, that person has left them, obviously, otherwise you wouldn't be seeing them.'

'Well, you might say it's out of a sense of corporate responsibility.'

'What, a kind of corporate pastoral care, do you mean?'

'Yes, in a way. Of course, it's not entirely altruistic.'

'No, I didn't think so, but how does the employer benefit at all?'

'Well, they don't want the employee badmouthing the firm around town.'

'No, but you can't prevent that.'

'No, you can't prevent it completely but you can try to . . . I don't know . . . head it off at the pass.'

'How do you do that?'

'You point out to them, gently, the ways in which it might not be all the firm's fault that things have turned out the way they have.'

'You mean, you implicate the economy?'

'Yes, that and the role they played themselves. Not everybody gets outsourced or downsized. Get them to ask themselves if they were really meeting their goals, earning their pay. Was there really any synergy between their personal style and the culture of the firm? . . . This is so weird.'

'These firms you deal with would all have different cultures, I suppose?'

'Yes, sure, but they all value success. Success is a core value of any corporate culture, any successful one. But I don't do that sort of work anymore . . . which is a bit of a relief.'

'What do you do now?'

'Oh, you know . . . all sorts of things.'

'Like what?'

'Well, for example, we just ran a series of two-day workshops at some of the major accounting firms to demonstrate to their staff how to turn social occasions into marketing opportunities, how to turn friends into clients. We try to get them to exploit their emotional intelligence, get them to see that their address books could be among their biggest assets. Simon, this is so weird . . . I feel so strange talking to you like this . . . nervous. We . . . we generally help professionals target other professionals in relevant markets.'

'You do what?'

'We . . . it's about professionals, placing them, targeting them. We fragmentise the market for them and—'

'Anna, do you hear yourself?'

'What?'

'Do you hear the way you talk? Do you feel anything when the words come out, or are you on automatic, spitting out this . . . shit?'

'What are you talking about?'

'Everything. Where do I start? With the powerful lure of the suffix "ise", maybe? *Fragmentise?*'

'Simon, what is it? What's your problem? I know you're criticising my . . . is "criticise" okay with you? Is it what I do or how I describe what I do? Fragmentise—it's a word. People use it. Jesus! This is so . . . surreal.'

'People might use it but it's ugly. Why not "fragment"? Look at the people who use it.'

'If people use it often enough, it's right. It becomes part of the language. Language is dynamic. You know that.'

'If the wrong thing is done often enough by enough people it becomes right?'

'I'm not saying that. It's not wrong. It's a word. You knew what I meant.'

'Anna, that's not how we were taught.'

'It's the way it is now. It's . . . how I speak.'

'You would never have said any of that when we were . . . us.'

'I wasn't working then.'

'You wouldn't have wilfully missed the point when we were—'

'Simon, I don't know anyone like the people we used to be. We were students then.'

'When people say, "We were students then", I'm never sure whether they're attempting to excuse the way they were then or the way they are now. Perhaps they mean, "We were students then, it was easier to care about doing the right thing"?'

'Simon, caring about the "right thing" is easy. But what do students ever really do about it?'

'What are they meant to do? They're students. To really change the world for the better they have to wait until they're grown up enough to marry a stockbroker.'

'Simon, I didn't come here to be lectured at or preached to.'

'No. Why did you come here?'

'I came here to find out why you did what you did.'

'I did it to get you to come here.'

Why was I doing this? It was as though I were two people, one angry and itching for a fight over anything, no matter how petty or how little it had to do with her, and the other just sitting opposite her in the visit centre listening incredulously to the first guy and unable to stop him. I had never thought to rehearse this conversation. As much as I had wanted her to come, rehearsing it had always seemed too humiliatingly futile, even to me. I had rehearsed only the outcome, the one in which she saves me.

She was right. It was incredibly surreal. We had not seen each other for ten years yet all I could do was to bicker with her while several feet away convicted murderers talked calmly to their loved ones. I heard my rant continue without knowing what had got me started. I think I was attacking the power of the stock market over the lives of ordinary people, something like that, attacking her husband, and attacking her for marrying him, and for everything else.

'They're slaves to the vagaries of a global casino which has no commitment whatsoever to, or any notion of, the common good.'

'Do you do what other people with these views do—demonstrate, join groups, picket the WEF or the WTO or whoever?'

'Anna, you have become one of those people who expect everybody to do what other people are doing. Even in protest you want uniformity. Well, I can't march in the street one of ten abreast shouting in unison with a fist in the air. It's like that line in Kundera—'

'Kundera! That's so eighties—'

'No, no. No, Christ no! Kundera, whether you like him or not, whether you liked him then but no longer do, you cannot say Kundera was the eighties. Steinbeck wasn't the thirties and Dickens wasn't the eighteen-hundreds. They were of their times but *for* the ages. Their writings are not products marketed for a brief time until they're out of vogue and discarded on the scrap heap. They're not silver scooters or hoola hoops, slinkies, Rubik cubes or breast implants. They're not trivial pursuits to be enjoyed when you think you need something new and amusing to fill the emptiness of your pointless job and your sham of a marriage.'

'Listen to you! Are you so crazy that you're angry at absolutely every institution going?'

'On a good day, yes.'

'Simon, when did you get so angry?'

'Anna, you're one of the few people I know who knew me when I *wasn't* angry. In fact, you're one of the few people I know.'

'You're angry with yourself and if I were you I would be too. You had everything going for you and you blew it.'

'Anna . . . What exactly does it mean to "blow it"? Have you "blown it" if you do anything for a living *other* than convince people that it was their fault they lost their job or that their friends are really clients or consumers in disguise? Is it possible to live a fulfilling life by doing something other than persuading people to gamble on shares in certain companies you really know nothing about?'

'Jesus, Simon! You can't take my son, for God's sake, and still claim some sort of moral superiority.'

'No, no, I can.'

'I don't know . . . Maybe it's a male thing but . . . you have more in common with my husband than you could possibly know.'

'You.'

'What?'

'We have years of you in common.'

'Not just me, it seems.'

'Yes . . . I'm sorry. I . . . I wasn't thinking of . . .'

'You know her very well. And it seems . . . so does he. I can't think of her name right now—'

'Angela. Her name is Angela, and I had nothing to do with her seeing—'

'What do I care what her fucking name is. She's the whore that you both . . . It's absolutely unbelievable. A whore!'

'Anna, get it straight. Her name is Angela. She's my friend and she's Joe's prostitute. To support herself she sleeps with many men, one at a time, for short periods in return for relatively small amounts of money. You, on the other hand, agreed to sleep with one man repeatedly, indefinitely, for a huge sum. Common interests, humour, shared world views, compatibility of temperament, affection, respect—they're not part of the equation for either of you. You both made compromises but you feel better attributing immorality to hers.'

Would I really hang myself to win an argument? That wouldn't be very clever and I am so clever, too clever for words, too angry to even have access to them. I can kill with them at twenty paces. She had her head in her hands. I thought that perhaps she was crying.

'Anna, I'm sorry. I didn't mean to . . .' She lifted her head up. There were tears.

'Simon, you've ruined everything for me. Why would you want to do that?'

'What have I ruined?'

'You took my son, for God's sake.'

'Let's be very clear about this. I picked him up from school. I gave him some chocolate milk and he had a sleep. He was never in any danger. You . . . you know that . . . It was wrong, a stupid, insane way to get your attention but I took good care of him.'

'You've ruined my marriage.'

'I didn't, Anna. You know I didn't. I simply shone a spotlight on two unhappy people going through the motions.'

'What right have you got to interfere in my life? You're in no position . . . What would you know? How can you even begin to—?'

'Anna, Joe went to see Angela about once a week. It wasn't me that sent him there.'

'You can't possibly—'

'I'm glad you still wear the bracelet. You got it fixed.'

'What? Yes, he was able to . . . This is too weird. Did you have my house bugged?'

'No. You had it fixed by the jeweller I bought it from. That's how I found out.'

'Found out what?'

'About your . . . affair.'

'I'm not having an affair.'

'Anna, I know you are.'

'But I'm not.'

'Then you were.'

'I wasn't. Anyway, it's none of your business.'

'That's true. That's my real problem, the one that led me here. But still . . .'

'Still what?'

'Someone, a man, not Joe, picked up the bracelet for you.'

'It might've been my father.'

'Might've been, but it wasn't.'

'That doesn't mean I'm having an affair.'

'No, it doesn't . . . not of itself.'

Neither of us spoke. She looked around the room, the visit centre at Port Phillip Prison. Turned away from me as she was, I couldn't see her face, but I knew she was crying.

There had been that weekend away at my parents' place in Sorrento. Then she was gone. It was over. For years I mentally revisited those last forty-eight hours looking for what it was I must have said or done. It was only later that I turned to trawling my memory for evidence that she had already decided some time before then to leave me. As was bound to happen, the images in my mind of what happened that weekend degraded with time; the light, the colours, the sounds, of those two days faded, until now I see clearly only the pathology of my concern with why she left me.

She sat there crying, not for me and my mistakes, but for hers, for her life exposed indelibly, painfully, before her, a life that had got away from her. How far was this, as I sat there in my prison uniform, afraid, unable to touch her, from the hypnagogic idyll that that been my home for about ten years.

'You know,' she said, and by this time I could not stem my own tears, 'I often thought of you ... well ... thought well of you. Your view of the world was like the glasses through which I looked at things, the papers, work ... "I wonder what Simon would say about that?" I'd think. Now I have to see you like this. What the hell happened to you? I don't even know why I agreed to come. It was emotional blackmail, probably your idea.'

'What?'

'I thought so well of you.'

'What was my idea?'

'Your psychiatrist said he thought you were suicidal. You would have known I wouldn't want that on my conscience. You know we had the media camped outside our house? ... He's my son.'

She got up to leave.

'Go and fuck yourself, Simon.' She turned and started walking.

'Anna, Anna. He *is* your son. Please listen to me ... about him. Forget me. To hell with me. Don't leave before we've talked about Sam. I'm a teacher. I know a little about kids ...' She turned around and stopped where she stood.

'Please, Anna ... sit down. I can't shout in here. I don't want to ... have this conversation in public.' She walked back slowly and sat down and I started talking for my life.

'You used to know me. Assume I deserve all of this, that it's due to my arrogance, vanity, egocentricity, stupidity ... criminality, if you like. Assume mental illness brought out by ... God knows what. Assume we never meant much to each other, me to you anyway.

Assume that I was just a page you quickly turned in a book you probably wish you could exchange, probably thought you had exchanged. Accept that whatever is going on between you and your husband is none of my business and that I don't even know the half of it. But do not assume that the years of coldness between you and your husband, the years of silences, the nearly total absence of animated, amicable adult interaction—do not assume this leaves your son untouched.

'There was a man—Shh! It's none of my business. It's Sam's business. This man, he might be . . . he might be the man you should be with. Is he a father? What kind of father is he? What kind of stepfather would he be to Sam? Shh! Don't say anything. None of my business. But you, you must have thought about all of this . . . and Sam. What kind of man would you like him to become? You must have had something in mind when you decided to have a child. You didn't have him for nothing, he's a human being, not a whim. Was it to have someone to look after you in old age, or was it simply to ensure the temporal extension of yourself in lieu of immortality? Or was it to have a friend, a real friend in a not very friendly world? So how tragic is it when the distance between you and him is born and starts to grow?

'Is it now, is this the time of the gestation of that wretched day when you realise that you don't recognise him? How did your little boy become this man? He's grown cold, sullen, disaffected. At first it was an act, a pose in early adolescence, a defence, a barrier against the world. Now he really is alienated. Does he ever feel anything deeply, strongly, and would you know if he did? You can't remember the last time he thought of you without being begged, bribed or threatened. You don't even know if he's happy. He's innately bright, but nothing and no one ever fostered his intellect or even his curiosity, so he just uses his intelligence as a weapon against others, against himself.

'But then, what did you offer him as a child? There was lip service to parenting fads, and many of the traditional values were mentioned occasionally, but what did he actually see? He saw space filled at times by absentee parents flitting like ghosts around the pauses between the arguments, saw his parents' lovers maybe, or traces of them, more or less distinct, and a domestic helper, a refugee from the latest country to reap the benefits of globalisation. Maybe the housekeeper is the most consistently available adult in his childhood world. No, no, don't rely on her. He'll forget her just as quickly as he will forget the few words she taught him of her native language.

'What does he see? He sees his parents straining, striving, to never have to rely on any other person. He'll deduce that it's because grown-ups have figured out that it's a cold and lonely place out there, that each of us is on our own and that no one but a fool ever genuinely does anything for anyone without expecting something in return. And if you're looking for something in return, why not see to it that you get back a little more than you gave.

'One day when he no longer is, if he ever was, the fastest gun on the block, or on any block, not anymore, and the wind has blown so much of the detritus of the times over the street where he lives, over where he lives and over where he was born, one day when his muscles ache, when his energy has ebbed, he will find himself trying to remember his parents. He will want to remember them. He should be able to remember them. He's not that old and, after all, he was there when, in their separate and conflicted ways, they pursued what was missing in their lives, missing in their home. They didn't mean any harm. They possibly meant well. He will want to remember them as he lies there, still and cold. But he won't be able to.'

'So now you're telling me how to save my son?'

'I've saved him once already.'

'What are you talking about?'

'Anna, he was drowning once.'

'What?'

'In your backyard swimming pool. He fell in wearing his school clothes. It was a hot summer day. I was there. I pulled him out. He was panicking. I gave him—'

'Yes, that's right. Your psychiatrist told me about this. He said you'd tell me this. I don't believe you.'

'Ask him. Ask him, Anna. Ask Sam about the time the gardener rescued him from the pool. He was frightened. He'll remember.'

'How come I didn't know about this?'

'I don't know. He dried off in the sun before you came home. Your housekeeper missed it. Joe wasn't home . . . I won't be there to rescue him next time. Maybe you'll save him. You can save him now.'

It is necessary in cross-examination to put to another party's witness all contrary facts to be alleged and inferences to be drawn in opposition to that witness's evidence. It's required both as a matter of fairness and to ensure for the trier of fact that the opposing cases are factually anchored to each other and are not permitted to float past one another like ships in the night. This requirement, Gina explained, is known as the rule in Browne v. Dunn. It means that, despite the burden of proof being on the prosecution at the trial, Gina would not be able to stay silent about my relationship with Anna until the end when she addressed the jury. She would have to give Anna the opportunity to deny it in cross-examination.

'There's no way out of it,' Gina told me.

'She'll deny it.'

'I know, but we'll be ready for that. We'll stress the intensity of your relationship with her when you were students, and all the reasons she has to deny the illicit reborn relationship, as against your lack of any conceivable reason, other than her request, to pick up her son from school. We've also got the fact of her recent visit to you here. It suggests some ongoing emotional involvement with you.'

'What about Angelique ... sorry, Angela? Surely this rule applies to her, assuming she's still treated as a "hostile" witness. And can't the fact of her visiting me here be used against her, against me?'

'You're right but ... they're not calling her.'

'Why not? Don't they trust her after the committal?'

'Maybe it's partly that but also ... didn't Alex tell you?'

'Tell me what?'

'Simon, I'm sorry. I thought he'd already ... She's been in an accident.'

Alex had been keeping it from me. He said he knew it would distress me and since there was nothing I could do to help her, he hadn't told me. As it was, he knew very little about it. He had been unable to contact her. He couldn't even tell me how he knew.

'Has she ... had she become a patient of yours?'

'No.'

'Had you ... were you seeing her?'

'Simon, I can't believe you're asking me that.'

'Do you think I'd say something to Gina? I wouldn't.'

'Simon, you're upset and you're being ridiculous.'

'Is Kelly a patient?'

'Kelly?'

'Her room-mate.'

'No, she's not a patient . . . and I'm not seeing her either.'

'But a patient told you about her accident, right? Come on, Alex!'

'Yes.'

'A man?'

'I've told you everything I—'

'It's Joe Geraghty, isn't it?'

No one would tell me what had happened to her. If Alex had kept the fact of the accident from me, maybe he was now hiding the details. Perhaps he did know the extent of her injuries and just wasn't telling me. I called her home for the first time since my arrest but the line had been disconnected. I lay awake wondering what had happened to my brave young friend. What risk had she taken now? I owed her an apology and more. I owed her an explanation and, for the sake of parity, many, many attempts to save her life. At least, I consoled myself, I had not been the cause of whatever had happened to her.

20

The Turk shivered. I knew that way of shivering. It had nothing to do with feeling cold, nothing to do with the temperature. I have shivered like that, talking with eyes averted to shop assistants and bank tellers. I've spent whole days travelling around the city on trains shivering the way Nazim the Turk shivered in my cell. He had found a guard who would let him in so long as I agreed and I had. I wanted to keep him on side in case I needed his assistance later. And, as far as one could, I liked him.

The Turk had taken a hit in the 'War on Drugs'. A dealer on the outside, prison life, the problems with his wife and now the rumours about her, had seen him become a user. To make matters worse, there was a heroin crisis, not just on the inside but in the real world as well. Everyone inside, even the non-users, knew about it because it had affected the price of everything on the black market, from gum to glue to protection. The price of heroin had gone up quite suddenly. It was harder to get and around two-thirds as pure when you got it. No one really knew why but everybody had a theory. Some said it was the Taliban's 'slash and burn' tactics. Others that it was a severe drought in Burma. Or the police. Whatever it was, it was making life inside even more unpredictable, even more violent, than before.

The Turk had taken to substituting other things for heroin, anything he could get his hands on. Crystal methamphetamine or ice, as it was called, became his substitute of choice but he also injected cocaine powder when he could. The particular problem with ice was its oiliness, which produced injection-related skin problems not usually associated with heroin. Perhaps worse than that were the psychiatric symptoms which, exacerbated by prison, could be fatal. He had become more paranoid, more anxious and more often more obviously psychotic.

He whispered to me, 'She's a bitch, hey, Fuck?'

'Who is?'

'My wife.'

'No, I'm sure she's not.'

'She is, Fuck. Open for business. Open all night. All day, all night.'

'No. Don't believe what these—'

'Say for me again. Your Turkish friend, Nazim.'

Quietly, with him breathing hot breath on my face in the tiny cell, I started to recite yet again Nazim Hikmet's 'Some Advice to Those Who Will Serve Time in Prison'. With tears in his eyes he hugged me, started to squeeze me.

'Nazim, it's okay. You can let—'

'Say again for me.'

'No.'

'Say again. Please. You say me again, hey you, Fuck?'

He wasn't letting go and I started again. He turned me around and when I struggled he held me tighter and put his hand over my mouth.

'Shut up. Just say again and again,' he whispered, and I thought of Angelique and of how often she must have felt like this when, at the very last minute, you stop resisting. You stand up and take it like a man. To think of abrasive trauma, fissures, contusions, thrombosed haemorrhoids, lacerations with bleeding and pain in prison is bad. To think of friendship is good. And I also recommend closing your eyes, trapping the tears and thinking of death.

21

Maria Manzano, Mrs Maria Manzano—who was she and how did she come to delay the beginning of my trial on the morning it was due to commence?

At the time Gina and I had expected to be in court listening to the prosecutor's opening to the jury, we found ourselves discussing the power of language, quite calmly, at least for a few moments there in the cells at the court. Criminal procedure everywhere in the world suffers from the same quite unavoidable problem. There is a tendency for people to hear a story once and, thereafter, to deem any deviation from that first telling, from the version they heard first, a deviation from the truth, to regard the first version as the true version against which other versions are measured. But since, by necessity, the prosecutor in a criminal trial has to go first or else there is no case to answer, there can never be any way around this. The judge or jury will always hear the prosecution's version first.

It was an academic observation Gina made in passing as we waited. 'People have to fight against it. Even lawyers,' she said, 'who really ought to know better, fall into these kinds of traps, following blindly, not thinking clearly. I saw examples of this in law school all the time. The very area of law we're waiting to deal with now is universally but quite inaccurately known by lawyers in Commonwealth jurisdictions as the "similar fact" rule, although the term "similar fact" actually refers specifically to an exception to a rule of exclusion.'

'What's that?'

'Okay, it's a rule, and we'll shortly be seeking to rely on it, which prevents or excludes the prosecutor from leading evidence for the purpose of establishing "discreditable disposition" on the part of the accused. Evidence of a "discreditable disposition" is highly influential on a jury. We say here it prejudices a jury against you. They say it helps them prove your guilt. In this case it's just a "try-on". They can't possibly expect to get this in.'

Maria Manzano was the mother of Carlo Manzano, the little boy who had gone missing while I was trying to improve his reading and boost his confidence. According to the prosecution, my 'discreditable disposition', as far as I could understand the alleged relevance of her evidence, was a tendency for me to be in some way connected to children who went missing.

'But Carlo's disappearance has nothing in common with me taking Sam.'

'I know, nothing in common with it but the fact that both boys went missing from their schools and, of course, you.'

'This is . . . crazy. It's completely unfair. It's something out of Kafka.'

'We'll fight the calling of any evidence concerning the disappearance of Carlo, or any kidnapped children, for that matter. The court has to weigh up the probative value of the evidence against its prejudicial value. Where the evidence is more likely to cause a jury to be prejudiced against you than it is to provide actual proof of the charges against you, that evidence has to be ruled inadmissible. Here it's an easy call.'

'Why?'

'Simon, have you read Mrs Manzano's statement? It's full of nothing but uncontentious and irrelevant facts. You, as his teacher, were providing Carlo with extra, remedial classes, after school. She knew about it and approved. At the end of one of these classes, Carlo went missing. You were the last one to see him. He's still not been found. She and her family were devastated. They continue to be. They're not over it. She doesn't think they ever will be. This has absolutely nothing to do with the charges against you. It's not evidence of any propensity on your part. It's just a nasty, sleazy and quite crude and clumsy attempt to poison the minds of the jurors, to somehow connect you causally and in a sinister way to the crime committed against Carlo. They want to carry on what the tabloids started.'

'If it's so obviously crude and clumsy, why are they doing it?'

'I don't know. I guess they think it's worth a try. The police were very, very angry, absolutely livid, after Angela's evidence at the committal. Now they're really determined to get you convicted. Even so, this is remarkably crude. It would make a great appeal point.'

The judge read Carlo's mother's statement and even I felt confident he was not going to let her evidence in. Gina requested a day to prepare a legal submission as to why he shouldn't. He gave her two hours.

The prosecutor never had a chance. Gina threw everything at him. She said that admitting Mrs Manzano's evidence would have the same effect as reversing the onus of proof, especially given the links to other children the tabloids had made at the time of my arrest and then again at the time of the committal. When both sides had finished addressing him, the judge delivered a ruling along the lines of the draft ruling Gina had handed up. The judge made it unambiguously clear that the prosecution was strictly prohibited from leading evidence of, or drawing any inference from, or raising in any way the disappearance of Carlo or any other child victims of any crime. The jury was impanelled and I tried to look as Gina had instructed me to look at the time of the committal. When all twelve of them were seated and ready for the commencement of proceedings, the judge adjourned the prosecution opening until the following day.

The prosecution opened its case the next morning. I'd heard it all before, but the jury hadn't. They listened attentively first to the prosecutor, then to Detectives Threlfall and Staszic. Staszic seemed even more stubbornly inflexible than at the committal. He was having difficulty hiding his hostility to me. He wasn't the only one.

Joe Geraghty, dressed in a navy suit, took the oath like a man swearing revenge but it wasn't till Gina's cross-examination that his composure deserted him. He chewed the vigour in the logic of her questions and spat it out in words dripping with frustration and pain.

'Mr Geraghty,' she asked him. 'You said you had received a note at work telling you that Sam would be returning late from a school excursion, didn't you?'

'Yes.'

'You don't have that note now, do you?'

'No.'

'In fact, you've never been able to produce that note, have you?'

'No.'

'And there's nobody from your former employer who can testify as to taking that message for you, is there?'

'No.'

'You know, don't you, that your son's teacher has said previously, and is going to give sworn evidence to this court, that Sam's class did not go on an excursion that day at all.'

'Yes, but somebody gave me the message—'

'You don't know who left that message, do you?'

'Well, I assumed it was my wife.'

'You don't know now that it wasn't from her, do you?'

'I only know what she tells me.'

'You don't always tell each other everything though, do you, Mr Geraghty?'

'I don't know what you mean.'

'I think you do.'

'Why don't you just tell me and stop showing everyone how clever—'

'Mr Geraghty,' the judge interrupted, 'please confine your answers to Ms Serkin's questions.'

'Mr Geraghty,' Gina continued, 'your marriage was not in the best of health, was it?'

'It has its ups and downs, like anyone's marriage.'

'Are you really saying that it was like anyone's marriage?'

'Yes . . . more or less.'

'But you were very dissatisfied within it, weren't you?'

'No, not especially.'

'You weren't?'

'No.'

'Mr Geraghty, you were seeing a prostitute approximately once a week for two years, weren't you?'

Joe Geraghty closed his eyes and shook his head.

'You're shaking your head. Are you saying "no"? Mr Geraghty, please answer the question, yes or no.'

'Yes. Yes, she was his girlfriend though, the defendant's girlfriend. But I didn't know that then.'

'Mr Geraghty, if a married man sees a prostitute once a week for two years, it suggests some distance between him and his wife, doesn't it?'

'Look, I know what you're trying to suggest here and it's quite, quite wrong. It's completely misleading. You're trying to mislead the jury.'

'Please, just answer my questions as I put them to you, Mr Geraghty.'

Joe looked ready to jump the box.

'My wife wasn't having an affair with him but the prostitute was. She conspired with him to kidnap my son from his school. She would've known he'd know how to do it.'

'Please, Mr Geraghty,' the judge interrupted. 'This will be over much sooner if you just answer the—'

'It's ridiculous, Your Honour. Where's the justice here? Everybody knows he's already kidnapped that little Italian boy and he's *still* missing.'

Nobody had warned Joe Geraghty about the inappropriately named 'similar fact' evidence rule. The prosecutor put his hand to his face before rising. 'Thank you, Mr Geraghty.'

'What the hell . . . You wanted the whole truth and nothing but—'

'Thank you, Mr Geraghty,' the judge said. 'You may step down now.'

'But, sir—'

'Mr Geraghty, we've heard enough from you for the moment. I'm asking you to step down.'

Joseph Geraghty stepped down utterly bewildered. The judge asked the members of the jury if they would like to stretch their legs in the jury room. At least some of them clearly understood what had just happened. When they had filed out, Gina, the judge and the prosecutor all agreed that the jury would have to be discharged. The trial was aborted. We were going to have to start again.

22

Exhausted almost to the point of tears, I was taken downstairs to the cells to wait for transport back to the prison. It was only a few days that had been lost but I couldn't bear the prospect of sitting there in the dock, the target of accusatory glances from twelve new jurors hearing afresh what I had done. One of the guards told me my lawyer would be coming down to see me before I left. I thought she would want to console me for having to go through it again. But walking towards me, she seemed too animated to be feeling the way I did.

'You never told me about the swimming pool,' she said.

'What?'

'He was drowning and you saved him, and in the family pool. Why didn't you tell me?'

'What difference does it make to the case?'

'Simon, it puts you in her home watching over him. You must have . . . you *had* to have had permission to be there. What other possible reason could you have for being there? Best of all, it's admissible for relevance and it also goes to your character. It makes you a hero.'

'Hardly a hero, Gina.'

'Either a hero or psychotic,' she said, smiling.

'You can be both, in fact.'

'Simon, this is serious. When we get another jury I want to call him.'

'Who?'

'Sam.'

'No. He's a little boy.'

'Simon, I really think—'

'Gina, no. Anyway, it was a long time ago. He won't remember.'

'Simon, he'll remember nearly drowning. Alex says he'll remember.'

'No, I don't want you calling him. I don't want him involved.'

'It's a bit late to think of that, isn't it?'

'What exactly are you saying?'

'Simon, don't be stupid. If Anna won't get you out of this, her son can.'

Could I ever prove to Anna that my feelings for her are not, as Alex insists, elements of a delusional condition, a madness? The burden of proof is almost impossible to meet. Almost. Alex, my friend, you're going to have to give her one last message. Tell her they wanted to call him. Tell her my lawyers wanted to call Sam. He would only have to tell the truth to be believed. This is a gift we adults don't have. All he has to do is tell the court the truth, what he remembers, and then according to Gina, the nightmare is over. But tell Anna I wouldn't let them put him through it. Tell her that.

They drive me and several others back to prison. Five of us rattle around in the back. Three are talking, two of us are lost somewhere in the world outside the van. The walls have been cleaned but not properly. You don't dare breathe deeply. A sudden stop or a pothole in the road and we are right back in it, maybe head first. How can I let Gina call Sam?

The smell of disinfectant punches you in the face as soon as you return. We are back later than normal. A jury took its time finding someone guilty and our transport was delayed. After being searched, I am taken, as always, back to my cell. The disinfectant smells stronger than ever. It tears at my skull. It will keep me from sleeping despite my exhaustion. The door is slammed shut, heavy, I close my eyes at the sound. No, Christ, no, not now. The Turk has found his way in. This has to stop.

'Nazim,' I whisper, but he doesn't answer. He lies on the cot.

'Get out!' I plead. Why did he have to come here, for what? For company, for comfort, for sex, or did he come to be talked out of it? He came with a gift, the disinfectant. He brought a bottle of it with him, a gift both in the bottle and the lesson in self-sufficiency. You don't need anyone else if you can swallow whatever life brings you. The Turk could. And now he won't move. Say goodbye me, you Fuck. No more afraid. Show you how. All good boys now, Mr Greer. All good boys now. All good boys.

part six

1

'Would you like to go first?'

I had to go first. It looked at the time like diabolically bad luck but it turned out to be a blessing in disguise. Sometimes they come in disguises. More often the disguises come first, alone, far too early and we have no choice but to inhabit them, grow older in them, get photographed in them for the glory of mantels and dressing tables, and then wait. We wait for the blessings to arrive and make themselves known to the disguises. I had to go first.

I stood up hoping that no one could notice the slight tremor that went from my hands to my notes. The tutor said I didn't have to stand if I didn't want to, whatever was most comfortable for me. I sat down again, cleared my throat and began to read.

'When I was a little girl, my mother tried to make me believe there was something special about me by constantly pointing out that my birthday, the first of November, was also All Saints' Day. For those not brought up Catholic, the Catholic Church celebrates a different saint every day of the year. Not only are there these three hundred and sixty-five saints, the ones mentioned in the official Canon, but there are several hundred more, many, if not most, of whom are almost forgotten. In addition, there are hundreds of would-be saints, or as my girlfriends at school called them, "Saint Wannabes", waiting to be added to the list. I wasn't very old when it occurred to me that All Saints' Day was really a kind of catch-all day designed to celebrate all of them and particularly all the ones we would otherwise feel guilty about forgetting. I took this to mean that being born on All Saints' Day did not at all, of itself, despite my mother's protestations, make me very special.

'When I put this to my mother she quickly came up with a new line of reasoning. There was indeed something inherently special about me, she assured me, because I shared my name with one of the most important women in the history of the world. My name, Anna, she said, was Italian for the name by which we know the mother of Mary. This new information did the trick, at least until my girl-friends and I started researching the whole matter of patron saints, particularly those who shared our names. Research at that time in our lives meant asking the nuns. Again for the uninitiated, patron saints are those saints who protect or have a particular interest in people in certain occupations, activities, or countries, or in people with specific ailments.

'It didn't take long for Hilary and Clare, my two best friends at school, to eagerly get back to me with what they breathlessly described as their big news about St Anne. I should have inferred from their glee that they hadn't discovered that St Anne was the patron saint of movie stars, supermodels or pop singers. But being as yet unacquainted with Schadenfreude, the feeling, let alone the word, I was totally unprepared when Hilary told me that St Anne was in fact the patron saint of housewives.

'Part of me didn't believe it and part of me believed it enough to cry face down in my pillow when I got home from school. I knew very little of the world but I knew that the world did not revere house-wives. My mother was one. I did not want to be a housewife. Further research confirmed that St Anne was indeed the patron saint of housewives and of Christian mothers, of childless women, and of women in labour. She was also the patron saint of miners and, inter-estingly, of Canada. My mother heard me sobbing in my bedroom and came to see what was wrong. That's when she told me for the first time about an Anna slightly closer to me than the mother of Mary.

'On the day that my mother was taken into hospital by a neigh-bour to give birth to me, my father received a telegram from his family in Italy informing him in the stop-start language of telegrams that his beautiful sister, his favourite sister, had died. They named me, Anna, after her. My mother once showed me a picture of my father as a little boy with his whole family, back in the small town in Italy he came from. She pointed out the little girl that was his sister, Anna, who was beautiful even as a child, and promised to get me my own copy of the photograph. I somehow suddenly felt quite a lot bet-ter. True to her word, she had a copy made for me. I often look at it still.

'But my appetite for learning had been whetted. A few days later, I was delighted to discover that of the sainted namesakes of my two best friends, St Hilary was the patron saint of snakebite victims and St Clare of Assisi was the patron saint of television, the story being that one Christmas when Clare of Assisi was too ill to leave her bed, she nonetheless managed to both see and hear Christmas Mass despite its taking place several miles away.

'Perhaps it was because of this early delight with learning that I am now at university continuing my education. A housewife can never know too much. Thank you.'

I sat down, too afraid to look at anyone. I started shuffling my papers, relaxing only when the tutor said, 'Thank you, Anna. Very interesting. Okay. Who's next?' At least it was over.

Next came a string bean of a boy in threadbare corduroy pants with stubble on his face who treated us to an exegesis on his love of the movies *A Clockwork Orange* and *Taxi Driver*. The blessing came next, after the stubbled corduroy string bean. A young man, clean-looking, dark hair, unostentatious in his dress, whom I hadn't remembered from the first tutorial the previous week, stood up and started talking, partly reading, partly performing, all without pretension, without ego. I had never seen anything like this before, not merely from someone my own age, but from anyone. I was mesmerised. The blessing was that I had gone first. I would not have been able to say anything aloud in public had I had to follow this young man. He was about to captivate the room.

His name was Simon. He stood up and began, '"Mom and Pop were just a couple of kids when they married. He was eighteen, she was sixteen and I was three."'

Then he paused and nobody knew where to look. It was as though he had expected this because he let us sweat it out, saying nothing, waiting a seemingly predetermined number of beats before continuing, before letting the rest of us off the hook. Then he continued.

'This is surely one of the great openings of the last hundred years. It's right up there with Kafka's, "Someone must have been telling lies about Joseph K., for without him having done anything wrong he was arrested one fine morning." But the subject of this professed autobiography was not a writer at all but a singer. In all likelihood, she didn't write the opening lines herself and, anyway, even if she did, it was not true. Her mother was eighteen, her father sixteen, and they never married.

'Her father, himself a musician, abandoned most of the usual rites of fatherhood almost upon her conception. The singer was born

Eleanora Harris. Her mother's parents had never married and Harris was her mother's father's surname. Her mother, said to have run a brothel, often sent Eleanora to live with relatives. At ten she was sent to live at the House of the Good Shepherd for Coloured Girls. Back home at eleven, she was raped by a neighbour before being sent back to the nuns. At twelve, a large full-bodied girl, she was herself working at a waterfront brothel where she distinguished herself from the other girls through her singing, sometimes to records, at other times a capella.

'Somewhere between twelve and fifteen she came to New York. This was in the late 1920s. Wilful, intelligent and high-spirited, she was never going to last long in domestic service—and with her mother's tacit approval, she again ended up in a brothel. She earned her first dollar as a singer in New York singing Fats Waller's "My Fate Is in Your Hands". She was then aged between fifteen and seventeen. It was around this time that she took her father's surname, becoming known in jazz clubs, and subsequently in the world, as "Billie Holiday".

'Because of the marginal position of jazz in our society, she is now probably better known, certainly to people born after 1970, more as an almost archetypal figure of "show biz" tragedy than as an artist. It didn't help that her repertoire comprised what were then largely pop songs which, like most pop songs of all eras, were often churned out and never meant to have much of a life beyond a few weeks' eager rotations on a jukebox or its successor. And to compound this still further, she was not in a position, at least in the early days of her career, to command even the best of these songs.

'Yet a few months before her inevitable premature death at forty-four, Frank Sinatra was moved to describe her as unquestionably the most important influence on American popular singing of the previous twenty years. What was it about her singing that made him say that?

'Like Louis Armstrong, her idol and musical role model, she often took liberties with written-down melodies, modifying them in subtle ways, rendering them more emotionally effective and more her own. To some extent, she was making the best of a limited vocal range which, even at her most supple and robust, was probably never much wider than fifteen notes. Also like Louis Armstrong, she seemed to have an impeccable sense of "swing", frequently illustrated in her trademark style of lagging slightly behind the beat. Her chosen inflections became the standard way of singing most of her repertoire, much of which became the standard repertoire for all jazz singers because of her.

'But her musicianship was greater than the sum of its parts as these might be identified by a musicologist. What lifts her at her best above almost everybody else in her field is the presence in her singing of genuine emotion without artifice. There are musically purer, smoother, silkier, more perfect voices, but they don't have the capacity to make you feel the singer's emotional intention within the song as easily as hers did. And she did this with bright, up-tempo, happy or sexy songs in the first half of her career just as much as she did with the now far better known melancholy songs she chose in the second half of her career as accompaniment to the alcohol, drug addiction and the brutality of too many men.

'There are many senses in which I shouldn't even know about her. I wasn't born when she was alive, and am even too young to have been touched by the periodic resurgence of interest in her. Like most of you, I belong to a generation that, to the extent that one can generalise about these things, takes pride in knowing almost nothing about what came before it while so far offering very little of substance to the world from within its own ranks. Personally, I am suspicious of the schmaltz which so often lurks within nostalgia—and with apologies to the young woman who spoke earlier—suspicious of hagiography. So why am I talking to you about Billie Holiday?

'We were set the task of presenting a piece of our own writing on any topic at all as long as it illustrated something of ourselves. I think you can tell a lot about people from what is important to them. Do they like art? What kind of art? How much do they like it, and why? Where did the liking come from? Provide the answers to these questions and you will have gone a long way towards revealing much of yourself. Ultimately, for all the expert criticism in the world, the test of something as subjective as music or literature or even a relationship is, as EM Forster put it, our affection for it. And conversely, the test of us is that for which we have affection. That is why you are apt to get upset when somebody you care about does not share your taste in music or movies or literature.

'I have to admit to having seen photos of the young, cheeky, sassy Billie Holiday that make me wish I could have known her, spent time with her, warned her against all that was coming and protected her from it. Many of her songs that I like most are not the ones the critics praise. They were recorded too close to her death and when I hear these songs I imagine taking her far away from the scene that was killing her and then feeding her, nursing her back to health.

'How much of my affection for her music can I really say is earned by the work and how much by the horror I feel at the circumstances of her life? To be absolutely, scrupulously honest, it is difficult to answer that accurately. Except to say that for a long time I knew and liked her music without knowing much at all about her life. The truth is, I started listening to Billie Holiday as a small boy because my mother liked her. It wasn't that my mother told me to like her but that as I was growing up I saw the importance of this woman's music to my mother. She has an illness that periodically leaves her bedridden. Listening to Billie Holiday makes her feel better; it always did. The first records I ever put on the family turntable were the Billie Holiday ones that I played for my mother. It was the only thing I could do for her.

'Unquestionably that adds to my affection for her music, but what about my mother's affection for it? She knew very little of Billie Holiday's life. When my mother listened to "I'm a Fool to Want You" from her bed after I'd moved one of the speakers into the hall so that she could hear the record player, she had no way of knowing the shocking details of the singer's life not long after the recording was made. Seventeen months after the song was recorded, the singer, emaciated and desperate for heroin, lay dying on a hospital bed. My mother would not have known about this. My mother might have known about the violent men in her life but probably not about the occasional affairs with women. I doubt she knew about the prostitution. But I can't be sure. You see, we didn't ever talk about Billie Holiday in my parents' house. Thank you.'

And with that he sat down. The girl sitting beside him must have wondered what she had ever done to deserve having to present her work immediately after him. I was sure that everyone else in the room was as impressed as I was, even if we didn't all quite know why.

He had chosen Billie Holiday—a long dead female African-American jazz singer, neither chicly obscure nor enjoying a return to anyone's notion of the prevailing fashion, musical or otherwise. It occurred to me that the choice might have been dictated by his desire to impress the women in the tutorial rather than by his real interest in her. As against this, there was a genuineness about him that was manifest in his revealing references to his mother and, implicitly, his father and their relationship with each other.

I was impressed. I was intrigued. I wanted to listen to Billie Holiday. I wanted to hear what he heard. More than this, the way he had spoken suggested untried worlds way beyond my father's ever-expanding bakery in which he baked biscotti, worlds away from my mother's saints, worlds beyond even all the floors of the Sir Robert Menzies School of Humanities, the 'Ming Wing' that housed us. This young man, Simon someone-or-other, was their ambassador. It was exciting to think of meeting people like this. But, of course, there were not people like this. There was only him. I didn't know that then. But had I known, I would not have done anything differently. For all the calm certainty, the maturity in his language and delivery, his intelligence and the unmistakable good looks they enhanced, there was a vulnerability and an honesty about him which I just assumed every woman in the room found irresistible. I knew I did even before he had sat down.

2

When the tutorial was over I made a point of standing next to someone I vaguely knew who seemed to know him. We all congratulated him. He had acquired something tantamount to instant celebrity with his tutorial paper, even if only among a handful of undergraduates. The small group, mostly women, went to the student union building, as it was then called, and I insinuated myself next to him in the queue to buy coffee. I let him pay for mine and he let me ask him about Billie Holiday.

'You'll probably think I'm stupid but—'

'Why would I think you're stupid?' he asked.

'Well, because of my paper for one thing and—'

'Your paper was good.'

'Oh, come on. You really don't have to say that. It wasn't.'

'No, really, Anna, I enjoyed it. I probably went a bit over the top with mine but I liked yours. It told us a bit about you and about all those saints. I know very little about that sort of thing.'

'About saints?'

'Yes, the religious ones.'

'What other ones are there?'

'Secular ones, canonised by someone other than the church. Some people might accuse me of beatifying Billie Holiday.'

'Well, to tell you the truth . . . I don't know anything about her . . . other than that she's something of a cultural icon.'

'Yeah, I suppose she is. And deservedly, I think. You should hear her some time.'

'I'd like that.'

I could not have been more obvious if I'd crawled under the table and torn at his jeans. He asked me to choose the time and the day, which was a little unfair, but when, as arranged, I met him later that night after the library had closed, and we went back to his place, I was glad he had. I had heard Billie Holiday before but never the way I heard her that night. I saw Simon again two nights later and then, abandoning all pretence at reticence, I agreed to let him take me to his parents' beach house at Sorrento, on the Mornington Peninsula, the following Saturday.

My parents were immediately charmed by his polite but quickly engaging warmth when he picked me up at home that morning. They would certainly have noticed, standing there on the front porch, that he opened and closed the car door for me. After we started for the coast he played the first of what would be a series of eclectic compilation tapes he made for me, many of which I still play. This one was a mix of Stephen Cummings, Billie Holiday, Bach and Microdisney. I sat beside him talking, laughing, listening and looking out at the bay. I was trying not to show my excitement or my nervousness. I was wearing a skirt and remember being concerned about my legs, particularly the way they seemed to expand against the car seat. Within half an hour it felt the most natural thing in the world to be sitting beside him there. I wanted the journey never to end. The traffic was light. It was a sunny day. I thought I might marry him.

The house was a single storey ranch style place on a half-acre block backing on to the beach. It would cost a fortune now but Simon told me the place had been in the family since before he was born. We had it to ourselves that day and it was that day that we made love for the first time. When I left him some two or so years later I told myself that I wanted to know other men, experience their bodies and the way they did things. That was true but largely irrelevant. It had almost nothing to do with my ending it but I knew it would sound reasonable enough to anyone but my parents or perhaps the nuns. It would sound reasonable enough should the other reasons, the real reasons, fade from my memory in years to come and should I need to remember why. There is no doubt a certain excitement in the very newness of a new relationship, but it is transitory. After a while the novelty of the novelty wears off and you have to resort to deceiving yourself about the quality of whomever you're knowing at the time. You do this in order to forgo another round of mechanical strategies, stop-start uncoordinated gropes and moves that leave you colder than being alone. It's a very dangerous time. You can ruin your life then in the time it takes to say 'I do'.

For all that, when I left there was some small element of truth in the pretext that I wanted to know other men. I just had not considered that their 'otherness' would always make them worse. Right from that first afternoon at his parents' beach house Simon could always satisfy me. It wasn't a matter of anatomy or athleticism, not alone. It was his way, his empathy with my body. He slid my skirt down to my ankles and made me sing like I'd never sung before and I kept on singing, amazing myself. He played me like a musical instrument. When you leave you never begin to consider the possibility that, in leaving the best you've had so far, you are leaving the best you will ever have.

I showered before we packed to go home that first time. Standing naked in front of the bathroom mirror brushing my hair, I saw Simon behind me just watching. For all that had just happened I was still far from relaxed enough around him to have him see me naked with equanimity and I was about to say something when he suddenly asked, 'Tell me about your aunt?'

'What?'

'Your aunt, Anna, your father's late sister.'

'What do you want to know?'

'Is there really a photograph of her as a little girl in Italy with your father and all his family?'

'Yes, my mother really did have a copy made for me,' I told him.

'I'd like to see it sometime.'

Along what road had his mind travelled in its journey from the sight of me naked in his parents' bathroom to his recall of my aunt's photograph? I asked him but he wouldn't tell me. I kept at him but he said he didn't know. He didn't know what made him think of her photo. I didn't believe him then. I came to believe him later. The Simon I knew then didn't lie.

Had he been looking at me brushing my hair in front of the dressing table mirror some ten years further on, he would have seen, under the reflection of a woman quite like the one he'd watched those years ago, photographs of her in different disguises, all elaborately framed and carefully assembled so as to appear a random assortment of snapshots of her life. The photographs were of me and my husband, me and my parents, one of his mother, but mostly they were of my son Sam—alone at various ages, or with us, or my parents. Home decoration was not among the few activities Joe and I undertook together. The choice and placement of these photographs was an exception, almost the only one. Both of us were involved in their collection and arrangement. It was done without much discussion, but the message was clear, as sharp as any of the images, a message to ourselves and to each other. This is who we are today. Get the picture?

Most of the photos had been staged, not merely posed for like the one of my father as a little boy in Italy, but staged. There were the wedding photos, of course, black and white and highly stylised. My sister, Sophie, and I had chosen the professional photographer after visiting several of them, looking at their folios and listening to their sales spiels.

'Anna . . . may I call you Anna? With the help of my assistant, I can guarantee to forever enable you to vividly and joyfully recapture the day.'

I heard the man say these words, he was the fourth photographer we had seen, and it was not that I thought of Simon but rather that I caught myself thinking *like* him. I found myself internally tearing apart the words he had used. With his assistant's assistance he could guarantee something. He needed help with the guarantee. And what was the something he needed assistance to guarantee? My eternal ability to joyfully recapture the day. Whatever it was that I was embarking on, his capture of it would be a source of delight forever. Simon would not have let this go but he had gone. He had been let go but still I heard the words as he would have heard them.

The photographer was paying more attention to Sophie than to me even though I was the reason we were there, but I resisted taking offence—after all, I was getting married. Sophie eventually talked me into choosing him over the other three we had seen earlier. Did we really like his work the best? I only know that he had secured Sophie's advocacy with the implied promise that there would be at least one man, a man on the payroll but still a man, and one critically important to the success of the day, who could be relied upon to flirt with her throughout the proceedings. But if her advocacy had helped, it was his vacuous, cliché-ridden language that had really swung things his way. For though I did not think of Simon, I did catch myself with Simon's cast of mind combing the photographer's language and it was a cast of mind I wanted violently to shed. I didn't want to be scrutinising this man's, nor any man's, language. I wanted to be one of those people who feel no shame in squealing with delight with her sister at certain of the photographs in his portfolio when he absents himself to answer the phone.

If I were not one of these more spontaneous, less hyper-analytical people, I wouldn't have been able to tolerate all those fittings for the bridal gown and bridesmaids' dresses, all those floral arrangement appointments, all those band interviews. I wouldn't have been able to go through with the whole thing, not just not with Joe, but not with any of the men I met after Simon, all of whom would have been able to converse smoothly, frictionlessly with the likes of this photographer. And I couldn't have married Simon, it would have been too stultifying. This meant marrying one of the others or not marrying at all. And I had to marry someone.

3

I had to marry someone in part because it was what my parents wanted for me. But to say that is to so discount what it was they wanted for me, and how badly they wanted it, as to be almost misleading. In their eyes, no accomplishment, no university qualification, no career, could replace marriage and children as the unquestionable reason for my being. I was a beautiful piece of ripe fruit, not too firm, not too soft, perfect for picking, which was going to spoil and rot at any moment, so 'now, now, now' was the optimum time, the only time. I was then twenty-two.

But it wasn't *just* that my parents wanted it for me. They had talked so much and for so long about me marrying that I had internalised their wants. I wanted it too and, as unbelievable as it is to me now, I had started to feel the first faint stirrings of panic, a panic that was only slightly mitigated by my awareness of its absurdity. There was always a younger version of me waiting, not in the wings but at the front door, whom no gentleman-caller could fail to miss. She was every year the winner of the 'Miss Junior Me' contest, a contest brought to me, to Sophie, and to each gentleman-caller, by my parents. And I, I was getting older than the winner by the minute. I had to get married there and then, and with Joe, or one of his many clones. They were the only men around, other than Simon, and I'd left him.

My parents', particularly my father's, delight was captured in many of the photographs taken at my wedding. Brushing my hair in front of the mirror and looking down at the array of photos on the dressing table, some of which were taken at the wedding, I thought of the professional photographer—he went out with Sophie a couple of times after the wedding—and I realised that he had indeed enabled me to vividly recapture that day. But not as he'd guaranteed, not joyfully. A photograph can capture more than the instant it freezes. It can capture the past that surrounds the instant.

It was from that past that I was suddenly rescued by a noise. It came from outside, downstairs, somewhere in the garden. Two men, grown men, were prowling around trying to photograph my son through the windows, trying to capture him forever, not just in an album but in the newspapers. The day before this, my son had been taken from us, just briefly and unharmed, but without our permission. It was now these men's job to capture my son and keep him forever a six-year-old victim of what they insisted was an epidemic of crime against children.

The telephone had been ringing all day as journalists from everywhere tried to get us to talk to them about the kidnapping. Would we consider a few minutes with Sam? I'd stopped taking the calls and though they hadn't stopped calling, it had never occurred to me that anyone would try a stunt like this. Joe wasn't home. He had taken his mother to visit Roger, his intellectually impaired brother. At least that's where he said he was going. He had left with her but the home they had put Roger in wasn't that far away. Joe should have been back by then. Perhaps he was still with his mother? He could have been anywhere. It had just recently been brought home to me what I suppose I should have long suspected. Joe had often been anywhere, and he could have been anywhere again. But he shouldn't have been there, he should have been home then. I shouldn't have had to face these photographers on my own. If we still shared anything it was an address and a son.

I raced downstairs, pulled Sam behind me, and drew the curtains.

'Sweetheart, do you want to go upstairs to your room?'

'No,' he said, a little afraid.

'Well, I'd like you to go upstairs now, okay?'

'No,' he kept repeating as I rushed around the house closing all the curtains. Alarmed at my response, he started to cry. I picked up the phone and called Joe on his mobile phone.

'Joe? Joe, it's me. Where are you? You've got to come home.'

'What's wrong? Why is Sam crying?' he asked.

'There are journalists . . . photographers trying to photograph him through the windows.'

'What?'

'Can't you hear me?'

'What are they doing?'

'It's the papers, Joe. The phone hasn't stopped. People want to see him, interview him.'

'Interview Sam?'

'Or us. I can't get rid of them.'

'Have you called the police?'

'I'm calling you, Joe. Are you coming home?'

I had been about to call the police but I hadn't got further than picking up the phone before I put it down again. I didn't want the photographers there but I didn't want the police there again either. They might have frightened Sam even more. And anyway, somehow, even though it was me who had known Simon, I was inclined to half blame Joe for what had happened. It wasn't rational. It was just how I felt. It was because of her, I suppose, because of the prostitute he'd been seeing, the prostitute who, it appeared, was also involved with Simon. I thought it was Joe's job to clear up this mess.

Joe's car came screeching to a halt in the garage in a way I suspect he had always wanted to drive it. Why else have a car like that? There are other ways of showing that you've made it. There are other cars, equally prestigious, with which you can demonstrate your success. He chose that car not just to show how well he had done (or how much he was capable of borrowing). Speed was the thing. It was almost everything. He was one of those people whose unconscious taste for violence was in the normal course of their lives channelled into their driving. But this was not a normal day.

On this day he could have the foreplay in his car and then open the door and step out for the real thing.

'Hey!' he called out, slamming shut the car door. Sam, who heard the car pull in, lifted the curtain above his head to look outside. He saw his father chasing the one remaining photographer. I regretted not calling the police. I looked through the curtains too, moving from room to room to follow Joe as he chased the photographer, Sam trailing behind me. Joe had to have been working out at the gym at least some of the time he claimed to have been. You didn't get to move as fast as he was moving simply through once-a-week sex with a prostitute. I could hear the fleeing photographer calling out to Joe, trying to mollify him. Had he realised how futile it was even to try, he might have run out into the street instead of further into our back garden.

'You fucking prick!' Joe yelled. Then he threw himself at him. In our back yard by the pool with Sam and me watching through the curtains, Joe lunged at him, using the man himself to break his fall. The man's camera fell on the stone paving around the pool.

'Mister, there's been a mistake,' I heard the photographer plead, breathing hard underneath my husband.

'No mistake, you fucking cunt. That's my son in there. He's crying.'
Sam's crying had stalled. Joe put his knee across the man's throat.

'I'm going to fucking kill you,' he screamed at the photographer.
Then he began punching him in the face again and again. I saw my
husband's fists going methodically, rhythmically, into the man's face,
splitting his skin and each time knocking the back of the photographer's head into the stone paving. And though my instinct was to
keep my son from seeing this, the truth is, it was not my only
instinct. My first instinct was to watch Joe. It was a kind of shocked
fascination. This was not one of those scenes for which one has time
to rehearse a response. On reflection, it was one from which you can
learn more about yourself than you might care to know by simply
replaying it and your part in it over in your mind.

What was it that made me stare transfixed for so long through
the window at my husband beating this man senseless? In part it
might have been my outrage at his assault on the already badly
breached peace and privacy of my little boy. But in part it must also
have been the simple human fascination of the train wreck or the car
crash or the wreck that was our own marriage, our lives, of which Joe
was then making an even bloodier mess. It was almost an epiphany.
Here was this crude man I had somehow married who was always
struggling to hide the essential animality that we both tried to pretend had not been inherited from his father, and all you had to do
was stand at the window and you could see it all come out. What did
Joe think he was doing? Was he defending his son, his wife, his
home? Was he proving himself to me or was he long past caring what
I thought of him? Was he trying to prove himself to himself or to the
world? Was his attack on this man a defensive reaction to what he
saw as an attack on his vital interests? If so, what were those interests? Sam—yes—but there was also the house, his property rights,
and there was also his self-image, which was so heavily dependent
on what others thought of him. So did I just stand there because I
wanted to see how much worse Joe could make everything for himself, how much more he could hurt himself? Was that the reason I
didn't call the police?

I didn't stand at the window for long. It was just long enough for
me to later remember that I had stood there watching Joe with the
photographer beneath him but not long enough for me to remember
what it was I was thinking or how my thoughts had travelled from
there to the realisation that, in his fury, Joe was going to kill him,
and that Sam was going to see it happen.

'Sam, upstairs to your room, right now,' I called to him, and when he didn't move: 'Sam, I'm serious. Upstairs, right now!' That is when he started crying again. And that is when I came to my senses. I rushed outside to stop Joe.

'Stop it, Joe! Get off him. You'll kill him!' I screamed.

But it was clear he wasn't stopping. My calling might even have infuriated him further. As I got closer I saw blood on Joe's fists and then on the photographer's face. I put my arms around Joe's shoulders as if in a bear hug, to try to pull him away, and the photographer, taking the opportunity afforded by Joe's temporary imbalance, managed to roll out from under him and get up. But then the idiot proceeded to reignite Joe's rage by reaching down to the ground to retrieve his camera. I was unable to hold Joe back when he saw this and he lunged at the photographer again.

'Joe, are you crazy?' I called out.

He knocked the camera from the photographer's hand and it fell again onto the stone paving. As the man, with blood streaming from him, took a few steps back, Joe started jumping on it, smashing it beyond recognition.

'Joe!' I called out, now hoarse. The photographer got past Joe and ran into the street. He was gone. His camera lay smashed at Joe's feet.

'Have you lost your mind?' I asked him. It was entirely rhetorical. From the look on his face, which had gone from fury to a kind of sad exhausted bewilderment, it was clear that, at least for a moment, he had.

I can understand that now: momentarily losing one's mind. I am even learning to sympathise with it. How hypocritical is it of someone to claim to be perplexed by someone else's momentary loss of themselves, when you, yourself, might be said to have lost your mind not for a moment, but for years, not so much lost your mind as lost something else, the name of which is not immediately apparent—call it your 'character'. After all, was not the life I'd been living a loss of character? And anyway, in attacking the photographer with such violence, was not Joe really giving a free rein to part of what *is* his character?

4

____

After almost two and a half years with Simon I was not the same person anymore. I had been spoiled. I had been educated. I had been programmed. After all the novels, the poetry, the music, the movies, the history and the politics he'd fed me, I was able to anticipate his attitude to most things. I had absorbed his thoughts and feelings. Inevitably, many of them even found their way into my university essays. I must have sounded incredibly well-read and intelligent all those years ago, at least to anyone who didn't know Simon. But, in truth, I rarely had much to contribute that hadn't come from him. It was all derivative. Perhaps that was it, the crux of it. Though it was never his intention, I wasn't any longer feeling augmented by him but diminished. In the couple that was us, Simon and me, I was pretty much an expendable echo, as all echoes are. That's how I was feeling by the end, by that last weekend at Sorrento.

His parents were there that weekend. I had just finished reading Doctorow's *The Book of Daniel*, a fictional account of what it would have been like to be the children of Ethel and Julius Rosenberg, the couple who were executed during the McCarthy era for conspiring to sell atomic secrets to the Russians. Simon had given it to me and there was some unspoken tension between us because I hadn't liked it enough, not as much as he had. Simon's mother was cooking dinner in the kitchen and had Billie Holiday turned up loud. We were reading on the bed with the door closed in the room we were always allocated whenever his parents were there too. When 'Strange Fruit' came on, Simon got up and opened the door a little.

'You know who wrote this song?'

'Cole Porter?' I said, continuing to flick through the book, not looking up.

'Cole Porter! . . . Are you serious?'

'No, I thought that was funny.'

'I suppose it is . . . in a way . . . Almost.'

'I've got no idea who wrote it. Are they famous? Should I know them?' I asked, still thumbing through the book.

'No, he's not what you'd call famous. He was a high school English teacher from the Bronx named Abe Meeropol. The story goes that sometime in the late thirties he saw a photo of a lynching and was so disturbed by it he wrote a poem that became "Strange Fruit".'

'It's a good song,' I said, continuing to flick through the book.

'A *good* song! It's better than that.'

'Oh shit, have I failed again?'

Simon had the good sense to ignore that. Maybe he saw better than I did that I was spoiling for a fight, even if he didn't really know why. He continued as though I hadn't said it.

'Not only is he the guy who wrote "Strange Fruit"—'

'Don't tell me,' I interrupted, 'he's also the guy that wrote "Anarchy in the UK"?'

'No, that was Irving Berlin. Abe Meeropol and his wife Anne were the couple who adopted the children of Ethel and Julius Rosenberg after they were executed.'

'Really?'

'Yep . . . unless it was Cole Porter.'

I closed the book and let it drop to the floor.

'Have to say,' I began, 'I really don't see what's so good about this book.'

'You're kidding. Weren't you moved?'

'Daniel was so horrible to his wife. And the father, the Julius Rosenberg character, he *was* guilty of conspiring to give atomic secrets to the Soviets. However naïvely humanitarian his motives, he did help them get the bomb. He wasn't just another innocent victim of McCarthyism. You don't find it convenient to remember that.'

'They would have got it anyway.'

'Maybe, but he helped them to get it sooner,' I said, getting bolder.

'Even if that's right, it doesn't necessarily implicate his wife and, anyway, they were both electrocuted, for God's sake. You can't defend that.'

'No, I don't, but you've just subtly changed the subject to capital punishment.'

'You're right. You're right, Anna, I have.'

'Fuck off, Simon.'

'What? What's wrong?'

I didn't know exactly what was wrong.

'You're patronising me,' I said. It felt good saying that, like I was on to something.

'How am I patronising you?' he asked, but I ignored him and kept going.

'It's not just that book. I don't see why you make such a big deal about Doctorow.'

'What about *Ragtime*?' he countered. 'It's clever, it's moving, it's—'

'It's derivative.'

'Whoa! I might have to ask you to step outside.'

Here was Simon, ever the champion of scepticism and independent critical thinking free of the tyranny of intellectual fashion, and for around two and a half years I had been agreeing, accepting every word of his as gospel. And there lay my problem. It *was* a gospel, the gospel according to St Simon. He had created his own orthodoxy.

'What do you mean it's derivative?'

'You ought to know, you're the one who put me on to Dos Passos. *Ragtime* is such a rip-off of *USA*. And what about Kleist's *Michael Kohlhass*? Doctorow practically uses the same name.'

'For who, Coalhouse Walker?'

'Yeah. The character serves exactly the same purpose.'

'Of course, that was intentional on Doctorow's part. Why do you think I gave it to you? I can't believe you're saying this. You loved *Ragtime*.'

'I read it before I'd read the other two.'

'And now you think it was wrong of you to have enjoyed it so much.'

'Simon, you're afraid to take my opinions seriously. Deep down you don't really think I'm bright enough for you.'

'Where the hell did that come from?'

At the time I didn't know exactly where it had come from. I don't even know if it was true. He was never patronising, quite the opposite. If anything, it was me that didn't think I was bright enough for him. But of course, that wasn't the whole story by any means. There was, after two and a half years, the intermittent desire for the kind of excitement that only comes from the attentions and the flattery of strangers. But that, too, was only part of what was driving me away. There was somehow all the time a certain heaviness attaching to Simon, not just in his thoughts and interests, but in his pleasure, his humour. Even the sex—which I only much later realised was the best I've ever had—was never light. The earth often moved but the curtains never swayed. It wasn't something he could help. He carried this heaviness with him like a birthmark.

It wasn't just his intelligence. Sure, nobody I knew made the connections between things that he did. Nobody I knew even talked about the things he talked about. There was more to it than even that. All his heroes, all his cultural references were born of oppression and, ultimately, defeat, be they people or ideas. The poets, the Billie Holidays, the Rosenberg kids and all the sweet little Abe Meeropols in the world—they hadn't stood a chance. But Simon was determined not to let them go. He had to save them all retrospectively, remember them all so that every day was All Saints' Day for him. His whole life was one huge, private quixotic struggle. He couldn't even find common ground with the formal institutions of the political left. He was almost more scathing of the left than the right.

'The right only do what they promise to do. It's the left who are the hypocrites. They're the ones who betray you,' he said.

But they weren't betraying *me*. I was only visiting the struggle. I didn't want to be a part. It was exhausting. I didn't identify with these people. Nobody else I knew did. I wanted to go back to being appealed to by advertisements. I liked knowing what people were wearing in glamorous places. I wanted to be free to ignore all the pain and suffering in the world.

Once, in the middle of recounting Simon's version of our history, his psychiatrist, Dr Klima, asked me to think back to the time I started planning to leave Simon. I don't remember exactly when I first began thinking about it but certainly by that weekend I knew I had to get out, the sooner the better. Simon's mother interrupted our conversation by calling out to him from down the hall. He had forgotten he was meant to have picked up some items she needed for dinner. I would have a shower to wash the beach off me while he took the car to do her shopping. He asked if we could continue later. It didn't matter anymore. What was to happen next wasn't what decided it for me. It only stopped me from explaining everything to Simon when I left him. I couldn't.

I met my husband within weeks, certainly within three months, of ending my relationship with Simon. I was going a little wild at the time. It didn't last long but it was uncompromising. I was staying out all night dancing at all sorts of places I'd never been to before, drinking too much, taking speed for the first time to keep me dancing, and sleeping with almost anything that asked. Joe asked. He was just one of many.

It felt so great to be free, free of constraints and free from concern for the unnamed cast of thousands in Simon's pantheon of saints and victims. Armed with big eyes, big breasts and a pancake-flat stomach, the attention I received from men, even bit-players, went as fast and as directly to my head as anything I ingested in those strobe-lit weeks. This was my brief incursion into the superficially glamorous world of what the social anthropologist might call the 'bimbo'. Always with the wind in my hair during one or other mood swing, I found myself behaving appallingly to people, even to my parents, even to Sophie. When one night at four am I tried cocaine with two much older men in the office of a nightclub, I got a little scared of my own reflection and decided I had to slow down. What scared me was how much I was changing.

But I slowed down slowly, forgoing the illicit substances but not the men, at least not initially. The plan was to keep having a good time while gradually crossing names off the list of gentleman-callers, one of whom happened to be Joe. It is astonishing to me now that Joe was the last man standing, the last name on the list. In retrospect, it probably speaks only to the quality of men I was dating, to my readiness to tolerate them, and to my parent-conditioned panic to transmute any half-decent boyfriend into a husband as soon as possible. And when I discovered that the penultimate gentleman-caller on my list was bragging, lying about having 'skewered' me—his term—up against a tree in St Kilda Road not far from the Shrine of Remembrance, Joe was looking pretty good. My parents liked him because he was Catholic, although it hadn't bothered them too much that Simon wasn't.

The night I agreed to see him exclusively I was momentarily touched by something he didn't even know I'd seen him do. He had taken me to an expensive restaurant in the city. A waiter greeted us at the door and asked for our coats. Seated first by the maître d, I turned to see Joe, who had just finished wrestling with his coat, hand it and an open bag of boiled sweets he'd dug out of a pocket to the first waiter. This struck me as disarmingly charming.

When Joe reached the table and sat down, I asked him about the bag of sweets but he didn't seem to want to talk about it.

'That's *his* tip then, isn't it?' he said, and then went on with uncharacteristic nervousness to compliment me on my dress, a compliment I couldn't return. Left to itself, Joe's innate dress sense tends to make him look a little foolish, although this is masked by his usual confidence and physical presence when you first meet him. When I told him that night that I thought we should make the relationship exclusive, he surprised me by saying that he thought we already had. He then asked me who else I'd been seeing while I was seeing him. I had to think fast and that's when I invoked Simon.

I told Joe that Simon and I had stayed in touch, but only as friends.

'It's only natural after two and a half years together, don't you think?' I asked.

'I don't know about that. After two and a half years it's only natural to wish your "ex" had never been born,' he shot back. Then I asked him if he would prefer it if Simon and I were not in touch at all.

'You can see who you like,' he said a little defensively. I responded with something so nauseatingly cloying and submissive that it misrepresented me, even then. I can't imagine saying it now to anyone. Joe took me at my word. Now, ten years later, as he tries to work out whether Simon had my permission to take our son from school, he can't shake the suspicion that I had been two-timing him with Simon, right from the start, before Sam, before we lost our first child, even before we were married. The nuns would say that I got what I deserved.

I sat opposite him in the restaurant that night and saw how much he wanted to believe me. Instead of pausing to consider where this need of his had come from, I reflected on how badly he was dressed. Immediately I chided myself for the shallowness of the thought. This young man, who had hurriedly given away his half-eaten bag of boiled sweets to the waiter, was trying to hide his boyishness in a man's clothes. If his sartorial sense is his only problem, I thought to myself, I can fix it. It was a moment of pity and I quickly got over it. I don't think I've pitied him again in nearly ten years. Until now.

I have felt so negatively about him for so long since then: anger and frustration chiefly, but also boredom, contempt, and sometimes embarrassment. The first time I was ashamed to be with him he had done nothing at all to deserve it. I should have pitied him and then, recognising the pity, I should have run for my life. Instead I went through various stages of kidding myself. Firstly that it, the embarrassment, was my fault, my problem, then that it was a one-off and it was unlikely I'd ever feel that way again, and finally, after a few weeks, that I hadn't really felt anything at all anyway. But, of course, I had.

5

Many marriages fail because the people in them don't realise before-hand just how hard it's going to be for them to make the compromises they are going to have to make. They know even before they marry that their spouses-to-be aren't perfect. They can list the imperfections, though only some of them. They suspect there are others.

Acceptance of them is the price they are prepared to pay for a lifetime with the countervailing virtues they impute to their partners, not the least of which is their partners' acceptance of them and their weaknesses. Yes, people know they are going to have to compromise; their choice is already a compromise. What they don't know is how *much* they are going to have to compromise. Even worse, they don't know how hard for them it is going to be to make the compromises they will have to make. I don't know that I've ever met anyone who has had the wisdom, the courage, to seriously consider how difficult it is going to be to live with the deficiencies of the person they are going to marry. That's how people get it wrong so often.

I was as blind as anyone else. Joe and I, not yet married, had just come out of a movie. It was a movie Simon would not have wanted to see and, had I still been with him, I would have pretended that I didn't care much whether we saw it or not. I took Joe's willingness to see it as evidence of a more relaxed attitude to these things, evidence of him being more broad-minded than Simon, more open to fun. The movie was inane. It should never have been made. I didn't know what to say. I was the one who had chosen it and I felt a little silly. Joe, on the other hand, though I wouldn't have admitted it at the time, seemed to have really liked it. Mind you, had he said something positive about it I would probably have interpreted this as politeness.

Back on the street after the movie, Joe, as if inspired, suddenly grabbed my arm and led me into a nearby Country Road store. Having teased him more than once about his taste in clothes, I was being given the opportunity to choose new ones for him. Money was no object, he told me. 'Go nuts.'

Perhaps it should have told me something about the depth of my feelings for him even then that I didn't consider this much of an offer but I went along with what he wanted because I didn't have any reason not to, not even one I could articulate to myself. Selecting some pants and shirts, I went to hold them up to him, but when a young salesman came up to us and offered to help, I suddenly felt a tremendous sense of relief, as if to say, 'Yes, this is not my business, not my problem, you deal with it,' and I fled to the far end of the store. What I'd seen, when I'd looked at him with the shirts on their hangers pressed to his chest, was a collage of eyebrows, larger than they'd ever been before, framing a stupid grin above a mountainous chest and shoulders which I knew no fabric, no design, no label, would make less stolid, less coarse. Later I'd tell myself that this very coarseness gave him a certain machismo one had to admire. But at that particular moment, with his grin and his dry-mouthed breath tumbling down onto my face, I had to get away.

We argued about it later. I had to deny again and again that my running away was exactly what it looked like, what it was. I virtually accepted his marriage proposal to prove I hadn't been embarrassed by him. He wouldn't remember how hurt he was at the time, I'm sure, especially now that so much else has overtaken it. You might be able to bludgeon him into recalling the events of that afternoon, but there's no way you could get him to recall his feelings, to *feel* how he'd felt. Perhaps it is this capacity to repress the memory of their feelings that explains, at least in part, the stubborn, relentless survival against the odds, generation after generation, of people like him. Perhaps it was simply that Joe became the final gentleman-caller, the last one there when the music stopped, through natural selection. Was that what I thought? Was that why I married him? Did I somehow think that his genes ensured survival?

Had I had any such thoughts about Joe's genes, I would have been wrong. Together we produced a son who couldn't last longer than seventeen days in this world. It's wrong to implicate Joe in this. I know that now and suspected it then. The baby's failure to survive three weeks had more to do with me than Joe, something I can never forget.

6

The ability to relive past emotional states is both an aptitude and a curse. It's a curse because it doesn't allow you to get on with your life. Every cut, every bruise, every rejection yields a harvest which is then stored. The pain is kept on ice and can be relied upon to taste as fresh as the day it was inflicted. Aptitude and curse, Simon had it in abundance. This didn't obligate me to stay with him forever. It didn't mean I couldn't start a new life with someone free of this curse. But it did mean I had to keep from him what it was that made me leave just when I did. Yes, I owed him a warning, an explanation, something that might have lessened the shock to him. But the way his psychiatrist, Dr Klima, tells the story, it's clear that neither he nor Simon ever considered that, as between telling him the truth about my timing and remaining brutally silent, the less hurtful option was the silence.

It was after that last weekend at Sorrento that I left Simon. I had been alone with him in our room late that Sunday afternoon trying to turn a discussion into an argument. My efforts were put on hold when Simon's mother called out from the kitchen to ask him where he'd put the food he was supposed to have picked up from the local supermarket. When Simon told her he hadn't gone yet, her over-reaction brought home to me the full import of his frequent insistence that I'd never really met his parents because they were always impersonating themselves in front of me. Simon and I hastily agreed that I would shower while he drove down to the supermarket. It was our last agreement as us.

Wearing a bathrobe and holding a towel and a small bottle of shampoo, I tiptoed down the hall. I could hear his mother in the kitchen chopping vegetables in a crisp determined rhythm over a Billie Holiday recording. William, Simon's father, was sitting in his chair in the lounge room, apparently oblivious to the rest of us, reading the weekend paper with a glass and a bottle of something on the table by his side. He was still wearing his bathrobe and slippers. I tried not to disturb either of them. I had never really felt comfortable with them. I was always too aware of the gulf between the image they tried to project and Simon's disdain for them. He had said it was better for him with both of them when I was there. And for me, when he was there. But he wasn't there then. And soon neither would I be.

For all that, not wanting to hurt them, I hoped Simon would be home before they realised I hadn't gone with him. I got into the shower. The water came rushing out with Billie Holiday and Lester Young's saxophone underneath it. Then another song from her. She sang with a sweet mischief.

> I fell in love with you the first time I looked into
> Them there eyes.
> You have a certain little cute way of flirtin' with
> Them there eyes.
> They make me feel happy
> They make me blue
> No stallin', I'm fallin'
> Going in a big way
> For sweet little you
> My heart is jumpin' you started somethin' with
> Them there eyes

You better watch them if you're wise
They sparkle, they bubble
They're gonna get you in a whole lot of trouble
Them there eyes.

I knew that one too well and hearing it didn't make leaving him any easier. We had danced to it and lots more in happier times. I knew which solos were Lester Young's and which were Sweets Edison's or Teddy Wilson's.

'Listen to Lester dance with her,' Simon would say.

With the shampoo thick in my hair I started swinging in time with her, just a little, under the water. That's when I noticed that the song had got louder. Was it Lester Young? He doesn't play on this. It was sudden. I rinsed the shampoo from my head, opened my eyes to find the bathroom door slightly ajar. There was no one there but I felt uncomfortable and ended the shower hurriedly. I closed the door and as I dried myself it occurred to me that I might not have closed it properly when I'd gone in. Still dripping slightly, I caught my reflection in the hall mirror as it followed me down the length of the hall back to our bedroom.

Through the window of the darkening room I saw Simon's car returning from the supermarket. He might have caught a glimpse of me, naked, in the light from his headlights as they panned across the room. It was then, in a trick of the light, that I saw the reflection of a figure in the window. It was startlingly sudden, sudden as the flash from a camera, sudden as the increase in the volume of Lester Young's solo when I'd been in the shower. I knew what it was, and more, I knew what it shouldn't have been. I was absolutely certain I had closed the door from the bedroom to the hall. And yet, somehow, the light from Simon's headlights had been reflected by the hall mirror back onto the bedroom window. I turned around and through a door that had been opened, I saw his father, William, in the hall. I felt sick. For just one moment, one ugly moment captured in my memory forever, I stood there and his bathrobe was open. It was unambiguous.

As I slammed the door shut in horror I heard Simon opening the front door. He had a short conversation with his mother and then came down the hall to find me.

'Tell your parents I can't eat dinner. I feel sick,' I said to him.

'What's wrong?'

'I've got a headache, nausea. It's like a migraine.'

I lay awake all night. The next morning I insisted that he drive me home before breakfast. Silent all the way in the car, I wouldn't take his call that night because I couldn't think what to say. I told my mother to tell him I was sick, too sick to come to the phone. When he called again the next day I told him I was feeling better but needed some space. I would call him. He called me five days later and I told him I thought we should end it. He came over and I told him again. He asked me if there was someone else. He was crying. I started crying and begged him not to make it any harder than it was. He said I didn't begin to know how much he loved me. Then he left and for close to two days I cried: cried for him, for me, for Billie Holiday, the Rosenberg kids and all the Abe Meeropols whose names were too hard to remember, even on All Saints' Day. Too hard to remember, let alone worship. And I found myself crying too for Mrs May Heywood, Simon's mother. Then ten years passed and because he could no longer bear the fact that, after all this time, I still had not begun to understand how much he loved me, without warning or permission, and having once been a teacher, Simon went back to school one fine afternoon and stole my son.

7

Charisma, in the original sense of the word, was a concept invoked by the church to overcome the frailty of men, particularly priests. Simply by uttering the words 'the gift of grace', even the most apathetic or hypocritical or even debauched priest could attain the charisma or divinely conferred power to offer parishioners communion with God. The young Joe Geraghty had a different sort of charisma, more grounded, more physical, far from divine and different in kind from that possessed by Simon Heywood. You would look at him and know he was going to achieve something with all that vigorous smooth-talking charm, limitless energy and relentless determination. The world was a giant apple to him and he was going to take the biggest bite possible out of it. His father had apparently tried to steal little bites while no one was looking but he kept getting caught with the most wretched of consequences. Joe, in contrast, was going to take a huge bite, maybe more than one, in full view of the world, right there in broad daylight, and get away with it. Joe was lucky enough to come of age at a time when audacity was the sweetener of choice, the honey for the apple, more valued than any ideals or qualifications, more valuable than anything but the apple itself.

Joe's broad muscular charisma, the easygoing charm, the semblance of love and admiration that was not predicated on me needing to do or say anything much to keep it going, the promise of ever increasing material comfort and concomitantly, status, and, *sotto voce*, the tiniest hint that everything on offer could easily go to someone else—it was all this and everything my parents could throw at me that had me choosing between commercial photographers for our wedding and not long after vomiting through my first trimester, the sadder for the realisation that charisma will sustain a relationship only in the way that strong coffee first thing in the morning will sustain a career.

I fell pregnant to Joe Geraghty too easily. That's what I thought when for three months I vomited so hard that, for the first time since childhood, I found myself praying for relief. Down on my knees with tears welling up in my eyes, I knelt more than once at the toilet bowl and prayed to St Anne to do whatever she had to do to end the nausea that had burrowed into me and made a home there.

'It's a shame, but . . . you know . . . it's what women go through,' Joe offered by way of empathy. 'It'll pass,' he added, and it did. It was a difficult labour and when the baby was finally born Joe was over the moon, ecstatic, triumphant. He'd wanted a boy. I just wanted to sleep. This angered Joe, who later blamed my post-natal exhaustion when I went on to have trouble feeding. My nipples were sore. I was sore. The baby was barely gaining weight. Extremely agitated, Joe accused me of not trying hard enough.

'You've got to put in, Anna,' he urged, as though he was the coach of a losing football team at half-time. He suggested we hire a wet nurse. That really made me feel good. Our mothers would visit and each of them, variously in their Italian or their Irish ways, were unable to hide their furrowed brows. In private I caught Joe muttering something under his breath about the baby and his brother Roger, the one they kept in an institution.

Continually on call, I grabbed the opportunity to sleep whenever it presented itself. Joe very quickly learned to get up and go to work around me. He had already left when I got up that morning. I splashed some water on my face and went to check on the baby as I always did. His hands were clutching fibres from the bedclothes. I saw that his nappy was wet with urine and stool. As I whispered his name in the half-light of his room, I thought his skin looked strange.

I picked him up and saw that it had taken on a leaden bluish colour, particularly the side he had been lying on. His lips were similarly discoloured, and out of them and out of his nostrils came a frothy mucus with a reddish tinge. His face was calm, his eyes slightly congested. Still half asleep, I wiped his face with a nearby cloth, thinking I could wipe it all clean, wipe it all away. I put him to my shoulder as if to burp him but he already wasn't breathing. I patted his back harder and harder. I rocked him faster and faster. We swayed together in the morning light. I didn't want to put him down because I was frightened that when I did I would see for the first time that he was clearly dead. Rocking him on my shoulder, we went to the phone in the other room.

'If you wish to speak to the police or ambulance service, press "one",' a recorded voice told me. I rocked him back and forth.

'All our operators are currently busy. You have been placed in a queue. Please be ready to nominate the emergency service you require. We apologise for the delay. An operator will be with you shortly.'

In my panic, in my shock, in my horror, I called for an ambulance and the police. I called Joe at work. I called my parents. I called Sophie. Sophie arrived first. I was still rocking him. It was she who took him off my shoulder. She put him back in his crib and told me to wash my hands and face. I did just as she told me, like a child. She followed me to the bathroom and as I splashed water on my face repeatedly I asked her, 'What do you think it is, Sophe? He . . . he looks terrible. He looks terrible.'

'Annie . . . sweetheart. You know . . . he's dead.'

When she said it I screamed in furious disagreement and ran to look at him. She got to the door of his room ahead of me and kept me out with her body. I screamed over her shoulder as she barred the door and this is the scene my parents faced when they arrived. It was a scene they could not have imagined.

There is a word for a child who loses his parents. There is no word for parents who lose a child, because it is too terrible to contemplate. Instead, if the child is young enough, there's an acronym that will always attach to the child—SIDS, Sudden Infant Death Syndrome. On his seventeenth day a confluence of factors overwhelmed my baby son and killed him. SIDS has always been around but it only acquired a name a few decades ago. The emergence of support groups is even more recent. My sister, Sophie, found out about them and tried to get Joe and me to sign up. I don't blame her for trying. I don't know what I would have done had she been the one to lose a child, but at that time she had no idea how far I was from being able to talk to strangers, how far I was from being able to talk to anyone. I was unable to make a cup of coffee. I didn't have the strength or the capacity to focus. The muscles of my arms and legs felt like jelly. Awake every night for hours, when the sun rose all I wanted to do was to sleep, but when it came to it, I couldn't. Instead I would drift aimlessly, listlessly, from room to room only to be startled every hour or so by a surge of panic, a tightness in my chest. A breathless hollow fear seemed to inhabit every cell of my body. I didn't want to eat. I didn't want to see anyone. All I wanted to do was cry. When Sophie or my mother came to visit they would find me sitting in my nightie sighing, heaving my very own soundtrack to the spontaneous images of the baby, the way he was when I last picked him up, silver blue and wet, that kept resurfacing in my mind.

Sophie had been the one to call my boss and tell him what had happened. The firm sent flowers but nobody from work came to the funeral. My friends, similarly, stayed away. There was just the priest, Sophie and my parents, Joe's mother, one of his sisters and his retarded brother, Roger. Someone, not Joe, had on his mother's instructions picked Roger up from the home they kept him in, put a tie around his neck and told him to stand still at the graveside. But try as he probably did, Roger couldn't manage to stay still. He shuffled back and forth as Joe's mother hung on to him with one hand, all the time whispering to him to keep quiet. But he couldn't do that either, and instead, talking over the priest, he said what everyone else was thinking.

'Just a baby . . . just a little baby, Mamma. Wasn't he?'

That night in bed when there was no one else around, Joe and I felt free to start on each other. He accused me of not taking to the baby.

'You thought he looked like Roger, didn't you?' he suddenly said in the darkness.

'What?'

'You thought he had eyes like Roger's.'

'What are you talking about? I never said that. You're the one who said that.'

'I said . . . I thought you were thinking that,' he said.

'What are you really trying to say, Joe?'

'Nothing . . . I'm just saying . . . You can't deny . . . I mean you of all people . . . you know . . . you had trouble breastfeeding.'

'Be very careful what you say next.'

'Fuck that! I don't have to be careful. He was my son too, you know. On the day of his funeral what do I have to be careful about? I did everything I was meant to do and I get pulled out of a breakfast meeting so you can tell me . . . tell me . . . he's dead. Suddenly, for no reason anyone can give me, our son is dead.'

I was flabbergasted. I didn't know where to start.

'*You* did everything you were meant to do. Come out and say it then. You blame me, don't you?'

'I'm not blaming anyone—'

'Oh, for fuck's sake, Joe, at least have the guts to make sense.'

'What do you mean?'

'You think he died because I was inadequate. Or was it deliberate, Joe? Tell me if this is how you explain it to yourself. He died because he wasn't fed enough. I deliberately didn't feed him enough because he looked too much like Roger and I didn't want him to be Roger and I didn't want me to be Roger's mother because I've seen Roger's mother and I know what she should have done years ago.'

'Shut your fucking mouth, Anna!'

'Is that pretty much it, Joe? Is that how you explain it all to yourself?'

'You've got a vicious fucking mouth, Anna. You know that?'

'*I'm* vicious? Well, what exactly did you mean when you said *you* did everything you were meant to do? What the hell does that mean? I didn't? And what exactly *were* you meant to do? What was your obligation in all this? The glory of the up and down, in and out for a few seconds before you fall asleep and then it's welcome to fatherhood. Like fatherhood was the only thing on your mind before nap time. Then you wake up to me swollen and throwing up for three months and all you can do is flee to the office, fast as the car will go, leaving the madonna on her knees at the toilet bowl. And at night time when you get home from the gym or drinks at the office, you throw your jacket on the couch, pour yourself another drink and start spouting pearls of wisdom like "we all do what we have to do" or some such shit while I'm still throwing up. You're a fucking animal.'

'A few seconds, is it?'

'What? That's the only thing you heard, isn't it? That's the only thing you heard me say, isn't it, Joe? What are you doing? What the hell do you think you're doing? Are you . . . Joe . . . no . . . Are you out of your mind?'

'A few seconds?'

'Get off me!'

'A few seconds, was it, Anna?'

'You're pathetic. Get off me!'

'We'll see about that, won't we? See who lasts . . . a few fucking seconds. I'm up for seconds, darling.'

'It wasn't a challenge. Joe, I don't want—'

'Hey, a talent, a class act like you . . . wouldn't still be here . . . if it was only ever . . . a few seconds.'

I was now on my front unable to move with him on top and inside me.

'Please . . . Joe,' I pleaded but he ignored me and kept going, not passionately, but furiously, like someone trying to beat a record. I closed my eyes, while he went for it, doing what he had to do. I closed my eyes and tried to concentrate on the perfect rhythm of his breathing and his cruelty, and all I could see behind my eyes was the baby, watching us through his small congested eyes, silver blue and wet. Joe stopped for a moment and turned me over. I was so unspeakably tired. He started going down on me with such fanaticism that I couldn't tell whether it was a demonstration or a punishment.

'Joe . . . Joe . . .' I whispered. 'What are you doing, Joe? That was our son today.'

He lifted his head. I reached for the bedside light. His face was red and he was crying, such a flood of tears and sobs as might move a stone. Then he buried his face in my breasts. Why couldn't I hold him or even caress the hair at the base of his head? The baby had had eyes like Roger's.

8

One night a few months later, Joe and I were at a meeting of a support group for parents who have lost children to SIDS. I looked around the room. There were mostly couples but there were also a few single people whose relationships had succumbed or were in the process of succumbing to SIDS. Though they each looked, almost to a mourner, like thoroughly decent people, I was desperate to get out of there as soon as possible and never to go back. An unbelievably tragic and random event had beaten them to a pulp and they were looking for solace in this suburban living room where a tall urn of boiling water waited on a card table beside a row of thin white empty cups and saucers, a jar of Nescafe, and some Tupperware holding somebody's coconut-sprinkled half-baked therapy.

I looked at Joe who, not getting much out of the grief counselling, had found a friend next to the coconut cookies and was in the process of handing out one of his business cards.

'Private client services,' I heard him say as he stood beside the shaky card table eating a cookie. 'Sounds impressive, but stripped of the jargon, my job is to put people in touch with the best mix of growth and security that's available at a given moment. That's it in a nutshell. Mmm . . . these are good, aren't they? But you gotta watch out for the crumbs.'

We had lost our son. I was still having trouble seeing the world as other than surreal, still having trouble sleeping. I wasn't crying. I was numb. During the occasional shafts of clarity, it became obvious to me that once I'd recovered a little, it would be better, for both our sakes, if we separated. We shared a tragedy that was no one's fault, but that was not enough to sustain the mistake that was our marriage. We were both still young.

At work, people, especially women, tiptoed around me. They didn't know how to approach me and so, for the most part, they didn't, notwithstanding that the firm styled itself 'the people people'. 'The people people', which had once described itself as being in the 'recruitment' business, then in 'personnel', then 'human resources', was a firm of management consultants specialising in 'outsourcing' and 'downsizing' counselling. It didn't take very long before you didn't hear 'the people people' anymore. You got used to it. We were, after all, 'the people people'.

I hadn't been at the firm very long when the slogan was introduced, and on being asked what I thought of it, I was generous with my praise lest it was me they were assessing and not the catchphrase.

There were bigger things in need of my tightrope-walking skills at the time. My immediate superior had developed an unwelcome interest in me. I would feel his hand on the small of my back at inappropriate moments. He would brush past me unnecessarily, his hands lingering everywhere, laugh and ask whether I'd stay where I was because he had to come back that way.

After a couple of months, I was sufficiently concerned to turn to a woman slightly senior to me and tell her what was happening. She said I was doing the right thing by ignoring it and that 'he tries it on with all the new girls'.

'But I'm not a secretary.'

'No, they don't have the choices that you have.'

'What choices?'

'You can go along with it—'

'Go along with it? You're kidding!'

'No. Many do.'

'Really?'

'Sure.'

'Go along with it, or what?' I asked.

'Ignore it. Ignore it for long enough and he'll get tired of it and go on to someone else.'

'What if I talked to him, said something to him about it?'

'I wouldn't do that if you want to stay. It's pretty good here. The pay is good. You can be happy here.'

'And if I ignore it, he'll stop sooner or later?'

'Yep.'

'And it'll still be possible to have a good working relationship with him?'

'I'm still here, aren't I?'

She was still there when my compassionate leave expired. She was still single, a director now, and afraid of nothing, not even the odour of my personal tragedy. At work she was the only one I could talk to. When months passed and still I hadn't recovered, I stopped going to support group meetings. Nothing was helping. In desperation I bowed to the urging of my family and Joe, and reluctantly agreed to taking a 'recuperative' holiday. Joe had been talking about Fiji. He was between deals.

'Might do us the world of good, recharge our batteries. Might be just what we need,' Joe lobbied.

What we needed was to separate. But it was easier to take the trip to Fiji and separate later than it was to start surreptitiously looking for a place to live. Just thinking about my parents' response to a separation was enough to get me on a plane to Fiji. And so instead of leaving Joe, I found myself accompanying him to Fiji for a bizarre vacation in which the hotel staff there treated us like honeymooners, at least initially. After a few days, someone must have noticed that I was going on long walks on my own and Joe was propping up the bar into the small hours of the morning without me and asking around where on the island paradise one could hire pornographic videos. He finally managed to get some with a local or at least a tropical flavour for us to watch in the privacy of our hotel suite. He ordered elaborate and colourful cocktails through room service and when they arrived replete with miniature umbrellas and swizzle sticks, he turned on the video for us to watch together in bed. I cannot imagine what he was thinking, or rather, I cannot imagine how he could think that any amount of gin, swizzle sticks and umbrellas and the sight of two oiled, hopelessly bored South East Asian women pretending to be excited by each other on a television screen could rejuvenate our marriage or anaesthetise me to the death of our son. He found it arousing and pleaded with me to 'live for the moment'.

Like the baby, the baby lived for a moment, I nearly said to him before telling myself, convincing myself, how much better things would be if I didn't say anything of the sort. After all, where was the harm in his trying to escape? Who was he hurting? So, we would separate later. He was hurting badly. Let him masturbate. There had been times when with my whole soul I detested him, and there would be again. There had been times when I had been overcome by paroxysms of contempt for him, and there would be again. But suddenly, seeing him there completely naked and unprotected on the bed, I felt a sadness for him. It was pity. In that moment I decided that in the remaining few days I would try to go along with him. There would be time enough for disappointment, policy statements, accusations and dissolution when we got back home. I would try to please him. I would fake it as much as was necessary. I would ride the waves of his puerile erotic fantasy with him. I would try to think of it as someone might who sleeps with a soldier on the eve of battle, the battle he would be going into when I left him. Where was the harm?

It was right there in me, all over again. We were back home when I realised I was pregnant. Joe opened a bottle of champagne. My mother fell to her knees, cried and thanked Jesus. I felt as if I'd been hit by a truck.

'I prayed for this, Anna, I actually prayed for this,' my mother told me.

'We all did,' Joe echoed.

I'd made an appointment for a termination. I had taken the telephone directory out of the cupboard, opened it and made an appointment, but I couldn't go through with it. The nuns had done my mother and father proud. But it wasn't just the nuns. Once I had told even Sophie, let alone Joe and my parents, I wasn't able to go through with it. My mistake, well, my second mistake, had been to tell anyone. I should have gone to the clinic as soon as I was sure, as soon as I'd missed my first period. It wasn't Sam yet then. It wasn't my beautiful son then. It wasn't anyone. But it was the end of any chance I had to start again, completely unencumbered.

One Saturday afternoon during the pregnancy I fell asleep on the bed to dream of a much older woman, a barely recognisable friend of my mother from church, bending over me in the half-light. As she drew circles on my stomach with a finger dipped in what looked like olive oil, she whispered, 'Three divinities from the Holy Trinity make one God. These three circles protect the life and development of a new being who will come into the world by the will of the Father, the Son and the Holy Ghost. Please grant . . .' I awoke but the whispering continued.

There really was a strange woman standing in my bedroom muttering about the Trinity. My mother, who was waiting anxiously in the kitchen, had paid her to come. Joe was listening to the football in another room. He let them in but stayed out of the argument that ensued between my mother and me. Later, Sophie thought it was all very funny.

'She's worried about you, that's all,' she said.

'Would *you* like it?'

'Hell, no! Just laugh it off. Forget about it.'

'But she actually paid that woman.'

'What kind of olive oil was it?'

'Sophie, you've got to get them off my back,' I said just as Joe walked in.

'Your sister's right, Anna. We need to find out what kind of olive oil it was. If she used ours, she's a thief and it won't work,' he said, biting into an apple. But at night, standing in his pyjamas as he finished brushing his teeth, he looked like an overgrown child, hopeful and trying to be good. I was reading on my side of the bed when he appeared at his side of the bed and said, apropos of nothing, 'I'm glad she did it. Why take chances?'

When the baby that is Sam was born, my mother and father, my husband and his mother, and my sister were overjoyed. The truth I have never been permitted to tell a soul is that I was not. Even so, I loved him immediately. And if great joy was absent, relief was not. Relief is what I felt every moment I went in to check on him, every morning when I woke up and he was still alive. It was years before I took for granted that he would be. I never did entirely.

I loved him dearly but I was not euphoric. I was conscious of how hard it would be to have to wait for my baby to grow old enough for the damage my leaving his father would do him to be so minimal that I could live with it.

9

Every day I would come home and burst with love and pride on seeing the adorable little boy I fed, clothed, bathed and read to—the little person I had produced—but still, every day without fail, I knew I had married a mistake. I was trapped in a house, smaller or bigger, depending on the market, but always a house inhabited by cavernous silences. I was forced to sleep beside, launder the clothes of, and be intimate with a crude, fairly simple man who showed few signs of having much of an inner life. The very routine of my circumstances meant that I was unlikely to meet someone new with whom I could commune, share my problems, someone who cared about me, about others, someone who could think. Certainly I was unlikely to experience any joyful abandon or elation in a future relationship. So, years later, when I thought I might have found it, it was completely unexpected.

I never expected to find myself warm, snug, smiling, tingling, glad to be alive, driving aimlessly at sunrise without anyone in the world knowing where I was. The streets beside me were just waking up. Deliveries were being made—flowers, newspapers, milk. Bakeries were lit and smiling complicitly. Everything was at once familiar and new. I had stayed out all night and I should have felt guilty, though not too guilty. I had been with a man but had not slept with him, much as we had both wanted to. We had barely kissed goodbye, and yet I felt a million dollars.

I needed to drive around until Joe was at work and the housekeeper had taken Sam to school. I had told Joe that I would be interstate for the firm and would leave my car at the airport. I drove to the other side of town and ordered coffee at a café I had read about in the epicure section of the paper. The café returned the compliment by providing that day's copy of the paper for its breakfast clientele to stain or steal. But I couldn't concentrate on reading. I was too alive. I ordered a huge cooked breakfast that I knew, even as I was ordering it, I would not be able to finish. It was more the desire to extend my stay in the café where jazz greeted people meeting other people for breakfast—artists, writers, musicians.

Had Simon been there he would have reminded me that few artists, writers and musicians can afford to eat breakfast out. Then he would have asked me if I wanted to join him in scouring the malls, supermarkets and shopping strips of Bentleigh, Croydon,

McKinnon or Box Hill looking for a Proust, Mahler or Matisse. He would have been right to gently mock my romanticisation of the neo-bohemian pretensions of the citizens of the left bank of the Yarra. I would have smiled, a little embarrassed, felt a little stupid and then I would have left him.

But Simon was not there and that morning in that café, life suddenly seemed fecund with possibility. I looked at the posters on the wall and, for at least a moment, took every one of them seriously. I would make it a point to get to more theatre, community theatre, avant garde interpretative dance masterclass workshops, all in performance spaces only walking distance from where I sat. Smell that coffee. Thank God people had continued to do things I'd never done. I could still get involved. I wasn't dead or even old. Another poster advertised a concert for Greenpeace. Maybe I would go. Maybe I would join. Maybe I would join Amnesty. People on this side of the river were definitely friendlier.

I thought that perhaps I might live on this side of the river one day but the thought dissolved before I got to whether it would be alone or with a new man, perhaps the man I had just been with. The arrival of the breakfast—eggs, bacon, tomato, hash browns and toast—had brought me back to earth a little. While it all looked and smelled just as it needed to in order to delineate the night before from the new day, the size of it reminded me of the reality of my situation. More than money and childlessness, what a woman needs for a second marriage is a pancake-flat stomach. It was the first time in years I had seriously thought of re-entering the market.

I hadn't been looking. I hadn't been looking for an affair or even for a way out. I'd gradually resigned myself to a half-life with Joe until Sam was older. How much older? I had no timetable and perhaps I was never really going to leave, but I needed the promise of it in some unspecified future. But then there came a cocktail party, another one associated with Joe's work that I hadn't wanted to go to because, if the people there thought well of Joe then they weren't worth spending time with, and if they didn't think much of him I wouldn't want to see that either. This particular cocktail party seemed to mean a lot to Joe.

'Why don't you wear that red dress? You know the one,' he called from the bathroom.

'No, which one?' I called back, genuinely not knowing.

'You know, the one I like. The red backless one with the . . . with the tits.'

'The tits are mine.'

'What?' he called.

'The tits are mine.'

'Come on, Anna. Don't get cute. We'll be late,' he called back impatiently. He was nervous. He kept changing his jacket. I'd been responsible for a complex about his dress sense and now he was unable to ask my opinion.

'That looks nice, Joe,' I volunteered.

'Yeah? It's got all this fucking cat hair all over it. How the hell does it get cat hair? We don't even have a cat,' he said, brushing his jacket brusquely with a lint remover.

I wasn't trying to be cute. The tits were mine but he thought of them as an asset of his to show off, like his house. Only, unlike his house, he'd owned them outright since the day he married me. We got in the car. He slammed his door shut and proceeded to drive like a man who expected to be refused admission if he were late.

'Joe Geraghty, this is Peter and Marian Simmonds. You know Peter, of course, and—'

'This is my wife, Anna, Anna Geraghty.'

'Pleased to meet you, Mr Sheere.'

'Please call me Donald.'

'Thank you.'

'This is my wife—'

'Oh, so pleased to meet you, Mrs Sheere. My husband has told me so much about you.'

'And I've told my husband so much about your husband. Haven't I, Don?'

'Oh, my word, yes. Joe has made quite an impression on my wife, and, more recently, on me. I've come to depend on him quite a lot. Oh, and this is Dr Michael Gardiner, on whom I depend even more than on Joe—he's my cardiologist. It's on account of his expertise that I'm still alive.'

'How do you do?' Dr Gardiner held out his hand. 'I have to tell you that Don doesn't really owe me anything, except perhaps my fee for the last consultation. He's rather prone to hyperbole, a condition notoriously difficult to treat.'

A waiter came up with a tray of drinks and momentarily arrested the flow of introductions. Once everyone was armed with a daiquiri, he continued.

'Joe and Anna Geraghty, this is David Buchanan. David is a partner at Kiersten, Emery, Hemmings.'

'How do you do, Anna and . . . Joe, is it?'

'Yes.'

'Very pleased to meet you . . . both. Donald tells me you're a broker with Gorman's team,' Buchanan offered.

'That's right.'

'And that you've done wonders for Mrs Sheere.'

'We just try harder,' Joe said, the merest suggestion of a smile acknowledging the compliment. He couldn't relax. This was work and he was working on a number of fronts—Joe was all front—among which control of his sphincters outranked control of his facial muscles. Besides, to have smiled broadly would have been to accord this neophyte too much importance.

'And what about your wife, Anna?'

'What about her?'

'Is she part of your team?' David Buchanan enquired.

'I beg your pardon.'

'Are you a broker too, Mrs Geraghty?' he asked me, smiling between sips.

'No, I'm not,' I smiled.

'Well, no, I've never seen a stockbroker who looked quite like you.'

'Well, thank you . . . I think.'

'Mrs Geraghty, I assure you—'

'Anna.'

'I meant it in the nicest possible way . . . Anna. You see in my—'

'You're a lawyer, aren't you?' Joe interrupted.

'Yes, I'm a partner at Kiersten, Emery, Hemmings . . . Joe, isn't it?'

I remember reading that the pride of a peacock is the glory of God while the nakedness of a woman is the work of God, something like that. I don't remember anymore who wrote it. Blake, maybe? Simon would know. He had probably referred me to it. I wasn't naked but David Buchanan looked at me as if I were, taking his eyes off me only to reassure himself that his plumage not only rivalled that of my husband but that it outshone it. Not only pride but vainglory, envy and malice, they were there a-plenty at the Sheere cocktail party that night. Hypocrisy was there somewhere too. I caught them only to the extent that I could process snatches of conversation in retrospect. A baby grand was too busy tinkling in and out and around melodies that, with each daiquiri, I was having increasing trouble placing.

'Mrs Geraghty, you're . . . um . . . Your husband has told me what line you're in but I . . .' Donald Sheere turned to me and hesitated.

'I work for a management consultancy firm.'

'Oh, really? Which one?' he asked, and I found myself delivering an impromptu public seminar on management consultancy generally and our firm in particular. And once Donald Sheere had asked me a few consecutive questions about my work, others in the crowd felt free, if not obliged, to show a similar interest.

'It's really come along, hasn't it? As a science, I mean,' Peter Simmonds chipped in earnestly. 'Indispensable tool of business nowadays. Certainly nowadays . . .'

All this attention seemed to be pleasing Joe. His asset was yielding a far higher than forecast dividend. He would have been content to let me dangle from the ceiling like a spinning mirror ball, fielding questions from men he either wanted to impress or depress while he went to work on Mrs Sheere. I shot glances his way occasionally just to check on how well he was doing. He seemed pleased with himself, that is, till David Buchanan placed his hand just below the small of my back. I was somewhat taken aback, so to speak, and didn't know how to react. So I waited and he waited, and so did his hand. To be brutally honest, I was a little excited by it, by the audacity of it as much as by anything special about David Buchanan. We were standing next to each other, part of a circle. Anyone could have seen what he was doing. Suddenly I thought I could feel the slightest movement of one of his fingers against my skin. Then he abruptly took his hand away, obviously seeing before I did that Joe was rejoining the circle. Joe made a point of putting his arm around me and before too long he was helping me on with my coat. When he walked a little away from me to say something privately to Mrs Sheere before leaving, I reached in my pocket with my right hand to find David Buchanan's business card. How he had managed that was beyond me but clearly he was reckless to the point of being dangerous, or even unhinged. Did he really think I was going to find the card, look at it and call him? I almost wanted to call him just to ask.

By the time we got home Joe was in a foul temper. It wasn't merely that he was convinced that I had been flirting. He felt he had gone to an important cocktail party and had lost. He had lost the cocktail party. By the time I had paid the babysitter and seen her out he was already in bed. I probably would have thrown out the business card there and then had I not felt that my having had it would infuriate him were he to see it in the rubbish bin. So I left it in my coat pocket and made a mental note to take it to work on Monday and throw it out there.

I thought about David Buchanan's business card for the first time on Monday when an unexpected call came through to me from reception, just before lunch.

'Anna Geraghty?'

'Yes.'

'This is Michael Gardiner. We met on Saturday night at the Sheeres?'

'Yes, Michael. How are you?'

'Fine, thank you. I wondered when you might be free to have lunch?' Persuading myself that he wanted, as the director of the cardiovascular department of a large public hospital, to talk about engaging our firm, I found myself agreeing to have lunch with him. I put the phone down and just sat there stunned for a moment. Then I tore Buchanan's card in two and threw it away. That's how it started with Michael.

10

It began with lunches, just long slow lunches with long intervals in between. In this way it was easy never to feel too guilty about any one of them. On the contrary, I felt somewhat exhilarated and almost—I am embarrassed now to remember it this way—almost noble. Noble precisely because nothing ever happened. Here I was having these long and irregular lunches with a softly spoken, attractive medical specialist and all we ever did was talk and eat.

We talked about art, theatre—he was a member of everything. He told amusing anecdotes about politicians and various celebrities, he knew people most other people never glimpsed outside a magazine or a newspaper. He might take my hand for a moment at the table or kiss me briefly on the cheek when we met or when we parted, but that was the full extent of it for nearly a year. His was an old world charm but its potency was very contemporary. He would preface a comment with, 'This is not something I could say easily to my wife,' and I would listen even more intently, the two of us slightly leaning toward each other. Had I thought about it, I would have realised that it was never clear why the thing he would then say next could not be said easily to his wife but, at the time, I didn't think about it. I was enjoying the experience too much. But I did wonder, why me? He could have ensnared just about any woman and I wasn't sleeping with him. I was nowhere near sleeping with him and it didn't seem to bother him at all. He never even broached the possibility. He saw something in me, he told me, something he rarely found in other people. I was smart enough not to ask what it was, defining it implicitly for myself as 'that something that he saw in me'. Simon would have liked the tautological certainty of that.

Then came the night that culminated with a sunrise which saw me, born again as someone else, driving north of the river to order an egregiously large breakfast at a café in Brunswick Street. Michael had phoned me a week before to ask whether I would like to join him for dinner. We had never had dinner together before; it had always been lunch. I asked about his wife and he said that she would be unable to join us. She would be out of town. He didn't mention Joe, either his inclusion—which would have been out of the question since Joe hadn't known about any of our lunches—or the require-ment for discretion. I told him that I would like to but that I didn't know what to tell my husband.

'Why don't you tell him the truth?' Michael said, after which there was a long pause.

'The truth . . . that's . . . interesting. What is the truth exactly . . . here?'

'The truth is, Anna . . . the truth is, I have never shown you any-thing but the utmost respect—'

'Well, yes, but—'

'That we talk very easily—'

'That's true.'

'We have had lunch together—what is it? Quite a few times now.'

'That's true.'

'Each time I feel as if I could keep talking to you forever.'

'Really?'

'Yes. You know that.'

'Michael, I—'

'The truth is, Anna, we're both constrained, we're married and this keeps me from seeing as much of you as I'd like, but you . . . you mean so much to me. Each time I see you for one of our lunches it's . . . well, it's the highlight of my week.'

'Really?'

'You know it is. And I'll go further. I think you quite enjoy them too.'

'Yes . . . I do.'

'Yes, to some people our relationship might seem a little uncon-ventional but, hell, we're unconventional people, aren't we?'

'Well, yes, I suppose that's . . . true.'

'I don't know Joe, but he's . . . he's probably more conventional than we are.'

'Yes . . . he is.'

'So, okay, you can't tell him the truth, or not the full truth about everything that goes on inside the complicated mind of the woman he's lucky enough to have snared. I understand this, but next week my wife will be away without me, and all I seem to want at the end of a long hard day is to have you over for dinner. I just want to have dinner with you. It's not such a crime, Anna, is it?'

'No.'

'I know you can't tell him that, so tell him something else.'

'What?'

'I don't know. Tell him you have to go interstate for work. You'll have a long unhurried dinner with me. We'll open a bottle or two, forget the time and when you're tired you can bid me goodnight and I can have a cab take you to a room I'll book for you in a hotel in the city. In the morning, you go to work and we'll both have had a very lovely time. I know it's a slightly unusual suggestion but—'

'What'll I do with my car?' I asked him suddenly, like a child. It slipped out and in letting it slip out I had, of course, said yes.

I lied Michael's lie to Joe. It made it easier to have had it virtually scripted, and once it was partially out, hanging in the air, there was no turning back. Joe didn't like it. I had never before spent a night away from him and, in retrospect, that might have been the problem. He was definitely suspicious, probably because of what, I now know, he was himself getting up to. He never actually accused me outright of lying about this sudden out-of-town work obligation, but it upset his equilibrium and we argued, but about other things, trivial things. Normally we barely interacted, and if we did it was not with any passion. But when our mutual recrimination reached a certain threshold, we fought, and then sometimes the words would get ahead of us. We would say what was on our minds and the volume would rise beyond that which the walls and doors were ever meant to absorb. Then Sam would hear. And while he probably didn't understand most of the words that got away from his parents, he knew well enough why they were said. Even a child not as bright as he was would have understood. Mum and Dad did not like each other very much.

When I vowed, soon after Sam was born, that I would do everything I could to protect him, I had meant that I would keep the walls from falling in on him, not that I would soundproof them. I had meant that I would stick it out with Joe until Sam was of such an age that the damage my leaving did to him was trivial compared to the damage I had incurred by staying till then, to say nothing of the damage I would suffer by staying permanently. He was my child and I was responsible for him. I owed him. But despite that, despite the hurt to him as he stood silently in doorways, listening and sensing the vibrations, so trapped was I feeling that I was going to escape for an unabbreviated evening with a charming, accomplished man, a man not of Joe's world, but of a world that really mattered.

It was also a world of antiques, a Victorian villa, a French garden. Money, yes. But somebody there had taste too. Probably his wife. Unexpectedly, it was not my conscience that troubled me, but my consciousness of my origins. What was the daughter of a migrant baker, a semi-literate peasant, doing here?

He served dinner himself. It had been prepared by their housekeeper before she left for the day. Why she hadn't opened her own Hungarian restaurant—she came from Budapest—was a question each course raised anew. Michael and I talked about many things, his work, his parents. His father had been dean of the medical faculty at the University of Melbourne many years before. We talked about my work, which he didn't belittle despite its unimportance compared to his own. What professional plans did I have? Only the vaguest. I was extremely bright, exceptionally capable, he told me. There was no telling how far I could go. But not that night. We drank too much and talked still more. A little after three in the morning I told him that I really needed to get some sleep.

He offered to drive me to the hotel in the city he had alluded to when he invited me but I lied and said I was fine to drive myself. He wrote down a number, which I assumed was the number of the room he'd booked, and apparently paid for, on a piece of paper and told me to give it to reception. They would show me to my room and have my car parked. I would not need to sign anything or give a name, even if I wanted room service. We stood close together at his front door and he told me how much he had enjoyed the evening.

He made me promise we would do it again.

'You promise me?' he said, running his fingers through my hair.

'Yes, I would like that. You do believe me?'

'I want to,' he said, now pulling me closer to him and embracing me. We stood there for a long time, not moving. The house was silent but for the loud ticking of a grandfather clock. He started patting me slowly, running his hand along my side. Then he placed the palm of his hand on the back of my head and guided my face towards his and we kissed. We kissed for a long time. He ran his hands all over my clothes, the small of my back to my thighs, my ribs to my breasts, everywhere. I could feel him. Once his inhibitions were completely abandoned, he kissed like a very hungry man.

'I'd better go, Michael.' He nodded and I turned and opened the door with two hands. I got into the car, started the engine and one of Simon's compilation tapes came on automatically, along with the heating. I had the piece of paper with the number Michael had written on it in my hand between my palm and the steering wheel. It was almost three-thirty in the morning. The city looked somehow different, as if I were observing it but without actually being in it. I parked my car at the entrance to the hotel, took a bag from the back, walked inside past a bar where two men stopped their conversation to watch me approach a tired subcontinental man at reception. I showed him the piece of paper.

'Hi . . . I was told to show you this?'

'Oh, yes, of course,' he said. 'Do you have a car you would like parked?'

'Thank you. Yes. I have a car,' I said, slightly slurring my words. 'I would like it parked.' I handed him my keys. I felt aroused. This was not my life.

Another man, almost a boy, spindly in his uniform, pale, with skin like china, densely populated by inexplicable phenomena, took my bag from me and stood a few polite steps away in the lift. With a quick glimpse he drank in as much of me as our relative positions permitted and for the next twenty or so floors we tried to hide the assumptions we were making about each other. He could probably smell the alcohol on my breath. We reached my room. He opened the door for me, put my bag down, fumbled for the lights and then stood there. I thought he might be waiting for me to make a pass at him. For a moment it even crossed my mind to try. I could make this boy do anything for me. Maybe I would test him. I reached into my bag and gave him twenty dollars.

'Thank you, ma'am. Have a pleasant night,' he said, closing the door behind him.

The room was huge. I tore off my clothes, theatrically laid out each item until I had covered one of the couches and stood naked on the king-size bed in front of a wall of mirrors. I ran the palm of my hand over my stomach and found it still pancake-flat. I was in the very heart of the city but the sounds of the night-time traffic couldn't hope to reach me. They didn't know where I was. I smiled at myself before making the room dark and burrowing into the bed.

11

After all the reading and talking about saints and sainthood by my girlhood friends and me, we were all of the opinion, even before we'd left school, that it wasn't worth it. We didn't want to be saints, none of us. The effort required was too great and the pay-off, so far as we could see from the earthly vantage of a Catholic girls' school, was too small.

Each of us had our own particular saints to look into either because we were born on their day or for some other perhaps even more arbitrary reason. My father was a baker, so I looked up the life of St Elizabeth of Hungary, one of the patron saints of bakers. Born to the king of Hungary in the first years of the thirteenth century, she was, at the age of four, promised to the eldest son of a duke. They were married when she was fourteen and he twenty-one. So far so good. She had known him throughout her premarital childhood and it is said she was very happy married to him. Elizabeth had three children. She devoted herself to prayer and charitable works, giving away much of her family's wealth. She turned the basement of the family castle into a hospital and personally helped to nurse the sick. This was all very compelling and easily pictured by a young girl at school.

I could imagine just how it all looked, the thirteenth-century Hungarian poor outside her castle every day waiting for her to provide food, money, even jobs. It was all going fairly well for her until she was twenty, when her husband died of plague on his way to join the Crusade to Jerusalem. This led me to look into the Crusades, only to discover that the 'good guys' sometimes had a relationship to goodness that might most tactfully be described as ambiguous. I started asking questions about Moslems and Jews. The questions were answered but always as briefly as possible and never encouraged. I wondered if I would ever meet a Moslem or a Jew.

When St Elizabeth learned at the age of twenty that she was a widow, a month after she became one, she was said to have been utterly distraught. Her family expected her to remarry. They didn't know that she and her husband had vowed that should one of them die before the other even while they were still young, the survivor would not remarry. It was a vow she intended to keep. Instead of remarrying, she moved to Marburg and, from her inheritance, established a hospice for the sick and needy. It was there that she came under the supervision of Konrad of Marburg, known for his scholarship, his asceticism and, as an inquisitor, for his severity with heretics. Konrad imposed a rigid discipline on Elizabeth which he enforced on occasion with 'physical chastisement'. For all that, Konrad was said to have helped her with the distribution of her funds to the poor and her care of the sick, traditionally a male domain at the time. Throughout it all Elizabeth worked tirelessly with humour and good grace. But whatever the state of her spirits, the constant work and the depredations of the life she led caused her health to deteriorate rapidly. She died a few years later at the age of twenty-four and was canonised only four years after that.

As romantic as it was, the story troubled me. Why didn't she help slightly fewer people, live a little better and die a lot older? 'What was the point of it?' I asked my mother.

'She was a saint. The woman was a saint!' was my mother's reply.

When I went to my father with Elizabeth's story, he said, 'Terrible, terrible isn't it, what some of the saints went through for us? Oh well . . . What're you gonna do, huh? Terrible. Don't think too much about this stuff, Anna *tesoro*.'

'But Dad, she was the patron saint of bakers!'

When I asked him about Moslems he screwed up his face as though he had just tasted something unexpectedly bitter or sour. He said they were backward people, strange and uncultured, but that I needn't worry because there weren't any here. When I asked him about Jews, he looked around from side to side before saying anything, as though he didn't want his answer to be overheard.

'You have to be careful of them.'

'Why?'

'Because they're everywhere. They turn up when you least expect it.'

'So?'

'So whatever they say, however sweet or clever the words, they're trying to trick you with their . . . *imbrogli*.'

'Trick you?'

'Trick you, or steal from you.'

'Why?'

'It's just how they are. I don't think they can even help it themselves. Too clever for their own good. It's their curse, I suppose. Always been that way.'

'Always? How come?'

'Since they killed the *bambino Gesú*.'

'Really, they killed Jesus?'

'*Oh, mio Dio*! Don't they teach you anything at school? The Jews killed *Gesú* in the biblical times. Now they trick you. Some of them can look like very nice people but sooner or later . . . it's a part of their cleverness. They're also mixed up with the *sindacato*.'

'Really, the mafia?'

For as long as I can remember, my father had always cursed the *sindacato* and I had always assumed he meant the mafia. But I later learned that *sindacato* meant trade union.

I have had two occasions as an adult to think about all of this. Once was when my father went back to visit the bakery he called his factory. He had sold it at least five years earlier and hadn't been back since. He had said that he'd been invited back but I doubted that. It was more likely that, despite his preoccupation with his investments, he was bored and suffering from what Sophie called new wave nostalgia. The first wave was for the old days back home. The second wave was for the old days at the bakery. Whatever it was that had made him take it, the trip down memory lane had not gone well for him. It had left him alternately angry and listless. My mother brought my father around to our place the following Saturday in the hope that, by playing with his grandson (Sam couldn't have been more than two at the time), my father might forget whatever it was about his visit to the factory that had upset him. Joe, as he often was when my parents came to visit, was out.

My father played a little with Sam but not with his usual gusto. When I asked him if anything was wrong, my mother, unable to contain herself any longer, blurted out that he had been this way since he'd been back to the factory.

'Did she ask *you*?' my father snapped at my mother.

'No, but I worry about you.'

'I'm alright,' he said, dismissively.

'What's wrong, Dad?'

What was wrong was that the bakery he had lovingly nurtured and expanded, the first of two he had ended up owning, had changed. It had become high-tech. There were computers and screens now and the old ovens had been replaced by new ones wired to the computers. None of the old guys were there anymore, not even the newer old guys. Strangers were working strange shifts in 'his factory', never touching the dough, never kneading it.

'They don't touch the bread,' he said. 'They never touch the bread.'

Icons appeared on computer screens providing options for every stage of the manufacturing process. Bread-coloured images appeared, permitting the operator to choose from a menu—Italian, French, rye, roll, loaf—and various oven temperature options. The operators didn't watch the ovens. They could monitor each stage of the process on the screen. Frequently, the computer failed to assess the precise nature of the raw material in the oven at the time and the loaves burned. There were large dump-bins near the ovens holding mounds of blackened loaves. The bakeries were now two of a small chain. It seems it was more efficient for the chain to just throw out the failed loaves and provide a standardised product from each of its stores in its standardised bags, each with a caricature of a short, stocky, southern European man holding a tray of baked goods in one hand and putting the thumb and two fingers of his other hand to his lips.

'They never touch the bread,' my father repeated.

The operators walked off the job even though the oven bells were ringing. They left it to the next shift to come and add the charred loaves to the mounds already in the dump-bins.

'They don't care,' my father began after a pause. 'One walks away from his mess not caring and a new one comes on and he doesn't care 'cause it's not his mess. They're not bakers, these people. I don't know what they are, these *musi gialli*, but they're not bakers. I'm telling you that for sure.'

'Are they Chinese?' I asked him.

'Most of 'em, some kind of *musi gialli*. They can't even speak English. I tried . . . you know . . . I saw them burning every third loaf and I tried to stop it. You know, to look into it. There must've been something wrong with the computer's instructions to the ovens. What do they call it? You know, the computer . . .'

'The software. The program.'

'Yeah. So I point it out to the manager. Even the manager's *muso giallo*. Can you believe it? I point to the burnt loaves and then to the computer and I tell him, "Something's going wrong here, Mr Ng." That's the name on his badge. Is it a joke? It's not even a name. And he just nods and says something about head office.'

'It's not your problem anymore, Dad.'

'I never had problems like that. I'm telling you that for sure. I would never have had all those *pagliacci*. You can't tell them what to do because they can't speak English. They can't fix the computers when they break. They don't even want to.'

'Don't blame it on the Asians, Dad. I hate it when you talk like that.'

'I know it's not their fault, they don't know bread. It's not their culture. They didn't have it till Marco Polo gave it to them. That's right, isn't it, Anna?'

'Dad—'

'You know whose fault it really is? It's the new owners. They don't care about the quality. They just want to get it out as fast as possible so they can sell more. I built that place, Anna, from nothing and now—'

'That doesn't make sense, Dad.'

'What doesn't make sense?'

'They must care about the quality to a certain extent. If the quality is poor, people will stop buying their bread and they care about that.'

'Who?'

'The new owners.'

'Ah, they don't care about quality, Anna. Are you kidding with me? They go into the bedroom with the *sindacato* and that's why they have all the Chinese, and then they make up lost sales with lower costs. You know what I mean.'

'No, I don't.'

'It's the new owners.'

'That doesn't make any sense, Dad.'

'It's the Bergs and the Steins. That's one of their old tricks. You know what I'm saying?'

'You're saying the new owners are Jewish and you blame them?'

'Sure.'

'Well, you would know if they're Jewish.'

'Sure they are.'

'What are their names?'

'What names?'

'The names of the people you sold the bakery to.'

'I can't remember that now. It's been years.'

'Do you remember if they had Jewish names?'

'They hid them, Anna. They're clever people. They always hide their names. They know how to do it. I'm telling you that for sure.'

'Dad, what do you mean, they hid them?'

'They don't use their real names. They use a company name.'

'So it was a company that bought the business from you?'

'Sure. It's not my fault. They offered a good price. How could I know the names behind the company?'

'But you're saying they were Jewish?'

'Anna, *principessa* . . . These people, it's what they do.'

The second time that I had occasion, as an adult, to think of Jews and of saints and martyrs, was more recent. I had left work early to pick Sam up from school. This wasn't something I usually did but the housekeeper was off that day and Joe had some reason for not being able to take Sam home. We had argued over whether Sam was old enough to walk home from school by himself. It was my view that he wasn't and I decided I'd pick him up, something I now wish I had done every day.

It gave me the opportunity to take an old bracelet in to a local jeweller for repair. It was just a simple bracelet Simon had given me but, despite the passage of time, I could never bring myself to stop wearing it. Somehow it had become a part of me, one of the few parts I hadn't wanted to change. From time to time it would break—sometimes the clasp, sometimes a link—but I always got it repaired. The first time it broke Simon and I were still together and, for a reason unknown to me then, Simon had wanted to take it to one particular jeweller to be repaired. I thought it might have been because the store was in a small shopping strip and looked like it could use the business. Whatever Simon's reason, that's where I'd been taking it whenever it needed fixing.

The old man, the suburban jeweller, and I knew each other to the extent of smiling a smile of recognition each time I went in there. I don't think I have ever been there for any reason other than to have Simon's bracelet repaired nor do I think I had ever brought Sam in with me before. The old man probably assumed I was coming in because of the bracelet. He had at times refused any payment, insisting that the repair hadn't taken him long. He always greeted me with a smile and a slight twinkle in his eyes. The twinkle was always there in this small man who never aged but seemed to have always been old. His hair was white and thin and he spoke quietly with a gentle Eastern European accent. The smile seemed to say that we shared a secret: the bracelet. I wondered then whether perhaps Simon had bought it from him all those years ago. Time had stood still in the little shop, as if trapped by history.

This time I walked in with the same bracelet in need of a similar repair but also with a little boy, my son. The man's smile was a little wider this time, the sparkle in his eyes a little brighter.

'Your son is getting bigger,' the old jeweller commented, looking at Sam, who had by this time gone to examine some watches, or more particularly the rotating watch stands that held them.

'Yes,' I smiled, to which the jeweller said nothing verbally but registered silent and clear approval through those shining eyes of his.

'It's the same bracelet again,' I said, taking it out of a plastic bag.

'Ah, yes. How could I forget it, this bracelet. You still like it, don't you?'

'Yes, I . . . it's simple but—'

'Very nice,' the jeweller interrupted softly. I wasn't sure whether he was finishing the sentence for me, telling me what he thought of it, or commenting on my continued fondness for something so unprepossessing.

Sam was rotating the watch spinner faster now and I asked him to stop.

'It's alright,' the old jeweller said, and Sam kept going, making it spin even faster.

'No, I'm sorry,' I said to him, and then called to Sam, 'Come on, Sam, come over here. Don't you want to see how the man is going to look at my bracelet? He has to look very carefully, more carefully than we normally do when we look at things.'

At this Sam came over quickly and stood quietly beside me at the counter. I ran my fingers through his hair as we watched the old man take a jeweller's magnifying glass and affix it to his eye.

'Of course, it's not that the links are so very small,' he began apologising, 'but my eyes . . . well, they're not so big anymore. They get smaller as I get older.'

'No, mine too,' I said too quickly, as though to assure him—I don't know what—that he wasn't that old, or that everybody's eyes deteriorated as they got older. The old man picked up a small pair of tweezers, hesitated, and put them down again. We watched in silence as he undid the button on his left shirt sleeve and began to roll it up his arm. Then he took the bracelet and the tweezers to the light of a lamp on the counter and for a moment everything was perfectly still. Sam was leaning in close as though a momentous discovery were about to be made and I stood behind him, suddenly loving him a little bit more for his deep interest in the jeweller's inspection of the bracelet. The two of them peered in at it and that was when I noticed for the first time that the jeweller had a series of numbers tattooed into the flesh of his forearm. It had never occurred to me that this old man I had been visiting periodically for ten or so years to have my bracelet fixed was a Jew, much less a Holocaust survivor. I'd never thought about his origins.

'It's this link here, of course, but maybe also this one next to it. I would tighten this one but the other one will probably break again.'

'Oh no! Really?'

'I probably have in the back . . . If you could leave it with me . . . I know how much you like this. I have a collection in the back of links and old bracelets. I am sure I could find a silver one very much like these to replace this one, the weakest one, but it will take some time to go through all of them to find the right one, the closest one. Can you leave it with me for a bit? My wife used to say, "Stop keeping this junk" but in this junk now might be the link that saves you. We can see. Can you leave it with me for a little bit?'

'Yes, of course.'

'I'm sure I'll have something for you,' he said.

'Oh, thank you . . . so much.'

'And for the little boy . . . what is his name?'

'Sam.'

'Sam! That's a good name. Do you like your name, Sam?'

'Yes,' Sam answered a little uncertainly.

'Then you like *my* name. Do you know why?'

'Cause it's your name too?'

'That's right, but they call me Samuel. Some of them . . . when they call. Anyway, Sam, for being such a good boy, for you I have something,' he said, reaching into a drawer under the counter. He handed Sam a boiled sweet wrapped tightly in cellophane.

'Is it alright I give him . . . ?'

'Oh sure, he eats worse than that every day at school. What do you say to the gentleman, Sam?'

'Why do you have a num—?'

'Say "thank you" to the gentleman, Sammy,' I said to shut him up.

'Thank you.'

'We'll have to go, I'm afraid.'

'So okay, you go and leave it with me. I'll find a link for you, and then you'll come back . . . with Sam,' he said, looking up at me. Sam had put the boiled sweet in his pocket and was transfixed by the number on the man's arm. I made a point of not looking at it, although I had never seen one before. Instead I looked back into his eyes. The gleam, the sparkle, was tiny but always there, like a permanent tear.

Outside on the window above the door it read in small print, 'Proprietor—Samuel J. Leibowitz'. I had never noticed it before. As soon as we had left the shop, Sam asked me why the man had a number on his arm. I didn't know where to start with the answer to that.

I thought that he was probably too young then to hear any kind of historical explanation. But I would have to tell him one day, even though I, myself, had trouble understanding how it could have happened. And if I didn't tell him, who would—my father? How would Joe explain it? It dawned on me with a certain horror outside the little jewellery store that I didn't know anyone I could trust to teach him even a tiny but accurate and unadulterated grain of the truth about man's capacity for inhumanity. I certainly couldn't. But wasn't I just like everybody else in this, and anyway, did what happened then still matter that much? Could we let it not matter that much? There were Simon's prints all over this sequence of thoughts. That bastard, that madman. One day he took my son, just like that. Now I see his prints all over my life.

I thought I'd have to tell Sam something but I didn't want to frighten him or give him nightmares. It was a problem I wasn't expecting, and as a parent I was ill equipped to deal with it. I was ill equipped and alone. The one thing I did know to tell Sam was that he mustn't say anything about the number on the jeweller's arm when we went back to collect the bracelet. But we didn't go back to collect the bracelet. Nor did I go on my own.

It was Michael Gardiner who picked up the bracelet for me. The cardiovascular clinic was not far from the jewellery shop. He insisted, a small favour. His efforts to have me agree to spend a weekend away with him were unsubtle and relentless. True, the attention was flattering, at times even embarrassing, and the prospect of being caught out was a little frightening. But, to be honest, it was a little exciting. More than that, it was distracting, and I wanted to be distracted. I was ready to be distracted. And it was guilt-free, at least thus far. I wasn't doing anything; he was. He was reeling me in. But I couldn't keep not doing anything. What the hell were all the squats and crunches for anyway? I had a pancake-flat stomach. I'd sweated for it. I wasn't dead yet. We agreed that I was to have a 'work-related conference', this time for an entire weekend, and we'd go away somewhere. We would fly somewhere. I had told Joe my lies. I was packed. I was nervous. I didn't know what to expect but I hadn't expected it not to happen. That was the Friday that Simon came rushing back into my life. All bets were off.

'Will passenger Anna Geraghty, passenger Anna Geraghty, please make her way to the information desk, passenger Anna Geraghty, please.'

It's never good, and always a little surreal, when they call your name over an airport's public address system. It was to get progressively more surreal. The message I was given at the information desk was so bizarre it defied understanding, let alone belief. Unable to wait for Michael to get there—he'd been held up—I called him on his mobile phone to explain.

'An old boyfriend of mine, from years ago, has apparently just taken my son from school. I have to go home immediately. I'm sorry . . . Yes, taken as in kidnapped . . . Yes, I'm serious. Why would I make something like this up? . . . Look, if I didn't want to go I'd tell you . . . I would . . . I certainly wouldn't come up with something like this . . . Michael, I'm telling you the truth. Where do you think? I'm in a cab right now . . . Going home . . . You've got to believe me. This is my son. It's got nothing to do with . . . No, it's got nothing to do . . . with us. I am calm . . . Well, you wouldn't sound too calm either if someone had just taken . . . No, I think he's okay but I want to see for myself obviously . . . completely out of the blue . . . Not for ten years . . . Really . . . Well, he was perfectly sane last time I saw him. A teacher . . . I told you . . . ten years . . . You're not serious? . . . Michael, for God's sake! No, no one else . . . I am not making any of this up, I wish I *were* . . . Nothing like this has ever happened to *you*! Nothing like this has ever happened to *me*! . . . Well, soon as I can but I just . . . I just want to see that he's alright. Well, yes, whenever my son is kidnapped I am apt to cry. Please, Michael, bear with me. I don't know what's going on.'

The reception cut out on my mobile phone in the back seat of the cab. As I wiped my eyes with a tissue I'd found in my bag the phone rang and, thinking it was either Michael or Joe, I hurried to answer. But it was neither of them. This was the first in a series of calls from a man whose mix of formality and intimacy, discretion and impertinence, was unlike any I had ever experienced. It was Dr Alex Klima. He had been put through to my mobile phone by one of the receptionists at work and he begged me not to hang up. He was Simon's psychiatrist and he wanted to talk to me about the madness that had alighted on my son and me. I took down his details. He couldn't really discuss it over the phone. Would I be able to meet him? I felt dirty.

'Can you stop the car, please?' I called to the driver, but we were still on the freeway and he showed no signs of even slowing.

'Will you pull over to the side of the road—stop the fucking car!'

This time he heard me. He pulled over and, with the cars whooshing past us, I opened the door and vomited in the emergency lane.

Sam was untouched other than by me. I wouldn't let him go. He didn't seem to know what the fuss was about. I sat him down and made him go through everything that had happened, moment by moment. It had been after school. He had been playing with a few boys in the school ground.

'Who were they?'

'Some boys.'

'Are they your friends?'

'I don't know.'

'Sam, this is important. What do you mean, you don't know? I know you're upset, but who were they?'

'I'm not upset.'

'Were these boys your friends?'

'I don't know. They're okay. They're older.'

'How much older?'

'Grade three and grade four and some grade two.'

'Did they make you do something?'

'No.'

'Anything?'

'No.'

'Did they make you go with him?'

'We played marbles.'

'Really, Sam, you can tell me the truth. Is that really—?'

'No.'

'It's not the truth?'

'They played marbles but I didn't really.'

'What did you do?'

'They wouldn't let me have a turn.'

'Were you upset?'

'No, I just watched and waited.'

'What were you waiting for?'

'My turn.'

'And what about going home?'

'I was waiting for Dad to pick me up.'

'And when Dad didn't come?'

'I went home with the other man.'

'But, Sam, what have we always said about strangers?'

'Don't talk to strangers. I know.'

'So why did you—?'

'He wasn't a stranger, Mum, I know him. I didn't do anything wrong. I'm not in trouble, am I?'

Sam insisted that Simon wasn't a stranger although he couldn't say who he was or where he'd seen him. It didn't make any sense but he seemed perfectly unharmed. He had played with a dog, been given some chocolate milk by a lady, and then had gone to sleep till the police came and then, after a little while, he saw his dad. Joe claimed that one of the receptionists at work had left him a memo of a phone call from the school informing him that Sam had gone on a school excursion and should be picked up somewhat later than usual. I shouted at him. I told him I didn't believe him. He couldn't produce the memo.

'Don't you fucking blame this on me!'

'Don't be angry, Dad. Dad, don't yell at Mummy, Dad.' Sam was crying. I put my arm around him.

'It's alright, my little Sam.'

'You've been seeing him again, haven't you?' Joe said.

'Don't be ridiculous.'

'Of course you have. How long?'

'Joe—'

'How long have you been seeing him?'

'Joe, I don't know what the hell is going on but it's not that.'

'Has this got something to do with the conference you were meant to be going to this weekend?'

'Joe, can we talk about this later? I just want to get him—'

'Just tell me the fucking truth!'

'I *am* telling you the truth. Please, just let me get him ready for bed and then maybe we can figure this out. I swear I don't know any more than you do.'

Once Sam was in bed, I spent about an hour trying to convince Joe that I had not been having an affair with Simon Heywood, and that I was as much at a loss to explain what was going on as he was. I told him I wanted to go and speak to Simon's parents, perhaps they could shed some light on what had led him to take our son. This was only partially a lie. I did go out that night to try to learn what had made him do it. I met Dr Alex Klima and for two hours I listened in silence as he told me all about Simon, and even a little about me.

On the way back home I stopped at the police station in St Kilda. The investigating officers weren't there. Simon was there but the police wouldn't let me see him. I didn't know if I wanted to see him. The sergeant at the desk confirmed that there had been a woman there too. She was somehow involved but she hadn't been charged. They had let her go. The woman was the prostitute Dr Klima had told me about. She was the link between Simon and my husband.

When I got home Sam was still asleep and Joe was drunk. I could smell it in the house as soon as I opened the front door.

'They still got your boyfriend locked up?'

'Joe, I know everything.'

'I'm sure you do. Maybe you can start telling me some of it.'

'You can cut it out, Joe. I know about her.'

'Who?'

'I know about your whore, Angelique.'

We lay beside each other in bed that night, two hostile strangers married to each other. I kept thinking about Simon, about what the psychiatrist, Alex Klima, told me had become of him. And about what Klima had suggested. He'd asked, pleaded, that I tell the police that Simon and I were having an affair and that Simon had had my permission to take Sam. This psychiatrist needed help himself if he thought I was going to tell the police that. He was just the sort of psychiatrist Simon would get: worldly, mellifluous, well-spoken and completely unhinged by a loyalty to Simon bordering on love. That would be the one, alright.

He had asked me if I would save Simon by telling the lie Simon wanted me to tell, a lie that even he, Klima, acknowledged could, would, cost me my marriage. 'So this is where we are now—all of us *separate* people,' he had said towards the end. What the hell right did he have to be critical of me, particularly on the very day that all his worldliness had come crashing down, the day his star patient had kidnapped my son? The gibe was unambiguous. If he thought this was the way to win friends and influence people, he was crazier than Simon.

'It had occurred to me,' he said, 'that it would not be possible for Simon to get you out of his system without him actually seeing you again, without establishing contact. My thinking was, with respect, that you could not help but disappoint him now. This might hurt him very much in the short run. It might even drive him back to his darkened bedroom. But after a while his despair over the reality of you, as opposed to his idealisation of you, would evaporate, and with it a lot of other things. I told him this. I think he was coming around to contacting you. I think you could have helped him—just by being the person you are, with your fears and weaknesses, and him seeing that you have them just like the rest of us. It would not have taken much. He nearly called you several times. You weren't to know. He nearly called you last night.'

To a background of arrhythmic snoring from a not entirely asleep Joe, I wondered what it was about me that Dr Klima held 'could not help but disappoint' Simon now. What was so disappointing about 'the reality of me'? And what kind of therapist, I wondered, permits himself to become the spokesperson for a crazy man, the spokesperson for one of his mistakes? The kidnapping of my son was Simon's doing and his psychiatrist's not-doing, and yet its undoing, according to the same psychiatrist, was my responsibility. Only I could help Simon now, he told me, and I didn't shout him down, I didn't storm out. I just sat there and listened to my former lover's passionate intermediary, this highly qualified, articulate stranger.

'You're the only one that can help him. He wants you to tell them that he is your lover, that he had your permission to take Sam. That is the only course that can save him now. Why would you want to save him? Because he's ill and because he's never stopped loving you. Among other things, he is ill *because* he's never stopped loving you. I'm not saying you owe him anything beyond that which we all owe each other. But when we are all finished being told that everyone out there must take responsibility for himself—what is it like when we get home? What is it like inside? He had been cast out and he had never done anything wrong, till now. You think it would be the end of everything to help him like this but it would only be the end of some things. What are you going to do? You're involved. You are finally involved, after all these years, and there is no way out of it. I nearly called you last night.'

Where do you find advocates like that? At times he even had me feeling sympathy for Simon, which was no mean feat given how angry I was with him for taking Sam. Just what the hell was he saying about Simon anyway, about his motivation? Was Simon really still in love with me or was he just unwell, pure and simple, and was this Dr Svengali trying to dress it up as something laudable, something a little flattering, at least to me? There was certainly nothing flattering in his depiction of my marriage. But even in that he attributed more fault to Joe than to me. A strangely likeable man, charming, even handsome in a distinguished sort of way; this was the man Simon had character-assassinating my husband on the day that Simon had chosen as perfect for taking my little boy.

14

Was Joe really asleep? Who was this woman, I wondered, and what was it about her that made him choose her not only above me but above all the women on display at the brothel he visited regularly? Dr Klima said it was always the same girl. That's my husband— faithful in his infidelity. But, of course, it wasn't really that. It was his stolidness, his woodenness. Simon had linked up with her too. She must have had something, this woman. No doubt she was younger than me. She had to be much younger. She probably hadn't had children, probably wasn't much more than a child herself. Was she slimmer than me or bigger breasted, or both? Was she more athletic or more supple? I'd done everything I could, given that I'd had a child. He wanted me to have a child. Everyone wanted me to have a child. I couldn't have worked out any more unless I'd quit my job and done nothing but work on myself. That's what models do. That's really what men want, not just men in the abstract, but the men you know, the men who once chose you, Joe and Simon. They want young girls who are professionally young girls. Girls who can't think, who can't talk, who can't even menstruate. They're not worth more than an hour but that's way more than Joe needs.

Maybe it was more than that. Simon, even half-mad, Simon would want more than that. Technique, it had to be technique. One learns by experience. I thought I'd had a lot of experience. But what kind of experience was it? Had I been too passive? Should I have experimented more? Had I been too concerned with my own pleasure, living for the moment and thinking I had forever to learn when really I had only until I got married, and I got married young because I wasn't about to spoil or rot. I was ripe fruit. I knew what they did to the fruit that ripened and rotted before it was picked. They crushed it into a concentrate, into instant spinster.

I wondered what would happen in the morning when Joe was tired of pretending he was asleep. He would have to talk. It would be the morning of the first day of the new era Simon had delivered to us when he took delivery of Sam. I lay on my stomach and exhaled involuntarily; I was apprehensive of what it would bring. Joe turned over and looked at me quizzically.

'Sorry. It's my stomach. I think my stomach is a little . . . upset,' I offered him.

'Would you like a cup of tea?' he counter-offered. He was feeling guilty and it caught me off guard. I was not accustomed to him feeling guilty.

'What?' I asked, buying time.

'Would you like a cup of tea? It might help settle your stomach.'

'No . . . only if you're having one.'

He got out of bed, put his slippers on and went downstairs to make us both a cup of tea. I watched him put his feet inside the slippers, slightly unbalanced, one foot at a time, slightly uncertain in his movements. It was seeing this action of his that made me suddenly feel so sorry for him. They were the slippers I had bought for Sam to give to him for Father's Day. What I felt was pity and a terrible sadness, and guilt. This was not what I wanted to feel right then. It was dangerous to feel that way in moments of truth. It would have been better to be angry with him for cheating, or at least to be steely. I had to think of the girl, the slut he preferred to me. Think of the whore. Don't think of the slippers. He kept the slippers for me. She didn't have to see him stumble into them. What did she do to him that he liked so much?

He came back upstairs with a cup of tea for each of us. He set mine down on the bedside table beside me and took his back to his own side where he got into bed and started sipping, slurping away. The slippers were gone. Thank God for that. I was better off without them. He said something but I didn't register the words, only the sound. I knew I'd better start. But what did I want to say?

'Joe.'

'Anna, what's going on?'

'Joe, we have to talk.'

'This guy Simon, you know him?'

'He was my boyfriend a long time ago.'

'Have you slept with him?'

'When we were going out. We went out . . . I don't know . . . ten years ago or something. I'd just finished going out with him when *we* met.'

'Are you sleeping with him now?'

'No.'

'Are you seeing him now?'

'Seeing him? No.'

'You're fucking lying, Anna. You're lying.'

'No, I'm not.'

'He says you're in a relationship. Simon says, "Fuck your ex-boyfriend behind your husband's back and steal his son".'

'Hey, don't talk to me about "behind your husband's back".'

'We're talking about Simon here.'

'Oh, are we? Have you spoken to him?'

'No, I haven't fucking spoken to Simon.'

'So what are you talking about?'

'The police.'

'The police?'

'The cops said you were fucking him.'

'Bullshit! Now *you're* lying. They didn't say that.'

'They said he says he was picking Sam up from school, picking up my son from school because . . . because you asked him to. Because you're still on with him.'

'Stop shouting. I'm not *on* with him. You'll wake Sam.'

'I'm not shouting.'

'You are.'

'You're fucking this Simon guy.'

'That's bullshit, Joe. I'm not.'

'Well, what's he doing picking up Sam ten years after you split up with him?'

'I don't know.'

'How can you look at me and lie like this? Do you think that I'm that fucking stupid? Do you think you're *that* much smarter than me that I'll believe any crap you give me?'

'Let go of me, Joe, let go of me.' I could see the frustration in his eyes. He had my arms and was squeezing. He wanted to hurt me.

'I'm not touching you. Christ, who could *that* be?'

'Let go of me.' The phone was ringing but he wouldn't loosen his grip. On the fourth ring he let go.

'Answer the phone, for fuck's sake. I feel sick.'

It was his mother. She could affect me the same way his slippers could, only more so. She had read about Sam and was crying. We had made the papers. I had my own parents' response to look forward to. Joe's mother wanted to see her grandson before she and Joe went off, as they regularly did, to visit her institutionalised younger son, Roger. Tell her about the whore, I thought, but didn't say. My breathing was shallow. Sam appeared at the doorway in his pyjamas. How much of the guilt I was feeling had I earned?

In the month or so that followed, Joe threw himself into a deal he was involved with. It was big. It was going to change everything but everything was already changed. He didn't believe me about Simon but the distraction of the deal kept him relatively quiet. There were, however, consequences of the kidnapping I couldn't escape. Among them was the pleasure of being interviewed by Detectives

Threlfall and Staszic. Despite the leering and brusqueness of Detective Staszic, the questions they asked were all of a kind I could answer truthfully and without embarrassment. I knew Simon Heywood. He had been my boyfriend at university but not since then. Yes, I was sure. I told them I resented the implication. Detective Staszic seemed to be able to live with that. He had to stifle a grin meant for other occasions.

Michael made what I thought was a perfunctory attempt to keep in touch. It bothered me that it was less to enquire about Sam's or my well-being than to sound me out about a weekend away, something I was not at all interested in so soon after what had happened. For one thing, a part of me felt that Sam's kidnapping was a punishment, or at least a warning. It was the sort of stunt the God I remembered went in for. After all, who knew better than Him how much Sam mattered to me? Still, I called Michael to try to at least arrange lunch, just to keep my hand in. He seemed to be very busy and we weren't able to schedule lunch. I wondered about that. Was he punishing me too?

It occurred to me that perhaps he genuinely was busier than usual. Joe certainly was, judging from his frequent explosions of verbal enthusiasm for the highly lucrative deal he said he could almost taste. It had something to do with private hospitals, health insurance, managed care and, of course, every businessman's god, Donald Sheere. There were phone calls and meetings at all times of the day and night. As it was, I was busy at work as well but it wasn't a lucrative deal that I could almost taste. It was the bitterness of all-day-stewed coffee repeating on me as I benefited from one opportunity after another to contribute to the marketing of 'the people people'. We have a newsletter that goes out to clients and to potential clients to keep them up to date with our desire to remind them that we exist. While nearly all of the senior people in the firm and some of the juniors were expected to draft pieces for the newsletter, it felt to me that the expectation was falling on me more often and more heavily than on many of my colleagues. And the more pieces I drafted, the more they got me to draft.

Joe was going to be away the weekend coming up. It was his firm's corporate retreat. Of course, it crossed my mind that he was lying and that he was taking his whore away for the weekend. I thought I would be able to gauge from his response to a few pointed questions where the truth lay. Did I care? I'd be able to judge this from my response to his response. So I asked him.

'You're not serious. Anna, you can't be serious?'

'Why? Under the circumstances it's not a stupid—'

'Just because you and the teacher were going away for the weekend doesn't mean—'

'Okay, think about it, Joe, and you don't need to be Einstein to figure it out—'

'Maybe not Einstein,' he interrupted, 'but it does help to be a teacher, doesn't it?'

'Oh, Jesus Christ, Joe! How does it make any sense that I'm having an affair with this man if the two of us plan to go away together for the weekend but then when the weekend comes we can't go because he's been arrested for kidnapping our son? Does that make any sense? Does it, Joe?'

'Anna, I never said I was Einstein or even a teacher but—'

'Joe, I'm sorry, I'm not trying to—'

'Maybe I only know one thing, but I really know it, and on the basis of it you're fucked. You know that?'

'Joe—'

'There was no conference.'

'What?'

'The weekend Sam was taken you weren't going to any work conference.'

'Joe, I think we both know why you're suspicious.'

'What the hell are you talking about now?'

'Well, I think her name is Angelique, but perhaps you have another name for her.'

'Jesus, Anna!'

'Do you have a special name for her?'

'You're changing the subject. You're very clever, aren't you?'

'Joe, I have to know this.'

'What?'

'When you see that woman . . . is it . . . are you protected?'

'Of course it is . . . was. It always has been . . . Anna . . . what . . . you do believe me?'

It was a fruitful line of questioning but its pursuit would have to wait until night time when we were alone. Sam was standing at the door listening to his parents arguing. Joe looked at me looking and then he saw him too.

In the event Joe really did go on a corporate retreat that weekend.

For years I had woken each morning and gotten out of bed in a state of denial, not simply denial of the act we were as a couple, but denial of the impossibility of keeping up the performance until Sam was old enough for the issue to be peripheral to the din of his own private concerns. The denial was the analgesic with which I palliated the mistake that was us. That is, until the day Simon took Sam, when I ran out of denials.

Every time I looked at Joe over breakfast, in the living room or in bed, I imagined him walking into that same brothel every week, week in, week out, for two years and being greeted by all the women there in their various states of tax-deductible undress: the lace, the hosiery, the underwear. He would have been going there longer than many of the women. Every time I looked at him I imagined this with only slight variations and I would feel ashamed, ashamed of him, ashamed of us. Then I would picture him with her and though my picture of her would change in each of my imaginings, her name was always the same: Angelique. I thought it probably wasn't even her real name, and that was right. I knew better than anyone else how capable Joe was of seeing a woman for two years and not knowing her real name, capable of not even being curious, and I was ashamed of that too.

I would picture them together. He was always the same but she was always changing. I couldn't get a grip on her. At times she was a blonde, then a brunette, redhead, dark and subcontinental; sometimes she was black. But in certain ways she was always the same. She was always younger than me. Younger and thinner. I could imagine him entering her from behind. He liked that. She'd be able to close her eyes or look away. That's what I did, always. I could imagine him going down on her. I had no trouble imagining that. I could even imagine the way he might talk to her. He would talk to her the way he spoke to young waitresses. Picturing him sweating over and into the ever-changing Angelique would make me very angry. I'd picture him this way as he buttered his toast in the morning in his underwear and I would want to lean over and hit him. But since Sam would hear or, worse, come in and see, I would just turn away from him, even when he was in mid-sentence about something quite innocent.

But there was one thing I wasn't able to imagine and that was how it was she pleased him. I didn't know what she could do, other than to be her, that would really work for him, really set him alight.

What exactly did she do to him for two years to keep him coming back so faithfully, other than not be me?

Joe had his own denial routine. Begun after Sam's kidnapping, it allowed him to ignore that he had, as he thought, been cuckolded for years by his wife and his predecessor. This denial was made possible in large part by money, in particular by the prospect of more of it, by the chase for it. But the chase and, by extension, the denial, seemed to come to a crashing halt the day he came home from his firm's corporate retreat.

His distress was apparent from the moment he marched into the house and straight up the stairs without responding to Sam's, 'Hi, Dad.' Something was clearly wrong. Normally, Joe couldn't resist playing with Sam the minute he got home. He would wrestle with him or cuddle him even when it was late and Sam was nearly asleep. But not that day. Curious, I went upstairs. Perhaps it had something to do with me. In the time it took to go from the kitchen to our bedroom I scanned my guilt for something he might have found out about me. Who at his firm knew anything about me? I was being paranoid. I didn't know any of those people and they didn't know me. What's more, they didn't know anyone who knew me, other than Joe, of course. Just before the top of the stairs who else they knew hit me so hard it hurt, and my palms grew a little moist. They knew Donald Sheere and he knew Michael Gardiner. Had Michael been talking? Surely not. I was panicking. I had to calm down.

Joe was agitated. He sat at the foot of the bed staring straight ahead of him at nothing, his eyes focused on the middle distance. His bag was on its side as though he had flung it or kicked it across the room.

'I didn't take enough clothes,' he said matter-of-factly without looking at me.

'What?'

'I didn't pack enough.'

'What's wrong, Joe? You look terrible.'

A colleague of his, a friend apparently, had been hurt at the retreat.

'Is it serious?'

'I don't know. I don't think so.'

'Who was it?'

'Mitch.'

'Mitch? Have I ever met him?'

'Mitch, Dennis Mitchell. You haven't met him. I don't think you've met him. He's a senior analyst.'

'Is he a friend of yours? I don't think . . . You've never mentioned him.'

Joe wasn't making much sense but I could wipe my palms. Whatever was wrong had nothing to do with me or Michael.

'Mitch. Dennis Mitchell. Mitch is a senior analyst. I've mentioned him. I mention him all the time.'

'Maybe to someone else.'

'Oh, don't start with me, Anna. I really wouldn't start with me today.'

'I'm sorry. Is he alright? Mitch . . . he's your friend?'

'Mitch and I work very closely together, very close. We're good friends. He's possibly my best friend at the firm. He's always looked after me. This house, most of the clothes you wear, they're all courtesy of Mitch. I have mentioned him. You should get down on your fucking knees and thank him, the way he's looked after this family.'

'Alright, calm down. Maybe you have mentioned him. What happened to him? You said it wasn't serious.'

'No, I don't think it is.'

'So what's wrong? You look terrible, Joe. You don't have to talk about it but if you're going to—'

'Anna,' he said, looking directly up at me for the first time, 'in the next few days, certainly by the end of the week, I'm going to be out of a job.'

'Why? What are you talking about?'

'They're going to get rid of me.'

'Is it Mitch?'

Joe let out a long breath. 'Mitch. Yep, Mitch.'

'Do they blame you for whatever happened to him? What happened to him? You didn't do something stupid to him, did you, Joe? You're too old for practical jokes. They're stupid and dangerous. I sure as hell don't want Sam—'

'It's got nothing to do with that. But thanks for the support.'

'Well, what are you talking about? Why are they going to get rid of you? You're doing so well for them.'

'Because I just stopped doing so well for them.'

'What do you mean? What about the deal, that health care business—?'

'You *were* listening.'

'Sure, it was health care, managed care, something . . . with Don Sheere and Sid Graeme.'

'Listen to you,' he said from the bed.

'What?'

'You meet him once and you're calling him Don.'

'Don, Donald, what about that deal? You said it was—'

'It's off. It's fallen through.'

'Really?'

'Really.'

'That doesn't mean they're going to get rid of you.'

'Couldn't you just take my word for something, for once in your life? There are some things you don't know better than me. Trust me on this. I'm finished there. They're finished with me.'

'There'll be other deals.'

'There won't be other deals!'

Joe explained what had happened. Some of it I'd already half heard before. He and Mitch had talked Gorman and the firm into underwriting a share issue by a health insurance company. The success of the issue—it was to fund a buy-up of private hospitals, the profitability of which was predicated on the introduction of US-style managed care legislation—depended on Donald Sheere, at Joe's urging, taking up a large parcel of shares. Unfortunately Sheere got wind of a development that threatened the passage of the legislation through the Senate and refused to go ahead with the purchase. This meant that the underwriting firm, Joe's firm, would have to take up the unsold shares. The cost to it would be huge. The firm had been talked into taking a beating by Joe and his friend and now they were going to have to pay for it with their jobs. That was the way Joe put it.

'But can't you explain to Gorman?'

'There's nothing to explain. We took a chance with the firm's money and it didn't come off.'

'But surely this sort of thing must happen all the time?'

'It does and people get iced all the time. And, anyway, this time it really was a lot of money. The firm is going to take a bath. We're through.'

'What are you going to do?'

'I thought I'd get drunk. What about you, got any plans?'

He believed that he was finished. I wasn't so sure. Perhaps he was exaggerating, perhaps he'd survive. I was wrong. By Thursday he was carrying boxes of papers from his car to the house.

'This is my career,' he said, holding aloft a few pieces of paper before stuffing them back into a cardboard file in the box.

'Why don't you call Donald Sheere?' I suggested. 'He's always . . . You said you get on well with him. Maybe he could help you.'

'Anna, it was his pulling out of the deal that cost me my job.'

'Well, maybe, but it was a business decision, right? I mean, it wasn't anything personal . . . was it?'

'No, it was business, strictly business. It's always business with guys like him. Even when it's personal, it's business.'

'What do you mean?'

'He doesn't want to know me now, I'm no use to him anymore.'

'You don't know that, Joe.'

'Anna, I know it. He won't even take my calls anymore.'

'You've tried calling him?'

'Of course I have. I tried to get him to change his mind, to stay in, to take the risk. But he said he didn't have to and he's right. It makes sense.'

'What do you mean?'

'He can always buy in again later if the legislation gets through the Senate. There's no reason for him to take the risk now.'

'Does he know what's happened to you? Maybe he doesn't know they've—'

'He'd know. If he gave it any thought, he'd know.'

'You can't be sure, and anyway, maybe he can help you with something else.'

'Anna, are you listening to me? He won't take my calls.'

I was having similar problems with Dr Gardiner. It seemed Anna and Joe Geraghty had been delisted. I tried calling Michael several more times and each time I was only able to leave a message. Anna Geraghty called. Joe was drinking every day.

'They can't just dismiss you summarily,' I said.

'Of course they can. I'm on contract.'

'Have you read the contract?'

'Nobody reads the contract. You don't have to read the contract to know you're fucked. *They draft* the contract. It's a fucking weapon.'

'Maybe you can sue them?'

'For what?'

'I don't know, but maybe you should take the contract to a lawyer.'

He assured me that this was a waste of time and I assured him that things couldn't continue as they were and when I said that, we both stopped for a moment and looked at each other. As I was saying it I hadn't meant what we both took me to mean at the moment that we both stopped to listen to the words as they hung in the air.

But nothing could continue the way it had been, even outside our marriage. Joe's mother, who had slowly been getting scattier, was suddenly substantially worse, I discovered, when I took Sam to see her. She was sitting in the kitchen in her dressing gown, her hair dishevelled, drinking a cup of tea.

'Annie, you're so early,' she said. The curtains were drawn and the lights were on.

'Do you want me to heat this up?' I called out to her as Sam swung his legs from one of her kitchen stools. She had gone to open the curtains.

'It's bolognese sauce. I told you on the phone I'd be bringing it. You like my bolognese.'

'Oh, I do, Annie, very much, but I can't eat that for breakfast.'

That was probably the first time I got a true sense of what was happening to her. It was five-forty in the afternoon. She had been asleep all day thinking it was night. She hadn't eaten. When I explained what time of day it really was she looked crestfallen, ashamed. Her eyes filled with tears. I went over to hug her and, seeing this, Sam came over to the two of us. He put his arms around our legs, gripping tighter and tighter as she sobbed. He buried his face in my skirt and then he was sobbing.

I pulled back and picked him up in my arms, which wasn't so easy anymore.

'Hey! There's nothing wrong. We're just happy to see each other, that's all,' I said.

'Oh no, there's nothing wrong,' Joe's mother chimed in, wiping her face against her sleeve. 'You're such a good boy, aren't you, such a lovely big boy. Here, open your palm out flat and close your eyes. I've got something for you,' she said, then reached over to a tin on the bench.

'There you are!' she said, placing a boiled sweet wrapped tightly in cellophane in his palm. 'You're a good boy, aren't you, Joey?'

'Dad is Joey. I'm Sam,' he corrected her, putting the sweet in his pocket.

'Why don't you have a shower and I'll boil the pasta,' I suggested quietly.

At home I told Joe how I had found his mother.

'It's not good, Joe.'

'I know.'

'She's worse than you think. She's really unwell. You know, she told me some story about the police rescuing her from an island. There was no convincing her that it was untrue.'

'It's true.'

'What do you mean, it's true?'

'It was a traffic island on the Nepean Highway. She was in a sea of traffic. The police found her there near Tommy Bent's statue. She was singing hymns, they told me.'

'Why didn't you tell me?'

'I don't know. It was the night before the retreat. There's been a lot going on. I must have forgotten.'

'Forgotten?'

'There's been a hell of a lot . . . I don't know, Anna . . . she's *my* mother.'

She was his mother and we were just as Dr Klima had described us, separate people, all of us separate. Joe had been to see a lawyer but the time for the appointment had come before he'd been able to find his employment contract within all his files and papers. He was to find the contract and then make another appointment. I found Joe searching for it among his papers. He looked up at me and I knew he felt like an idiot.

I started thinking about Michael; what had happened to make him change so suddenly? He had wanted me fiercely, with a self-destructive hunger that was literally palpable. I called him again, more out of curiosity than anything else, but he failed to return the call.

There was, however, somebody who was bombarding me with phone calls. It was Simon's archangel, Dr Alex Klima. At first he was calling me to see whether I would tell their lie. When it became obvious that I was unwilling to become a martyr to his favourite patient's madness, he went for something less. Would I agree to visit Simon?

'Anna . . .' he entreated.

'No, Dr Klima, you listen to me,' I whispered from my desk.

'You should call me "Alex" by now.'

'You shouldn't be calling me at all.'

'Yes,' he said with a certain sadness. 'Don't you think I know that?'

'Alex, I'm angry with him. You didn't know him when I did, before he was . . . sick. He was so sane, so bright.'

'Anna, you mustn't punish him for becoming unwell.'

'Nor should I sacrifice myself for him and reward it. I'm sorry, Alex. You're a nice man. I can tell. But you're asking, *he's* asking, way too much. I can't do it. Please excuse me. I don't mean to be rude but I really have work to do. Goodbye now.'

'Goodbye, Anna.'

I put the receiver down and sat there for a moment before someone went past my door and reminded me I had better get down to work. I had to stick with the one thing and finish it before starting something new. That was the way to maximise my efficiency. 'It's Not What You Know but Who You Know'. No. I couldn't bring myself to write that, not now. What else? What about 'Getting More Out of the Most—Ten Handy Tips for Performance Assessments'? I was too tired for ten. What about seven? What about five? Could I get away with five? What could I get away with? I was getting older. A man once wanted me quite desperately, now he wouldn't return my calls. Less and less could I get away with.

16

Sam came home from school with a note from his teacher asking me or Joe to call her. This was the second such note. Was it the virtually unattended birthday party we had invited his class to, his parents' arguing, or his paternal grandmother's unravelling before his eyes that had led to whatever it was that had led to the note? Apparently Sam had become uncharacteristically inattentive and disruptive in class following Simon's offer of chocolate milk and Joe's reduction of the photographer in our back yard to a bloody pulp.

'What's he done?' I asked his teacher, a pretty young woman, younger than me, gentle and concerned, of Greek extraction. Sam had always seemed to like her. We were lucky Sam was in her class, the other mothers had said at the end of the previous year.

'Well, he's been calling out, a lot . . . lately.'

'What do you mean, lately?' I asked the young teacher.

'Well, since the . . . since the troubles.'

Since 'the troubles', she had said, not being able to even say the word 'kidnapping', so afraid, as the school had informed us in a carefully worded letter, were they of saying anything that might cause us offence and provoke litigation.

'What, he's been calling out since the beginning of inter-religious hostilities in Ireland?' It was an off-the-cuff smartarse remark of the kind Simon could've made. The taste one gets for them resurfaces in moments of stress.

'Pardon me?' the young teacher asked, completely at a loss.

'I'm sorry, you said since "the troubles", which is the name given to the Catholic–Protestant conflict in Ireland. I'm sorry, I was just being flippant. Things have been—'

'No, I'm sorry, for my insensitivity. Geraghty? Of course, Sam Geraghty. I have to admit I'm not always up to date with my world events. Have you lost family recently in Northern Ireland? Did Sam know the deceased directly or is it a sort of . . . vicarious pain? We can schedule grief counselling if you like. It can be for the whole family if you think it would help everyone . . . or anyone.'

Sam had been calling out at school, sometimes the answers to questions, sometimes silly comments to get a laugh. He'd also been accused of pushing some of the other kids. He had never been at all like this before. I vacillated between denying everything his teacher had said, blaming the school, blaming Simon or Joe or both of them and their little *puttana*, as my father would have put it, before finally settling on blaming myself as a mother.

17

Joe had found his employment contract and had gone back to see his lawyer. He took the finding of the contract as some kind of turning point in his luck. But it wasn't. It turned out that, technically, he wasn't actually employed by the firm he had been working for. Instead, he was contracted to another company which, his lawyer suspected, probably held a contract with the stockbroking firm he'd been working for.

'I've never heard of this other company, the company I'd signed a contract with. Can you believe it?'

'It doesn't matter,' I said. 'If your lawyer can find an angle—what do they call it?—A "cause of action". I think they call it that—then you can sue the other company.'

'I already thought of that. I asked him if I could sue the other company but he said it was a shelf company.'

'What does that mean exactly?'

'It's a "two dollar" company. Even if you sue it and win, it doesn't have any assets. There's no point suing it.'

'So you can't sue the real firm because you didn't have a contract with it, and the other company, the one you did have a contract with, doesn't have any money?'

'That's what he's telling me.'

'I'm sorry I recommended you see a lawyer. He's probably going to charge you for this.'

'Yeah, right. See how fast I pay. Anna, there's something I've got to tell you and you're not going to like it.'

'Tell me anyway.'

'Look, Anna, if I could hold off telling you I would but . . . I mean, I know you're going to leave me anyway—'

'You've got another woman, I mean other than . . . not just Angelique?'

'No, it's got nothing to do with that. I wish it did.'

'Yeah, I bet you do.'

'Oh for Christ's sake, Anna.'

'You kiss her . . . You pay your money, you kiss her; God knows where you kiss her, and then you come home and kiss—'

'Anna, how long has it been since you kissed me, since we kissed each other?'

'Sam . . . you fucking bastard.'

'What do you mean, Sam? What about him?'

'You come home from her . . . once a week . . . and you kiss him goodnight.'

'Do you know where your Simon has been?'

'I haven't seen him for ten years.'

'I'll tell you one place he's been. He's been with her. He's been with her too. So . . . add it up, Anna. He's as filthy as I am and just as unfaithful. That's your teacher for you. But you didn't deny him the way you denied me. He had no cause to see her or anyone like her, whereas I had you. And if I'm unfaithful, so is he, and so are you. And if I'm unclean, so is he and then, of course, so are you. And you come home and you kiss Sam goodnight too. So don't stand there all fucking holier than thou like you're our lady of the stuck-up virgin bitches because you're no fucking better than me. Except that you've got a job.'

'You'll get one, Joe. You just—'

'Do you want to hear what I'm trying to tell you? We need money. We're going to have to get some money pretty quickly.'

'We can tighten our belts for a while, till you get a good job.'

'I need one hell of a good job, and quickly.'

'You'll get a job, Joe, but you've got to stop putting all your eggs in one basket.'

'I've no idea what that means but—'

'Your whole idea of yourself, your self-esteem, is entirely dependent on how much money you've got.'

'No more than anyone else's.'

'That's not true. I'm not like that.'

'Oh, Anna, come on. You're not serious. You married me for money, for a start.'

'That's not true. You didn't have much when I met you.'

'No, not a lot, but you took a chance because you knew I was going places and sooner or later you'd be able to live very, very well.'

'No, you're wrong, Joe. Money has never been that important to me. Yes, it's nice to be able to live well but—'

'Well, I'm glad you feel that way because we're probably going to lose the house.'

'What are you talking about? We *own* the house.'

'No we don't. We haven't paid off the mortgage. And since I lost my job I'm not going to be able to keep up the payments for very long unless something very good comes up pretty quickly.'

'How long have we got?'

'I don't know. It depends. Not long.'

'Well, how long? What does it depend on?'

'I don't know. I'll have to work some things out. I'll have to sell everything but even then it's just a matter of time. All the credit cards are maxed out, mine anyway. That's one of the things I wanted to talk to you about.'

'You're talking about using your credit cards to make mortgage repayments? How long do you think you can keep doing that?'

'Not long. That's what I'm telling you.'

'But we own the house.'

'Anna, do you have any idea of anything? What do you think our equity is in this place?'

'I don't know.'

'You don't want to know.'

'Joe, I want to know.'

'How do you think it was we could just move in here overnight, into a place like this, near the beach, with all these bathrooms and empty fucking bedrooms waiting to be filled by the kids we never had or the kids we had who died?'

'How much?'

'How much what?'

'How much is our equity in the house?'

'We'd be lucky if we owned twenty-five per cent of it ourselves.'

'Oh my God!'

'That's why the repayments are so high.'

'Isn't there someone you can talk to?'

'Who can I talk to, Jesus?'

'But you know so many people in investment, in the finance industry. Can you talk to someone at the bank?'

'Anna, I don't have a job. How can I talk to them if I don't have a job? What can I possibly offer them?'

'I have a job. Do you want me to talk to someone at the bank?'

'You can't talk to someone at the bank.'

'Why the hell not? Because I'm a woman? Joe, this is no time for macho—'

'Anna, for Christ's sake, don't give me that feminist bullshit now.'

'Why can't I talk to someone at the bank?'

'Because your name is not even on the title. The house and the mortgage, it's all in my name.'

'Joe! What are you saying?'

'Well, what did you think, Anna? You think *I'm* an idiot when I can't find the stupid contract? Do you remember signing anything at the time we bought this place?'

'No.'

'Anything at all?'

'No.'

'Well now, how big an idiot are you? Think yourself lucky you're not responsible for the debt.'

'What? My father gives *us* the deposit for the house and you go and put it in *your* name, not both our names? Is that what you're telling me?'

'Yes.'

'You're a fucking bastard, Joe! And you've got the gall to tell me you were doing me a favour? I'm not that much of an idiot. Don't you think I know the debt is covered by the house, not by you? Jesus, you're despicable.'

'Well, when wasn't I, Anna?'

'Is there anything we actually own outright?'

'Just my car.'

'*Your* car! What about *my* car?'

'Do you remember paying for that, remember signing anything? I bought it for you.'

'I thought the money . . . I thought it all came out of our joint account.'

'It did. I put down the deposit and all the payments came out of the joint account.'

'That's where my salary goes, into the joint account,' I said incredulously.

'Then you were helping to pay off your car. It worked out better tax-wise, believe me—'

'Joe, you're a fucking bastard.'

'Yeah? You didn't think so till I lost my job.'

'I just didn't say it.'

'No, well, you didn't say it till I lost my job.'

'What about all those shares? You used to brag about making money from following your own advice. What about them?'

'I borrowed to buy them. You're not responsible for that debt either . . . Look, I know you're going to leave me sooner or later and I know that losing the house isn't going to—'

'We're not going to lose the house, Joe. There's my salary. What about that?'

'It'll take more than your salary.'

'Look, you can't expect me to have the answer straight away. You've just dumped this news on me.'

'Well, I couldn't think of a gentle way of telling you we're going to lose the house.'

'Let me think about it. Just let me . . . We'll figure something out.'

18

At work it occurred to me to try to get through to Donald Sheere myself. A call from me might be unexpected enough to excite his curiosity. I tried a number of times over the next few days but my calls were all fielded by minions skilled in doing just that. While I was at it I tried calling Michael again, to similar effect. Surprisingly, my failure to get through to either was less distressing than I would have thought. Somehow the loss of the lover I never really had was being palliated by the impending loss of the house I never really had, and vice versa. The total pain was proving to be less than the pain of either of them alone.

For all that, I was curious about what it was that had turned Michael off like that. Was it that he didn't want to be involved with someone whose family was suddenly helping to sell his patient's tabloids? Was he really so unaccustomed to being stood up, was that the reason? Could his pride not tolerate coming second, second not to my husband, but to my kidnapped son? Or did the news of the kidnapping only confirm his worst suspicions, that I had been seeing someone else all along and that that someone, Simon, had been caught in sordid circumstances, taking my son from school? Michael Gardiner would not have wanted any part of that. Was it that, or was it a little of everything? Or did he just find someone else, someone else with a pancake-flat stomach, someone younger, and was it crêpe-flat?

Joe busied himself selling shares he had originally borrowed to pay for and applying the proceeds to repay other loans in order to get more credit and so on in a desperate and admittedly enervating attempt to delay our day of final reckoning. It occupied so much of his time and thought that he was, in a sense, able to justifiably claim exhaustion as an excuse for not looking for another job. He told me to trust him, which did not really mean that he wanted my trust. It was too late for him to really mean that. What he meant was that he didn't want me to bother him while he rearranged the deckchairs on the *Titanic*. Any suggestion that he look for a job, however quietly and sympathetically offered, was regarded as carping and treated as a *casus belli*.

The first of the Simon-related legal proceedings, the one they called the committal hearing, was approaching. Joe and I were forced to spend time with Simon's prosecutors so that they might get our stories straight. We were warned that when the hearing started, the press interest in us, in my alleged relationship with Simon, and in Joe's relationship with the prostitute Angelique, would intensify. It was against this background that I went to see my father.

I chose a time I knew my mother would be out. She went shopping every Monday, Wednesday and Friday morning. It was a vocation. Food had to be fresh, she insisted. My father was delighted to see me but was disappointed I had come without Sam.

'Where is my grandson? Where is Sam?'

'He's at school, Dad. It's a school day. I have something to talk to you about.'

'Is something wrong? Is it Sam? What's wrong?'

'Nothing is wrong with him. He's fine. It's not Sam but . . . Dad, we're in some trouble now and I—'

'What trouble? *Polizia*?' he laughed.

'No, don't be stupid, Dad.'

'I was joking. Anna, *tesoro*, what is it? You look like . . . in your face . . . it's serious?'

'I don't know where to start—'

'Anna, tell me! You want me to have another heart attack?'

'Dad, I don't think I've ever asked you for anything—'

'I give you everything.'

'I know you have, Dad, but—'

'This about money?'

'Yes, it is, but also—'

'That's good. I'm relieved. If it's money it's okay. You can always get more money. If you work hard you get some money. Anna, I'm relieved, *tesoro*. I thought maybe something was wrong with Sam and I—'

'Dad, will you let me finish?'

'You finished. You need money. How much?'

'Dad, it's not as simple as that.'

'Why not?'

'Dad . . . Joe lost his job.'

'Why?'

'It's complicated.'

'So we sit down and you tell me.'

'He talked the firm into doing something which ended up costing the firm a lot of money. They lost a whole lot of money and so they took it out on him.'

'Was it . . . honest?'

'What do you mean, honest?'

'Was it *legale*?'

'Of course it was legal.'

'Anna, calm yourself. You know I'm going to help you every way I can. But you hear on the news about these things with the big companies' . . . *casini*. I just want to know the . . . everything.'

'Okay, well, I guess you're going to know everything.'

'Good.'

'Dad, you remember I've told you that I'm going to have to go to court to testify about Simon taking Sam? It's coming up soon.'

'But that didn't have nothing to do with you.'

'Yes, and that's what we have to tell them.'

'So? So there's nothing you can say wrong. I still can't believe it. I liked that Simon. You think you know people. He fooled all of us, eh!'

'Dad, Joe is going to have to testify too.'

'Okay, so he has nothing to hide either. Okay?'

'It's not quite that simple.'

'Why?'

'Dad, when Simon picked up Sam from school that day he took him back to his place.'

'Yes, I know you said he didn't touch him or nothing. He didn't touch him, did he?'

'No, but . . .'

'But what? Anna, what did he do?'

'Nothing, but . . . there was a woman there.'

'Where?'

'At Simon's place.'

'So? Did she touch him? *She* didn't touch him, did she?'

'No, no, she didn't touch him. In fact, it seems that . . . she was actually the one who called the police.'

'So? So what about the woman? We should thank her.'

'Dad, she's . . . a prostitute.'

'Oh, Simon. Anna, it happens with men. Yes, I read it in the paper. The woman Simon was with was a prostitute. But still . . . we should thank her, yes? She didn't give Sam drugs or nothing?'

'No drugs. Chocolate milk, I think. Dad, Joe knows her.'

'What do you mean?'

'Joe's been seeing this woman once a week for about two years.'

'The *puttana*?'

'Yes.'

'*Che bastardo*! *Va a mori ammazzato*! Anna, I'm very sorry, *tesoro*.'

My father came to me and hugged me.

'You're a beautiful girl. You know that. I don't understand him . . . It's . . . it's the way men are. They . . . I'm sorry. She was in it with him, this *puttana*? It's not making sense. Then why did she call the police?'

'I don't know, but I had to tell you. It's going to come out.'

'What?'

'It'll be in all the papers . . . that Joe knew this woman. I wanted to tell you first, and Mum. Dad, Joe and I . . . we have problems, big problems in our marriage.'

'You can get over it.'

'We're probably going to lose the house.'

'Why? Joe will get another job.'

'We're mortgaged up to the roof.'

'You tell him to come and see me, honest, man-to-man. I help you with the roof. He'll tell me how much you need until he can get a good job.'

'Why do you need *him* to tell you? I know how much we need.'

'How much do you need?'

'It's a lot. We own very little. Joe took out a second mortgage.'

'Anna, I tell you. He talks to me and I help him till he finds a good job.'

'Jesus, Dad, it's not that simple.'

'Why not?'

'I think he's planning to leave me.'

'Why do you think this?'

'Dad, he was seeing a prostitute once a week for two years.'

'He's a stupid man, Anna. You mustn't think about it. You should make him happy. Try to make him happy—'

'Dad!'

'It's with him . . . *la virilità* . . . *le palle*. Make him feel a man. He can feel you think he's a . . . *buffone, pagliaccio*. It's why you have only one kid.'

'Dad, it's a terrible marriage.'

'I didn't choose him, you did. I just pay for the wedding. He comes to me, man-to-man . . . if he tells me the truth with the numbers I will help him till he can get a good job. You won't lose the house. Also, you have to change your way with him and start to make him happy, like a man again. Maybe you shouldn't be working.'

'Dad, I'm the one with the job!'

'Yes, alright. Is true. He should tell me where the deposit on the first house has gone.'

'This isn't going to work.'

'Anna, you have to try.'

'Look how quickly you're forgiving him everything.'

'I was not forgiving him everything. You must do that. But now we have to face all what is now.'

'What about . . . ?'

'The *puttana*.'

'Well, yes, that.'

'Anna, I am sad for you. But what can we do? You chose him. He is your husband and my grandson's father. I will do everything I can for you, *tesoro*.'

'And if he leaves?'

'You can make him stay. You're not an old woman.'

'What if I don't want him?'

'You chose him. Not me.'

'I know. You just paid for the wedding.'

'*Si*.'

'But it doesn't have to stay like this.'

'I know, Anna. It's what I'm telling you.'

'No, I'm not talking about luring him away from some whore. I'm talking about a separation—'

'No!'

'Or divorce.'

'No!'

'Dad, I might not have any say in it.'

'You can have your say.'

'But maybe it's for the best anyway. I could start again and—'

'*Non si fa così*. No divorce. It's not our way.'

'Dad, I haven't been religious for years. You said you'd help me.'

'I will help you. I told you. Make him feel a man. You have a son, Anna. Joe is the father. You have to grow up whether you like it or not. Don't be seeing Simon anymore.'

'What are you talking about? I wasn't seeing Simon.'

'But Joe thinks so, yes?'

'Yeah, but he's wrong.'

'Anna, *tesoro*. Make him happy and he finish with the *puttana*. He comes to me with numbers on paper and I help him with the house.'

'That's not going to happen. He won't talk to you about any of this.'

'Then he won't get the money. He was always too much a big man in the stock market. He is a *buffone* . . . with a *puttana*. *Bastardo*. He has to come to me and then I give him the money.'

My father could not begin to understand that Joe would never go to him for money, that he'd rather lose the house twice over than humble himself before him. 'Ask that Italian peasant, and you're not on the title, are you kidding?'

19

Prosecuting Simon was easier if you didn't know him. If you had ever known him, you would be far more interested in trying to understand why he had done what he did. And Dr Klima certainly knew him. Moreover it was his job to understand him, not to judge him. But it wasn't his job to like Simon and that he so obviously did made me warm to the psychiatrist in unlikely circumstances. I even envied Simon his Dr Klima. I could have used some well-trained and softly spoken professional, a cross between someone standing in loco-parentis and an advocate. But this was not our way.

I was mock examined and cross-examined in various people's offices. I was even shown the inside of an empty court room. It was apparently as much as they were allowed to do but it doesn't ade-quately prepare you for the real thing: a court room filled to capacity with lawyers in action, a real judge, inexplicable court staff, a thirsty public and a thirstier media. The real thing also contained Simon.

There was some kind of guard or prison officer on either side of him. It was absurd. He didn't look very different at all, which height-ened the absurdity of him being guarded. He wore a suit and was, maybe, a little thinner than I remembered him. I raised the Bible in my right hand and swore by almighty God something to do with truth but my voice faltered in front of all those people. They would not understand how out of character it was for Simon to have done what he did. Nor were the proceedings designed to elicit that sort of information. The fact was that he had taken Sam without my per-mission and God only knew why. Obviously things must have gone terribly badly for him since we had been together. There was no other explanation that would deliver my gentle, funny, quixotic, Byronesque university boyfriend to the dock between two guards.

The prosecutor, Mr Henshaw, asked straightforward questions and I responded with straightforward answers. We had been a cou-ple at university around ten years ago. We had gone out for around two years. I had barely, if at all, seen him since those days. Yes, that made it impossible for us to have had any kind of relationship, let alone a romantic relationship, since then. No, he did not have my permission to take my son from school that day or any day. No, I was at a loss to explain why he had done it. That was the only occasion we looked at each other at the same time. It hurt and I looked away. Mr Henshaw's questions were over. What a relief it was to be able to tell the truth.

There were no questions about his gentleness back then or about his sense of humour. I could have told them how we met after his tutorial paper on Billie Holiday. There were no questions about his mother or about the poets he read or about Doctorow, Dos Passos and Abe Meeropol. I wasn't given the opportunity to tell the magistrate how Simon had had a silver bracelet designed for me or how, back then anyway, he possessed a rigorous clarity of thought and an intol-erance of cant which I had often tried to adopt in the subsequent years without consciously remembering that these too were his gifts to me along with the bracelet. They were gifts which, if properly cared for, could have gone some of the way towards assuaging the loneliness I bore at home and at the office, but which, instead, were buried underneath piles of every intervening day's leavings and self-deceits. By the time I had sworn on the Bible to tell the truth or that much of it called for by Mr Henshaw's questions, only the bracelet was called upon regularly.

But neither, it seemed, had Simon called upon these other gifts much recently either. What he had done made no sense and, worse than that, he was probably going to be telling the world that I had been unfaithful to my husband with him and that my husband had regularly been unfaithful to me with a prostitute they shared. Some of this was true, some of it was not, but I could not think what it was I had done to deserve the humiliation of any of it.

Simon's lawyer, a Ms Serkin, whom Mr Henshaw privately referred to as Gina, questioned me next. She was a perfectly groomed woman some ten or so years older than me, maybe a little more. She was polite enough, businesslike in her manner, but not what anyone would call friendly. She seemed bright and competent. She would have had to interview Simon about all this over and over. I wondered if she believed him, especially since her questions didn't really get to the heart of the matter. She was asking me questions about my relationship with Simon ten years ago. All her questions drew me to saying complimentary things about Simon and positive things about the relationship, but I had never denied any of that. None of it had anything to do with his taking of Sam that day and although I had no qualms about answering her questions, Mr Henshaw objected to them. Argument as to their relevance allowed me to tune out and reflect on the dissection of our relationship by lawyers in a court room full of strangers.

If Dr Klima was in court he made no attempt to talk to me. I didn't see him but I was too apprehensive about the proceedings to remember to look out for him. This was something I only thought about later when, looking at myself in the pages of the newspaper, I wondered how long it would take for people to forget about this. There would be people I had known at school, people who had known Simon and me as a couple from our student days, who would never forget. If we met up at seventy, they would remember that there was something murky, criminal and vaguely scandalous in my past. Was it this, the scandal that had made me suddenly repugnant to him, to Michael?

I thought of him only at odd moments, moments when my mind

strayed from work and I caught myself staring blankly into a distance blocked out by the wall in front of me. Caught also, that's what I felt anyway, by the new girl, a graduate from some school of communications that hadn't existed when I was at university. While I no longer really expected Michael to call, neither did I expect to receive another spate of calls from Simon's Dr Klima. Perhaps they were precipitated by my evidence at the committal hearing. But surely they must have expected me to say what I said. I was only telling the truth, after all. Whatever his motivation, I did eventually—out of sympathy for him, I suppose, as a former fellow 'unrequited' caller—get around to phoning him back. The straws they were grasping at were becoming more and more untenable. He told me, in all seriousness, that Simon had followed Sam and our housekeeper from Sam's school to our home one day and had seen Sam, fully clothed, fall into our swimming pool and not surface till Simon dragged him out. If Simon hadn't intervened, Dr Klima explained, it's likely that Sam would have drowned. I reminded him that he had told me this before, that it was still too horrible to contemplate, and that it was also too ridiculous to believe. Why hadn't Sam told me about it? I said goodbye just as the young communications graduate walked past me and smiled. Communications. My father wanted to know when Joe was going to talk to him. We were going to lose the house.

20

One darker than black night, a fierce, deranged wind fell upon the city and upon me as I stood in an unfamiliar street. I had been there once before but then it had been with Joe and it was he who'd been tense. This time it was me, strafed and ridiculed by the wind, who was the supplicant. For all that I was embarrassed, nervous to the point of an arid tongue, I was unable to imagine any consequences arising from what I was about to do that were sufficiently dire to prohibit it. It would be a crash course in communication.

I rang the intercom and waited. The carefully manicured bushes, all dressed up for other occasions but with nowhere to go to escape the beating, convulsed in the wind. Only the massive pillars supporting the open gates to the Sheere mansion remained unmoved.

Eventually a small middle-aged foreign woman, a housekeeper, opened the front door. They must have been expecting someone or she'd have screened me on the intercom. I trudged up the drive.

'Hello, my name is Anna Geraghty,' I said, shivering and dishevelled. 'I was wondering if I might have a few moments with Mr Sheere?'

'Sorry, what did you say your name was again?'

'Mrs Anna Geraghty.'

'Is he expecting you?'

'No, not really. He knows me and my husband, Joe, Joe Geraghty, and I need to speak to him quite . . . suddenly, no, not suddenly but . . . er . . . urgently. It's so terribly windy, isn't it?'

'Mrs?'

'Geraghty,' I offered again.

'Garatee,' she said, looking for the approbation I gave her immediately with a little smile of unearned gratitude.

'Please, just a moment.' The woman closed the door sufficiently to attach a chain to it. The sound of her footsteps attenuated with her retreat into the cavernous interior. After some minutes she returned, took the chain off the door and opened it.

'This way, please, Mrs Garatee,' she said as she led me across the mottled white marble floor of the foyer into a private study slightly off to one side. I didn't remember seeing it on the perfunctory and perhaps obligatory tour of the house we had been given on our earlier visit. The room seemed very masculine to me, all wood panelling and leather chairs. In place of the usual photographs of children or grandchildren there were plaques recognising the family's charitable works.

'Mr Sheere will be with you shortly.'

True to his housekeeper's word, within thirty seconds Donald Sheere imposed himself on the room with all the weight of his wealth. My knees weakened. What the hell did I think I was doing there? He closed the door behind him firmly.

'Mrs Geraghty, to what do I owe this pleasure?'

'Please, call me Anna. I must apologise for this intrusion. I've tried to phone you a number of times but I haven't been able to get through.'

'What can I do for you, Anna?'

'I . . . I came to see if you could help my husband, Joe. He's lost his job. Gorman got rid of him and his friend when you pulled out of that health insurance company share issue.'

'Yes, I heard.'

'Mr Sheere, he's out of work and we can't service our mortgage.

It's only a matter of time before we lose the house. You bear some responsibility—'

'Mrs Geraghty—Anna. I made a strictly commercial decision to opt out of that purchase. It was based on the best information available to me at the time. That Joe lost his job on account of it is unfortunate. But it's not my fault. These things happen. It's part of the game. Joe's a good broker. One of the others will pick him up. Gorman had to do what he did and so did I. There's nothing personal in any of it.'

'There is something personal, Mr Sheere. I have a son—'

'Ah yes, that . . . that must have been a terrible experience, even if you knew the man who took—'

'I knew him ten years ago, not—'

'Mrs Geraghty, it's none of my business. It's your business, and Joe's.'

'He doesn't have any business, Mr Sheere. That's why I'm here.'

'What do you want me to do?'

'Can't you help him . . . with a job?'

'Anna, there'd be nothing I could say to Gorman that—'

'I don't mean that—'

'I'm not a stockbroker, Mrs Geraghty. I don't have any need to employ a dealer. I'm sorry, I can't help you.'

I sat in the car for a moment, more in shock at what I had tried than in the way it had turned out.

On the way home I called into Sophie's. Unusually for her, she was home. And alone. Unusually for her also, she looked concerned when she saw me.

'You look terrible,' she said. 'Anna, what's wrong? What's wrong? Come here, big sister. What's wrong, sweetie? Why are you crying?'

'I'm so sorry you . . . I'm just . . . I'm so stupid.'

'Oh, Anna, what are you talking about? I wish I had your . . . you never do the stupid things I do all the time. You're so . . . level-headed. You've got your life so . . . together.'

'Are you kidding, Sophe? I'm married to a man the public knows via the newspapers as the man who was having an affair with his son's kidnapper's whore. My life is . . . My marriage is a wreck the public gets to view every so often. It'll be on display soon again during Simon's trial.'

'You're married and you've got Simon. I always liked Simon.'

'What are you talking about? I haven't got Simon.'

'Maybe not now but—'

'Doesn't anyone fucking believe me?'

My family didn't believe that I hadn't been having an affair with Simon. Not that this meant, as far as my parents were concerned, that I didn't have to let him languish in prison rather than admit the infidelity. Family honour and the sanctity of marriage is what one had to protect, not one's lover. Joe was the husband, the provider, and he had to be forgiven. Mind you, not if they knew I wasn't on the title of the house.

'But you have him,' she said. Sophie was crying too.

'Who?'

'You'll always have him to love and he'll always love you.'

'Who?'

'Sam.'

21

I was soon to be given cause to wonder yet again at Simon's luck to have so dogged an advocate as Dr Klima, so dogged I even contemplated threatening to complain to the police if he didn't stop phoning me. But I didn't. However irritating his persistence, he was too reasonable a man to threaten to set the dogs on to. And this time he was being even cleverer than usual.

'Mrs Geraghty, I know what you must be going through at the moment so I can imagine the effect on you and your blood pressure of a phone call from me.'

'How good is your imagination, Dr Klima?'

'Too good, I'm afraid.'

'Then I guess you must be either very brave or stupid.'

'I'm certainly the latter. Anna, I'm calling you for both grave and selfish reasons. And knowing how much you don't want to hear from me, I've fortified myself with a liberal dose of scotch for the purpose.'

Maybe I was going crazy but now he even talked like Simon. It was this acknowledgement of self-interest that piqued my curiosity. What was in it for him? He wanted insurance against guilt. He said he knew I would be sceptical about what he was going to say to me but, for his own sake, he had to tell me that he suspected Simon was contemplating suicide. This was not something that had occurred to me, but when he forced me to think about it, it seemed far from out of the question. He was telling me because he thought a visit from me might bring Simon back from the precipice, at least for a while. There was nothing he could do if I didn't believe him, if I thought it was a trick, but if he didn't try one last time to get me to visit Simon and then Simon did take his own life, his failure to try would plague his conscience for the rest of his days.

Was it a trick? I didn't know. But if it were, in placing this responsibility on me, it worked. The failure to try would plague his conscience for the rest of his days. What would Simon's suicide do to my conscience for the rest of my days if I didn't see him? How dare Klima assume that I would be able to live with it with equanimity? Or was he presuming precisely the contrary?

So tiring is the drive from my office in the city to Port Phillip Prison at Laverton that you barely register the manifest evil at the heart of the building's architecture when you get there. I was nervous. I had never been anywhere like this before. What if I visited him and it didn't save him? Dr Klima had said I needed only to reaffirm to Simon just how much our student relationship had meant to me. I had already done that publicly in cross-examination at the committal hearing. Presumably it wasn't enough. As supportive as it might be to talk to Simon in prison about the good old days, what if that wasn't enough? What if it didn't work? Alex Klima's conscience might be clear, but what about mine? I could say the very words that lost him, or I could fail to say the precise words needed to save him. This was not my responsibility; it was Klima's. I wasn't his psychiatrist. I was his victim. I was just the one he said he loved, and I felt tricked and angry.

Already at reception, where you signed in, placed your belongings in your visitor's locker, and were searched, there was a nauseating smell. It was like some kind of industrial detergent or disinfectant. I had smelled it before but I couldn't place it. It wasn't confined to reception. Despite having to walk outside across a desolate compound to get there, once you were inside the visit centre you were again assaulted by it.

I had seen him in court but now up close he looked worse. He wore a powder blue plastic uniform. It was like a one-piece body suit. The sound of plastic rubbing against plastic drowned the words that accompanied our handshake. He had to endure a cavity search before and after meeting me, he would tell me in passing.

I looked around the room at the other prisoners and their families. It was entirely surreal being there and I said so. Then, to make matters worse, as if they weren't bad enough already, we started to argue. It was almost as though we were a married couple. We argued about his taking Sam. We argued about our past relationship. And like a couple of pedants, we argued about the correct use of words in the media, and about the ignorant self-righteousness of certain university students. I became tearful. He apologised and when he did it all poured out of me and I blamed him for everything, things I didn't articulate, things he couldn't have known about. I even blamed him for the pain that must have driven his mother to visit us and talk to Joe. I did this not only because he had taken my son or because he eerily knew so much about me—little things like where I'd had my bracelet fixed—I did it in large part because he had apologised and nobody else had done that. I didn't know people who did that anymore.

We argued about Angelique. Her real name was Angela and I didn't want her to have a real name. I told him how often and how well I used to think of him, that his reason had become a template for my world view. This was true but it was also true that it was a template, which, for one reason or other, I didn't use often enough. When we split up, I had felt liberated, free to observe the world and draw my own conclusions, freehand, free to call upon the legacy of Simon's thinking, or not, as I saw fit. In telling him that this had been the case right up until the day he befouled his standing with me by taking Sam, I was hurting him with the truth, which was an uncharacteristic way for me to hurt people. But I was angry, he was vulnerable and it was his turn to become my victim. Tearful, angry and embarrassed, I told him to go fuck himself and got up to leave.

I wanted to get out of there as fast as I could, to distance myself from the nauseating smell, the claustrophobia, the misery that dwelt in the visit centre. I stood up and began to walk away. And just as Simon had managed to reintroduce himself into my life, so with the same device did he get me to turn around and sit down again. The device was Sam.

First he disarmed me by owning to all manner of madness and irrelevance that I might want to impute to him as a person. Then he proceeded to talk about Sam with such searing feeling that I could not but hear him out.

'Do not assume the years of coldness between you and your husband, the nearly total absence of animated, amicable, adult interaction—do not assume this leaves your son untouched.'

His eyes hadn't changed, piercing, intelligent, he counted on you falling into them and not getting out.

'Don't say anything. None of my business. But you, you must

have thought about all of this. And Sam. What kind of man would you like him to become? You must have had something in mind when you decided to have a child. You didn't have him for nothing, he's a human being, not a whim. Was it to have someone to look after you in old age, or was it simply to ensure the temporal extension of yourself in lieu of immortality? Or was it to have a friend, a real friend, in a not very friendly world? So how tragic it is when the distance between you and him is born and starts to grow.

'Is it now, is this the time of the gestation of that wretched day when you realise that you don't recognise him? How did your little boy become this man? He's grown cold, sullen, disaffected. At first it was an act, a pose in early adolescence, a defence, a barrier against the world. Now he really is alienated. Does he ever feel anything deeply, strongly, and would you know if he did? You can't remember the last time he thought of you without being begged, bribed or threatened. He's innately bright, but nothing and no one ever fostered his intellect or even his curiosity, so he just uses his intelligence as a weapon against others, against himself.

'But then, what did you offer him as a child? There was lip service to parenting fads, and many of the traditional values were mentioned occasionally, but what did he actually see? He saw space filled at times by absentee parents flitting like ghosts around the pauses between the arguments, he saw his parents' lovers maybe, or traces of them, more or less distinct, and a domestic helper, a refugee from the latest country to reap the benefits of globalisation.

'He saw his parents straining, striving, to never have to rely on any other person. He would have deduced that it was because grown-ups had figured out that it was a cold and lonely place out there, that each of us was on our own and that no one but a fool ever genuinely did anything for anyone without expecting something in return. And if you were looking for something in return, why would you not see to it that you got back a little more than you gave.'

'So now you're telling me how to save my son?'

'I've saved him once already.'

'What are you talking about?'

'Anna, he was drowning once.'

'What?'

'In your backyard swimming pool. He fell in wearing his school clothes. It was a hot summer day. I was there. I pulled him out. He was panicking. I gave him—'

'Yes, that's right. Your psychiatrist told me about this. He said you'd tell me this. I don't believe you.'

'Ask him. Ask him, Anna. Ask Sam about the time the gardener rescued him from the pool. He was frightened. He'll remember.'

'How come I didn't know about this?'

'I don't know. He dried off in the sun before you came home. Your housekeeper missed it. Joe wasn't home . . . I won't be there to rescue him next time. Maybe you'll save him. You can save him now.'

This was vintage Simon. I left the visit centre and walked back across the compound to reception and the car park, shell-shocked by what he'd said and blind to my surroundings. I sat in the car for a while just staring into space before heading back to the city. Sam's mother had meant well, hadn't she? I had some Billie Holiday in the car somewhere. It was just a matter of finding it.

22

Joe wasn't going to talk to my father. He just wasn't. He had too much contempt for him. And then there was the small matter of the house being in his name only. What if my father wanted to look at the title?

'He's too embarrassed to talk to you now. He feels so demeaned being unemployed. Wait till he gets a job. He'll talk to you then. He'll get one soon, you know he will,' I lied to my father when I went to see him. 'The thing is, we need help now.'

I was crying. It wasn't an act. I was terrified of losing the house. It wasn't altruism either. Despite not being on the title, I knew I'd be awarded at least half the house were we to separate. Sam had been traumatised enough. I didn't want him to have to move.

My father had transferred funds from an investment account into his cheque account in anticipation of what he thought was his impending talk with Joe, a talk I knew was never going to happen.

I came home with a cheque for $100 000. It was Joe my father wanted to lambast, not me.

'My first girlfriend,' Joe said, 'my first real one, you know, the first one you're really stuck on, that you never forget, the one you never really get over, her name was Kirsty, Kirsten. She was *alright* and I was . . . I was alright too . . . back then. You should've seen me. I was king of the whole damn school and . . . everything. You would've, even you would've liked me then.'

He was drunk. I could smell it when I walked into the room and he didn't try to hide the evidence; a glass with ice, a two-thirds empty bottle of Teacher's and some incoherent reminiscences. It used to be Chivas. This was how Joe dealt with our straitened circumstances.

'But then . . . I don't know . . . her uncle died or some bullshit,' he continued, 'and her father said she wasn't where she was meant to be, which was true because she was with me but it wouldn't have made any difference. I mean, how did her being with me cause her uncle to die? He'd taken too many sleeping pills.'

'Joe, why are you telling me this?'

'Her father gave her a good talking to and we . . . broke it off. Just like that! Cunt!'

'Joe, why are you telling me this . . . about your first girlfriend's father and all this—'

'Your father just called.'

'What did he want?'

'He wanted to talk to me.'

'To you? Didn't you take the call?'

'I was busy.'

'Where were you when he called?'

'I'd just got home.'

'Were you with your mother all that time?'

'Are you checking up on me?'

'I've never been able to stop you doing whatever you want.'

Sometimes, lately anyway, I noticed that I could sound like a bitch when I really hadn't meant to. Even I heard it that way but once Joe had there was nothing I could say to put everything back together.

'I'm going to have to find a place for her.'

'Who, your mother?'

'Yep.'

'What happened? Has something happened, Joe?'

'She can't be left alone. I've got to find somewhere that can take her but all those places really cost, that's if you can even find one with any room, one where they don't fucking bathe them in kerosene.'

'Oh, Jesus, did she get lost somewhere again?'

'She set fire to the curtains.'

'Oh, fuck. How?'

'She was in the kitchen, cooking. You know the window near the stove?'

'Oh no, not those curtains?'

'She said she just turned around for a moment and all of a sudden . . . I don't think that's what happened at all. I think she had something on the stove, and then left the room for some reason and forgot all about it. She denies this but all the food was burnt. It wasn't just those curtains that had caught fire.'

'I can cook for her, Joe. She doesn't have to cook. She could just heat it up.'

'You already cook for her.'

'Yes, but I could make something for her each day and label it, "Monday", "Tuesday", et cetera.'

'She'd forget you'd done it and anyway, there's nothing to stop her setting fire to the place with your food. She's not choosy about her fuel.'

'But she'd just have to put it in the microwave.'

'You know those wheat-filled heat packs you put on sore muscles?'

'Yeah.'

'They're meant to go in the microwave for, I don't know . . . two minutes. She put hers in for two hours. There was smoke coming out of the kitchen when I got there.'

'When was this?'

'A couple of weeks ago.'

'Why didn't you say something?'

'I don't know. You were out when I got home and then Sam was upset and . . . I probably forgot.'

'You didn't forget. Come on, Joe. How can I help if you don't tell me?'

'How are you going to help her if I do tell you?'

I couldn't say anything at the time but I knew exactly how I was going to help him. It was time to deposit my father's cheque. I told Joe I was expecting a raise at work, a raise and a bonus. I said we were all getting one. It was a stupid thing to say because even the combination of the two would be insufficient to keep up the repayments on the mortgage for long or to pay for a place in a retirement home for his mother. But it was all I could think of on the spur of the moment and I had to do or say something to give him enough hope to stop drinking long enough to look for some kind of job, long enough to do something to help his mother. She couldn't live with us. Not even we could. He said he couldn't go back to the bank again to talk about reducing the repayments still further until he could tell them he had a job. He did promise to keep looking. Then he asked me why I hadn't suggested that my firm try to place him. I didn't know what to say. It honestly hadn't occurred to me.

'Well, it had occurred to *me*.'

'Then why didn't you . . . you should've said.'

'Don't give me that. I know why you didn't suggest it.'

He was right to be angry about this. I didn't have an answer for him, not one that would placate him.

'Come on, Joe, do you really think I'd rather lose the house than risk the embarrassment of my colleagues knowing you were out of work? People are losing their jobs all over the place. I see it every day.'

But that wasn't the embarrassment he was referring to and both of us knew it.

'I'm sorry. I'll think of someone suitable and I'll set up an appointment for you as soon as possible. Jesus, it's not like they don't owe me a favour.'

'Anna, I'm not anyone's favour.'

'I didn't mean it like that. You know how many hours I've put into that place and . . . I just meant they don't appreciate me. Not for the work I do.'

'But they're giving you a raise, right—and a bonus?'

'Yes, they are. They are, but . . . they're giving it to everyone.'

We agreed that in the meantime he would keep the appointments he'd made for job interviews. He was also to take his mother to look at retirement homes. I told him not to worry about the cost. He had to find the best place for her as soon as possible. His mother needed more than a little persuasion. She kept insisting she was able to take care of herself. Then when he finally did get her to agree at least to come and look at some of the places with him, she suddenly changed her mind all over again, ostensibly because their first appointment was for a Sunday. Sunday was the day she went to visit her other son, Roger. Joe told her that Roger could miss a week but still she resisted. What if they visited Roger later that day? No, it had to be the same time every week, otherwise Roger got upset. That she often visited him on a Saturday didn't seem to matter. It was as though there was something sacred about seeing him on a Sunday. Both Joe and I had our final appointments with Simon's prosecutor in the coming week. I got Joe's mother to agree to look at the retirement home with Joe on the Sunday. I offered to visit Roger myself at the regular time in her place. She had wanted me to take Sam along but I went alone. I got Sophie to stay with Sam. She had said he was the only thing that could get her up before noon on a Sunday.

Roger was sitting in a chair half facing the window. I could see Joe in him. Another patient, a cigarette in his hand, was standing nearby, rubbing himself against a chair.

'Uh . . . Roger, hi. Hi, Roger . . . You know . . . You remember me?'

'You're Annie. Joe's girlfriend.'

'Yes, that's right. I'm Joe's wife.'

'Yes, Annie. I know. So pretty, Annie. We're so lucky, aren't we?'

'Why, Roger? Why are we lucky?'

'Joe calls me, he says, "Hi Roger-Dodger", and I'm the one. I'm Roger-Dodger.'

'Why are we lucky, Roger . . . Dodger?'

'Mum says we're so lucky, Annie.'

'Why?'

'Mum says we're so lucky to have you. So pretty and she loves little Sam. I have pictures. I have pictures. My mum gives me pictures. Little pictures . . . of little Sam . . . and little baby . . .'

'Who's the baby?'

'Jesus. You silly! Where's Mum? Annie, where's Mum?'

'She couldn't come today.'

Joe managed to find a place that his mother seemed to like, at least at the time she saw it. There was a vacancy but they had two other people who were interested. They wanted $20 000 in advance. He promised them he would be back the next morning with the money. I went to the bank that afternoon and deposited my father's cheque. Back home, I wrote one of my own for $20 000 made out to the retirement home, and gave it to Joe.

I had to decide which of my colleagues was going to get Joe as a client. Nobody ever liked being given a member of a colleague's family as a client. It put extra pressure on you. It was like having someone from the firm watch you while you worked and then report on you and, worst of all, the consequences of the job placement would come back to you in instalments five days a week after that. Since it all really boiled down to luck and to how well Joe sold himself at interviews, all my potential choices were equally good, or ungood, as Orwell warned we might say. So I decided to set him up, while I still had authority over her, with the young communications graduate.

My father was still waiting to hear from Joe. That he'd given me a cheque for the amount we needed urgently had not lessened his determination to, as he put it, make Joe learn the hard way. Joe, on his part, wasn't going anywhere near him. Fortunately, my father wasn't home when I dropped in to see them that evening. Had he been, he would have started on me about not hearing from Joe. My mother would have tried to calm him down but ultimately she would have backed off when he told her to. She did as she was told. That's how their marriage worked. That's how it had worked for decades. Talking over coffee about Sophie's biological clock, as my mother was wont to do, I asked her why they hadn't had more children. She said she hadn't wanted more although my father had. He had wanted a son.

'But you had to have slept together more than twice.'

'That's not a subject for mother and daughter.'

'Mum, what are you telling me?'

'I'm not telling you anything.'

'You've been a practising Catholic all your life, haven't you?'

'Of course I have.'

'So then—'

'Anna, there are ways to not get pregnant. It was a trade-off. You get used to it.'

My father's unexpectedly early return home saved my mother's face from reddening further. But it did nothing for mine.

'So where's Joe? He has to come and talk to me like a man. Why don't he come, Anna? I give you the cheque. Why don't he come?'

He was getting angrier by the word. Stupidly, I tried to mollify him with the truth.

'Dad, he's ashamed to talk to you.'

'I know all that. I know he don't have a job. But he has to be a man.'

'Yes, but there are things you don't know, things he's embarrassed about.'

'What things?'

'Well, the title, you see—'

'The title, there's a mortgage, I know all that.'

'Yes, but . . . I'm not on it. That's what he's—'

'What? What do you mean you're not on it?'

'Dad, the house is . . . It's entirely in his name, and the bank's, I suppose. I'm not on the title.'

'The *bastardo*, he did this to you? I'll kill him, I'll kill him! It's not too late, I'll fix him.'

There was nothing I could do to stop him shouting so I left.

Simon's trial was starting the following week. I was due to have my final briefing or preparation session with the prosecutor at around the time of the appointment I'd made for Joe with my young colleague. My story hadn't changed but my comfort in telling it had and I wondered if the prosecutor noticed. Of course, I didn't tell any of them I'd visited Simon. Nonetheless something about my manner, about the way I gave my evidence, must have made them all a little wary. Mr Henshaw reminded me about Ms Serkin's cross-examination at the committal hearing.

'Do you remember how she asked you that whole long series of detailed questions concerning your relationship with Simon in your student days?' he asked.

'Yes.'

'Well, she's going to do that again, you know.'

'So, I'm meant to tell the truth, aren't I? And, anyway, you said those questions weren't relevant.'

'Yes, but they might be deemed relevant by the trial judge. Ms Serkin will use them to try to make it sound more likely that you were still, that is at the relevant time, having an affair with Simon.'

'But I wasn't.'

'No, but if a jury thinks you were, they will also think it more likely that Simon did have your permission to pick Sam up from school. It raises, or helps to raise, a reasonable doubt. We don't want that.'

'Look, I'm . . . I'm only telling the truth. It's all I've ever done.'

'That's all we want,' Mr Henshaw said, before a new addition to their team, a woman I'd not seen before, suddenly put her hand on my wrist and said, 'Anna, there's the truth and . . . the truth. If you really want to see this animal locked up for a long time, you don't have to agree that your earlier relationship was quite so peachy.'

I looked at this woman for a moment.

'Have we met?'

23

I was giving Sam his dinner when Joe came home after his interview with my young colleague, way after. He had obviously stopped off somewhere to drink the rest of the afternoon away.

'How did you find Celéste?' I asked him.

'She's good but she's eleven.'

'Is she, Dad?'

'No, Dad's joking. Aren't you?'

'Yes, I'm only joking.'

'She's young but she's determined. She's very keen.'

'Oh, I thought so,' he said, and that was all we said about it until Sam was in bed. Then he took his dinner out of the microwave and ate it standing up while I did the dishes.

'Anna.'

'Uh-huh.'

'The money, the advance for the retirement home.'

'Uh-huh.'

'Where did you get it?'

'I told you, we got a raise.'

'And a bonus?'

'Yes, that's right.'

'Everyone?'

'Pretty much everyone, uh-huh.'

Then he slammed his plate down and the food rose and fell, not all of it falling back on the plate.

'What the fuck is going on?' he shouted.

'What's wrong? What are you talking about?'

'Anna, are you going to tell me the truth, about anything?'

'I don't understand, what are you talking about?'

'I spent about two hours today with your colleague, the lovely Celéste. She's really going places, right?'

'Joe, she's at least as good as anyone else there.'

'Probably better than some, right?'

'For sure.'

'Then why didn't she get any fucking raise? Why didn't she get a bonus?'

'You asked her about that?'

'Yes, I asked her about that,' he said at the top of his voice. 'She didn't get anything and she hasn't heard of anyone else there getting anything. She said it's not even the right time of the year for it. You got your bonuses at the end of the financial year. So are you going to tell me where you now want me to think the money is coming from? I don't know what your game is but—'

'How did you even get to talking to her about that?'

'Well, to be honest, Anna, I had money on my mind when I walked in there. Then Celéste started asking questions about lifestyle. What are my main avenues of expenditure? Well, I thought of the mortgage, of course. But even before that came to mind, right at the forefront, right before my very fucking eyes, was my mother's retirement home. It's funny, isn't it? I walk into my wife's place of business, am greeted by this gorgeous kid, with hair and a cleavage you could build a country estate in, and all I can focus on is my dear mother's retirement home.'

'Why?'

'Because not long before my appointment I got a call from them.'

'Oh no. Is she alright?'

'The cheque bounced!'

Sam was standing quietly in the kitchen doorway. His pyjama bottoms were wet.

My cheque had bounced. My father must have stopped his.

Joe, even when on the verge of an alcohol-induced stupor, as he frequently was then, was still sometimes able to cross-examine me to within an inch of my life. He had caught me lying about where the twenty thousand dollars for the retirement home was supposed to be coming from. He pressed me for the truth and the truth was that I wasn't so good at thinking on my feet. At first, without it making any sense, he suspected that Simon was somehow meant to have come up with the money but hadn't. The trial was days away. Joe would be called yet again to give his version of events and he was particularly Simon-conscious. It didn't take me long to convince him it had nothing to do with Simon. Joe didn't know where the money was supposed to be coming from and he didn't know why his son was picked up from school one day by my ex-boyfriend of a decade earlier. He was just attributing the things he couldn't explain to a single cause. Joe was using Occam's razor, Simon's weapon of choice. But if the money wasn't coming from Simon, who was it supposed to be coming from? I wasn't fast enough. I panicked and grasped at the truth, yet again. I must remember to stop doing that.

'There's nothing sinister in it, Joe.'

'Then tell me.'

'I got the money from my father.'

'Anna, don't bullshit a bullshitter. Your father wanted me to beg him for it. He wouldn't have given you a bean till I did. And maybe not even then.'

'Well, I did the begging for you, Joe. And he lent me one hundred thousand beans.'

'So why did the cheque bounce?'

'He must've . . . He'd been at me for days wanting to know why you still hadn't been to see him. The only thing I could think of telling him was that you were embarrassed about me not being on the title. When I told him that he went berserk. He must've stopped the cheque he'd given me.'

'You idiot, Anna. He'll hold that against me forever, that jumped-up little—'

'Watch it, Joe. I'm one of them too. So is your son.'

'Well, you shouldn't have fucking gone to him for help!'

'Joe, I'd tried everything else. He was our last resort.'

'You'd tried everything else? What the fuck does that mean?

What had you tried?'

'Lots of things. Just take it from me, Joe, I'd tried everybody else.'

'Who else had you tried?'

'Joe, I . . . I even tried Sheere.'

'What? You asked Donald Sheere? Are you telling me you asked Donald Sheere?'

'Yes.'

'You asked Donald Sheere? Are you out of your mind?'

'Think about it, Joe. After all the money you've made for him and his wife, the ungrateful bastard pulls out of an attempt by you to make him still more and you lose your job and our house on account of it. Why shouldn't I ask him for help?'

'How did you even get through to him? He wouldn't take my calls.'

'He wouldn't take mine either.'

'Anna, what did you do?'

'I . . . I went to his house.'

'You went to his house?'

'Yes.'

'Jesus, Anna! Uninvited?'

'Joe, what did I have to lose?'

'My reputation.'

'Oh, come on, Joe, be—'

'What happened?'

'I saw him.'

'Oh fuck!'

'I told him what had happened to you.'

'He would've known that.'

'I told him about the house, how we could lose the house.'

'Oh Jesus! Anna, you've humiliated me. I spent years, literally years, cultivating that relationship and in one visit you—'

'Joe, listen to yourself. He sold you out and you're still worried about—'

'Anna, there was nothing personal in what he did. It was business. He had to do it. I can't believe it! My wife goes to this man and airs our dirty laundry.'

'Joe, you said you were finished.'

'And you were primed to believe me, for perhaps the first time since we got married.'

'Joe, do you really think—'

'What did he say?'

'Well . . . He heard me out and he said you were . . . he said you were a good man . . . and that he liked working with you and—'

'Really? He said that?'

'Yep. He said that . . . and that he was sorry that things had turned out the way they had. I told him we were going to lose the house and he said he was sure that wouldn't happen, that you would be . . . back on top again very soon. He had no doubt about that, but there was nothing he could do.'

'You begged him. Oh Jesus, you begged him.'

'Joe, I didn't. I didn't.'

'You humiliated me for nothing. More than nothing. This is going to cost more than a hundred thousand. I already had ideas to put to him. You didn't know that. He would've backed me if you hadn't made me look pathetic to him. They hate losers. You never beg them. You've got to offer them something they want. Jesus! What on earth made you think he would help you? Why would he do anything for you?'

'He owed you, Joe. I thought it was worth trying.'

'Well, it wasn't, was it?'

'That's why I went to my father. I had no one else to turn to.'

'And he let you down too.'

'Yes, he let me down too.'

24

Sam was wetting his bed every night and waking. The trial started. Joe was due to give his evidence ahead of me. He might well have been drinking the morning he testified. I'd gone to work but it wouldn't have surprised me. I thought it all the more likely after he'd precipitated a mistrial and the discharge of the jury by his mention of Carlo, Simon's missing student, which the judge deemed irrelevant or overly prejudicial or something. Everything was going to have to start again.

Without telling Joe, I went to see someone from the bank that held the mortgage over our home. I explained the situation. He was sympathetic but ultimately he only allowed us a further reduction in repayments for four months, after which, if we could not resume repayment at the original rate, the bank would be forced to sell the house. Joe was visiting my office for regular meetings with Celéste. It nauseated me. The trial was due to start again when Joe finally put the only thing he owned outright, his car, on the market. The money would go to pay for his mother's accommodation at the retirement home.

It was around this time that I again heard from Dr Alex Klima.

'Alex, you know I could report you to the judge and to your professional association. You really do try my patience, you know.'

'I could say you tried one of mine.'

'You wouldn't though, would you? It wouldn't be worthy of you. Listen, since you're harassing me, can I get your professional opinion?'

'Of course.'

'This doesn't mean I owe you anything, right?'

'You don't owe me anything.'

'It's about Sam. To be honest . . . I'm worried about him. He's wetting his bed. He's crying—'

'I'm happy to talk to you about him, but at least until the trial is over, I think it might be better if you talked to someone else.'

'Why, are you going to say it's my fault?'

'Oh, Anna, we always say it's the mother's fault. You know that.'

'Well, that's a relief. I thought sometimes it's the ex-girlfriend's fault.'

'Seriously, Anna, if you're really concerned I could give you the names of some colleagues who specialise in children.'

'I thought you specialised in children.'

'Is this making you feel better?'

'Isn't that your job?'

'Yes, I am supposed to make somebody feel better. It happened once. I remember it well.'

'Now you are trying to make me feel sorry for you so that I'll do or say something for your friend. Alex, things have been terrible for me. I'm not going to visit him again. Please don't ask me for anything because—'

'Anna, I didn't call to ask you for anything. I called to tell you something, for what it's worth. It's a sign of something—an altruism bordering on mental illness, misguided love maybe. Call it what you will.'

'What are you talking about?'

'Sam.'

'What about him?'

'I don't know why it took this long to come out but Simon's lawyer only now found out—she didn't find out—I told her—about

Simon rescuing Sam from the swimming pool.'

'That again.'

'You still haven't asked Sam?'

'No, it doesn't make any sense. There's already too much craziness going on around him.'

'Well Gina, Gina Serkin, Simon's barrister, wants to call Sam as a witness.'

'No. No way. You can't. You fucking bastard. Is this blackmail—'

'Hold on. Firstly it's not up to me.'

'Who's it up to?'

'Simon.'

'Then he's evil. This is worse than taking him in the first place.'

'Anna, I'm calling to tell you that Simon won't permit Gina to call Sam as a witness.'

'I'm meant to be grateful for this, I suppose?'

'You should be. Calling Sam to give evidence about the swimming pool incident would greatly increase Simon's chances of acquittal.'

'Simon made it up.'

'Anna, talk to your son. Ask him. He'll remember. Ask him about the time the gardener fished him out of the swimming pool. He was very shaken. He won't have forgotten it. Then ask him if this was the same man who collected him from school that day, who gave him chocolate milk and let him play with his dog. Ask him.'

This time Joe managed to give his evidence without aborting the trial. It wasn't a matter of either of us learning from our mistakes. The mistakes we could make were by no means limited to those we had already made. He felt better having given his evidence, and now, he said, he was free to go to court every day and sit, as he put it, 'in the audience', so the jury could see the stolen boy's father.

The night before I was due to give my evidence, I dreamed that I had to go to visit Joe's brother, Roger, again. In the dream I walked in as I had before, with the smell of the place sickening me. I kept having to walk around looking for Roger but I couldn't find him anywhere. I turned to see one of the patients, the one who was smoking, rubbing himself against the back of an empty chair, and I wanted to look away, to walk away, but I felt obliged not to, however much I wanted to run like hell out of there. Before I could leave in good conscience I had genuinely to try as hard as I could to find Roger. So, despite my repulsion, I walked up to and then in front of the man. He said nothing but continued rubbing himself. Up close I saw him smile at me. It was Michael Gardiner rubbing himself, and the chair in front of him which had appeared empty from the back had Sam sitting in it, swinging his legs as he sometimes did in Joe's mother's kitchen. I raced over to hug him, to take him away. He didn't appear distressed at all but he looked up at me and said, 'Where's Mum? Yeah, but where's Mum?' I woke up with my heart pounding, got out of bed and rushed into Sam's room and just stood there till I'd calmed down. I didn't sleep the rest of the night.

I wasn't due to give evidence till midday at the earliest. It was school holiday time and I drove Sam to my parents' house. My mother came to the door when she heard the car pull up. I had finally taken Dr Klima's advice. I had asked him.

'Sam, you've never had an accident in the pool, have you?'

'No.'

'No, I didn't think so.'

'I haven't, really, I haven't.'

'I believe you, Sam,' I said, giving him a big hug. I didn't want to release him.

'I always go before I get in the pool.'

'What? Say that again, sweetie. What did you say?'

'I don't ever do it in the pool anymore.'

'Sammy, sweetie, I want to ask you a question and I want you to have a good hard think before you answer. It's important, but you won't be in any trouble whatever the answer is, okay?'

'Okay.'

'You know how you're not supposed to go into the pool without an adult watching?'

'I don't. I really don't, Mum.'

'I know you don't, sweetie, but think hard and tell me, did you ever fall in by mistake?'

'Yep.'

'You did?'

'It was a hot day . . . but it was an accident. I—'

'What happened?'

'My ball fell into the pool. I tried to make it float back by paddling the water and I fell in, in my school clothes.'

'What happened then?'

'I was scared. I swallowed all this water and I was out of breath and I was scared.'

'What happened then?'

'He came into the pool and got me out and I got my breath back.'

'Who did?'

'The gardener. It wasn't my fault because the ball—'

'Sam, was that man, the gardener, the same man who picked you up from school the day Dad was late?'

'Yes. He has a dog, Mum. We played with his dog. Can we get a dog like the gardener's dog? He was middle-sized and he was grey. Can we get one, maybe?'

'Maybe.'

My mother came to the door when she heard the car pull up. I took Sam to the door and she hugged him the same way I did, putting one hand at the back of his head and squeezing her other arm around him. It was the first time I had noticed that we both did this. For all that she couldn't say, to me anyway, and probably to Sophie, as a grandmother she was completely unrestrained. I'd given him a devoted grandmother. Would he remember his times with her? Grandmothers don't get much of a press these days. Perhaps they never did. Even the grandmother of God, St Anne, doesn't get a mention in the Bible proper. She doesn't turn up till an unreliable second century document and even then, once she's given birth to Our Lady, she vanishes, right out of the Apocrypha, a grandmother for eternity and the patron saint of Christian mothers.

Mind you, I'd had my doubts about St Anne from the time I learned that my aunt and namesake, my father's late older sister, had died in Italy from complications in childbirth which, I intuited from the way it was barely discussed in my childhood, was tinged with shame. If St Anne could let Zia Anna down, then any saint can let you down. And if the saints could let you down, who couldn't?

St Elegius, the patron saint of jewellers, must have been distracted or else unable to intervene at the suburban jewellery store I had for years been taking my bracelet to for repairs. A board had replaced a plate glass window. I was on my way home to change for court when I saw it. With time to kill before midday, I thought I'd stop. I'd been meaning to go there anyway. The shop was empty but for the old man, as it always was.

'Mr Leibowitz,' I said as he greeted me with his smile, 'were you burgled?'

'The police say burglary but . . . I don't know . . . it doesn't feel like burglary in the air.'

'What do you mean?'

'The window was smashed but nothing was taken. What kind of burglar does that?'

'Maybe the alarm scared them away.'

'Maybe, but I don't think so. I think in the air sometimes I can smell it.'

'What?'

'Europe. Europe in the thirties . . . You've come about your favourite bracelet, yes? But you're wearing it.'

'No, I didn't come about the bracelet, but to ask about the window.'

'That is very kind of you. Your bracelet, it is well? It's like family. It was born here and now it brings your little boy here and while it's—how can I put it?—it's not the most expensive piece ever to come through here, it is probably the most cared about. I do remember. It has a story to it that I don't really know but . . . apart from the man who came to pick it up not long ago there was also the much younger man who had himself aged. He came in asking about your bracelet, the man who had bought it for you all those years back.'

'You remembered him? How could you possibly have remembered him after all that time?'

'He was a memorable fellow. He came in all those years ago wanting to buy a silver bracelet for his girlfriend. He looked at all the silver bracelets I had but he was a student and didn't have much money and it saddened him. We got talking about his girlfriend. The boy was *meshugah* for her, for you. He saw the number on my arm and we talked for a couple of hours about the war, politics, history, all sorts of things. He was a nice boy. At the end of it I told him I would make him a silver bracelet, design it myself, and let him have it cheap. This was how your bracelet was born. That is why I don't forget him.'

'And you've been losing money on it ever since.'

'But you keep coming back, and sometimes with your son.'

'And you never charge.'

'It's not his son, is it? Ah well, it's none of my business but, as I said, everybody loves that bracelet.'

'I do.'

'And so did the other man, the man who picked it up recently.'

'Oh, he did, did he?'

'Look after your boy,' the jeweller called out to me as I left his jewellery store.

At home, Joe surprised me with a reprise of his assertion that there had been no work conference that fateful weekend.

'It was a lie, Anna. I happen to know there was no conference. You were going away with Simon, weren't you?'

'You're not on about that again, are you? If Simon and I were planning to go away together for a dirty weekend, why would he go and kidnap Sam? It doesn't make sense. Don't you see that?'

Joe was silent. It had finally sunk in. I couldn't have been going away with Simon. Joe filled the electric kettle and switched it on. He stood there waiting for it to boil. He looked across at me.

'It's Buchanan, isn't it?'

He was getting close.

As I sat at the dressing table, in front of a photo of a woman and a man which the wedding photographer had promised would enable them to 'forever joyfully recapture the day', and looked in the mirror at a likeness of that woman preparing to go to court, I knew he was getting the picture, indistinct though it was. My unintended dismemberment of him was complete.

25

I drove, parked the car, survived the onslaught of photographers outside the court, and swore on the Bible, all as if in a dream. Dutifully I repeated my story at Mr Henshaw's request. I might have sounded too practised but at least it was over. I was exhausted. All I had to do now was to get through Gina Serkin's cross-examination and live the rest of my life with the consequences.

She asked all the questions we'd been expecting, questions designed to show how close Simon and I had been ten years earlier, how in love we'd been. And just as I had for Mr Henshaw, I told the truth. I had loved him. He had marked my life forever. She asked good questions but not enough of them. There was so much more that she could have got out of me, so much more that would have shown the jury just who he was and what we were together. I'd been programmed, long before him, to receive saints and martyrs and he had them all for me: Billie Holiday and Abe Meeropol and the others. She should've asked me about Abe Meeropol. I remembered it all. He wrote songs under the name Lewis Allen, the name under which he is credited as the author of 'Strange Fruit'. He adopted the Rosenberg kids after their parents were electrocuted. You had to really love Abe Meeropol. My mind wandered. It roamed. I wanted to sleep until, all of a sudden, she brought me back with her best question yet.

'Mrs Geraghty,' she began, 'I put it to you that you were in fact in an illicit relationship with Simon Heywood on the day in question.'

Other than my son, there was only one person on earth who

claimed to love me above everyone else, and he was unwell and I was being asked to convict him. I looked over at him now.

'Mrs Geraghty? . . . Mrs Geraghty? Do you understand what I am putting to you?'

'Your Honour, do I have to answer that question?'

'Yes, Mrs Geraghty, you do have to answer . . . Mrs Geraghty?'

The judge was asking me to grade all the major decisions of my adult life. He seemed to be saying that I, a victim, had to confess my mistakes, the big ones, to the world in a crowded court room, and let the consequences fall where they may.

'Mrs Geraghty,' he persisted, 'are you thinking about your answer or are you indeed refusing to answer?'

I never did get used to being called by Joe's mother's name. The judge seemed to be getting angry. 'Mrs Geraghty?' he asked again.

part seven

I was seven years old, almost eight, when my father came home with a dog. It was beautiful—a full-blood, pure-bred schnauzer with shaggy grey hair and twinkling brown eyes so full of intelligence, so alive with personality, that he seemed at once more of a playmate than a pet. He was a gift, my father said. But he was a gift my mother could do without and she erupted at my father for bringing him home. Who was going to care for it? Who was going to wash it, feed it, walk it? When I said that I would, my mother rattled off a list of things I had started and then given up. It was an impressive list for one so young. It would have been nice to have kept up any one of them but then none of them had provided the instant reward this dog did.

'Who will train him?'

'He's already trained,' my father said.

'Who will pay for him?' my mother asked. When my father said that he would pay for the upkeep of the dog, I thought, as a child would and because I wanted the dog so badly, that with that, all outstanding issues had been resolved in favour of us keeping the dog. But instead it brought forth a verbal blitz from my mother, a storm of thunder against which reason, humour and sentiment were powerless. Reason, humour and sentiment were my father's tools.

This was so typical of my father, she bellowed, all care and no responsibility. Who had asked him to bring a dog home? Who was going to care for the back lawn now, not that he ever did? This was another attempt to cast her as the disciplinarian, wasn't it? He wasn't even meant to be there now. When she said that, my attention shifted away from the dog for the first time since my father's arrival.

She asked him, or really told him, to use the doorbell in future and not to just let himself in. Otherwise she would have to change the locks. And he was to keep to the arranged times and not to turn up just when he felt guilty. He said now she was finally talking about something she knew about. And she said what was the dog if not a bribe, and he said the dog was a dog and that, as far as guilt was concerned, she was the one who had started this, but she said no, she was just the one who had ended it. Neither of them was listening to the other. She yelled at him to get out or she would call the police. He said it was still his house too and she pushed him. He said, 'Not in front of the . . .' and pushed her back. He called out goodbye and said that he would be back when my mother had calmed down. I ran out after him to the front gate, crying, and the dog ran after me.

'Dad! Dad!' I screamed, and my father turned around, squatted down at the gate, hugged me and wiped the tears from my face. The dog was barking. 'What's his name, Dad? You didn't tell us his name. Does he have a name?'

'Yes, little one. He has a name.'

'What's his name?'

'Empson.'

2

Empson was a refugee. Your little dog, an innocent victim of the upheaval in your life, suddenly found himself thrust into a suburban war zone or, if not a war zone, then at least the scene of the spontaneous clashes that erupted whenever my father came to visit us and of which we were the major casualties. Children of separated parents always hope their parents will reconcile. Well, we did, anyway, my sister and I. For what it's worth all these years later, we did love your dog and we quickly came to think of him as ours. Even our mother came to love him, I think, despite the manner of his arrival, which seemed to symbolise to her much of what she thought was by then wrong with our father. The truth, at least when looked at from her perspective, is that it was inconsiderate of him not to check with her first before bringing home a dog, particularly since he wasn't living there anymore. It wouldn't have helped him had she learned, as she subsequently did, that Empson was the dog of one of his patients, the newly famous one, who had just been arrested for kidnapping a child.

Without being or needing to be a psychiatrist herself, she had long thought our father was getting too involved with his patients. That she was right nobody knows better than you. Broadly in agreement with his world view, she was nevertheless more pragmatic than him, less resistant to compromise with the prevailing ethos, less eager to go into battle for what she believed. She wanted someone else to fight the good fight against the introduction of managed care, partly, I think, because it took up too much of his time and attention and partly, I suspect, because she knew that sooner or later, it would be introduced anyway. And then, not only would his efforts have been futile, but his practice would suffer disproportionately on account of what would be seen as his Ludditism. She's sounding more and more reasonable, isn't she? There was much more to it than that. She eventually got even more reasonable having been, for a while, far less. But at the time, she was the one who didn't want us to have the dog despite us being just crazy about him. He was our first pet, excluding a quickly dead goldfish, and I suppose he served as a tangible manifestation of our absent father's love for us. But a girl grows up, first romantic and then cynically hip and forever tyrannised by her own concerns. With these acting on her as an anaesthetic, she acclimatises to what she comes to label offhandedly, like a latter-day Holden Caulfield, as her 'parental problems'. You can't have known much about the circumstances of your dog and his new owners. There was a time, an important time, when you had so much more of our father's attention than we did and we really missed him, especially at first, and especially me. Not as much as now though.

Did you know he had children or how many he had? Did you know they were girls? Did you know that we grew up knowing of you primarily as 'that nut who destroyed your father'? But now, knowing all about you and knowing that our parents' problems were born before you came into our father's life, I know that our mother's method of identifying you gave you much more credit, or should I say blame, than you deserved. For all the time and effort that he put into you, his importance to you was far greater than your importance to him, at least in the sense of influencing the way things turned out for each of you. Don't you agree? It's in your interests to agree. Or will you say you don't know?

I wonder, for example, if you know how old he was when he left

Czechoslovakia? Do you know anything about his parents or the world they came from? Compared with the maelstrom they lived through, even your problems pale. His parents, whom I never knew, were married before the war. In 1941 they and their two children were sent to the ghetto at Łódz, in Poland. As I understand it, the younger of the two children died in the ghetto. The older child went with them to Auschwitz and died there. Miraculously, both my grandparents survived the Holocaust. Can you imagine living through that, being separated, herded like animals, starved, slaving in workshops beside the chimneys as they belched out the smoke of your gassed and burned children, along with the thousands of other Jews they belched out, twenty-four hours a day, day after day, till shortly before the end of the war? I have trouble imagining how they coped even after the war, when they managed to find each other and start again. How can people possibly start again after that?

My grandparents were educated middle-class professionals. He was a doctor, she a teacher of languages. They were non-communist Jewish leftists, children of the enlightenment, for all the good it did them. After the war, they went back to Prague and tried to integrate into a society that had let them and their families be rounded up and taken away. Now that almost all of their families were gone, distant cousins whom they barely knew grew in importance, in closeness. In between attempts to find out who was left, they had to go about their lives, with the numbers still on their arms, and try to re-establish careers, professional lives, amongst neighbours who resented their survival.

When Czechoslovakia slid into communism in the 'victorious February' of 1948, my grandparents, by all accounts, did not yet feel part of whatever passed for normal society to fear the change. Even to mourn the mysterious death of the foreign minister, Jan Masaryk, was a self-indulgence they couldn't fully allow themselves. My grandmother had a distant relative, some sort of cousin or cousin's cousin whom the war had brought closer and he was a communist, a leading member of the Party. Whether this encouraged any optimism I can't say but if it had, it would have been short-lived. The cousin or cousin's cousin turned out to be Rudolf Slánsky, the deputy prime minister and general secretary of the Czech Communist Party. I don't know how well they knew him or even if they ever met him. Having read up about him, I can tell you that my father would have been born around the time, almost to the day, that Slánsky and his thirteen co-defendants went on trial for being 'Trotskyist-zionist-titoist-bourgeois-nationalist' traitors, spies and saboteurs, enemies of the Czechoslovakian nation, of its people's democratic order, and of socialism. Eleven of the fourteen defendants were Jews. The trials were quite literally scripted. All the 'actors' had to learn and rehearse their lines. Apparently when the trial judge inadvertently skipped a question, Slánsky covered for him, answering the question the judge had meant to ask. Eventually they all confessed. Eleven of them were executed and their property was appropriated for the families of newly promoted apparatchiks.

By the time my father was two, around one hundred and fifty thousand people had been imprisoned by the regime. It was in this climate of informers, denunciations, arbitrary arrests, blacklists and unswerving, uncritical, unthinking loyalty to the Party that my father grew up, in this climate and against the background of his parents' wartime experiences. Those most at risk from the regime's caprice were the intelligentsia, non-communist leftists—seen as bourgeois class enemies—and the Jews. My grandparents on my father's side were all three. This was the world into which your psychiatrist was born. I thought you might want to know.

By the early to mid 1960s, things had relaxed slightly. My father was about twelve or thirteen when his parents managed to leave Czechoslovakia and settle here, bringing with them three or four suitcases filled to the brim with nothing, some tertiary qualifications of almost no value here, a lonely, cynical, bookish teenage son with faltering English, and each with his own custom-made memories of the nightmare of twentieth-century Europe. That the boy would one day grow up and be your psychiatrist should seem incredible to you, much more incredible than hearing from one of his daughters out of the blue some twelve or so years after he might be said to have saved your life.

I was seven years old, almost eight, when my father came home with a dog but could not stay. My mother shouted. The dog barked. The children cried, first at the sound of their parents' raised voices and then at the sight of their parents pushing each other. You know the scene. You can imagine it; I know you can. We sure as hell needed something. Empson was a good place to start. There were many arguments, before and after my father left home, many before and after the one about Empson, but that one, the argument about whether or not we could keep a dog—and he was such a cute dog—that one stands out.

It stands out, I suppose, because I had such a vested interest in the outcome that I felt responsible for it. And from there, of course, for a little girl anyway, it is a short road to feeling responsible for the whole mess that was your parents' youthful decision to bind themselves to each other and then to procreate so that other innocent people might not only witness it, but be bound too in a way that is, perhaps, more inescapable than anything else this side of death. After all, you can change your hair length and colour, change your name and even the shape of your nose, but you can never change the identity of your parents. You heard your parents argue. You saw them push each other and worse. I know you did. How could I possibly know that? I could know it through your stepson. You're very open with him. But that's not how I know it. He's another story. I'll get to that, I'll tell you that one too.

3

When I turned eighteen I became entitled to my share of my father's estate. It won't surprise you that he had nothing to leave, no assets, no money to speak of. I say it won't surprise you but I don't know the extent to which you've ever considered what you cost him financially. Certainly the divorce took it out of him, but almost immediately after you were arrested your father stopped paying him and then, if anything, he started devoting even more of his time to you, what with the trips to Laverton and everything. There was less time left for his other patients. Even before you came along, for some reason, he didn't seem to have had enough full-fee paying patients. It hadn't always been that way but my mother admits, when pushed, that his practice had got too quiet even before you arrived on the scene. So all there was for me to inherit were his genes and his book. You've seen the book; I'm sure you have. It's not so much a book as a journal.

It seems he began it purely as a journal, a personal record of his private thoughts, but over time it seemed to have mutated into a memoir of everything that was going on in his life. He seems to have included notes about his patients, and not just you. At the beginning there are merely allusions to various patients, but by the end there are detailed notes about specific patients and specific sessions. You might be flattered to know you dominate the journal right to the end. There's a while there where you're more the subject than he is. Not just your sessions either, although they're faithfully recorded as well.

You would find parts of it interesting as a record of yourself at the time, everything from throwaway lines to deeply held convictions.

This is how I come to know about you and your parents and even their friends, Henry and Diane Osborne. This is how I come to know that you heard your parents argue and that you saw much worse than that. I know about your mother's depression and how, as a boy, you tried to treat it with music, in particular with Billie Holiday. In fact, as I lay on my bed reading about your mother, I sort of half pictured her looking like Billie Holiday, as ridiculous as that might sound. When I thought about it later it occurred to me that your mother might well have been one of the whitest middle-class women ever to set foot on her son's forehead, ever to lie back, close her eyes in the suburban day, and listen to that black singer. But, for all that, from what I've gleaned from the journal, she was the Billie Holiday of your family of origin. Unless it was you.

I don't mean to embarrass you. This is all highly personal and not easily characterised as my business, but you and your story, your history, your taste, views and opinions seemed to have become an integral part of my father's business. His business became part of his history and when he left me his history it became my business. Sometimes he must have taken down what you said as you were saying it. That's the way it looks. Do you remember reciting the opening to 'Howl' by Allen Ginsberg to him one day? My father didn't know it. Do you remember?

> *I saw the best minds of my generation destroyed by*
> *madness, starving hysterical naked,*
> *dragging themselves through the negro streets at dawn*
> *looking for an angry fix . . .*

Every first year English literature student knows it. You'll be pleased to know your stepson knows it. You said to my father, 'I never even saw the best minds of my generation. They had to have been there somewhere but they were too well disguised, hidden, blanketed, overshadowed and overwhelmed by their intoxication with a fearsome self-interest to be recognised as the best of anything.'

The two of you then went on to explore the prevailing culture of every man for himself and to commiserate with each other over the demise of liberalism and its concern for the common good. You speculated about how much anger, how much alienation it would take to persuade society to reinvent the wheel, the commonweal. He attributes the pun to you. I read all this and wondered who was getting the therapy. At the bottom of that day's entry in my father's journal, almost as an afterthought, my father had written, 'There is anger on the streets. You see it mostly inside cars.'

I said every first-year student knows the opening to 'Howl'. I was a first-year student very, very recently. They should know it. They don't. It's probably worse than in your day. Or do we all say that? Does everybody say that things are worse than in 'their day'? Or do they say that things are better? Allen Ginsberg wrote 'Howl' in the mid 1950s. Were you saying that your generation had it worse than his or that they were themselves worse people? If people live long enough, 'their day' encompasses lots of other peoples' days and when you take account of geographical differences, that sort of talk becomes pretty meaningless. Was your day my father's day? Was my father's day his parents' day? In his day he lived for a while under a kind of Stalinism. In his parents' day people lived under Hitler and went up, up and away out of chimneys as smoke. That's how it was in their day.

So were things better or worse for you? Maybe you were just bleating on because your father was paying my father to listen to you? What was your problem, anyway?

In my day we never had Father's Day, not after I was ten. Do you remember the way, just before Father's Day, all those chain hardware stores used to advertise electric drills and circular saws on television? When I was about eleven I gave my mother a gift certificate from one of those hardware stores for her birthday to the value of sixteen dollars. She asked me what I thought she should buy with it. I told her she should put it towards an electric drill or a circular saw and she started to cry.

Within a few years of my father's death, the official line, the one sanctioned and promoted by my mother, saw my father partially rehabilitated. He went from being bad to sad and a little mad. You were increasingly implicated. But she didn't know about the journal or, if she did, she hadn't read it.

While the journal is filled with you and with details of your thoughts concerning everything from your relationships, your parents and Anna, thoughts of and reflections on Billie Holiday, William Empson, Eliot, Swinburne, deconstructionism, neo-classical economics, Nazim Hikmet, EL Doctorow and Abe Meeropol, you were not the only one to get a moment in the sun. You were not even the only patient he wrote about other than in a professional capacity. But, on balance, I would have to say you were his star patient and not only because you made it into the papers, or because of the time you took up, or even because of the money he lost on you. I say it really, I suppose, because of his great fondness for you. It's clear from the journal. He liked you and he agreed with so many of your views. They were his views. Possibly, he was comforted to hear them coming from you the way he did, by which I mean that not only was he impressed and maybe even charmed or entertained by your eloquence, but because you held many of the same opinions, he felt less alone in his.

The problem for him, at least before the kidnapping, might have been that, while he recognised that you were unhappy and unwell, I think he couldn't help but feel that there was some part of you, some part bound inextricably to your illness, which everybody could do with a little more of. Not the melancholy, of course, nor even the capacity for quips and one-liners ('Give me lithium or give me death,' remember?). Perhaps it was just what he more than once described as a mixture in you of acuity and romanticism that made most other people's versions of sanity appear hollow compromises, or evasions. Perhaps it was just your capacity to love in spite of the evidence. He identified this unambiguously as part of your illness and yet I suspect he felt that a lot of people could do with suffering this symptom occasionally.

At one point in there, apparently apropos of nothing but near in time to a session with you, he quotes another psychiatrist. I don't know whether he ever put it to you. 'Illnesses of mood distort and magnify what is human; they do not destroy it.' It's the last entry on an otherwise normal day that included a session with you. He doesn't mention you near it but it has a forgiving quality to it and you were probably the one most in need of his forgiveness. I stress that this entry dates from before the kidnapping when there was less to forgive. He wasn't meant to be in the business of bestowing or withholding forgiveness but, with you, he was far too willing to cross the line, right from the start. It was not enough for treatment to have been the primary purpose of your relationship. It should have been the sole purpose. When you kidnapped Sam, everyone's illness was magnified. But what would I know? I know just enough to know that a few undergraduate courses in psychology qualify me only for more undergraduate courses in psychology.

4

My father had another patient who earned himself extracurricular entries, a gambler. He didn't like him. You and my father on your walks could sound like two old army buddies agreeing with each other till the early hours beneath the on-again, off-again neon beer advertisement in the window of some seedy bar, but this man was an antagonist. In one of the earliest entries concerning him, my father noted that the man had told him that, much to his dislike, people were always abbreviating his surname, Mitchell, and calling him Mitch. Thereafter in the journal my father only ever referred to him as Mitch. And, if that's a bit obscure, he once wrote, 'Mitch again today. Unpleasant, angry. Warrants sympathy. Not forthcoming.'

I take the last part to mean that the sympathy this man warranted wasn't forthcoming. Mitch himself was actually quite forthcoming. To read his story, albeit through my father's eyes, is to see that he was clearly an intelligent man who had suffered terribly. I'm surprised by the dislike my father seemed to take to him and equally how well he was able to maintain his professional demeanour with him despite it. Could the man tell that my father didn't like him?

There's no evidence to suggest my father ever told you anything about him or, indeed, about any of his other patients, and nor should he have. If you're wondering why he took such a dislike to this gambler, I can assure you it had nothing to do with his gambling. My father wasn't any kind of puritan and one of the few things he and Mitch seemed to agree about was that gambling was the least of this man's problems. If anything, I think my father rather enjoyed Mitch's gambling stories. They would get this man talking and once he started he wouldn't stop.

Mitch was or had been some sort of senior analyst with a stock-broking firm in the city. Is this ringing a bell? There's no point being coy or hiding anything now and, anyway, there's always the chance that you already know some of it. Remember, I don't know exactly what you know. Mitch worked for a time for the same firm as Anna's husband, Joe. They often worked closely together. But before you get too excited, firstly, it was no coincidence that Mitch and you both became his patients, and secondly, my father's dislike of the man shouldn't be misinterpreted as further evidence of his loyalty to you, not that you need any. Mitch seemed to dislike Anna's husband more than you ever could have. I'm not sure you ever disliked him. Mitch certainly did. They worked together on some big deal which, when it fell through, left both men 'exposed', by which I mean it left them unemployed. Mitch seemed to hold Joe in some way responsible for this. To make matters worse, Mitch had, at about the same time, badly injured himself at some work retreat and he seemed to hold Anna's husband responsible for that too. A certain time after this he started seeing my father.

By then managed care, which my father had opposed publicly, had already been introduced. I find it completely endearing that he could ever have thought that a few well-written articles or letters could even momentarily slow the juggernaut of civil society's dismantling, which they were calling 'reform' at the time. Well, that's the way I describe it. I am my father's daughter, after all. Anyway, your stepson calls me a 'sell-out' or a 'capitulationist'. What he means is that he's more radical, read 'virtuous and wise', than me, and that what I see as pragmatism is really a moral or political cop-out. Well, what do you want? We're students. We're still naïve enough to think we can change things, still young enough to think we've got time.

The deal that cost Mitch and Anna's husband, Joe Geraghty, their jobs when it fell through wasn't just another deal. It was going to be the first deal to provide a windfall gain consequent upon the introduction of managed care. Mitch was therefore, at least for a time, depending on the failure of my father's quixotic project, the one that wasn't you.

It probably won't surprise you that it wasn't their difference over the health system that gave rise to my father's dislike of Mitch. Not as far as I can gauge. That might have been enough for me or for a young hot-head like Sam, but it wasn't for my father. Each of them knew, fairly early on, where they stood on the issue, that is, on opposite sides. My father made sure Mitch knew but he already did when he started seeing him. Mitch wasn't ideologically committed to any particular system of health-care provision. He wasn't ideologically committed to anything much at all. He had chosen my father through a recommendation, not one from Joe Geraghty but, in a way, through him.

It seems that after his accident and the breakdown of his marriage, Mitch had sought the physical comfort of a woman who, unlike his wife, was going to stick with him through thick and thin, at least till the one-hour appointment was up. He and Joe Geraghty had once, in happier times, visited the brothel she worked in together. It was there that he called when the times, his times, became decidedly unhappier. The woman he got to visit him regularly told him, without mentioning names, that she was in love with a man who needed help with legal fees. That was you. Mitch, in turn, told her the sad story of his life and she recommended a psychiatrist, your psychiatrist, my father.

The effort my father made to keep his dislike of Mitch to himself was not reciprocated. Mitch did not share your fondness for my father and he didn't try to hide it. But for some reason, he kept coming back. He couldn't bring himself either to terminate therapy or to see another therapist. Why?

It's tempting for a daughter to speculate that, for all his irritability and his contempt for my father and psychiatry, this man, Mitch, was getting some relief or comfort from his sessions with him. It's so tempting for a daughter to think this that I am not prepared to discount it entirely. My father, on the other hand, was never so tempted. For him Mitch's loyalty could be summed up in a word much less technical than 'transference' or whatever it was that you and Dad had for each other: Angelique.

Putting it simply—and this is the way my father put it, so don't get angry with me—what Anna was to you, Angelique was to Mitch; by which he didn't mean that Anna was your callgirl. He was talking about obsession. I'm sure he would forgive you if you wanted to say something about you having the last laugh, but he's not here anymore. You've only got his daughter, one of them, here and I won't forgive you if you say anything about having the last laugh, no matter how much I might need your help now.

The only link Mitch had to Angelique was my father. After her accident he had no way of contacting her without getting her phone number or real name from him. Faced with my father's refusal to divulge these, Mitch kept coming back to him, week after week, for more antidepressants, more cognitive therapy and for another spin of the wheel, another roll of the dice. There was always a chance, however small, that my father would either relent or else let something drop, some hint or clue which would lead him to her. But when the weeks and then months passed and there was no pay-off, Mitch decided to play his trump card.

He explained to my father that he had some money, thousands of dollars, that belonged to Angelique and that if my father didn't help him contact Angelique he, Mitch, wouldn't be able to get the money to her. They had won the money together just before her accident. As compelling as it must have sounded to my father, he told him 'no dice', or words to that effect. But Mitch was no idiot and he was a major league obsessive, almost up there with you. My father was of the opinion that, in addition to Mitch's obsession with Angelique, his need to see her, there were other things going on. The desire to see her wasn't merely or even barely some sort of sexual need, not in the conventional sense, anyway. Since Mitch's accident at his firm's corporate retreat he was an extremely bitter man. He was angry about so many things, not just the accident. His wife had been consistently unfaithful to him even before the accident. In particular, he was angry about what he perceived as his almost complete powerlessness. Not only did he no longer have any economic power or power to attract the opposite sex, but—and this must be the ultimate disempowerment—he had even lost the ability to help people, particularly Angelique. He was nothing, just a drain on society, an angry drain at that. A competitive man, or at least a man who had for years toiled at the coalface of competition, in the 'helping' game, at least in the 'helping Angelique' game, he was being beaten, or at least frustrated, by my father. Not only that, but for as long as my father refused to help him contact her, Mitch wouldn't even get to be a player.

But he had a sum of money with which he intended to apply leverage. My father described it as a test of strength for this man, a tug of war, a test of wills. Each session he would bring the money, some thirty thousand dollars in cash. He would try to give it to my father or leave it in his rooms at the end of the session but my father would refuse either to accept it or to give Mitch Angelique's telephone number. The truth was that since her accident he had been unable to contact her himself. You, obviously, couldn't have known where she was and her housemate had either moved out or neglected to pay the phone bill or both. Angelique had vanished. But this man, this angry, physically broken, insistent man and his bag of money would not go away.

It is well documented in his journal how my father came to think that it made sense to do what he then did. There is a logic to it and yet I read it and shake my head wondering how he could have done what he did. Perhaps you'll understand it better than I do. What happened was this. Realising eventually that my father was never going to intentionally divulge Angelique's whereabouts, Mitch came by my father's consulting rooms while he was absent—perhaps he was visiting you—and left the money for him with the receptionist he shared with a number of other doctors.

This money and much that surrounds it is all part of a trail that leads to you. You wonder how it can lead to you when you've never even met this man, Mitch? Well, for a start, as I told you, the money represented Angelique's winnings. When the two of them swapped stories and Angelique told him of her boyfriend's problem paying for his legal defence, Mitch taught her or helped her to gamble her way into thirty thousand dollars at the Casino. The money was Angelique's, Mitch insisted. It was for the lawyer defending her boyfriend, defending you, that is. You see, there was a period of some weeks, at least, when my father and, therefore, I guess, you, thought that your lawyer, my father's new friend Gina, would cease to represent you after Legal Aid threatened to withdraw its funding for your case. Although this fear ultimately proved to be unfounded, it persisted for a number of weeks and during that time, my father was seriously worried about what would happen.

By the time his concern about Legal Aid was resolved by Gina, Mitch and Angelique had already made their assault on the coffers of the Casino and, as you might know, it was from there—no doubt giddy with her good fortune, delivered more or less as Mitch had promised—that she pulled out into an oncoming car. Mitch took the money when the ambulance took her.

It was my father's intention to simply give the money back to Mitch at their next session, but there wasn't one. Mitch left a message after hours cancelling his next scheduled appointment. He didn't request an alternative time. He wasn't planning to come back. My father left him a number of messages asking him to reschedule and telling him that he had to take the money back. Mitch didn't take any of the calls despite it being likely from his own earlier description of his life that he was home. Nor did he return any of them. My father, it seemed, had lost him as a patient but gained thirty thousand dollars.

You might be wondering why Mitch, having failed in his attempt to use the money to lever a reconnection with Angelique, would stop trying and instead leave the money with my father. My father clearly wondered about this. He thought that Mitch simply wanted the money to reach her even if he, Mitch, wasn't able to. This struck my father as indicative of a selflessness and a nobility he would not have credited Mitch with, and that, in turn, did nothing for my father's feelings of guilt for having disliked him.

Of course, implicit in this interpretation is the implication that Mitch regarded my father as a man of sufficient integrity to be relied upon to get the money to Angelique and not to keep it for himself. It was an implication my father never commented on, not in the journal anyway. It also assumes, as Mitch had assumed all along, that my father was actually capable of contacting her. Mitch had always assumed either that Angelique was one of Dad's patients or else that he was one of her clients. Mitch's assumptions about their relationship were, as you know, of course quite wrong and so was his conclusion. Dad was never able to find her after her accident, try though he did.

But nor did he like holding on to the money. It made him uncomfortable for all sorts of reasons. For a start, he didn't have the facilities to store thirty thousand dollars securely in his rooms. Carrying it around wasn't an acceptable alternative and neither was stashing it somewhere in his none-too-salubrious recently rented two-bedroom place in East St Kilda.

I remember that place well. People think that children don't notice relativities in income, living conditions and circumstances, but the act of noticing is itself relative. My sister and I remembered a time when our father did not live in circumstances where you could smell the fried cooking smells of some of the forty other apartments, where you could follow the rhythms of other people's domestic arguments, hear their radios and televisions, their use of the bathroom and know the precise bodily function being fulfilled, or hear the strained night-time groans that were less mysterious than we wanted them to be. Children often sit on the floor. They know the feel of carpet better than adults do. No one needs to tell them that the floor beneath them is not as clean anymore, that it is harder, more coarse, closer to the slab that supports everything tenuously. Money would have been conspicuous there. It was no place to house thirty thousand dollars in notes.

But for a while he alternated between keeping the money at home and keeping it in his rooms without telling anyone. Then, when your trial was over, he gave it to someone, someone he thought would understand why, someone who probably would have understood had he perhaps explained it differently.

I don't know whether you're still in touch with her, probably not. It was all a long time ago. Perhaps you didn't have that kind of relationship with her, but my father spoke, or rather, wrote, so well of her that it's not out of the question that you did. It sounds like she did a great job for you.

5

I contacted her first, that is, before I contacted you. It was logistically harder but emotionally easier. My thinking was that if she would agree to see me she had to be at least civil. How does a member of the public contact a judge? I knew she'd been made a judge, not merely because my father had predicted it but because I'd called the Victorian Bar to ask for her and they'd told me. I called the County Court and eventually got on to her associate who offered to transmit a message. What was the message? How about, 'My father is still dead, but I'm an adult woman now. Can I talk to you about him?' That's not so far from the message I left. I said my name was Rachael Klima, daughter of Alex Klima. Can I come and talk to you?

A considerable time elapsed without any reply. I vacillated between calling again and giving up. Maybe the associate hadn't given her the message? There was no way to get to her other than through her associate. I wouldn't have minded if she was busy. I expected that, but surely I deserved some kind of response, for my father's sake, if not just out of politeness.

When her associate finally called me back he apologised on her behalf. 'Her Honour has had a backlog of judgments to write.'

'Oh,' I said. What is anyone meant to say to that?

She didn't look like a judge, or not like the stereotype of a judge. She was too attractive, still too young and female to fit the stereotype. Just as she'd done well for you, you'd done well for her, although it wasn't as though she was immediately appointed to the bench a week or two after your acquittal. There were many other cases, other triumphs, professional triumphs anyway.

She invited me to sit down and offered me coffee which I refused because I was too nervous to hold a cup with confidence. I wanted to establish a good enough rapport with her to enable me to ask her certain questions, most of which were really only half formulated. More perfectly imagined was the sense of calm I hoped to get from her answers.

'I'm sorry for the delay in getting back to you.'

'No, that's quite alright. I'm sure you must be . . . very busy.'

'My associate said you were a law student.'

'No, no, I'm majoring in psychology.'

'Not doing any law subjects at all?'

'No, psych and English mainly, some politics.'

'So you weren't looking for career advice in the law?'

'No . . . no, hardly.'

'Well, that's a relief . . . I suppose.' She seemed about as uncomfortable as I was.

'Why a relief . . . Judge?'

'Please, Rachael, call me Gina. I knew your father when you were a little girl.'

'Thank you.' I smiled, still nervous.

'It's a relief because the truth is, I don't know what advice to give a young aspiring lawyer. Try to be in the right place at the right time, perhaps. I don't know.'

'Do you mean try to get good cases?'

'Yes, that's a start. It's always good advice to be lucky, isn't it? Always was.'

'Was Simon Heywood's case a case worth getting?'

'In many ways. It was high profile but it was also high stress.'

'Higher stress than usual?'

'Yes, in many respects.'

'Why?'

'Oh boy!' she exhaled. 'Where do I start? Simon himself made it harder.'

'Really? Why? Was he difficult?'

'No, not really, hardly ever difficult. It's just that . . . there was a tendency to . . . this might sound strange . . . there was a tendency, at least for your father and me, a tendency to identify with him. Not with what he had done but—'

'Not with what he was *accused* of, you mean?'

'Yes, quite. Not with what he was accused of, but with Simon himself. So, as unpleasant as it is to see any of your clients, or nearly any, in prison, it was that much more unpleasant in Simon's case. Firstly, his circumstances were worse than usual, and then, I suppose . . . it was easier to see yourself in him.'

'Why?'

'Why were his circumstances worse than average or why was it easy to see one's self in him?'

'Well . . . both, I suppose.'

'His circumstances were worse than most because he had been in solitary confinement in the maximum security section of one of the largest prisons in the state for over a year and he hadn't been tried yet.'

'And why was it easier to identify with him?'

'I'm not sure what you know about Simon Heywood but—'

'My father kept a journal.'

'You've read the journal?'

'More than once. That's how I came to be here.'

'So then you know pretty much . . . everything.'

'I know a version of some of the things my father chose to put down. It can seem random, sometimes cryptic.'

'I don't doubt it. What can I tell you?'

'Why was it easier to identify with Simon Heywood than with other clients of yours? Because he's middle class?'

'No, there Rachael you're making assumptions about me *and* my clientele.'

'I'm sorry, I didn't mean to—'

'That's alright. Firstly, I have to make it clear that I didn't identify with Simon anywhere near as much as Alex, your father, did. One of the problems I had with your dad was the extent to which he took Simon on, not as a case, but as a cause. To me Simon was always a case and only a case. But he was a difficult case. In addition to his worse-than-usual circumstances and the tabloid publicity that comes with any child-related crime, he was so eminently likeable. It made it harder to be unemotional, harder to concentrate on forensic matters.'

'I'm sorry, but I still don't get it, not fully. What's wrong with liking him?'

'Well, to start with, all advocates, every one of them and I don't care how experienced they are, have a tiny little voice inside them that must be silenced at all costs. It's a voice that nestles somewhere deep inside them and surfaces only when they are up on their feet in court and about to speak. Then it screams, "You're ill-prepared. A few hours ago you were home asleep in bed in a foetal position. You are good at that. Do that!" And it's at precisely this time that you have to open your case.

'Now, if on top of this, you feel too much for your client, he's at real risk. The same applies to surgeons. Surgeons shouldn't operate on people they care too much about. It wasn't easy not liking Simon too much. Your dad couldn't do it. There was a friendship there. He liked him too much.'

'And you didn't?'

'I had a job to do. I wasn't there to be his friend. I wasn't there to make him feel good about himself. I was there to get him acquitted.'

'Well, you certainly did that.'

'No. It wasn't me.'

'What do you mean?'

'Two other women did that.'

'What other women?'

'Simon had a . . . a friend called Angela. You might have read about her in your dad's journal. She did a lot for Simon. She told a couple of different stories to the investigating detectives, another one at the committal hearing and was conveniently unavailable at the trial.'

'Unavailable?'

'She was in an accident and wasn't able to—'

'Oh yes, the accident. And the other woman?'

'I thought you read the journal? It's all in there.'

'One version of it.'

'Are you cross-examining me or your father retrospectively?'

'I'm sorry, Judge, I was—'

'Gina.'

'Sorry, Gina. I don't mean to sound as though—'

'No, Rachael, *I'm* sorry. You ask anything you like. I shouldn't be defending him, not to you, not after all these years.'

'I don't know. Maybe you should. But this other woman you mentioned—you mean Anna?'

'Yes, Anna. When it came time for me to cross-examine her, she changed her story.'

'What did she finally tell them?'

'Well, I don't know what is in the journal you've been reading but the way I remember it, and you can check my memory against the newspaper records—'

'No, that won't be necessary.'

'Rachael, dear, you don't have to defend your father either, not to me . . . All along, that is to the police, at the committal hearing and as far down the track as her evidence-in-chief at the trial, Anna's story had been that she hadn't seen Simon since they'd been university sweethearts. Then, all of a sudden in cross-examination, she showed a reluctance to repeat it. She tried not to answer the question, the all-important one about a romantic relationship with Simon way after university. So I put it to her, as I was obliged to, that she had been having an illicit relationship with her old boyfriend, Simon Heywood, and that, in fact, Simon hadn't taken Sam, her son, illegally because he'd had her permission to take him.

'She stalled as long as she could and then, when told by the judge that she couldn't refuse to answer, she said yes. She said it was true. In re-examination the prosecutor put the question to her again and again. She tried not to answer and again the judge ordered her to.'

'Did she repeat that Simon had her permission?'

'No, she didn't. The prosecutor reminded her that she was under oath. He asked her if she understood the gravity of a charge of perjury. She said she did and then she changed her story back again. She told the jury that Simon hadn't had her permission to take Sam. When asked why she had answered differently under cross-examination, she said that she'd felt sorry for him, seeing him there in the dock. She said that he was fundamentally a good person and that it would be criminal for him to spend years of his life in a prison. She effectively started a plea on his behalf.'

'She wasn't charged with anything, was she?'

'You mean perjury?'

'Yes.'

'No. No. She told one lie and then quickly took it back. But that was all she had to do to free him.'

'What do you mean?'

'By showing such reluctance to answer the question, then vacillating the way she did, first denying Simon had permission to take Sam, then lying, then coming back to her original story, she'd effectively torpedoed the prosecution case. Her own credibility was shot. Her performance was entirely consistent with our case that she was ashamed of the affair with Simon and was lying in order to save face and her marriage. There was enough reasonable doubt to drive a truck through. She really managed it all with one lie which she then took back in time to protect herself.'

'Don't you mean she only needed to tell the truth once?'

'Listen, Rachael, you've read the journal. You don't have to be coy about this. I know the real truth now.'

'I'm sorry. I'm not following you.'

'What a lawyer suspects and what she knows are not necessarily the same thing and when they're not the same thing, the difference between the two can be crucial.'

'So my father only gave you the version Simon wanted the court to believe. He never actually told you the real truth?'

'God no! He knew better than that.'

'Was that why ... Was that why the relationship, yours with him, ended?'

'Oh boy!' Gina exhaled again. 'This isn't what you expect after a long day in court. Look, Rachael, would you like to have dinner with me, maybe sometime next week?'

I wasn't going to turn that down and so began an irregular series of dinners, coffees and drinks with my new friend, Judge Serkin. I say my friend. I'd like to think that we were friends but who ever knows what people are to each other, right? Isn't that one of the things Dad was always on about to you, the ambiguity of relationships? Was I just using Gina to find out more about my father? Was she using me, perhaps, to expiate some kind of guilt she felt about what she had or hadn't done to my father? Maybe she just wants to pair me off with her son? She's mentioned him quite a few times. I've told her I'm sort of taken. I don't know anymore. Why am I asking you? I'm not. Forget it.

6

I met her for dinner that first time. After we'd ordered a drink but before we'd ordered the food, she explained one of the practice rules of the Victorian Bar. It requires that where a barrister learns during a hearing from the client (or a witness called on the client's behalf) that the client (or one of his witnesses) has lied to or misled the court, the barrister must then refuse to take any further part in the case unless the client authorises him to inform the court of the lie.

Our drinks had arrived. A waiter was hovering, waiting to take our food order but Gina either didn't see him or else ignored him.

'That is the rule now and it was the rule then, at the time of Simon Heywood's trial. I wanted the case. I was grateful to your father for recommending me to Simon, and I didn't want to lose the brief or the case. I didn't want to have to return the brief and let someone else take it. I'm not embarrassed to admit that a case like that was exactly what my career needed at the time.'

Then she noticed the waiter and what sounded like the beginnings of a self-defence or self-apologia, a spirited off-the-cuff plea in mitigation of something she hadn't yet decided to confess, not to me anyway, was put on hold.

'Your father was an unconventional man. That's part of what I liked about him.'

'And part of what you didn't?'

'He crossed the line within his own profession. That was his prerogative.'

'But you disapproved?'

'I don't know that it was my place to approve or disapprove.'

'Maybe it wasn't your place to disapprove of it professionally but—'

'Professionally, he was just a client's psychiatrist. He wasn't even a witness. He was never going to be.'

'But personally?'

'Personally? . . . Personally, your father was one of the finest men I've ever met.'

'And he disappointed you by deceiving you about Simon, telling you that Simon had always had Anna's permission to take Sam?'

'No. Firstly, as I think I've told you, he never said that.'

'Maybe he didn't actually say it but he let you believe—'

'Rachael, it wasn't that, that wasn't the problem. Hell, I knew, I mean I strongly suspected that Simon had taken the little boy without permission.'

'And you were insulted that my father could let you believe—'

'No, no. He knew that I knew . . . or suspected.'

'Suspected that you knew?'

'Knew that I suspected. I couldn't actually positively know or I'd have to give the case back. He knew that.'

'So . . . I don't get it. What was the problem?'

'Anna,' she said, taking a sip of her drink.

'What?'

'Anna was the problem.'

'Oh God! You're not going to say what I think you're going to say?'

'I don't know, what do you think I'm going to say?'

'What do you mean, Anna was the problem?'

'Alex, your father, and I had a tacit understanding.'

'Gina, is this going to make me feel sick?'

'Rachael, do you think I'm going to say something about your father's sex life?'

'Are you?'

'No, of course not. Your father and I did not have that kind of tacit understanding. What I mean is that we both knew that I had a fair idea that Simon wasn't telling me the truth and that whatever I might suspect, he, Alex, wasn't ever to confirm it or I'd have to drop the case.'

'Yes, okay, but what does this have to do with Anna, with my father and Anna?'

'Alex had crossed the line with respect to Simon long before I was involved.'

'Involved with my father?'

'Involved in the case. You see, at first, it seemed just . . . I don't know . . . diligence, no, more than that . . . a quite extraordinary dedication to his patient, a remarkable knowledge of him and a dangerous understanding of him.'

'Dangerous?'

'Rachael, maybe I'm being wise after the event or perhaps I'm not being wise and it's just that he's . . . your father isn't here now to point it out.'

'I'm not following you.'

'You're majoring in psychology, aren't you?'

'Trying to.'

'What is it called when a patient shifts certain emotional reactions onto the therapist and—'

'Transference.'

'Yes, transference.'

'Are you saying Simon experienced transference with respect to my father?'

'I don't know if he did but that's not what I'm saying. I'm saying your . . . I'm saying Alex experienced a certain reverse transference with respect to Simon. Look, I'm a lawyer, not a psychiatrist or a psychologist, but your father's capacity for empathy . . . Maybe it's possible for a therapist, or anyone . . . to empathise too much.'

'Let me make sure I'm understanding you. You're saying Dad empathised with Simon to the point of identifying with him and, in some way, absorbed his obsession with Anna Geraghty?'

'No, I'm not saying that. I'm not saying he empathised to the point of identifying with him and I'm certainly not saying he shared or in any way took on Simon's obsession with Anna.'

'So, what are you saying about him . . . and Anna?'

'When he socialised with Simon, when he went out for drinks with him, or walked with him, with him and Simon's friend, Angela—that was his business. It was unprofessional, contrary to his discipline and he knew it, but that was his business. But when, after Simon's arrest, he persisted in calling Anna, in trying to get her to tell the police that Simon had her permission to take her son, that was my business.'

'Why?'

'He could have been charged with all sorts of things, attempting to pervert the course of justice, hell, anything. She could've sought a restraining order against him.'

'But he wasn't your client. Simon was.'

'Rachael, I . . . I loved him.'

'Did you?'

'Oh yes. Of course I did. Didn't you know that?'

'I'd hoped you did.'

'Wasn't it clear from the journal, I mean? Didn't he know? He would have—'

'You had a conflict of interest.'

'What? What do you mean? Why do you say that? Did he write that in the—?'

'Simon's interests and my dad's interests; they weren't the same.'

'Well, yes, but . . . I don't see what you're getting at.'

'It was in Simon's interest to have my dad convince Anna to say whatever was necessary to get him, Simon, acquitted. It was in my father's interest to have nothing to do with her or, at least, as little as possible. In advising them both you can't—'

'No, you're wrong. Firstly, it was in Simon's interests not to have your father harassing—'

'Harassing?'

'Leaving himself open to allegations of harassment, intimidation of a witness. If the prosecution had any idea how many times Alex spoke to her or even how many times he *tried* to speak to her . . . leaving aside what it would have done to Alex in terms of criminal liability, in terms of his professional standing, it would have been disastrous for Simon's case.'

'Why?'

'Because it would have looked to a jury like your father was doing exactly what he was doing—trying to get this woman to lie for a friend, a friend who'd once been a patient.'

'But you're saying she did lie.'

'Well, not exactly.'

'Gina, I don't give a shit about the legal niceties. You knew what you knew and I don't care. I'm talking about my father.'

'I'm talking about him too . . . and I never do anymore. I don't know anyone who knew him.'

'Anyone else.'

'Else?'

'I knew him. You know me.'

'Yes, you were his little girl.'

'I was just one of two.'

'He talked about you.'

'Please, I don't mean to sound rude but . . . don't change the subject.'

'I thought you'd want to know what he said about—'

'Of course I do. You know I do, but I have to understand this. Anna said enough of what Simon needed her to say?'

'Yes.'

'You think my father talked her around?'

'He . . . I don't know that Simon would have been acquitted without him.'

'So it worked.'

'Alex took a huge risk, a stupid risk.'

'It paid off.'

'For Simon.'

'That's why you broke it off.'

'Well—'

'You were angry at him, so you broke it off.'

'I was angry. But that wasn't the reason.'

'Then why did you break it off with him? You loved him. He loved you.'

'Is that what he said? Is that what it says in the—'

'Why did you break it off with him?' I asked her. She took a sip from her glass, put two fingers to her lips and exhaled through the gap between them, like someone who had once smoked habitually. Then she spoke.

'You're going to have to put yourself in my position and, because we're talking about your father, I don't know if you're going to be able to. You're a young woman, Rachael, you've got your whole life ahead of you and—'

'Uh-oh.'

'What?'

'Well, you know you're in trouble when someone prefaces something they're about to say with, "You've got your whole life ahead of you."'

'Why?'

'Because it means the speaker is about to patronise you, to make all sorts of assumptions about you based on your youth and one of them is almost always that your pain is somehow worth less ounce for ounce than that of someone who was born earlier.'

'Rachael, I'm not discounting your pain. You're very quick to make assumptions.'

'Really? I thought I was being restrained. Blame it on my youth.'

'Rachael, it won't do you any good being angry with me, especially if you want my perspective on your father.'

'With respect, Your Honour, how many times can he die? I know the end of the story. I'm the sequel. And, anyway, I don't mean to make this sound like a trade negotiation but this is a two-way exchange of information. As you can imagine, he wrote about you in the journal.'

'Rachael, why are you angry with me?'

'I don't know . . . Because he's dead.'

'And because I'm not?'

'No, because you knew him better than I did; because he didn't love my mother anymore and because of something you were about to tell me before I snapped at you, something bad, something hard for you to say, to me, something which I'd find easier to understand if I had more of my life behind me.' On the last few words I was choking back tears I had promised myself not to show her. She took my hand and I was gone for all money, a sobbing mess of a half-orphan, no longer the young sophisticate I was pretending to be. Then the waiter came with our meals and she took her hand away.

7

What she would tell me does, I suppose, on reflection, make sense. At the time of your arrest and consequent need for her legal services, she was a divorced woman in her early forties with two children under ten. Although she already knew my father, this was the time when they re-entered each other's lives with unambiguous significance. The picture she painted of him made sense and yet, or maybe because it made sense, it sat uncomfortably with me. A handsome, unconventional man, a gentle medically educated iconoclast, cultured, with a certain old world charm but no *meshuggener*; that's what she fell for and probably what my mother fell for originally as well. That's what we all fell for. You too fell for this only in your case he seemed to be acting on a promise that was, for all the rest of us, only implied. He was going to make everything alright for you. Yes, he would love the rest of us and, yes, he would fight to save the public health system from the grasp of faceless men who wanted to turn everybody's ill-health into gold. But for you, he would go into battle every day, and the greater your problems, the deeper into them he would dive, risking his own well-being for yours. I think, at least for a time, you were the measure, yours was the case by which he would judge himself. If he failed you, he had failed. And why choose you for this august role? He chose you because he saw in you so much of himself, too much of himself.

So it flattered her that he would choose her to represent you. It was about the highest compliment he could pay her advocacy skills. And initially his dedication to your problems was admirable. And yes, everybody knew, by which I mean that my dad and she and, of course, you, knew that you had taken Anna's Sam without anyone's permission and that he couldn't tell her you had and that she couldn't ask or even admit her suspicion that you had. And maybe, as long as she didn't quite know, maybe it was forgivable to just once make contact with Anna and try to convince her that, for all your obsession-fuelled spur-of-the-moment recklessness, the greatest crime in all this would be to let you be convicted and die in prison.

Once, maybe he could do it once. Once was wrong, once was crazy, once was still a one-time breach of just about anything you can think of. But he didn't do it once. Anna was not interested in saving you, not at first, not at all, and that you wanted him to keep trying to get her to change her mind shouldn't have mattered. You were in prison, you were in extremis. This was not the time to take instruction from you, legal instruction maybe, but not an instruction to commit professional suicide.

When Gina learned that my father had been, not once, but repeatedly in contact with Anna, she was furious. Had Anna wanted to, she could have brought charges against your psychiatrist. They might have stuck too, in which case it would have meant not only the end of his practising career but possibly prison for him as well. It would have been disastrous for your case too. This isn't my opinion. This was what Gina said. What fun the prosecution would have had with the knowledge that the defendant's psychiatrist had attempted to bribe or intimidate or coerce the defendant's ex-girlfriend, mother of the kidnapped child, into changing her evidence, that he had attempted to pervert the course of justice. Gina said that she had pointed this out to him more than once and always very forcefully. But still, he kept calling her, calling Anna.

She told me that she was furious with him not merely because of the risks he was taking with your case and with his own career and indeed with his liberty. She said she came to realise she was furious at him because of what his repeated calls to Anna were doing to her, Gina. Anna could save you, she could save my father by not telling the police about his calls, but she could not save Gina, she could not save Gina from seeing something she had been closing her eyes to. Dad wasn't well.

And this was where she asked me to try for a moment to forget that he was my father and to put myself in her position. She had come out of what could best be described as a stale marriage but, she said, could at worst be much more colourfully described than that. The man she had married had given her two children before revealing himself to be competitive, insecure and selfish and not the man she thought she was getting. It was years before Gina had finally summoned up enough courage to leave him. While she didn't say she was positively reconciled to remaining on her own indefinitely, she said she was well aware before she left him that it was a distinct possibility. She left him anyway, taking her two children with her. She was renting a place and trying to keep her practice going when my father walked back into her life, this time in a starring role. Without ever saying anything to this effect, he was going to save her life too.

He brought her a high-profile, career-making case which he would, in his way, be working on with her. He was a dinner companion, a warm and worldly, intelligent, available professional man. But in persisting with his attempts to persuade Anna to perjure herself on your behalf, he was revealing something about himself she didn't want to see. For what does it say about a man that he will act so imprudently, even for a good cause, so detrimentally to himself and to those people he has a much greater obligation to help? It says, 'Do not invest too heavily here. This man is unwell.'

So she pulled away, just a little. But my father could tell she was becoming slightly distant. She wasn't a good enough actress to hide it. He broached it with her and, at first, she denied it. He implored her not to let any problems between them compromise her work for you. Then they argued. She said there weren't any problems between them other than his suggestion that her work on your case could be affected by her relationship with him. This, she now concedes, was untrue but at the time, she was unwilling to name their other problems. She had no qualms insisting he cease all attempts to contact Anna. That came within her professional purview. But how do you tell someone you love, a psychiatrist, someone who had been going to take care of you, that you have concerns for his mental health? They were both under enough stress already. You saw to that, as did the rest of their work, their exes and maybe even their children.

She said she was putting off sorting things out with him till your case was finished. But then came the bag of money he gave her and that ruined everything. You know where this money came from. It was the money Mitch had dumped on my father. It was the money he had helped Angelique win. Unable to contact Mitch or Angelique, my father decided after a while to apply it to your defence, as Angelique had intended, which meant giving it to Gina.

It's not clear from his journal whether this was a carefully considered use of the money or a spur of the moment decision. However he arrived at it, it was a grave miscalculation and I heard the way Gina received it. I had not wanted to hear the way she received it and it took two further meetings before she was able to get me to shut up and listen, before she was able to get me to stop defending him.

He arrived at her home one evening when they were meant to be going out for dinner. Her children and the constraints that went with them were at her mother's and when he gave her the money in a bag, her response was consequently unconstrained. Where did he suddenly get this money? Wasn't he short of money and why was he suddenly giving it to her? None of his answers, as true as they were, made things any better. The money was, in a roundabout way, from Simon, he told her. Don't laugh. There's a way in which it was. Angelique had Mitch help her get the money to cover your legal expenses and Mitch had entrusted my father with it when he couldn't find Angelique. My father, having tried unsuccessfully to call Mitch, was then giving it to Gina. But it seemed there was no way to make any of this sound reasonable and it only further contributed to her picture of my father as unstable. She told him she was already getting paid to defend you, that Legal Aid was paying for it. He said he knew that but the Legal Aid scale of fees was way below what a privately funded client would pay and that, anyway, she was working around the clock on the case and wasn't charging for even half the time she was putting in. The money he had brought would help redress the imbalance. But it was a bag with $30 000 in notes and the truth, as it came out of my father, with his description of his angry, mysterious, uncontactable patient, sounded fantastic to the point of bizarre.

She was suddenly being forced to confront all her doubts about him. Her response was explosive. It is still emotional, even in the retelling but it's no longer red hot and out of control. At the time, in addition to her disillusionment, her disappointment in him, there was the insult to her and the squalidness of the whole thing. She had fallen in love with him and there he was turning up with a bag full of money, ostensibly on your behalf. She had never threatened to withdraw from your case. On the contrary, when there had been a bureaucratic glitch, when Legal Aid had tried to pressure you to enter a plea of guilty by threatening they'd withdraw funding if you didn't, she had gone into battle to ensure that your trial was funded irrespective of the plea.

It was one thing, she said, to be a little obsessive in his 'pastoral' care for you, one thing to try to persuade Anna to lie for you, but this money in a bag, this was something else altogether. She even wondered about the ethics and legality of accepting the money. An honest lawyer, despite the popular stereotype, will run a mile to get away from a pile of money in a brown paper bag. And if he was prepared to jeopardise her career and reputation this way, what did it say about the sincerity of his feelings for her? She was bewildered and hurt. How had she allowed herself to fall in love with him? Her judgment with respect to men was obviously still suspect. The hunger that lives in a failed marriage had snuck up on her and impaired her discrimination. She said that this was what she was thinking at the time, and at that time, it might even have been that night, she broke it off with my father.

The way she told it, it made sense for her to have the doubts she had and to end it. The way he wrote about it, it made sense for him to give her the money. He was devastated when she ended it. He hadn't seen it coming at all. Whether or not they would have made a successful couple, I'm in no position to say. When one first meets her, or should I say when I first met her, she seemed too cold for him, not warm enough. Not warm enough for the father I remember from my childhood. But she warms up and, after a while, she talks about him with a tenderness I cannot always bear. It makes the way their relationship ended all the more tragic.

Why didn't they talk more? I'm guessing he was too hurt, too embarrassed to plead his own case with anything like the vigour with which he'd pleaded yours. People who are in the business of saving the world don't get ditched by their girlfriends. It's inconsistent with their self-image, I suppose. And for Gina, the money was the last straw. The man was clearly unwell. Given enough breathing space, one or both of them might have been able to put it all in context. But it seems there was no breathing space.

8

My father had received a letter from Mitch. 'You've failed me. I'm not coming back,' it announced. My father, concerned about his emotional state, phoned him a number of times but Mitch was either always out or just not taking the calls. He was anxious to identify the specific nature of Mitch's dissatisfaction and either address it or, at least, recommend another psychiatrist. The only response his calls could elicit was another letter from Mitch reiterating that he wasn't coming back to see him and that he should stop phoning him. 'You've failed me and I'm finished with you,' it concluded. Again my father left messages and again they went unanswered.

It was then my father took the unusual step—in fact it was unprecedented other than in your case—of making a house call. Without warning and despite Mitch's hostility to him, my father drove to the address on Mitch's file. He rang the doorbell and waited. He waited for quite some time. He had in mind, I suppose, that Mitch was partially incapacitated. It's not clear from the journal what my father was going to say. Maybe, as he waited for the door to open, he didn't know either. But the door didn't open.

Dad was going to leave when through the curtain he saw a light on somewhere deep inside the house. Something possessed him to lean against the front door and when he did, it moved slightly. He called out through the gap several times but there was no answer. After waiting a little while longer he pushed the door again, tentatively. Its progress was being impeded by something. My father called out to Mitch a few more times before forcing the door wide open. When his further calls were met with silence he stepped inside the house. There he saw what had been somehow jammed up against the door. It was, my father wrote, Mitch's cane or walking stick. My father recognised it from their sessions. It was all very strange. Apprehensively, and calling out 'hello' as he went, he made his way to the only room with a light on. It was an upstairs bedroom and the bedside lamp burned hot, illuminating in the bed the man referred to in the journal as Mitch, nearly too cold to be alive and no longer with thoughts too sad for dreaming. Unconscious, he lay there still and still there in new flannel pyjamas, the cellophane and cardboard packaging strewn on the floor. That's how my father found him.

The paramedic in the ambulance my father called could not tell him which hospital they were taking Mitch to. The closest, he said, might still be on ambulance bypass. Sufficient hospital beds were not a government priority. The paramedic didn't say that. My father did.

Gina hadn't known anything about this at that time. How could she have? How could she have known? She could have called him. Why didn't she call him? When the jury finally came back with their verdict and found you 'not guilty', whether it was through Gina's skill or Anna's momentary *entrechat* between her honesty and your liberty, Gina could have called my father. But she didn't call him on that late afternoon. I can barely imagine the afternoon your nightmare ended. He wasn't in court. He couldn't be there which was, in itself, a minor tragedy. Did you have a chance, near the climax of it all, to wonder why?

He couldn't be there because, not knowing what time the jury would be ready to return its verdict, he was frantically busy trying to find out which hospital an overdose victim, a former patient of his, a one-time analyst in a stockbroking firm, Dennis Mitchell, had been taken to. And when he'd located the hospital, it took him a while to determine Mitch's condition. The enquirer, he had to explain, was the patient's former psychiatrist. He was also the one who had found him and called the ambulance and, yes, the one who'd prescribed the sleeping pills he'd overdosed on. The duty ER physician informed my father that they'd got him in time and that he'd be alright.

That my father found Mitch, that no one else was visiting him, might go a long way toward explaining why it was that, evidently, given the new pyjamas, Mitch or Mr Mitchell had opted to determine 'check out' time for himself. But it did not explain, not to my father, why he, my father, had not anticipated such an eventuality by taking more care with Mitch when he was still keeping his appointments. However hard he might have taken the suicide or attempted suicide of any of his patients, this one seemed to have delivered an extra blow, what you might call a guilt-edged guilt.

In part, this was due to the note. Mitch had left a note. In it he blamed his ex-wife, the Family Court, his former boss, Sam's father, Donald Sheere, the character who ran the work retreat at which he was injured—he listed a cast of thousands. He blamed them all for what had befallen him, for what he was about to do. The cast included my father, and not as a bit-player either. My father kept the note. He explains in the journal that he wanted to analyse it more carefully. He thought it might prove of some assistance if Mitch eventually came back to him for treatment. And if he didn't, if he saw some other psychiatrist, it could be of value to him.

When Gina didn't receive any message of congratulations from my father after your acquittal, she assumed his silence was born of a rejected man's injured pride. He, or maybe even you, should be so incredibly proud of me for the restraint I showed as I sat there, gripping one hand with the other, and Gina told me her sorry interpretation of his silence. What happened, what exactly happened when, standing in the dock, you were referred to for the last time as 'the prisoner' and asked by the judge's associate to stand to take the jury's verdict? I can imagine a court room in the city some twelve years ago filled to the gills with representatives of the media and members of the public who happened to be in the right place at the right time and just couldn't believe their luck almost as much as they were not going to believe yours. I can easily imagine a packed room lined with wood panelling which has, since its construction, absorbed so many waves of anxiety and fear that it has lost the capacity to absorb those about to compete with the rising din from people whose excitement exceeds the level they are institutionally permitted to exhibit. It is here that you are led to the dock.

The judge enters and everyone stands, then the jury enters and only you stand. The foreman of the jury—I'm assuming it was a man because had it been a woman, I'm sure Dad would have mentioned it—is asked if the jury has reached a verdict on all of the charges. He says 'yes' and as each of the charges is put to him he responds, 'not guilty'. Were there gasps? Did your eyes moisten? Were your parents there? They must have been, surely? Did you want to shout or cry? I can even imagine you wanting to make some sort of speech or public declaration, a plea on behalf of pedantic, lying child-stealers everywhere. I can imagine all and any of that, believe me. I wish I'd been there to see it. Really, I do. I really wish I'd been there, if not for the drama of the moment then at least to fly the flag, so to speak, to represent all the Klimas who couldn't be there but without whom you would still be in prison.

While I have no trouble imagining the day or even the hour of your acquittal, I cannot for the life of me, or of him, imagine why you didn't insist that Gina call him. Did you have a drink with her? Did you go out and drink yourself spastic for three days straight only to find yourself hungover wearing the clothes you were wearing at the time of your arrest, at the time someone else's six-year-old child was asleep at your feet?

One can also imagine the period immediately subsequent to your release. Your family would have welcomed you back, at least briefly, although, from what I've read about them, and given the mud, the ignominy you'd traipsed through the house, the prodigal son's welcome would've worn thin not long after the flashes from the cameras of the press waiting outside the court had faded. You left messages for Dad from your parents' place but he didn't want to call you there. Well, he was reluctant to call you there. To your credit, you did set about trying to find Angelique. As for the clandestine meetings with

Anna Geraghty, you know what my father made of that, don't you? Maybe you don't. But is this more or less what happened?

That's more or less the way Sam tells it, that part of it. Have you ever heard Sam's version? You'd like it. He doesn't spit it out, not exactly. It takes a while before he's comfortable enough with someone new, but then it tumbles out of him like a chivalric romance of yore. I'm someone new. How do you do? We were going to meet sooner or later.

9

Sam is quite uncharacteristically uncynical about the story of his mother, his still young and beautiful mother and how she overcame convention in the public eye of a court room at the eleventh hour to save her childhood sweetheart, letting the loose renegade thread of her never-ending affection for you snare the yarn of her stultifying marriage and completely unravel it. The formal resurrection of the relationship between you and Anna and your subsequent renaissance, that bit gets glossed over. Not so in the journal, where my father described the gradual beginnings of the reconciliation of Anna and you as 'a marriage between your enduring obsession and her pragmatism'. Why pragmatism? Well, I'm guessing it's because by the time you were acquitted, Sam's father, Joe, had been all but destroyed in most respects, and whoever she'd really had waiting in the wings—the one Sam has always been permitted, even encouraged, to think was you—well, this white knight had slunk out the back with the chorus when the house lights were turned on again. And I'm not getting the part about Joe Geraghty, Sam's dad, from the journal. I get that from Sam himself.

You see, I'm the one you and his mother get to only hear about, the mysterious one you never meet. He stays over at his girlfriend's place all the time. He's even been away with her a couple of times for weekends yet you and Anna have never even met her. Now you know why, and I can tell you, it hasn't been easy. He obviously never even knew you had a psychiatrist, and I wasn't going to tell him, however much he could have benefited from an explanation. He's very sweet, your stepson. He tries to appear detached about such things, but he's not very good at it, which makes him all the more cute.

He tries to pretend that he's not in the least put out by the fact that, not only have I never shown the slightest interest in meeting the two of you, but I actively come up with excuses not to. I know it hurts him and, believe me, I hate doing anything that's even remotely likely to hurt him but, given our family histories, I haven't really felt I could.

It's actually your fault we met in the first place. It was your influence he says that got him to take psychology in first year. What were you thinking? That's not actually where I met him but it's where I became aware of him—initially as just a sweet, very good-looking young man who seemed most obviously uncomfortable only when he was having difficulty playing down his own earnestness. It was a very big class and at first I didn't even know that the name, Sam Geraghty, which I'd seen a little above my own on various noticeboards, belonged to him. That it did I learned later, without making any special effort, I might add. I'm human and that weakness sufficed. The academic year was ending and I think maybe we smiled at each other in doorways and corridors a few times. He says he doesn't even remember that but I don't believe him. He's a terrible liar. But I'm not.

Was it really him, this man who looked so good in every sense of the word? It had been towards the middle of that year that I first read my father's journal and learned about the Sam Geraghty my father's patient had taken from school one afternoon twelve years earlier. Not that it really mattered to me whether he was the same Sam Geraghty or not. I liked the look of him anyway. So I couldn't lose. That was my thinking. I'll admit I was a little cavalier, I suppose, because I didn't really think it was him. Of course, the realisation after just a short conversation that he was Sam Geraghty did nothing to dampen my growing enchantment. I wanted to swallow him whole. Who could blame me? Pretty much anyone but you. You know what it is like to be so fuelled by something that everything you do is an error waiting to be discovered.

Before I knew it, it was the full-blown undergraduate courting catastrophe. We would lie beside each other on a couch or on the floor and his past would take shape before my eyes as he spoke about it. Do you remember such a time? It seems to come when you're still young enough to be telling it for the first time but already old enough to need to tell it. It comes around the time you and your lover regularly pretend to be nonchalant about each other's nakedness, it comes around the time you laugh yourselves to tears in bed in the dark, singing the very worst pop songs of your shared youth, the more esoteric the better. Yes, you remember. You're going to implore me to hang on to these memories with all my might. There'll be no other time like this, right? Somewhere in all this we started filling in the dots of our lives for each other, as one does. Everyone has some story, right? But it's very few people who get caught out not knowing that they're getting it wrong. They're getting their own story wrong and they don't realise it. Sam and I, we were never entirely strangers. I knew he had some of it wrong. You saw to that.

He became quite confessional after a short time and I learned about his parents' break-up and the alleged kidnapping, all of which I already knew the truth about, and I was kind of sad for him and a little disgusted with you and Anna for keeping up the lie all these years. Perhaps because my interest in his past was more than polite, he began to tell me about his troubled relationship with his father.

He told me how, as a little boy, he had seen his father viciously assault someone by the swimming pool in the family's back yard. He'd heard sounds coming from the back while he was inside. A photographer was trying to take pictures of him or the house for one of the tabloids. It was after you'd taken him. His mother tried to keep him from the window but he sneaked a look and then, when Anna apparently had to rush out to keep Joe from killing the guy, little Sam pulled back the curtains and watched the whole thing. He saw his father rain blows on the man, on the man's face with his fists. He remembered what he described as a sea of red. How does a small child process that, the sudden creation of a sea of red issuing from a man's face as a result of the incessant hammering of the mallet at the end of each of his father's trunk-like arms? He has dreamed about it, and not merely as a kid, but as an adult too. Did you, did Anna, think he would forget? But whatever you thought about their relationship, you still encouraged, pressured, Sam to see his father. 'I love you, Sam, but I'm not your father,' you would say. Then Anna would chime in, 'Yes, sweetheart, you only have one father. He loves you very much . . . in his own way.' Was that to assuage your guilt?

He knew he had only one father. His father was the guy whose fists could turn a man's face to liquid before a child's horrified and disbelieving eyes. He was the one who had the suspended sentence hanging over his head for years after that assault. Was that what Anna meant by Joe loving Sam 'in his own way'? I have no doubt that Sam grew up a little scared of him. Could you not see that or was it that you would let nothing stand in the way of a little time alone together without the boy? His father drank, enough for a little boy to notice. Didn't anyone else notice? Then there was the bizarre succession of what Sam says

Joe variously called 'second', 'new' or 'other' mums. He says it was as though his father was getting them out of a catalogue, trying them out, then returning them. Did you know that from his bedroom in a few of the places Joe lived, Sam could hear his father and these women have sex on the other side of the wall and that for a long time he tried to pretend to himself it was the sound of cats outside his window? When he couldn't fool himself any longer, he took to putting the pillow over his head and singing the pop songs of the day to himself till the final cry that signalled an at least temporary halt in his father's desperate attempt to dull the pain that drove him to live like that.

But for all the unpleasantness of one night a week and every second weekend with his father, the packaged food, the strained good humour, for all that Sam hated it, he felt guilty and even ashamed that he did. Joe was trying and Sam knew that he was. It was just that his father completely failed to 'get' him. From as far back as Sam can remember, his father never understood him, well before he was a teenager and was meant to be misunderstood. It was as though the two of them weren't related. Each birthday or Christmas, Joe would give him some elaborate and obviously expensive toy which had the effect of rubbing his face in their failure to have any kind of relationship that was not simply one that went, however politely, through the motions. Sam would always pretend to like the gift but he knew that Joe knew that he really didn't. These gifts, sad bribes—call them what you will—would sit in boxes on the floor of the room allocated to Sam each time his father moved from one place to another. It got to where the boxes would overflow and the gifts would spill out onto the carpet and break under the feet of a little boy trying to find the bathroom in the dark, while in the next room his dad was attempting to fuck his way out of this year's rented accommodation into a brighter future, a golden past, some heaven that did not resemble the way things actually were.

Then there were the times when, fuelled by drink, Joe would decide to share some insights with his boy, insights into Sam's mother, and more often into you. He seemed to hold you responsible for pretty much everything except cholera, and particularly for the distance between him and Sam. In a way, there was something in this. It wasn't that you or even Anna were turning Sam against him by speaking ill of him. Quite the opposite. Sam has spoken of how much the two of you would plead with him to go to Joe's. But such is Sam's affection and regard for you and, from what I've read of you in the journal, such is his emulation of you, that Joe, however obtuse he is, could not have but seen it. Sam is just too much like you and too little like his father. Or should I say that he's more like Anna than he is like Joe? But the way my father tells it, if Sam is more like Anna than he is like Joe, at least in terms of Sam's interests and his sensibility, it is because she has taken on so much of you. Am I unfair to her? Do I flatter you? Whatever the case, the things that made me fall for him—beyond his looks which, excepting his stature, clearly come from Anna—equally clearly do not come from Joe. How can I be so sure of this? Well, even apart from what Sam himself says, which, as we know, can be wrong, I've seen Joe Geraghty for myself. I'll get to it. I promise.

As far as I know, you and Anna exhibited a discretion Sam's father and the new 'mothers' could not be relied upon to match. Sam never heard the two of you writhing at night. If he ever did, he hasn't mentioned it to me. But he heard you. You cried out in the middle of the night and the sound of your cries would wake him. It distressed him far more than the sounds from his father's various bedrooms over the years. And it didn't really help much when his mother explained why you cried out and from where the nightmares came, that they were a legacy of your time in prison. The explanation meant that there was no reason you should ever stop crying out in the night and it did more than this. It forced a critical re-examination of the myth he was inheriting, the myth of Anna and Simon. What does it say about his mother that she would let Simon, the Simon he loved more than his own father and that she too was always meant to have loved more than his father, rot in prison for even one day, let alone for however long it was? If his mother could abandon Simon while weighing up her options, who else could she abandon and under what circumstances? What would it take for his mother to abandon him? What if he stopped bringing home good marks? What if he didn't practise the piano? I'm not saying these fears are your fault.

As long as he heard you cry out in your sleep someone was going to have to explain the nightmares to him. And you were probably right to eventually disregard Anna's advice not to write about your time in prison. I'm sure she genuinely thought writing about it would only bring it all back to you but since it had obviously never left you, and the book no doubt kick-started your academic career, I think we can safely say she was mistaken. She would have to admit that now, wouldn't she? As ever, she was just trying to be practical. You really should have talked to someone professionally. In the absence of that, it makes sense to have written it all down. Wouldn't Dad have said that?

The question of Mitch's intention exercised my father's mind excessively. Mitch had taken too many pills in too short a space of time to continue living. That was straightforward; a conclusion reached by way of the empirical and quantitative side of medical science. 'What was his intention, Dr Klima?' my father himself asked on many occasions as though he might respond, 'Bear with me, will you, I'll just go and look that up.' Had Mitch meant to kill himself? You bet he had. Dad knew it, at least in the same way, I suppose, that Gina knew that you did not have permission to take Sam to your home.

But that wasn't really knowing. That was only suspecting strongly. Other than by asking Mitch, and he didn't want to talk to my father, how could he know? Through a note. One in four suicides leaves a note. That's the average. The presence or absence of a note is indeterminative, of course, unless the note evinces an intention explicitly or implicitly. The note can just say 'goodbye'. That's enough. It can attempt to explain. Few notes attempt to explain and even fewer succeed in providing any real explanation. Usually they're banal, which tends to make them, in their context, perhaps the most haunting documents imaginable. These are the ones written as though the suicide has just stepped out to buy some bread and milk and is leaving some hastily dashed-off instructions: take care, study hard, sorry for ducking out but it seemed like the best thing to do, I've fed the dog, so tired of this, be good to yourself.

Virginia Woolf began the second of two suicide notes to her husband by exonerating him.

> *Dearest,*
> *I want to tell you that you have given me complete*
> *happiness. No one could have done more than you have*
> *done.*
> *Please believe that.*

But you probably already knew that.

Mitch had written a note. If the attempt was genuine you have to think about the mind of the man whose last act of communication with the world was a note like his. How much anger must he have had inside him to write, not to his son—he had a son—but to the world at large, excoriating just about everybody he'd ever known and blaming them for his problems. On the other hand, it might not have been a genuine attempt. It might have been a *cri de coeur*. He hadn't answered his phone for weeks. He'd left his front door open. Perhaps he was counting on somebody, it could even have been my father, finding him in time as he lay there in his new pyjamas.

Better than a note is a previous attempt. A previous suicide attempt is the best predictor. My father made a note of a British study that showed that almost forty per cent of successful suicides have a history of previous attempts. But none of this guarantees anything. Sixty per cent of successful suicides are not known to have made serious attempts to take their own lives before their first and last attempt.

My father had had suicides before and he'd have them again. Goes with the territory, right? No, wrong. This one was different. My father was damned. He tortured himself wondering if he should have seen it coming, if he should've made his house call sooner, if he should've tried harder to get him back into therapy, if he should've referred him to another therapist. Or if he should've had him committed.

But there were no apparent grounds for having him committed. There are a lot of angry people out there and a lot of unhappy ones. Very few unhappy ones kill themselves. In his journal, Dad quotes a Hungarian-born psychiatrist, Thomas Szasz: 'Happiness is an imaginary condition, formerly often attributed by the living to the dead, now usually attributed to adults by children, and by children to adults.' No, Mitch did not present as a suicide risk.

11

I searched everywhere for a while looking for a note from Sam. I thought he might want to explain what the hell was going on. I cried for a few days, probably because, in reality, part of me had actually already figured it out. But we make the phone calls, leave the messages and then visit the haunts, at first in hope, and then more in homage. Don't you agree? It's only after this that we start to mentally retrace the last steps.

It might sound incredible to you but I think our problems began with a political argument. I say incredible not because politics is not important to either of us. It is. We're both intellectually, and even emotionally, politically engaged. It's incredible because, fundamentally, we agree politically on very nearly everything. He credits you with his political awareness, which is a credit to him. When I've told him this, he's said that my telling him is a credit to me. So, with all this mutual appreciation, where did things go wrong?

The peculiar striations that define someone's personality are too numerous to know, no matter how close the observer. A person we think we know can suddenly become someone else when previously hidden strands of their character are called to the fore by circumstance. Sam might have been intellectually, and even emotionally, politically engaged but he was never likely to become politically active. This much I could have predicted. What I couldn't have known was how he was going to react to me telling him I was thinking of doing something as trivially party-political as handing out how-to-vote cards at the impending federal election. I didn't ask him if he wanted to do it with me, knowing full well that he wouldn't, but from the strength of his response I thought, possibly flattering myself, that he might feel a little threatened by my contact with other men in the party.

'You're jealous, aren't you? Admit it,' I gently taunted before I'd registered the sternness of his countenance.

'Jealous of what?'

'Of the time I'll be forced to spend in the company of all those serious young men working their way up the party machine.'

'The ladder.'

'What?'

'You work your way up a ladder, not a machine.'

'Really, what do you do with a machine?'

'You get caught in it.'

That wasn't it. He didn't feel threatened. He was disappointed, disappointed in me. My sudden need to be politically involved was to him a shocking betrayal, not political, but personal. We didn't do that sort of thing. We were loners, not 'joiners'. That was the deal, or part of it, and I was reneging. It wasn't even all that important to me. I thought maybe I might meet one like-minded interesting person, male or female. It wasn't meant to signal any dissatisfaction with him. I was just thinking out loud. It was just an idea I'd had.

'Are you doing this for political reasons or social reasons?'

'I'm not even sure I'm doing it.'

'But if you do?'

'I don't know . . . a little of both. Political really . . . mainly.'

'Really?'

'Why do you say that like it's the wrong answer?'

'Hey, you decide . . . what's right for you.'

'What does that mean? You want to get rid of this government.'

'Of course I do but . . .'

'But what?'

'I don't know . . . Buchanan. It's fucking Buchanan.'

'Well, you're going to vote for him.'

'I'm voting against the government.'

'It's the same thing.'

'It's not the same as actually campaigning for him.'

'It's just, you know . . . how-to-vote cards. I'm not even sure I'd—'

'Rachael, how could you even contemplate it? Buchanan is so . . . where do I start?'

'Oh, that's right, your mother or Simon or someone said he's sleazy. Well, they're all sleazy. And what do they mean by that anyway? What was the story? He made a pass at your mother or something ten or twenty years ago? Didn't everybody? Let's assume he's the biggest womaniser on either side of politics. Frankly, that doesn't bother me, and—'

'It's more than that. Look at him on television. He sweats insincerity. What do you like about him?'

'He's not the government.'

'So vote for him by all means, but, for God's sake, don't campaign for him! He's like the mob that's in but less so. Name one policy of his you like. You can't.'

He had me there and with every second I cast about, my mind flailing for a policy I positively liked, I looked more naïve, more juvenile, more like what I was. I just liked the idea of being part of something bigger than me and my arts degree, my interstate mother and sister and my dead father. Then I came up with a policy, one policy.

'The Patients' Bill of Rights. He's said he'd introduce a Patients' Bill of Rights to stop people getting ripped off by health insurance companies. You're in favour of that, aren't you?'

'Yes, but look how long it took you to think of it.'

'Well, that's not *his* fault.'

'No, but you're the one who wants to campaign for him. And maybe it *is* his fault.'

'Why?'

'Because he only came up with a Patients' Bill of Rights when he was pushed and even then all he's really said is that he'll consider it. If he does consider it he won't legislate it and if he does it'll have loopholes big enough for the health insurance companies to drive their ambulances through. Did you know he also agrees to limiting compensation for medical negligence and for work injury? He's in the pocket of the insurance industry like all the rest of them.'

'So, Sam, if he's that bad, how come you're going to vote for him?'

'Because the other side is worse.'

'Well, at least he *says* the right things.'

'Oh, Rachael, by all means vote for him but as you look around for something to believe in, don't shout "Eureka" when your eye falls on him.'

'This is all about your insecurity, isn't it?' I shouted. I was hurt and I was wrong.

I was wrong because, while there probably was some element of insecurity in his response, it was far from what all this was about. I was hurt because he'd exposed in me a need to find something to belong to. But he was hurt too. He was hurt and angry that I needed to belong to something bigger than us.

So with both of us hurt, we argued more and our voices grew louder. We said things we shouldn't have said. I told him he needed to form his own opinions and not rely on his mother and stepfather to tell him what to think. It was around that time, give or take a few gratuitous expletives and insults, that he walked out.

12

'Give me a psychotic any day,' my father began a passage which I think, no, I'm sure, was about you. 'The problem with this man,' he wrote, 'was that he was too reasonable. He was too likeable. He made too much sense. One could easily have been him.' He's writing about you and yet he lapses into past tense.

After Anna had done the right thing by you, made you an honest, or should I say, a not guilty man, and the two of you started . . . what . . . courting, my father seemed to feel that he'd lost you. See the way he switches to past tense? It might sound strange, but I think he thought that he'd failed you. He saw your obsession with Anna as an illness, or a symptom of one. He was meant to cure you of it. When you were acquitted and free and everybody, and especially you, started behaving as though you really had been having an affair with her, he felt defeated, maybe even cheated.

But it's possible to fool a therapist, even a good one, isn't it? When you first came to him, or rather, when you first came to each other, my father didn't think you were all that unwell. Your concern for others was, he thought, inconsistent with serious depression. The extent of your illness became impossible to ignore only when you decided to include kidnapping in your decalogue of moral imperatives. It was a deterioration Dad had been unable to predict.

He wrote about you that within you a highly developed sense of morality, of empathy, coupled with a vigorous almost muscular rationality, was continuously at war with a disorder characterised by an obsessive longing for Anna, chronic feelings of emptiness, fears of abandonment and, fleetingly, by intense periods of anger, all of which made you feel greatly ashamed. This madness (my word for it, not his) he felt was, in part, the cost of so much time spent seeing things too clearly. It's a cost most people know instinctively is too high. 'The illumination is not worth the candle,' my father writes wryly. So most of us get by by not seeing things too clearly. Everything is a little blurred but, being always this way, people don't notice it and we say that each of them is a picture of mental health.

I would like to have discussed your case with my father. I think his writing permits me to at least speculate that you were a classic victim of what Durkheim calls *anomie*, the situation that pertains when all traditional social bonds and all genuine social life have been destroyed. Doesn't that sound like you at that time? As Fromm points out, for *anomie* to be removed, it's not enough simply for someone to be fed and clothed. There must be some not insignificant coincidence of interests between those of society and those of the individual. Unfortunately, consumption and competition, which are what currently drive society, have never been valued highly by you. I would like to have talked to him about that.

Dad was interested in the question of how people respond to the burden of unremitting acuity. That might be part of the explanation for his tremendous interest in you. More and more as I make my way through the journal I see him talk about a division between those people who are burdened by the clarity with which they see the world and those who are not. For those who are not, any semblance of emotional stasis or equilibrium is threatened only by things particular to them. If they, personally, can avoid poverty, substance abuse, sexual abuse, unemployment, divorce, physical illness, random violence or moving house, they might well feel and be considered mentally healthy.

But what about the other group, those who, even if only fleetingly and from time to time, are encumbered by their perception of the way the world really is? This group presented a problem for my father. Was he really prepared to categorise only the fortunate and simple or obtuse as mentally healthy? Most people are not all that fortunate and not that simple. Was he really prepared to deem the vast majority of people mentally unwell?

Naturally, he was dissatisfied leaving things like this, and here is where Seligman and Beck first make their way into the journal. Did he ever talk to you about Marty Seligman? He and Aaron Beck were the Empsons of cognitive therapy. If he didn't talk to you about them, he would have eventually. It was Seligman who came up with the concept of 'learned helplessness'.

Sometime in the sixties, Seligman devised an experiment in which a group of dogs were exposed to a series of mild and random electric shocks under conditions in which the dogs were unable to avoid the shocks. Each time before receiving a shock, the dogs would hear a warning tone. The conditions were then changed so that, each time they heard the warning tone, they would now be able to avoid the shock by jumping over a low bar. Seligman was expecting that the dogs would learn that the tone meant an impending shock and that they would then know to jump over the bar whenever they heard it. This wasn't what happened.

When the dogs heard the tone they just whimpered, lay down in front of the bar and accepted the shock. Seligman concluded that the first stage of the experiment—the one where there was nothing the dogs could do to escape the shock—had 'taught' them to be helpless. Without any apparent way of controlling their circumstances, the dogs became resigned to their fate. This state of hopeless resignation Seligman called 'learned helplessness'.

My father hypothesised that many, if not most, of those people who were neither fortunate nor obtuse learned to be helpless. This is how a huge proportion of society goes through each day. Whatever you think of this, it certainly accounts for those people who recognise the way things really are both in the world and in their lives and who do nothing about it. They do nothing because they feel helpless. You flirted with helplessness for a long time and then acted decisively to change your circumstances. You thrashed about, got yourself locked up and then manipulated your way back into the mainstream. What can we learn from you? Nothing, you *were* unwell.

There's a huge gap of some twelve or so years in my knowledge of your illness. Perhaps you are not ill at all anymore? The way Sam tells it, with the exception of your nightmares—a legacy of your time in prison—you have lived pretty much happily ever after. I know that he would think that, in the couple that has been us, Sam and me, I have been the naïve one. But I don't quite believe that you walked out of prison, smiled for the cameras and for your family and lived happily ever after. Nothing is ever that smooth. In the grafting of you to Anna and to her then little boy, you would have experienced at least moments of rejection. And there would always have been the worry that if Anna could ditch her husband, her son's father, for a crazy obsessive with a dubious history—you used to drink, you were chronically out of work, and you stole her son—if she could leave him for you, then perhaps her eyes might not remain permanently fixed on you either? When does a woman with twenty-twenty vision close her eyes to the next best thing? You think I am unfair? I am, and yet you know that she was seeing someone when you took Sam and that it wasn't you. When no one else knew, it was easy to kid yourself that, in taking a chance on her after all that had happened, you weren't crazy. But now, well there's the problem.

13

My mother and elder sister live interstate and the quality of their advice is—I try to be objective—unreliable. My father is famously not alive. Sometimes, seeing myself this way, I act like a child. I let a day and a half go by after Sam and I had that ridiculous argument without making any attempt at reconciliation. What marked the passing of the day and a half was not me not contacting him but him not contacting me. I wasn't going to call him. He'd been the one to walk out. You can guess at around what age I stopped growing up.

Knowing my lecture timetable, Sam knew when I wouldn't be in. (I rarely miss classes. You can say what you like but I'm not so inse-cure that I need to affect indifference to my courses.) He was therefore able to get into the student residence I live in, he has a key to my room, when I wasn't there. I'd been practising a sort of punc-tuated self-restraint. I wouldn't call him before lunchtime and then, having survived to lunch, not before dinner and so on. When I came home that day racked with doubt about the wisdom of not having called him, I was overjoyed to find he had left a bunch of flowers and a card for me.

The card was soppy, at least objectively. Subjectively, it was just what I needed. In it he asked me to call him when I got home. I was so relieved that we were about to make up and that it was he who'd made the first move. There was nothing now to be gained by waiting further. As soon as I'd read the card I kicked off my shoes, flung myself on the bed and picked up the phone to call him.

'Hey, it's me,' I said to his answering machine. 'Pick up. I love the flowers. I love the card even more. Where are you? Answer the phone, you rotten bastard. I'm impatient to make up ... No? You're really not there? Where are you? Okay. Call me as soon as you get this.'

I waited but he didn't call. I waited some more, not unhappy, just impatient. I left another message, several more on his mobile phone, and started reading for an essay. I began to worry, but looking again at the flowers and the card, I told myself not to be stupid. I tried him one more time, leaving him a message asking him not to call me because I was about to go to bed.

In the morning I tried his home and mobile numbers from campus after two back-to-back classes, again without success. I grabbed something to eat and then went back home. I tried both his numbers again a few times, leaving increasingly frantic messages. I couldn't understand why I wasn't hearing from him. We weren't fighting anymore. I hadn't dreamt the card or the flowers. I wondered whether I should be calling the police or at least some of his friends. That was the first time I seriously thought of calling Anna or you. I didn't know exactly where she worked but I thought I could get hold of you through the university. I looked at the flowers. There's nothing ambiguous about six long-stemmed roses. I was starting to panic. I picked up the phone. I was going to call you or the police. As I tried to decide which, I noticed the card. It was lying on the desk, between the flowers and the journal. Then it hit me with an almighty thud and I put the phone down. Now I knew I was right to panic.

The journal, Dad's journal, was on my desk, naked on my desk, near the card and the flowers. I never left it there. I kept it in the top drawer of my desk. I religiously returned it there every time after reading it. He'd found it. He must have gotten bored while waiting for me, found it, started reading it, and then, realising what it was, taken it away. He must have taken it home, read it and left it on my desk when he returned it. Now he knows everything, or thinks he does.

14

The first thing you notice is the size of the man, his frame. He's a big man. Sam is tall but his father is wider, broader. He was sitting at his desk under a blinking strip light in the showroom where 'Moon River' in muzak form was leaking out of tiny strategically-placed speakers. Perhaps on hearing it, one was meant to think of *Breakfast at Tiffany's*. I don't know why they played it. There had to be a story behind the casting of George Peppard opposite Audrey Hepburn. So miscast, like Joe Geraghty. You look at Joe and it's not true to say you can't see any of him in Sam but, as his father, he's so miscast. He should have been Sam's uncle. I wanted to see him before he saw me. Even sitting down, I could see how big he was.

I knew where he worked because Sam had told me one day as we drove past it together on our way somewhere. 'My father works there,' he'd said matter-of-factly, pointing across me toward the passenger window out on to the Nepean Highway. I looked and read, 'Laffenden's New and Used Cars'. It's where Reg Hunt used to be when I was growing up. Do you remember that stretch? 'A mile of cars,' it used to say. He might have already told me that his father sold cars but I hadn't remembered.

You could be wondering why, in looking for Sam, I chose to try Joe Geraghty first, I mean ahead of you and Anna, especially given that Sam had at times been almost estranged from him. The prospect of meeting him was far less intimidating for me than the prospect of meeting Anna and, especially, meeting you. Sam's father had had nothing to do with my father and so, unlike you two, was connected to me only through Sam. It was a connection less weighty in significance for me. And, anyway, Sam had more than once said that he would like to try to get to know his father better, or words to that effect. I thought he'd be even more motivated now, after reading my father's journal.

He would now know that he'd been fed a lie about the circumstances of his parents' break-up. He would know that, contrary to what he'd been led to believe, his mother hadn't really left his father for her university sweetheart. She'd been seeing someone else. It was only when this someone else didn't come through that she decided to cast her vote against Sam's dad and in favour of the man whose unhealthy obsession with her had upset the applecart in the first place. Sam had grown up not knowing that his father was, in a sense, taking the rap for you. Joe had always been cast as the gross, bad, insensitive husband, the professional fornicator. It occurred to me that after reading the real story, Sam might have been moved to contact his father. When I still hadn't heard from Sam at one in the morning I resolved to stop by Laffenden's New and Used Cars the next day to see if anyone there knew where he was. It's impossible to get to sleep until your mind settles on a plan of some sort, no matter how desperate it is. You know the way it works. You know the drill.

After you notice the man's size, you notice the way he looks at you. Well, you do if you're a young woman. The spider and the fly come to mind. He approached me with a smile. I was nervous, less nervous than had it been you, but, nonetheless, nervous. He wouldn't have known. As far as he was concerned, I was there to look at the cars. But I knew. What I didn't know was how to start talking to this man, a stranger, about his son and about his divorce ten or twelve years earlier, in a car showroom. So I turned away to bury my gaze through a driver's window deep into a cloth interior, taupe, they probably called it. Then I smelled him: aftershave, a cloud of aftershave in a scent with just a hint of man. The cloud was about to burst.

'Beauty recognises beauty,' he said.

'Pardon me?'

'I think, and I hope you'll forgive me for telling you what I think, but I think that a young woman should drive a car that makes her feel beautiful and a beautiful car can do that. It *will* do that. I'm Joe. You are?'

'I'm . . . Rachael.' He took my hand, shook it, holding on for too long.

'That's a beautiful name. Almost biblical. Rachael, what are you driving now? No, on second thoughts, let me guess—'

'No, please don't . . . don't guess.'

'You're a young woman. You needn't be ashamed of your car. You have to work your way up to your "dream" car. I had a car once, Rachael . . . Well, no, that *was* my dream car. I don't know much about art but she had curves straight out of the Bauhaus school. They used to say it would offend the eye to change one thing about her. And performance! She could perform. Really. From zero to a hundred in 6.4 seconds. Even I'm not that fast. You know what I'm saying? But she was a roadster, the Audi TT roadster. It had a top speed of 243 kilometres per hour. She purred. But my point here, Rachael . . . my point . . . my point is that she wasn't my first car by any means. Just my dream car. So whatever you're driving now, and it doesn't matter, you've got to be allowed to dream. Now, I saw you looking at this one here and if this helps you dream . . . Shall we? I'm not really supposed to . . . We could . . . Oh hell! Who would even know? Would you like to try her on the road, just for a little while?'

The way it was happening I wasn't going to get a word in, not about his son, not about anything. Suddenly I was in the driver's seat of a car whose make I hadn't even registered, not saying a word, with him and his aftershave beside me. He spoke only to offer directions. He had me turn right from the Nepean Highway into North Road and then to the end where he suggested I try the turning circle in the car park at the beach. When I pulled to a stop he looked at me and that's when I got really nervous. This wasn't what I'd had in mind.

'Rachael,' he started.

'Joe,' I interrupted. 'I'm Sam's girlfriend.'

'Sam . . . My son?'

'Yep.'

'Jeez . . . he never . . . well, son of a gun! Where's he been hiding you?'

'Well, it's funny you should mention hiding.'

Someone out there is going to buy themselves a brand new car with a taupe cloth interior and the reverberations of a conversation held in a car park overlooking an overcast sea, a conversation wherein a salesman was dumbstruck for much of the time as a version of his life was played back to him by a much younger woman he'd never before met. A man who is easily comical is easily tragic. Joe Geraghty listened to me as I explained, firstly, who I was: the younger daughter of his ex-wife's husband's deceased psychiatrist. When he had absorbed that, he heard how I'd met his son at university, and how, after reading my father's journal, I came to know more about Sam's parents, and particularly his stepfather, than Sam ever would. And when Joe realised, not without some shock, just how much I knew, he asked me, almost fearfully, 'What do you want?'

It was as though he was frightened that I might want to blackmail him or else use that part of his life against him in some way. Perhaps it was because it had already been used against him. Were not those no longer recent transactions of the market and the heart, over which he'd had about as much control as over the weather, still being used to keep the second bedroom in every apartment he moved into gapingly empty? And there's no amount of aftershave can fill a room that has no people in it.

I told him I had come to see if he could help me. I wanted to find

Sam. I explained about the fight we'd had, how we'd made up by correspondence and how then, when I'd been at a loss to explain why I wasn't hearing from him, I'd discovered my father's journal out of place.

'So, he's read the journal, so what? What's it got to do with me? Your father couldn't have written anything about me. He didn't even know me. I was the fucking victim in that circus. I'll never understand Anna. Never did. And Simon Heywood . . . I don't know . . . I really don't know. The fucking lunatic reads poetry and everyone thinks he's Christmas. Sam does. Sam thinks he's Jesus on a stick. He fucking kidnapped him! Okay, so he pulled him out of a swimming pool when he was little. Anyone would've done that. What kind of a monster would he have been if he hadn't? When I had money Anna . . .

'I've got to get the car back on the floor. Rachael, you seem to know so much. I don't know why you thought you'd find him with me.'

'Because he's going to see things differently now, the past and . . . I know he's going to want . . . He'd already talked about wanting to spend more time with you.'

'Really?'

'Yes.'

'He really said that?'

I drove us back to the car yard. He asked for my number and he told me he would call me if he heard from Sam, on the condition that I called him when I found him.

'Maybe we could . . . I mean the three of us, when you've patched things up, maybe we could all grab a bite together or something.'

'That would be nice, Mr Geraghty.'

'Joe.'

'That would be nice, Joe, assuming Sam still wants to have anything to do with me. Maybe you could put in a good word?'

He nodded and I began to walk away when, after a few steps, I heard him say quietly, 'Sorry for your loss.'

'So you don't think I've got much chance then?' I turned and asked.

'No, it's not . . . I meant . . . your father.'

I had made it all the way back to my car when I realised there was something I'd never understood from reading the journal and listening to Sam. Why hadn't Joe told him the truth? Why, sooner or later, amidst the alcohol-fuelled rants against the faithless Anna, why had he never told Sam that Anna had been seeing someone other than you, and that you really had kidnapped Sam? I went back to the yard to ask him but he was busy with a customer, a woman.

'Are you kidding?' he said to the woman. 'Too masculine! This is the exact model my wife drives. My hand to God. I never see her; she's always out in this car. Rachael, long time no see. This is my daughter-in-law. Be with you in a moment, honey.'

The woman gestured that she would make way for me to talk privately with him but I said I would wait.

'My daughter-in-law, God bless her, she's a university student. She's got all the time in the world.'

I walked around the floor refusing all the entreaties of the sales personnel. Eventually, after the woman had left with a fist full of brochures, I got to ask him. He thought for a moment and sighed, 'Right from the time he was a kid . . . I don't know, it's . . . It's just one of those things. Sam always seemed to . . . to really like him.'

'Who?'

'Simon. It's like they just clicked and I . . . What was I going to say? You love your son. You want him to be happy. What was I going to say?'

He said this without looking at me. He couldn't look at me.

'Rachael, honey, we've . . . we've got a sales meeting,' he said looking at his watch. 'You call me. I'll be waiting.'

15

The last time I saw my father it was late at night. My sister and I were staying over at his place. It was a Sunday night and our mother was to come the next morning and take us to school. He would some-times need to get to work earlier than we had to be at school. Some patients could only see him before they started work. My mother said that it was interesting that he had these early morning patients on the mornings after his daughters had stayed the night with him. The comment was probably just one of her scatter-gun attacks on him, not said with much thought given to us, but it made me wonder why he didn't want to take us to school. I don't know whether he really had a patient the next morning on that occasion or not. I'm sure he would have had them once but by that time his practice was in poor health.

The last time I saw my father, it was late at night. I don't know what time it was but it was very late, not just late for little girls but late for everyone. My sister was asleep in our room and I got up to get a glass of water. He was sitting in the living room in the dark wearing his pyjamas and dressing gown. I could just discern his outline. I went up to him and sat on his knee.

'Hi, Dad,' I said quietly.

'Hi,' he said. I asked him what he was doing and he said he was just thinking. I sat there for a while, neither of us saying anything. Then I got up off his knee and went to get my glass of water from the kitchen. I looked at him sitting there on my way back to bed and I fell asleep. Maybe you could tell me about the last time you saw him.

I was always going to contact you sooner or later. Sam has made it urgent and the urgency has made me crazy. I've been to your house. I've sat outside and I've waited for the smallest sign of him. I have to tell him, or someone has to, if he won't talk to me, that it wasn't what I think he thought it was. My initial interest in him, our relationship—it has nothing to do with you and my father. It may not make any difference to what happens to us but it matters to me that I tell him I wasn't using him to get closer to my father. It's him I want to be close to. I should have told him sooner about our connection but once I hadn't told him at the outset, there was never a time when it didn't seem far too late, and, paradoxically, when it didn't seem there was always still time. Until now, that is, when it really is too late. The losses that are your own fault are the ones that hurt the most and the longest.

When I couldn't find him through his father, the two of you seemed the obvious choice. Actually you were always the obvious choice. But his car wasn't outside your place that night, and when I looked there first thing the next morning and it still wasn't there, I thought again of going to the police and reporting him missing. I was about to leave when the front door opened and I saw you, the remarkable Simon I had heard and read so much about. You walked out to the letterbox and got the paper.

I watched you walk back inside and waited for you to close the door behind you. When the door didn't close I thought of getting out of my car and walking in. I was going to, when you came out again carrying a large box and got into the car in the drive. It can't have been more than seven-thirty in the morning. It occurred to me that the box contained food or groceries or whatever for Sam. He wasn't staying with you but you knew where he was. You were taking it to him. All I had to do was follow you in the car. I would meet you and at the same time try to explain myself to Sam. You might need to explain a few things yourself. He's just found out that you'd kidnapped him.

You drove away from the direction of his place and I followed never more than two cars behind you, confident that my expectations were about to be confirmed. You stopped outside a little terrace house opposite a park. From my car I could hear you crunching the pebbles in the path as you walked to the front door. You hadn't seen me.

————

I'm always on the lookout for small stones. At first Sam thought this very strange and even gently mocked me for it. He said that I probably wanted them to throw at the windows of the old Radley house. Remember Boo Radley? Sam took to calling me Scout for a while there and asking me, 'Didn't anyone ever teach you never to harm no mockingbird?' But when I told him the reason for the small stones he stopped calling me Scout and took instead to bringing me stones in little bags, a few times anyway. He'd come over with them. After a while, he wouldn't even mention them. I'd find a bag with a few stones a day or so later.

My father is buried in the Jewish section of the Springvale cemetery, the only place on earth where it is always raining. Jews don't bring flowers to a grave. They bring stones. Who knew? I didn't start visiting him there till I could drive. Sam would offer to come with me. I always declined. He asked if it was because he wasn't Jewish and I told him that was ridiculous. I'm only half-Jewish myself and, since it's not on my mother's side, many would say I'm not Jewish at all. Even my father, who had Jews on both sides, was never at all religious, as far as I know.

I don't think he could read Hebrew and maybe he couldn't but there were some Hebrew letters in one of his journal entries towards the end. It's all Greek to me but I showed them to someone who could read Hebrew. The man wasn't certain but it seemed, he said, that my father had written 'as if' in not very confident Hebrew. When I asked him its significance, he couldn't tell me. It so intrigued me that my father would write anything in Hebrew, let alone something as cryptic as this, that I couldn't just let it go and I finally got the closest thing to an answer that I am likely to get. There is an ancient Jewish tradition that holds that if someone saves the life of a single human being, it is 'as if' he has saved the whole world. My father had written this in his journal in the period after Mitch's suicide attempt, in what might have been an argument he was having with himself. I try hard not to overinterpret every random thought he ever jotted down all those years ago. But this one, in Hebrew, could not have been random.

Let's take it at its worst and say that he should have seen Mitch's suicide attempt coming. He dropped the ball. But he saved him anyway, even if only by chance. And didn't he save you? If you were as he described in his journal, in saving you hadn't he saved what he thought was best in man? So he lost his battle against the local introduction of US-style managed care. But he did save someone who is crazy enough to go on fighting the good fight and passionate enough to breathe some of his fervour into the next generation. Or did the negative side of the ledger drag along the ground when he took a trial balance? Health care, his failing practice, his failed marriage, the end of his relationship with Gina and then his near failure of Mitch—these were things you could touch, as well as feel.

He records less about himself and his own quotidian life and, increasingly, as the journal goes on, more of his reflections on the current state of the world. He wrote, 'Whether temporary or not, I can't say, but for some time now the culture of every man for himself has so triumphed that any concern for the common good is referred to a psychiatrist. Emotionally we live in the darkness of the shadows of ourselves. We are always cold and, for the most part, we don't know why.

'I keep looking for the footprints of the small steps forward man was taking but they have vanished. The Enlightenment is over. It doesn't take a genius to see this. I am not, by any means, the best of the ones who used to believe. I am just the last. Fundamentalism, be it religious or of the market variety, is everywhere and everywhere there is a reaction to complexity, an attempt to ignore the contradictions and conundrums of our existence. People crave the simplicity of easily assimilable black and white paradigms and any blurring, any ambiguity, is viewed with hostility.'

This is the sort of thing he was writing. Occasionally, the entries are preceded or followed by a clipping from a newspaper. This one has above it an article about a fire in an institution for the intellectually impaired. Nine intellectually impaired residents were incinerated. An inquiry found the government guilty of neglect. The sprinkler system was found to be faulty. It hadn't been examined or maintained for years and nine men, nine of those least able to care for themselves, met a horrible death. There is a scribbled comment next to the clipping: 'It wasn't neglect. Governments have relinquished their responsibility for the provision of health and welfare and education to the user. It is "user pays", and so these users paid.'

16

I thought you could lead me to him. So I sat in my car and watched anxiously as you carried the box you'd put in your car to the front door of the little terrace house with the pebble path and rang the doorbell. I should not, of course, have expected Sam to open the door. If he was staying at someone's house then it was likely that that someone would be the one to open the door. But, even so, when it wasn't Sam my heart sank, and it sank still further when I saw it was a woman. She was a woman I had never seen before and I felt sick. This was what came from acting on hunches and following people. You got to know things you didn't want to know. It didn't make any sense. Sam had female friends and even a couple of ex-girlfriends, but I knew or at least had met them all. This wasn't one of them. I was thinking that he couldn't possibly be seeing anyone else, not yet, and then I realised that Sam wasn't there at all and that I had followed you to a place that had nothing at all to do with him.

I should have been relieved by this realisation. But I wasn't because it was immediately overtaken by what, sitting there behind the wheel of my car, I saw next. What I saw was you embracing and kissing her.

I was outraged. There was no telling what I would have done had I been able to get out of the car in time. After all that you had put my father through, not to mention all the others with your insufferable obsession with Anna, you then have to go and cheat on her. 'You bastard, you fucking bastard,' I shouted on my father's behalf from inside my car. No one could hear me.

One in four leaves a note. This means three in four suicides do not leave notes. So it's more likely that a suicide won't leave a note than that he will. Most notes seem like parodies of notes anyway. They can embarrass you with their banality. If your last act of communication with the world was as banal as some suicide notes, you'd want to kill yourself too. But what if the note is so long we don't even recognise it as a note? You think I'm hysterical to think he intended to die. You're too motivated to think otherwise. You want, you need, to think it was an accident. Gina is similarly motivated but she's not as far gone as you. She thinks he meant to. She hasn't said it in so many words but I know that's what she thinks.

Depression is at the throbbing heart of most suicides. His first mistake was to treat his own depression himself. The records show things clearly enough. He was treating himself with Prozac, a selective serotonin reuptake inhibitor or SSRI. Presumably because it wasn't working, he switched to one of the more classical anti-depressants still being used in this country at that time, Nardil, which isn't an SSRI but a member of the family of drugs known as monoamine oxidase inhibitors or MAOI. In changing his medication, he started taking Nardil too soon. The level of SSRI was still too high in his bloodstream, causing a fatal synergy with the MAOI. That's what killed him. It's called 'serotonin syndrome'. This is not his daughter's speculation twelve years after the fact. That's what the coroner's report shows. He didn't wait long enough after finishing the Prozac before starting the Nardil.

Who should have known better the half-lives of these drugs than a practising psychiatrist? Who should have known better the toxic and even fatal consequences of getting it wrong? Who should have known better the foolishness of treating your own mental illness? Come with me to the Jewish section of the Springvale cemetery. We'll stand in the rain with a handful of small stones and you can tell me it was an accident.

Perhaps when he wrote this it was also by accident:

'This is the single greatest achievement of the last twenty-five years, better than Prozac or Zoloft—the enslavement of millions of people, under the aegis of globalisation, to the tyranny of an unregulated market and an unprotected economy, and calling it a blow for freedom.

'From every corner they come to the city. And in every city from every corner they come, day after day—unknowing, broken and heartsick moving things, to look for the work that is no longer there, the steady, adequately rewarded work. But it is gone. It has gone to countries where toil is dirt-cheap. Do not be mistaken, do not be blinded by the glare of the everywhere-lights, cruelly never not on. There is no warmth to them. It is a cold and brutish age.'

17

One in every four leaves a note. The last time I saw my father it was late at night. I sat on his lap and then I went to get a glass of water. I should've stayed. I should never have got off. When was the last time you saw him and why wasn't it later than that? Gina doesn't think it was an accident. She thinks it was intentional. That's what she thinks now that I have told her what I know. She didn't say so but I know that's what she thinks. She can't remember anymore exactly why she didn't see him again either. She tries not to think about it but when I look at her over dinner I know that the question lingers with her still. That's why three weeks after I last saw her, she sent me a cheque for the money he'd left with her. As much as I could use it, you know I can't keep it.

My sister won't accept that it was intentional. She says that the coroner's report only indicates that his reasoning was likely to be impaired. The facts accumulate until there are enough of them to constitute a history. The history, like all histories, supports conflicting views.

———————

I thought you would lead me to Sam so I sat in my car and watched anxiously as you carried a box to the terrace house with the pebble path. You rang the doorbell, the door opened and from my car I saw you kiss the woman who opened the door. I didn't know the woman. I'd never seen her before. She was pretty. Too young to be your mother, and you have no sister, but she let you in like she knew you. I waited, almost apoplectic, while you disappeared inside. The door was left open and in a moment you came back carrying empty pots and pans which you put back in your car. Then you went back to the front door where she met you and closed the door behind her so that the two of you were standing outside on the doorstep. You locked your arm in hers, her one free arm. The hand of her other arm gripped a cane. Even with the cane she walks with a heavy limp.

I know this because I watched the two of you walk, arm in arm, slowly and with difficulty twice around the park, stopping only to feed some crusts from a bag to the sparrows. And it was only when you were halfway around the first time that I began to cry. I wasn't angry anymore. I knew who this woman was and I knew that Anna knew who she was and why you were there. It was Angelique, the woman you called Angel.

I've nearly called you so many times. Sam is missing still, and I am still missing my father. So it seemed like the perfect time. Especially now, because I know what to do with the money Gina sent me. It's hers. I don't know how badly injured she was or whether, as my father would've predicted, her incapacity was exacerbated by a health care system that had both eyes on the bottom line rather than on her.

I think that, next to my sister and me, you probably miss him most. The three of us are what's left of his life's work. Especially you. How did it go? 'If you save a life . . .' Will you help me get in touch with Sam? You tend to know where he is when nobody else does.

I want to know if you will help me with something else. I'd like to read you the last entry in Dad's journal. Its meaning is far from clear, but given your closeness to him and your expertise, you perhaps have a better chance of knowing what it means than anyone else. It might mean nothing at all. I don't know.

> *The pleasure lives there when the sense has died.*
> *The pleasure lives there when the sense has died.*
> *Sired, hired, inspired, fired, mired, tired.*
> *I reasoned, but it will not rhyme.*
> *There are some for whom the pleasure cannot live when the*
> *sense has died.*

What do you make of it?

Acknowledgements

For their help in various ways (sometimes unknown to them), the author wishes to express his gratitude to: the Australia Council for the Arts, the Bevilacqua family, Andrea Brookes, Craig L. Brookes, Sarah Chalfant, Nikki Christer, Barbara Cirignano, Virginia Fay, Doug Ferguson, Simone Ford, Rick Goldberg, David Grace, Julie Grau, Carmen Gurner, Deborah Gurner, Fred Gurner, Jack Gurner, George Halasz, Liv Perlman Handfield, Toby Handfield, Trevor Hildebrand, Mark Irving, Jo Jarrah, Wendy Koleits, Dorothy Kovacs, Susan Lehman, Mark Lock, Peter Marfleet, Liz Marley, Lena Martin, Ross Martin, Martine Murray, Zoë Pagnamenta, Janine Perlman, the Prostitutes' Collective of Victoria, Glen Ramos, Nos Sacks, Saud A. Sadiq, Rod Saunders, Suzie Sharp, Ted Woodward, Andrew Wylie and Brent Young.

An early version of Part One appeared in *Granta*, and thanks are owed to Ian Jack, Liz Jobey and Sophie Harrison for their help in its preparation.

Harry Perlman deserves to be singled out for the critical attention he lavished on the many incarnations of this book over the years of its creation. His close reading and thoughtful advice proved invaluable, and cannot be repaid in words alone.

Permissions

Excerpt from 'God Has Pity on Kindergarten Children', from *The Selected Poetry of Yehuda Amichai* by Yehuda Amichai, translated by Chana Bloch and Stephen Mitchell, used with permission of University of California Press.

Excerpt from 'The Love Song of J. Alfred Prufrock' (on page 10), from *Collected Poems 1909–1962* by T.S. Eliot, used with permission of Faber and Faber.

Excerpt from 'To Speak of Woe that is in Marriage', from *Collected Poems* by Robert Lowell, used with permission of Faber and Faber.

'Celebration' © 1980 EMI Longitude Music Co. Used by permission of EMI Music Publishing Australia Pty Limited. All rights reserved.

'Some Advice to Those Who Will Serve Time in Prison', from *Poems of Nazim Hikmet* by Nazim Hikmet, translated by Randy Blasing and Mutlu Konuk. Translation © 1994, 2002 by Randy Blasing and Mutlu Konuk. Reprinted by permission of Persea Books, Inc. (New York).

'Them There Eyes' by Maceo Pinkard, William Tracey and Doris Tauber © Copyright 1930 by Bourne Co. Copyright renewed. This arrangement © Copyright 1993 by Bourne Co. All rights reserved. International copyright secured.

Excerpt from 'Howl', from *Howl* by Allen Ginsberg, Penguin Books.

While all efforts have been made to contact copyright holders of material used in this work, any oversights will be gladly corrected in future editions.